STRAY BULLETS

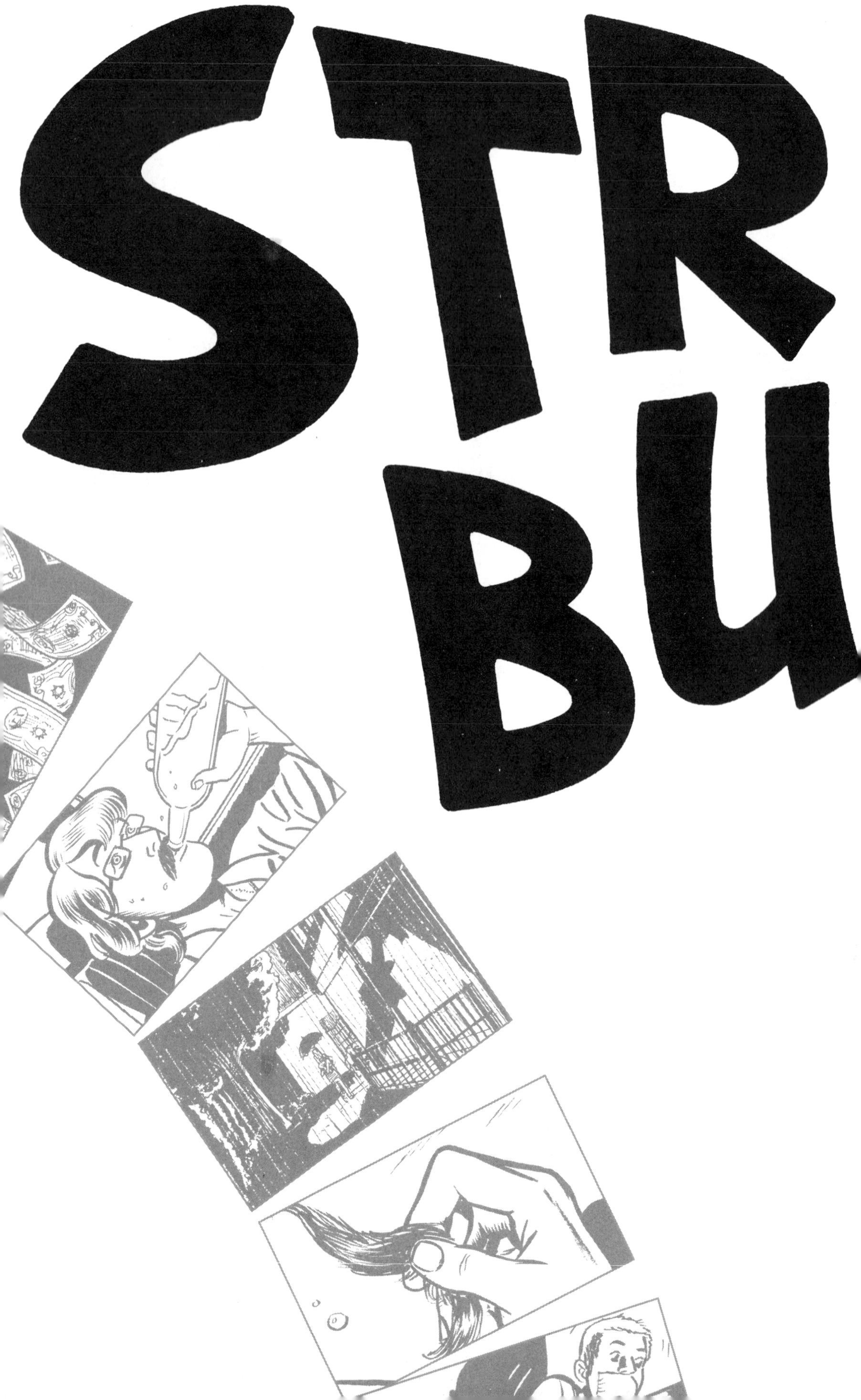
STR
BU

AY LLETS

PART THREE

"THE QUEEN OF PALM COURT"

by

DAVID LAPHAM

MARIA LAPHAM

EL CAPITÁN

STRAY BULLETS:
SUNSHINE & ROSES, PART 3

by
DAVID LAPHAM

•

PRODUCED AND EDITED BY
MARIA LAPHAM

AN
EL CAPITÁN
PRODUCTION

SERIES DESIGN BY
DAVID LAPHAM   MARIA LAPHAM

COPY EDITED BY
RENEE MILLER

COVER COLORS BY
DAVID LAPHAM

IMAGE COMICS, INC.

Robert Kirkman—Chief Operating Officer
Erik Larsen—Chief Financial Officer
Todd McFarlane—President
Marc Silvestri—Chief Executive Officer
Jim Valentino—Vice President

Eric Stephenson—Publisher/Chief Creative Officer
Corey Hart—Director of Sales
Jeff Boison—Director of Publishing Planning
  & Book Trade Sales
Chris Ross—Director of Digital Sales
Jeff Stang—Director of Specialty Sales
Kat Salazar—Director of PR & Marketing
Drew Gill—Art Director
Heather Doornink—Production Director
Nicole Lapalme—Controller

IMAGECOMICS.COM

CONTENTS

POP

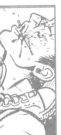

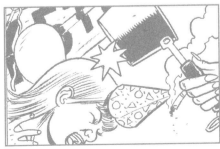

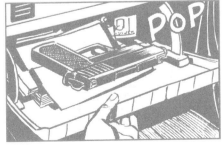

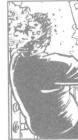

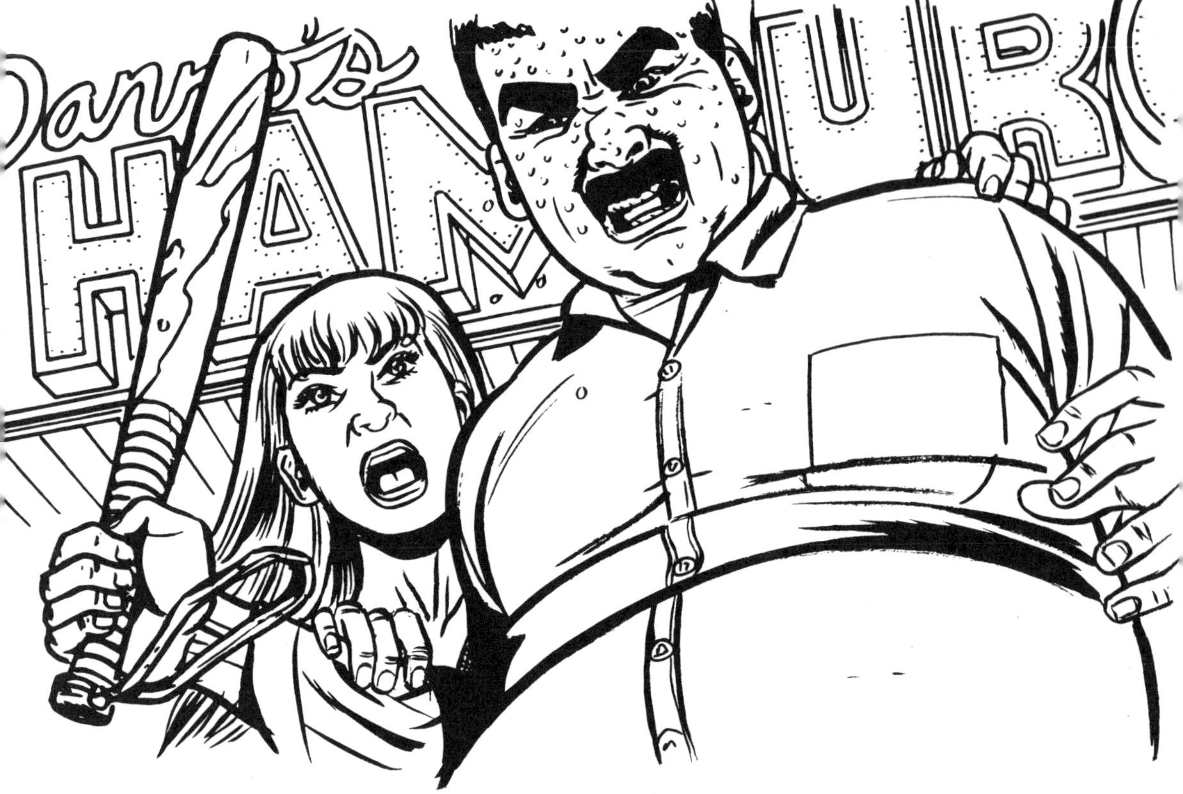

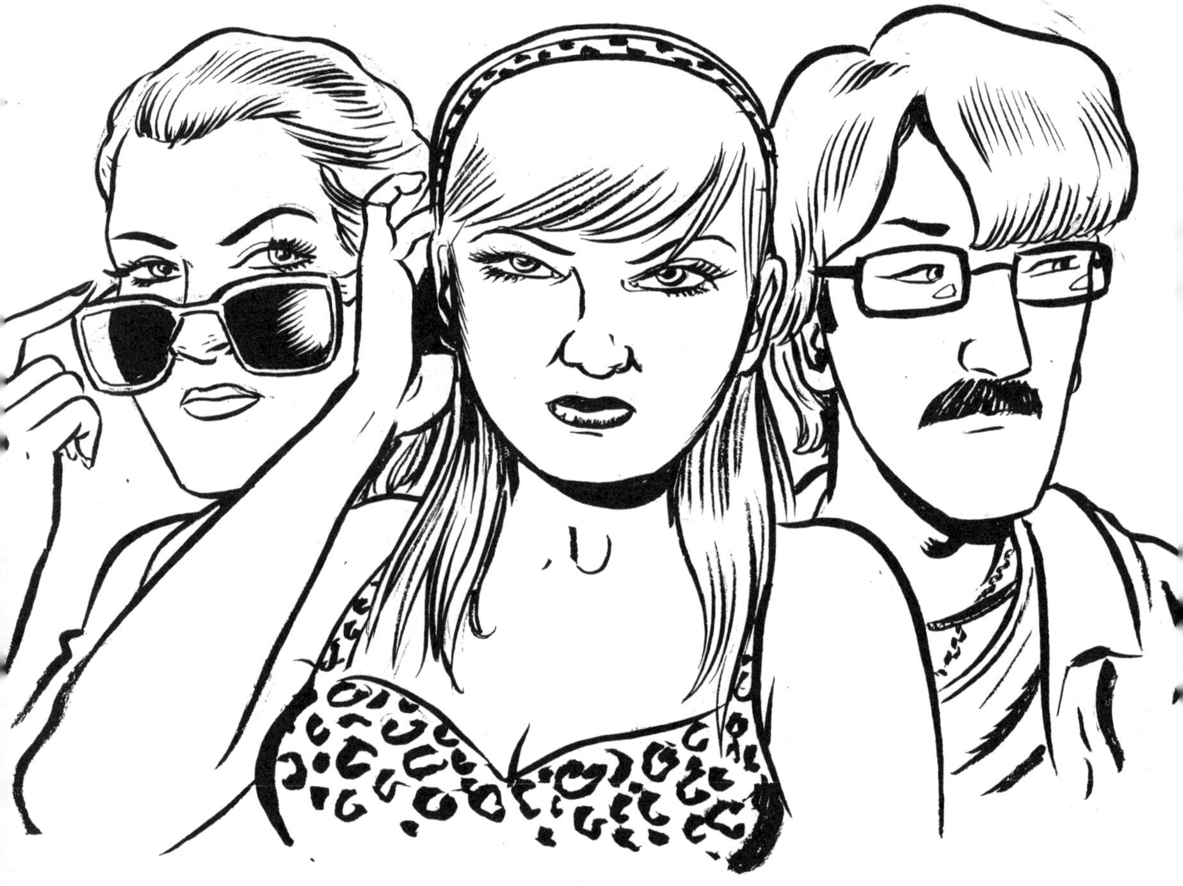

STRAY BULLETS

"Annie's an entrepreneur!"

1

"THE QUEEN OF PALM COURT"

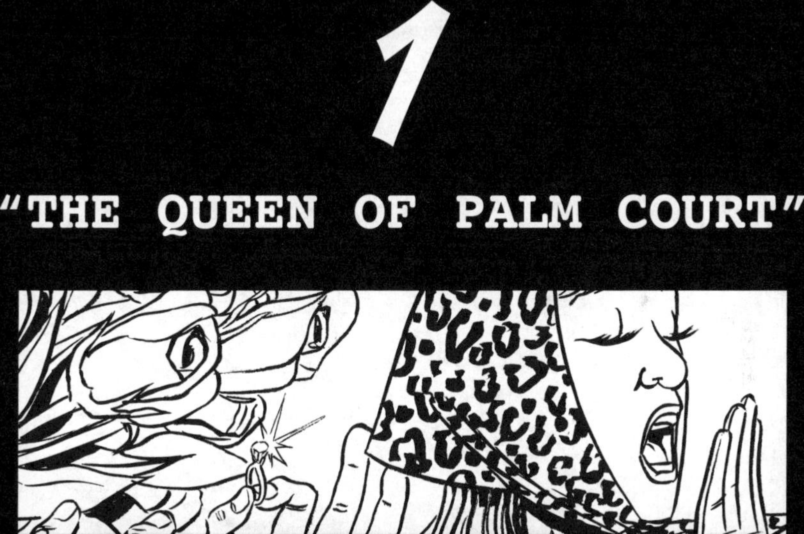

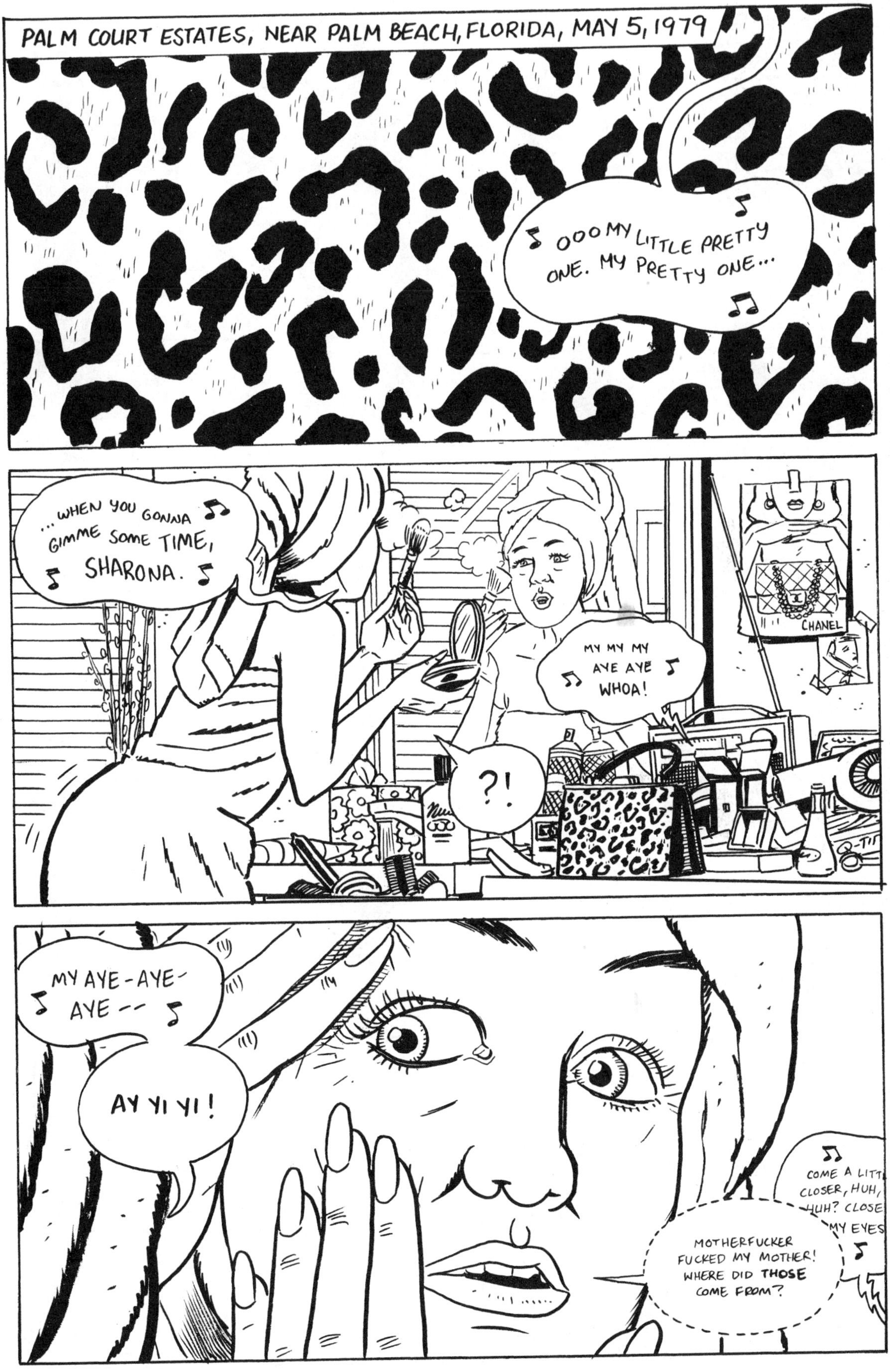
PALM COURT ESTATES, NEAR PALM BEACH, FLORIDA, MAY 5, 1979
OOO MY LITTLE PRETTY ONE. MY PRETTY ONE...
...WHEN YOU GONNA GIMME SOME TIME, SHARONA.
CHANEL
MY MY MY AYE AYE WHOA!
?!
MY AYE-AYE-AYE--
AY YI YI!
COME A LITT CLOSER, HUH, HUH? CLOSE MY EYES
MOTHERFUCKER FUCKED MY MOTHER! WHERE DID **THOSE** COME FROM?

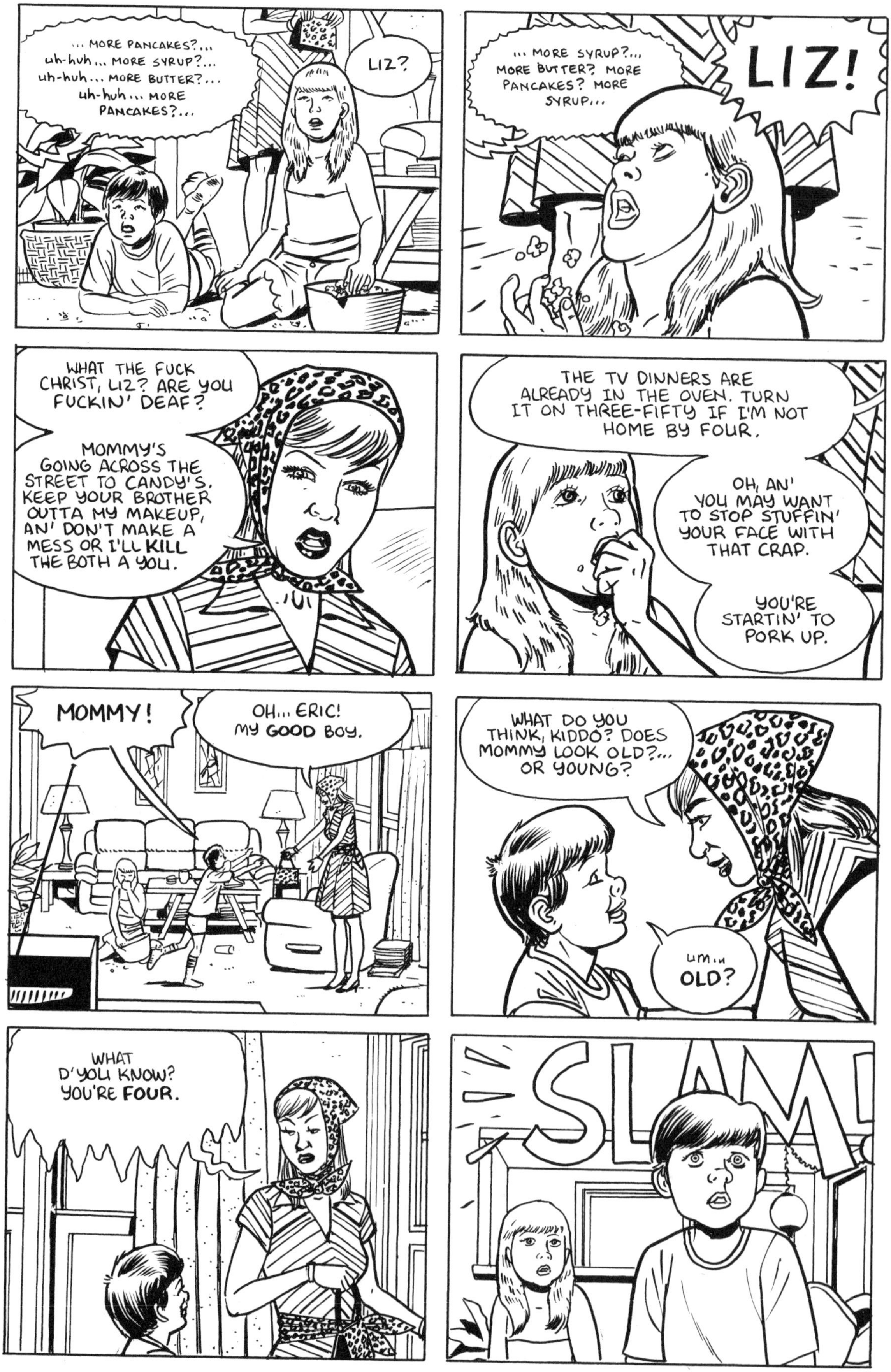
... MORE PANCAKES?... uh-huh... MORE SYRUP?... uh-huh... MORE BUTTER?... uh-huh... MORE PANCAKES?...
LIZ?
... MORE SYRUP?... MORE BUTTER? MORE PANCAKES? MORE SYRUP...
LIZ!
WHAT THE FUCK CHRIST, LIZ? ARE YOU FUCKIN' DEAF?
MOMMY'S GOING ACROSS THE STREET TO CANDY'S. KEEP YOUR BROTHER OUTTA MY MAKEUP, AN' DON'T MAKE A MESS OR I'LL KILL THE BOTH A YOU.
THE TV DINNERS ARE ALREADY IN THE OVEN. TURN IT ON THREE-FIFTY IF I'M NOT HOME BY FOUR.
OH, AN' YOU MAY WANT TO STOP STUFFIN' YOUR FACE WITH THAT CRAP.
YOU'RE STARTIN' TO PORK UP.
MOMMY!
OH... ERIC! MY GOOD BOY.
WHAT DO YOU THINK, KIDDO? DOES MOMMY LOOK OLD?... OR YOUNG?
UM... OLD?
WHAT D'YOU KNOW? YOU'RE FOUR.
SLAM!

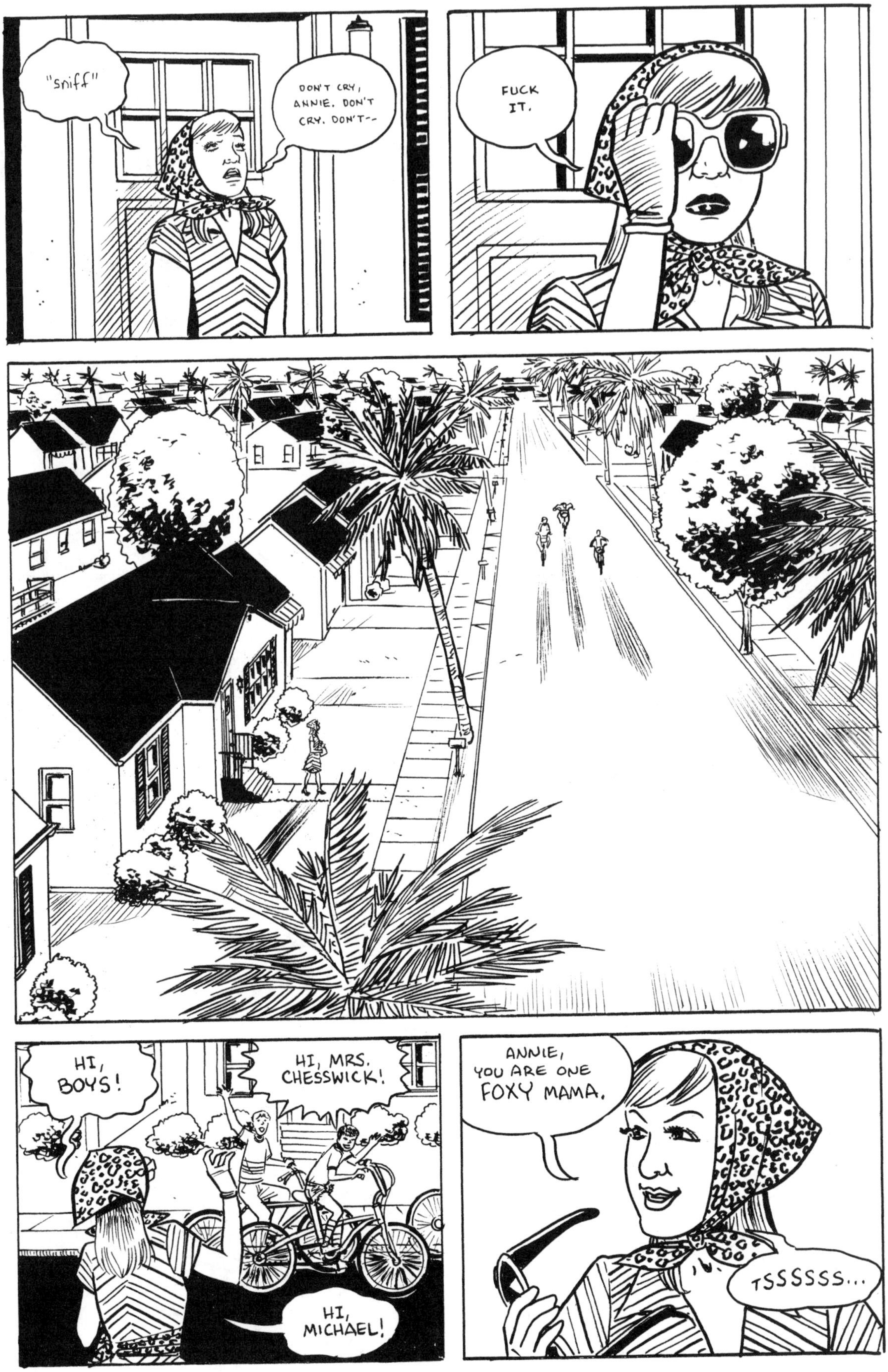
"sniff"
DON'T CRY, ANNIE. DON'T CRY. DON'T--
FUCK IT.
HI, BOYS!
HI, MRS. CHESSWICK!
HI, MICHAEL!
ANNIE, YOU ARE ONE FOXY MAMA.
TSSSSSS...

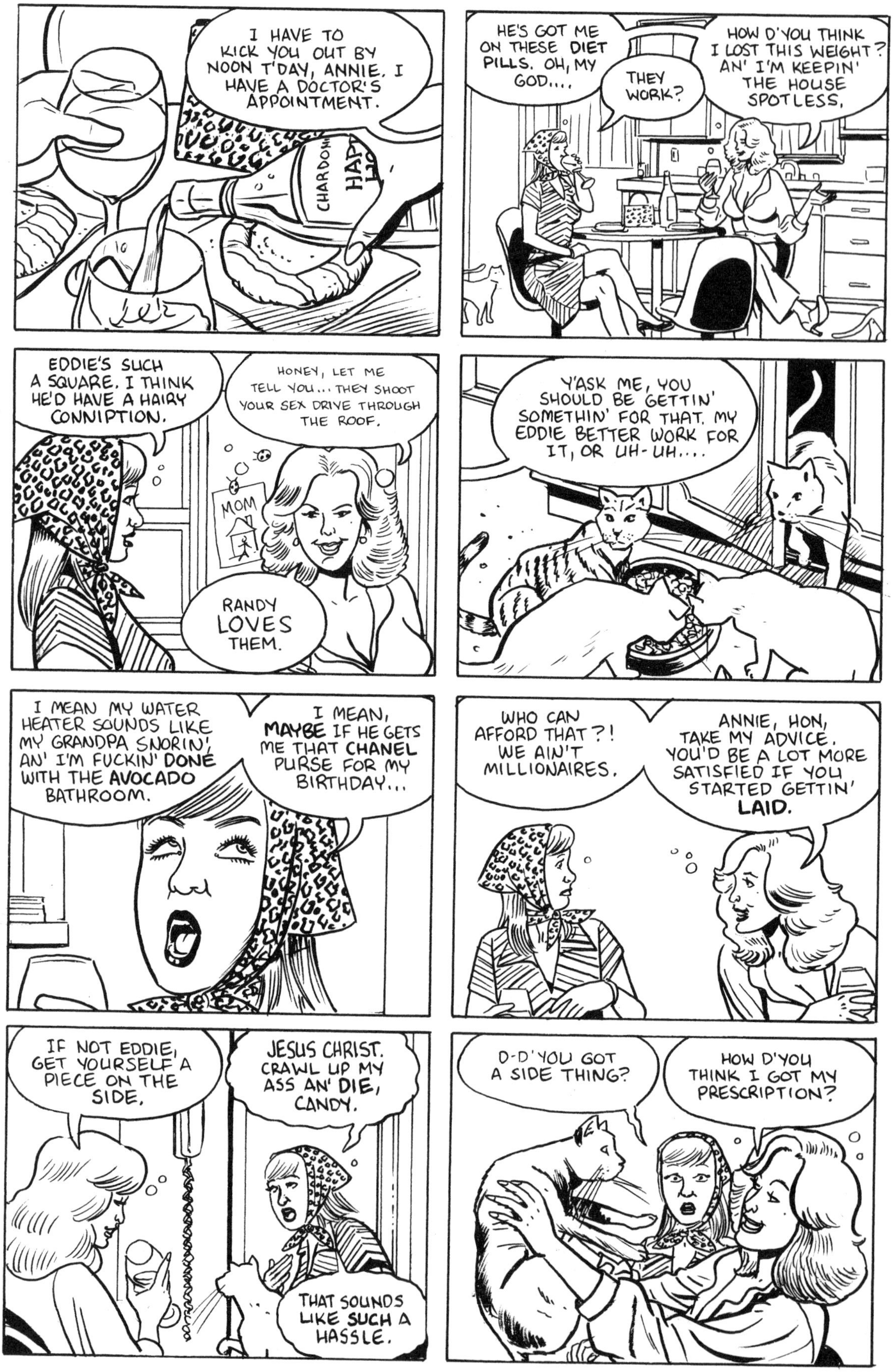
I HAVE TO KICK YOU OUT BY NOON T'DAY, ANNIE. I HAVE A DOCTOR'S APPOINTMENT.
CHARDON
HAP
HE'S GOT ME ON THESE DIET PILLS. OH, MY GOD....
THEY WORK?
HOW D'YOU THINK I LOST THIS WEIGHT? AN' I'M KEEPIN' THE HOUSE SPOTLESS.
EDDIE'S SUCH A SQUARE. I THINK HE'D HAVE A HAIRY CONNIPTION.
HONEY, LET ME TELL YOU... THEY SHOOT YOUR SEX DRIVE THROUGH THE ROOF.
MOM
RANDY LOVES THEM.
Y'ASK ME, YOU SHOULD BE GETTIN' SOMETHIN' FOR THAT. MY EDDIE BETTER WORK FOR IT, OR UH-UH....
I MEAN MY WATER HEATER SOUNDS LIKE MY GRANDPA SNORIN', AN' I'M FUCKIN' DONE WITH THE AVOCADO BATHROOM.
I MEAN, MAYBE IF HE GETS ME THAT CHANEL PURSE FOR MY BIRTHDAY...
WHO CAN AFFORD THAT?! WE AIN'T MILLIONAIRES.
ANNIE, HON, TAKE MY ADVICE. YOU'D BE A LOT MORE SATISFIED IF YOU STARTED GETTIN' LAID.
IF NOT EDDIE, GET YOURSELF A PIECE ON THE SIDE.
JESUS CHRIST. CRAWL UP MY ASS AN' DIE, CANDY.
THAT SOUNDS LIKE SUCH A HASSLE.
D-D'YOU GOT A SIDE THING?
HOW D'YOU THINK I GOT MY PRESCRIPTION?

LATER...

VVRUMMM

KLIK
KLIK
KLIK
KLIK

♪ ...OFF TO OUTER SPACE WE'RE LEAVING MOTHER EARTH... ♪

FUCK, PLEASE, FUCK, PLEASE, FUCK, PLEASE, FUCK--

GOD-DAMN!

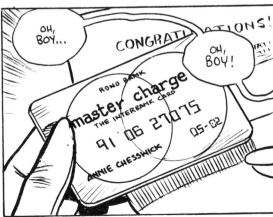

OH, BOY...

CONGRATULATIONS!

OH, BOY!

RONO BANK
master charge
THE INTERBANK CARD
91 06 27075
05-82
ANNIE CHESSWICK

THERE ARE NOW ONLY ONE HUNDRED AND TWELVE DAYS TO SAVE EARTH FROM...

BACK SOON!

9

2:15 P.M....

WORTH'S

MAY'S

MAY'S

WEAR

?

COFFEE HUT

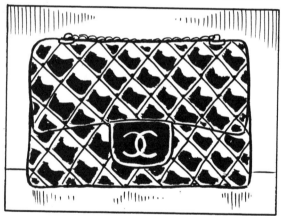

FUUUUUCK...

COFFEE H

HELLO?... MASTER CHARGE? I NEED A CREDIT LIMIT INCREASE....

YEAH, I KNOW I JUST ACTIVATED IT....

PHONE
PHONE
PHONE

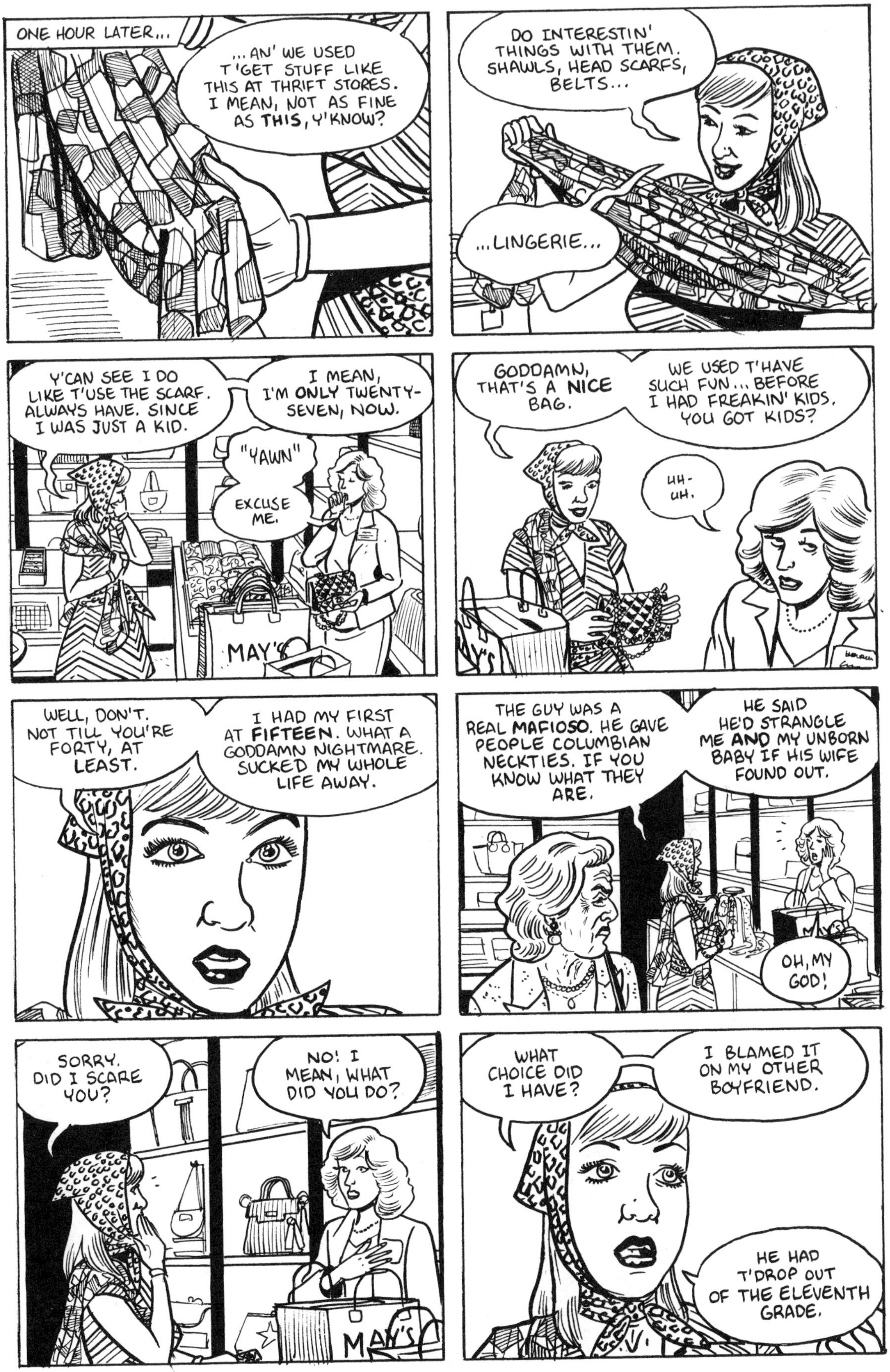
ONE HOUR LATER...
...AN' WE USED T'GET STUFF LIKE THIS AT THRIFT STORES. I MEAN, NOT AS FINE AS THIS, Y'KNOW?
DO INTERESTIN' THINGS WITH THEM. SHAWLS, HEAD SCARFS, BELTS...
...LINGERIE...
Y'CAN SEE I DO LIKE T'USE THE SCARF. ALWAYS HAVE. SINCE I WAS JUST A KID.
I MEAN, I'M ONLY TWENTY-SEVEN, NOW.
"YAWN"
EXCUSE ME.
MAY'S
GODDAMN, THAT'S A NICE BAG.
WE USED T'HAVE SUCH FUN... BEFORE I HAD FREAKIN' KIDS. YOU GOT KIDS?
UH-UH.
WELL, DON'T. NOT TILL YOU'RE FORTY, AT LEAST.
I HAD MY FIRST AT FIFTEEN. WHAT A GODDAMN NIGHTMARE. SUCKED MY WHOLE LIFE AWAY.
THE GUY WAS A REAL MAFIOSO. HE GAVE PEOPLE COLUMBIAN NECKTIES. IF YOU KNOW WHAT THEY ARE.
HE SAID HE'D STRANGLE ME AND MY UNBORN BABY IF HIS WIFE FOUND OUT.
OH, MY GOD!
SORRY. DID I SCARE YOU?
NO! I MEAN, WHAT DID YOU DO?
MAY'S
WHAT CHOICE DID I HAVE?
I BLAMED IT ON MY OTHER BOYFRIEND.
HE HAD T'DROP OUT OF THE ELEVENTH GRADE.

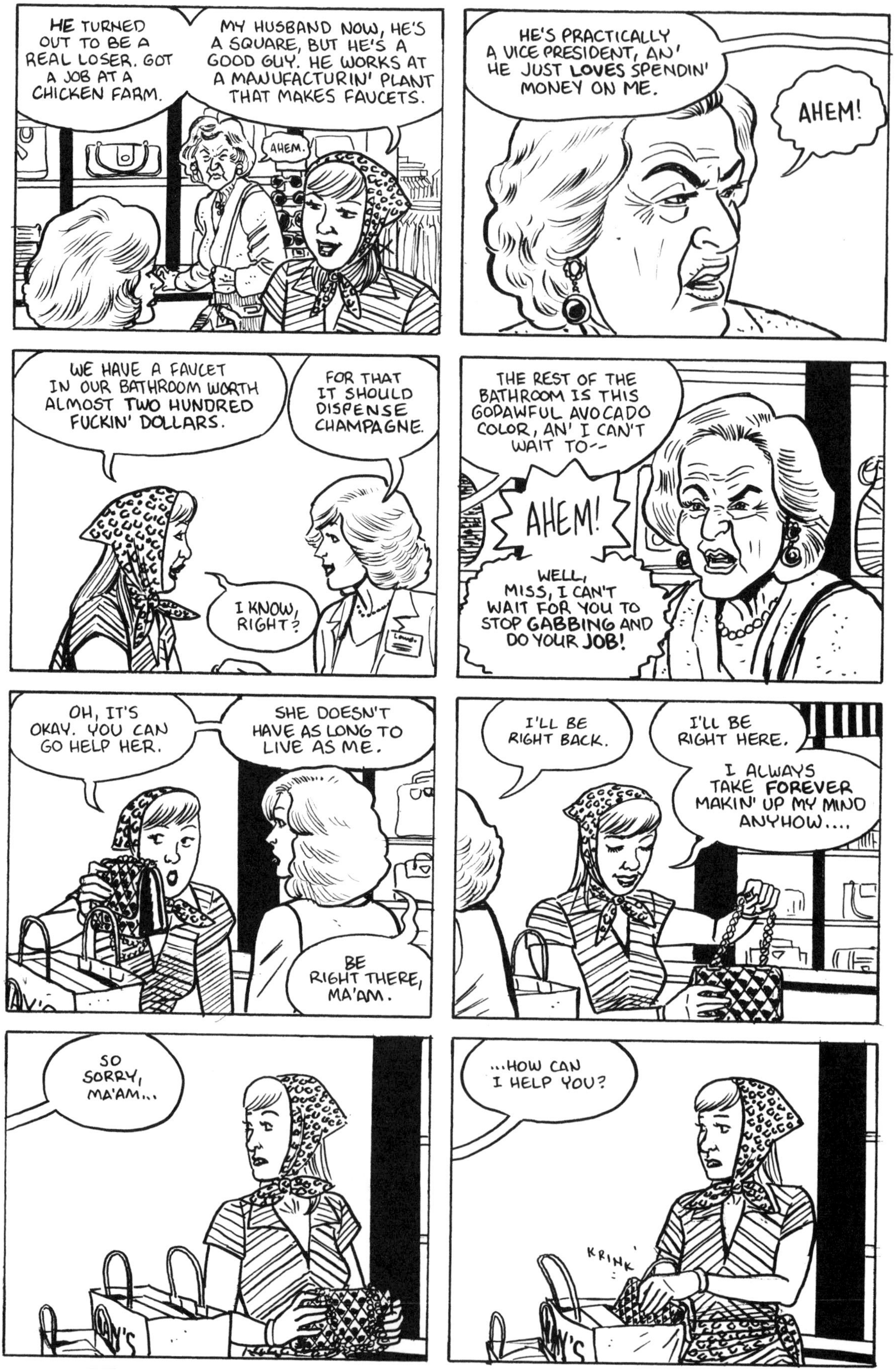

HE TURNED OUT TO BE A REAL LOSER. GOT A JOB AT A CHICKEN FARM.
MY HUSBAND NOW, HE'S A SQUARE, BUT HE'S A GOOD GUY. HE WORKS AT A MANUFACTURIN' PLANT THAT MAKES FAUCETS.
AHEM.
HE'S PRACTICALLY A VICE PRESIDENT, AN' HE JUST LOVES SPENDIN' MONEY ON ME.
AHEM!
WE HAVE A FAUCET IN OUR BATHROOM WORTH ALMOST TWO HUNDRED FUCKIN' DOLLARS.
FOR THAT IT SHOULD DISPENSE CHAMPAGNE.
I KNOW, RIGHT?
THE REST OF THE BATHROOM IS THIS GODAWFUL AVOCADO COLOR, AN' I CAN'T WAIT TO--
AHEM!
WELL, MISS, I CAN'T WAIT FOR YOU TO STOP GABBING AND DO YOUR JOB!
OH, IT'S OKAY. YOU CAN GO HELP HER.
SHE DOESN'T HAVE AS LONG TO LIVE AS ME.
BE RIGHT THERE, MA'AM.
I'LL BE RIGHT BACK.
I'LL BE RIGHT HERE.
I ALWAYS TAKE FOREVER MAKIN' UP MY MIND ANYHOW....
SO SORRY, MA'AM...
...HOW CAN I HELP YOU?
KRINK

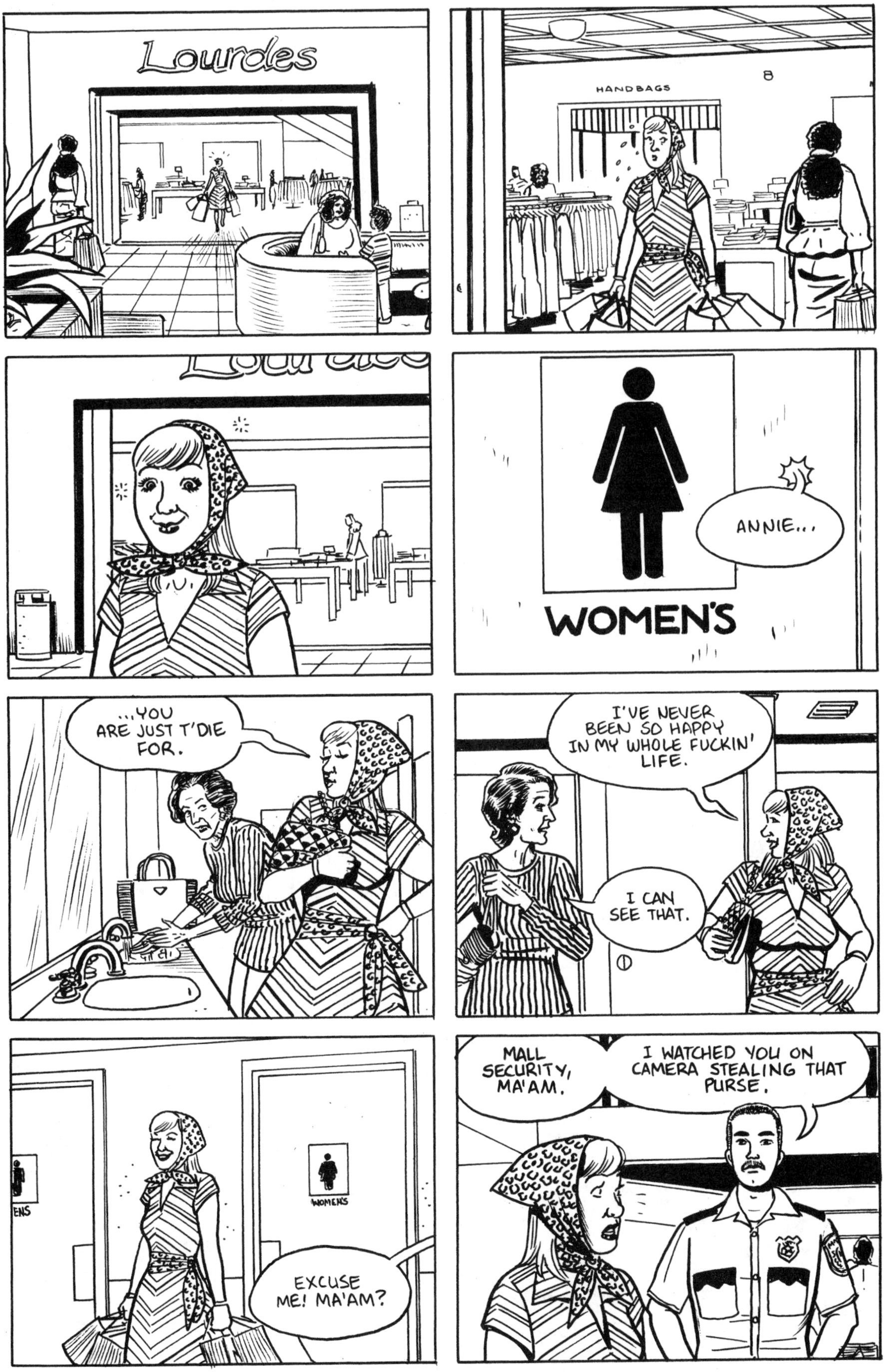
Lourdes
HANDBAGS
ANNIE...
WOMEN'S
...YOU ARE JUST T'DIE FOR.
I'VE NEVER BEEN SO HAPPY IN MY WHOLE FUCKIN' LIFE.
I CAN SEE THAT.
WOMEN'S
EXCUSE ME! MA'AM?
MALL SECURITY, MA'AM.
I WATCHED YOU ON CAMERA STEALING THAT PURSE.

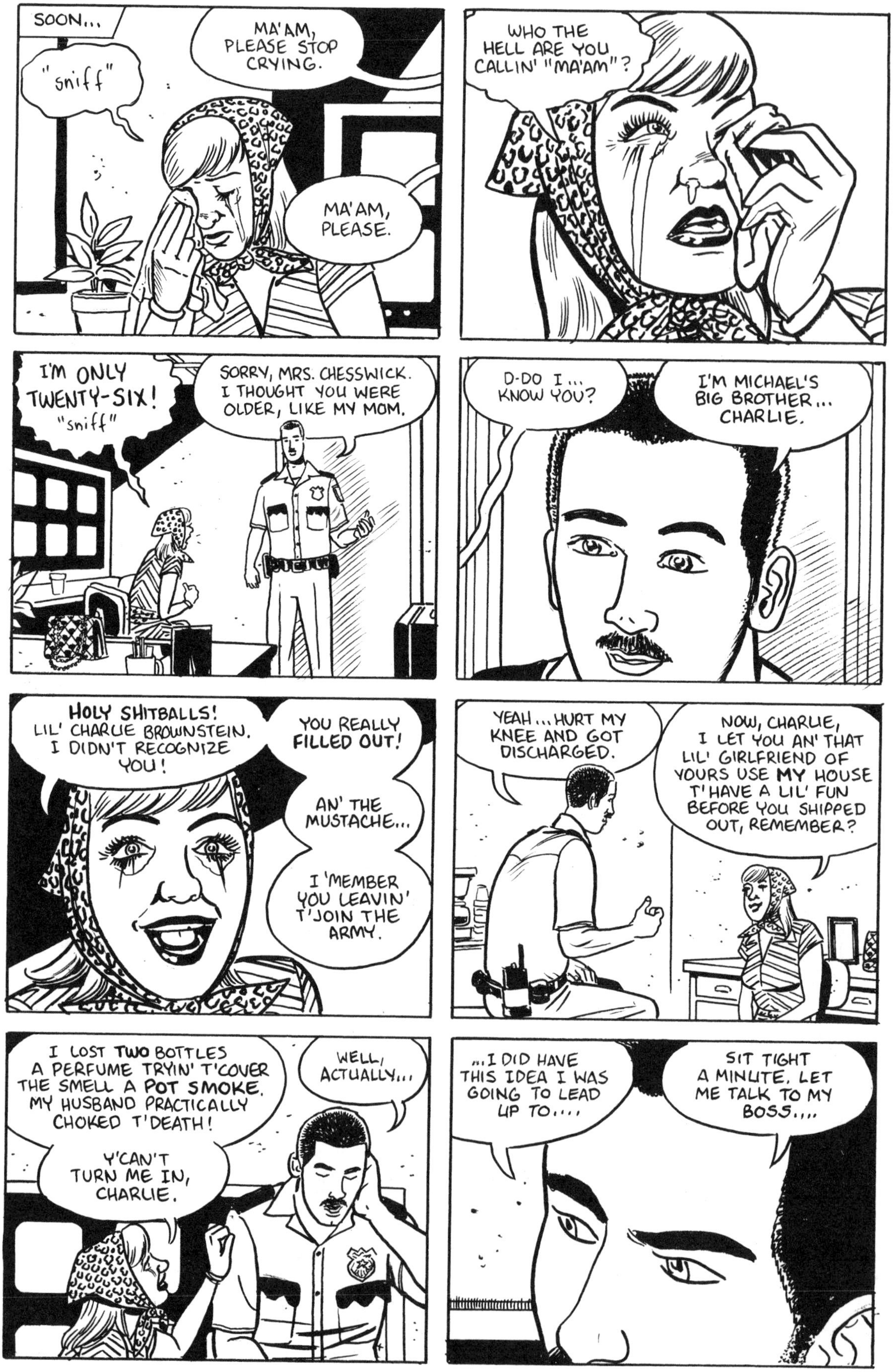
SOON...
"sniff"
MA'AM, PLEASE STOP CRYING.
MA'AM, PLEASE.
WHO THE HELL ARE YOU CALLIN' "MA'AM"?
I'M ONLY TWENTY-SIX! "sniff"
SORRY, MRS. CHESSWICK. I THOUGHT YOU WERE OLDER, LIKE MY MOM.
D-DO I... KNOW YOU?
I'M MICHAEL'S BIG BROTHER... CHARLIE.
HOLY SHITBALLS! LIL' CHARLIE BROWNSTEIN. I DIDN'T RECOGNIZE YOU!
YOU REALLY FILLED OUT!
AN' THE MUSTACHE...
I 'MEMBER YOU LEAVIN' T'JOIN THE ARMY.
YEAH... HURT MY KNEE AND GOT DISCHARGED.
NOW, CHARLIE, I LET YOU AN' THAT LIL' GIRLFRIEND OF YOURS USE MY HOUSE T'HAVE A LIL' FUN BEFORE YOU SHIPPED OUT, REMEMBER?
I LOST TWO BOTTLES A PERFUME TRYIN' T'COVER THE SMELL A POT SMOKE. MY HUSBAND PRACTICALLY CHOKED T'DEATH!
Y'CAN'T TURN ME IN, CHARLIE.
WELL, ACTUALLY...
...I DID HAVE THIS IDEA I WAS GOING TO LEAD UP TO....
SIT TIGHT A MINUTE. LET ME TALK TO MY BOSS....

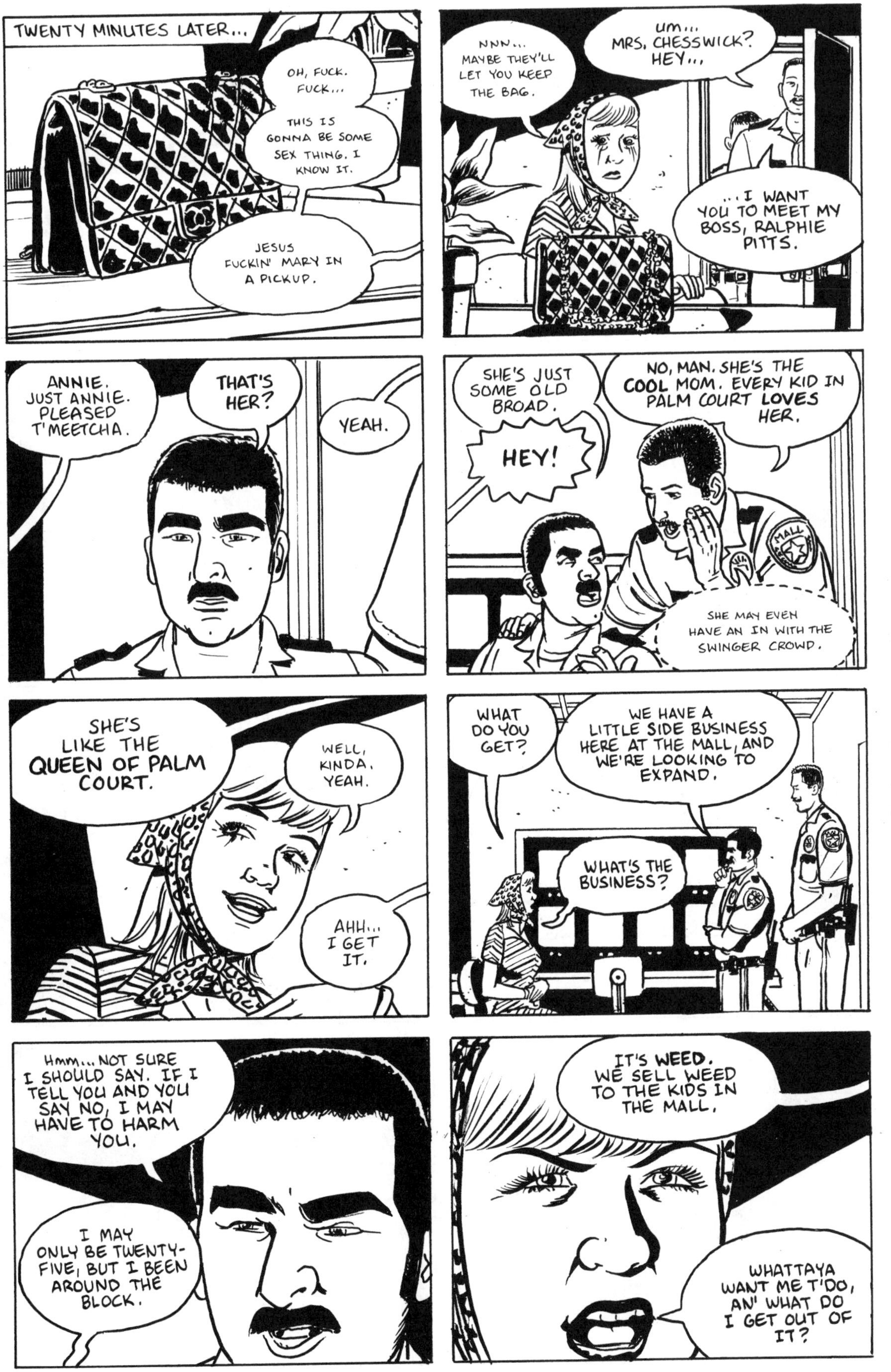
TWENTY MINUTES LATER...
OH, FUCK. FUCK...
THIS IS GONNA BE SOME SEX THING. I KNOW IT.
JESUS FUCKIN' MARY IN A PICKUP.
NNN... MAYBE THEY'LL LET YOU KEEP THE BAG.
UM... MRS. CHESSWICK? HEY...
...I WANT YOU TO MEET MY BOSS, RALPHIE PITTS.
ANNIE. JUST ANNIE. PLEASED T'MEETCHA.
THAT'S HER?
YEAH.
SHE'S JUST SOME OLD BROAD.
NO, MAN. SHE'S THE COOL MOM. EVERY KID IN PALM COURT LOVES HER.
HEY!
SHE MAY EVEN HAVE AN IN WITH THE SWINGER CROWD.
SHE'S LIKE THE QUEEN OF PALM COURT.
WELL, KINDA. YEAH.
AHH... I GET IT.
WHAT DO YOU GET?
WE HAVE A LITTLE SIDE BUSINESS HERE AT THE MALL, AND WE'RE LOOKING TO EXPAND.
WHAT'S THE BUSINESS?
HMM... NOT SURE I SHOULD SAY. IF I TELL YOU AND YOU SAY NO, I MAY HAVE TO HARM YOU.
I MAY ONLY BE TWENTY-FIVE, BUT I BEEN AROUND THE BLOCK.
IT'S WEED. WE SELL WEED TO THE KIDS IN THE MALL.
WHATTAYA WANT ME T'DO, AN' WHAT DO I GET OUT OF IT?

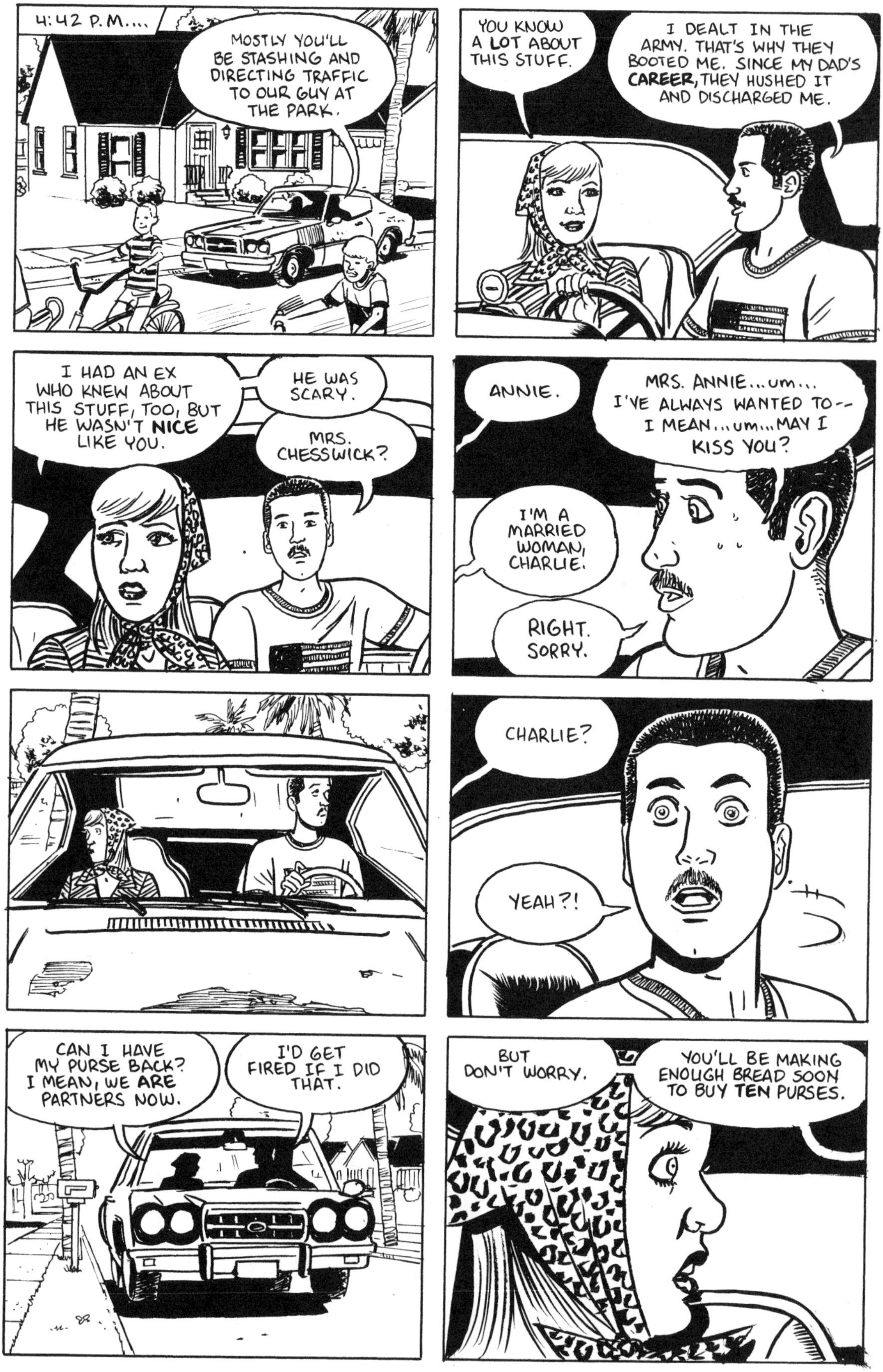
4:42 P.M....
MOSTLY YOU'LL BE STASHING AND DIRECTING TRAFFIC TO OUR GUY AT THE PARK.
YOU KNOW A LOT ABOUT THIS STUFF.
I DEALT IN THE ARMY. THAT'S WHY THEY BOOTED ME. SINCE MY DAD'S CAREER, THEY HUSHED IT AND DISCHARGED ME.
I HAD AN EX WHO KNEW ABOUT THIS STUFF, TOO, BUT HE WASN'T NICE LIKE YOU.
HE WAS SCARY.
MRS. CHESSWICK?
ANNIE.
MRS. ANNIE...um... I'VE ALWAYS WANTED TO-- I MEAN...um...MAY I KISS YOU?
I'M A MARRIED WOMAN, CHARLIE.
RIGHT. SORRY.
CHARLIE?
YEAH?!
CAN I HAVE MY PURSE BACK? I MEAN, WE ARE PARTNERS NOW.
I'D GET FIRED IF I DID THAT.
BUT DON'T WORRY.
YOU'LL BE MAKING ENOUGH BREAD SOON TO BUY TEN PURSES.

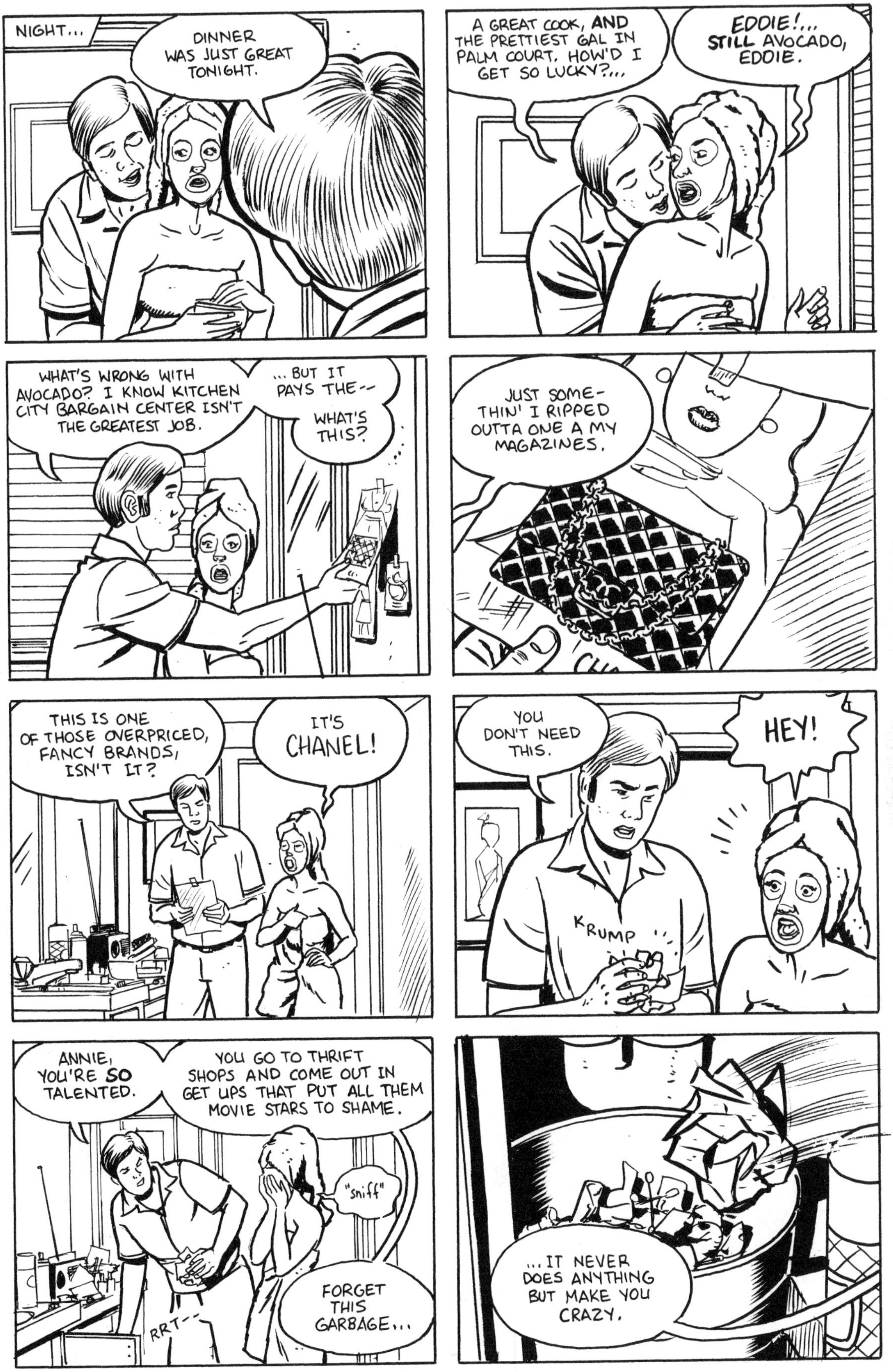
NIGHT...
DINNER WAS JUST GREAT TONIGHT.
A GREAT COOK, AND THE PRETTIEST GAL IN PALM COURT. HOW'D I GET SO LUCKY?...
EDDIE!... STILL AVOCADO, EDDIE.
WHAT'S WRONG WITH AVOCADO? I KNOW KITCHEN CITY BARGAIN CENTER ISN'T THE GREATEST JOB.
...BUT IT PAYS THE--
WHAT'S THIS?
JUST SOME-THIN' I RIPPED OUTTA ONE A MY MAGAZINES.
THIS IS ONE OF THOSE OVERPRICED, FANCY BRANDS, ISN'T IT?
IT'S CHANEL!
YOU DON'T NEED THIS.
HEY!
KRUMP
ANNIE, YOU'RE SO TALENTED.
YOU GO TO THRIFT SHOPS AND COME OUT IN GET UPS THAT PUT ALL THEM MOVIE STARS TO SHAME.
"sniff"
RRT--
FORGET THIS GARBAGE...
...IT NEVER DOES ANYTHING BUT MAKE YOU CRAZY.

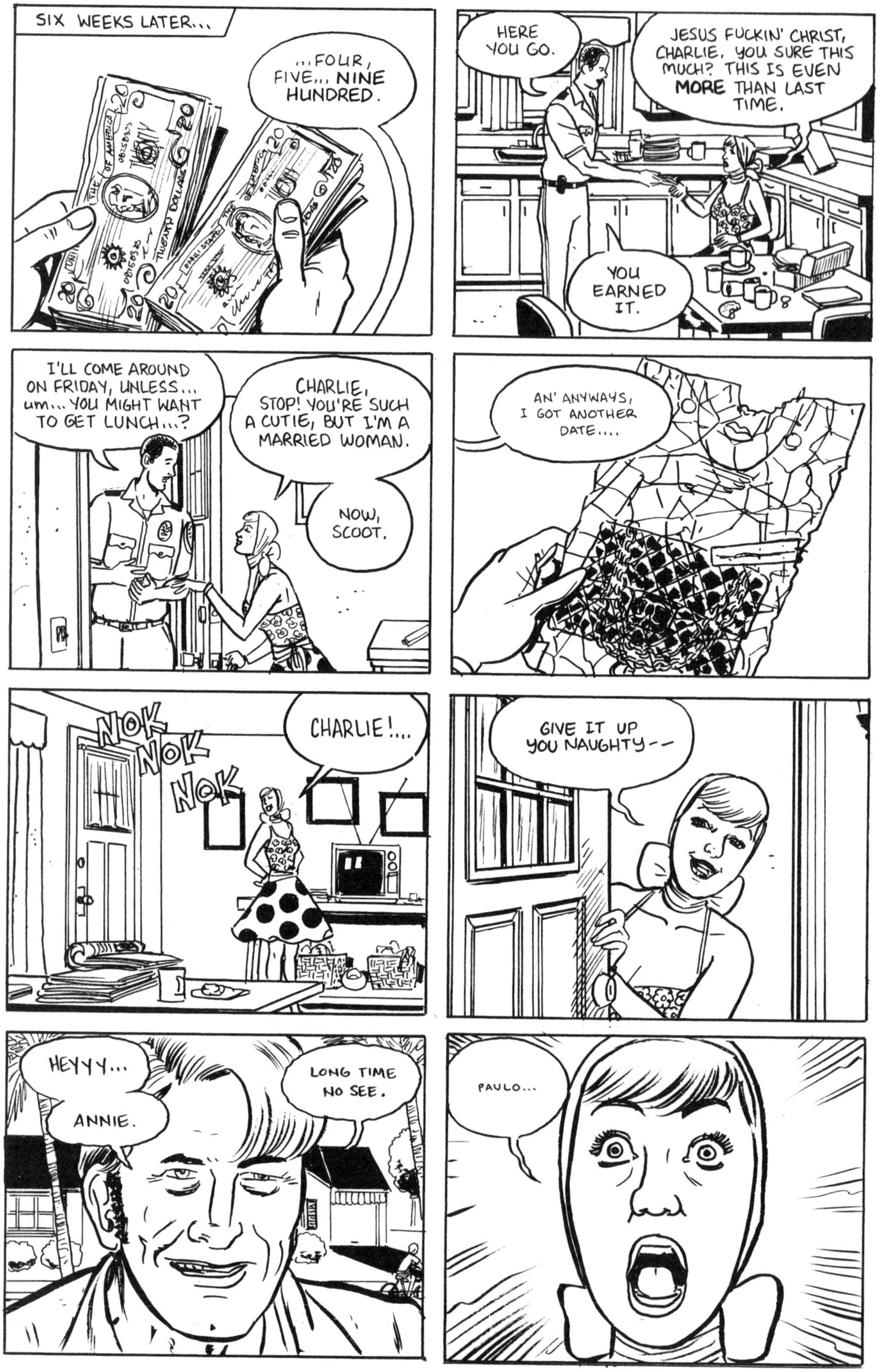
SIX WEEKS LATER...
...FOUR, FIVE... NINE HUNDRED.
HERE YOU GO.
JESUS FUCKIN' CHRIST, CHARLIE. YOU SURE THIS MUCH? THIS IS EVEN MORE THAN LAST TIME.
YOU EARNED IT.
I'LL COME AROUND ON FRIDAY, UNLESS... um... YOU MIGHT WANT TO GET LUNCH...?
CHARLIE, STOP! YOU'RE SUCH A CUTIE, BUT I'M A MARRIED WOMAN.
NOW, SCOOT.
AN' ANYWAYS, I GOT ANOTHER DATE....
NOK NOK NOK
CHARLIE!...
GIVE IT UP YOU NAUGHTY--
HEYYY...
ANNIE.
LONG TIME NO SEE.
PAULO...

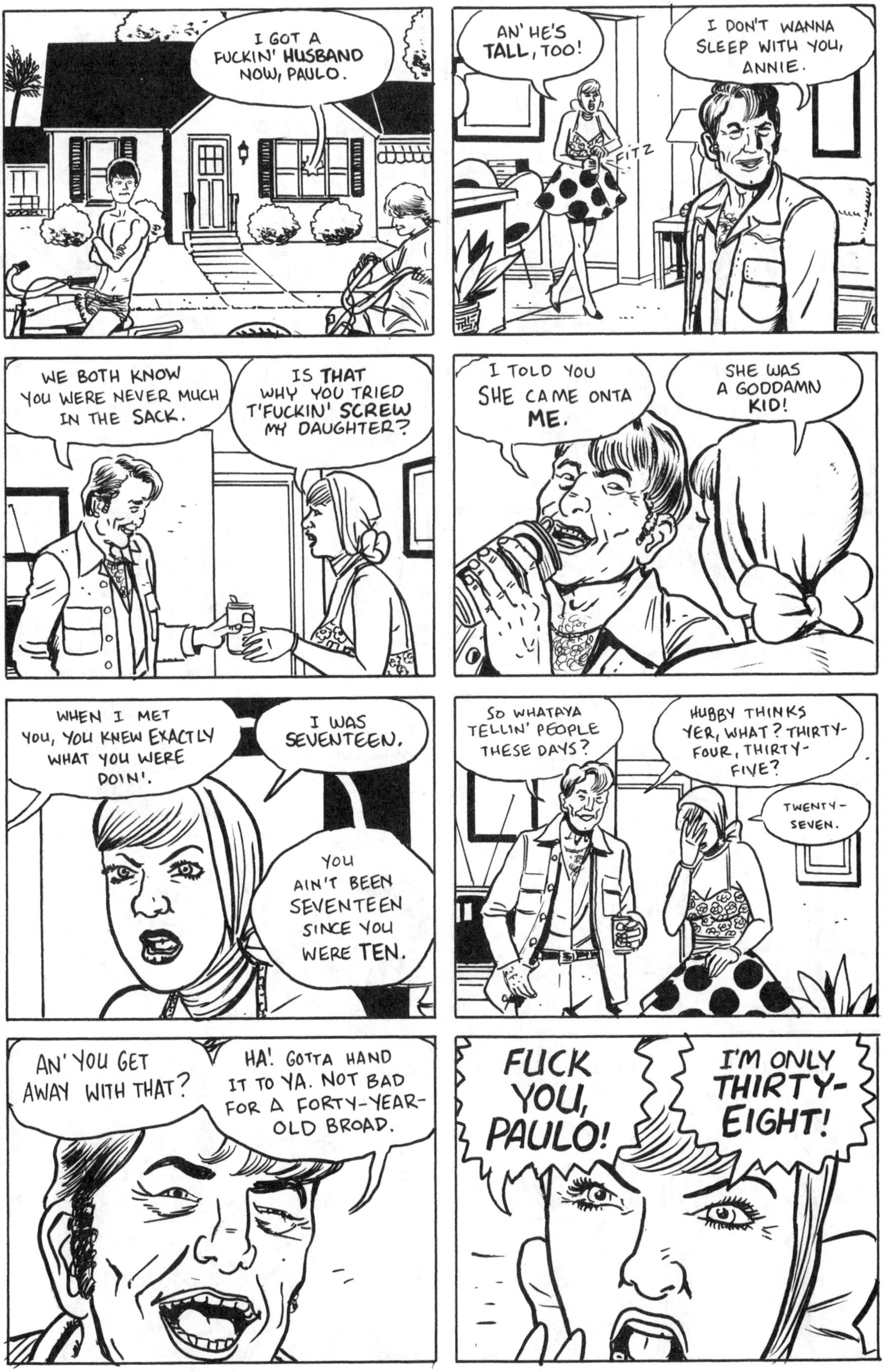
I GOT A FUCKIN' HUSBAND NOW, PAULO.
AN' HE'S TALL, TOO!
FITZ
I DON'T WANNA SLEEP WITH YOU, ANNIE.
WE BOTH KNOW YOU WERE NEVER MUCH IN THE SACK.
IS THAT WHY YOU TRIED T'FUCKIN' SCREW MY DAUGHTER?
I TOLD YOU SHE CAME ONTA ME.
SHE WAS A GODDAMN KID!
WHEN I MET YOU, YOU KNEW EXACTLY WHAT YOU WERE DOIN'.
I WAS SEVENTEEN.
YOU AIN'T BEEN SEVENTEEN SINCE YOU WERE TEN.
SO WHATAYA TELLIN' PEOPLE THESE DAYS?
HUBBY THINKS YER, WHAT? THIRTY-FOUR, THIRTY-FIVE?
TWENTY-SEVEN.
AN' YOU GET AWAY WITH THAT?
HA! GOTTA HAND IT TO YA. NOT BAD FOR A FORTY-YEAR-OLD BROAD.
FUCK YOU, PAULO!
I'M ONLY THIRTY-EIGHT!

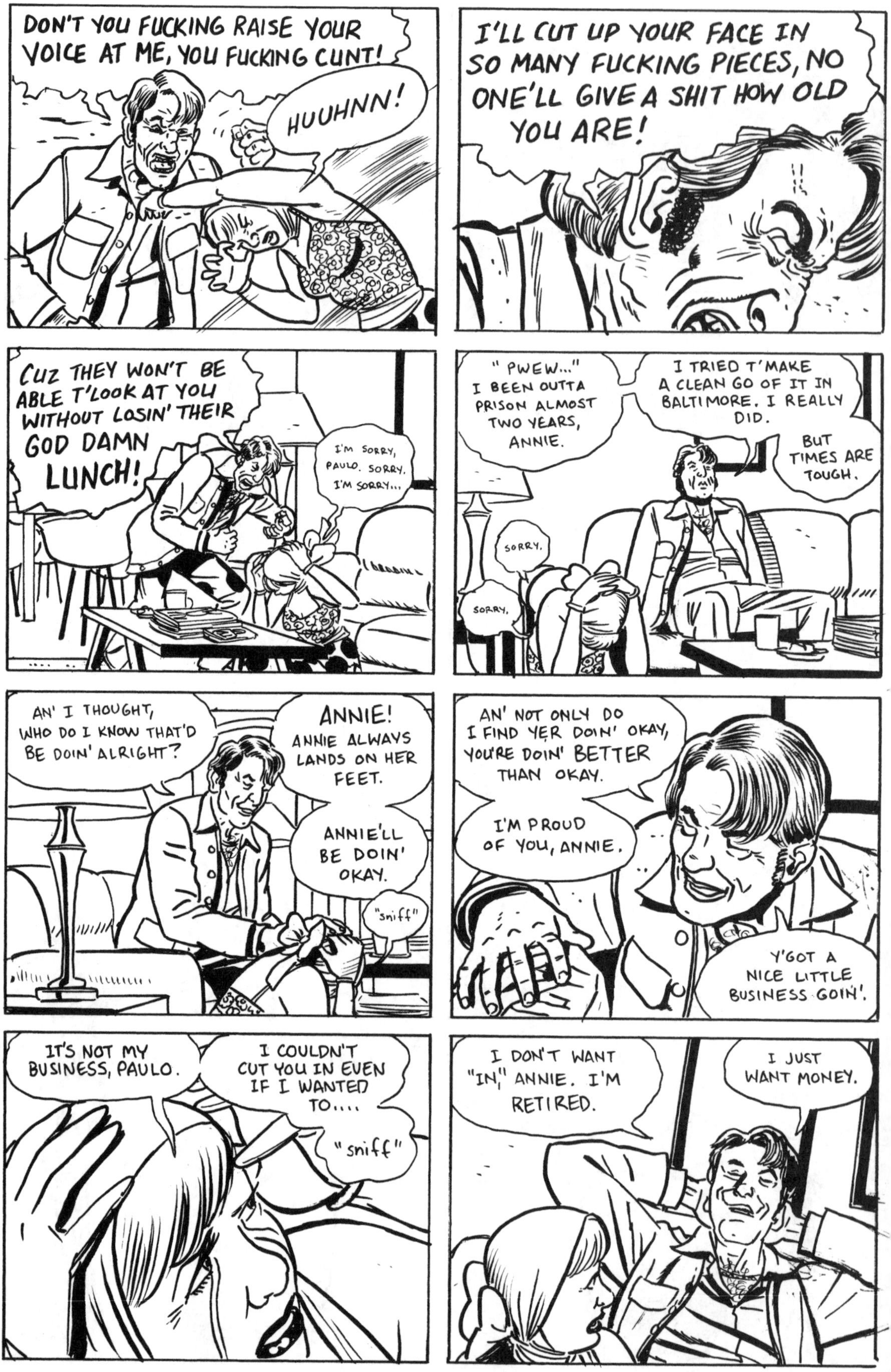
DON'T YOU FUCKING RAISE YOUR VOICE AT ME, YOU FUCKING CUNT!
HUUHNN!
I'LL CUT UP YOUR FACE IN SO MANY FUCKING PIECES, NO ONE'LL GIVE A SHIT HOW OLD YOU ARE!
CUZ THEY WON'T BE ABLE T'LOOK AT YOU WITHOUT LOSIN' THEIR GOD DAMN LUNCH!
I'M SORRY, PAULO. SORRY. I'M SORRY...
" PWEW..." I BEEN OUTTA PRISON ALMOST TWO YEARS, ANNIE.
I TRIED T'MAKE A CLEAN GO OF IT IN BALTIMORE. I REALLY DID.
BUT TIMES ARE TOUGH.
SORRY.
SORRY.
AN' I THOUGHT, WHO DO I KNOW THAT'D BE DOIN' ALRIGHT?
ANNIE! ANNIE ALWAYS LANDS ON HER FEET.
ANNIE'LL BE DOIN' OKAY.
"sniff"
AN' NOT ONLY DO I FIND YER DOIN' OKAY, YOU'RE DOIN' BETTER THAN OKAY.
I'M PROUD OF YOU, ANNIE.
Y'GOT A NICE LITTLE BUSINESS GOIN'.
IT'S NOT MY BUSINESS, PAULO.
I COULDN'T CUT YOU IN EVEN IF I WANTED TO....
"sniff"
I DON'T WANT "IN," ANNIE. I'M RETIRED.
I JUST WANT MONEY.

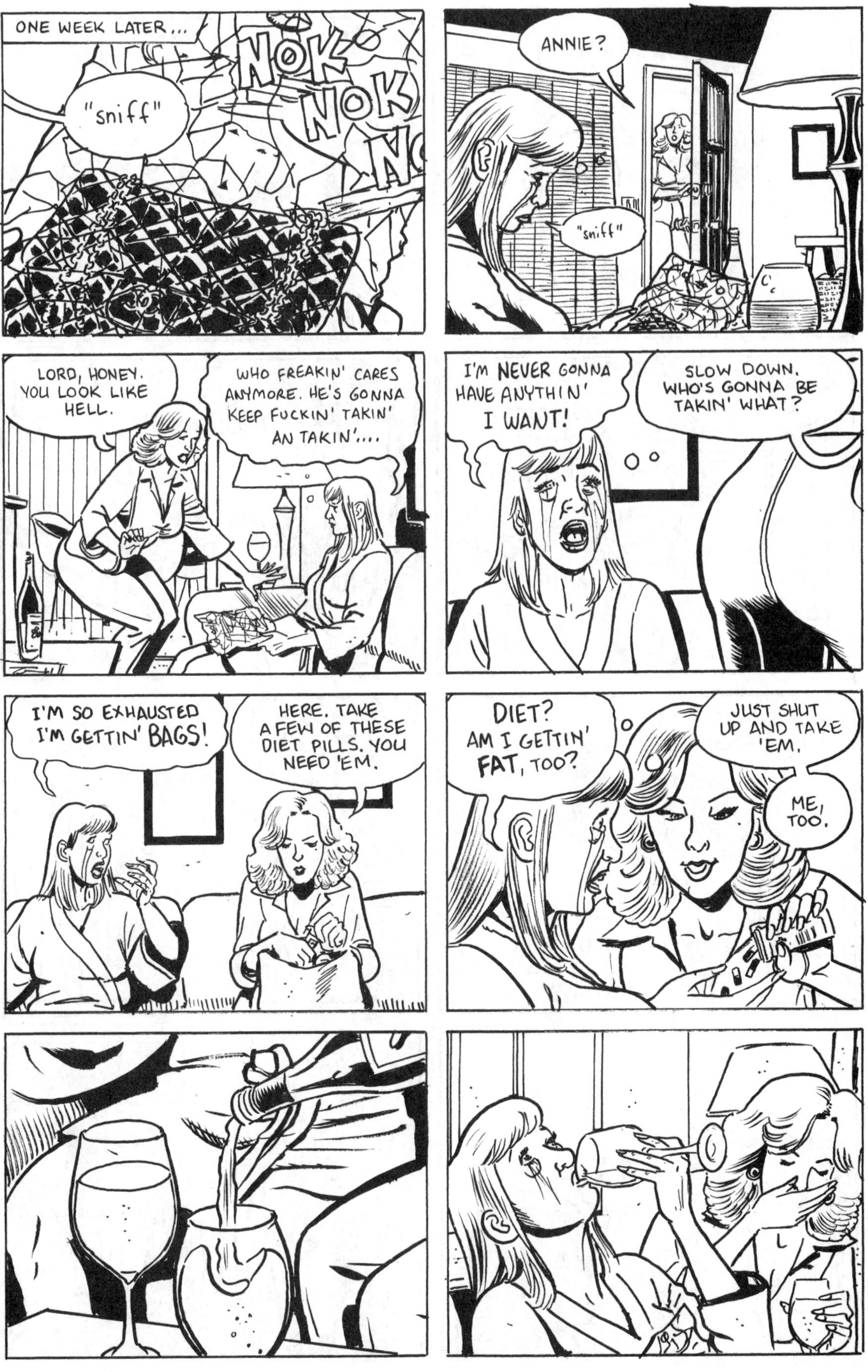
ONE WEEK LATER...
NOK NOK N
"sniff"
ANNIE?
"sniff"
LORD, HONEY. YOU LOOK LIKE HELL.
WHO FREAKIN' CARES ANYMORE. HE'S GONNA KEEP FUCKIN' TAKIN' AN TAKIN'....
I'M NEVER GONNA HAVE ANYTHIN' I WANT!
SLOW DOWN. WHO'S GONNA BE TAKIN' WHAT?
I'M SO EXHAUSTED I'M GETTIN' BAGS!
HERE. TAKE A FEW OF THESE DIET PILLS. YOU NEED 'EM.
DIET? AM I GETTIN' FAT, TOO?
JUST SHUT UP AND TAKE 'EM.
ME, TOO.

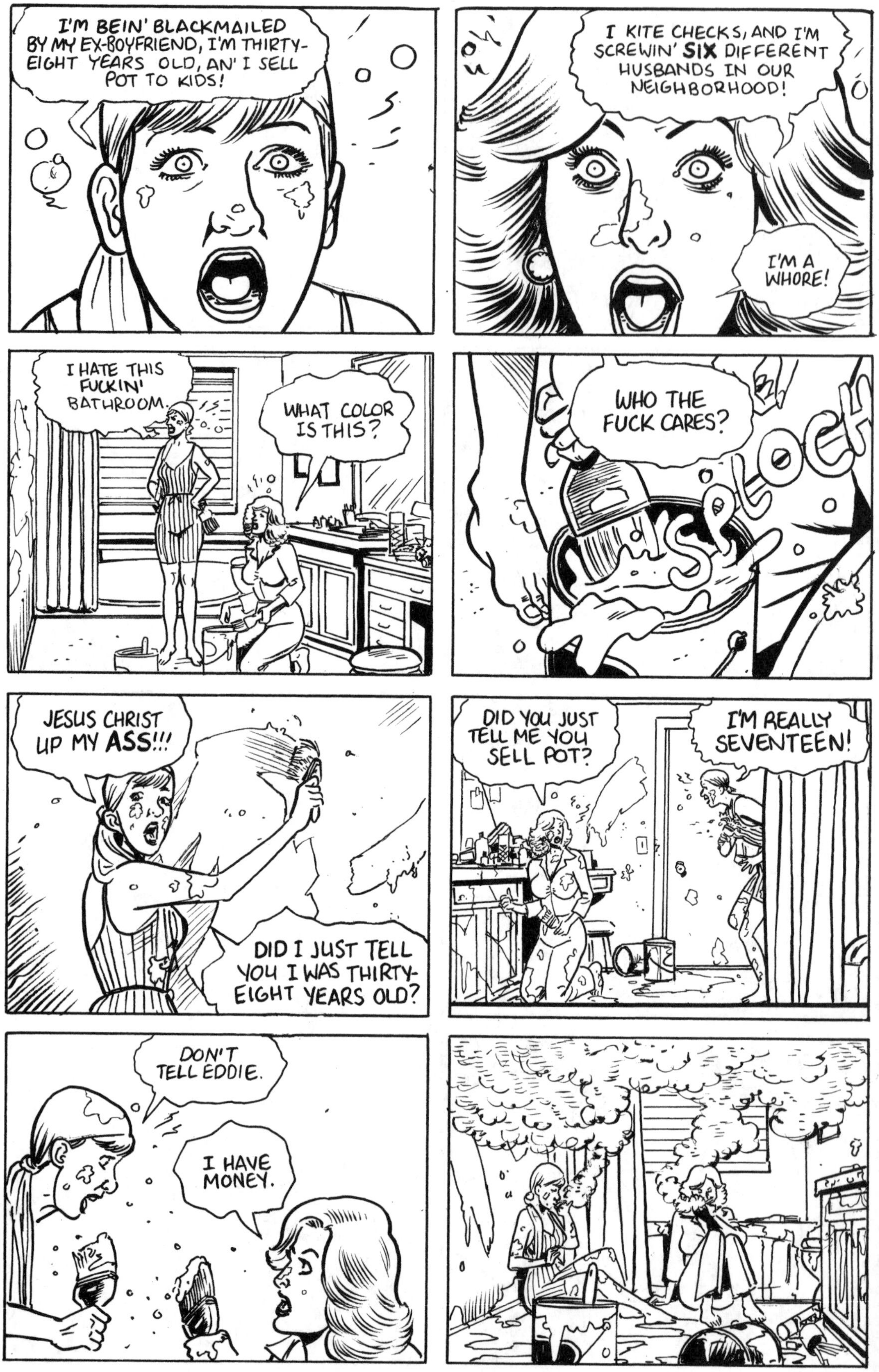
I'M BEIN' BLACKMAILED BY MY EX-BOYFRIEND, I'M THIRTY-EIGHT YEARS OLD, AN' I SELL POT TO KIDS!
I KITE CHECKS, AND I'M SCREWIN' SIX DIFFERENT HUSBANDS IN OUR NEIGHBORHOOD!
I'M A WHORE!
I HATE THIS FUCKIN' BATHROOM.
WHAT COLOR IS THIS?
WHO THE FUCK CARES?
SPLOCH
JESUS CHRIST UP MY ASS!!!
DID I JUST TELL YOU I WAS THIRTY-EIGHT YEARS OLD?
DID YOU JUST TELL ME YOU SELL POT?
I'M REALLY SEVENTEEN!
DON'T TELL EDDIE.
I HAVE MONEY.

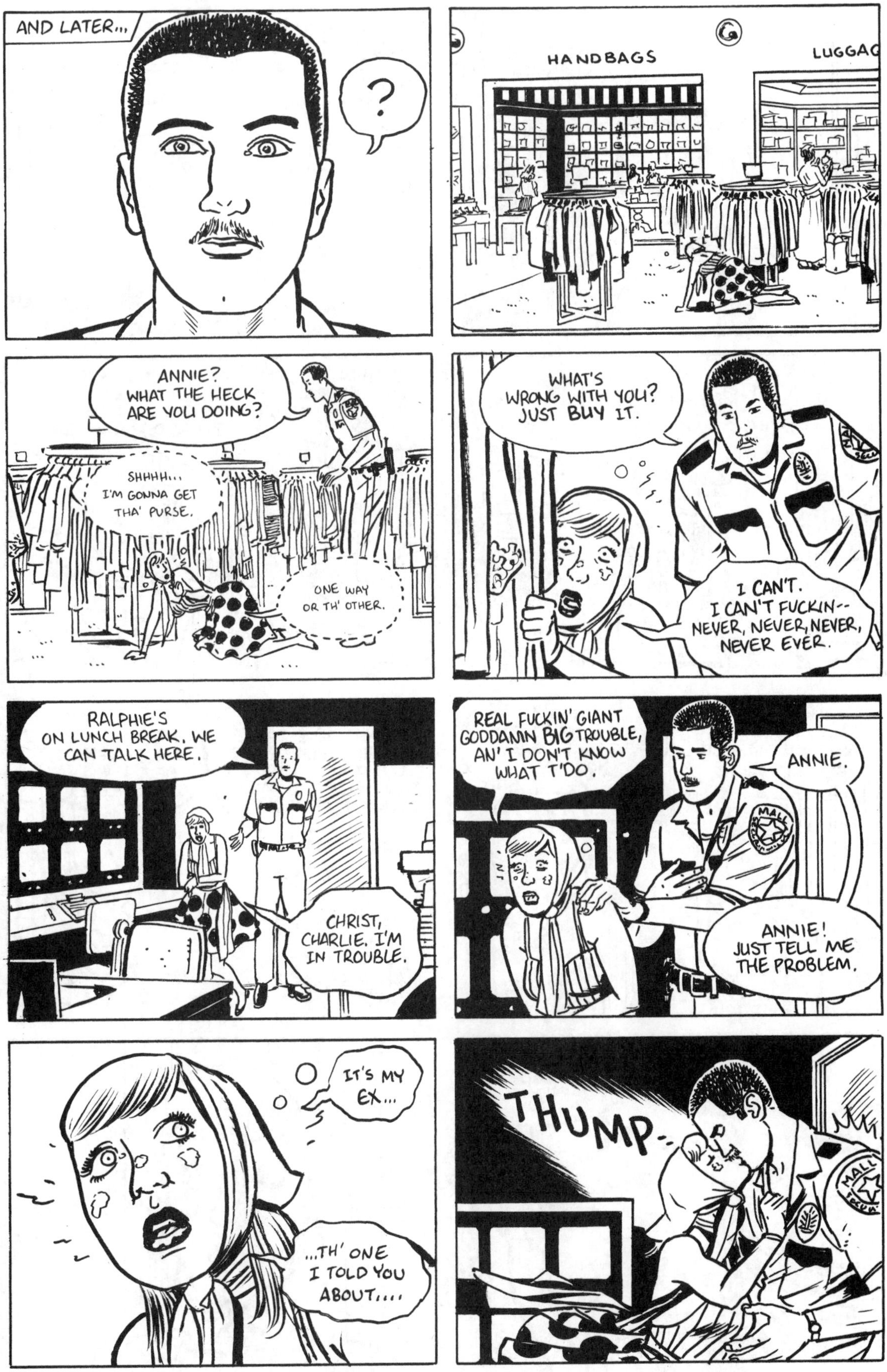
AND LATER...
?
HANDBAGS
LUGGAG
ANNIE? WHAT THE HECK ARE YOU DOING?
SHHHH... I'M GONNA GET THA' PURSE.
ONE WAY OR TH' OTHER.
WHAT'S WRONG WITH YOU? JUST BUY IT.
I CAN'T. I CAN'T FUCKIN-- NEVER, NEVER, NEVER, NEVER EVER.
RALPHIE'S ON LUNCH BREAK. WE CAN TALK HERE.
CHRIST, CHARLIE. I'M IN TROUBLE.
REAL FUCKIN' GIANT GODDAMN BIG TROUBLE, AN' I DON'T KNOW WHAT T'DO.
ANNIE.
ANNIE! JUST TELL ME THE PROBLEM.
IT'S MY EX...
...TH' ONE I TOLD YOU ABOUT....
THUMP

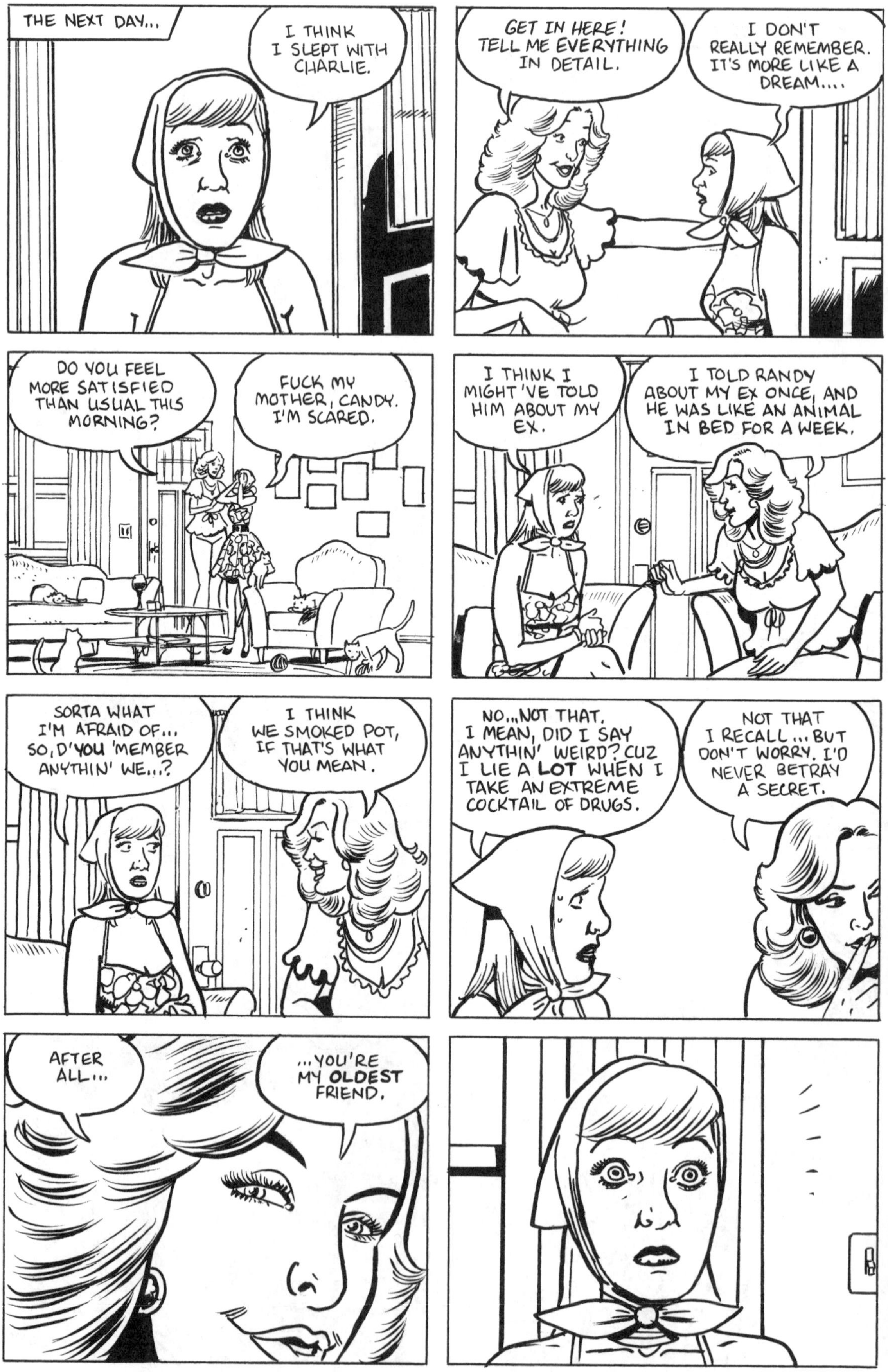
THE NEXT DAY...
I THINK I SLEPT WITH CHARLIE.
GET IN HERE! TELL ME EVERYTHING IN DETAIL.
I DON'T REALLY REMEMBER. IT'S MORE LIKE A DREAM....
DO YOU FEEL MORE SATISFIED THAN USUAL THIS MORNING?
FUCK MY MOTHER, CANDY. I'M SCARED.
I THINK I MIGHT'VE TOLD HIM ABOUT MY EX.
I TOLD RANDY ABOUT MY EX ONCE, AND HE WAS LIKE AN ANIMAL IN BED FOR A WEEK.
SORTA WHAT I'M AFRAID OF... SO, D'YOU 'MEMBER ANYTHIN' WE...?
I THINK WE SMOKED POT, IF THAT'S WHAT YOU MEAN.
NO...NOT THAT. I MEAN, DID I SAY ANYTHIN' WEIRD? CUZ I LIE A LOT WHEN I TAKE AN EXTREME COCKTAIL OF DRUGS.
NOT THAT I RECALL... BUT DON'T WORRY. I'D NEVER BETRAY A SECRET.
AFTER ALL...
...YOU'RE MY OLDEST FRIEND.

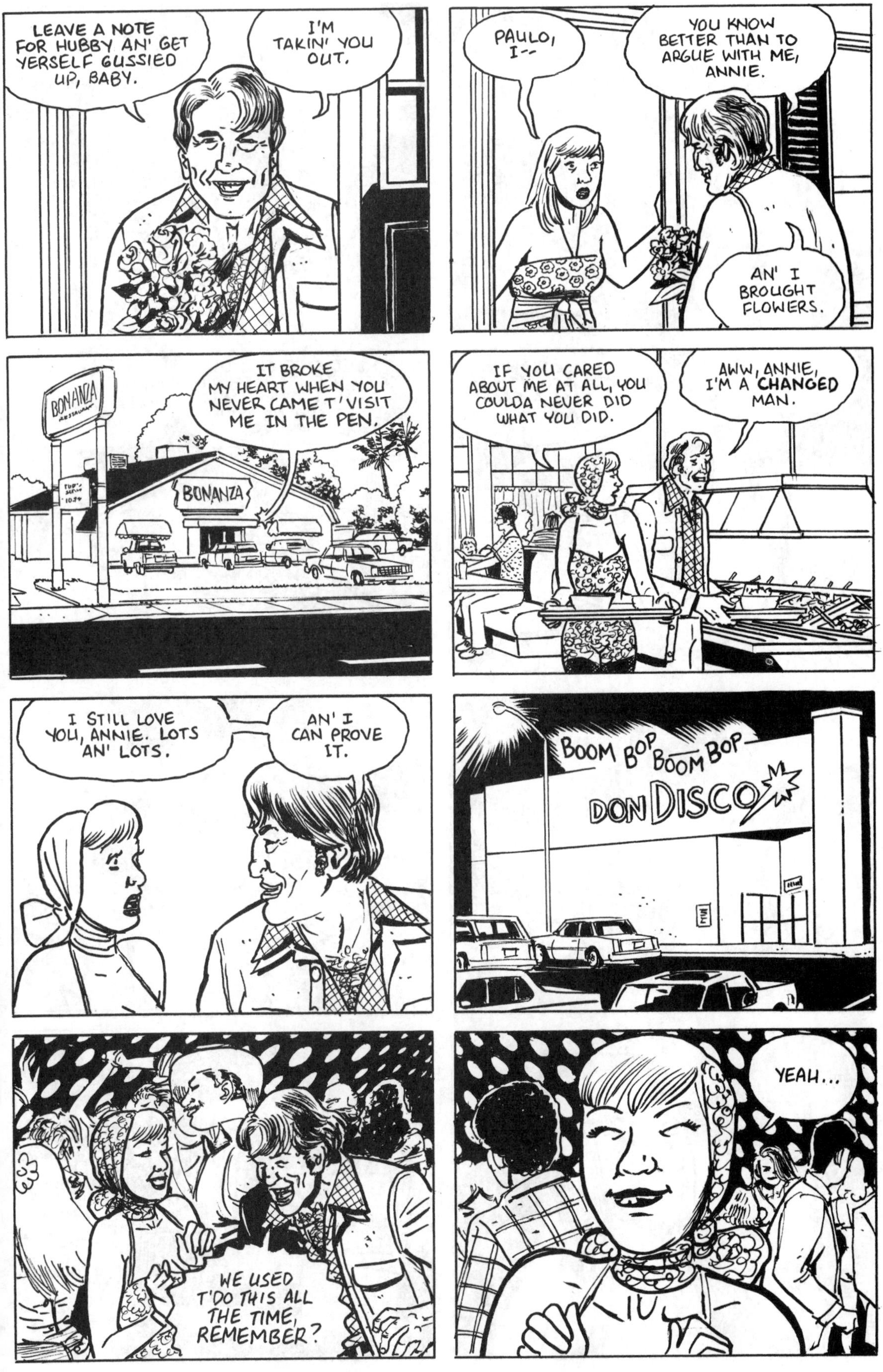
LEAVE A NOTE FOR HUBBY AN' GET YERSELF GUSSIED UP, BABY.
I'M TAKIN' YOU OUT.
PAULO, I--
YOU KNOW BETTER THAN TO ARGUE WITH ME, ANNIE.
AN' I BROUGHT FLOWERS.
BONANZA
BONANZA
IT BROKE MY HEART WHEN YOU NEVER CAME T'VISIT ME IN THE PEN.
IF YOU CARED ABOUT ME AT ALL, YOU COULDA NEVER DID WHAT YOU DID.
AWW, ANNIE, I'M A **CHANGED** MAN.
I STILL LOVE YOU, ANNIE. LOTS AN' LOTS.
AN' I CAN PROVE IT.
BOOM BOP BOOM BOP
DON DISCO
WE USED T'DO THIS ALL THE TIME, REMEMBER?
YEAH...

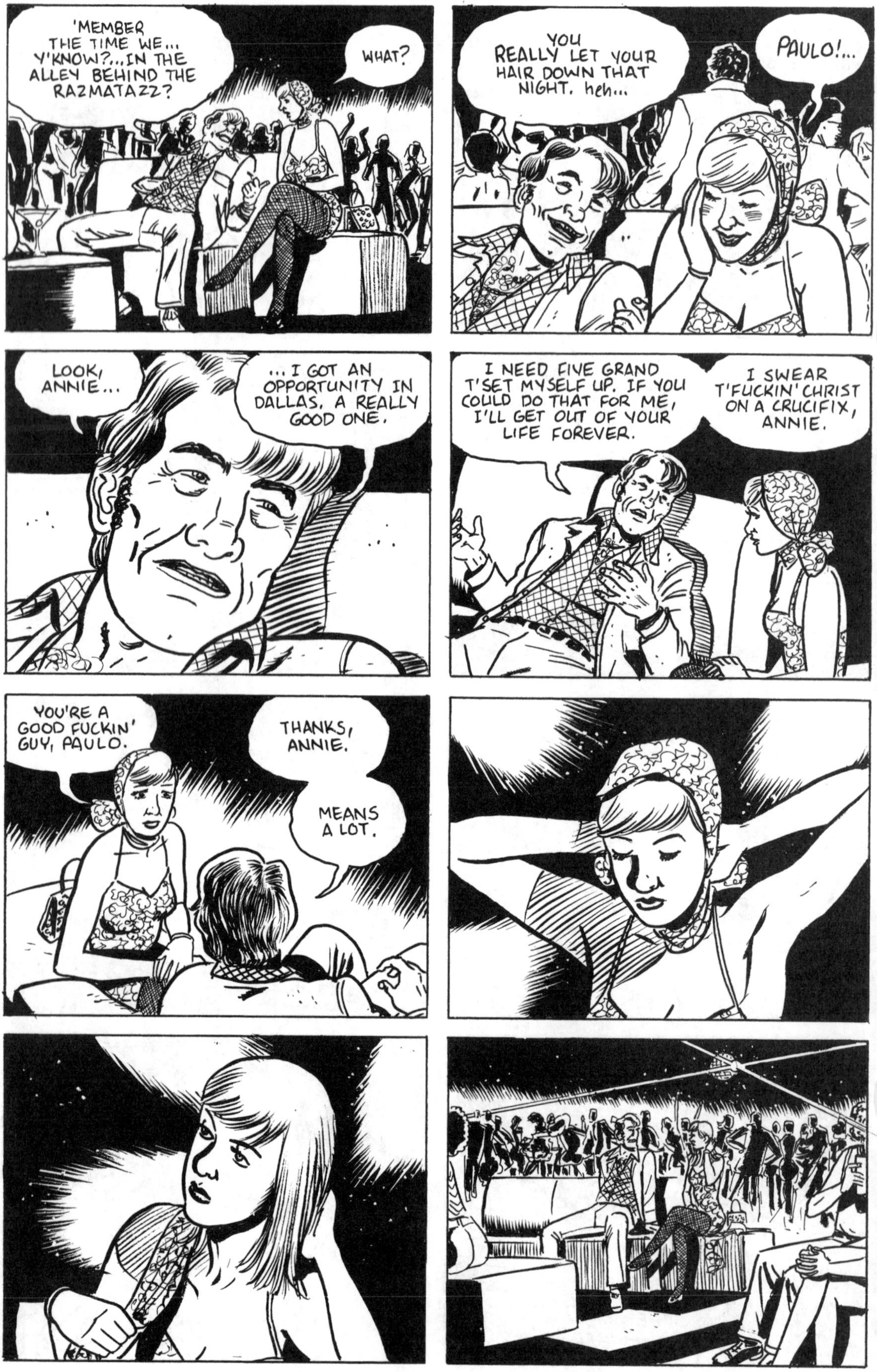
'MEMBER THE TIME WE... Y'KNOW?...IN THE ALLEY BEHIND THE RAZMATAZZ?
WHAT?
YOU REALLY LET YOUR HAIR DOWN THAT NIGHT. heh...
PAULO!...
LOOK, ANNIE...
...I GOT AN OPPORTUNITY IN DALLAS. A REALLY GOOD ONE.
I NEED FIVE GRAND T'SET MYSELF UP. IF YOU COULD DO THAT FOR ME, I'LL GET OUT OF YOUR LIFE FOREVER.
I SWEAR T'FUCKIN' CHRIST ON A CRUCIFIX, ANNIE.
YOU'RE A GOOD FUCKIN' GUY, PAULO.
THANKS, ANNIE.
MEANS A LOT.

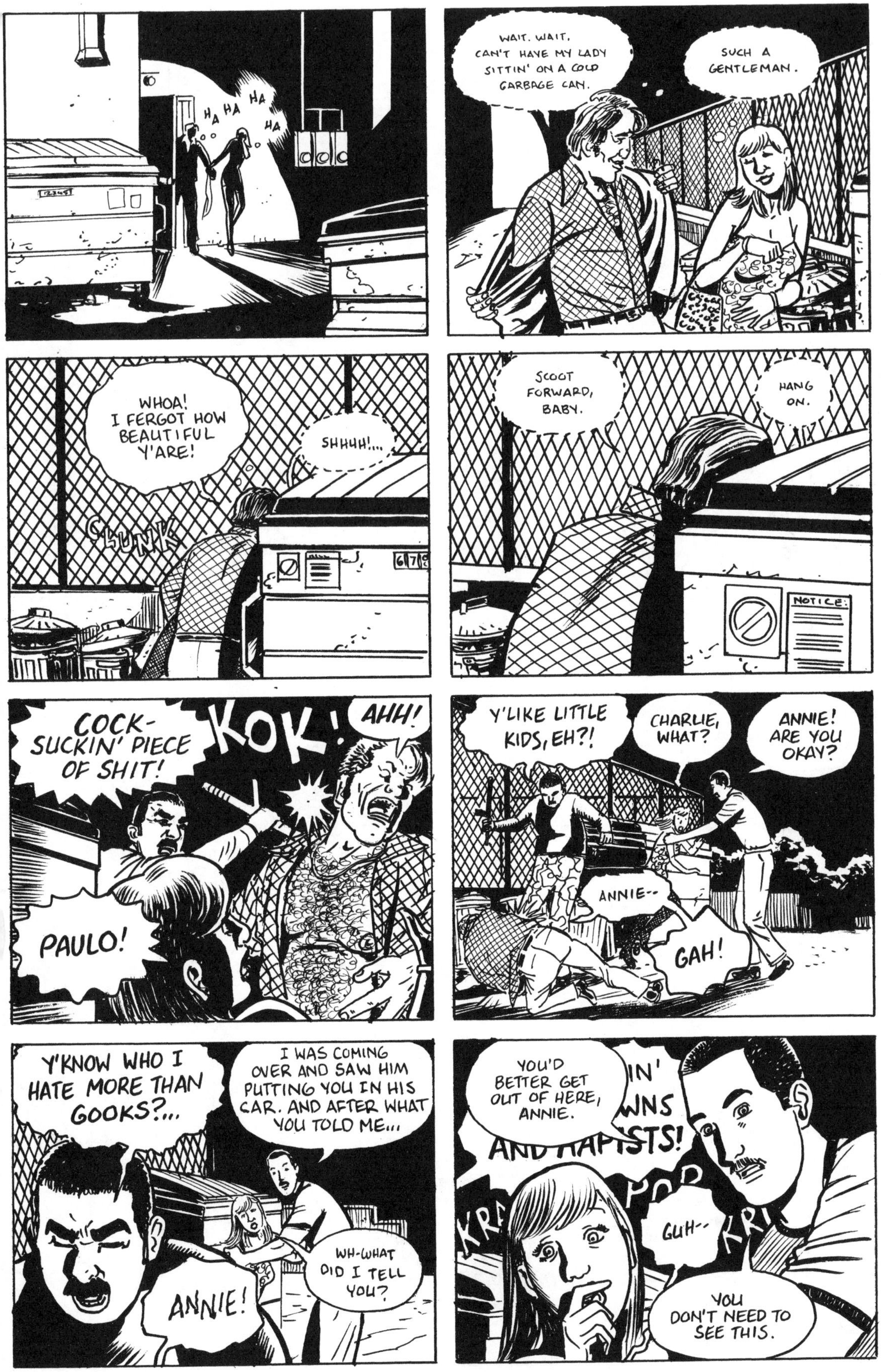

HA HA HA HA HA
WAIT. WAIT. CAN'T HAVE MY LADY SITTIN' ON A COLD GARBAGE CAN.
SUCH A GENTLEMAN.
WHOA! I FERGOT HOW BEAUTIFUL Y'ARE!
SHHHH!...
CLUNK
SCOOT FORWARD, BABY.
HANG ON.
COCK-SUCKIN' PIECE OF SHIT!
KOK!
AHH!
PAULO!
Y'LIKE LITTLE KIDS, EH?!
CHARLIE, WHAT?
ANNIE! ARE YOU OKAY?
ANNIE--
GAH!
Y'KNOW WHO I HATE MORE THAN GOOKS?...
I WAS COMING OVER AND SAW HIM PUTTING YOU IN HIS CAR. AND AFTER WHAT YOU TOLD ME...
ANNIE!
WH-WHAT DID I TELL YOU?
YOU'D BETTER GET OUT OF HERE, ANNIE.
GUH--
YOU DON'T NEED TO SEE THIS.

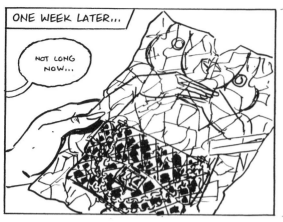

ONE WEEK LATER...

NOT LONG NOW...

...I GUESS.

ANNIE, IT'S SO GOOD TO SEE YOU. HOW ARE YOU DOING?

I'M GETTIN' BY, CHARLIE.

LOOK, THE LESS YOU KNOW THE BETTER, BUT REST EASY. YOU WON'T **EVER** HAVE TO WORRY ABOUT THAT GUY AGAIN.

CHARLIE... YOU REALLY SHOULDN'T'VE. REALLY...

I **LOVE** YOU, ANNIE.

I'D DO ANYTHING FOR YOU.

OH! RALPHIE GOT TIPPED THAT THE COPS ARE ON TO US.

NOW, I DON'T WANT YOU TO WORRY. NOTHING IS GOING TO HAPPEN, AND I'D TAKE THE FALL BEFORE I LET ANY-THING HAPPEN TO YOU, BUT IT'S BEST YOU STEP AWAY FOR A WHILE. A SILLY PURSE AIN'T WORTH JAIL.

heh... YEAH...

WHAT ABOUT YOU, CHARLIE?

WE'LL SHUT THINGS DOWN TILL THE HEAT COOLS. WE MOVED OUR STASH TO THE BASEMENT OF MY GREAT GRAMMY'S NURSING HOME WHERE THE COPS'LL **NEVER** FIND IT.

AND SO...

HELLO, POLICE...?

28

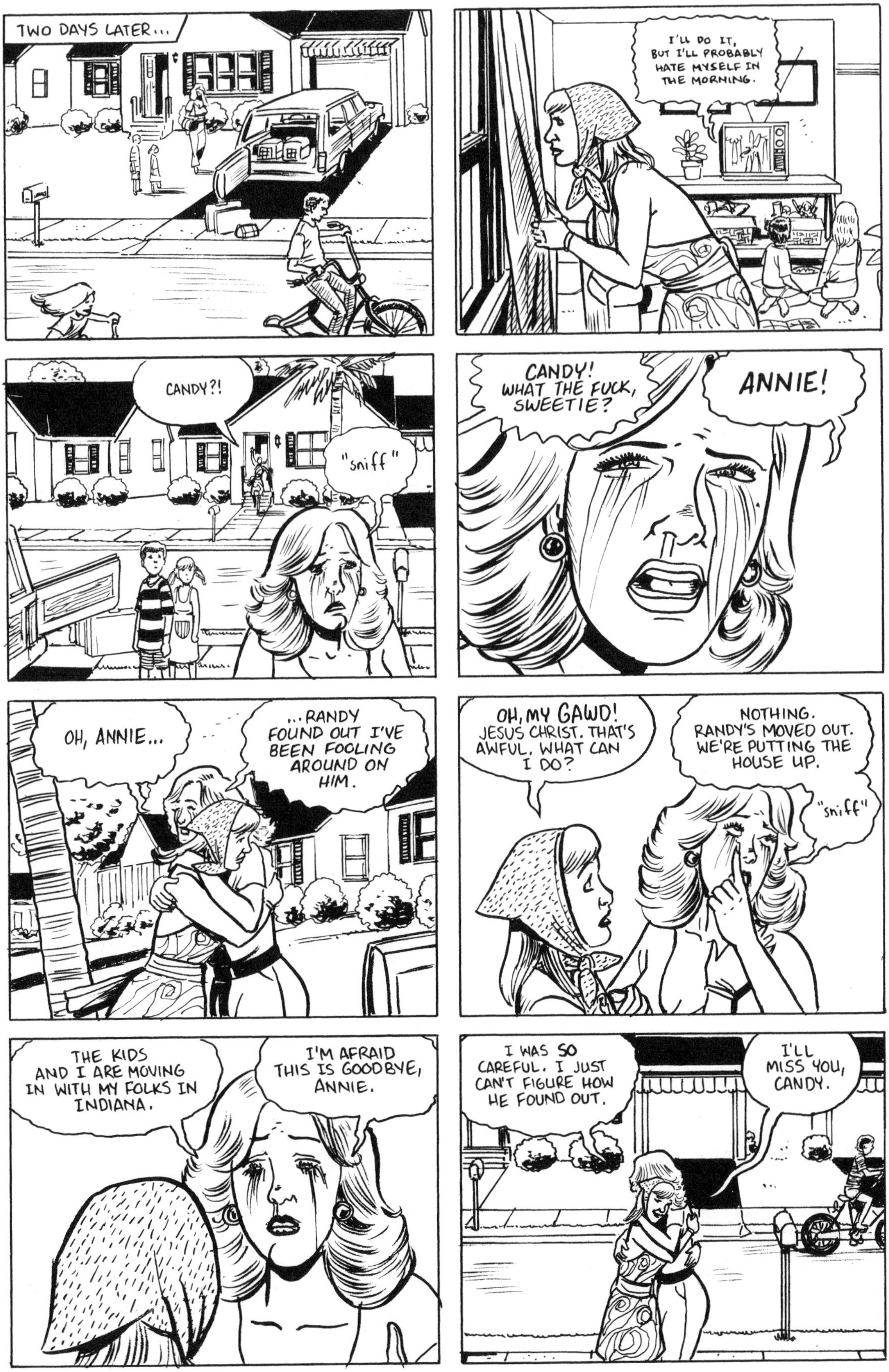
TWO DAYS LATER...
I'LL DO IT, BUT I'LL PROBABLY HATE MYSELF IN THE MORNING.
CANDY?!
"sniff"
CANDY! WHAT THE FUCK, SWEETIE?
ANNIE!
OH, ANNIE...
...RANDY FOUND OUT I'VE BEEN FOOLING AROUND ON HIM.
OH, MY GAWD! JESUS CHRIST. THAT'S AWFUL. WHAT CAN I DO?
NOTHING. RANDY'S MOVED OUT. WE'RE PUTTING THE HOUSE UP.
"sniff"
THE KIDS AND I ARE MOVING IN WITH MY FOLKS IN INDIANA.
I'M AFRAID THIS IS GOODBYE, ANNIE.
I WAS SO CAREFUL. I JUST CAN'T FIGURE HOW HE FOUND OUT.
I'LL MISS YOU, CANDY.

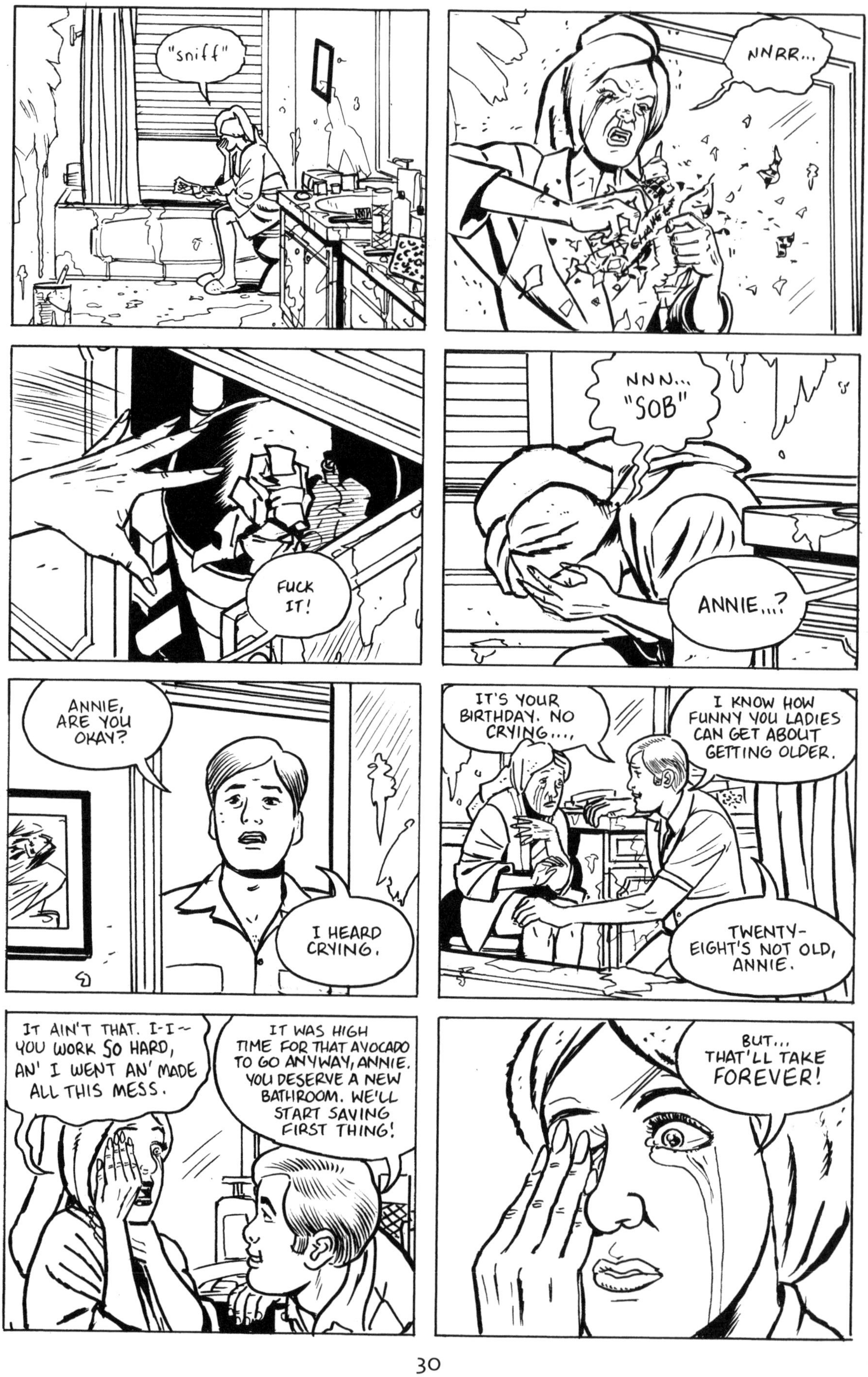
"sniff"
NNRR...
FUCK IT!
NNN... "SOB"
ANNIE...?
ANNIE, ARE YOU OKAY?
I HEARD CRYING.
IT'S YOUR BIRTHDAY. NO CRYING...,
I KNOW HOW FUNNY YOU LADIES CAN GET ABOUT GETTING OLDER.
TWENTY-EIGHT'S NOT OLD, ANNIE.
IT AIN'T THAT. I-I-- YOU WORK SO HARD, AN' I WENT AN' MADE ALL THIS MESS.
IT WAS HIGH TIME FOR THAT AVOCADO TO GO ANYWAY, ANNIE. YOU DESERVE A NEW BATHROOM. WE'LL START SAVING FIRST THING!
BUT... THAT'LL TAKE FOREVER!

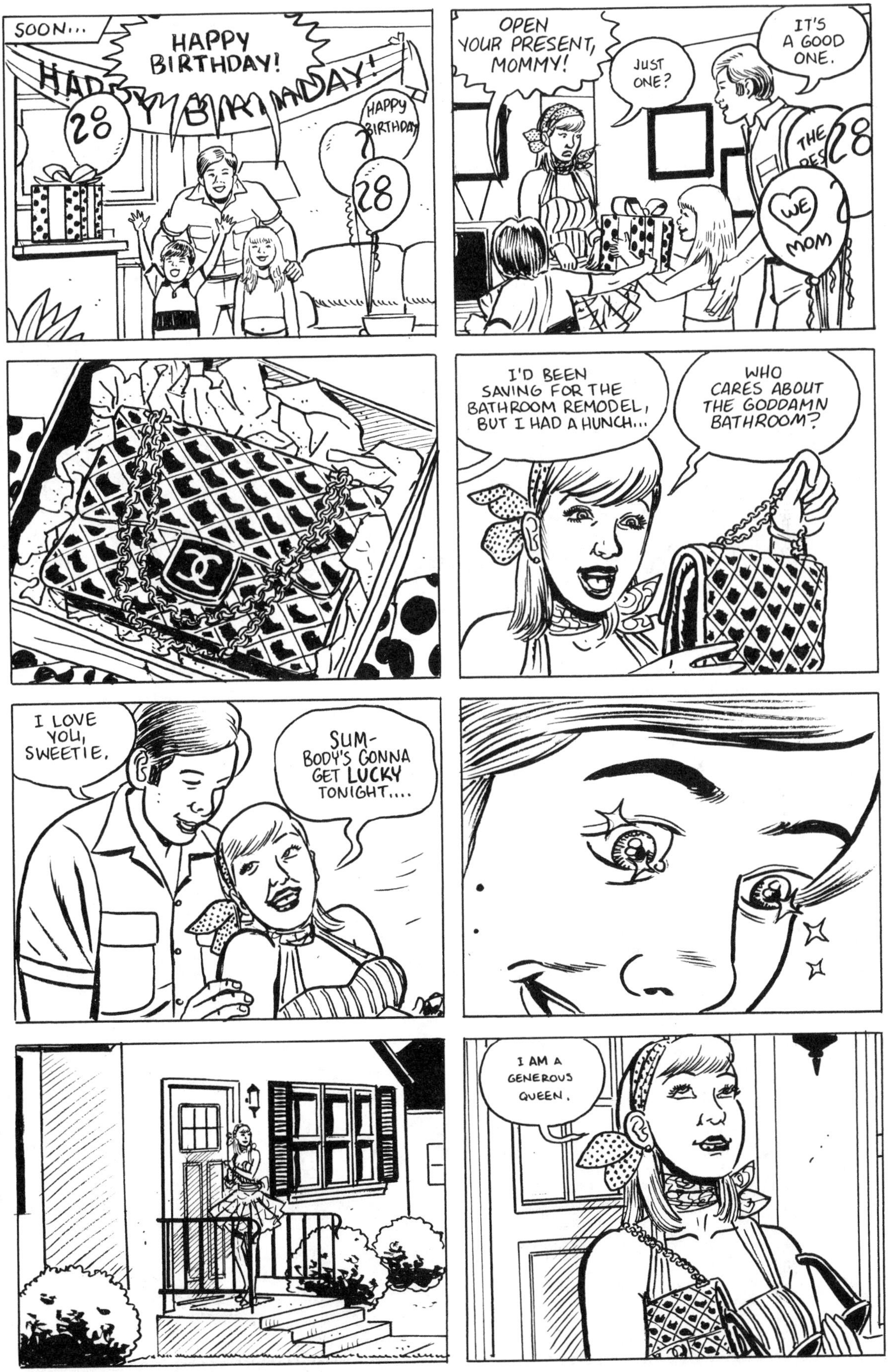
SOON...
HAPPY BIRTHDAY!
HAPPY BIRTHDAY!
28
HAPPY BIRTHDAY
28
OPEN YOUR PRESENT, MOMMY!
JUST ONE?
IT'S A GOOD ONE.
28
WE MOM
I'D BEEN SAVING FOR THE BATHROOM REMODEL, BUT I HAD A HUNCH...
WHO CARES ABOUT THE GODDAMN BATHROOM?
I LOVE YOU, SWEETIE.
SUM-BODY'S GONNA GET LUCKY TONIGHT....
I AM A GENEROUS QUEEN.

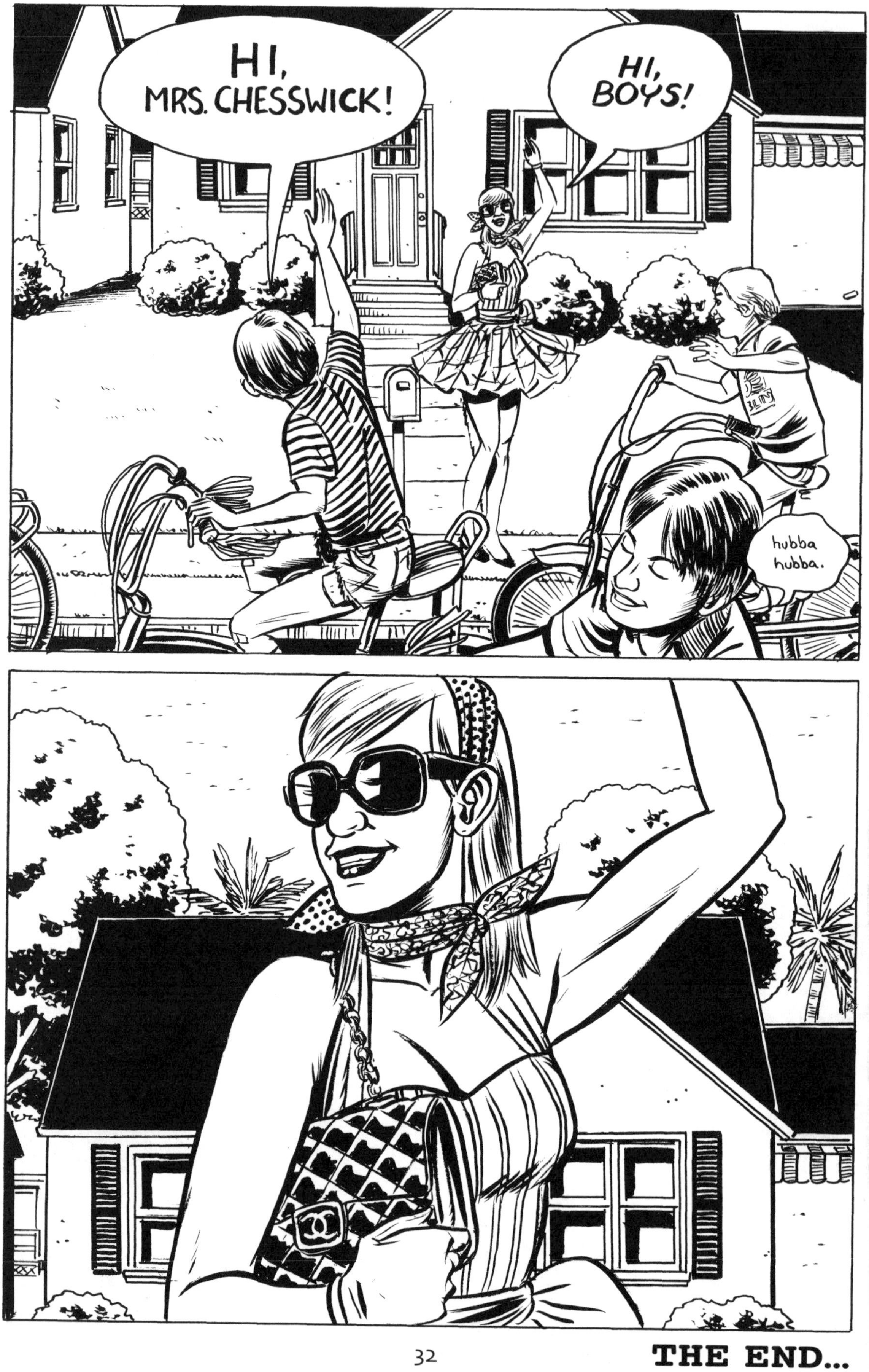
HI, MRS. CHESSWICK!
HI, BOYS!
hubba hubba.

THE END...

2
"THE BROKEN HAND OF FATE"

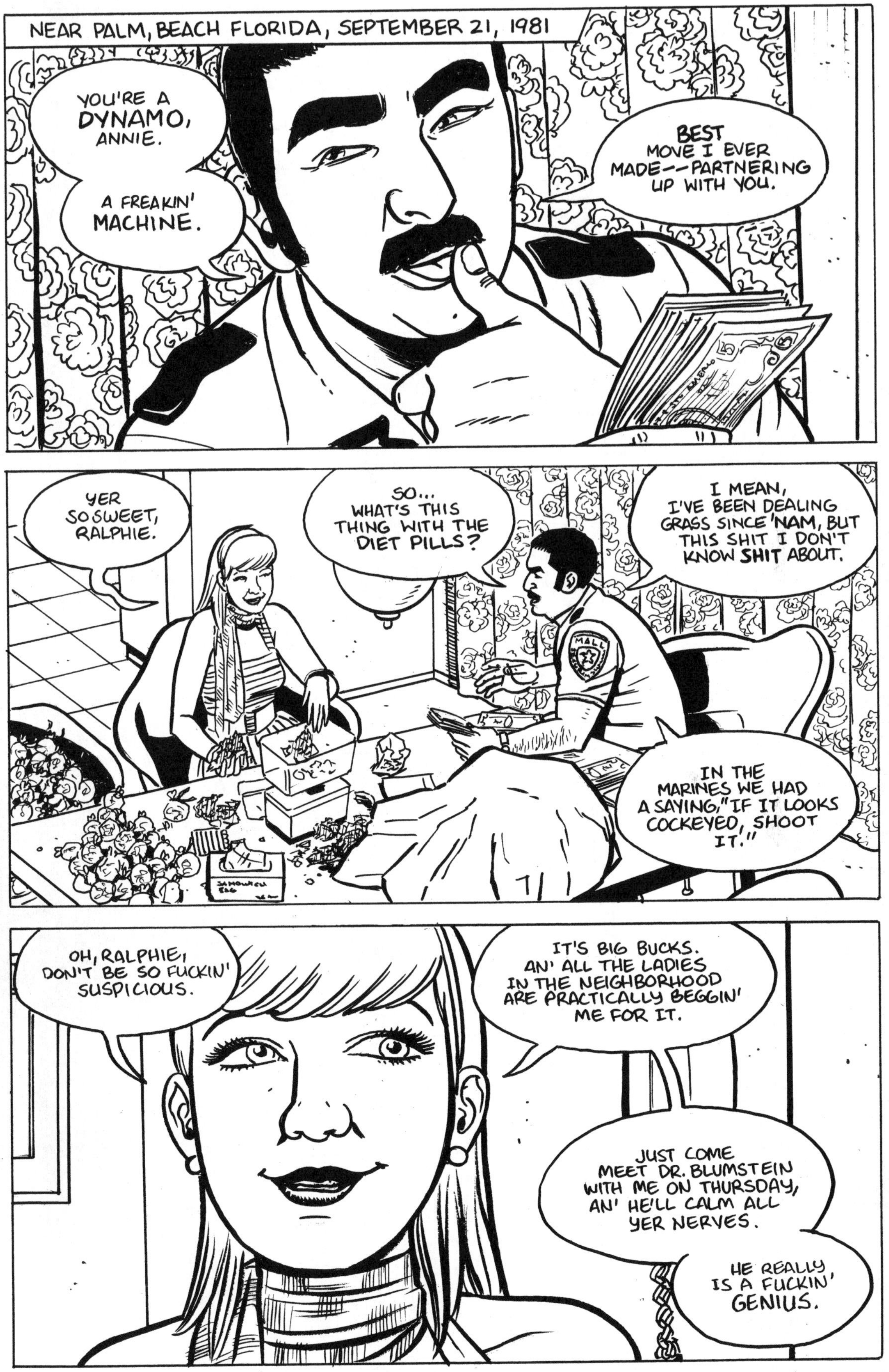
NEAR PALM, BEACH FLORIDA, SEPTEMBER 21, 1981
YOU'RE A DYNAMO, ANNIE.
A FREAKIN' MACHINE.
BEST MOVE I EVER MADE--PARTNERING UP WITH YOU.
YER SO SWEET, RALPHIE.
SO... WHAT'S THIS THING WITH THE DIET PILLS?
I MEAN, I'VE BEEN DEALING GRASS SINCE 'NAM, BUT THIS SHIT I DON'T KNOW SHIT ABOUT.
IN THE MARINES WE HAD A SAYING, "IF IT LOOKS COCKEYED, SHOOT IT."
OH, RALPHIE, DON'T BE SO FUCKIN' SUSPICIOUS.
IT'S BIG BUCKS. AN' ALL THE LADIES IN THE NEIGHBORHOOD ARE PRACTICALLY BEGGIN' ME FOR IT.
JUST COME MEET DR. BLUMSTEIN WITH ME ON THURSDAY, AN' HE'LL CALM ALL YER NERVES.
HE REALLY IS A FUCKIN' GENIUS.

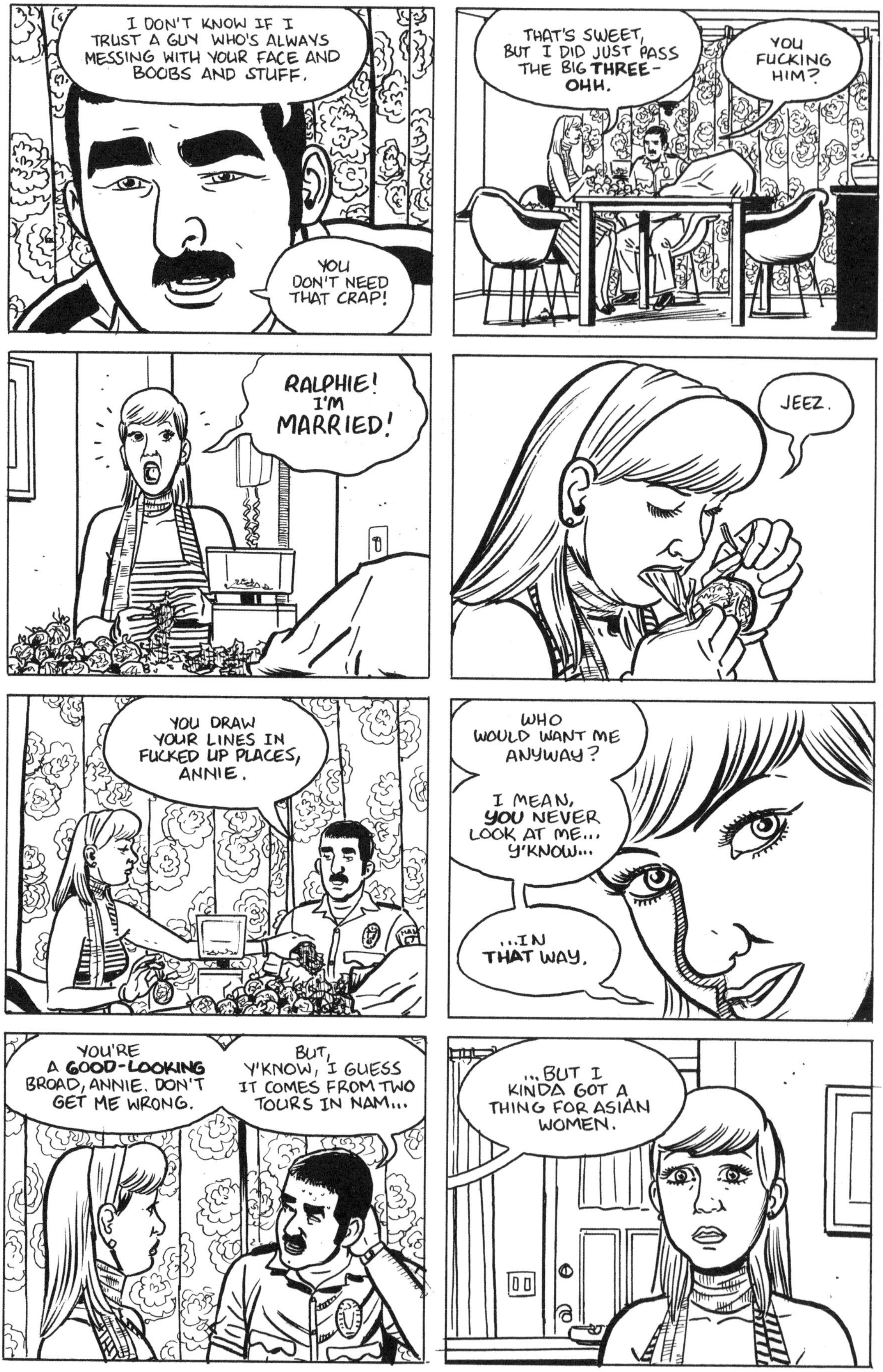
I DON'T KNOW IF I TRUST A GUY WHO'S ALWAYS MESSING WITH YOUR FACE AND BOOBS AND STUFF.
YOU DON'T NEED THAT CRAP!
THAT'S SWEET, BUT I DID JUST PASS THE BIG **THREE-OHH.**
YOU FUCKING HIM?
RALPHIE! I'M MARRIED!
JEEZ.
YOU DRAW YOUR LINES IN FUCKED UP PLACES, ANNIE.
WHO WOULD WANT ME ANYWAY?
I MEAN, **YOU** NEVER LOOK AT ME... Y'KNOW...
...IN **THAT** WAY.
YOU'RE A **GOOD-LOOKING** BROAD, ANNIE. DON'T GET ME WRONG.
BUT, Y'KNOW, I GUESS IT COMES FROM TWO TOURS IN NAM...
...BUT I KINDA GOT A THING FOR ASIAN WOMEN.

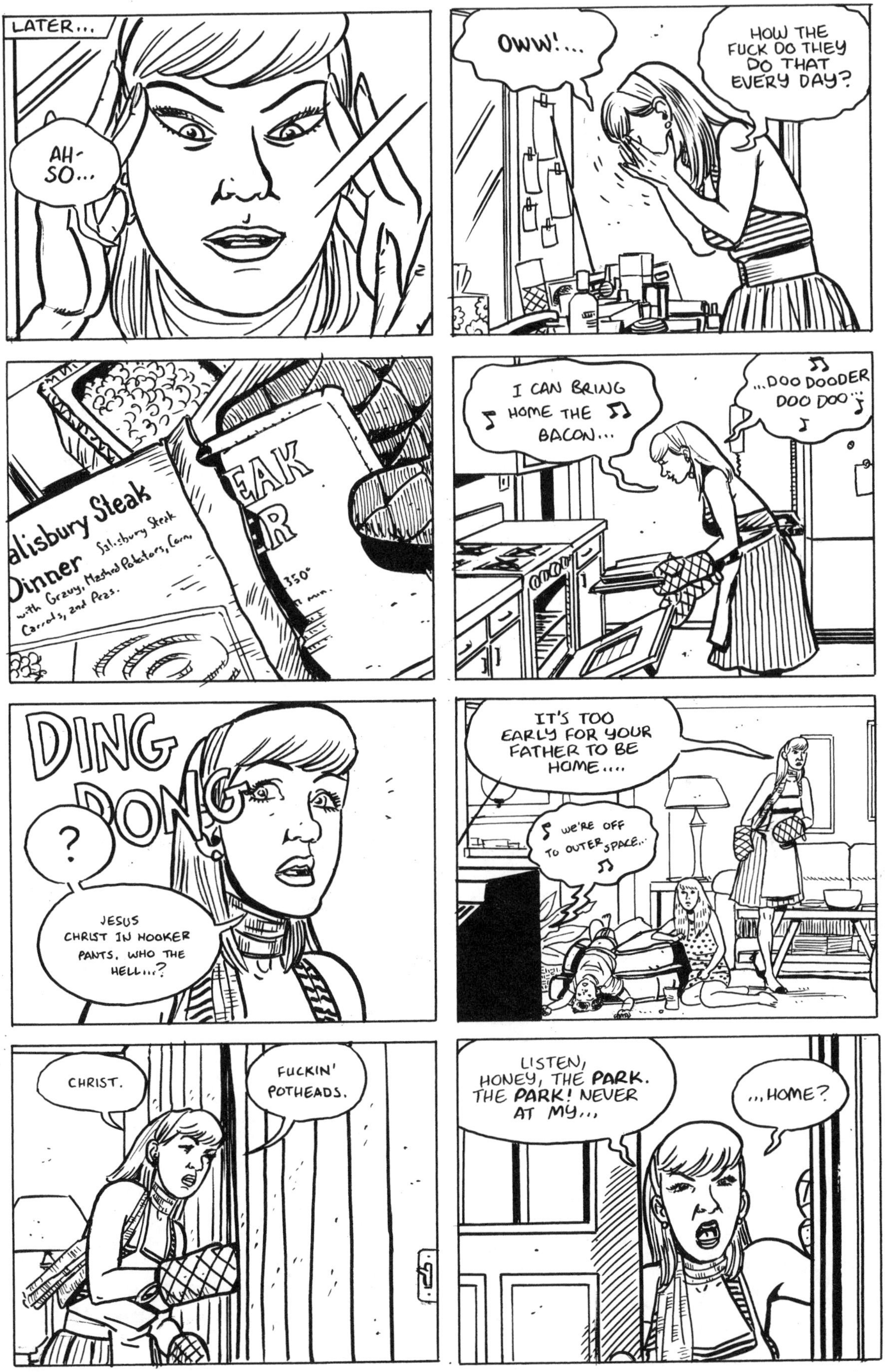
LATER...
AH-SO...
OWW!...
HOW THE FUCK DO THEY DO THAT EVERY DAY?
Salisbury Steak Dinner Salisbury Steak with Gravy, Mashed Potatoes, Corn, Carrots, and Peas.
EAK
R
350°
I CAN BRING HOME THE BACON...
...DOO DOODER DOO DOO...
DING DONG
?
JESUS CHRIST IN HOOKER PANTS. WHO THE HELL...?
IT'S TOO EARLY FOR YOUR FATHER TO BE HOME....
WE'RE OFF TO OUTER SPACE...
CHRIST.
FUCKIN' POTHEADS.
LISTEN, HONEY, THE PARK. THE PARK! NEVER AT MY...
...HOME?

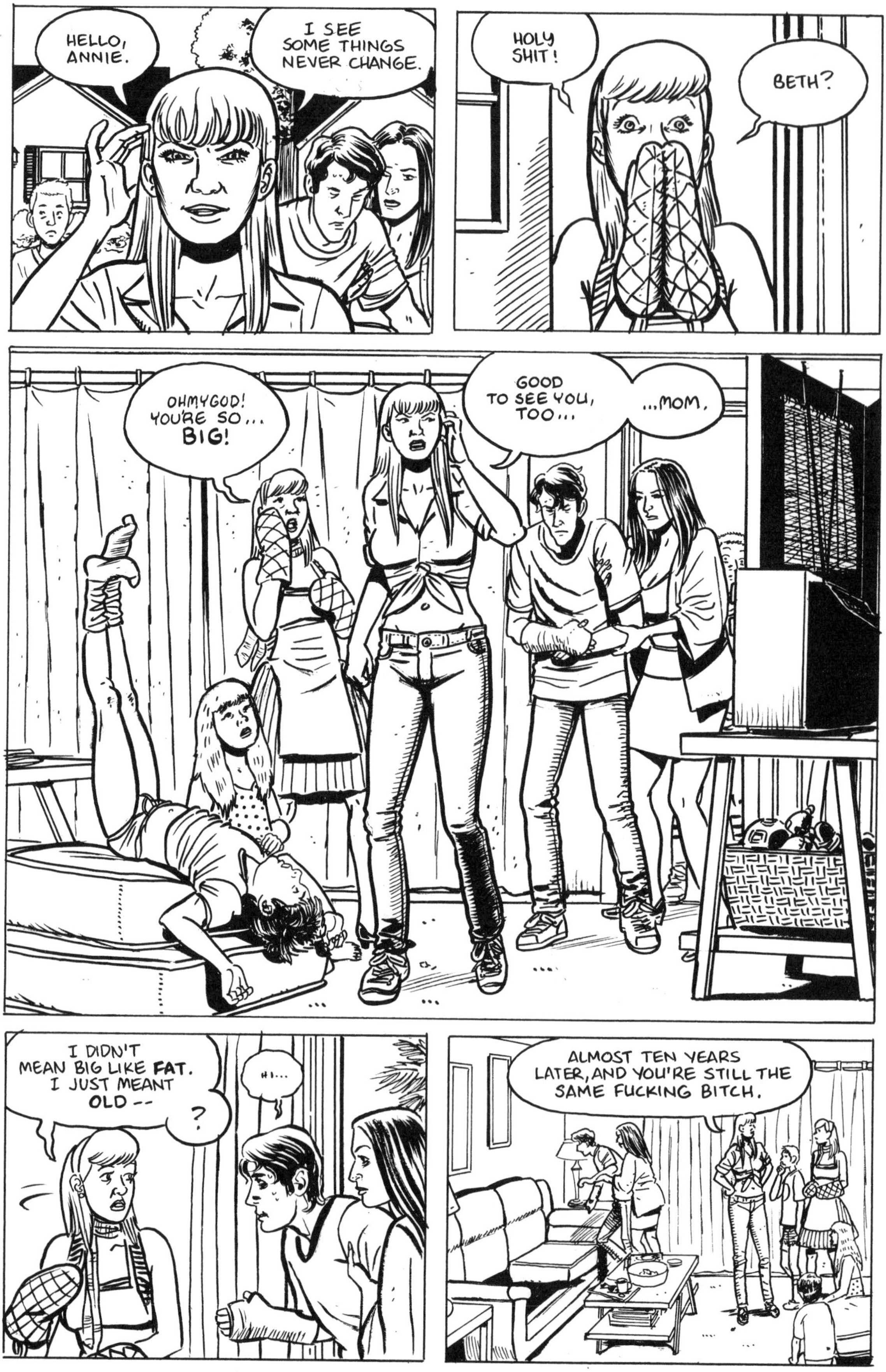
HELLO, ANNIE.
I SEE SOME THINGS NEVER CHANGE.
HOLY SHIT!
BETH?
OHMYGOD! YOU'RE SO... BIG!
GOOD TO SEE YOU, TOO...
...MOM.
I DIDN'T MEAN BIG LIKE FAT. I JUST MEANT OLD --
?
HI...
ALMOST TEN YEARS LATER, AND YOU'RE STILL THE SAME FUCKING BITCH.

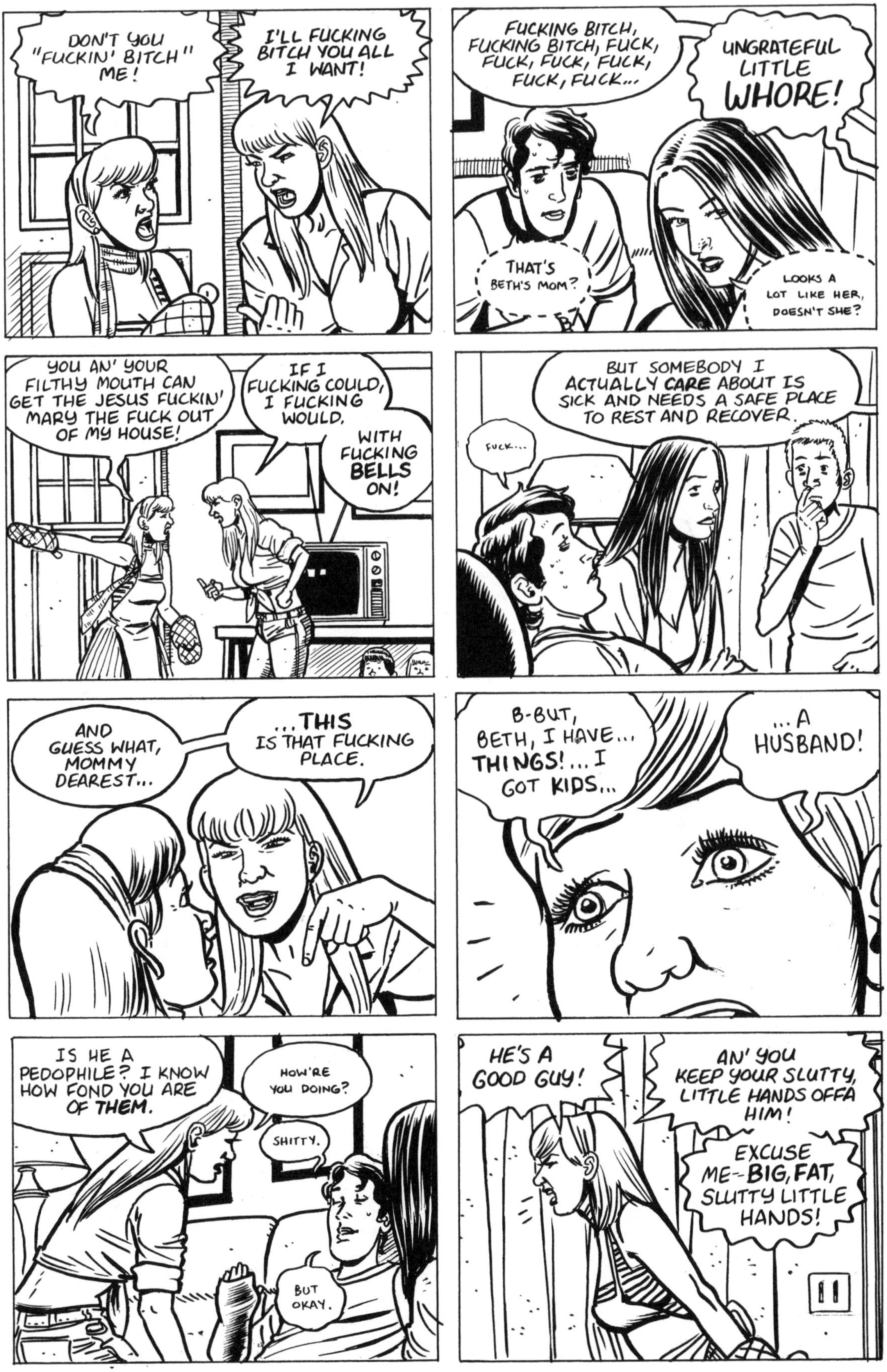
DON'T YOU "FUCKIN' BITCH" ME!
I'LL FUCKING BITCH YOU ALL I WANT!
FUCKING BITCH, FUCKING BITCH, FUCK, FUCK, FUCK, FUCK, FUCK, FUCK...
UNGRATEFUL LITTLE WHORE!
THAT'S BETH'S MOM?
LOOKS A LOT LIKE HER, DOESN'T SHE?
YOU AN' YOUR FILTHY MOUTH CAN GET THE JESUS FUCKIN' MARY THE FUCK OUT OF MY HOUSE!
IF I FUCKING COULD, I FUCKING WOULD.
WITH FUCKING BELLS ON!
BUT SOMEBODY I ACTUALLY CARE ABOUT IS SICK AND NEEDS A SAFE PLACE TO REST AND RECOVER.
FUCK...
AND GUESS WHAT, MOMMY DEAREST...
...THIS IS THAT FUCKING PLACE.
B-BUT, BETH, I HAVE... THINGS!... I GOT KIDS...
...A HUSBAND!
IS HE A PEDOPHILE? I KNOW HOW FOND YOU ARE OF THEM.
HOW'RE YOU DOING?
SHITTY.
BUT OKAY.
HE'S A GOOD GUY!
AN' YOU KEEP YOUR SLUTTY, LITTLE HANDS OFFA HIM!
EXCUSE ME--BIG, FAT, SLUTTY LITTLE HANDS!

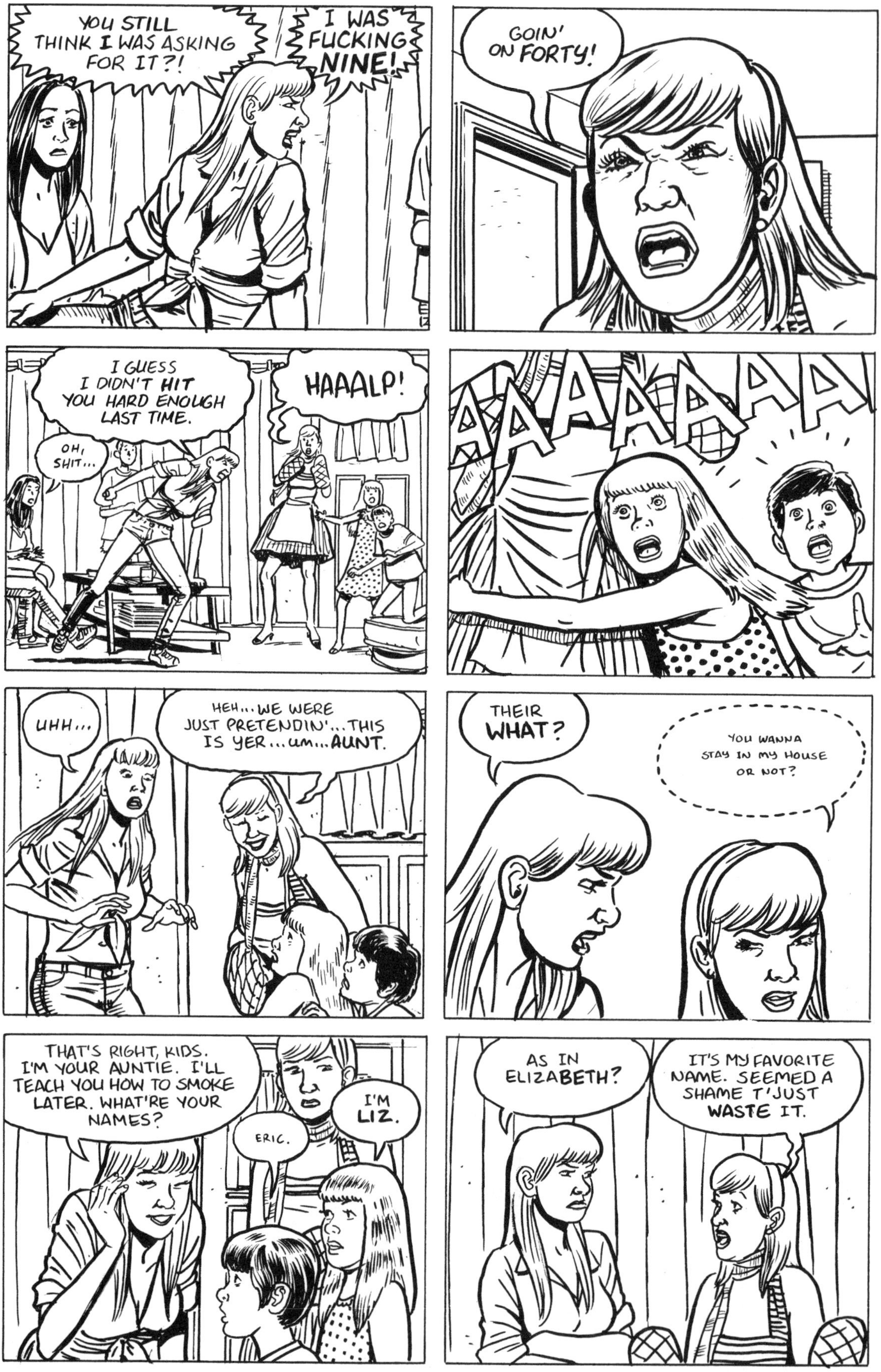
YOU STILL THINK I WAS ASKING FOR IT?!
I WAS FUCKING NINE!
GOIN' ON FORTY!
I GUESS I DIDN'T HIT YOU HARD ENOUGH LAST TIME.
OH, SHIT...
HAAALP!
AAAAAAA
UHH...
HEH... WE WERE JUST PRETENDIN'... THIS IS YER... UM... AUNT.
THEIR WHAT?
YOU WANNA STAY IN MY HOUSE OR NOT?
THAT'S RIGHT, KIDS. I'M YOUR AUNTIE. I'LL TEACH YOU HOW TO SMOKE LATER. WHAT'RE YOUR NAMES?
ERIC.
I'M LIZ.
AS IN ELIZABETH?
IT'S MY FAVORITE NAME. SEEMED A SHAME T'JUST WASTE IT.

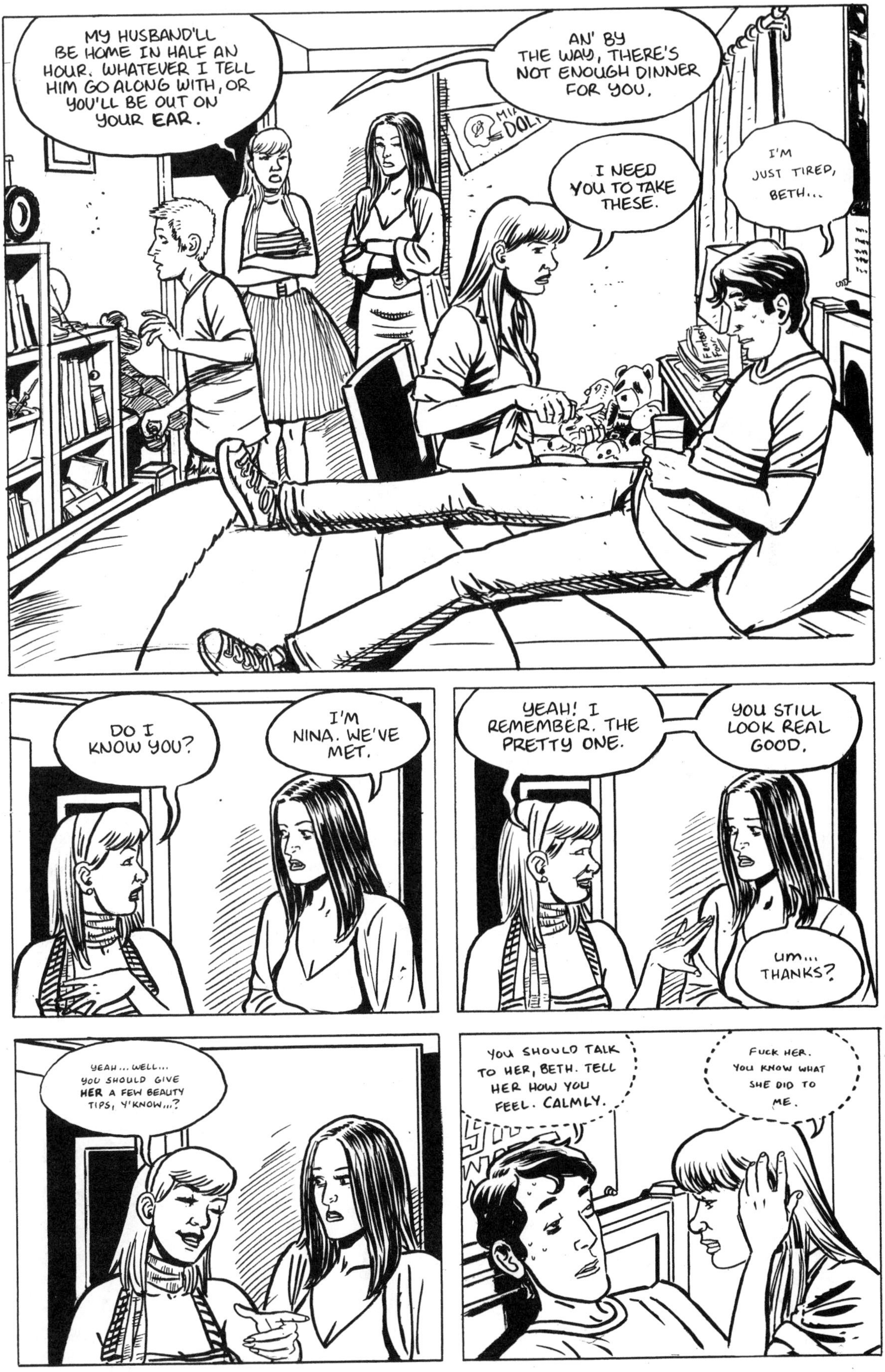
MY HUSBAND'LL BE HOME IN HALF AN HOUR. WHATEVER I TELL HIM GO ALONG WITH, OR YOU'LL BE OUT ON YOUR EAR.
AN' BY THE WAY, THERE'S NOT ENOUGH DINNER FOR YOU.
I NEED YOU TO TAKE THESE.
I'M JUST TIRED, BETH...
DO I KNOW YOU?
I'M NINA. WE'VE MET.
YEAH! I REMEMBER. THE PRETTY ONE.
YOU STILL LOOK REAL GOOD.
UM... THANKS?
YEAH... WELL... YOU SHOULD GIVE HER A FEW BEAUTY TIPS, Y'KNOW...?
YOU SHOULD TALK TO HER, BETH. TELL HER HOW YOU FEEL. CALMLY.
FUCK HER. YOU KNOW WHAT SHE DID TO ME.

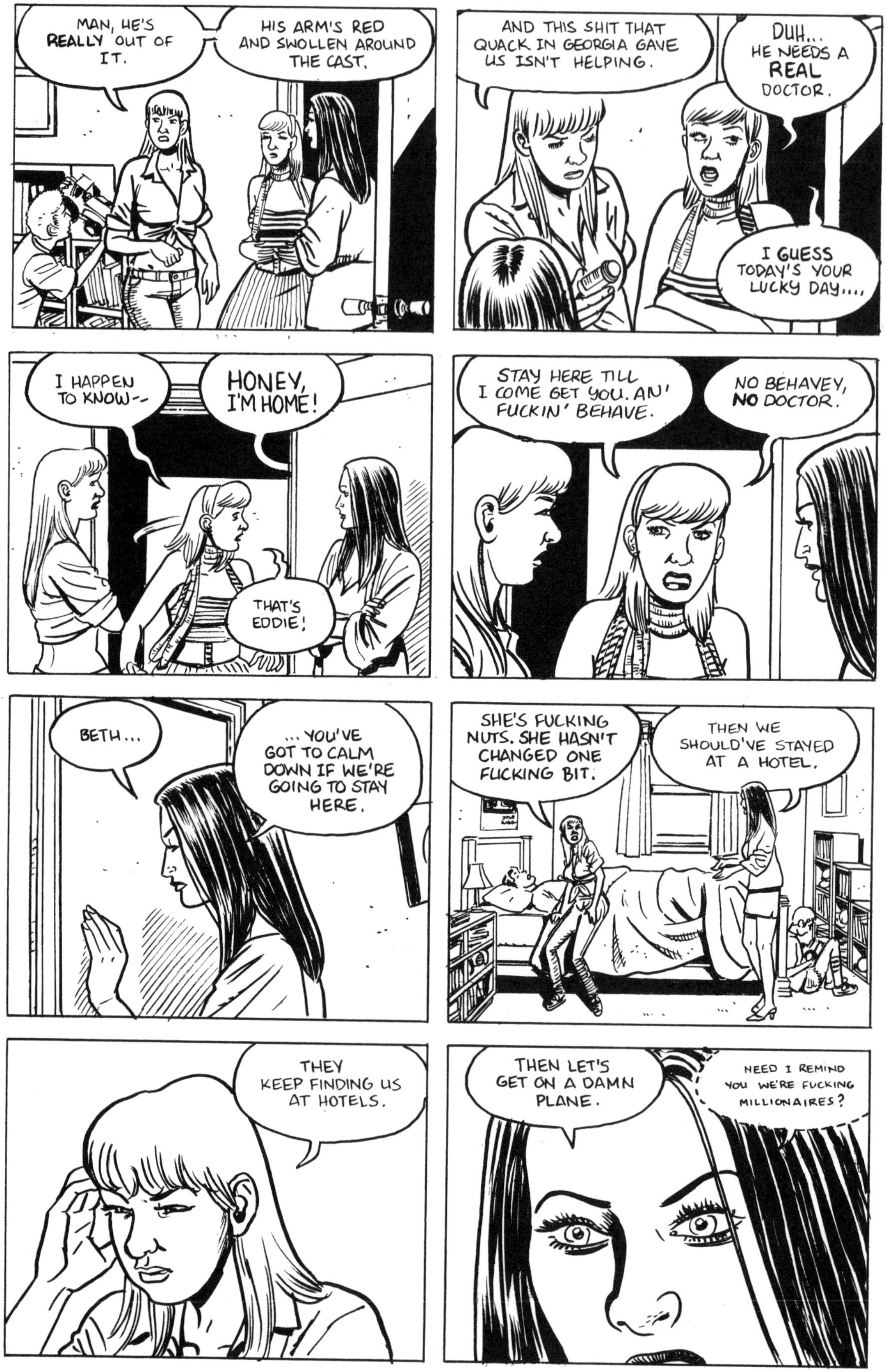
MAN, HE'S REALLY OUT OF IT.
HIS ARM'S RED AND SWOLLEN AROUND THE CAST.
AND THIS SHIT THAT QUACK IN GEORGIA GAVE US ISN'T HELPING.
DUH... HE NEEDS A REAL DOCTOR.
I GUESS TODAY'S YOUR LUCKY DAY....
I HAPPEN TO KNOW--
HONEY, I'M HOME!
THAT'S EDDIE!
STAY HERE TILL I COME GET YOU. AN' FUCKIN' BEHAVE.
NO BEHAVEY, NO DOCTOR.
BETH...
...YOU'VE GOT TO CALM DOWN IF WE'RE GOING TO STAY HERE.
SHE'S FUCKING NUTS. SHE HASN'T CHANGED ONE FUCKING BIT.
THEN WE SHOULD'VE STAYED AT A HOTEL.
THEY KEEP FINDING US AT HOTELS.
THEN LET'S GET ON A DAMN PLANE.
NEED I REMIND YOU WE'RE FUCKING MILLIONAIRES?

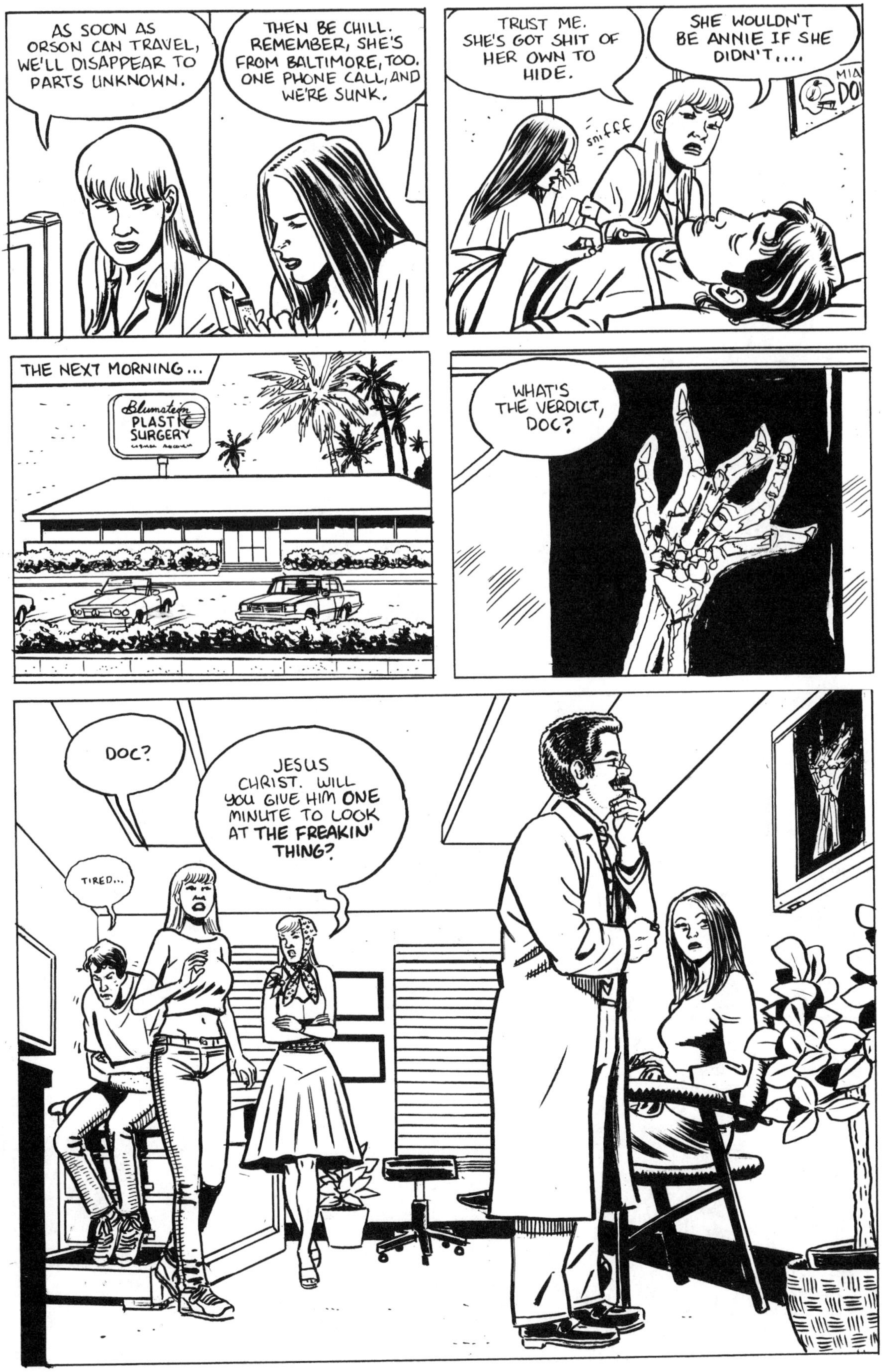
AS SOON AS ORSON CAN TRAVEL, WE'LL DISAPPEAR TO PARTS UNKNOWN.
THEN BE CHILL. REMEMBER, SHE'S FROM BALTIMORE, TOO. ONE PHONE CALL, AND WE'RE SUNK.
TRUST ME. SHE'S GOT SHIT OF HER OWN TO HIDE.
SHE WOULDN'T BE ANNIE IF SHE DIDN'T....
sniffff
THE NEXT MORNING...
Blumstein PLASTIC SURGERY
WHAT'S THE VERDICT, DOC?
DOC?
JESUS CHRIST. WILL YOU GIVE HIM ONE MINUTE TO LOOK AT THE FREAKIN' THING?
TIRED...

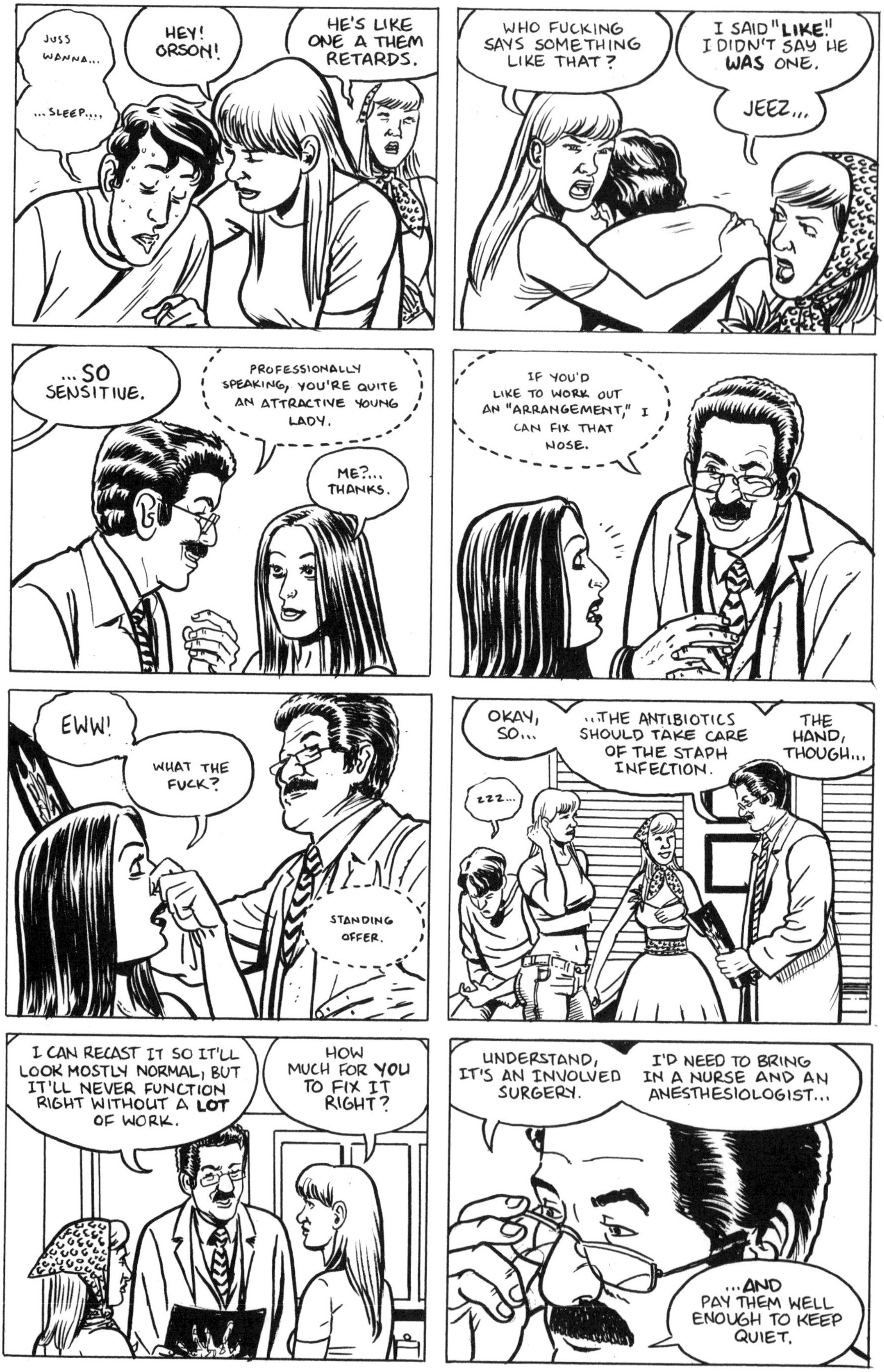
JUSS WANNA...
...SLEEP...
HEY! ORSON!
HE'S LIKE ONE A THEM RETARDS.
WHO FUCKING SAYS SOMETHING LIKE THAT?
I SAID "LIKE!" I DIDN'T SAY HE WAS ONE.
JEEZ...
...SO SENSITIVE.
PROFESSIONALLY SPEAKING, YOU'RE QUITE AN ATTRACTIVE YOUNG LADY.
ME?... THANKS.
IF YOU'D LIKE TO WORK OUT AN "ARRANGEMENT," I CAN FIX THAT NOSE.
EWW!
WHAT THE FUCK?
STANDING OFFER.
OKAY, SO...
...THE ANTIBIOTICS SHOULD TAKE CARE OF THE STAPH INFECTION.
THE HAND, THOUGH...
ZZZ...
I CAN RECAST IT SO IT'LL LOOK MOSTLY NORMAL, BUT IT'LL NEVER FUNCTION RIGHT WITHOUT A LOT OF WORK.
HOW MUCH FOR YOU TO FIX IT RIGHT?
UNDERSTAND, IT'S AN INVOLVED SURGERY.
I'D NEED TO BRING IN A NURSE AND AN ANESTHESIOLOGIST...
...AND PAY THEM WELL ENOUGH TO KEEP QUIET.

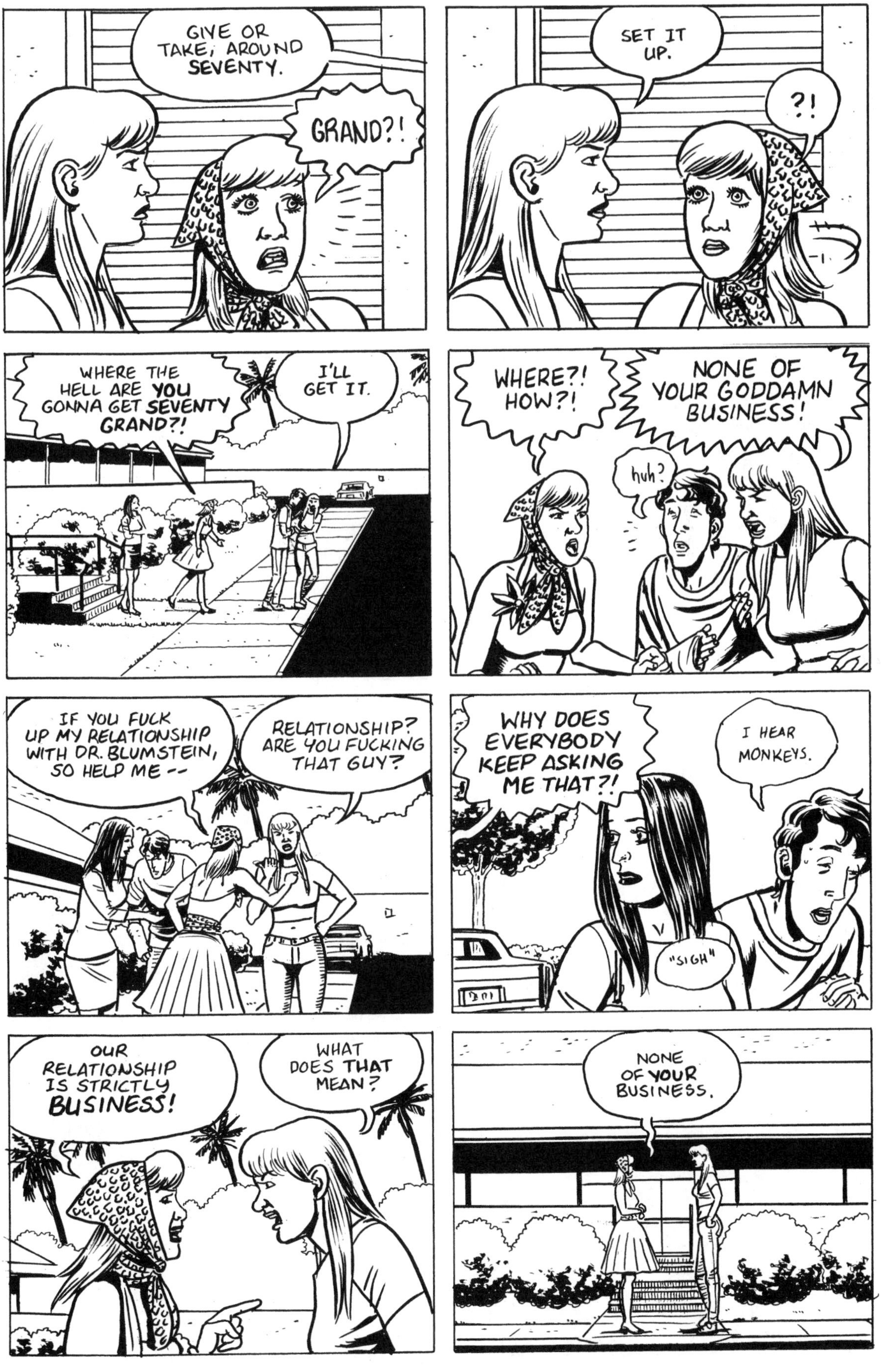
GIVE OR TAKE, AROUND SEVENTY.
GRAND?!
SET IT UP.
?!
WHERE THE HELL ARE YOU GONNA GET SEVENTY GRAND?!
I'LL GET IT.
WHERE?! HOW?!
NONE OF YOUR GODDAMN BUSINESS!
huh?
IF YOU FUCK UP MY RELATIONSHIP WITH DR. BLUMSTEIN, SO HELP ME --
RELATIONSHIP? ARE YOU FUCKING THAT GUY?
WHY DOES EVERYBODY KEEP ASKING ME THAT?!
I HEAR MONKEYS.
"SIGH"
OUR RELATIONSHIP IS STRICTLY BUSINESS!
WHAT DOES THAT MEAN?
NONE OF YOUR BUSINESS.

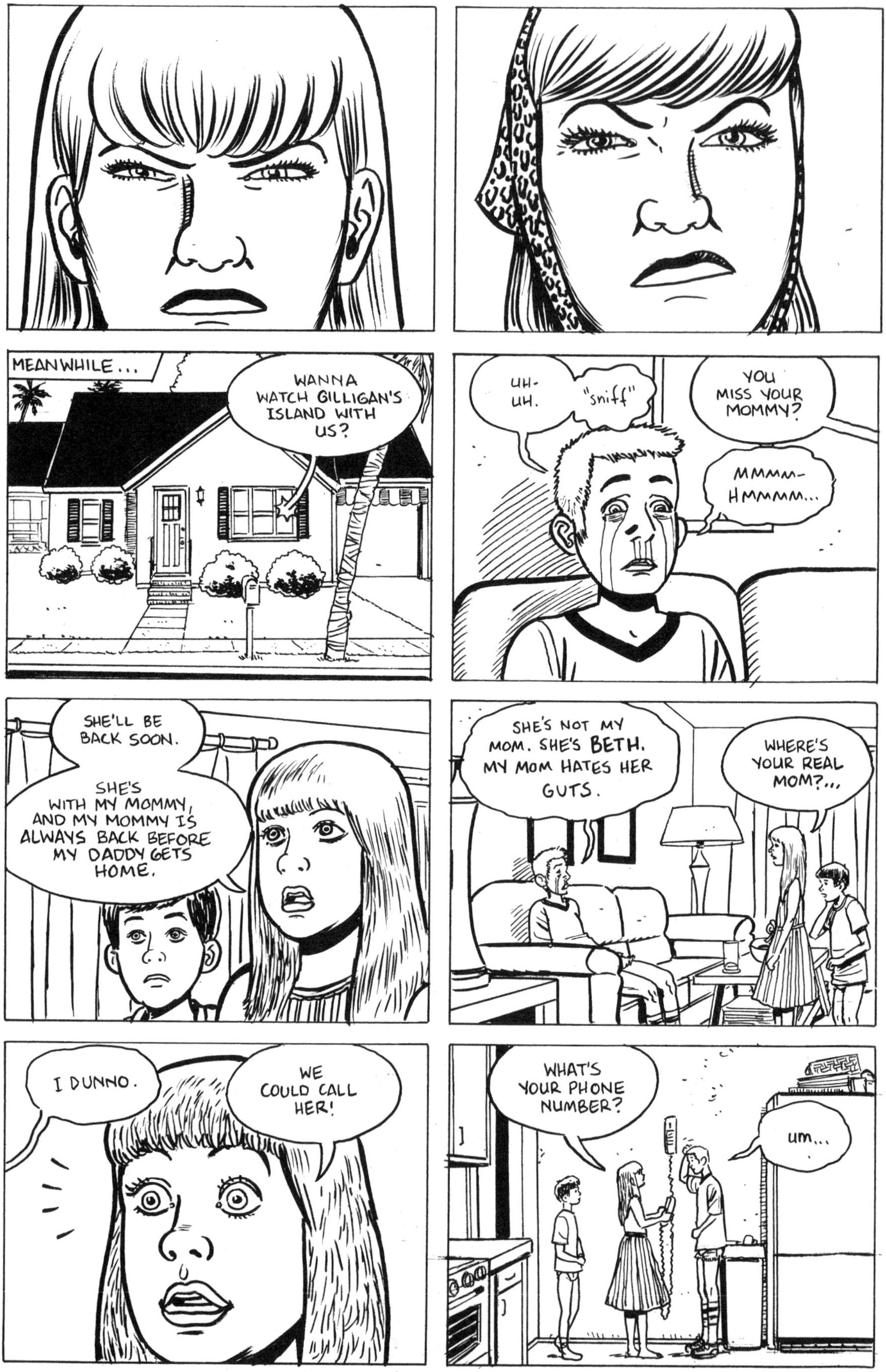
MEANWHILE...
WANNA WATCH GILLIGAN'S ISLAND WITH US?
UH-UH.
"sniff"
YOU MISS YOUR MOMMY?
MMMM-HMMMM...
SHE'LL BE BACK SOON.
SHE'S WITH MY MOMMY, AND MY MOMMY IS ALWAYS BACK BEFORE MY DADDY GETS HOME.
SHE'S NOT MY MOM. SHE'S BETH. MY MOM HATES HER GUTS.
WHERE'S YOUR REAL MOM?...
I DUNNO.
WE COULD CALL HER!
WHAT'S YOUR PHONE NUMBER?
um...

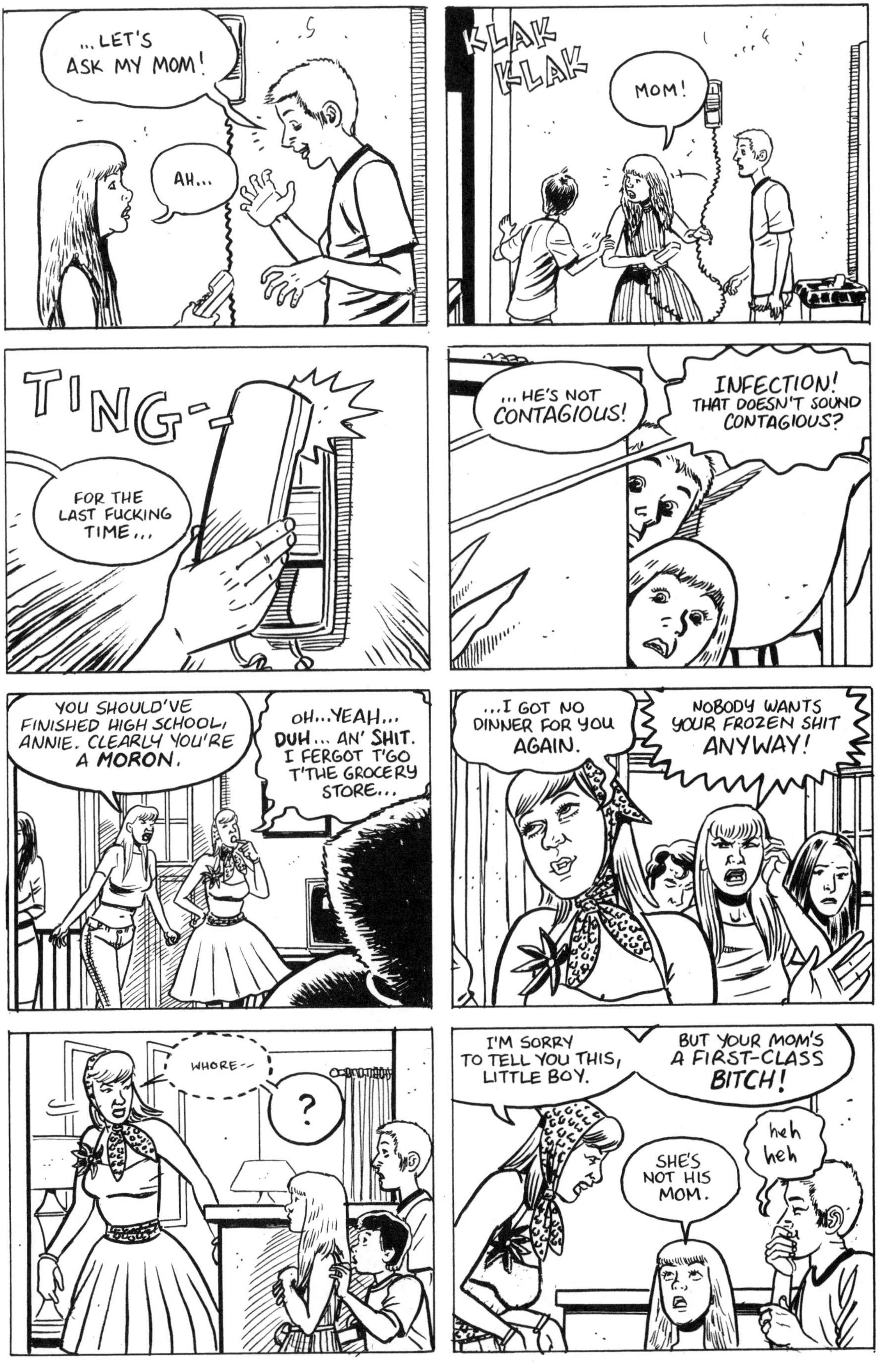
...LET'S ASK MY MOM!
AH...
KLAK KLAK
MOM!
TING-
FOR THE LAST FUCKING TIME...
...HE'S NOT CONTAGIOUS!
INFECTION! THAT DOESN'T SOUND CONTAGIOUS?
YOU SHOULD'VE FINISHED HIGH SCHOOL, ANNIE. CLEARLY YOU'RE A MORON.
OH...YEAH... DUH... AN' SHIT. I FERGOT T'GO T'THE GROCERY STORE...
...I GOT NO DINNER FOR YOU AGAIN.
NOBODY WANTS YOUR FROZEN SHIT ANYWAY!
WHORE--
?
I'M SORRY TO TELL YOU THIS, LITTLE BOY.
BUT YOUR MOM'S A FIRST-CLASS BITCH!
SHE'S NOT HIS MOM.
heh heh

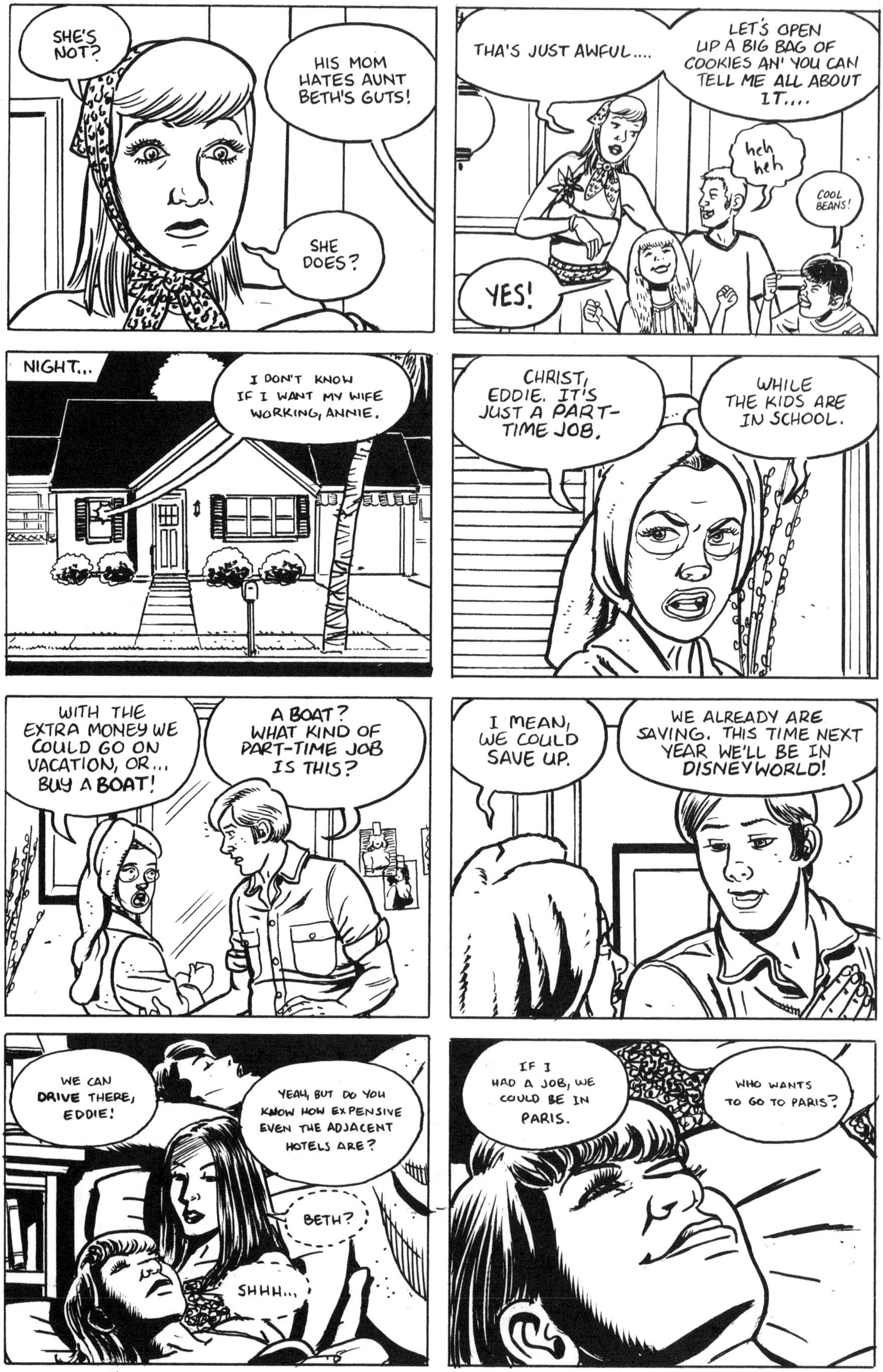
SHE'S NOT?
HIS MOM HATES AUNT BETH'S GUTS!
SHE DOES?
THA'S JUST AWFUL....
LET'S OPEN UP A BIG BAG OF COOKIES AN' YOU CAN TELL ME ALL ABOUT IT....
heh heh
COOL BEANS!
YES!
NIGHT...
I DON'T KNOW IF I WANT MY WIFE WORKING, ANNIE.
CHRIST, EDDIE. IT'S JUST A PART-TIME JOB.
WHILE THE KIDS ARE IN SCHOOL.
WITH THE EXTRA MONEY WE COULD GO ON VACATION, OR... BUY A BOAT!
A BOAT? WHAT KIND OF PART-TIME JOB IS THIS?
I MEAN, WE COULD SAVE UP.
WE ALREADY ARE SAVING. THIS TIME NEXT YEAR WE'LL BE IN DISNEYWORLD!
WE CAN DRIVE THERE, EDDIE!
YEAH, BUT DO YOU KNOW HOW EXPENSIVE EVEN THE ADJACENT HOTELS ARE?
BETH?
SHHH...
IF I HAD A JOB, WE COULD BE IN PARIS.
WHO WANTS TO GO TO PARIS?

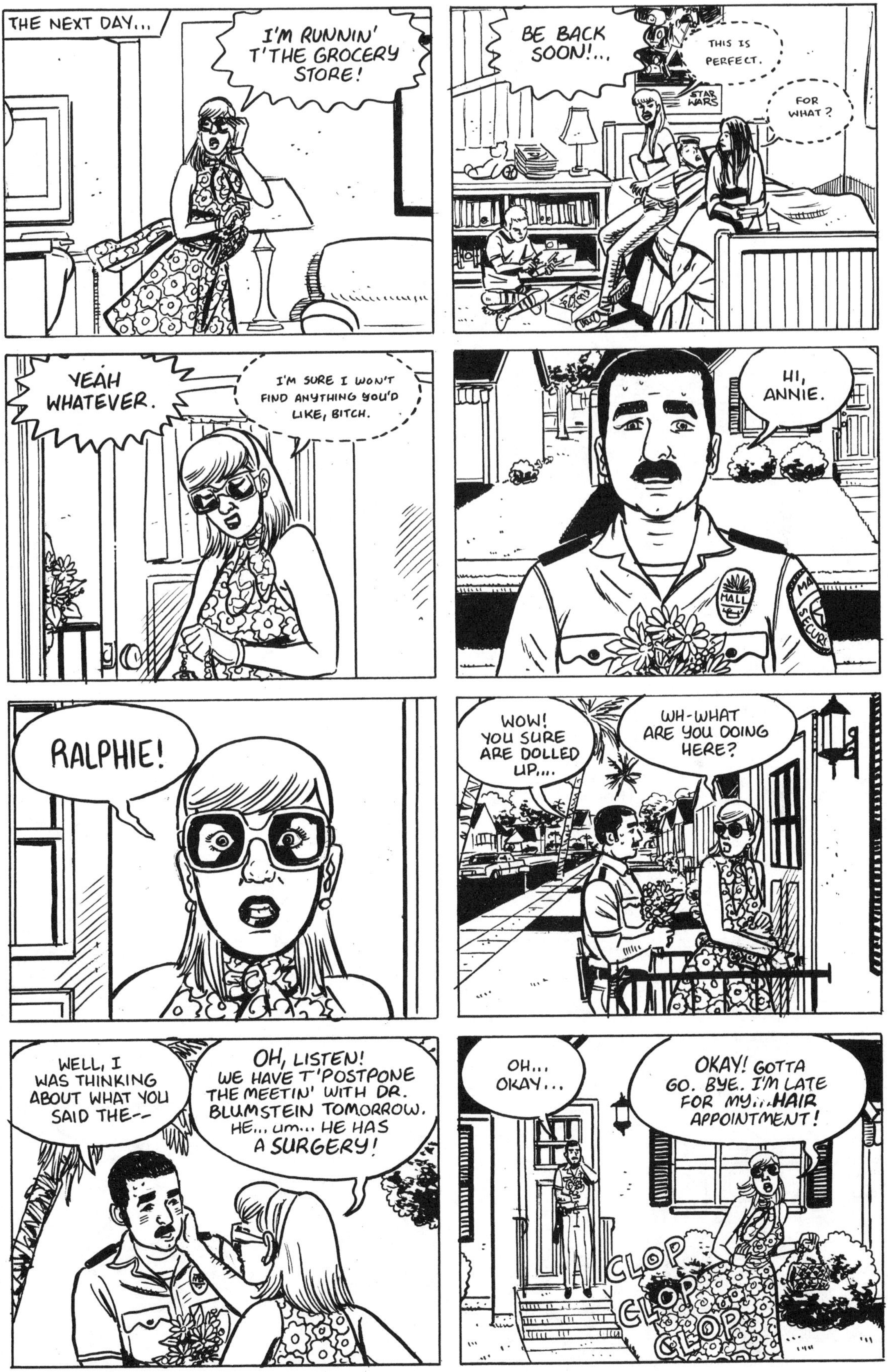
THE NEXT DAY...
I'M RUNNIN' T'THE GROCERY STORE!
BE BACK SOON!...
THIS IS PERFECT.
FOR WHAT?
STAR WARS
YEAH WHATEVER.
I'M SURE I WON'T FIND ANYTHING YOU'D LIKE, BITCH.
HI, ANNIE.
MALL
RALPHIE!
WOW! YOU SURE ARE DOLLED UP....
WH-WHAT ARE YOU DOING HERE?
WELL, I WAS THINKING ABOUT WHAT YOU SAID THE--
OH, LISTEN! WE HAVE T'POSTPONE THE MEETIN' WITH DR. BLUMSTEIN TOMORROW. HE... um... HE HAS A SURGERY!
OH... OKAY...
OKAY! GOTTA GO. BYE. I'M LATE FOR MY... HAIR APPOINTMENT!
CLOP CLOP CLOP

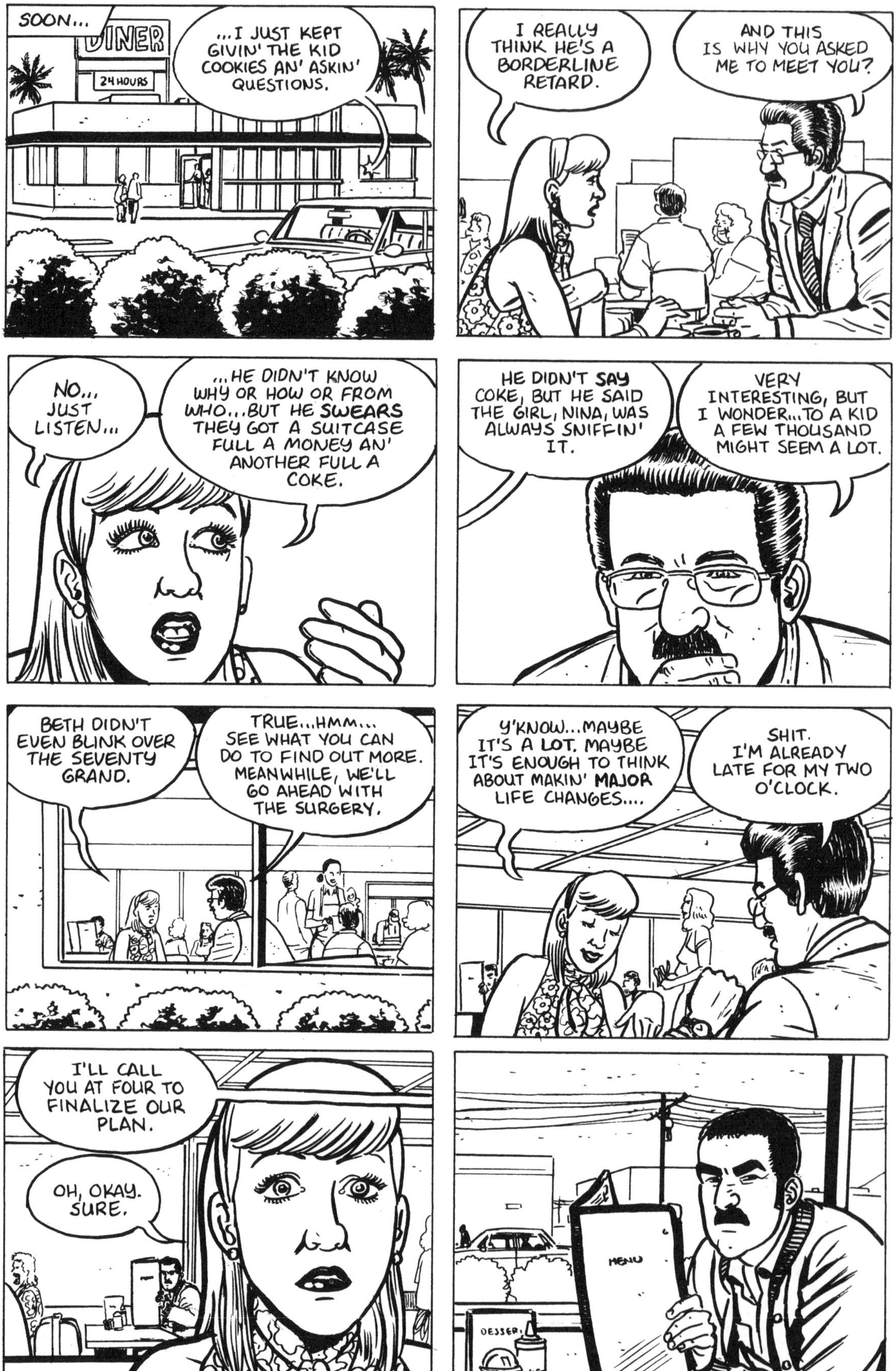
SOON...
DINER
24 HOURS
...I JUST KEPT GIVIN' THE KID COOKIES AN' ASKIN' QUESTIONS.
I REALLY THINK HE'S A BORDERLINE RETARD.
AND THIS IS WHY YOU ASKED ME TO MEET YOU?
NO... JUST LISTEN...
...HE DIDN'T KNOW WHY OR HOW OR FROM WHO...BUT HE SWEARS THEY GOT A SUITCASE FULL A MONEY AN' ANOTHER FULL A COKE.
HE DIDN'T SAY COKE, BUT HE SAID THE GIRL, NINA, WAS ALWAYS SNIFFIN' IT.
VERY INTERESTING, BUT I WONDER...TO A KID A FEW THOUSAND MIGHT SEEM A LOT.
BETH DIDN'T EVEN BLINK OVER THE SEVENTY GRAND.
TRUE...HMM... SEE WHAT YOU CAN DO TO FIND OUT MORE. MEANWHILE, WE'LL GO AHEAD WITH THE SURGERY.
Y'KNOW...MAYBE IT'S A LOT. MAYBE IT'S ENOUGH TO THINK ABOUT MAKIN' MAJOR LIFE CHANGES....
SHIT. I'M ALREADY LATE FOR MY TWO O'CLOCK.
I'LL CALL YOU AT FOUR TO FINALIZE OUR PLAN.
OH, OKAY. SURE.
MENU

MEANWHILE...

SHE'S NEVER GOING TO SAY SORRY, Y'KNOW?

WHO'S ASKING? I JUST WANNA FUCK UP HER WORLD.

SURE...

YEAH... THERE'S ALL KINDS OF DESIGNER SHIT HERE.

CLOTHES, BAGS...SHIT HUBBY'D NEVER NOTICE.

SHE'S GOING OUT OF HER MIND CUZ SHE'S GOT MONEY AND CAN'T SPEND IT.

UH HUH...

Sniff

YOU COULD JUST TRY AND TALK IT OUT, Y'KNOW?

YOU CAN ONLY CALL SOMEONE A FUCKING BITCH SO MANY TIMES.

SOMEPLACE THE KIDS...

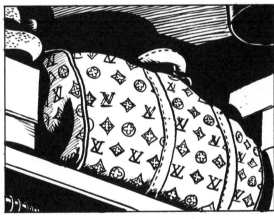

ANNIE'S AN ENTREPRENEUR!

51

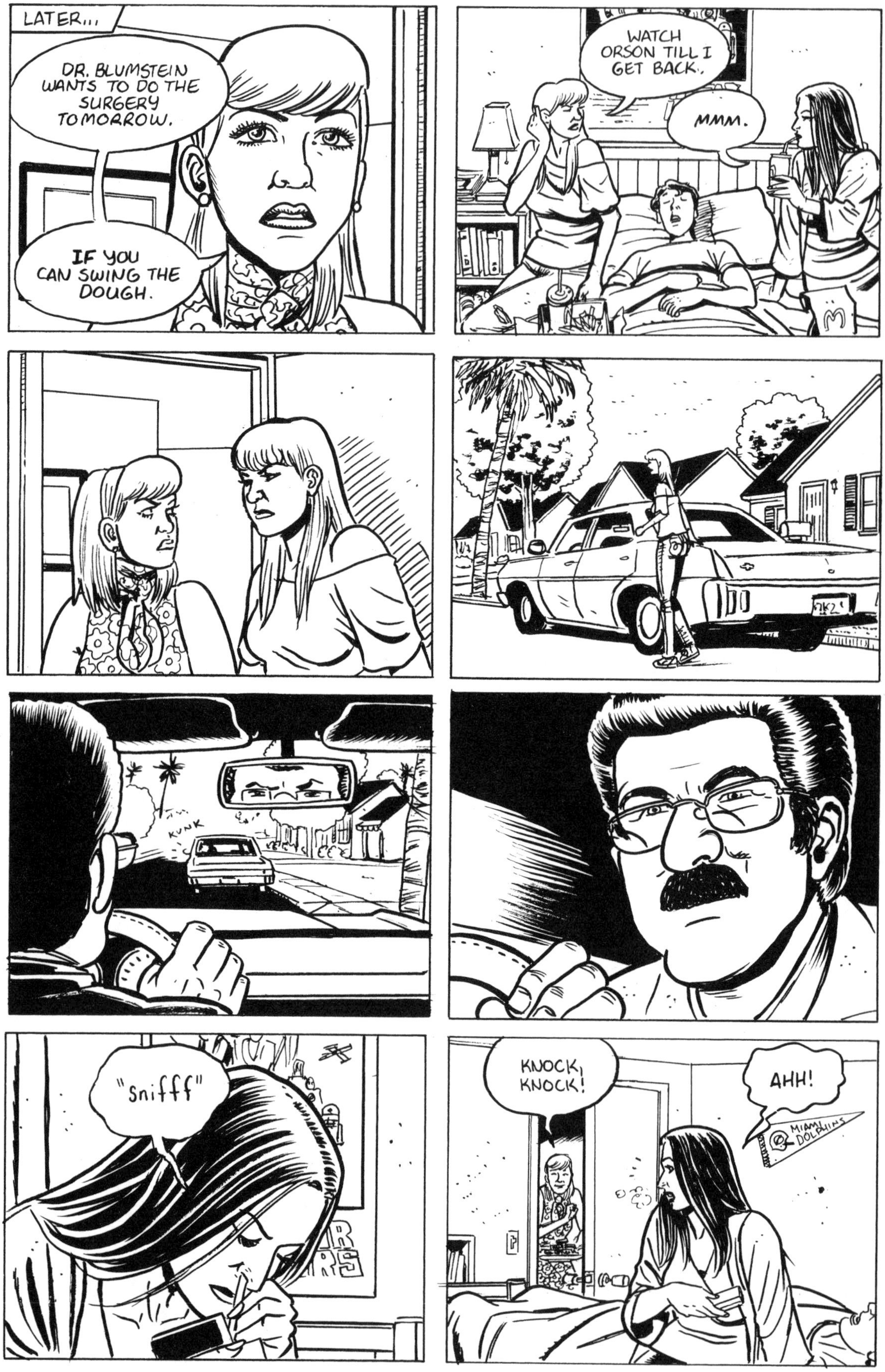
LATER...
DR. BLUMSTEIN WANTS TO DO THE SURGERY TOMORROW.
IF YOU CAN SWING THE DOUGH.
WATCH ORSON TILL I GET BACK.
MMM.
KUNK
"Snifff"
KNOCK, KNOCK!
AHH!
MIAMI DOLPHINS

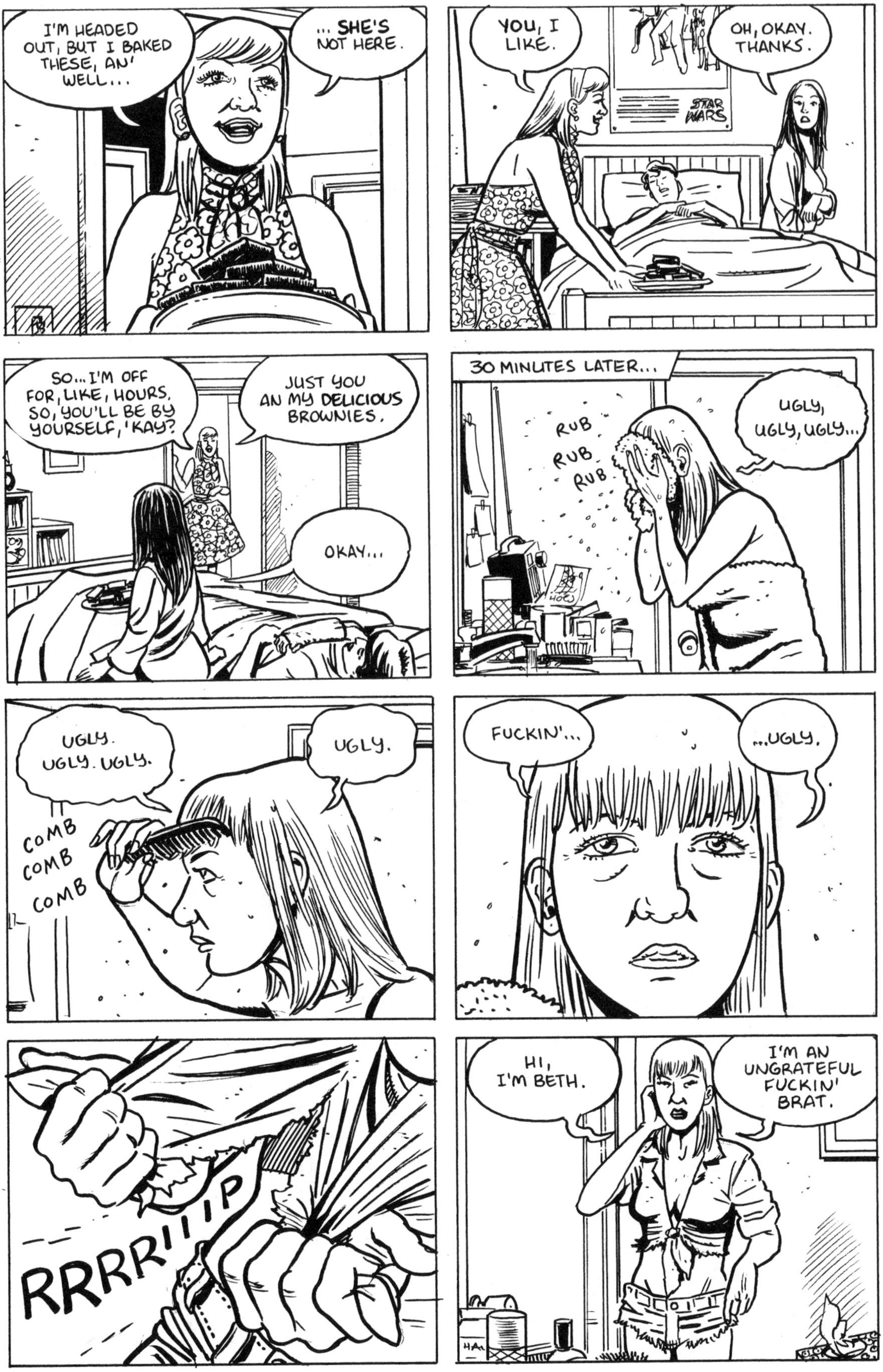
I'M HEADED OUT, BUT I BAKED THESE, AN' WELL...
... SHE'S NOT HERE.
YOU, I LIKE.
OH, OKAY. THANKS.
STAR WARS
SO... I'M OFF FOR, LIKE, HOURS, SO, YOU'LL BE BY YOURSELF, 'KAY?
JUST YOU AN MY DELICIOUS BROWNIES.
OKAY...
30 MINUTES LATER...
RUB RUB RUB
UGLY, UGLY, UGLY...
UGLY. UGLY. UGLY.
UGLY.
COMB COMB COMB
FUCKIN'...
...UGLY.
RRRRIIIP
HI, I'M BETH.
I'M AN UNGRATEFUL FUCKIN' BRAT.

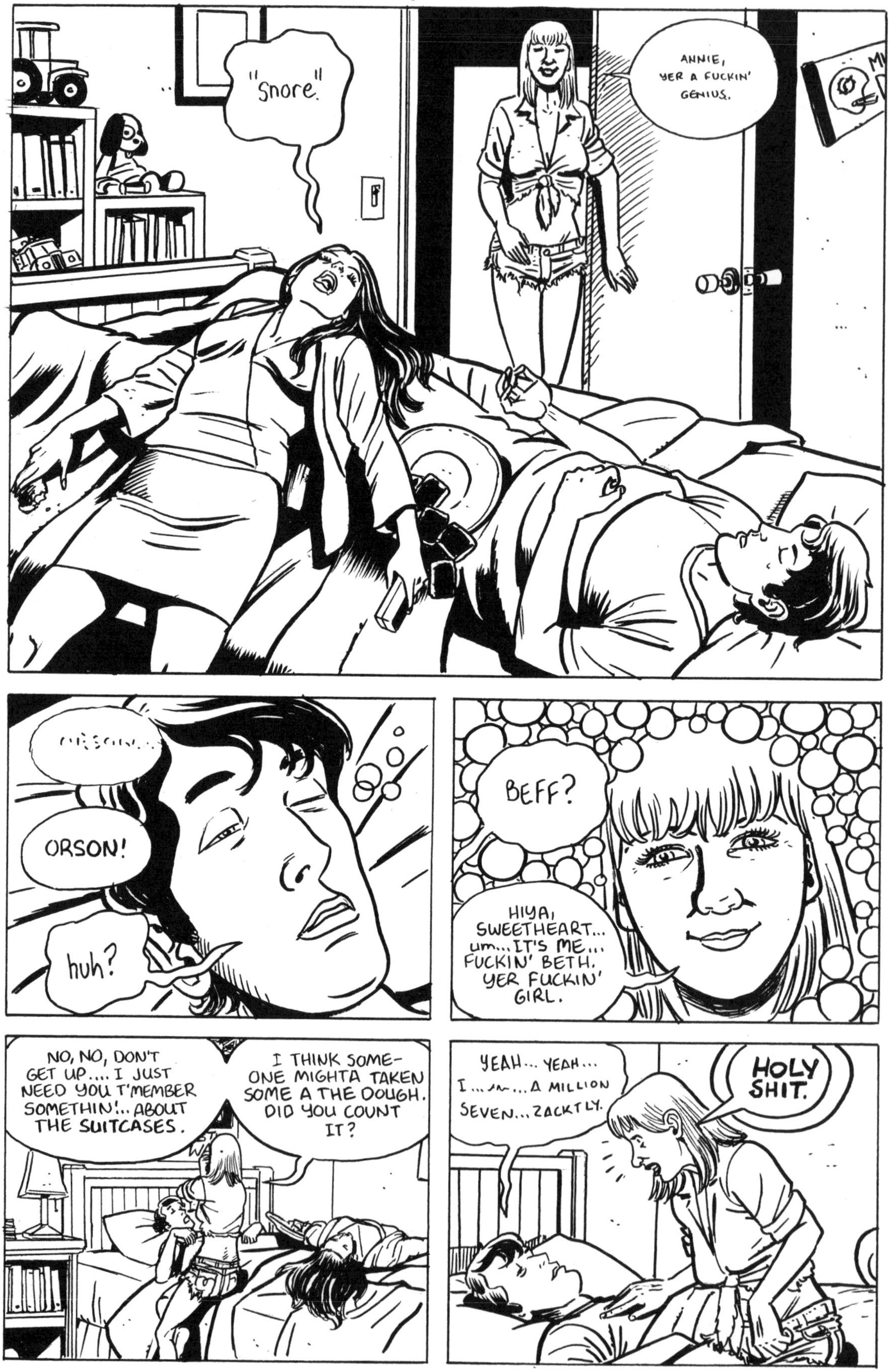
"snore"
ANNIE, YER A FUCKIN' GENIUS.
ORSON!
huh?
BEFF?
HIYA, SWEETHEART... um... IT'S ME... FUCKIN' BETH. YER FUCKIN' GIRL.
NO, NO, DON'T GET UP.... I JUST NEED YOU T'MEMBER SOMETHIN'... ABOUT THE SUITCASES.
I THINK SOME-ONE MIGHTA TAKEN SOME A THE DOUGH. DID YOU COUNT IT?
YEAH... YEAH... I... um... A MILLION SEVEN... ZACKTLY.
HOLY SHIT.

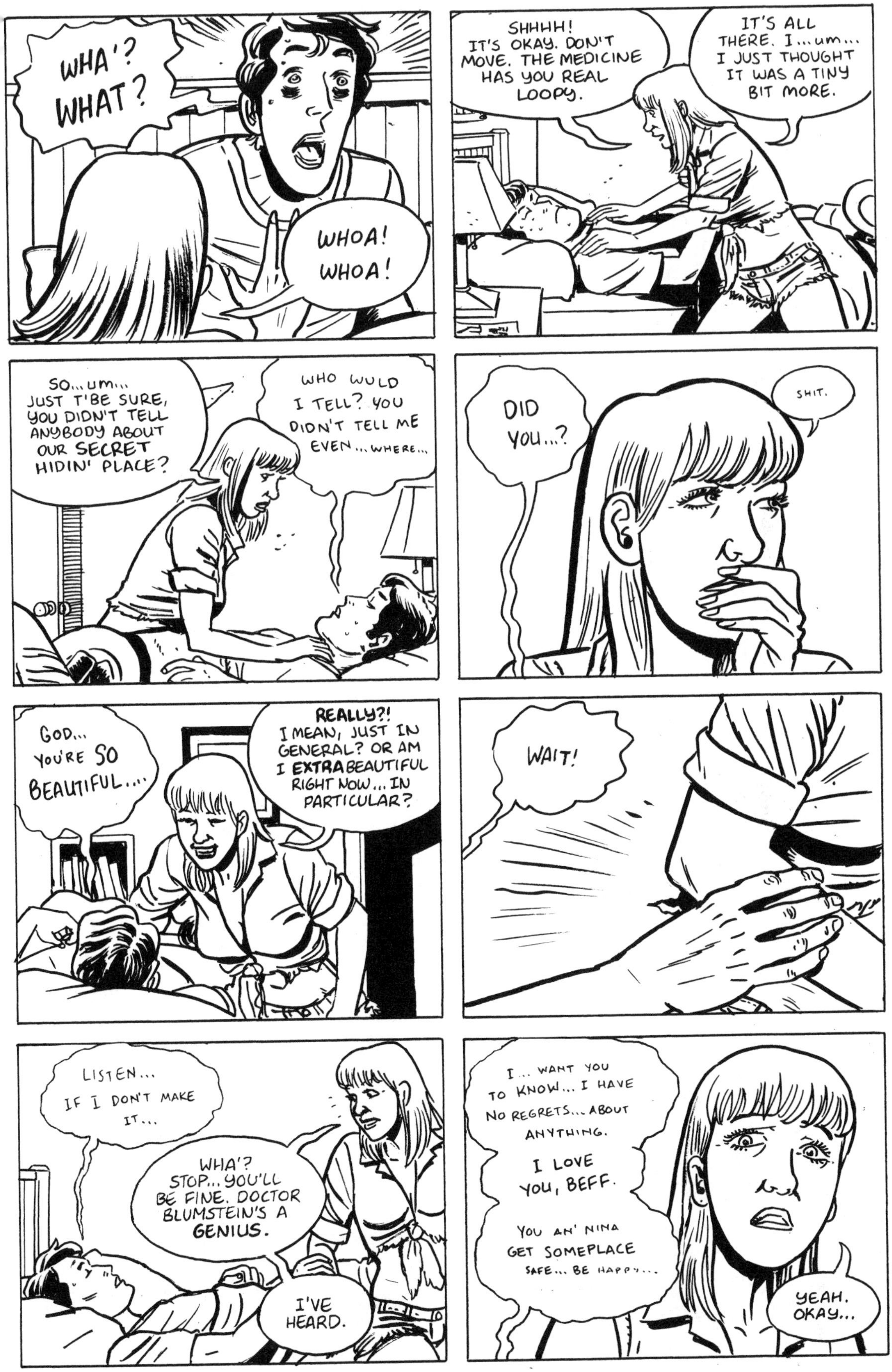
WHA'? WHAT?
WHOA! WHOA!
SHHHH! IT'S OKAY. DON'T MOVE. THE MEDICINE HAS YOU REAL LOOPY.
IT'S ALL THERE. I...um... I JUST THOUGHT IT WAS A TINY BIT MORE.
SO...um... JUST T'BE SURE, YOU DIDN'T TELL ANYBODY ABOUT OUR SECRET HIDIN' PLACE?
WHO WULD I TELL? YOU DIDN'T TELL ME EVEN... WHERE...
DID YOU...?
SHIT.
GOD... YOU'RE SO BEAUTIFUL....
REALLY?! I MEAN, JUST IN GENERAL? OR AM I EXTRA BEAUTIFUL RIGHT NOW... IN PARTICULAR?
WAIT!
LISTEN... IF I DON'T MAKE IT...
WHA'? STOP... YOU'LL BE FINE. DOCTOR BLUMSTEIN'S A GENIUS.
I'VE HEARD.
I... WANT YOU TO KNOW... I HAVE NO REGRETS... ABOUT ANYTHING.
I LOVE YOU, BEFF.
YOU AN' NINA GET SOMEPLACE SAFE... BE HAPPY...
YEAH. OKAY...

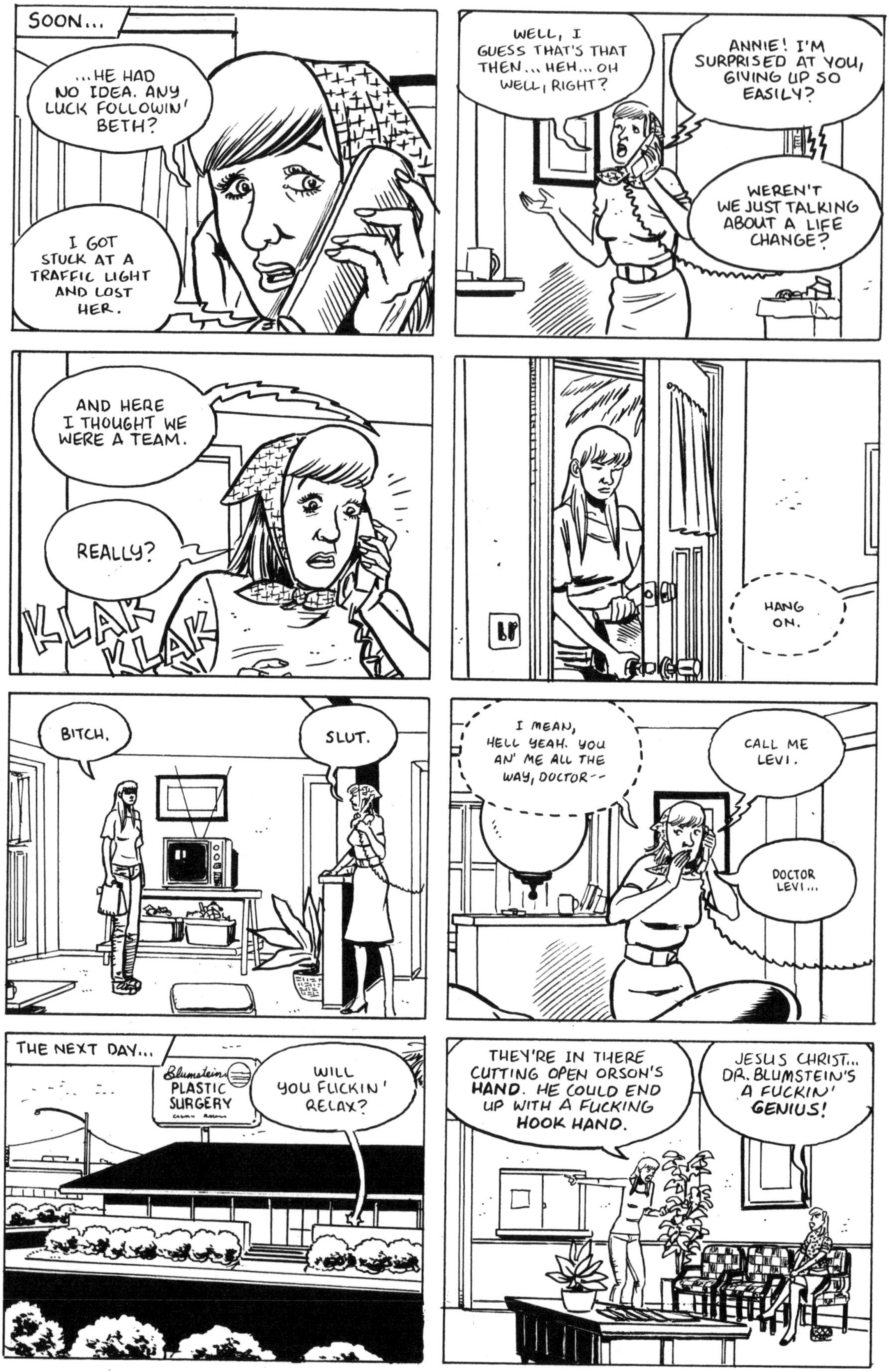

SOON...
...HE HAD NO IDEA. ANY LUCK FOLLOWIN' BETH?
I GOT STUCK AT A TRAFFIC LIGHT AND LOST HER.
WELL, I GUESS THAT'S THAT THEN... HEH... OH WELL, RIGHT?
ANNIE! I'M SURPRISED AT YOU, GIVING UP SO EASILY?
WEREN'T WE JUST TALKING ABOUT A LIFE CHANGE?
AND HERE I THOUGHT WE WERE A TEAM.
REALLY?
KLAK KLAK
HANG ON.
BITCH.
SLUT.
I MEAN, HELL YEAH. YOU AN' ME ALL THE WAY, DOCTOR--
CALL ME LEVI.
DOCTOR LEVI...
THE NEXT DAY...
Blumstein's PLASTIC SURGERY
WILL YOU FUCKIN' RELAX?
THEY'RE IN THERE CUTTING OPEN ORSON'S HAND. HE COULD END UP WITH A FUCKING HOOK HAND.
JESUS CHRIST... DR. BLUMSTEIN'S A FUCKIN' GENIUS!

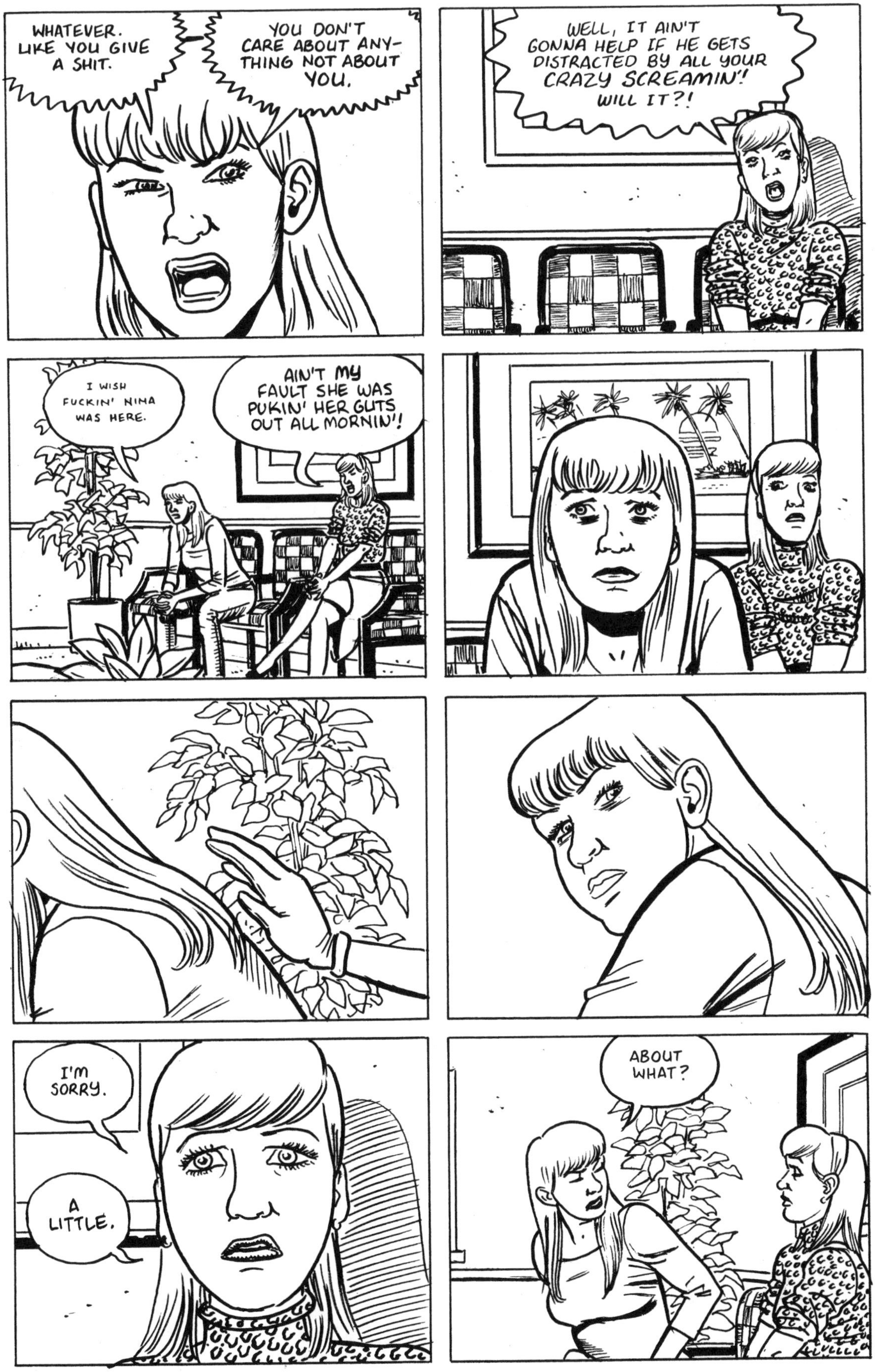
WHATEVER. LIKE YOU GIVE A SHIT.
YOU DON'T CARE ABOUT ANY-THING NOT ABOUT YOU.
WELL, IT AIN'T GONNA HELP IF HE GETS DISTRACTED BY ALL YOUR CRAZY SCREAMIN'! WILL IT?!
I WISH FUCKIN' NINA WAS HERE.
AIN'T MY FAULT SHE WAS PUKIN' HER GUTS OUT ALL MORNIN'!
I'M SORRY.
A LITTLE.
ABOUT WHAT?

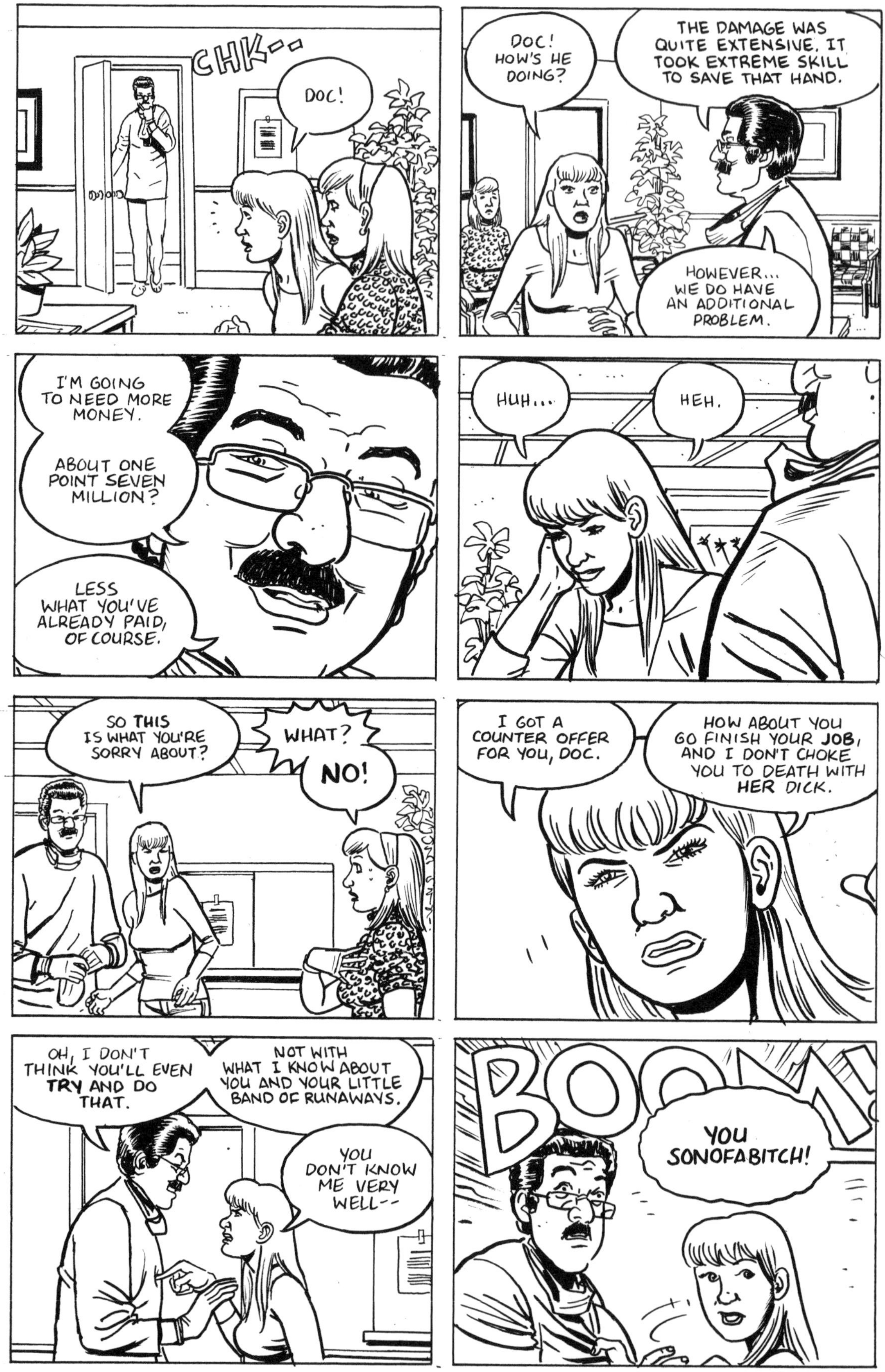
CHK--
DOC!
DOC! HOW'S HE DOING?
THE DAMAGE WAS QUITE EXTENSIVE. IT TOOK EXTREME SKILL TO SAVE THAT HAND.
HOWEVER... WE DO HAVE AN ADDITIONAL PROBLEM.
I'M GOING TO NEED MORE MONEY.
ABOUT ONE POINT SEVEN MILLION?
LESS WHAT YOU'VE ALREADY PAID, OF COURSE.
HUH...
HEH.
SO THIS IS WHAT YOU'RE SORRY ABOUT?
WHAT?
NO!
I GOT A COUNTER OFFER FOR YOU, DOC.
HOW ABOUT YOU GO FINISH YOUR JOB, AND I DON'T CHOKE YOU TO DEATH WITH HER DICK.
OH, I DON'T THINK YOU'LL EVEN TRY AND DO THAT.
NOT WITH WHAT I KNOW ABOUT YOU AND YOUR LITTLE BAND OF RUNAWAYS.
YOU DON'T KNOW ME VERY WELL--
BOOM!
YOU SONOFABITCH!

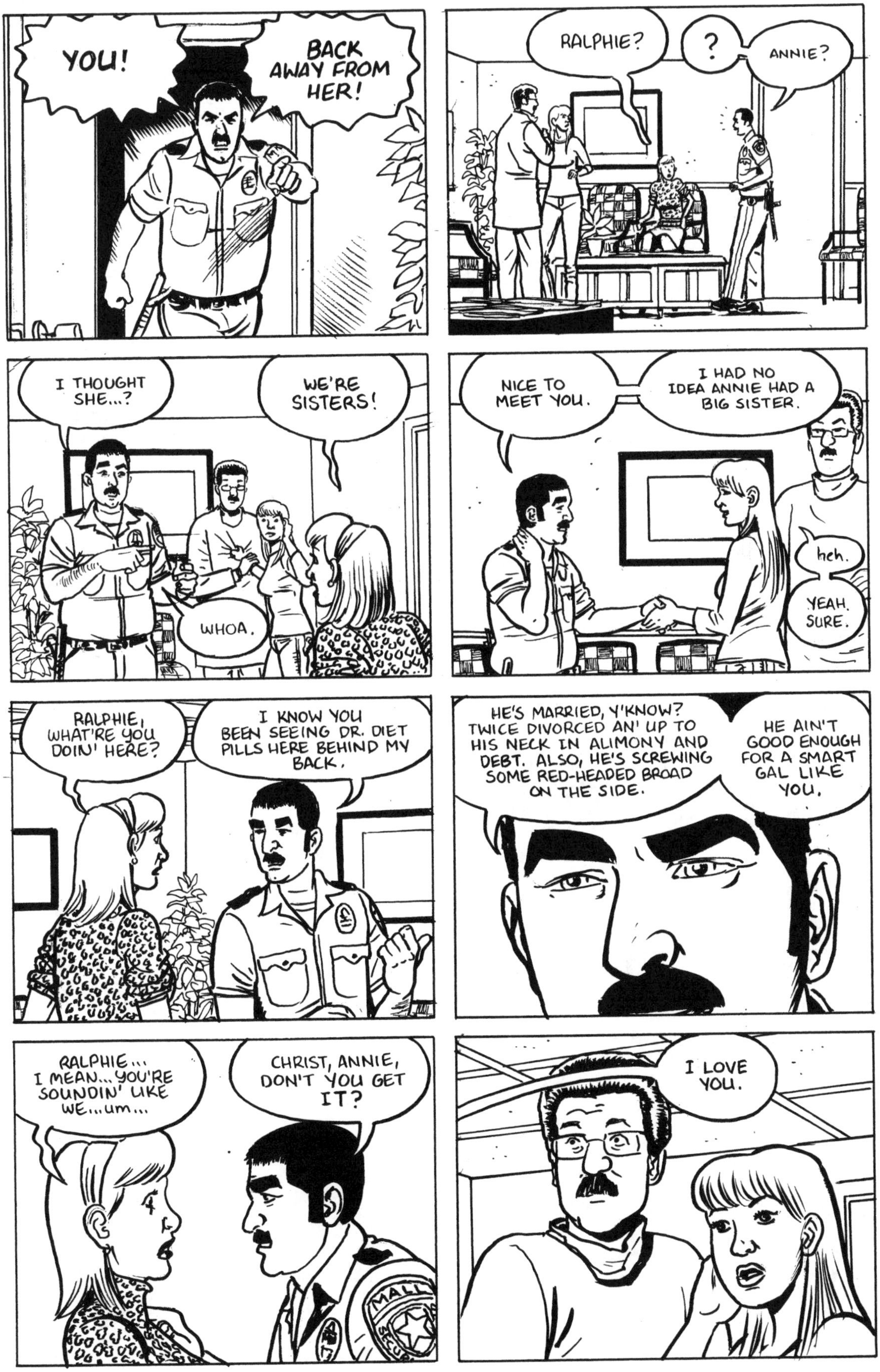
YOU!
BACK AWAY FROM HER!
RALPHIE?
?
ANNIE?
I THOUGHT SHE...?
WE'RE SISTERS!
WHOA.
NICE TO MEET YOU.
I HAD NO IDEA ANNIE HAD A BIG SISTER.
heh.
YEAH. SURE.
RALPHIE, WHAT'RE YOU DOIN' HERE?
I KNOW YOU BEEN SEEING DR. DIET PILLS HERE BEHIND MY BACK.
HE'S MARRIED, Y'KNOW? TWICE DIVORCED AN' UP TO HIS NECK IN ALIMONY AND DEBT. ALSO, HE'S SCREWING SOME RED-HEADED BROAD ON THE SIDE.
HE AIN'T GOOD ENOUGH FOR A SMART GAL LIKE YOU.
RALPHIE... I MEAN... YOU'RE SOUNDIN' LIKE WE...um...
CHRIST, ANNIE, DON'T YOU GET IT?
I LOVE YOU.

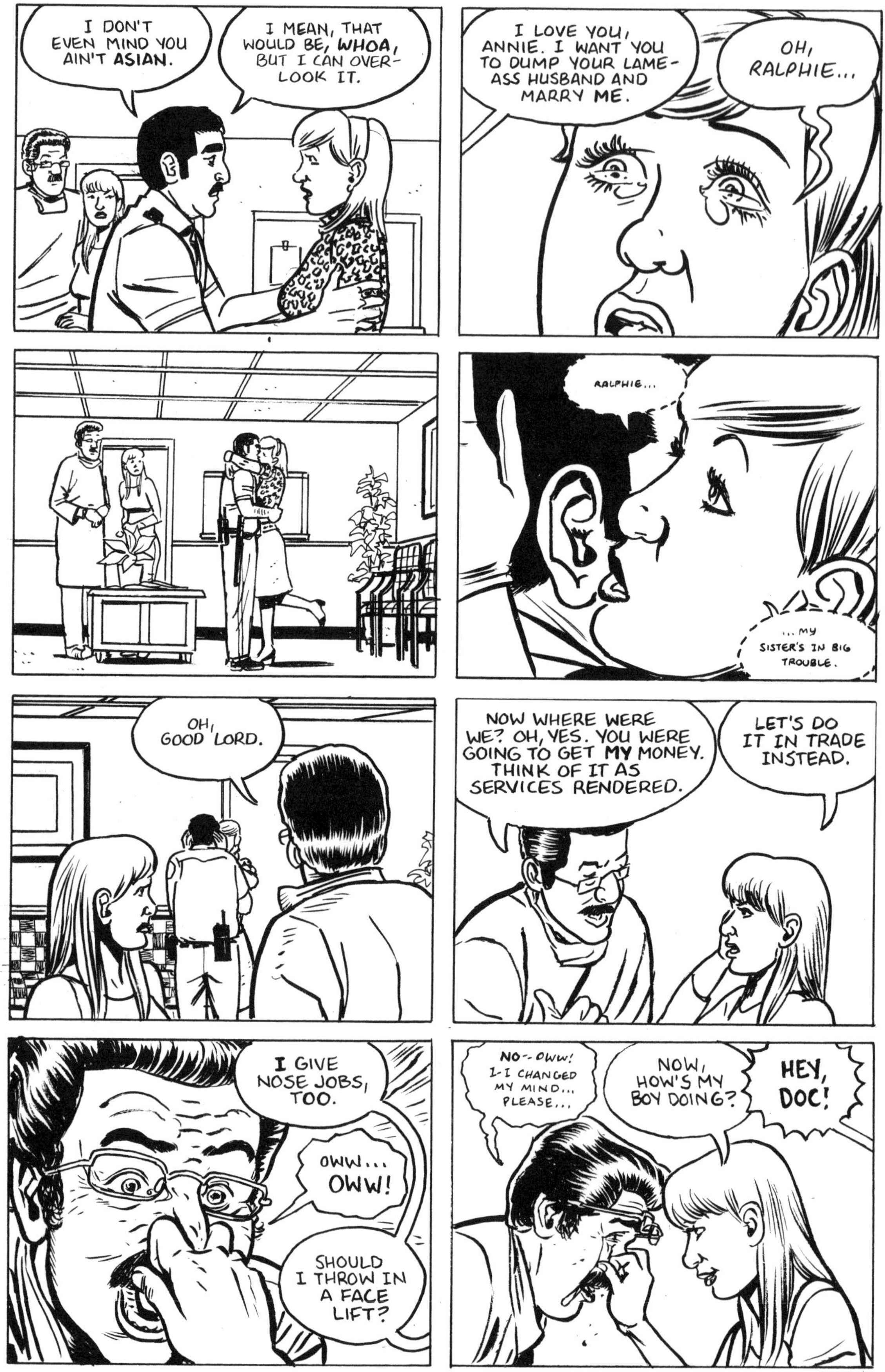

I DON'T EVEN MIND YOU AIN'T **ASIAN**.
I MEAN, THAT WOULD BE, **WHOA**, BUT I CAN OVER-LOOK IT.
I LOVE YOU, ANNIE. I WANT YOU TO DUMP YOUR LAME-ASS HUSBAND AND MARRY **ME**.
OH, RALPHIE...
RALPHIE...
...MY SISTER'S IN BIG TROUBLE.
OH, GOOD LORD.
NOW WHERE WERE WE? OH, YES. YOU WERE GOING TO GET **MY** MONEY. THINK OF IT AS SERVICES RENDERED.
LET'S DO IT IN TRADE INSTEAD.
I GIVE NOSE JOBS, TOO.
OWW... **OWW!**
SHOULD I THROW IN A FACE LIFT?
NO--OWW! I-I CHANGED MY MIND... PLEASE...
NOW, HOW'S MY BOY DOING?
HEY, DOC!

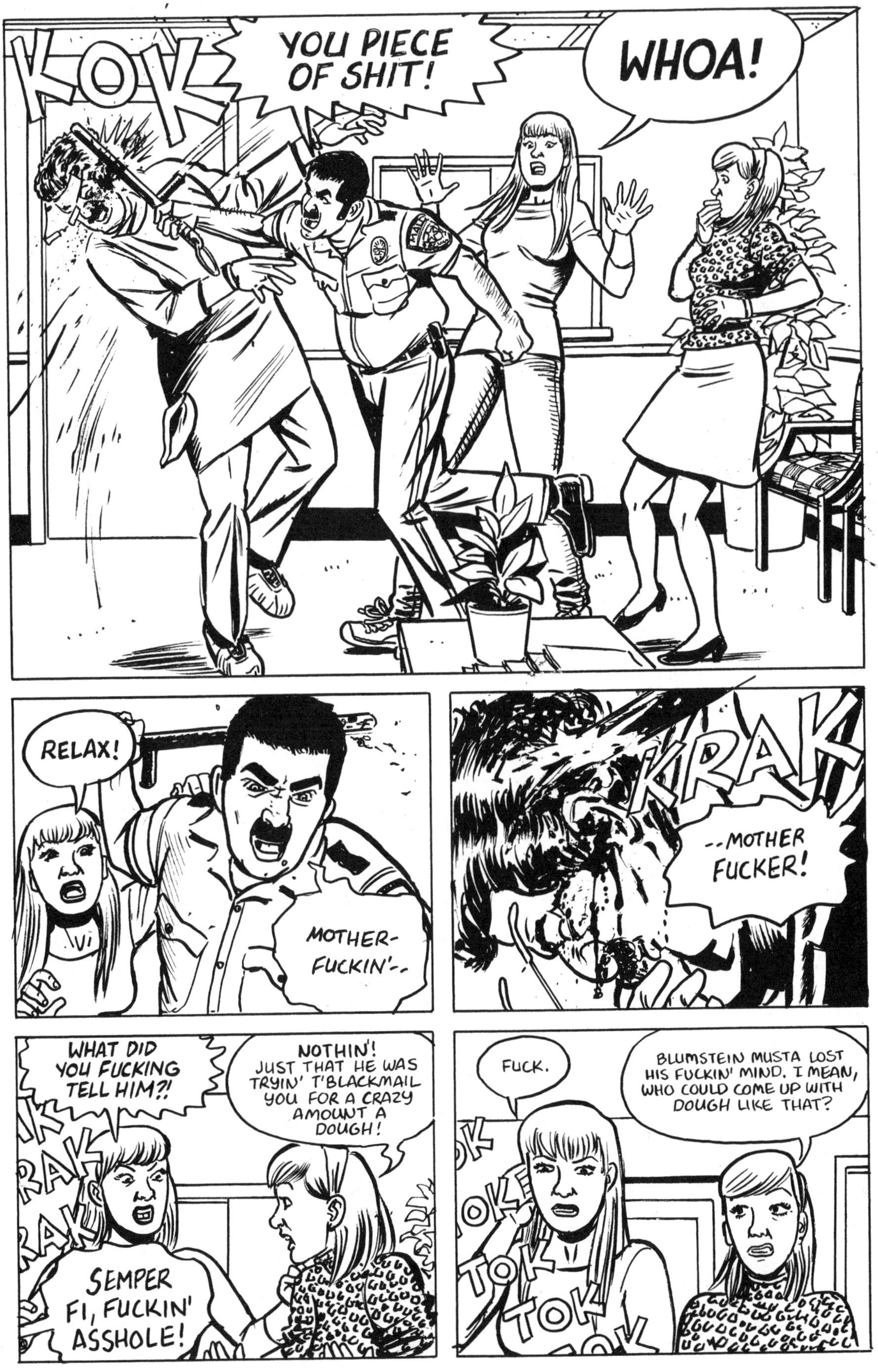
KOK
YOU PIECE OF SHIT!
WHOA!
RELAX!
MOTHER-FUCKIN'--
KRAK
--MOTHER FUCKER!
WHAT DID YOU FUCKING TELL HIM?!
NOTHIN'! JUST THAT HE WAS TRYIN' T'BLACKMAIL YOU FOR A CRAZY AMOUNT A DOUGH!
KRAK
SEMPER FI, FUCKIN' ASSHOLE!
FUCK.
BLUMSTEIN MUSTA LOST HIS FUCKIN' MIND. I MEAN, WHO COULD COME UP WITH DOUGH LIKE THAT?
TOK TOK

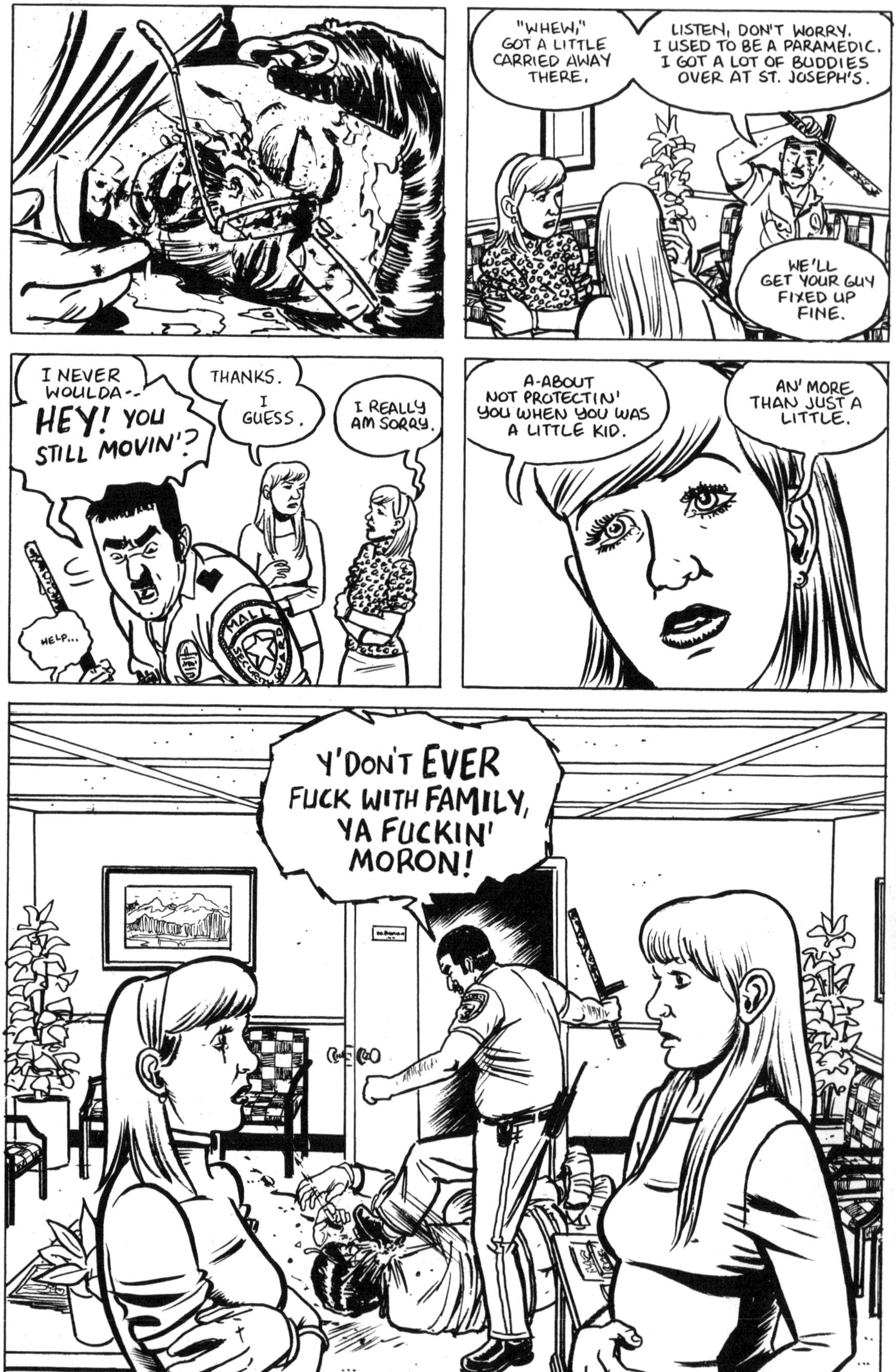
"WHEW," GOT A LITTLE CARRIED AWAY THERE.
LISTEN, DON'T WORRY. I USED TO BE A PARAMEDIC. I GOT A LOT OF BUDDIES OVER AT ST. JOSEPH'S.
WE'LL GET YOUR GUY FIXED UP FINE.
I NEVER WOULDA--
HEY! YOU STILL MOVIN'?
THANKS. I GUESS.
I REALLY AM SORRY.
HELP...
MALL SECURITY GUARD
A-ABOUT NOT PROTECTIN' YOU WHEN YOU WAS A LITTLE KID.
AN' MORE THAN JUST A LITTLE.
Y'DON'T EVER FUCK WITH FAMILY, YA FUCKIN' MORON!

THE END...

3

"ALL SMILES"

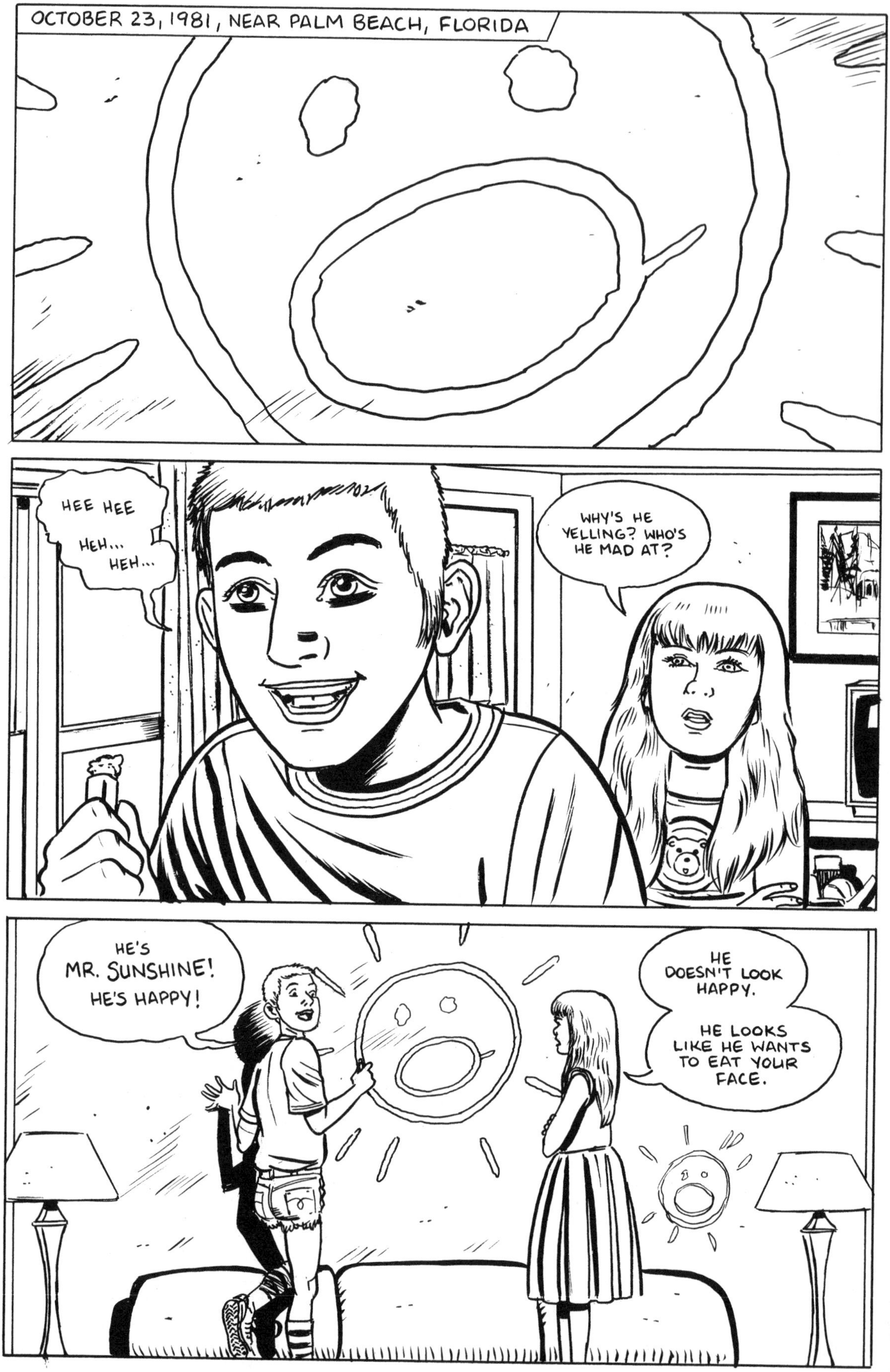

OCTOBER 23, 1981, NEAR PALM BEACH, FLORIDA
HEE HEE HEH... HEH...
WHY'S HE YELLING? WHO'S HE MAD AT?
HE'S MR. SUNSHINE! HE'S HAPPY!
HE DOESN'T LOOK HAPPY.
HE LOOKS LIKE HE WANTS TO EAT YOUR FACE.

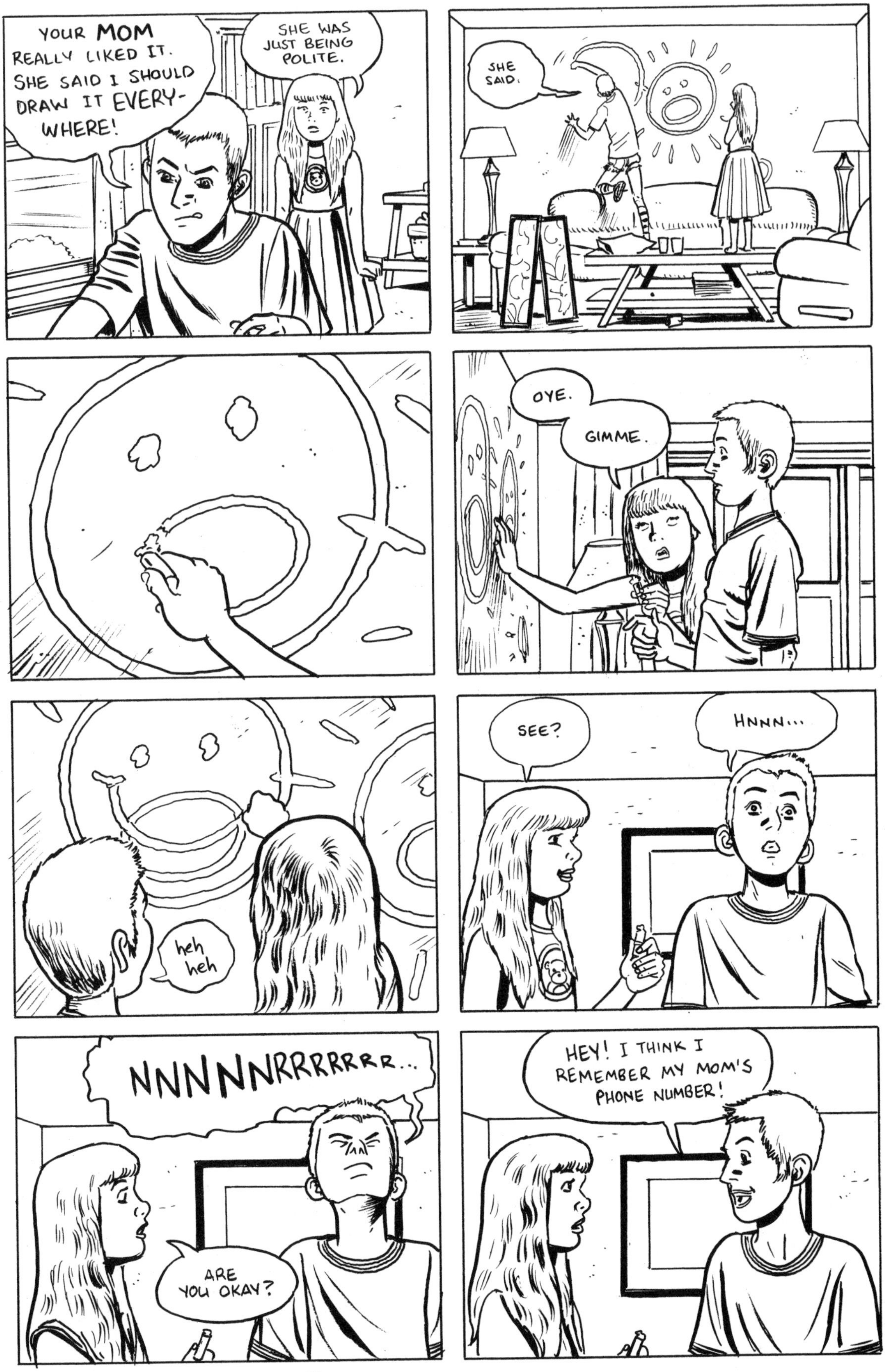
YOUR MOM REALLY LIKED IT. SHE SAID I SHOULD DRAW IT EVERY-WHERE!
SHE WAS JUST BEING POLITE.
SHE SAID.
OYE.
GIMME.
heh heh
SEE?
HNNN...
NNNNNRRRRRR...
ARE YOU OKAY?
HEY! I THINK I REMEMBER MY MOM'S PHONE NUMBER!

MEANWHILE...

I NEVER WANTED TO BE A MOM.

NOT EXACTLY EARTH-SHATTERING NEWS, ANNIE.

PLEASE TAKE A NUMBER

25

BLACK FOREST

I WAS FIFTEEN!

IF MY DAD NEVER FOUND OUT LIKE HE DID, I NEVER WOULDA EVEN **HAD** YOU.

GEE, THANKS.

NOW SERVING

2 2

JUST TRYIN' T'BE FUCKIN' HONEST.

TWENTY-THREE?!

BUT... Y'KNOW... I WAS **SUPPOSED** T'BE THE MOM.

AN' I MEAN, **YOU** AIN'T THE ONE WHO KNOCKED ME UP.

THAT WOULD BE FUCKIN' WEIRD. Heh.

AN' PRETTY IMPOSSIBLE.

DO YOU HAVE A **POINT**, ANNIE?

YEAH!

I'M TRYIN' T' APOLOGIZE FER BEIN' A CRAPPY MOM!

TWENTY-FOUR?!

IF YOU THINK THAT MEANS WE'RE GOING TO START PEEING IN FRONT OF EACH OTHER...

WHO'S ASKIN'?!

TWENTY-FIVE?!

66

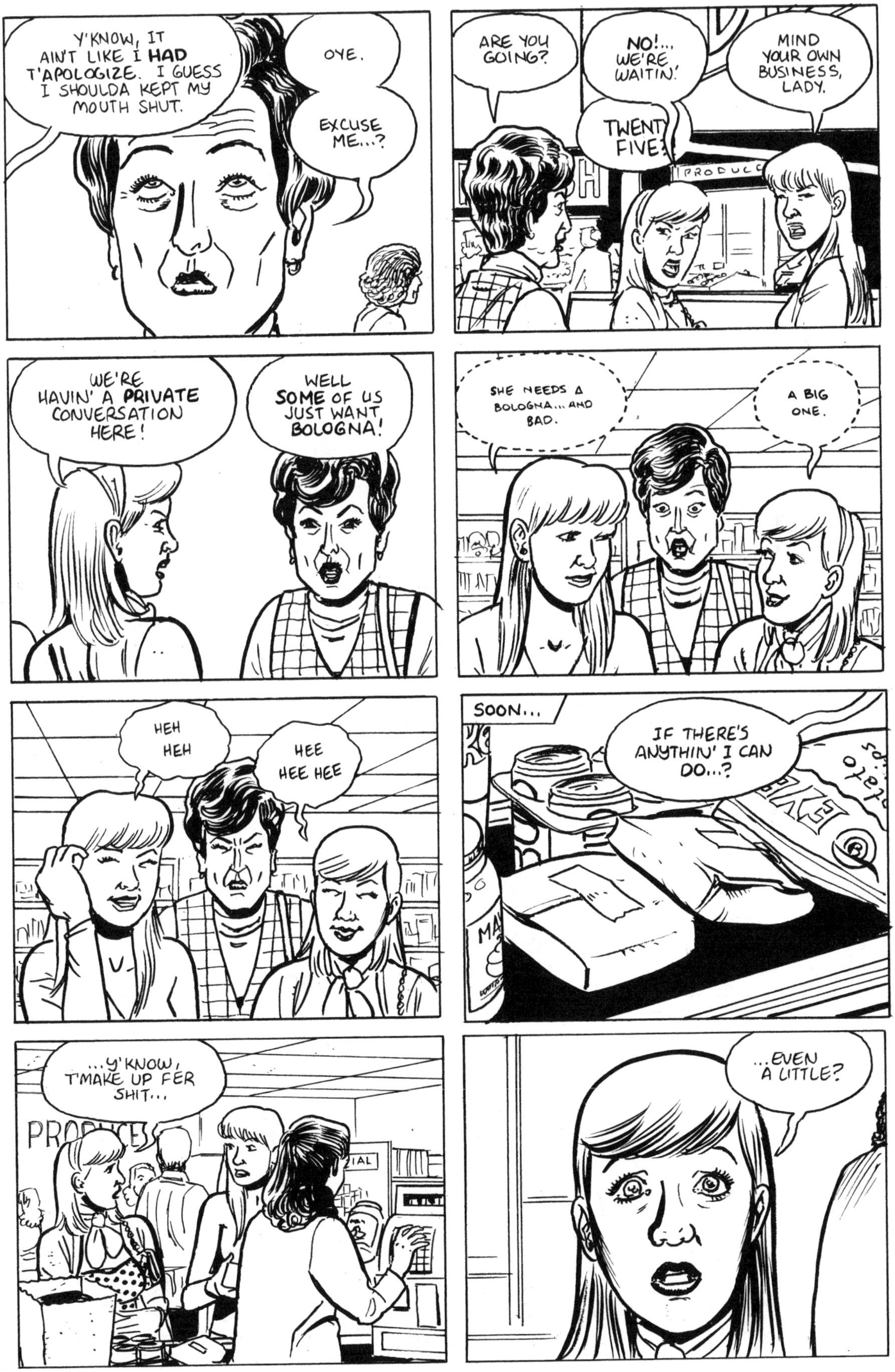
Y'KNOW, IT AIN'T LIKE I HAD T'APOLOGIZE. I GUESS I SHOULDA KEPT MY MOUTH SHUT.
OYE.
EXCUSE ME...?
ARE YOU GOING?
NO!... WE'RE WAITIN'.
TWENTY FIVE?
MIND YOUR OWN BUSINESS, LADY.
PRODUCE
WE'RE HAVIN' A PRIVATE CONVERSATION HERE!
WELL SOME OF US JUST WANT BOLOGNA!
SHE NEEDS A BOLOGNA... AND BAD.
A BIG ONE.
HEH HEH
HEE HEE HEE
SOON...
IF THERE'S ANYTHIN' I CAN DO...?
...Y'KNOW, T'MAKE UP FER SHIT...
PRODUCES
...EVEN A LITTLE?

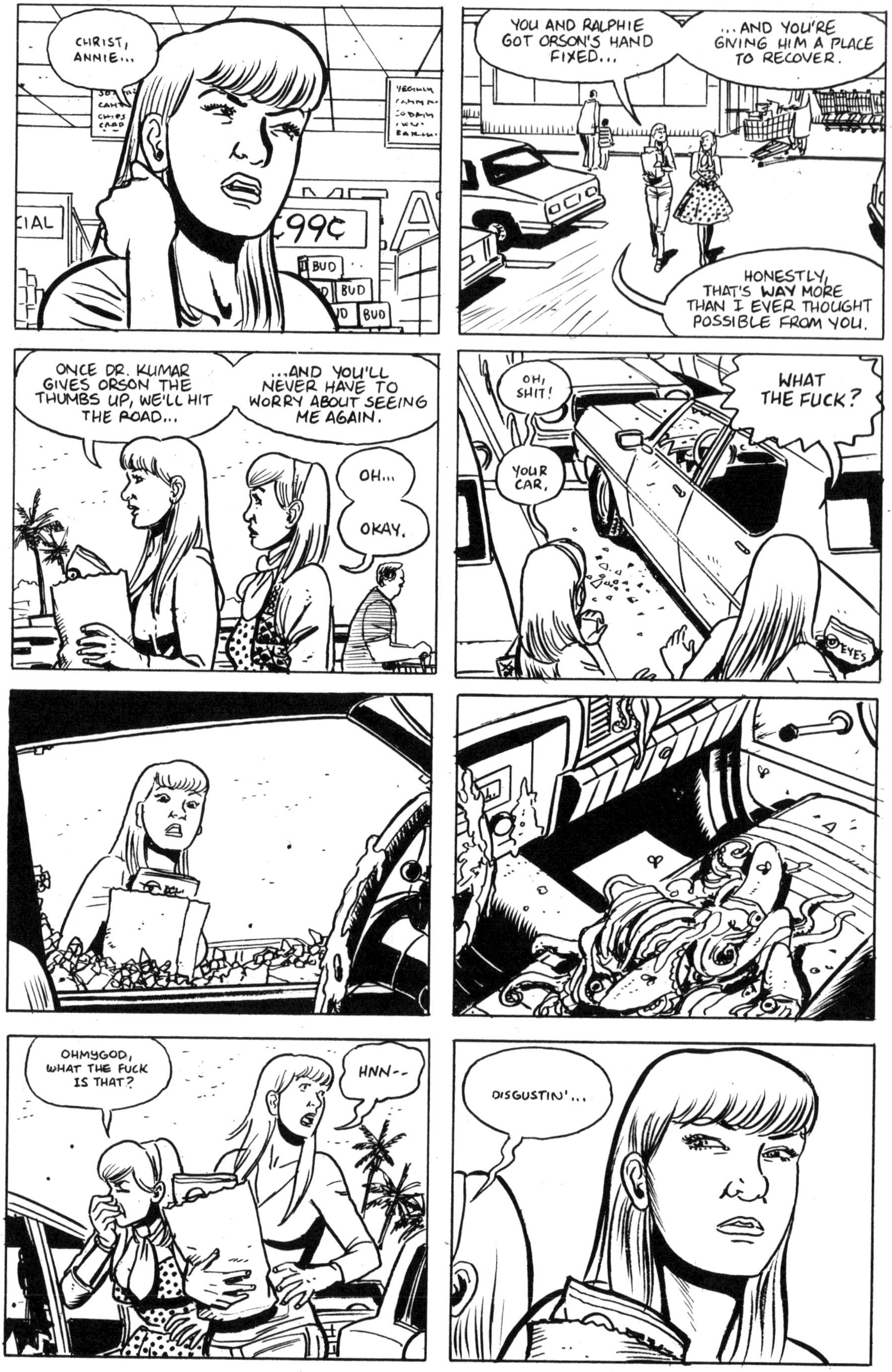
CHRIST, ANNIE...
CIAL
99¢
BUD
YOU AND RALPHIE GOT ORSON'S HAND FIXED...
...AND YOU'RE GIVING HIM A PLACE TO RECOVER.
HONESTLY, THAT'S WAY MORE THAN I EVER THOUGHT POSSIBLE FROM YOU.
ONCE DR. KUMAR GIVES ORSON THE THUMBS UP, WE'LL HIT THE ROAD...
...AND YOU'LL NEVER HAVE TO WORRY ABOUT SEEING ME AGAIN.
OH...
OKAY.
OH, SHIT!
YOUR CAR.
WHAT THE FUCK?
EYES
OHMYGOD, WHAT THE FUCK IS THAT?
HNN--
DISGUSTIN'...

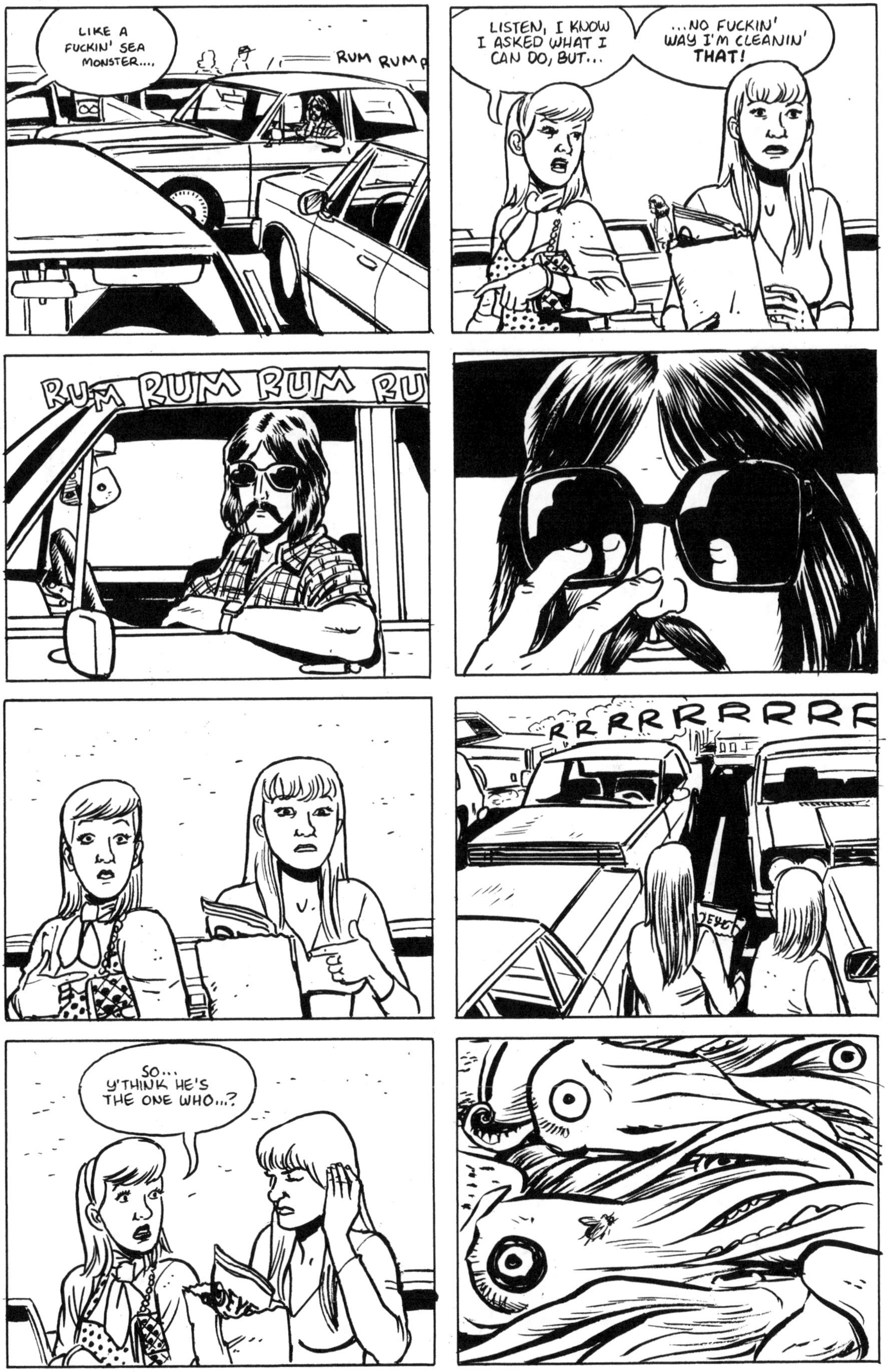
LIKE A FUCKIN' SEA MONSTER....
RUM RUM
LISTEN, I KNOW I ASKED WHAT I CAN DO, BUT...
...NO FUCKIN' WAY I'M CLEANIN' THAT!
RUM RUM RUM RU
RRRRRRRRRR
SO... Y'THINK HE'S THE ONE WHO...?

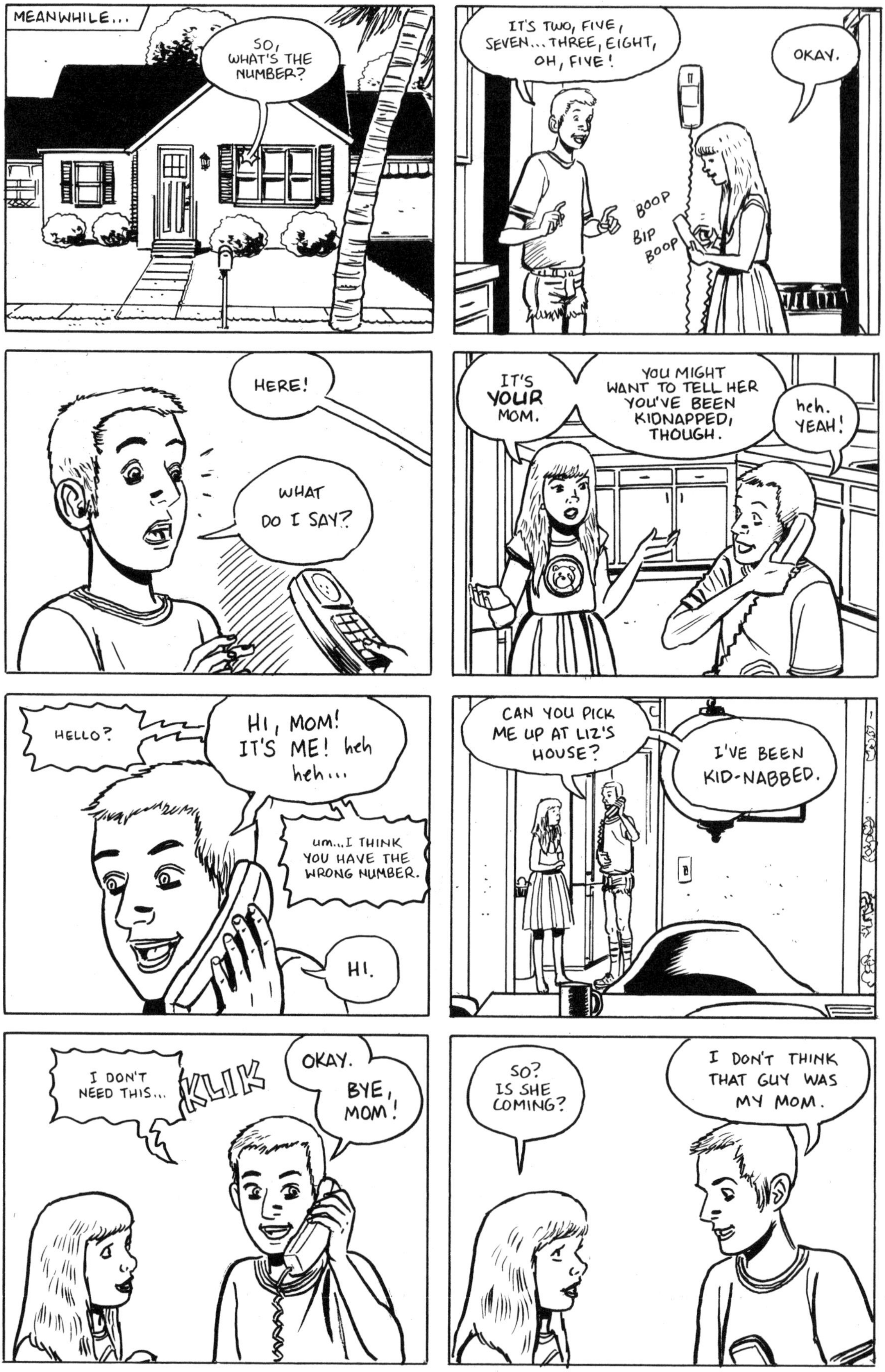
MEANWHILE...
SO, WHAT'S THE NUMBER?
IT'S TWO, FIVE, SEVEN... THREE, EIGHT, OH, FIVE!
OKAY.
BOOP
BIP
BOOP
HERE!
WHAT DO I SAY?
IT'S YOUR MOM.
YOU MIGHT WANT TO TELL HER YOU'VE BEEN KIDNAPPED, THOUGH.
heh. YEAH!
HELLO?
HI, MOM! IT'S ME! heh heh...
um...I THINK YOU HAVE THE WRONG NUMBER.
HI.
CAN YOU PICK ME UP AT LIZ'S HOUSE?
I'VE BEEN KID-NABBED.
I DON'T NEED THIS...
KLIK
OKAY.
BYE, MOM!
SO? IS SHE COMING?
I DON'T THINK THAT GUY WAS MY MOM.

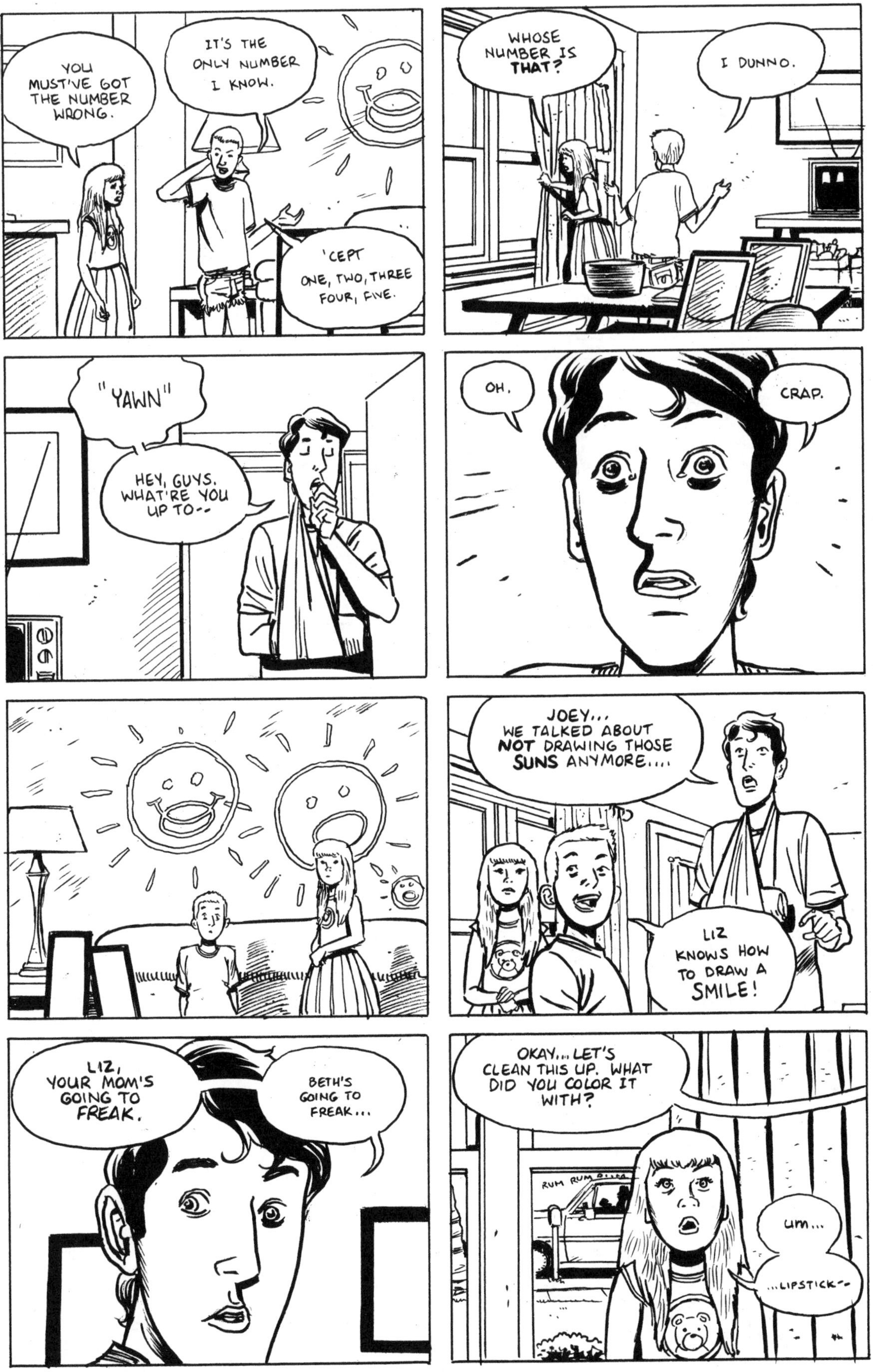
YOU MUST'VE GOT THE NUMBER WRONG.
IT'S THE ONLY NUMBER I KNOW.
'CEPT ONE, TWO, THREE FOUR, FIVE.
WHOSE NUMBER IS THAT?
I DUNNO.
"YAWN"
HEY, GUYS. WHAT'RE YOU UP TO--
OH.
CRAP.
JOEY... WE TALKED ABOUT NOT DRAWING THOSE SUNS ANYMORE....
LIZ KNOWS HOW TO DRAW A SMILE!
LIZ, YOUR MOM'S GOING TO FREAK.
BETH'S GOING TO FREAK...
OKAY... LET'S CLEAN THIS UP. WHAT DID YOU COLOR IT WITH?
um...
...LIPSTICK--

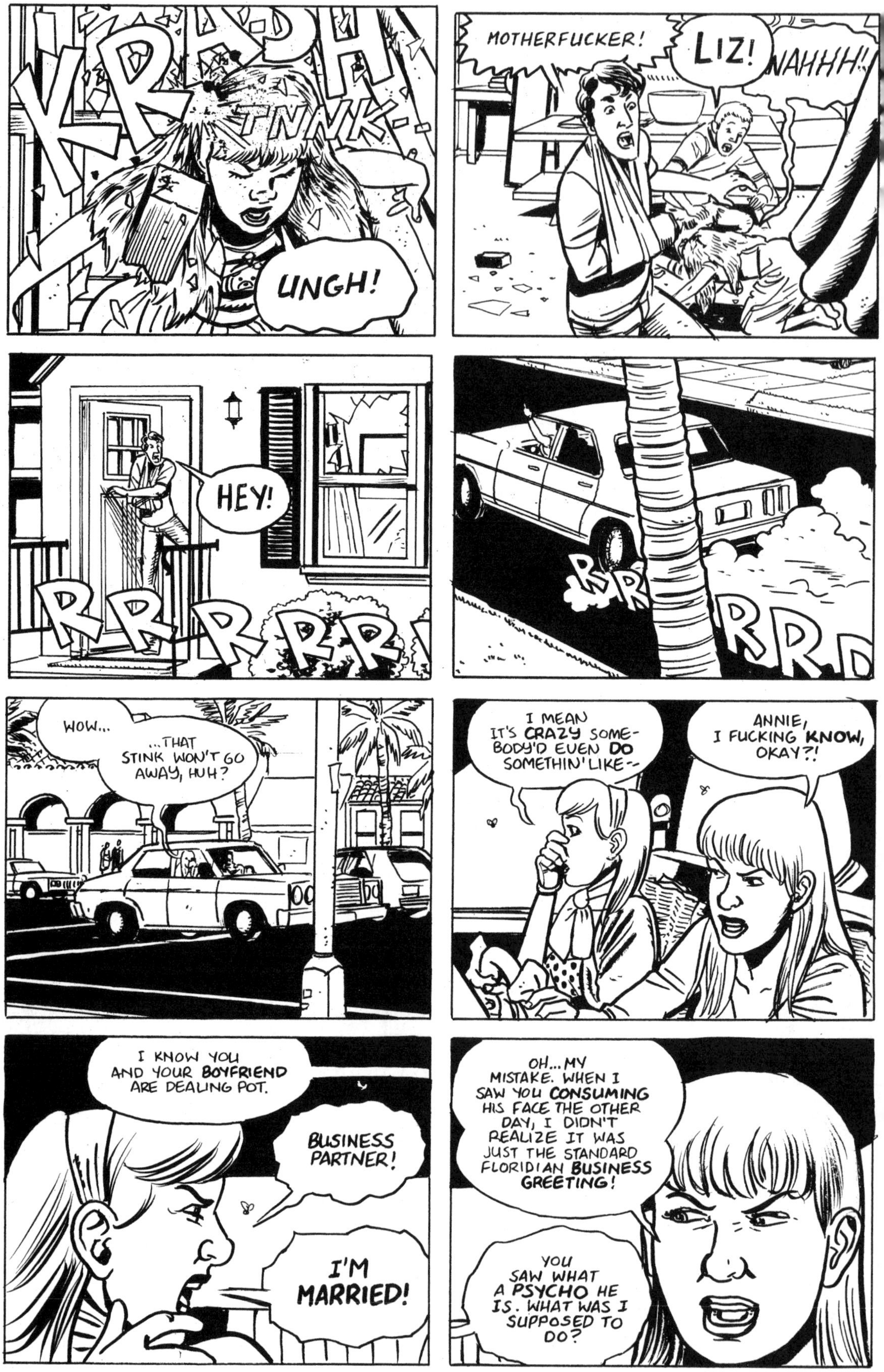

KRASH
TNNK-
UNGH!
MOTHERFUCKER!
LIZ!
NAHHH!!
HEY!
RRRRRR
RRRRRD
WOW...
...THAT STINK WON'T GO AWAY, HUH?
I MEAN IT'S CRAZY SOMEBODY'D EVEN DO SOMETHIN' LIKE--
ANNIE, I FUCKING KNOW, OKAY?!
I KNOW YOU AND YOUR BOYFRIEND ARE DEALING POT.
BUSINESS PARTNER!
I'M MARRIED!
OH... MY MISTAKE. WHEN I SAW YOU CONSUMING HIS FACE THE OTHER DAY, I DIDN'T REALIZE IT WAS JUST THE STANDARD FLORIDIAN BUSINESS GREETING!
YOU SAW WHAT A PSYCHO HE IS. WHAT WAS I SUPPOSED TO DO?

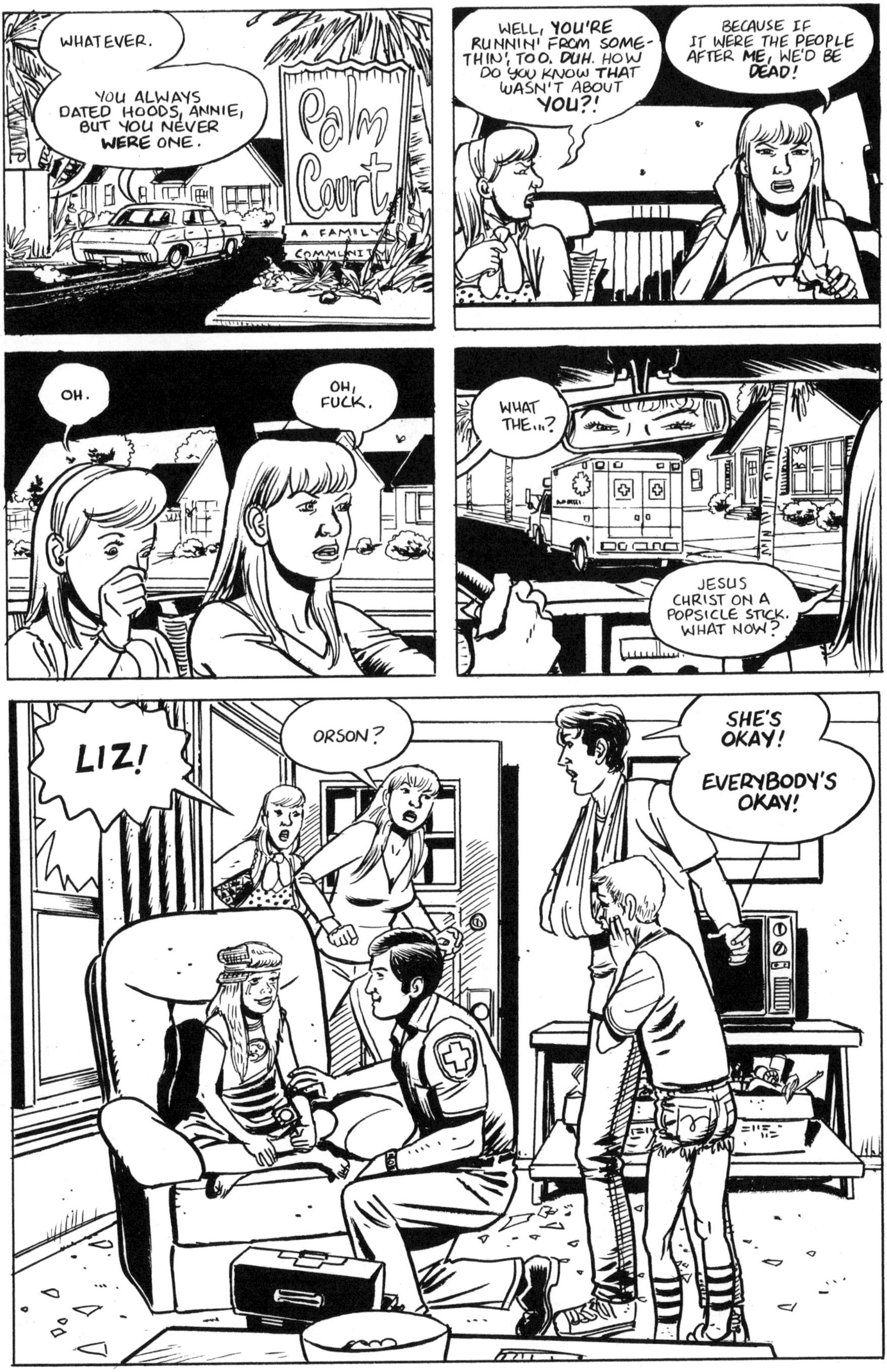
WHATEVER.
YOU ALWAYS DATED HOODS, ANNIE, BUT YOU NEVER WERE ONE.
Palm Court
A FAMILY COMMUNITY
WELL, YOU'RE RUNNIN' FROM SOMETHIN', TOO. DUH. HOW DO YOU KNOW THAT WASN'T ABOUT YOU?!
BECAUSE IF IT WERE THE PEOPLE AFTER ME, WE'D BE DEAD!
OH.
OH, FUCK.
WHAT THE...?
JESUS CHRIST ON A POPSICLE STICK. WHAT NOW?
LIZ!
ORSON?
SHE'S OKAY!
EVERYBODY'S OKAY!

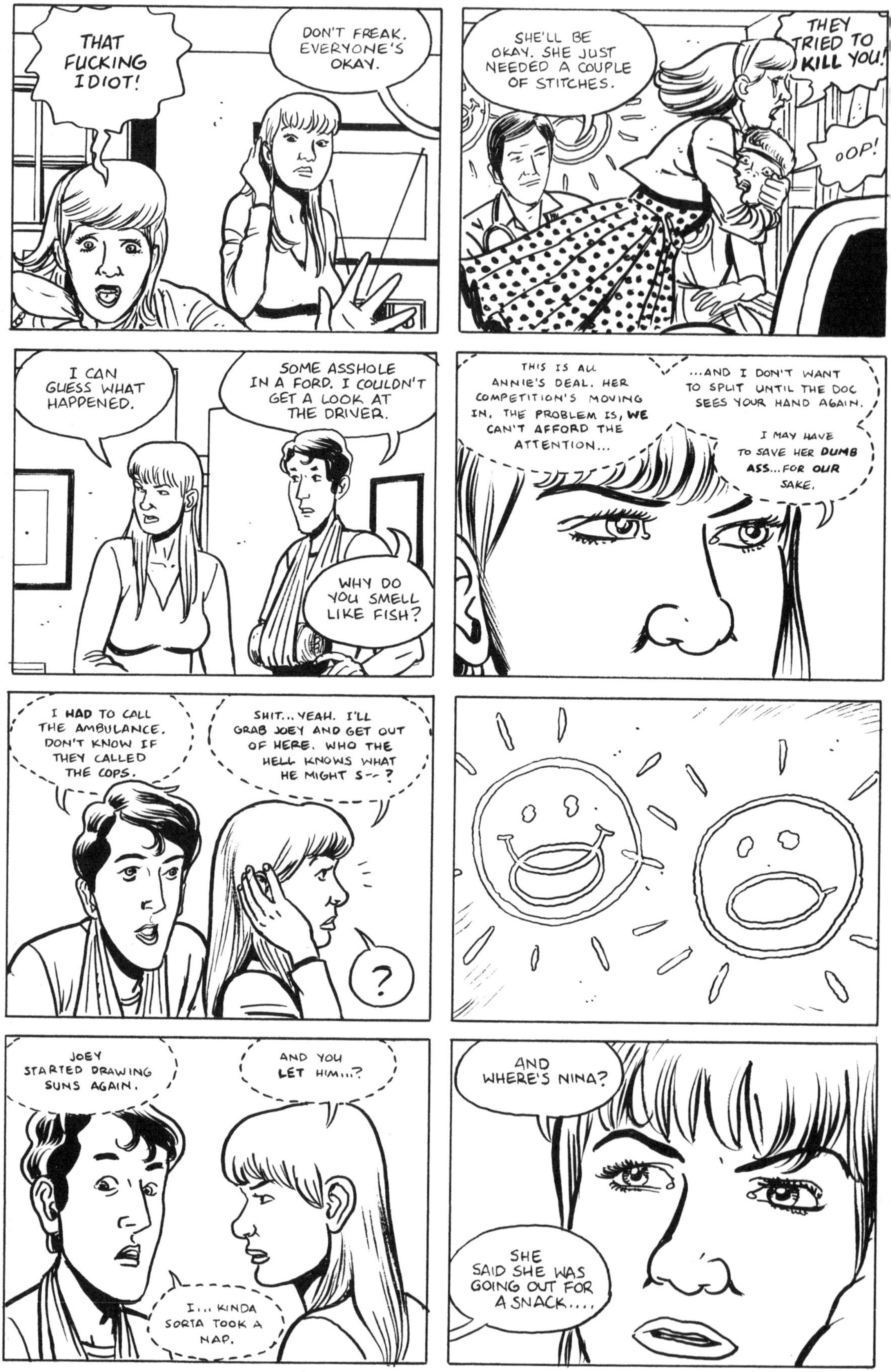
THAT FUCKING IDIOT!
DON'T FREAK. EVERYONE'S OKAY.
SHE'LL BE OKAY. SHE JUST NEEDED A COUPLE OF STITCHES.
THEY TRIED TO KILL YOU!
OOP!
I CAN GUESS WHAT HAPPENED.
SOME ASSHOLE IN A FORD. I COULDN'T GET A LOOK AT THE DRIVER.
WHY DO YOU SMELL LIKE FISH?
THIS IS ALL ANNIE'S DEAL. HER COMPETITION'S MOVING IN. THE PROBLEM IS, WE CAN'T AFFORD THE ATTENTION...
...AND I DON'T WANT TO SPLIT UNTIL THE DOC SEES YOUR HAND AGAIN.
I MAY HAVE TO SAVE HER DUMB ASS...FOR OUR SAKE.
I HAD TO CALL THE AMBULANCE. DON'T KNOW IF THEY CALLED THE COPS.
SHIT...YEAH. I'LL GRAB JOEY AND GET OUT OF HERE. WHO THE HELL KNOWS WHAT HE MIGHT S--?
?
JOEY STARTED DRAWING SUNS AGAIN.
AND YOU LET HIM...?
I...KINDA SORTA TOOK A NAP.
AND WHERE'S NINA?
SHE SAID SHE WAS GOING OUT FOR A SNACK....

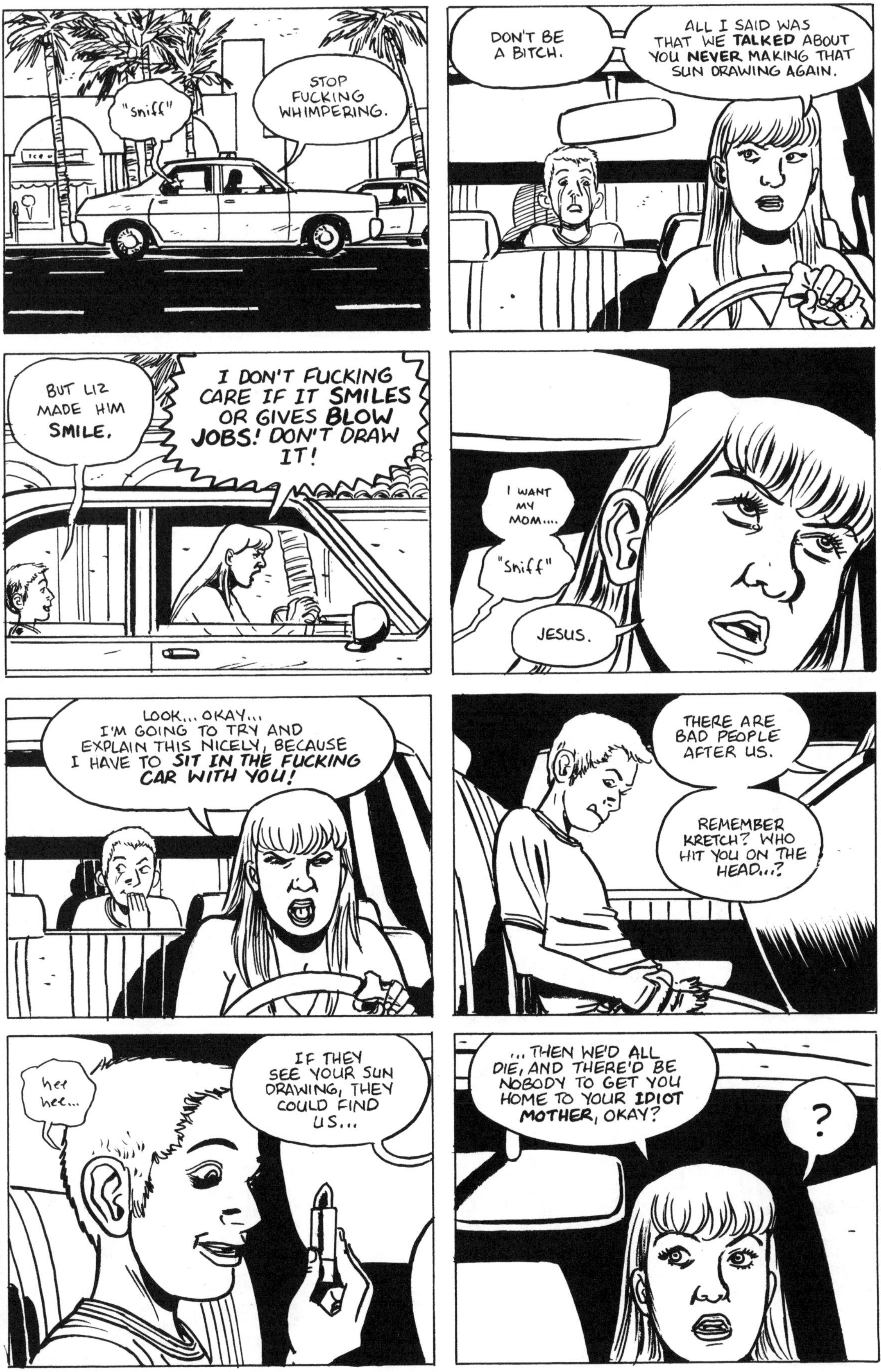
"sniff"
STOP FUCKING WHIMPERING.
DON'T BE A BITCH.
ALL I SAID WAS THAT WE TALKED ABOUT YOU NEVER MAKING THAT SUN DRAWING AGAIN.
BUT LIZ MADE HIM SMILE.
I DON'T FUCKING CARE IF IT SMILES OR GIVES BLOW JOBS! DON'T DRAW IT!
I WANT MY MOM....
"sniff"
JESUS.
LOOK... OKAY... I'M GOING TO TRY AND EXPLAIN THIS NICELY, BECAUSE I HAVE TO SIT IN THE FUCKING CAR WITH YOU!
THERE ARE BAD PEOPLE AFTER US.
REMEMBER KRETCH? WHO HIT YOU ON THE HEAD...?
hee hee...
IF THEY SEE YOUR SUN DRAWING, THEY COULD FIND US...
...THEN WE'D ALL DIE, AND THERE'D BE NOBODY TO GET YOU HOME TO YOUR IDIOT MOTHER, OKAY?
?

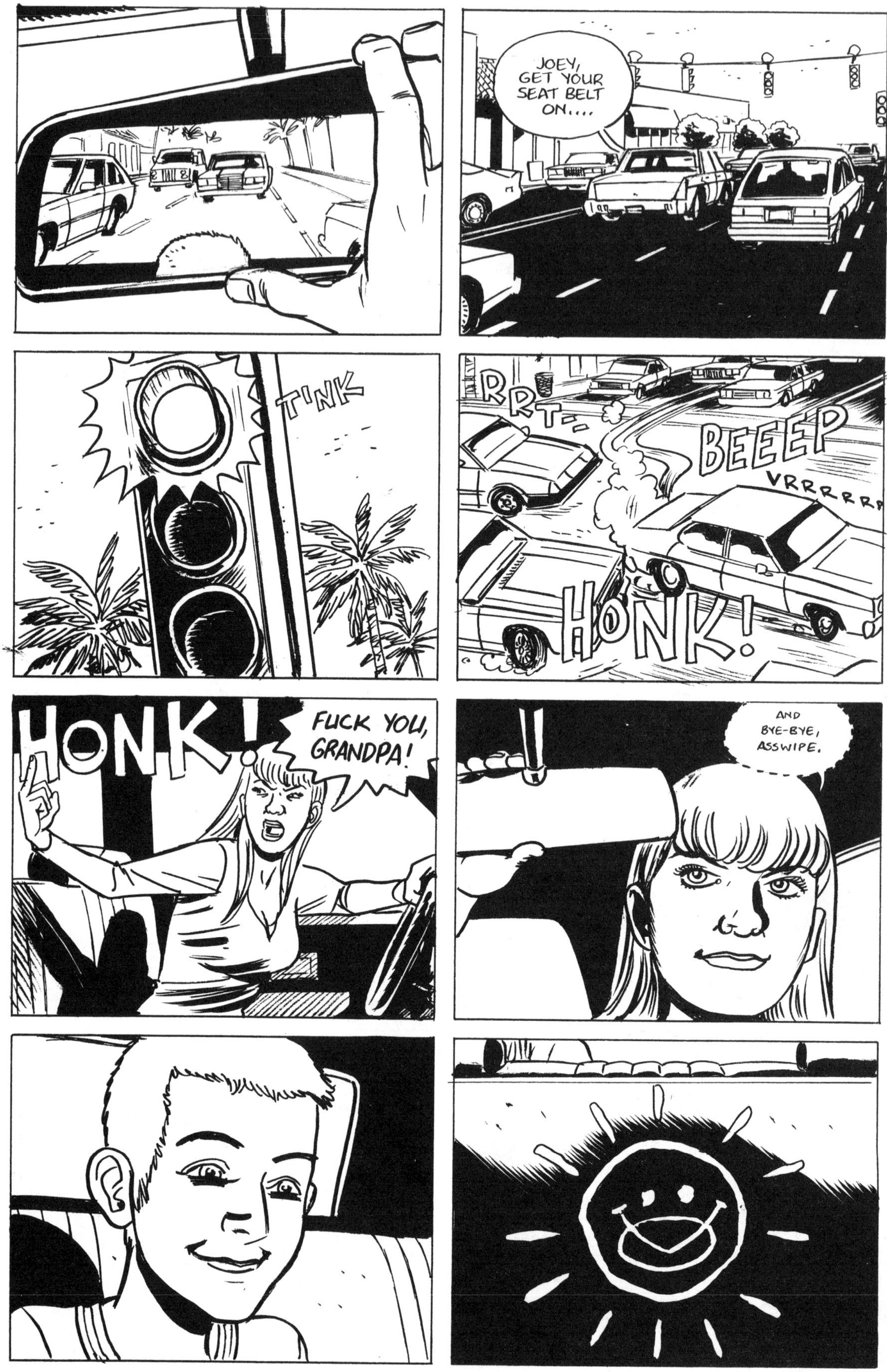

JOEY, GET YOUR SEAT BELT ON....
TINK
RRT-.
BEEEP
VRRRRRRR
HONK!
HONK!
FUCK YOU, GRANDPA!
AND BYE-BYE, ASSWIPE.

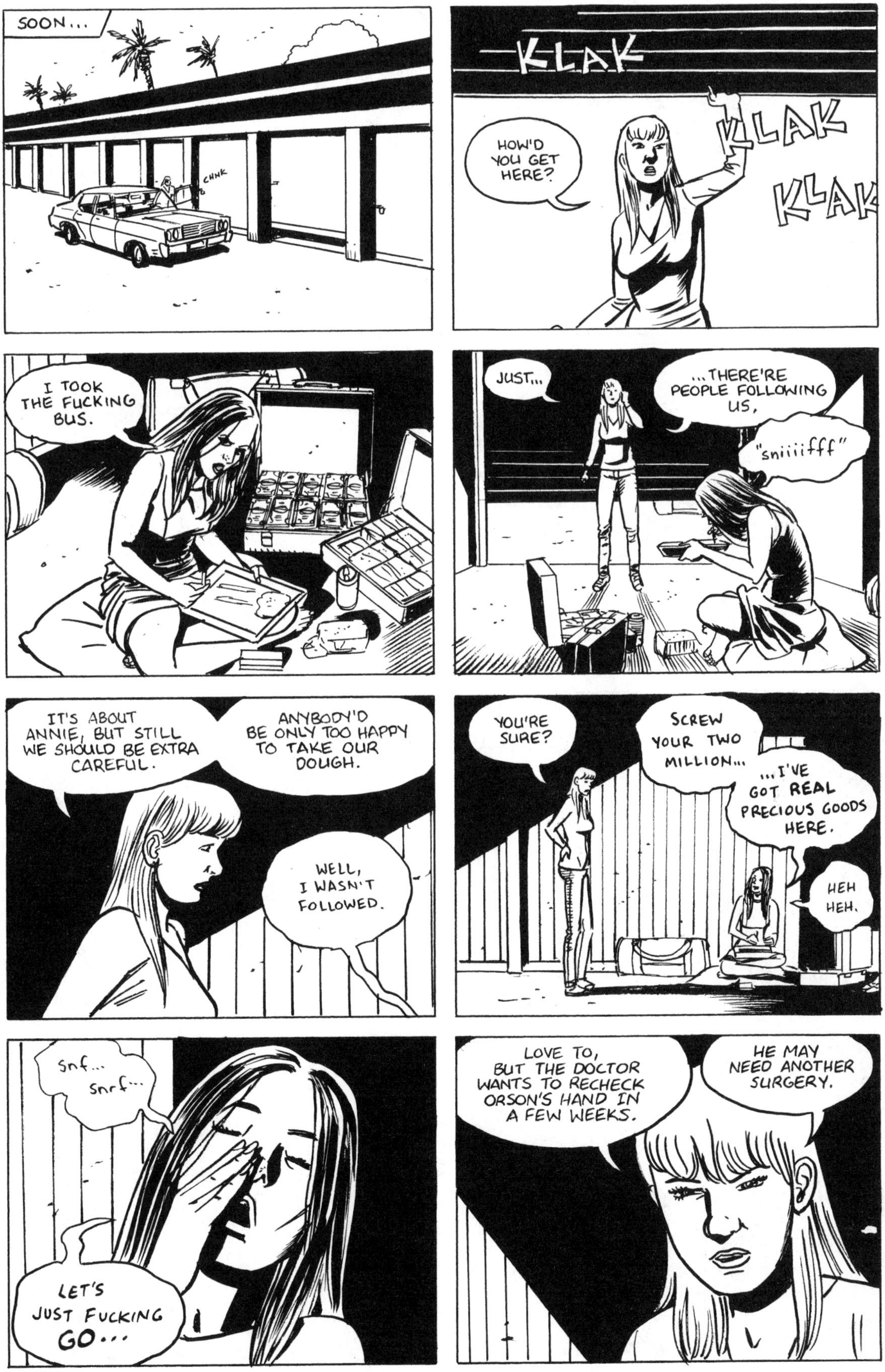
SOON...
CHNK
KLAK
HOW'D YOU GET HERE?
KLAK
KLAK
I TOOK THE FUCKING BUS.
JUST...
...THERE'RE PEOPLE FOLLOWING US,
"sniiiifff"
IT'S ABOUT ANNIE, BUT STILL WE SHOULD BE EXTRA CAREFUL.
ANYBODY'D BE ONLY TOO HAPPY TO TAKE OUR DOUGH.
WELL, I WASN'T FOLLOWED.
YOU'RE SURE?
SCREW YOUR TWO MILLION...
...I'VE GOT REAL PRECIOUS GOODS HERE.
HEH HEH.
Snf... snrf...
LET'S JUST FUCKING GO...
LOVE TO, BUT THE DOCTOR WANTS TO RECHECK ORSON'S HAND IN A FEW WEEKS.
HE MAY NEED ANOTHER SURGERY.

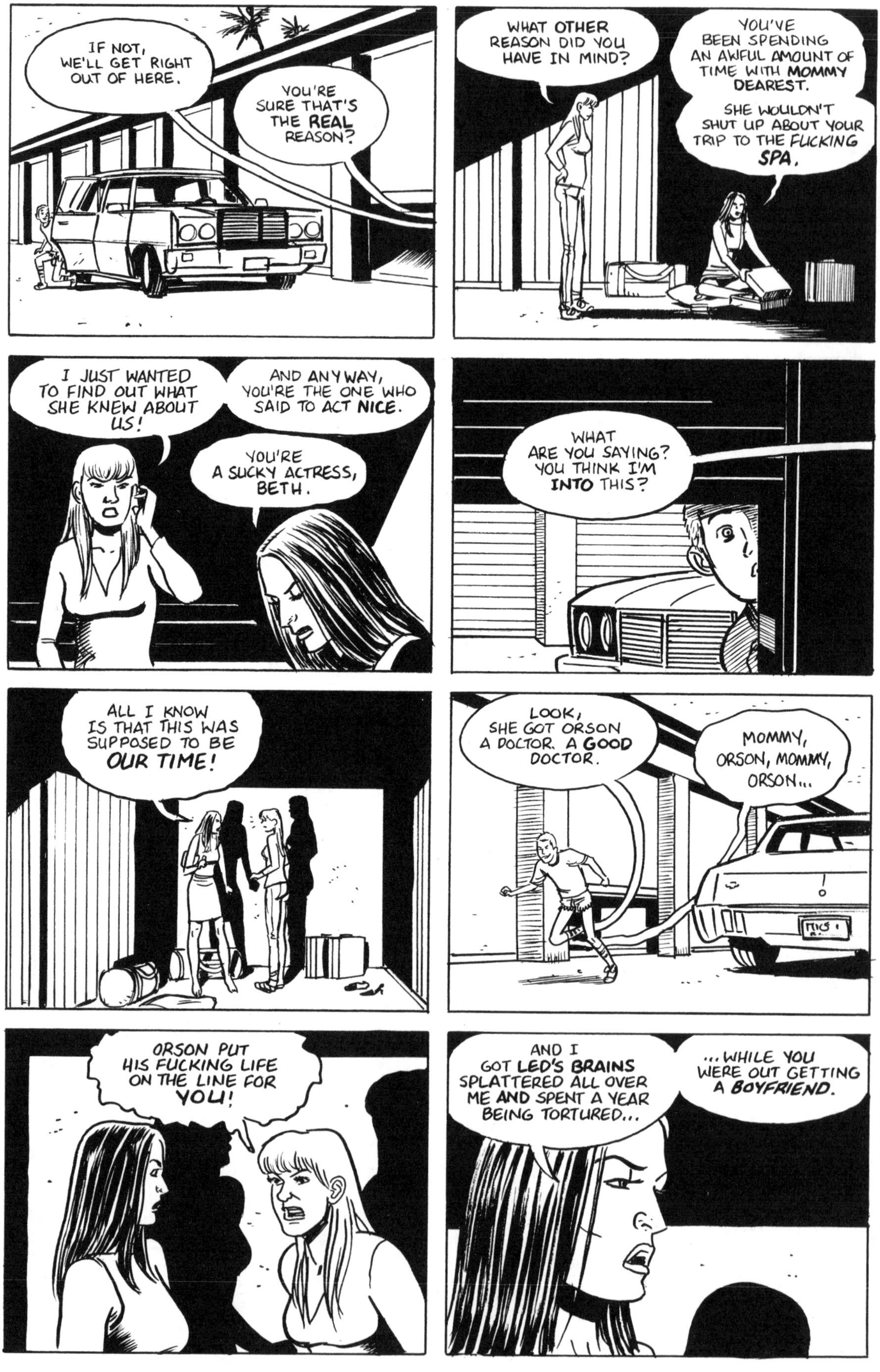
IF NOT, WE'LL GET RIGHT OUT OF HERE.
YOU'RE SURE THAT'S THE **REAL** REASON?
WHAT **OTHER** REASON DID YOU HAVE IN MIND?
YOU'VE BEEN SPENDING AN AWFUL AMOUNT OF TIME WITH **MOMMY DEAREST**.
SHE WOULDN'T SHUT UP ABOUT YOUR TRIP TO THE *FUCKING* **SPA**.
I JUST WANTED TO FIND OUT WHAT SHE KNEW ABOUT *US!*
AND ANYWAY, YOU'RE THE ONE WHO SAID TO ACT **NICE**.
YOU'RE A SUCKY ACTRESS, BETH.
WHAT ARE YOU SAYING? YOU THINK I'M **INTO** THIS?
ALL I KNOW IS THAT THIS WAS SUPPOSED TO BE ***OUR TIME!***
LOOK, SHE GOT ORSON A DOCTOR. A **GOOD** DOCTOR.
MOMMY, ORSON, MOMMY, ORSON...
ORSON PUT HIS FUCKING LIFE ON THE LINE FOR **YOU!**
AND I GOT **LED'S BRAINS** SPLATTERED ALL OVER ME **AND** SPENT A YEAR BEING TORTURED...
...WHILE **YOU** WERE OUT GETTING A ***BOYFRIEND***.

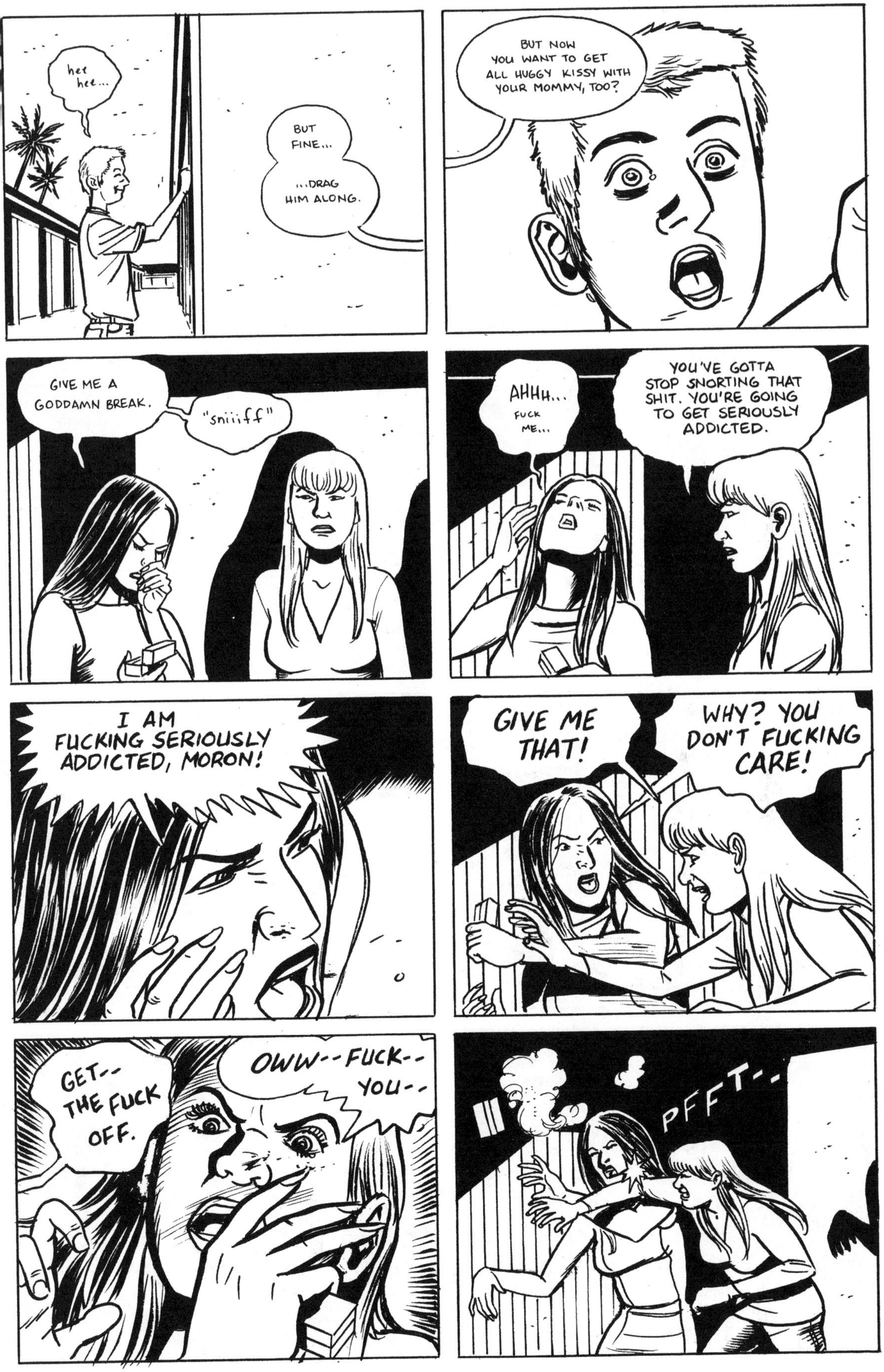
hee hee...
BUT FINE...
...DRAG HIM ALONG.
BUT NOW YOU WANT TO GET ALL HUGGY KISSY WITH YOUR MOMMY, TOO?
GIVE ME A GODDAMN BREAK.
"sniiiff"
AHHH... FUCK ME...
YOU'VE GOTTA STOP SNORTING THAT SHIT. YOU'RE GOING TO GET SERIOUSLY ADDICTED.
I AM FUCKING SERIOUSLY ADDICTED, MORON!
GIVE ME THAT!
WHY? YOU DON'T FUCKING CARE!
GET-- THE FUCK OFF.
OWW--FUCK-- YOU--
PFFT--

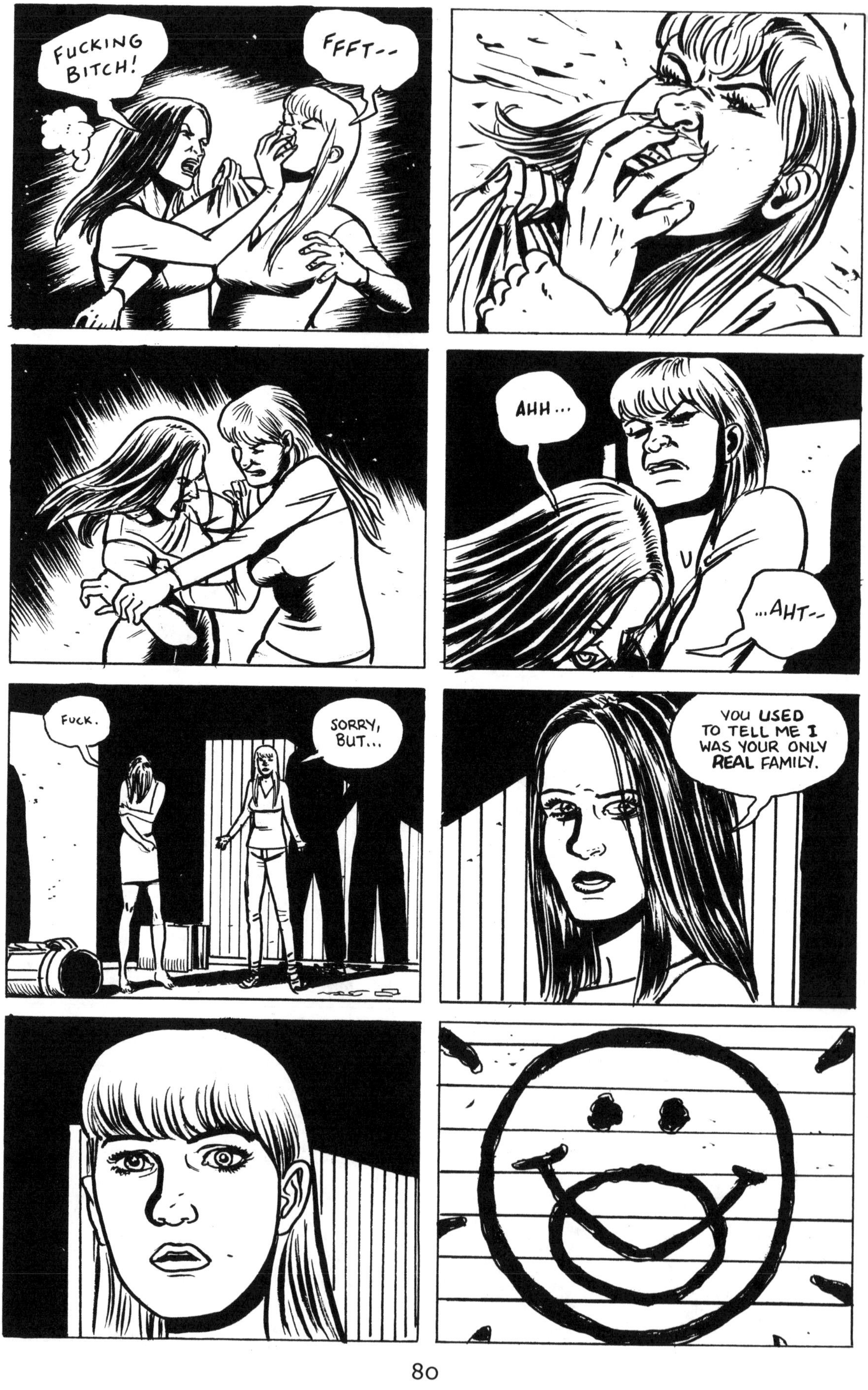

FUCKING BITCH!
FFFT--
AHH...
...AHT--
FUCK.
SORRY, BUT...
YOU USED TO TELL ME I WAS YOUR ONLY REAL FAMILY.

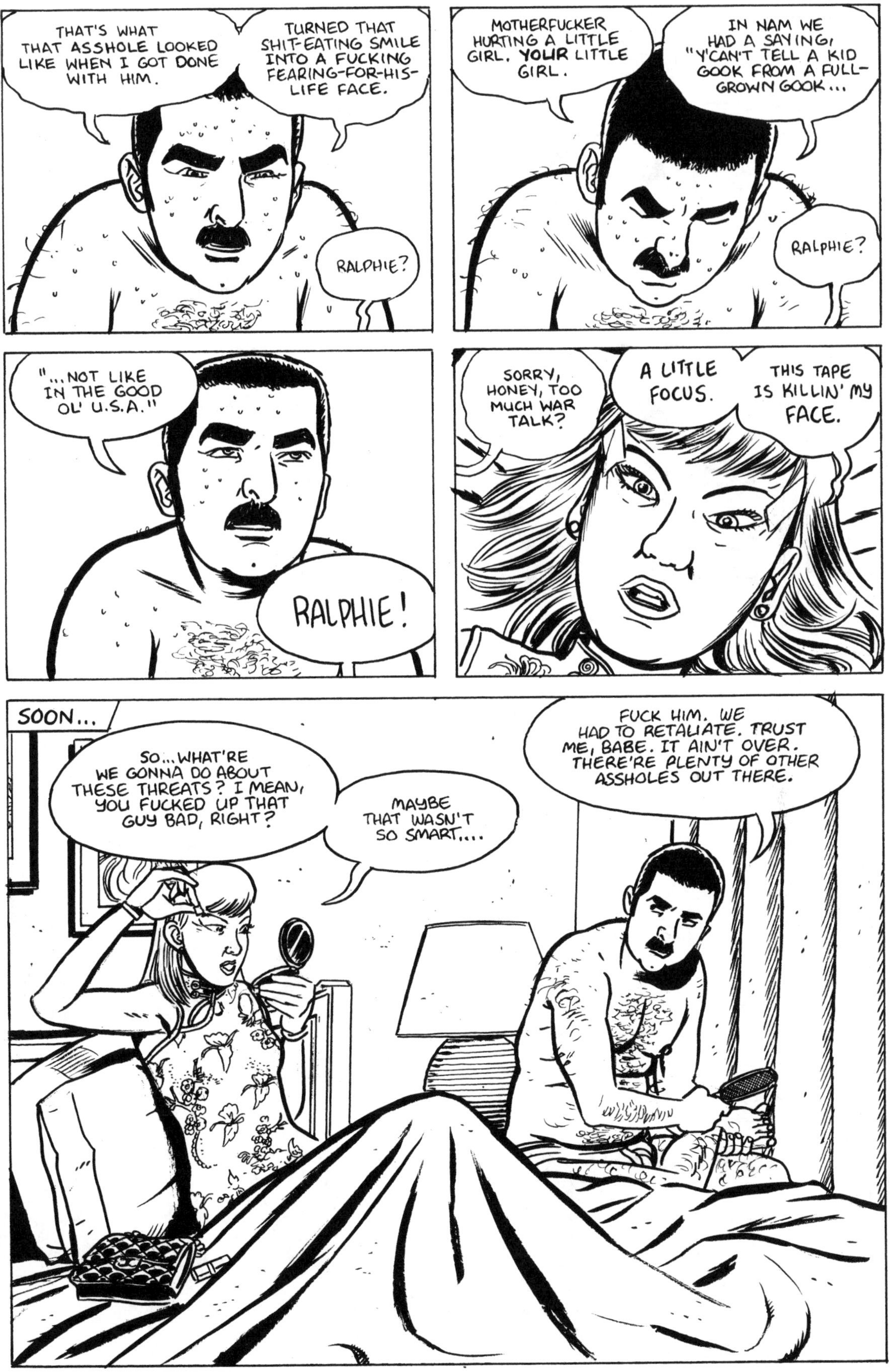
THAT'S WHAT THAT ASSHOLE LOOKED LIKE WHEN I GOT DONE WITH HIM.
TURNED THAT SHIT-EATING SMILE INTO A FUCKING FEARING-FOR-HIS-LIFE FACE.
RALPHIE?
MOTHERFUCKER HURTING A LITTLE GIRL. YOUR LITTLE GIRL.
IN NAM WE HAD A SAYING, "Y'CAN'T TELL A KID GOOK FROM A FULL-GROWN GOOK...
RALPHIE?
"...NOT LIKE IN THE GOOD OL' U.S.A."
RALPHIE!
SORRY, HONEY, TOO MUCH WAR TALK?
A LITTLE FOCUS.
THIS TAPE IS KILLIN' MY FACE.
SOON...
SO...WHAT'RE WE GONNA DO ABOUT THESE THREATS? I MEAN, YOU FUCKED UP THAT GUY BAD, RIGHT?
MAYBE THAT WASN'T SO SMART....
FUCK HIM. WE HAD TO RETALIATE. TRUST ME, BABE. IT AIN'T OVER. THERE'RE PLENTY OF OTHER ASSHOLES OUT THERE.

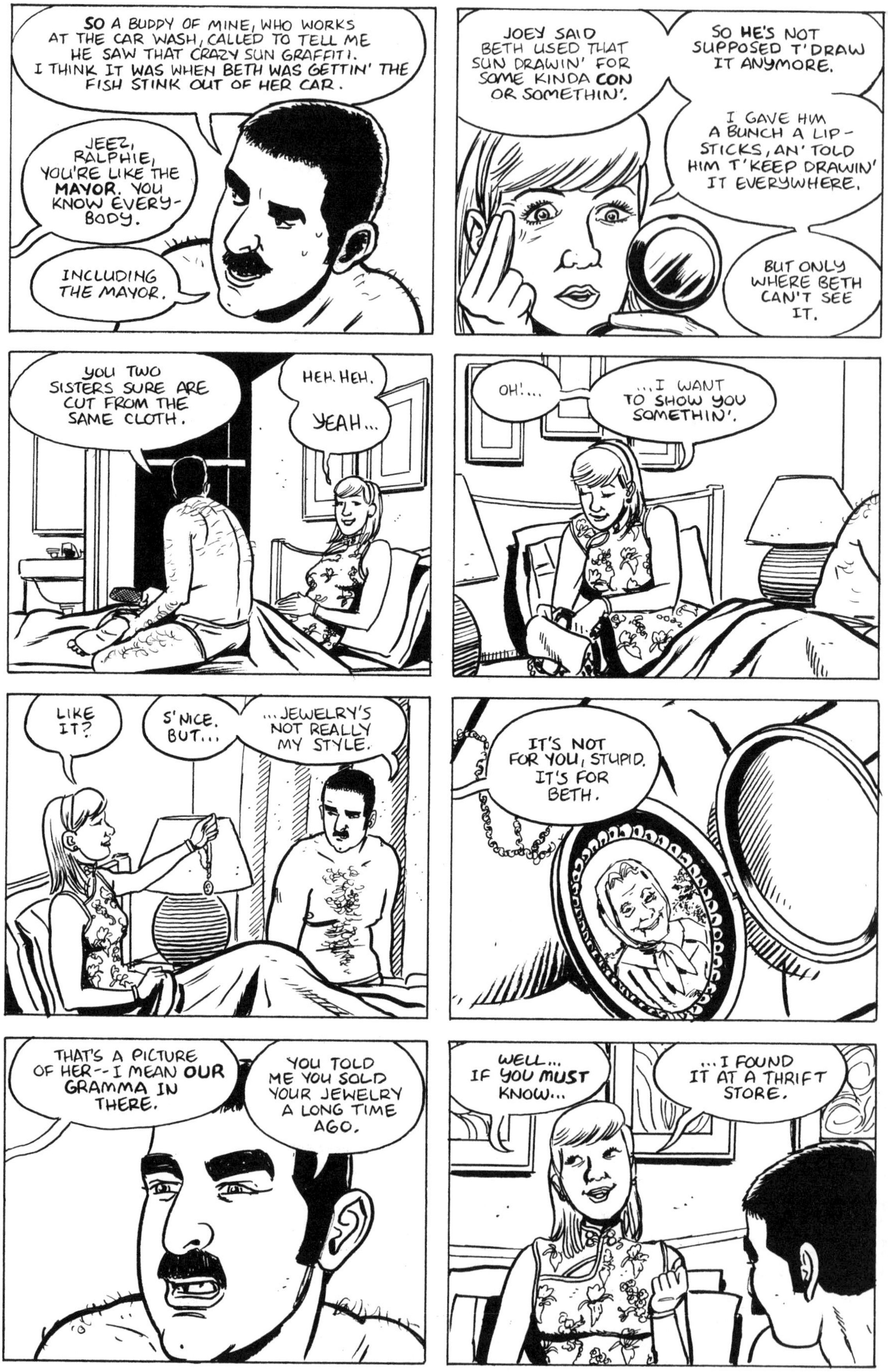
SO A BUDDY OF MINE, WHO WORKS AT THE CAR WASH, CALLED TO TELL ME HE SAW THAT CRAZY SUN GRAFFITI. I THINK IT WAS WHEN BETH WAS GETTIN' THE FISH STINK OUT OF HER CAR.
JEEZ, RALPHIE, YOU'RE LIKE THE MAYOR. YOU KNOW EVERY-BODY.
INCLUDING THE MAYOR.
JOEY SAID BETH USED THAT SUN DRAWIN' FOR SOME KINDA CON OR SOMETHIN'.
SO HE'S NOT SUPPOSED T'DRAW IT ANYMORE.
I GAVE HIM A BUNCH A LIP-STICKS, AN' TOLD HIM T'KEEP DRAWIN' IT EVERYWHERE.
BUT ONLY WHERE BETH CAN'T SEE IT.
YOU TWO SISTERS SURE ARE CUT FROM THE SAME CLOTH.
HEH. HEH.
YEAH...
OH!...
...I WANT TO SHOW YOU SOMETHIN'.
LIKE IT?
S'NICE. BUT...
...JEWELRY'S NOT REALLY MY STYLE.
IT'S NOT FOR YOU, STUPID. IT'S FOR BETH.
THAT'S A PICTURE OF HER--I MEAN OUR GRAMMA IN THERE.
YOU TOLD ME YOU SOLD YOUR JEWELRY A LONG TIME AGO.
WELL... IF YOU MUST KNOW...
...I FOUND IT AT A THRIFT STORE.

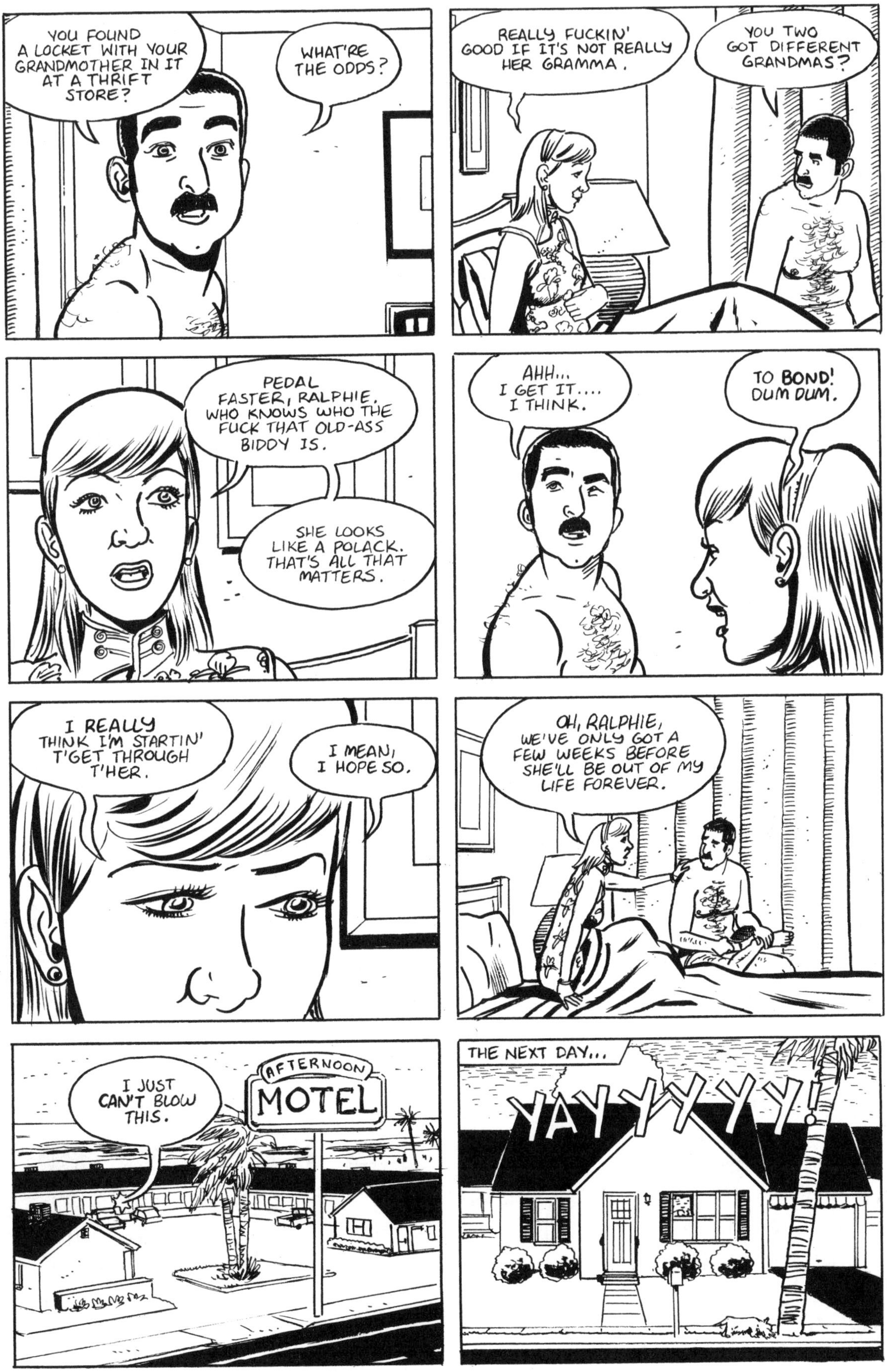
YOU FOUND A LOCKET WITH YOUR GRANDMOTHER IN IT AT A THRIFT STORE?
WHAT'RE THE ODDS?
REALLY FUCKIN' GOOD IF IT'S NOT REALLY HER GRAMMA.
YOU TWO GOT DIFFERENT GRANDMAS?
PEDAL FASTER, RALPHIE. WHO KNOWS WHO THE FUCK THAT OLD-ASS BIDDY IS.
SHE LOOKS LIKE A POLACK. THAT'S ALL THAT MATTERS.
AHH... I GET IT.... I THINK.
TO BOND! DUM DUM.
I REALLY THINK I'M STARTIN' T'GET THROUGH T'HER.
I MEAN, I HOPE SO.
OH, RALPHIE, WE'VE ONLY GOT A FEW WEEKS BEFORE SHE'LL BE OUT OF MY LIFE FOREVER.
I JUST CAN'T BLOW THIS.
AFTERNOON
MOTEL
THE NEXT DAY...
YAYYYYY!

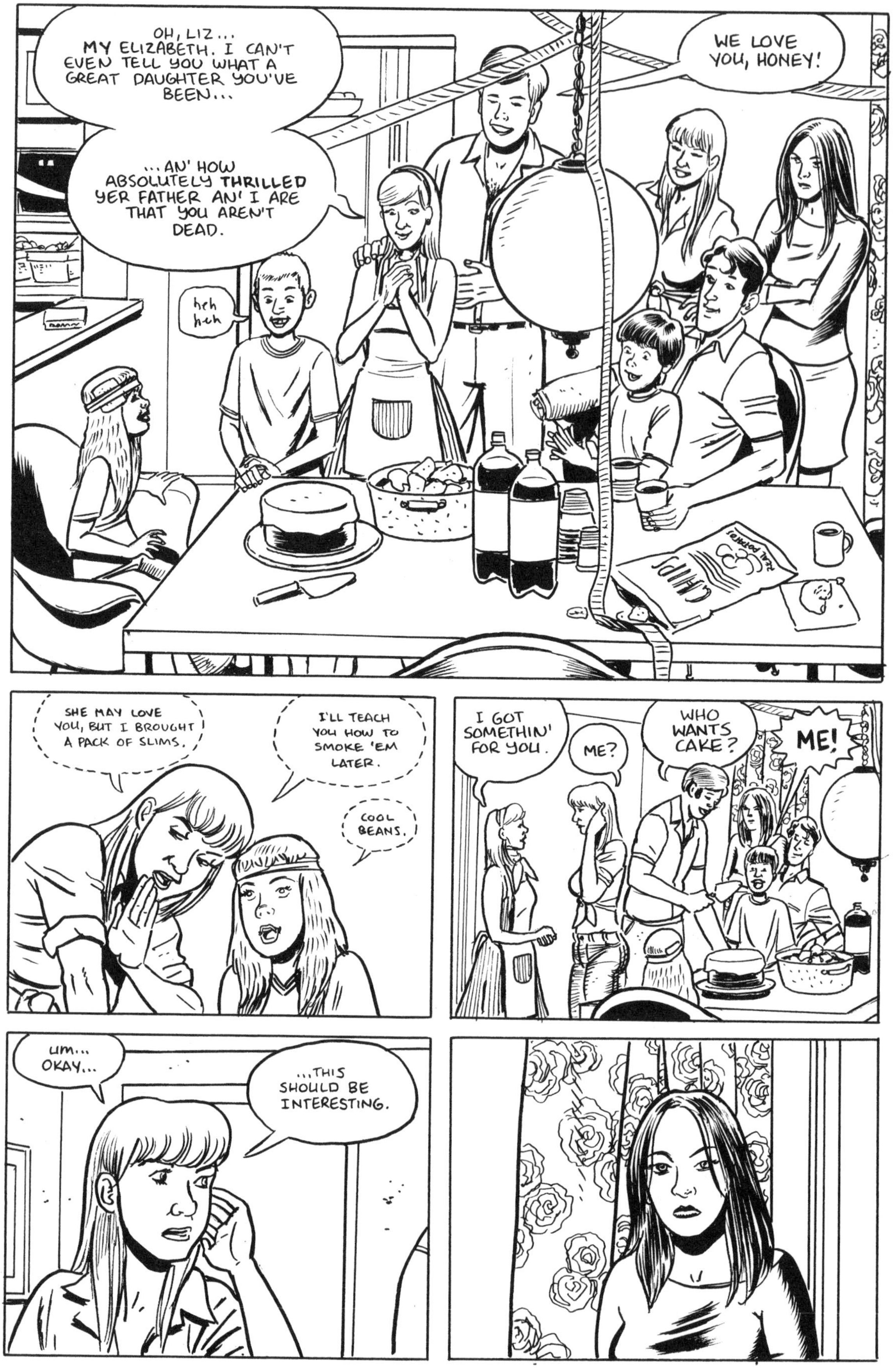
OH, LIZ... MY ELIZABETH. I CAN'T EVEN TELL YOU WHAT A GREAT DAUGHTER YOU'VE BEEN...
...AN' HOW ABSOLUTELY THRILLED YER FATHER AN' I ARE THAT YOU AREN'T DEAD.
WE LOVE YOU, HONEY!
heh heh
CHIPS
SHE MAY LOVE YOU, BUT I BROUGHT A PACK OF SLIMS.
I'LL TEACH YOU HOW TO SMOKE 'EM LATER.
COOL BEANS.
I GOT SOMETHIN' FOR YOU.
ME?
WHO WANTS CAKE?
ME!
UM... OKAY...
...THIS SHOULD BE INTERESTING.

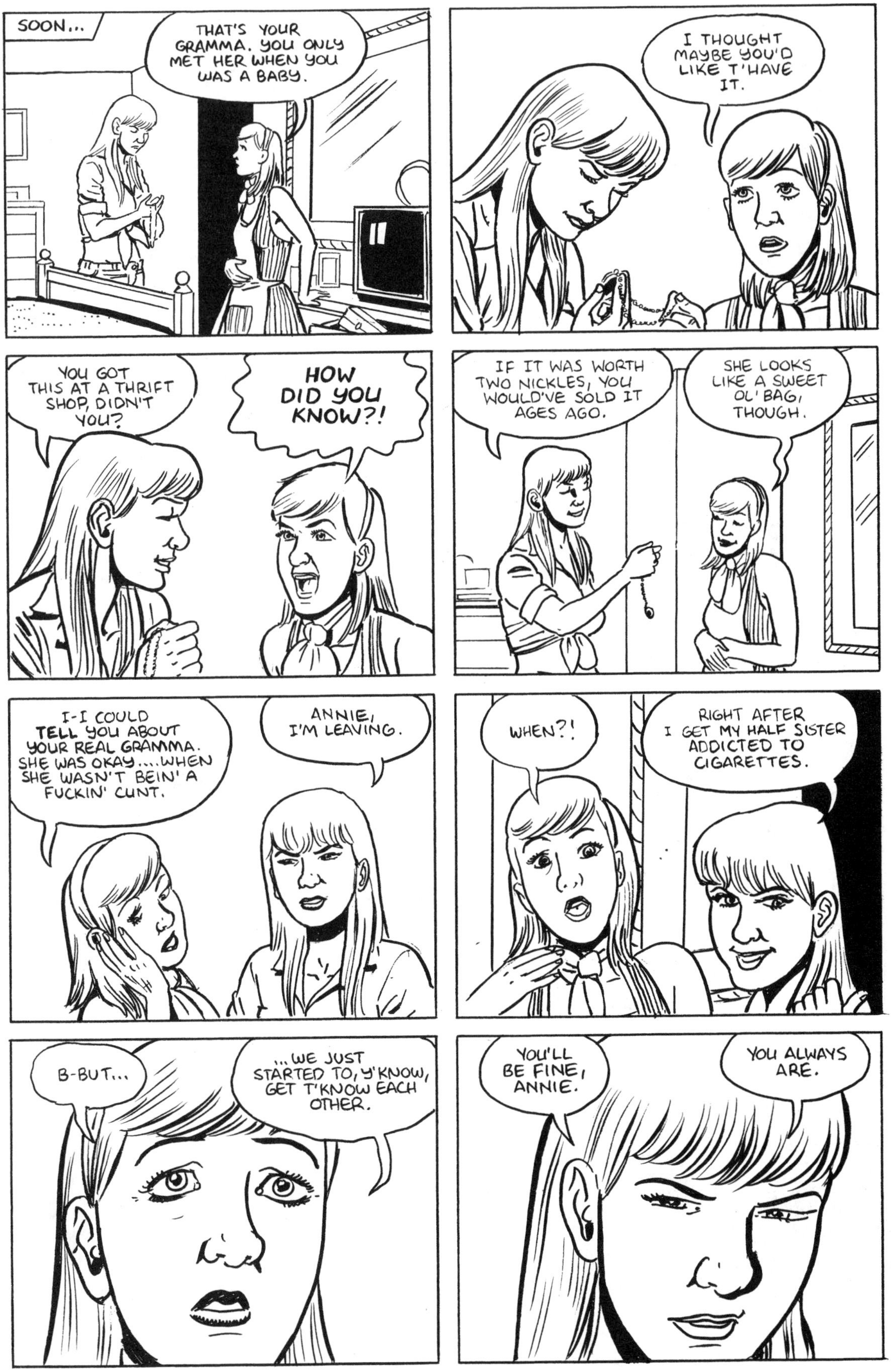
SOON...
THAT'S YOUR GRAMMA. YOU ONLY MET HER WHEN YOU WAS A BABY.
I THOUGHT MAYBE YOU'D LIKE T'HAVE IT.
YOU GOT THIS AT A THRIFT SHOP, DIDN'T YOU?
HOW DID YOU KNOW?!
IF IT WAS WORTH TWO NICKLES, YOU WOULD'VE SOLD IT AGES AGO.
SHE LOOKS LIKE A SWEET OL' BAG, THOUGH.
I-I COULD TELL YOU ABOUT YOUR REAL GRAMMA. SHE WAS OKAY....WHEN SHE WASN'T BEIN' A FUCKIN' CUNT.
ANNIE, I'M LEAVING.
WHEN?!
RIGHT AFTER I GET MY HALF SISTER ADDICTED TO CIGARETTES.
B-BUT...
...WE JUST STARTED TO, Y'KNOW, GET T'KNOW EACH OTHER.
YOU'LL BE FINE, ANNIE.
YOU ALWAYS ARE.

FOUR MINUTES LATER...

C'MON...
C'MON...PICK
UP...

BRRRRIIING

BRRRRIIIING

HELLO?

SHE'S LEAVIN'!
SHE'S FUCKIN' LEAVIN'
IN A FEW MINUTES,
RALPHIE!

OH, HEY, BABE.
I GOT ANOTHER WEIRD
SUN SIGHTING. THIS
ONE AT A STORAGE--

DID YOU
NOT FUCKIN'
HEAR ME?!

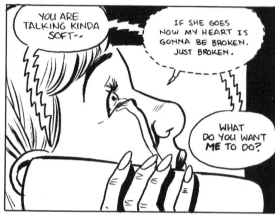

YOU ARE
TALKING KINDA
SOFT--

IF SHE GOES
NOW MY HEART IS
GONNA BE BROKEN.
JUST BROKEN.

WHAT
DO YOU WANT
ME TO DO?

YOUR
DAD LOOKS LIKE
HE'D HAVE A STICK
UP HIS BUTT ABOUT
THIS...

... BEST
NOT TO PRACTICE
WHEN HE'S
AROUND.

SHHT--

YOU'RE
THE COOLEST,
AUNT BETH.

I'M GLAD
MOM NAMED
ME AFTER
YOU.

NOW
CAN WE
LIGHT IT?

PSST!
BETH!

HANG
ON A SEC,
KIDDO.....

SHE'S A
REALLY COOL
KID.

HARD TO BELIEVE
YOU AND BIG BORING
IN THERE SPAWNED
HER.

WE HAVE
A PROBLEM.

RALPHIE'S
HERE. HE SAYS IT'S
URGENT HE SPEAK TO
US ALL.

RALPHIE?
BUT HUSBAND'S
HOME....

UP THE
BLOCK...

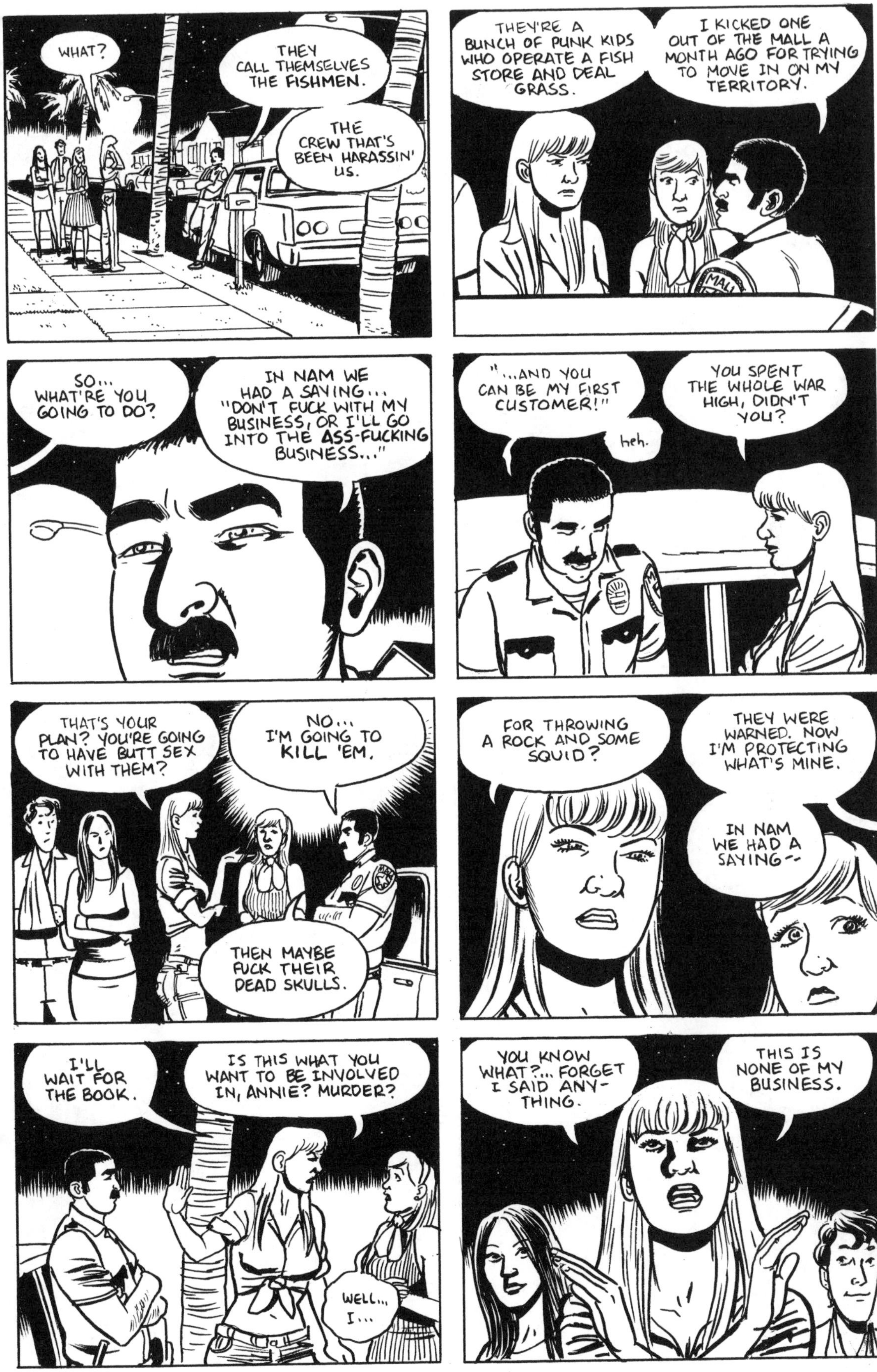
WHAT?
THEY CALL THEMSELVES THE FISHMEN.
THE CREW THAT'S BEEN HARASSIN' US.
THEY'RE A BUNCH OF PUNK KIDS WHO OPERATE A FISH STORE AND DEAL GRASS.
I KICKED ONE OUT OF THE MALL A MONTH AGO FOR TRYING TO MOVE IN ON MY TERRITORY.
SO... WHAT'RE YOU GOING TO DO?
IN NAM WE HAD A SAYING... "DON'T FUCK WITH MY BUSINESS, OR I'LL GO INTO THE ASS-FUCKING BUSINESS..."
"...AND YOU CAN BE MY FIRST CUSTOMER!"
heh.
YOU SPENT THE WHOLE WAR HIGH, DIDN'T YOU?
THAT'S YOUR PLAN? YOU'RE GOING TO HAVE BUTT SEX WITH THEM?
NO... I'M GOING TO KILL 'EM.
THEN MAYBE FUCK THEIR DEAD SKULLS.
FOR THROWING A ROCK AND SOME SQUID?
THEY WERE WARNED. NOW I'M PROTECTING WHAT'S MINE.
IN NAM WE HAD A SAYING--
I'LL WAIT FOR THE BOOK.
IS THIS WHAT YOU WANT TO BE INVOLVED IN, ANNIE? MURDER?
WELL... I...
YOU KNOW WHAT?... FORGET I SAID ANY-THING.
THIS IS NONE OF MY BUSINESS.

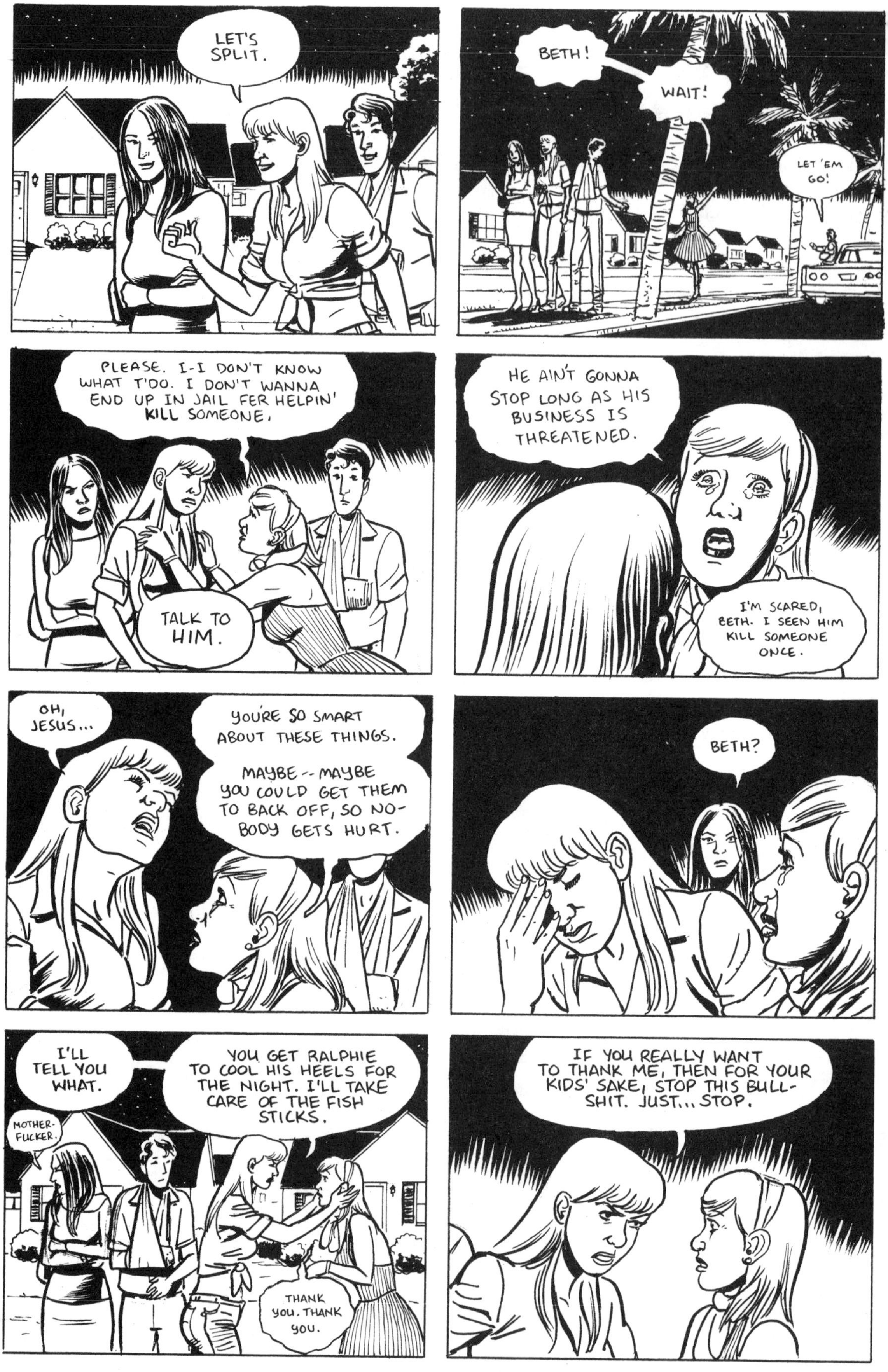
LET'S SPLIT.
BETH!
WAIT!
LET 'EM GO!
PLEASE. I-I DON'T KNOW WHAT T'DO. I DON'T WANNA END UP IN JAIL FER HELPIN' **KILL** SOMEONE.
TALK TO HIM.
HE AIN'T GONNA STOP LONG AS HIS BUSINESS IS THREATENED.
I'M SCARED, BETH. I SEEN HIM KILL SOMEONE ONCE.
OH, JESUS...
YOU'RE SO SMART ABOUT THESE THINGS.
MAYBE -- MAYBE YOU COULD GET THEM TO BACK OFF, SO NO-BODY GETS HURT.
BETH?
I'LL TELL YOU WHAT.
YOU GET RALPHIE TO COOL HIS HEELS FOR THE NIGHT. I'LL TAKE CARE OF THE FISH STICKS.
MOTHER-FUCKER.
THANK YOU. THANK YOU.
IF YOU REALLY WANT TO THANK ME, THEN FOR YOUR KIDS' SAKE, STOP THIS BULL-SHIT. JUST... STOP.

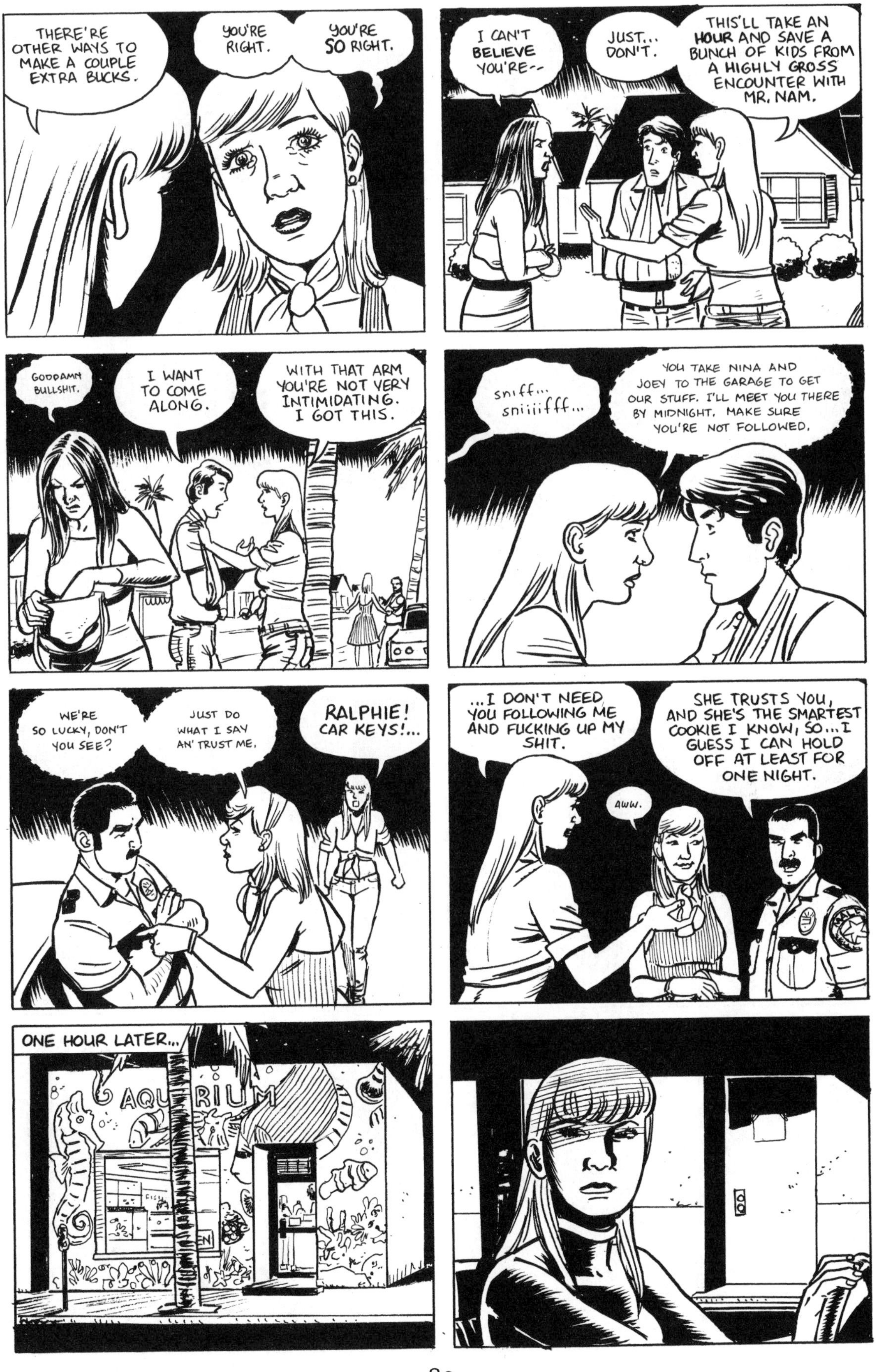
THERE'RE OTHER WAYS TO MAKE A COUPLE EXTRA BUCKS.
YOU'RE RIGHT.
YOU'RE SO RIGHT.
I CAN'T BELIEVE YOU'RE--
JUST... DON'T.
THIS'LL TAKE AN HOUR AND SAVE A BUNCH OF KIDS FROM A HIGHLY GROSS ENCOUNTER WITH MR. NAM.
GODDAMN BULLSHIT.
I WANT TO COME ALONG.
WITH THAT ARM YOU'RE NOT VERY INTIMIDATING. I GOT THIS.
sniff... sniiiifff...
YOU TAKE NINA AND JOEY TO THE GARAGE TO GET OUR STUFF. I'LL MEET YOU THERE BY MIDNIGHT. MAKE SURE YOU'RE NOT FOLLOWED.
WE'RE SO LUCKY, DON'T YOU SEE?
JUST DO WHAT I SAY AN' TRUST ME.
RALPHIE! CAR KEYS!...
...I DON'T NEED YOU FOLLOWING ME AND FUCKING UP MY SHIT.
AWW.
SHE TRUSTS YOU, AND SHE'S THE SMARTEST COOKIE I KNOW, SO... I GUESS I CAN HOLD OFF AT LEAST FOR ONE NIGHT.
ONE HOUR LATER...
AQUARIUM

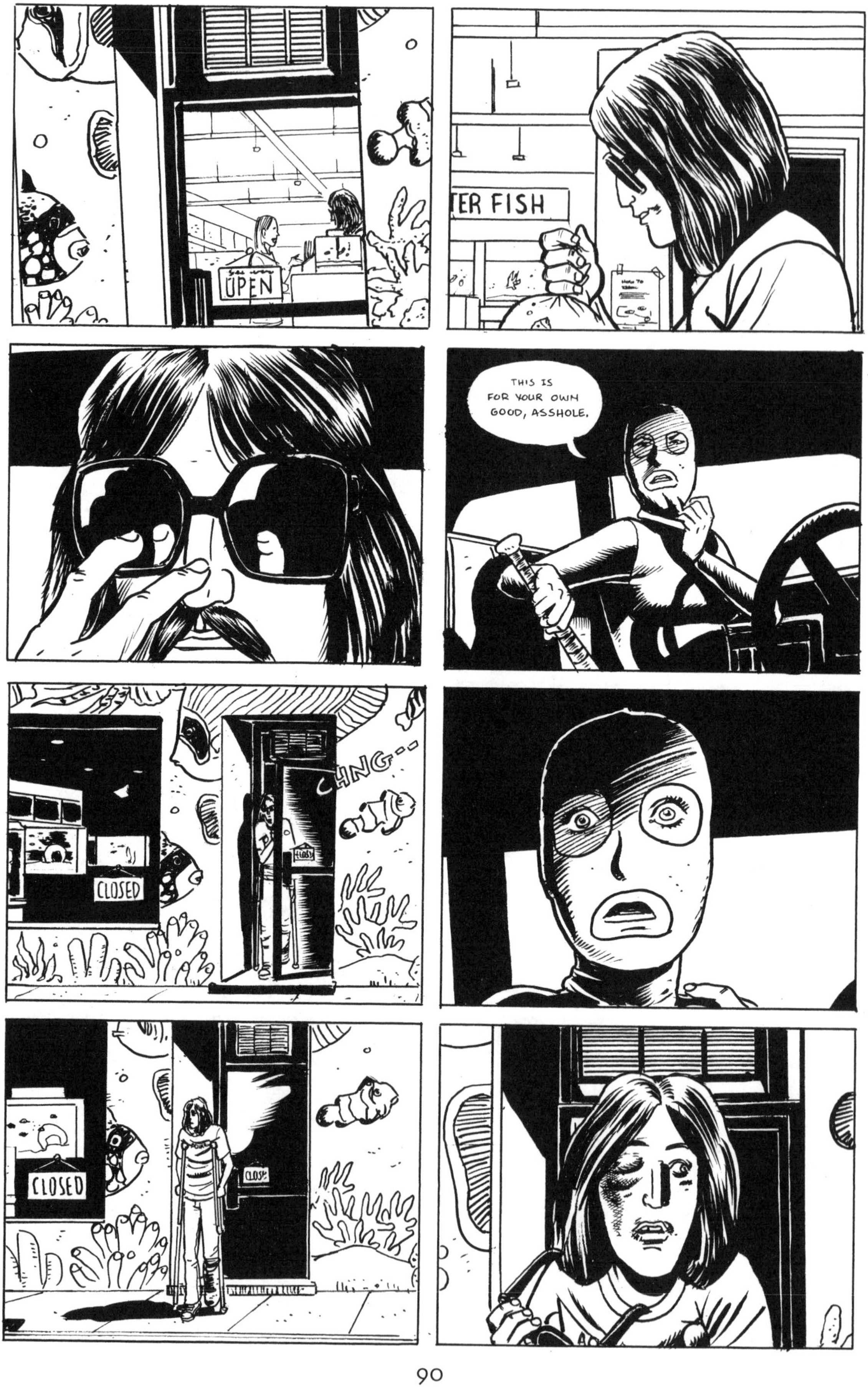
UPEN
TER FISH
THIS IS FOR YOUR OWN GOOD, ASSHOLE.
CHNG--
CLOSED
CLOSED

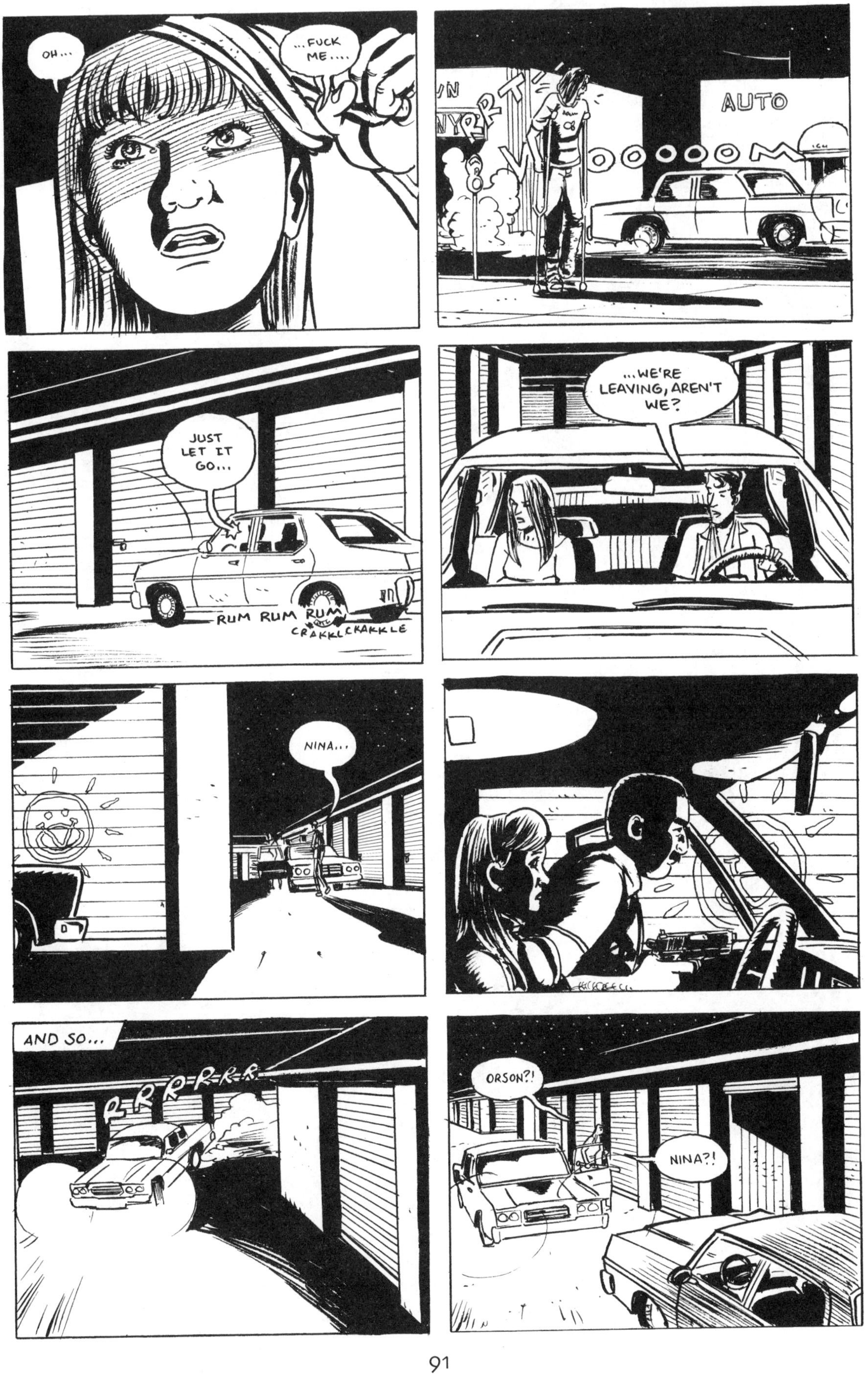

OH...
...FUCK ME....
VROOOOOOM
AUTO
JUST LET IT GO...
RUM RUM RUM
CRAKKLCKAKKLE
...WE'RE LEAVING, AREN'T WE?
NINA...
AND SO...
RRRRRRR
ORSON?!
NINA?!

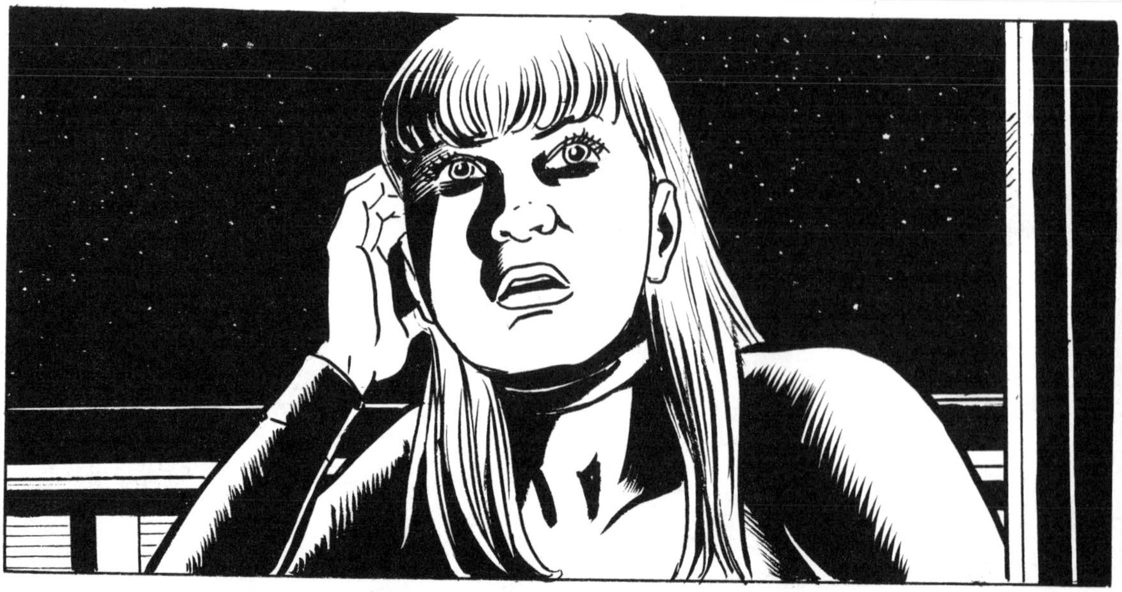

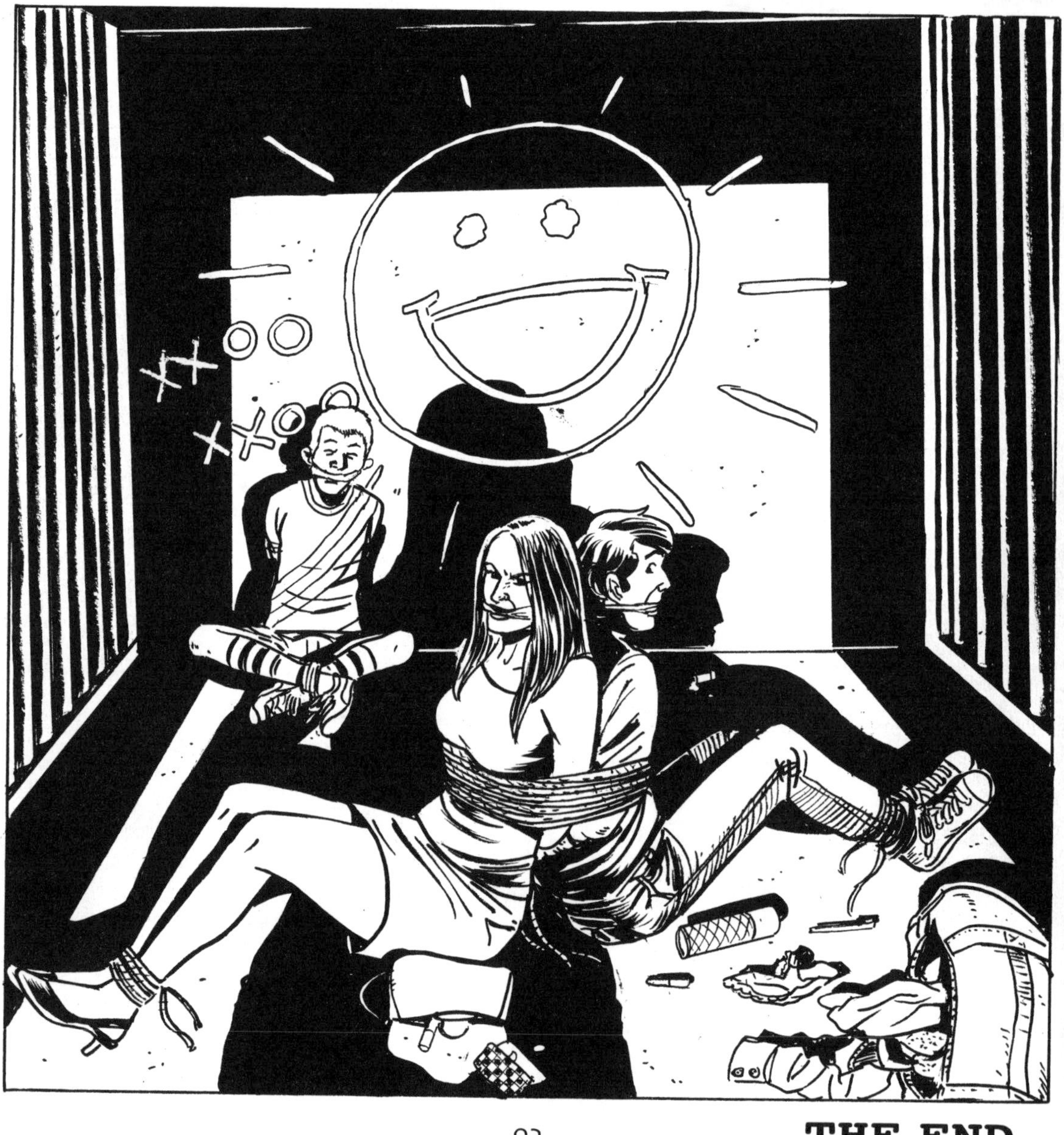

THE END...

4

SPAWN OF AMY RACECAR

OR

"The Great Delusion Contusion Confusion Reunion...of Our Time"

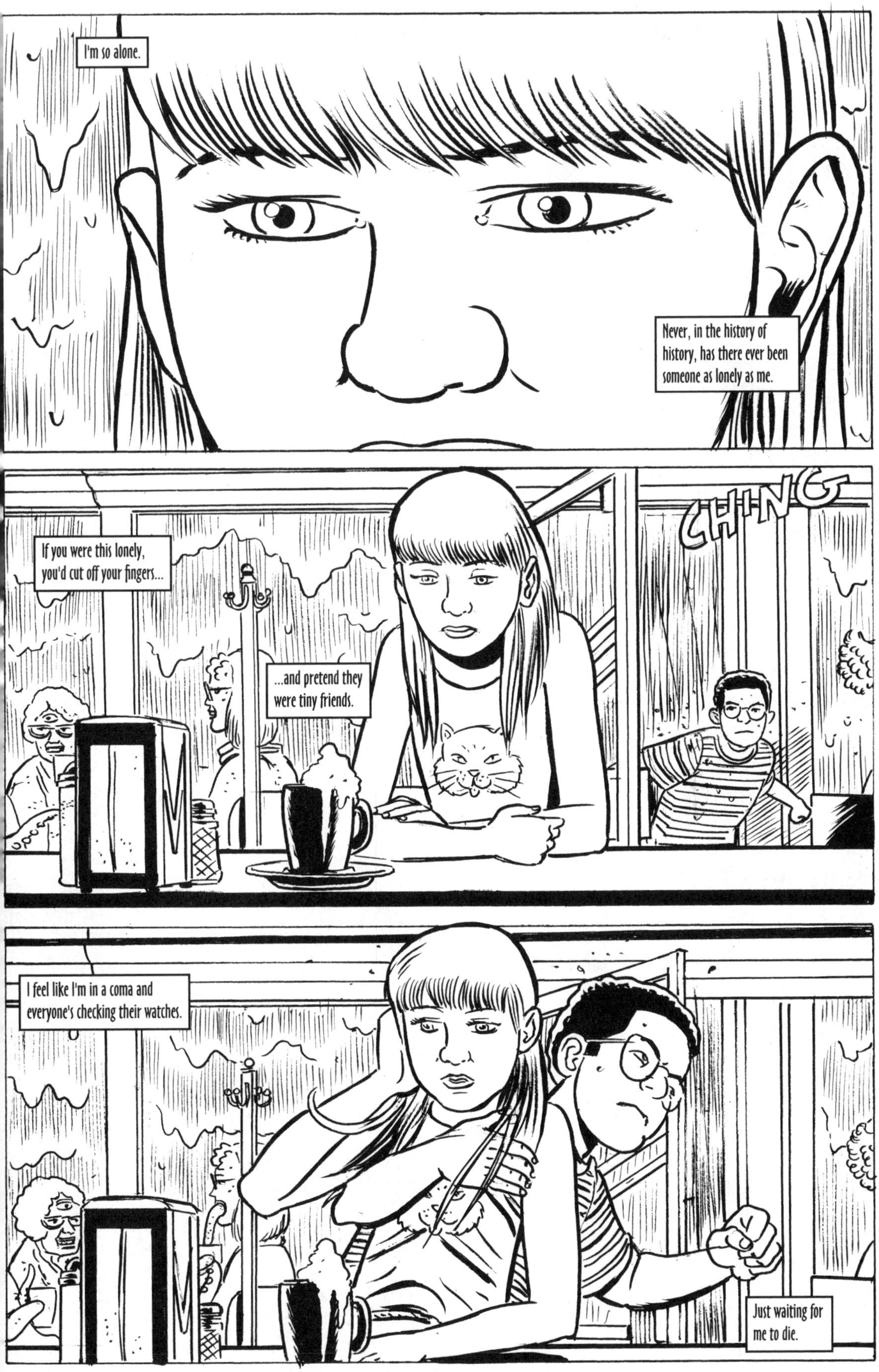
I'm so alone.
Never, in the history of history, has there ever been someone as lonely as me.
If you were this lonely, you'd cut off your fingers...
...and pretend they were tiny friends.
CHING
I feel like I'm in a coma and everyone's checking their watches.
Just waiting for me to die.

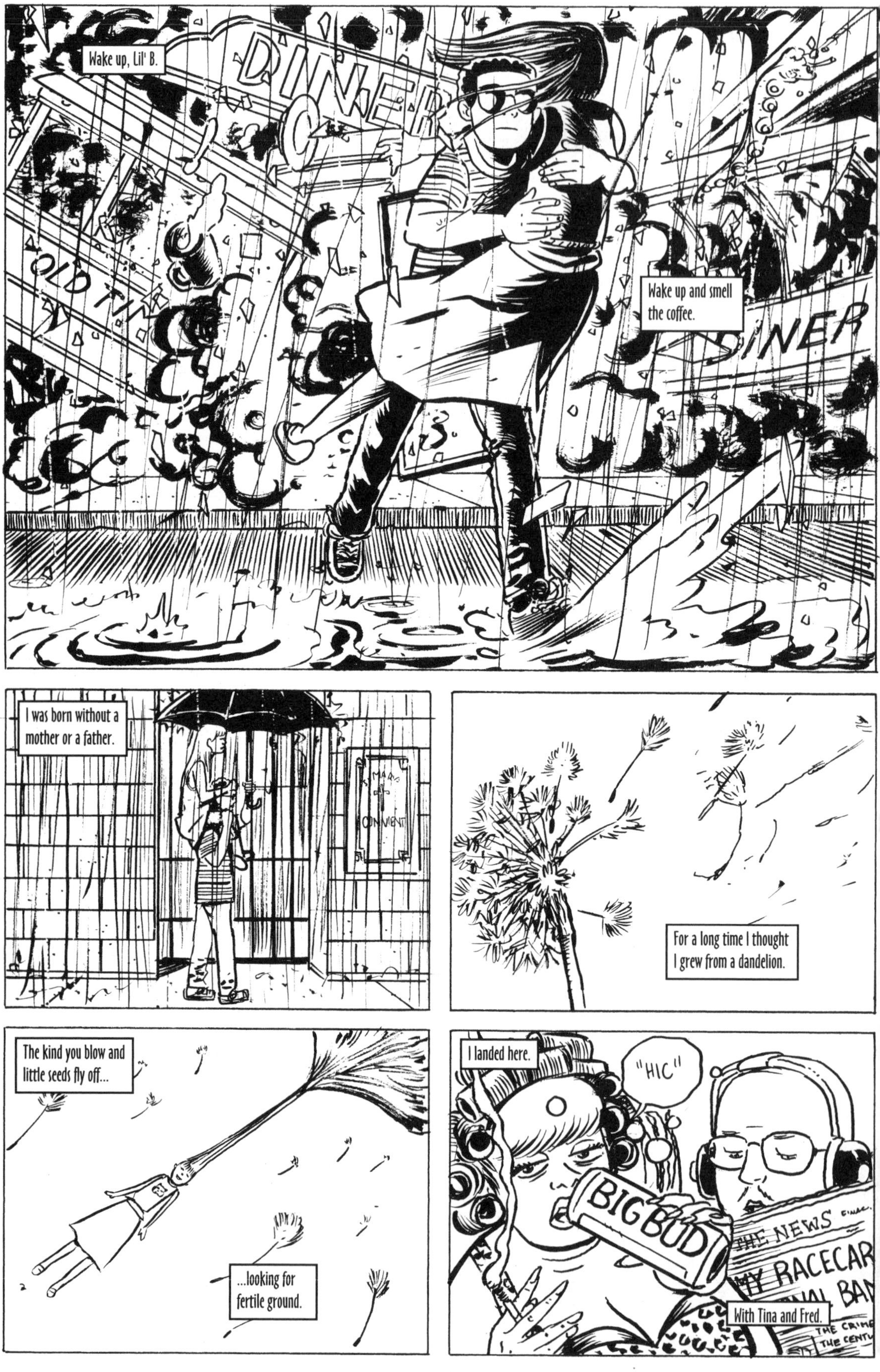
Wake up, Lil' B.
DINER
Wake up and smell the coffee.
DINER
I was born without a mother or a father.
For a long time I thought I grew from a dandelion.
The kind you blow and little seeds fly off...
...looking for fertile ground.
I landed here.
"HIC"
BIG BUD
THE NEWS
With Tina and Fred.

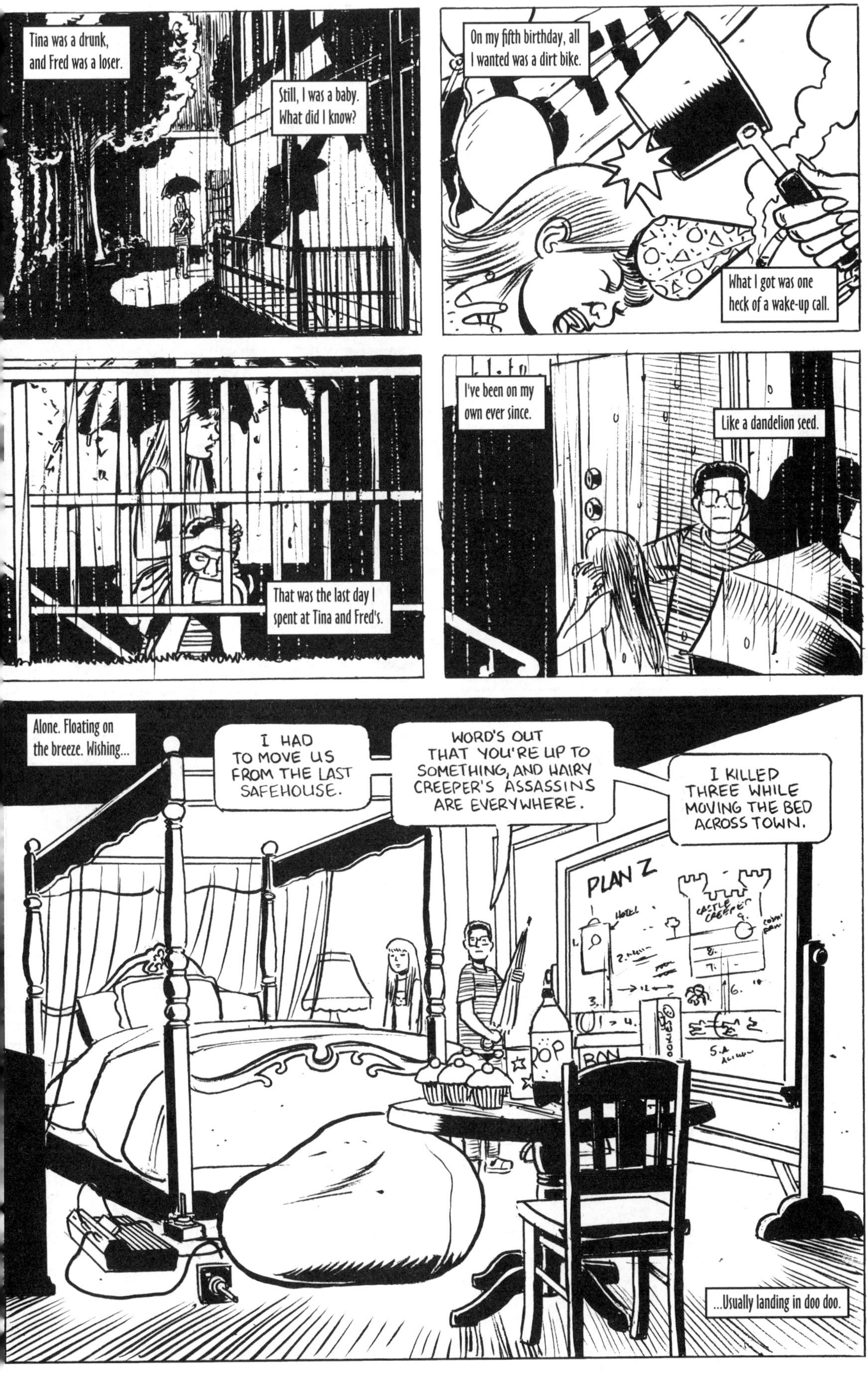
Tina was a drunk, and Fred was a loser.
Still, I was a baby. What did I know?
On my fifth birthday, all I wanted was a dirt bike.
What I got was one heck of a wake-up call.
That was the last day I spent at Tina and Fred's.
I've been on my own ever since.
Like a dandelion seed.
Alone. Floating on the breeze. Wishing...
I HAD TO MOVE US FROM THE LAST SAFEHOUSE.
WORD'S OUT THAT YOU'RE UP TO SOMETHING, AND HAIRY CREEPER'S ASSASSINS ARE EVERYWHERE.
I KILLED THREE WHILE MOVING THE BED ACROSS TOWN.
PLAN Z
HOTEL
CASTLE CREEPER
POP
...Usually landing in doo doo.

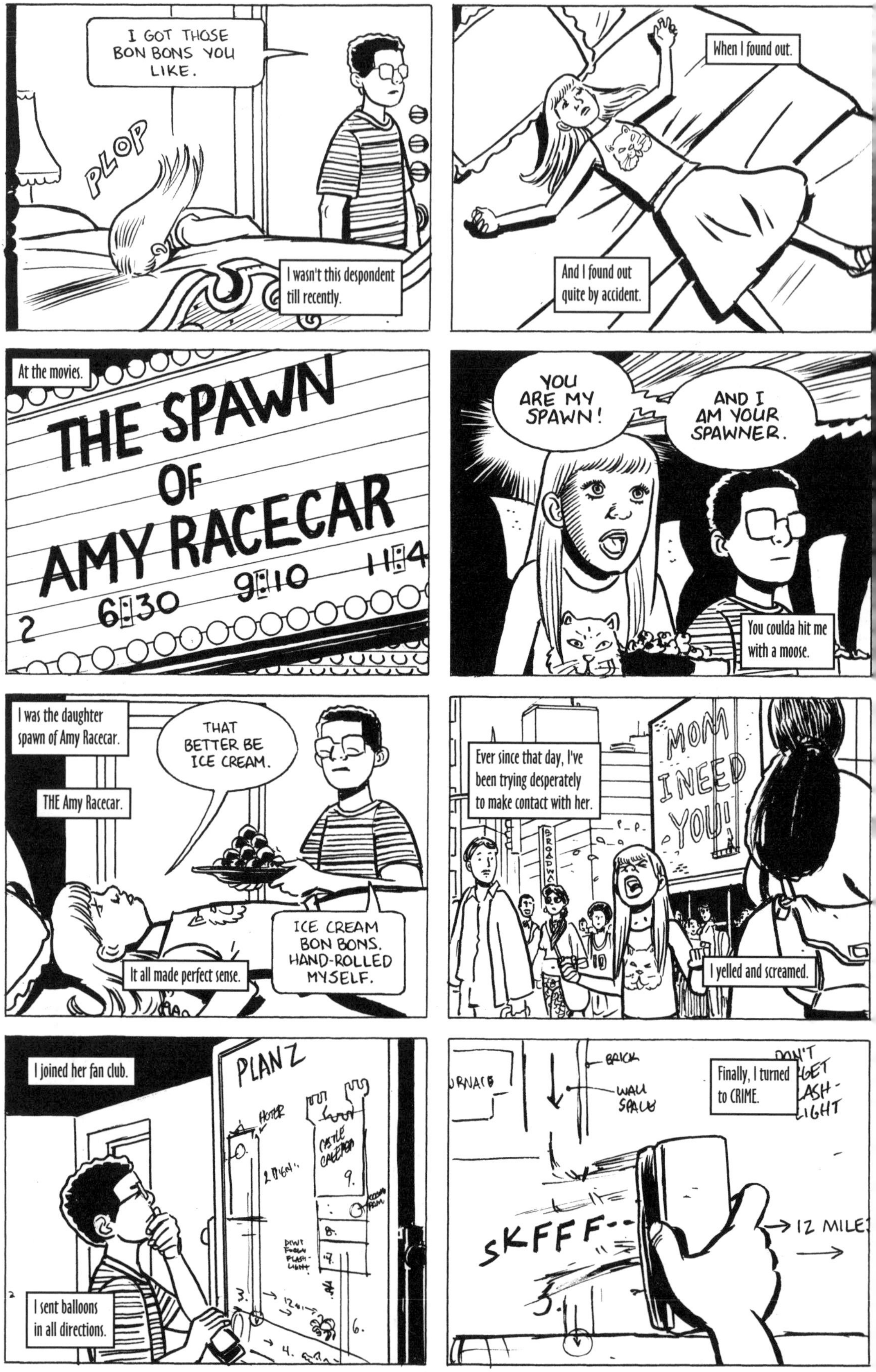

I GOT THOSE BON BONS YOU LIKE.
PLOP
I wasn't this despondent till recently.
When I found out.
And I found out quite by accident.
At the movies.
THE SPAWN OF AMY RACECAR
2 6:30 9:10 11:4
YOU ARE MY SPAWN!
AND I AM YOUR SPAWNER.
You coulda hit me with a moose.
I was the daughter spawn of Amy Racecar.
THE Amy Racecar.
THAT BETTER BE ICE CREAM.
It all made perfect sense.
ICE CREAM BON BONS. HAND-ROLLED MYSELF.
Ever since that day, I've been trying desperately to make contact with her.
BROADWAY
MOM I NEED YOU!
I yelled and screamed.
I joined her fan club.
PLANZ
I sent balloons in all directions.
Finally, I turned to CRIME.
BRICK
SKFFF--

PLAN Z²

HOTEL

CONVENT

CASTLE CREEPERS
9.

BASEMENT
DUNGEON
COSMIC PRINCE

1. DIG
8. 10 FEET STEEL
10 FEET CONCRETE

GIANT SPIDERS
6. DIG

GATORS

Despite being the most notorious thief in the known universe, Amy Racecar had failed to do ONE THING.

Break into Castle Creepers, the impenetrable home of gangster Hairy Creepers...

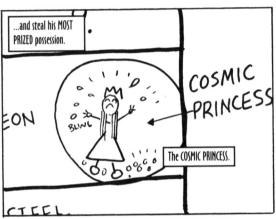

...and steal his MOST PRIZED possession.

COSMIC PRINCESS

EON

BLING

The COSMIC PRINCESS.

STEEL

A girl whose tears literally turn to pure gold.

Her misery single-handedly funds the Creeper Empire.

This is simply the most complex plan I've ever devised.

And I've devised some doozies.

KREE E

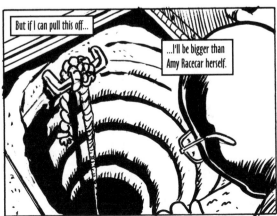

But if I can pull this off...

...I'll be bigger than Amy Racecar herself.

And then she'll HAVE TO pay attention to me.

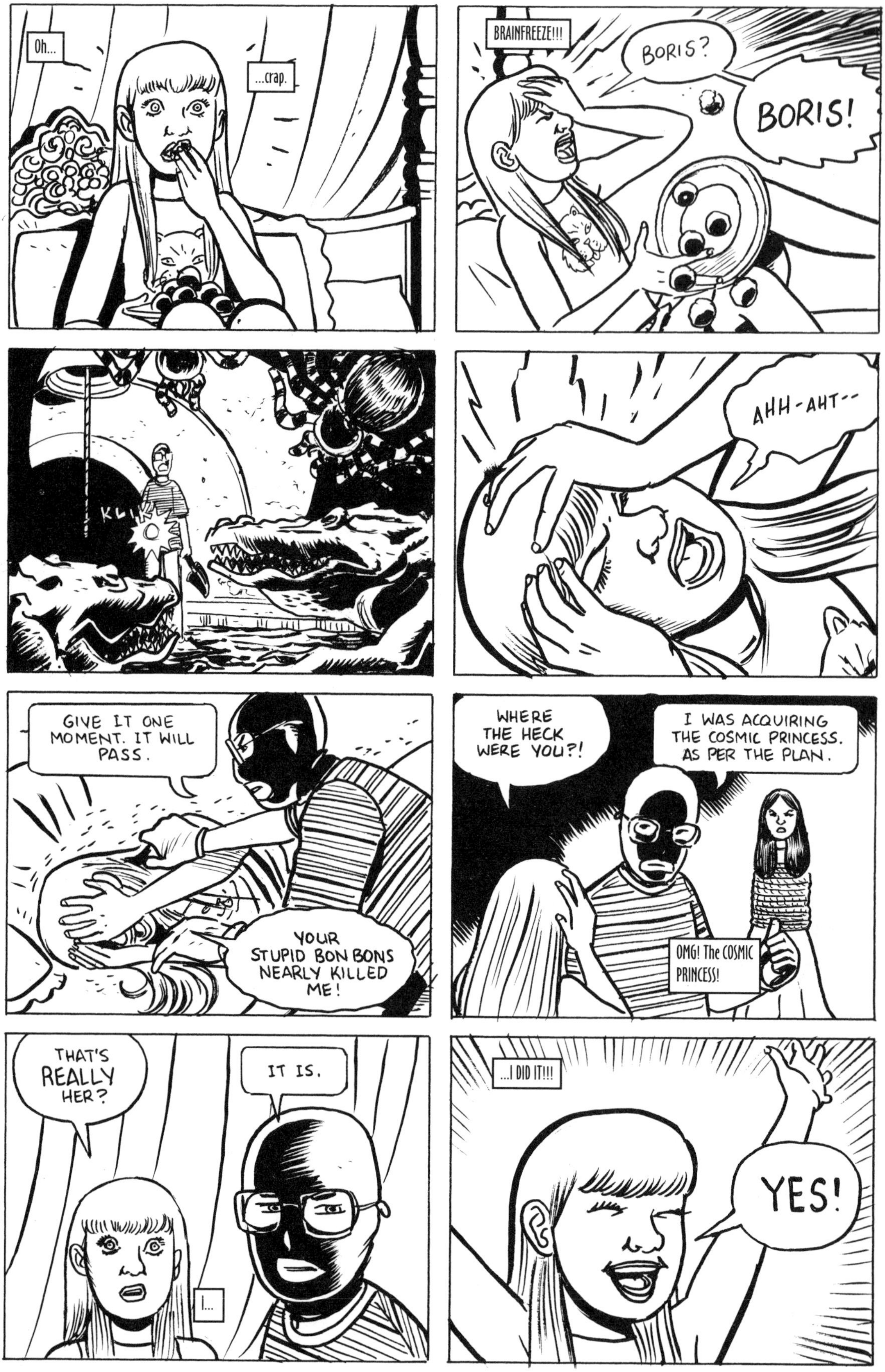
Oh...
...crap.
BRAINFREEZE!!!
BORIS?
BORIS!
KLIK
AHH-AHT--
GIVE IT ONE MOMENT. IT WILL PASS.
YOUR STUPID BON BONS NEARLY KILLED ME!
WHERE THE HECK WERE YOU?!
I WAS ACQUIRING THE COSMIC PRINCESS. AS PER THE PLAN.
OMG! The COSMIC PRINCESS!
THAT'S REALLY HER?
IT IS.
I...
...I DID IT!!!
YES!

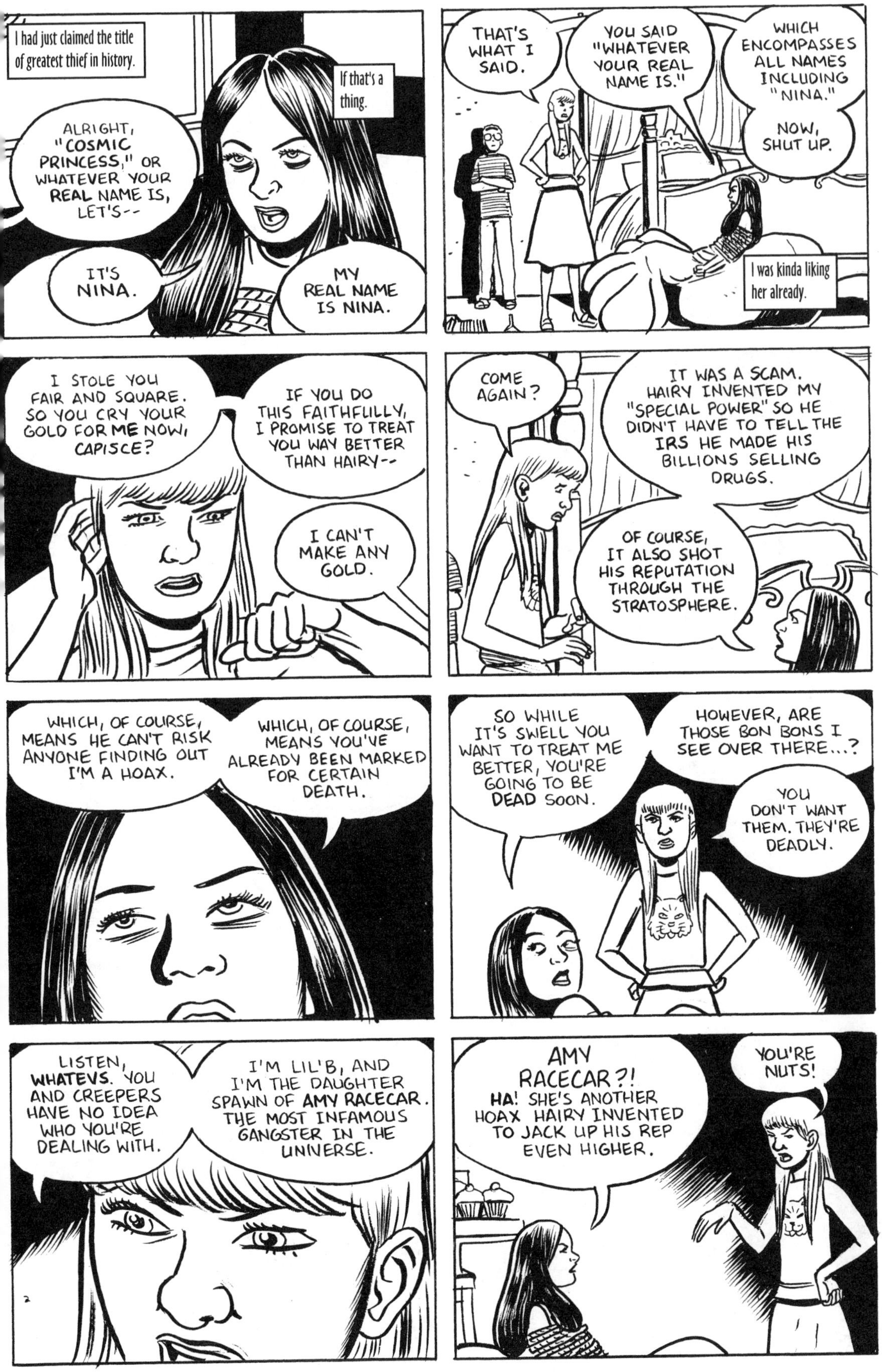
I had just claimed the title of greatest thief in history.
ALRIGHT, "COSMIC PRINCESS," OR WHATEVER YOUR REAL NAME IS, LET'S--
If that's a thing.
IT'S NINA.
MY REAL NAME IS NINA.
THAT'S WHAT I SAID.
YOU SAID "WHATEVER YOUR REAL NAME IS."
WHICH ENCOMPASSES ALL NAMES INCLUDING "NINA."
NOW, SHUT UP.
I was kinda liking her already.
I STOLE YOU FAIR AND SQUARE. SO YOU CRY YOUR GOLD FOR ME NOW, CAPISCE?
IF YOU DO THIS FAITHFULLY, I PROMISE TO TREAT YOU WAY BETTER THAN HAIRY--
I CAN'T MAKE ANY GOLD.
COME AGAIN?
IT WAS A SCAM. HAIRY INVENTED MY "SPECIAL POWER" SO HE DIDN'T HAVE TO TELL THE IRS HE MADE HIS BILLIONS SELLING DRUGS.
OF COURSE, IT ALSO SHOT HIS REPUTATION THROUGH THE STRATOSPHERE.
WHICH, OF COURSE, MEANS HE CAN'T RISK ANYONE FINDING OUT I'M A HOAX.
WHICH, OF COURSE, MEANS YOU'VE ALREADY BEEN MARKED FOR CERTAIN DEATH.
SO WHILE IT'S SWELL YOU WANT TO TREAT ME BETTER, YOU'RE GOING TO BE DEAD SOON.
HOWEVER, ARE THOSE BON BONS I SEE OVER THERE...?
YOU DON'T WANT THEM. THEY'RE DEADLY.
LISTEN, WHATEVS. YOU AND CREEPERS HAVE NO IDEA WHO YOU'RE DEALING WITH.
I'M LIL'B, AND I'M THE DAUGHTER SPAWN OF AMY RACECAR. THE MOST INFAMOUS GANGSTER IN THE UNIVERSE.
AMY RACECAR?!
HA! SHE'S ANOTHER HOAX HAIRY INVENTED TO JACK UP HIS REP EVEN HIGHER.
YOU'RE NUTS!

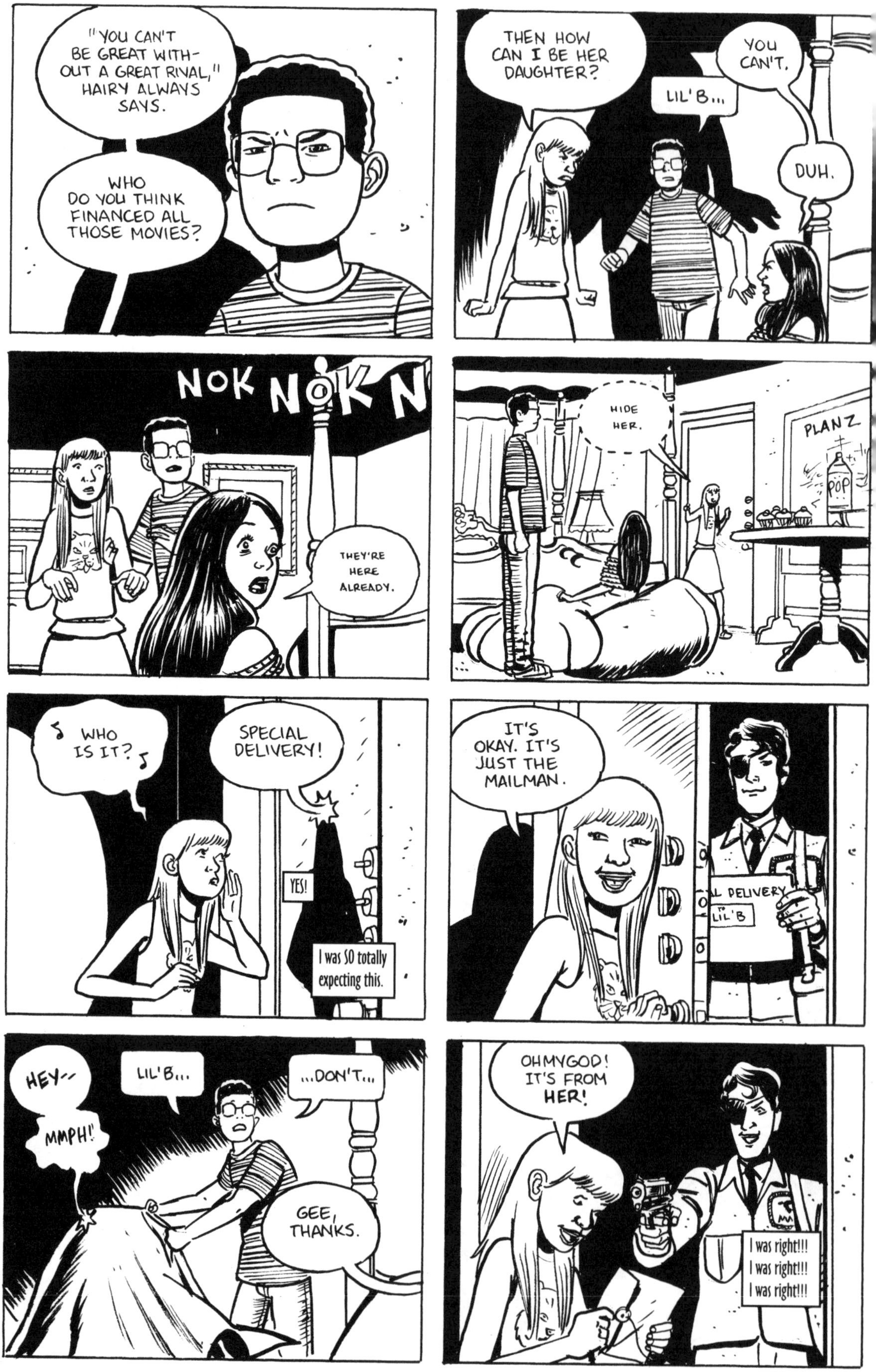
"YOU CAN'T BE GREAT WITH-OUT A GREAT RIVAL," HAIRY ALWAYS SAYS.
WHO DO YOU THINK FINANCED ALL THOSE MOVIES?
THEN HOW CAN I BE HER DAUGHTER?
LIL'B...
YOU CAN'T.
DUH.
NOK NOK N
THEY'RE HERE ALREADY.
HIDE HER.
PLANZ
POP
WHO IS IT?
SPECIAL DELIVERY!
YES!
I was SO totally expecting this.
IT'S OKAY. IT'S JUST THE MAILMAN.
L DELIVERY TO LIL'B
HEY--
MMPH!
LIL'B...
...DON'T...
GEE, THANKS.
OHMYGOD! IT'S FROM HER!
I was right!!! I was right!!! I was right!!!

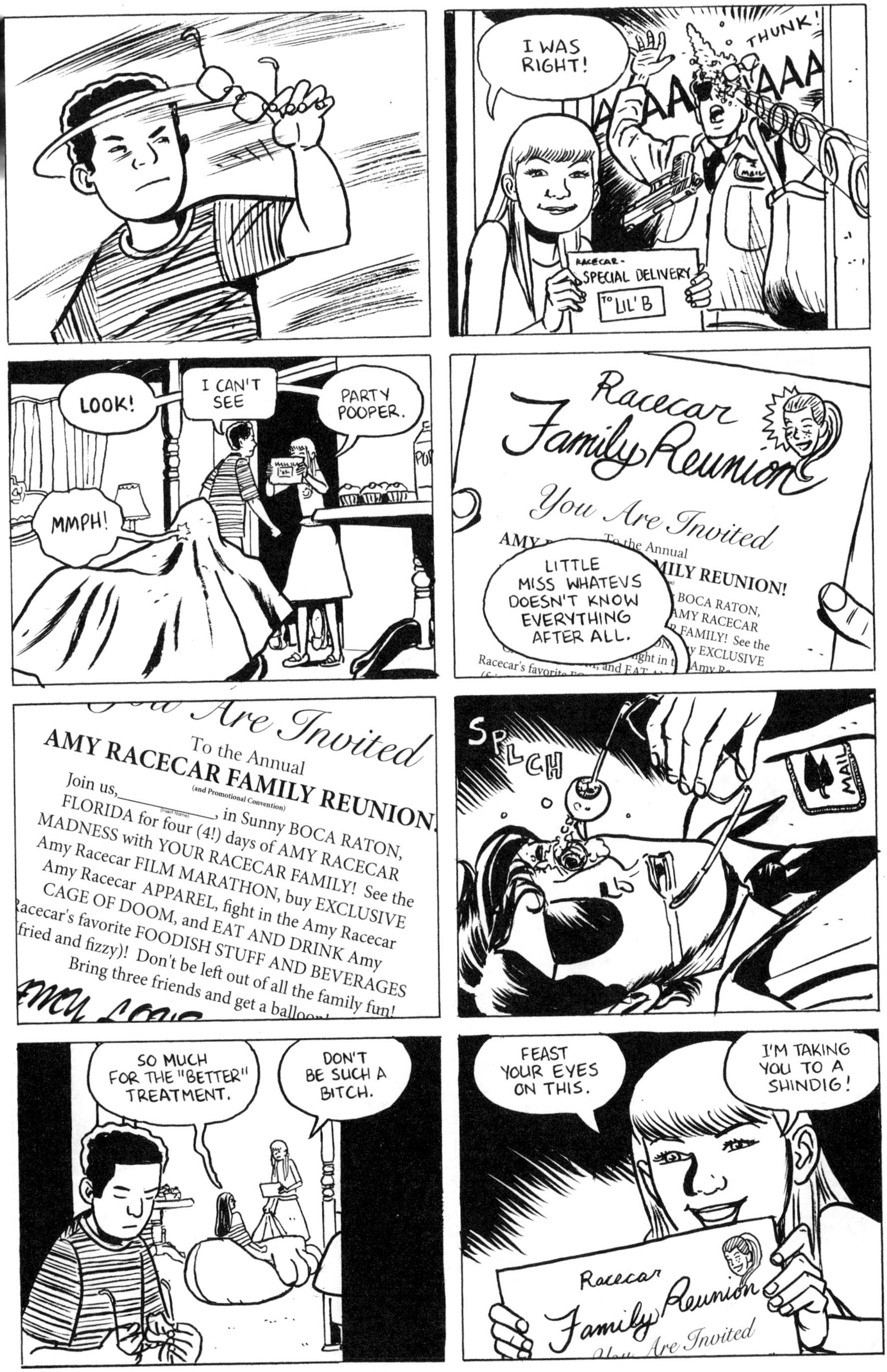
I WAS RIGHT!
THUNK!
AAAAAAA
RACECAR - SPECIAL DELIVERY
TO LIL' B
LOOK!
I CAN'T SEE
PARTY POOPER.
MMPH!
Racecar Family Reunion
You Are Invited
LITTLE MISS WHATEVS DOESN'T KNOW EVERYTHING AFTER ALL.
You Are Invited
To the Annual
AMY RACECAR FAMILY REUNION!
(and Promotional Convention)
Join us, ________, in Sunny BOCA RATON,
(Insert Name)
FLORIDA for four (4!) days of AMY RACECAR
MADNESS with YOUR RACECAR FAMILY! See the
Amy Racecar FILM MARATHON, buy EXCLUSIVE
Amy Racecar APPAREL, fight in the Amy Racecar
CAGE OF DOOM, and EAT AND DRINK Amy
Racecar's favorite FOODISH STUFF AND BEVERAGES
(fried and fizzy)! Don't be left out of all the family fun!
Bring three friends and get a balloon!
SPLCH
MAIL
SO MUCH FOR THE "BETTER" TREATMENT.
DON'T BE SUCH A BITCH.
FEAST YOUR EYES ON THIS.
I'M TAKING YOU TO A SHINDIG!
Racecar Family Reunion
You Are Invited

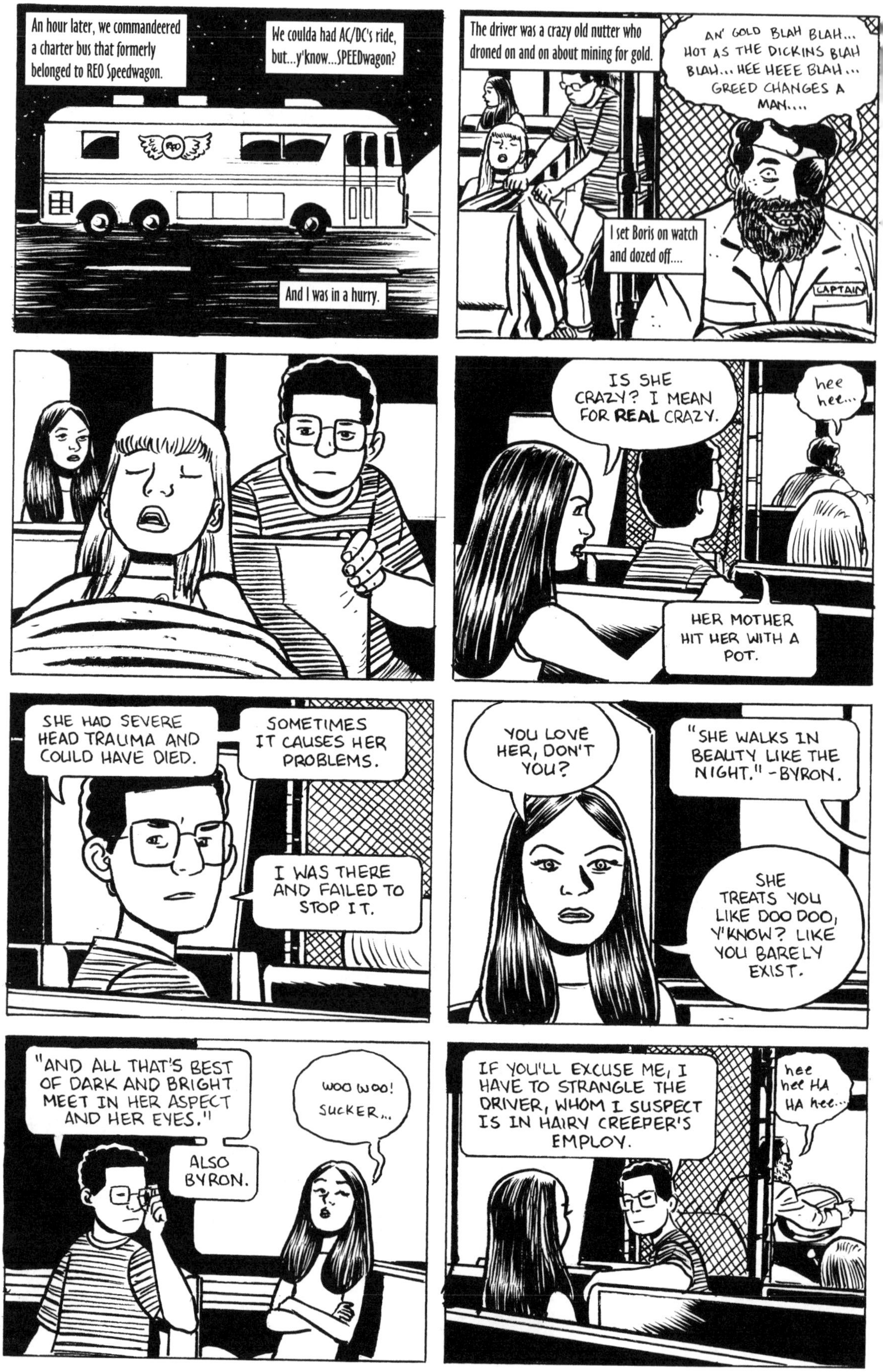
An hour later, we commandeered a charter bus that formerly belonged to REO Speedwagon.
We coulda had AC/DC's ride, but...y'know...SPEEDwagon?
REO
And I was in a hurry.
The driver was a crazy old nutter who droned on and on about mining for gold.
AN' GOLD BLAH BLAH... HOT AS THE DICKINS BLAH BLAH... HEE HEEE BLAH... GREED CHANGES A MAN....
I set Boris on watch and dozed off....
CAPTAIN
IS SHE CRAZY? I MEAN FOR **REAL** CRAZY.
hee hee...
HER MOTHER HIT HER WITH A POT.
SHE HAD SEVERE HEAD TRAUMA AND COULD HAVE DIED.
SOMETIMES IT CAUSES HER PROBLEMS.
I WAS THERE AND FAILED TO STOP IT.
YOU LOVE HER, DON'T YOU?
"SHE WALKS IN BEAUTY LIKE THE NIGHT." -BYRON.
SHE TREATS YOU LIKE DOO DOO, Y'KNOW? LIKE YOU BARELY EXIST.
"AND ALL THAT'S BEST OF DARK AND BRIGHT MEET IN HER ASPECT AND HER EYES."
ALSO BYRON.
WOO WOO! SUCKER...
IF YOU'LL EXCUSE ME, I HAVE TO STRANGLE THE DRIVER, WHOM I SUSPECT IS IN HAIRY CREEPER'S EMPLOY.
hee hee HA HA hee...

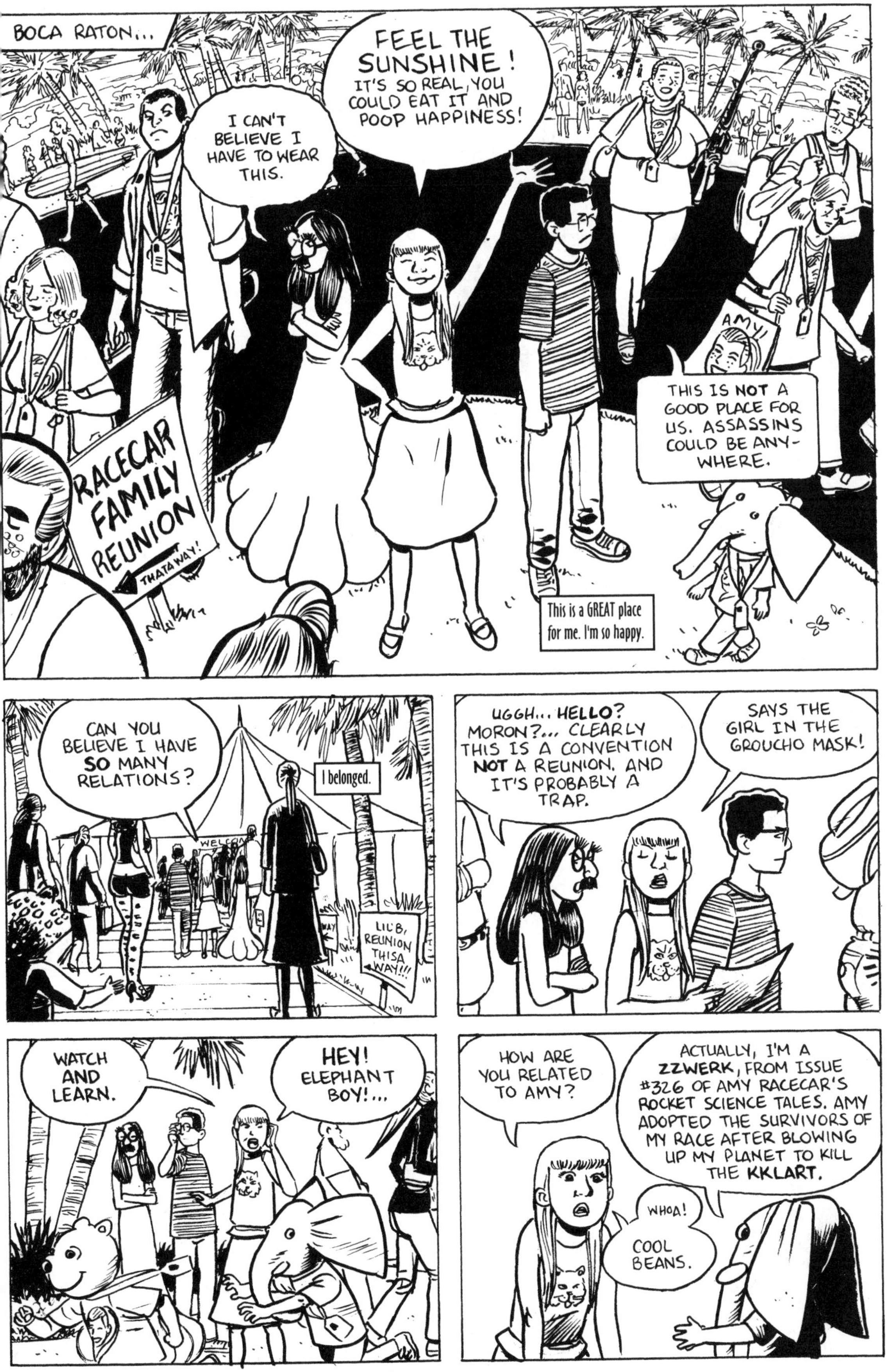
BOCA RATON...
I CAN'T BELIEVE I HAVE TO WEAR THIS.
FEEL THE SUNSHINE! IT'S SO REAL, YOU COULD EAT IT AND POOP HAPPINESS!
THIS IS NOT A GOOD PLACE FOR US. ASSASSINS COULD BE ANYWHERE.
AMY!
RACECAR FAMILY REUNION
THATA WAY!
This is a GREAT place for me. I'm so happy.
CAN YOU BELIEVE I HAVE SO MANY RELATIONS?
I belonged.
LIL'B, REUNION THISA WAY!!!
UGGH... HELLO? MORON?... CLEARLY THIS IS A CONVENTION NOT A REUNION. AND IT'S PROBABLY A TRAP.
SAYS THE GIRL IN THE GROUCHO MASK!
WATCH AND LEARN.
HEY! ELEPHANT BOY!...
HOW ARE YOU RELATED TO AMY?
ACTUALLY, I'M A ZZWERK, FROM ISSUE #326 OF AMY RACECAR'S ROCKET SCIENCE TALES. AMY ADOPTED THE SURVIVORS OF MY RACE AFTER BLOWING UP MY PLANET TO KILL THE KKLART.
WHOA!
COOL BEANS.

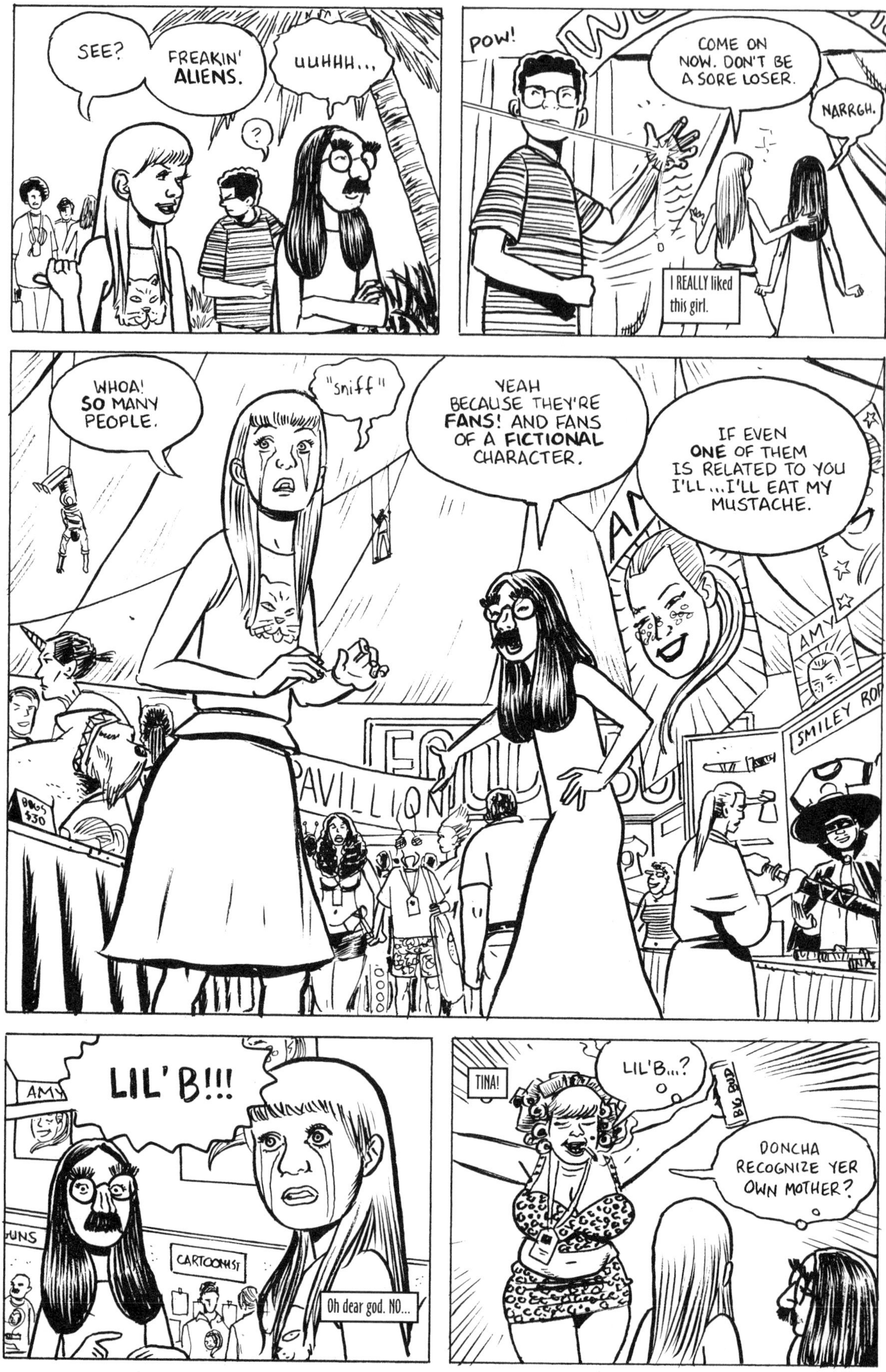
SEE?
FREAKIN' **ALIENS.**
UUHHH...,
?
POW!
COME ON NOW. DON'T BE A SORE LOSER.
NARRGH.
I REALLY liked this girl.
WHOA! **SO** MANY PEOPLE.
"sniff"
YEAH BECAUSE THEY'RE **FANS!** AND FANS OF A **FICTIONAL** CHARACTER.
IF EVEN **ONE** OF THEM IS RELATED TO YOU I'LL...I'LL EAT MY MUSTACHE.
PAVILLION
AMY
SMILEY ROP
BOGS $30
LIL' B!!!
AMY
CARTOONIST
Oh dear god. NO...
TINA!
LIL'B...?
BIG BUD
DONCHA RECOGNIZE YER OWN MOTHER?

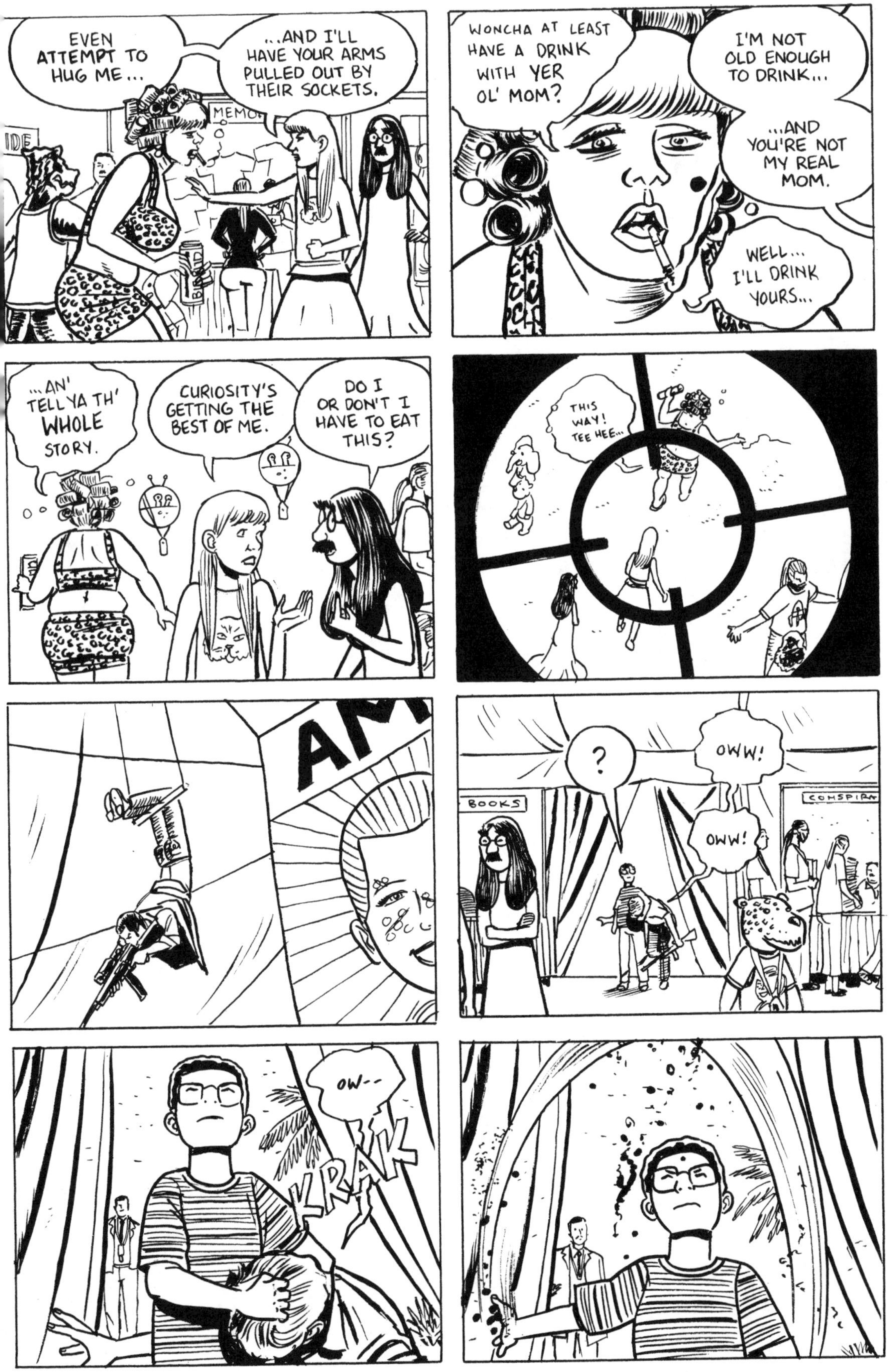
EVEN ATTEMPT TO HUG ME...
...AND I'LL HAVE YOUR ARMS PULLED OUT BY THEIR SOCKETS.
MEMO
WONCHA AT LEAST HAVE A DRINK WITH YER OL' MOM?
I'M NOT OLD ENOUGH TO DRINK...
...AND YOU'RE NOT MY REAL MOM.
WELL... I'LL DRINK YOURS...
...AN' TELL YA TH' WHOLE STORY.
CURIOSITY'S GETTING THE BEST OF ME.
DO I OR DON'T I HAVE TO EAT THIS?
THIS WAY! TEE HEE...
AM
?
OWW!
BOOKS
OWW!
OW--
KRAK

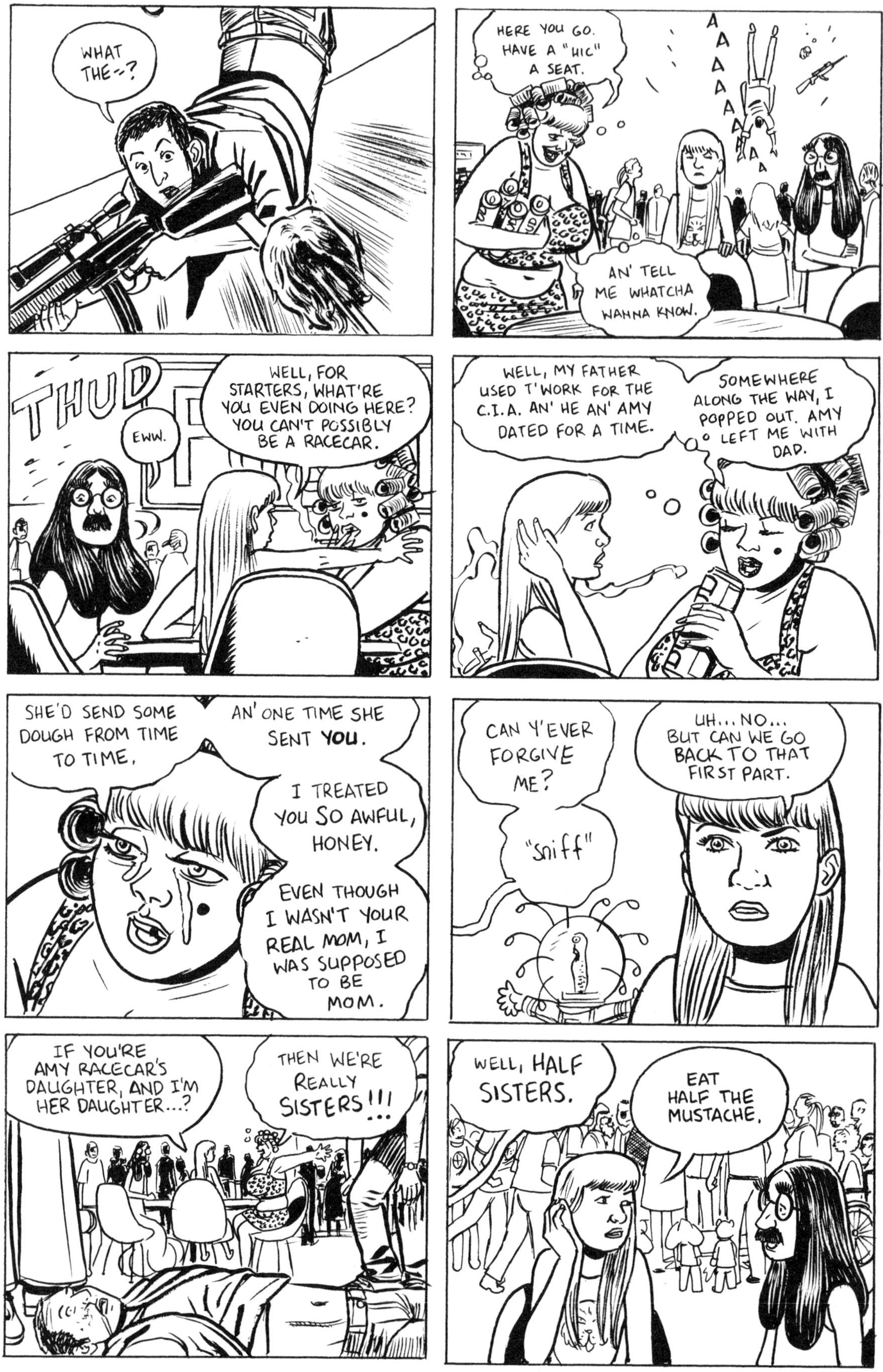
WHAT THE--?
HERE YOU GO. HAVE A "HIC" A SEAT.
AAAAAAAAA
AN' TELL ME WHATCHA WANNA KNOW.
THUD
EWW.
WELL, FOR STARTERS, WHAT'RE YOU EVEN DOING HERE? YOU CAN'T POSSIBLY BE A RACECAR.
WELL, MY FATHER USED T'WORK FOR THE C.I.A. AN' HE AN' AMY DATED FOR A TIME.
SOMEWHERE ALONG THE WAY, I POPPED OUT. AMY LEFT ME WITH DAD.
SHE'D SEND SOME DOUGH FROM TIME TO TIME.
AN' ONE TIME SHE SENT YOU.
I TREATED YOU SO AWFUL, HONEY.
EVEN THOUGH I WASN'T YOUR REAL MOM, I WAS SUPPOSED TO BE MOM.
CAN Y'EVER FORGIVE ME?
"sniff"
UH... NO... BUT CAN WE GO BACK TO THAT FIRST PART.
IF YOU'RE AMY RACECAR'S DAUGHTER, AND I'M HER DAUGHTER...?
THEN WE'RE REALLY SISTERS!!!
WELL, HALF SISTERS.
EAT HALF THE MUSTACHE.

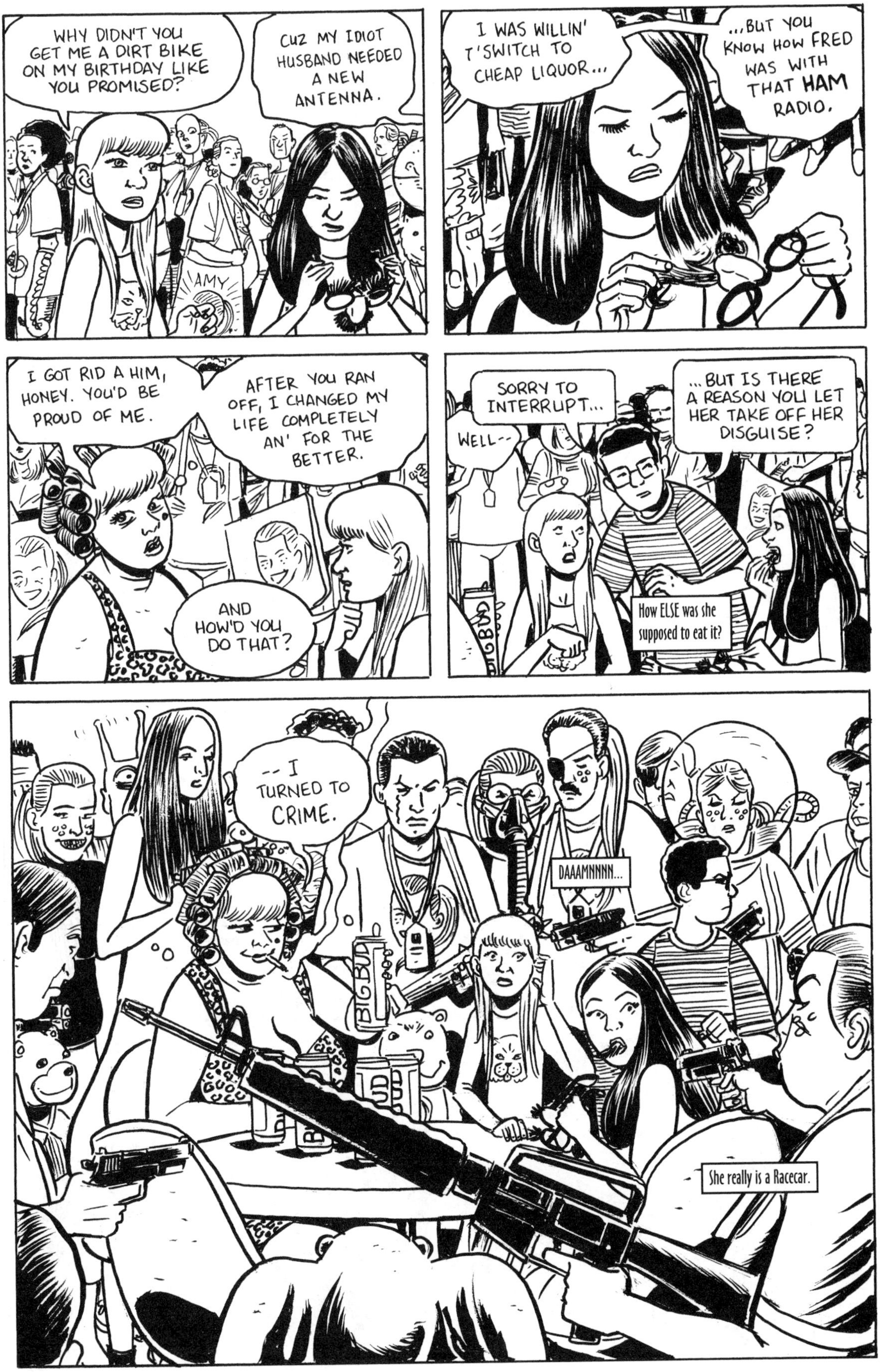
WHY DIDN'T YOU GET ME A DIRT BIKE ON MY BIRTHDAY LIKE YOU PROMISED?
CUZ MY IDIOT HUSBAND NEEDED A NEW ANTENNA.
AMY
I WAS WILLIN' T'SWITCH TO CHEAP LIQUOR...
...BUT YOU KNOW HOW FRED WAS WITH THAT HAM RADIO.
I GOT RID A HIM, HONEY. YOU'D BE PROUD OF ME.
AFTER YOU RAN OFF, I CHANGED MY LIFE COMPLETELY AN' FOR THE BETTER.
AND HOW'D YOU DO THAT?
WELL--
SORRY TO INTERRUPT...
...BUT IS THERE A REASON YOU LET HER TAKE OFF HER DISGUISE?
How ELSE was she supposed to eat it?
BIG BUD
-- I TURNED TO CRIME.
DAAAMNNNN...
BIG BUD
She really is a Racecar.

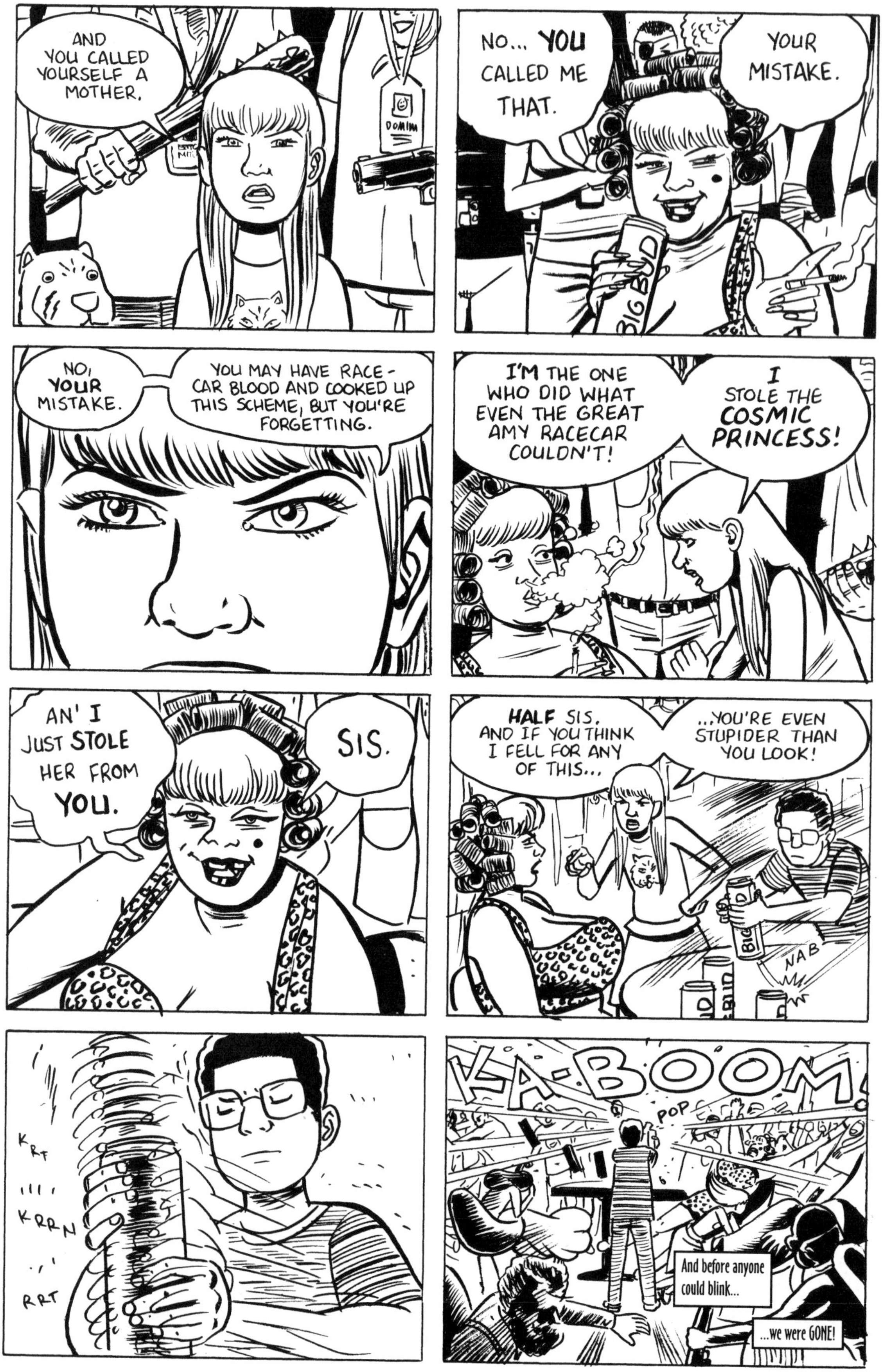
AND YOU CALLED YOURSELF A MOTHER.
NO... YOU CALLED ME THAT.
YOUR MISTAKE.
BIG BUD
NO, YOUR MISTAKE.
YOU MAY HAVE RACE-CAR BLOOD AND COOKED UP THIS SCHEME, BUT YOU'RE FORGETTING.
I'M THE ONE WHO DID WHAT EVEN THE GREAT AMY RACECAR COULDN'T!
I STOLE THE COSMIC PRINCESS!
AN' I JUST STOLE HER FROM YOU.
SIS.
HALF SIS. AND IF YOU THINK I FELL FOR ANY OF THIS...
...YOU'RE EVEN STUPIDER THAN YOU LOOK!
NAB
KRT
KRRN
RRT
KA-BOOM!
POP
And before anyone could blink...
...we were GONE!

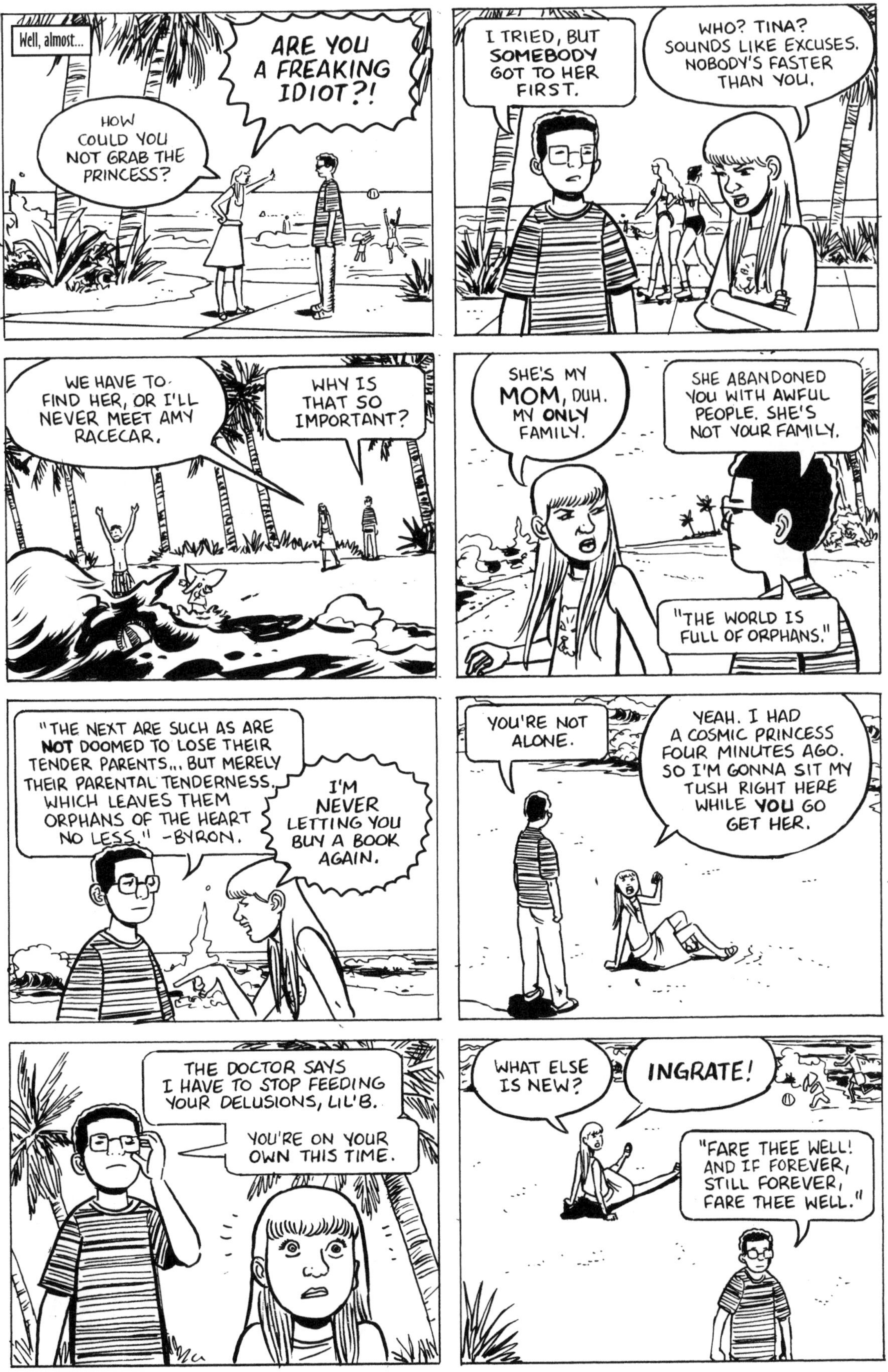
Well, almost...
ARE YOU A FREAKING IDIOT?!
HOW COULD YOU NOT GRAB THE PRINCESS?
I TRIED, BUT SOMEBODY GOT TO HER FIRST.
WHO? TINA? SOUNDS LIKE EXCUSES. NOBODY'S FASTER THAN YOU.
WE HAVE TO FIND HER, OR I'LL NEVER MEET AMY RACECAR.
WHY IS THAT SO IMPORTANT?
SHE'S MY MOM, DUH. MY ONLY FAMILY.
SHE ABANDONED YOU WITH AWFUL PEOPLE. SHE'S NOT YOUR FAMILY.
"THE WORLD IS FULL OF ORPHANS."
"THE NEXT ARE SUCH AS ARE NOT DOOMED TO LOSE THEIR TENDER PARENTS... BUT MERELY THEIR PARENTAL TENDERNESS, WHICH LEAVES THEM ORPHANS OF THE HEART NO LESS." -BYRON.
I'M NEVER LETTING YOU BUY A BOOK AGAIN.
YOU'RE NOT ALONE.
YEAH. I HAD A COSMIC PRINCESS FOUR MINUTES AGO. SO I'M GONNA SIT MY TUSH RIGHT HERE WHILE YOU GO GET HER.
THE DOCTOR SAYS I HAVE TO STOP FEEDING YOUR DELUSIONS, LIL'B.
YOU'RE ON YOUR OWN THIS TIME.
WHAT ELSE IS NEW?
INGRATE!
"FARE THEE WELL! AND IF FOREVER, STILL FOREVER, FARE THEE WELL."

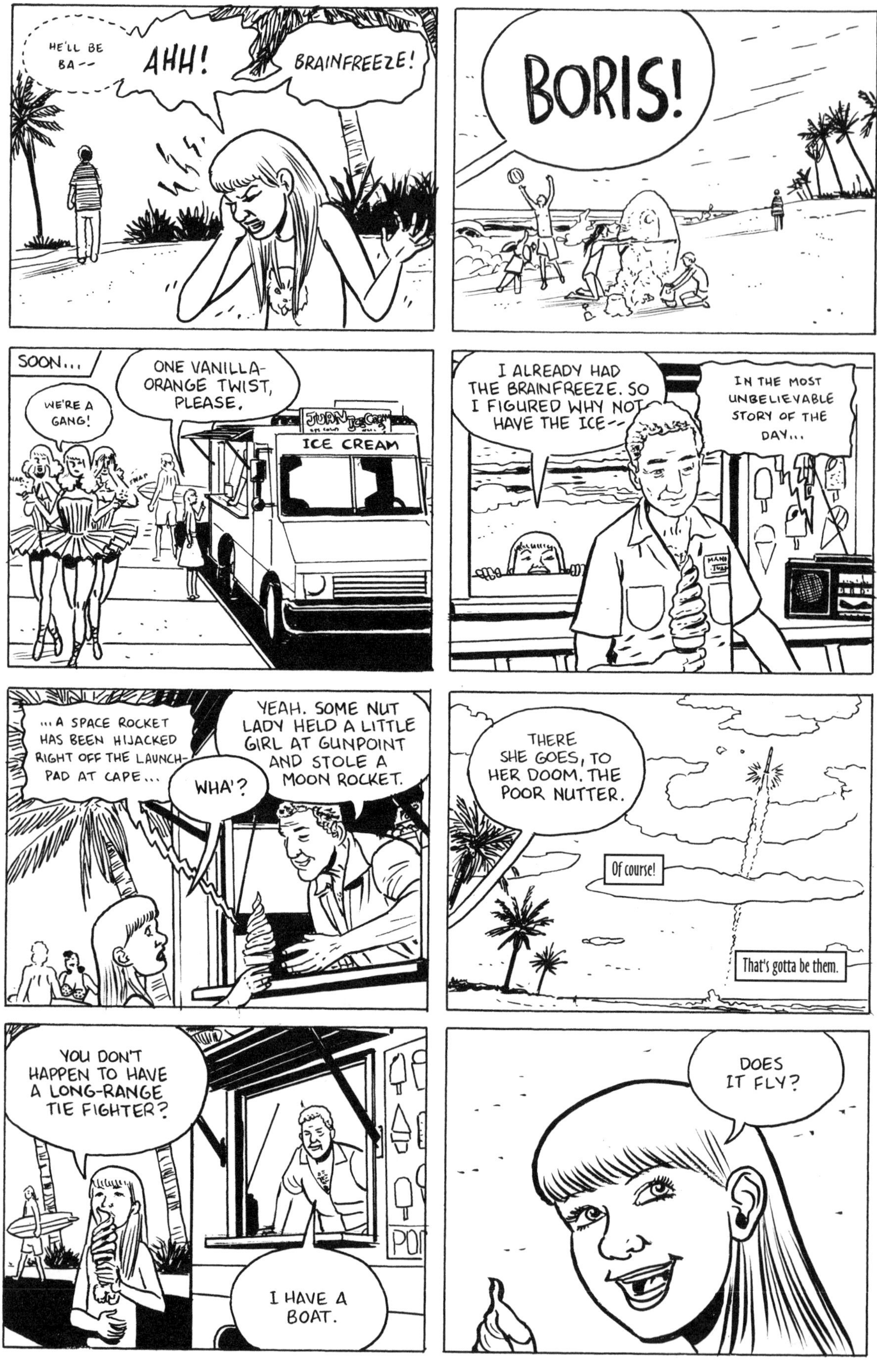
HE'LL BE BA--
AHH!
BRAINFREEZE!
BORIS!
SOON...
WE'RE A GANG!
ONE VANILLA-ORANGE TWIST, PLEASE.
ICE CREAM
I ALREADY HAD THE BRAINFREEZE. SO I FIGURED WHY NOT HAVE THE ICE--
IN THE MOST UNBELIEVABLE STORY OF THE DAY...
...A SPACE ROCKET HAS BEEN HIJACKED RIGHT OFF THE LAUNCH-PAD AT CAPE...
WHA'?
YEAH. SOME NUT LADY HELD A LITTLE GIRL AT GUNPOINT AND STOLE A MOON ROCKET.
THERE SHE GOES, TO HER DOOM. THE POOR NUTTER.
Of course!
That's gotta be them.
YOU DON'T HAPPEN TO HAVE A LONG-RANGE TIE FIGHTER?
I HAVE A BOAT.
DOES IT FLY?

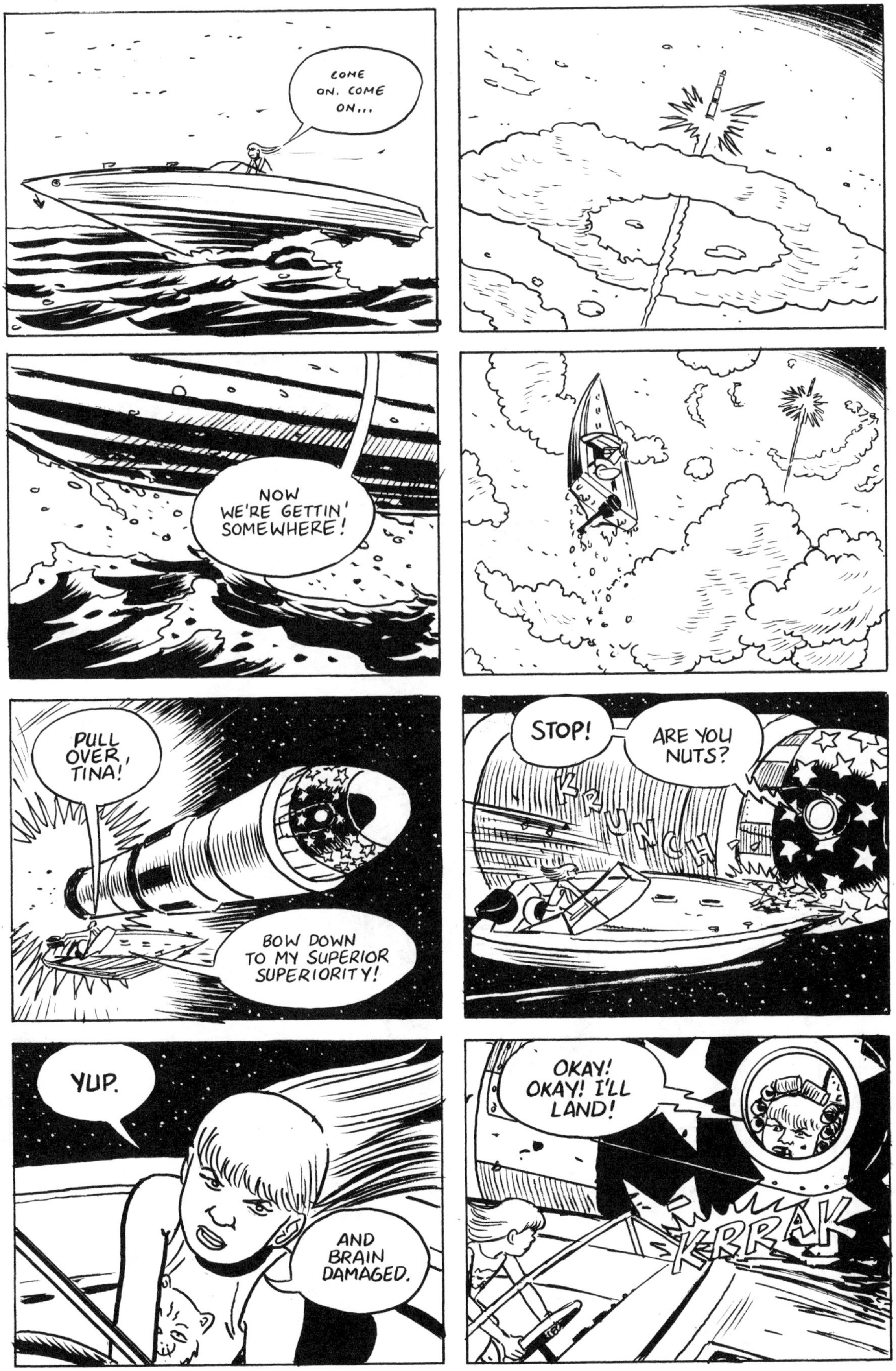
COME ON. COME ON...
NOW WE'RE GETTIN' SOMEWHERE!
PULL OVER, TINA!
BOW DOWN TO MY SUPERIOR SUPERIORITY!
STOP!
ARE YOU NUTS?
KRUNCH
YUP.
AND BRAIN DAMAGED.
OKAY! OKAY! I'LL LAND!
KRRAK

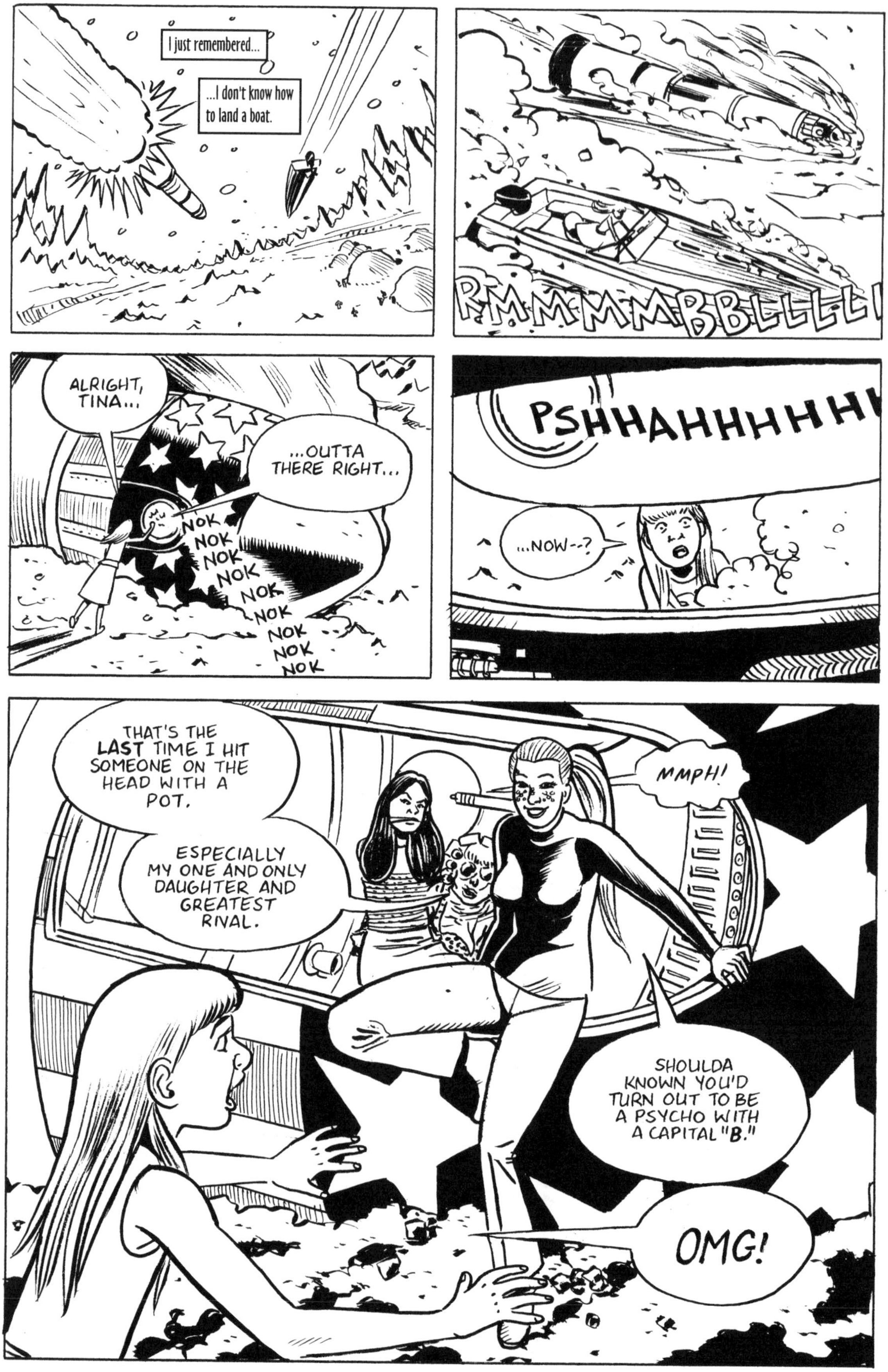
I just remembered...
...I don't know how to land a boat.
RMMMMMBBLLLLL
ALRIGHT, TINA...
...OUTTA THERE RIGHT...
NOK NOK NOK NOK NOK NOK NOK NOK NOK
PSHHAHHHHHH
...NOW--?
THAT'S THE LAST TIME I HIT SOMEONE ON THE HEAD WITH A POT.
ESPECIALLY MY ONE AND ONLY DAUGHTER AND GREATEST RIVAL.
MMPH!
SHOULDA KNOWN YOU'D TURN OUT TO BE A PSYCHO WITH A CAPITAL "B."
OMG!

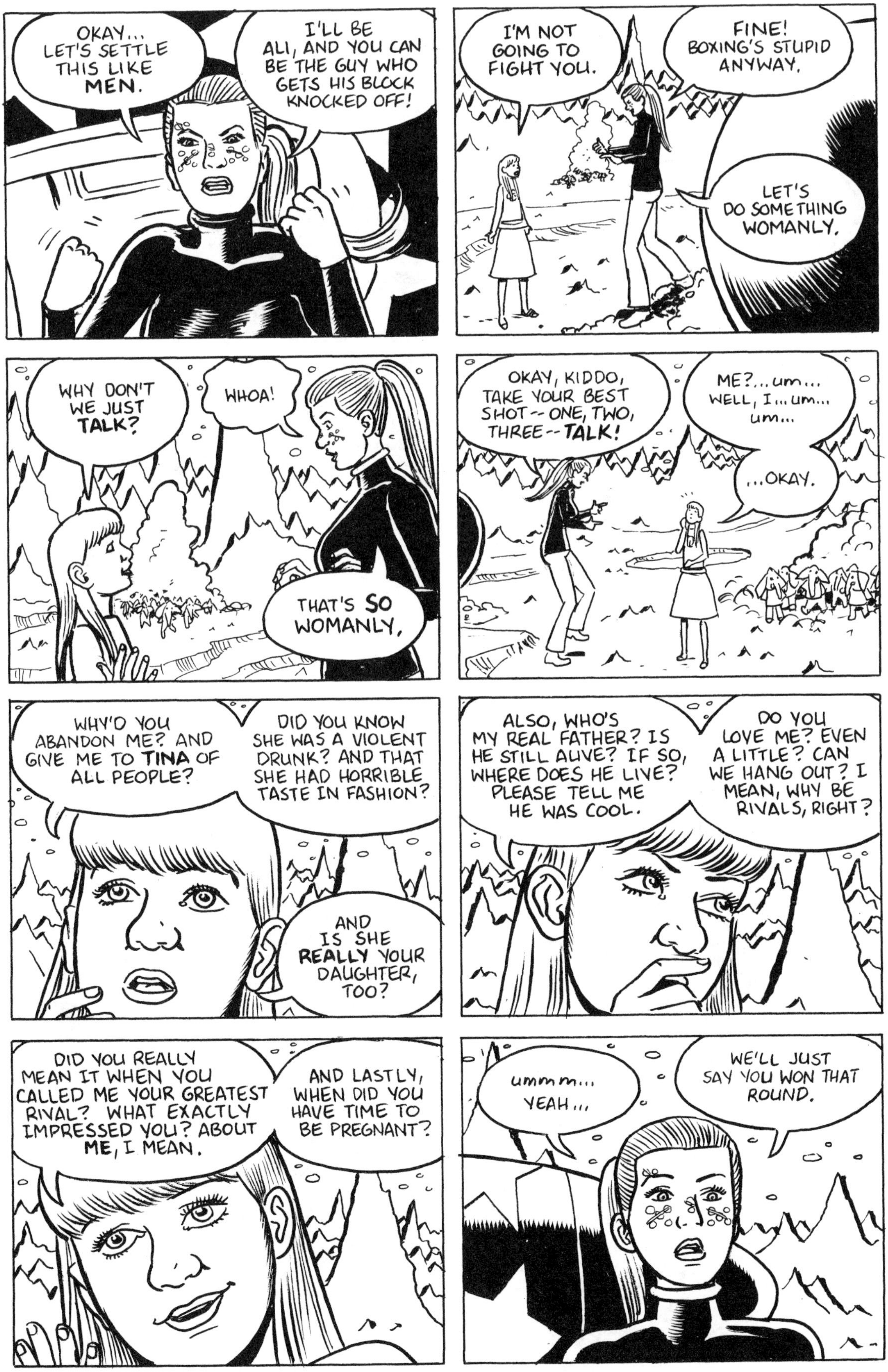

OKAY... LET'S SETTLE THIS LIKE **MEN**.
I'LL BE ALI, AND YOU CAN BE THE GUY WHO GETS HIS BLOCK KNOCKED OFF!
I'M NOT GOING TO FIGHT YOU.
FINE! BOXING'S STUPID ANYWAY.
LET'S DO SOMETHING WOMANLY.
WHY DON'T WE JUST **TALK**?
WHOA!
THAT'S **SO** WOMANLY.
OKAY, KIDDO, TAKE YOUR BEST SHOT -- ONE, TWO, THREE -- **TALK**!
ME?...um... WELL, I...um... um...
...OKAY.
WHY'D YOU ABANDON ME? AND GIVE ME TO **TINA** OF ALL PEOPLE?
DID YOU KNOW SHE WAS A VIOLENT DRUNK? AND THAT SHE HAD HORRIBLE TASTE IN FASHION?
AND IS SHE **REALLY** YOUR DAUGHTER, TOO?
ALSO, WHO'S MY REAL FATHER? IS HE STILL ALIVE? IF SO, WHERE DOES HE LIVE? PLEASE TELL ME HE WAS COOL.
DO YOU LOVE ME? EVEN A LITTLE? CAN WE HANG OUT? I MEAN, WHY BE RIVALS, RIGHT?
DID YOU REALLY MEAN IT WHEN YOU CALLED ME YOUR GREATEST RIVAL? WHAT EXACTLY IMPRESSED YOU? ABOUT **ME**, I MEAN.
AND LASTLY, WHEN DID YOU HAVE TIME TO BE PREGNANT?
ummm... YEAH...
WE'LL JUST SAY YOU WON THAT ROUND.

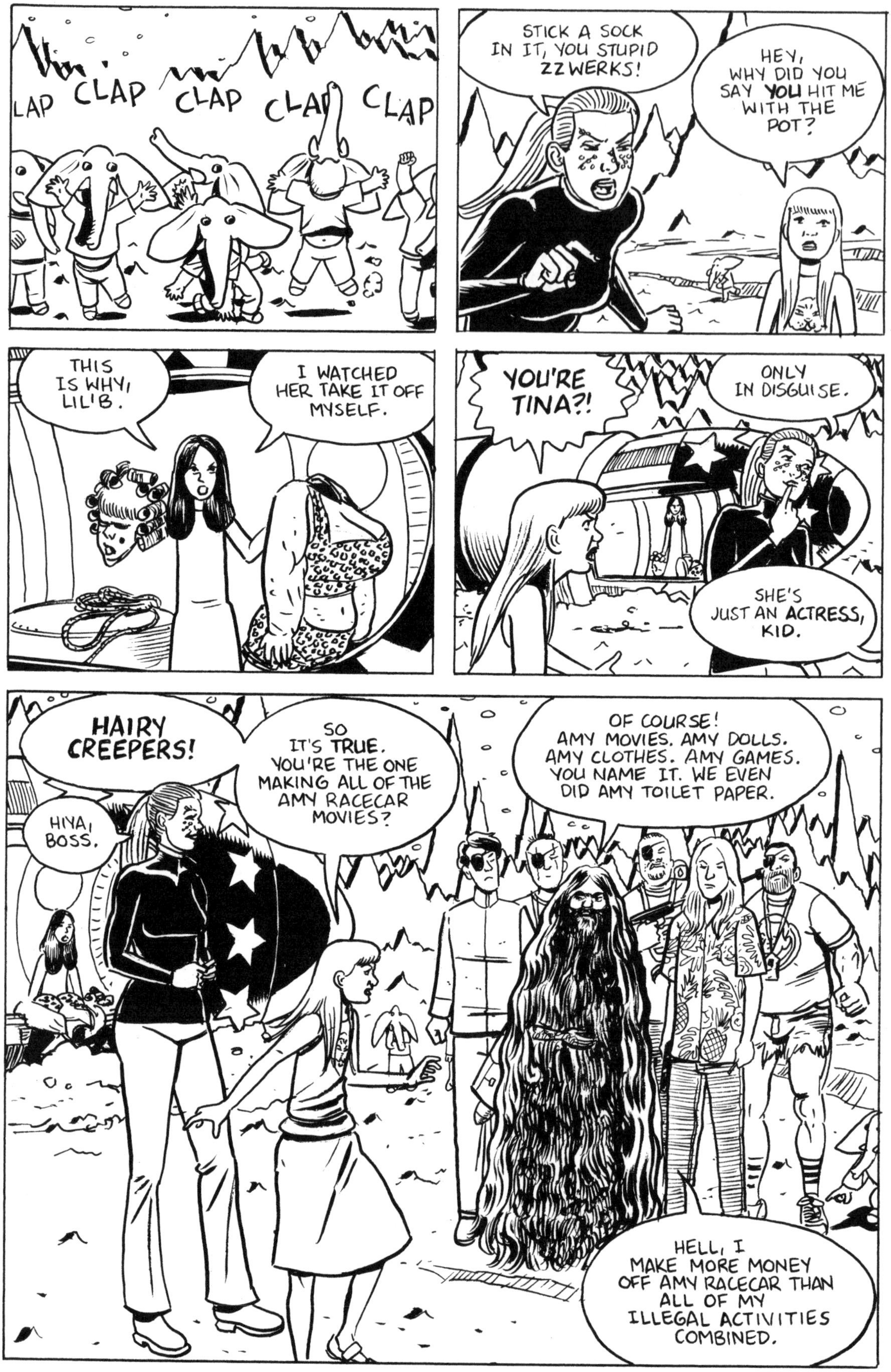
CLAP CLAP CLAP CLAP CLAP
STICK A SOCK IN IT, YOU STUPID ZZWERKS!
HEY, WHY DID YOU SAY YOU HIT ME WITH THE POT?
THIS IS WHY, LIL'B.
I WATCHED HER TAKE IT OFF MYSELF.
YOU'RE TINA?!
ONLY IN DISGUISE.
SHE'S JUST AN ACTRESS, KID.
HAIRY CREEPERS!
HIYA, BOSS.
SO IT'S TRUE. YOU'RE THE ONE MAKING ALL OF THE AMY RACECAR MOVIES?
OF COURSE! AMY MOVIES. AMY DOLLS. AMY CLOTHES. AMY GAMES. YOU NAME IT. WE EVEN DID AMY TOILET PAPER.
HELL, I MAKE MORE MONEY OFF AMY RACECAR THAN ALL OF MY ILLEGAL ACTIVITIES COMBINED.

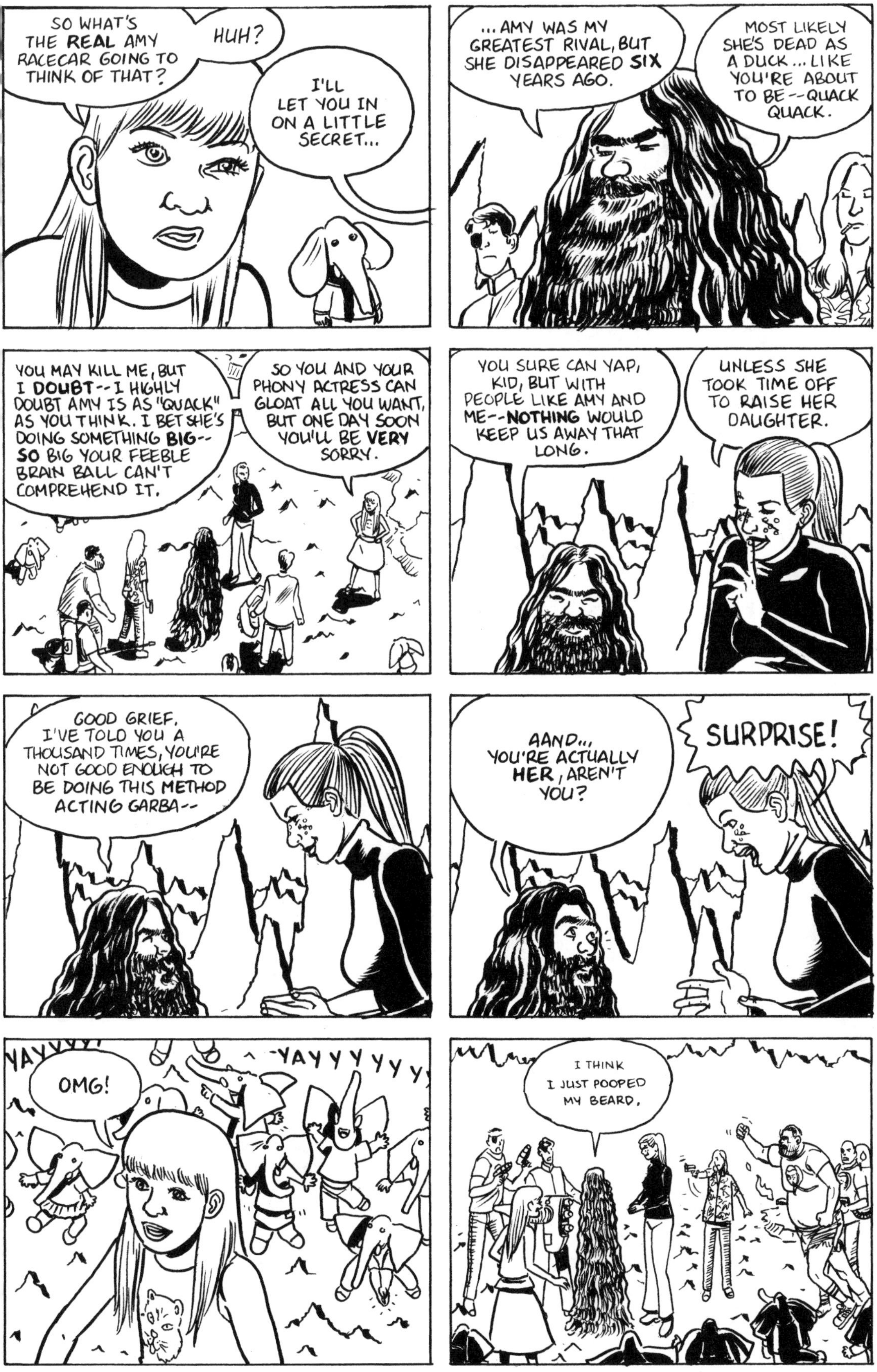
SO WHAT'S THE REAL AMY RACECAR GOING TO THINK OF THAT?
HUH?
I'LL LET YOU IN ON A LITTLE SECRET...
...AMY WAS MY GREATEST RIVAL, BUT SHE DISAPPEARED SIX YEARS AGO.
MOST LIKELY SHE'S DEAD AS A DUCK... LIKE YOU'RE ABOUT TO BE--QUACK QUACK.
YOU MAY KILL ME, BUT I DOUBT--I HIGHLY DOUBT AMY IS AS "QUACK" AS YOU THINK. I BET SHE'S DOING SOMETHING BIG--SO BIG YOUR FEEBLE BRAIN BALL CAN'T COMPREHEND IT.
SO YOU AND YOUR PHONY ACTRESS CAN GLOAT ALL YOU WANT, BUT ONE DAY SOON YOU'LL BE VERY SORRY.
YOU SURE CAN YAP, KID, BUT WITH PEOPLE LIKE AMY AND ME--NOTHING WOULD KEEP US AWAY THAT LONG.
UNLESS SHE TOOK TIME OFF TO RAISE HER DAUGHTER.
GOOD GRIEF, I'VE TOLD YOU A THOUSAND TIMES, YOU'RE NOT GOOD ENOUGH TO BE DOING THIS METHOD ACTING GARBA--
AAND... YOU'RE ACTUALLY HER, AREN'T YOU?
SURPRISE!
YAYYY!
YAYYYYYYY
OMG!
I THINK I JUST POOPED MY BEARD.

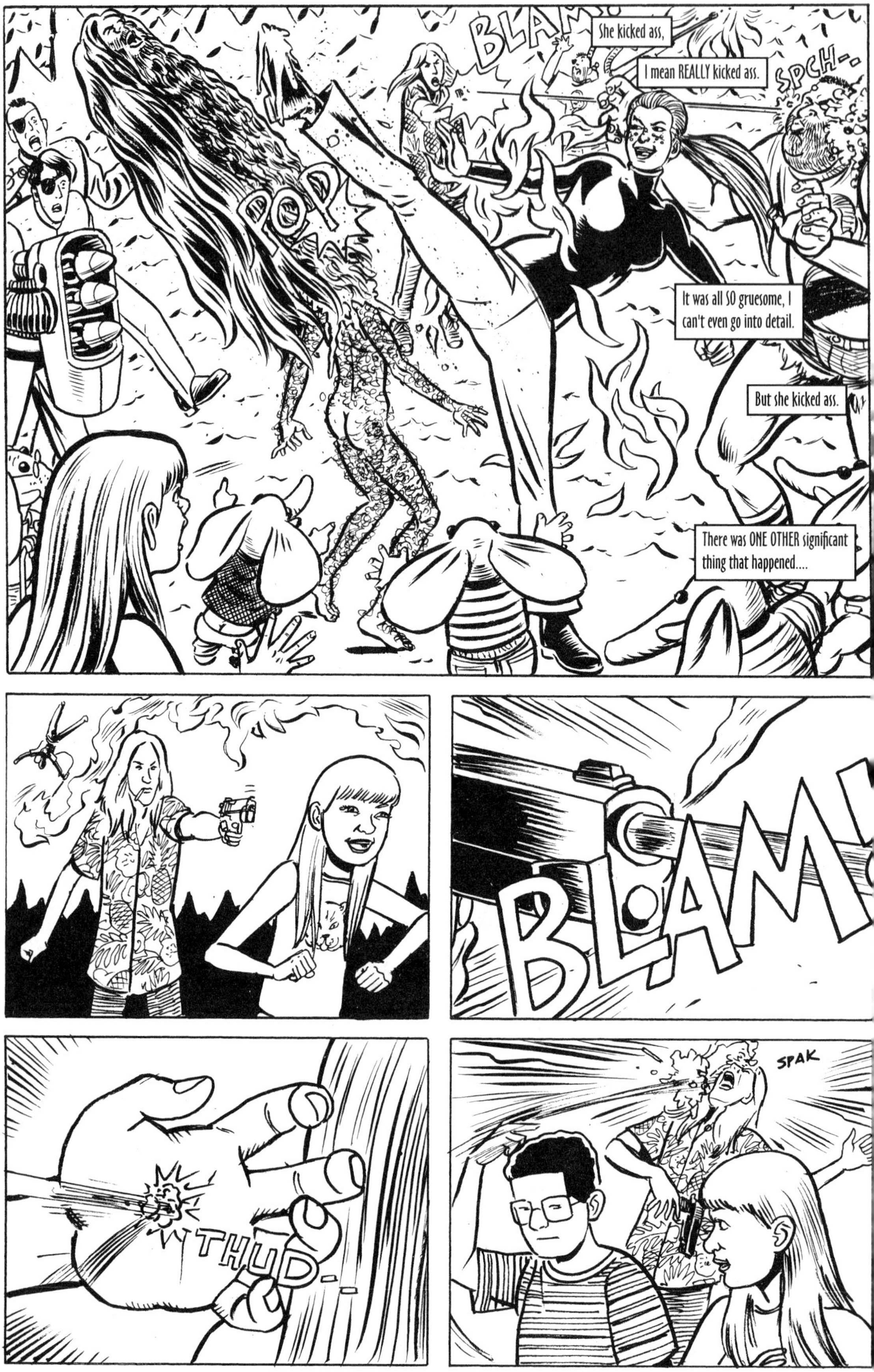
BLAM!
She kicked ass,
I mean REALLY kicked ass.
SPCH--
POP
It was all SO gruesome, I can't even go into detail.
But she kicked ass.
There was ONE OTHER significant thing that happened....
BLAM!
THUD--
SPAK

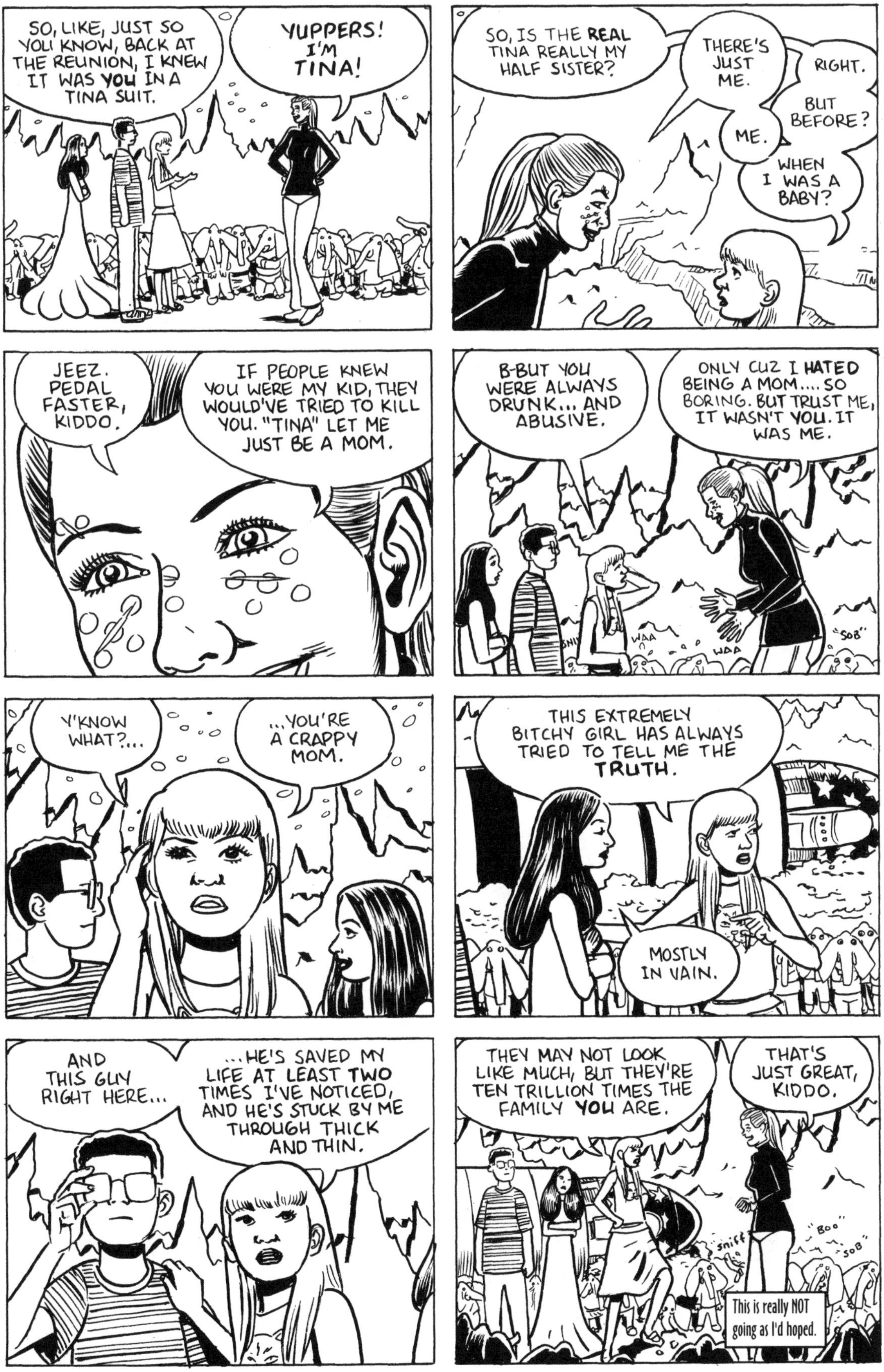
SO, LIKE, JUST SO YOU KNOW, BACK AT THE REUNION, I KNEW IT WAS YOU IN A TINA SUIT.
YUPPERS! I'M TINA!
SO, IS THE REAL TINA REALLY MY HALF SISTER?
THERE'S JUST ME.
RIGHT.
BUT BEFORE?
ME.
WHEN I WAS A BABY?
JEEZ. PEDAL FASTER, KIDDO.
IF PEOPLE KNEW YOU WERE MY KID, THEY WOULD'VE TRIED TO KILL YOU. "TINA" LET ME JUST BE A MOM.
B-BUT YOU WERE ALWAYS DRUNK... AND ABUSIVE.
ONLY CUZ I HATED BEING A MOM.... SO BORING. BUT TRUST ME, IT WASN'T YOU. IT WAS ME.
WAA
WAA
"SOB"
Y'KNOW WHAT?...
...YOU'RE A CRAPPY MOM.
THIS EXTREMELY BITCHY GIRL HAS ALWAYS TRIED TO TELL ME THE TRUTH.
MOSTLY IN VAIN.
AND THIS GUY RIGHT HERE...
...HE'S SAVED MY LIFE AT LEAST TWO TIMES I'VE NOTICED, AND HE'S STUCK BY ME THROUGH THICK AND THIN.
THEY MAY NOT LOOK LIKE MUCH, BUT THEY'RE TEN TRILLION TIMES THE FAMILY YOU ARE.
THAT'S JUST GREAT, KIDDO.
sniff
"BOO"
"SOB"
This is really NOT going as I'd hoped.

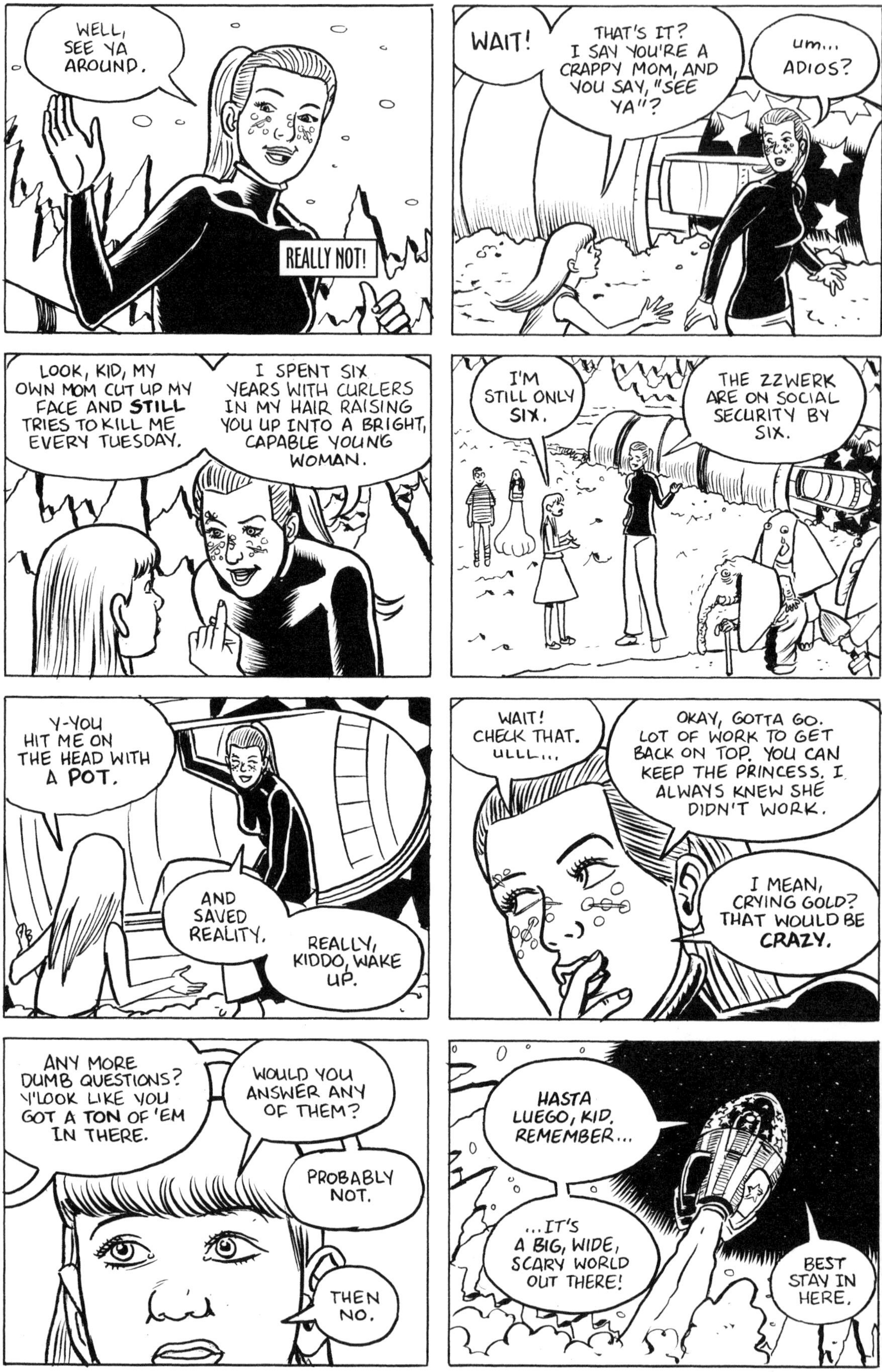
WELL, SEE YA AROUND.
REALLY NOT!
WAIT!
THAT'S IT? I SAY YOU'RE A CRAPPY MOM, AND YOU SAY, "SEE YA"?
um... ADIOS?
LOOK, KID, MY OWN MOM CUT UP MY FACE AND STILL TRIES TO KILL ME EVERY TUESDAY.
I SPENT SIX YEARS WITH CURLERS IN MY HAIR RAISING YOU UP INTO A BRIGHT, CAPABLE YOUNG WOMAN.
I'M STILL ONLY SIX.
THE ZZWERK ARE ON SOCIAL SECURITY BY SIX.
Y-YOU HIT ME ON THE HEAD WITH A POT.
AND SAVED REALITY.
REALLY, KIDDO, WAKE UP.
WAIT! CHECK THAT. ULLL...
OKAY, GOTTA GO. LOT OF WORK TO GET BACK ON TOP. YOU CAN KEEP THE PRINCESS. I ALWAYS KNEW SHE DIDN'T WORK.
I MEAN, CRYING GOLD? THAT WOULD BE CRAZY.
ANY MORE DUMB QUESTIONS? Y'LOOK LIKE YOU GOT A TON OF 'EM IN THERE.
WOULD YOU ANSWER ANY OF THEM?
PROBABLY NOT.
THEN NO.
HASTA LUEGO, KID. REMEMBER...
...IT'S A BIG, WIDE, SCARY WORLD OUT THERE!
BEST STAY IN HERE.

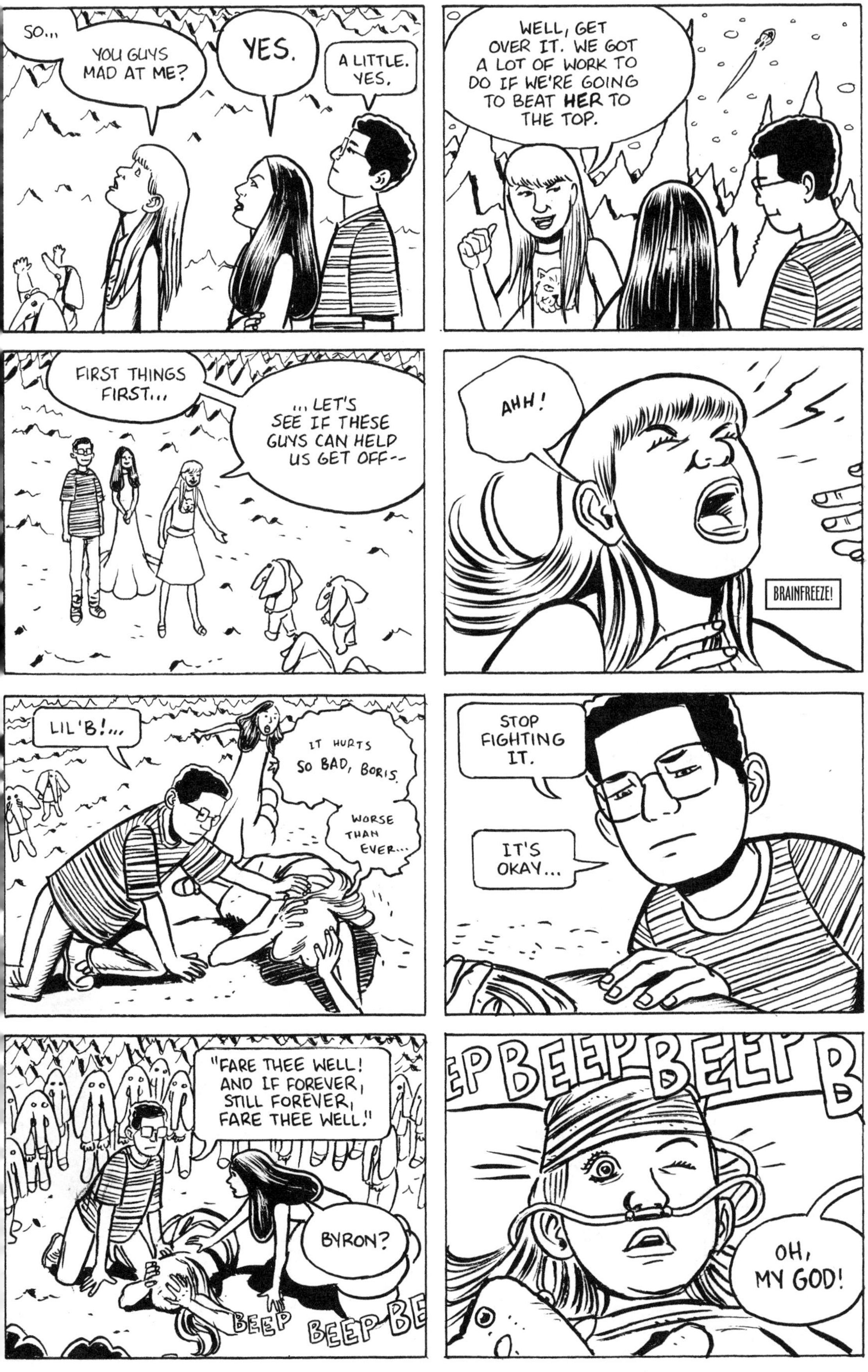
SO...
YOU GUYS MAD AT ME?
YES.
A LITTLE. YES.
WELL, GET OVER IT. WE GOT A LOT OF WORK TO DO IF WE'RE GOING TO BEAT HER TO THE TOP.
FIRST THINGS FIRST...
...LET'S SEE IF THESE GUYS CAN HELP US GET OFF--
AHH!
BRAINFREEZE!
LIL'B!...
IT HURTS SO BAD, BORIS.
WORSE THAN EVER...
STOP FIGHTING IT.
IT'S OKAY...
"FARE THEE WELL! AND IF FOREVER, STILL FOREVER, FARE THEE WELL."
BYRON?
BEEP BEEP BE
EP BEEP BEEP BEEP B
OH, MY GOD!

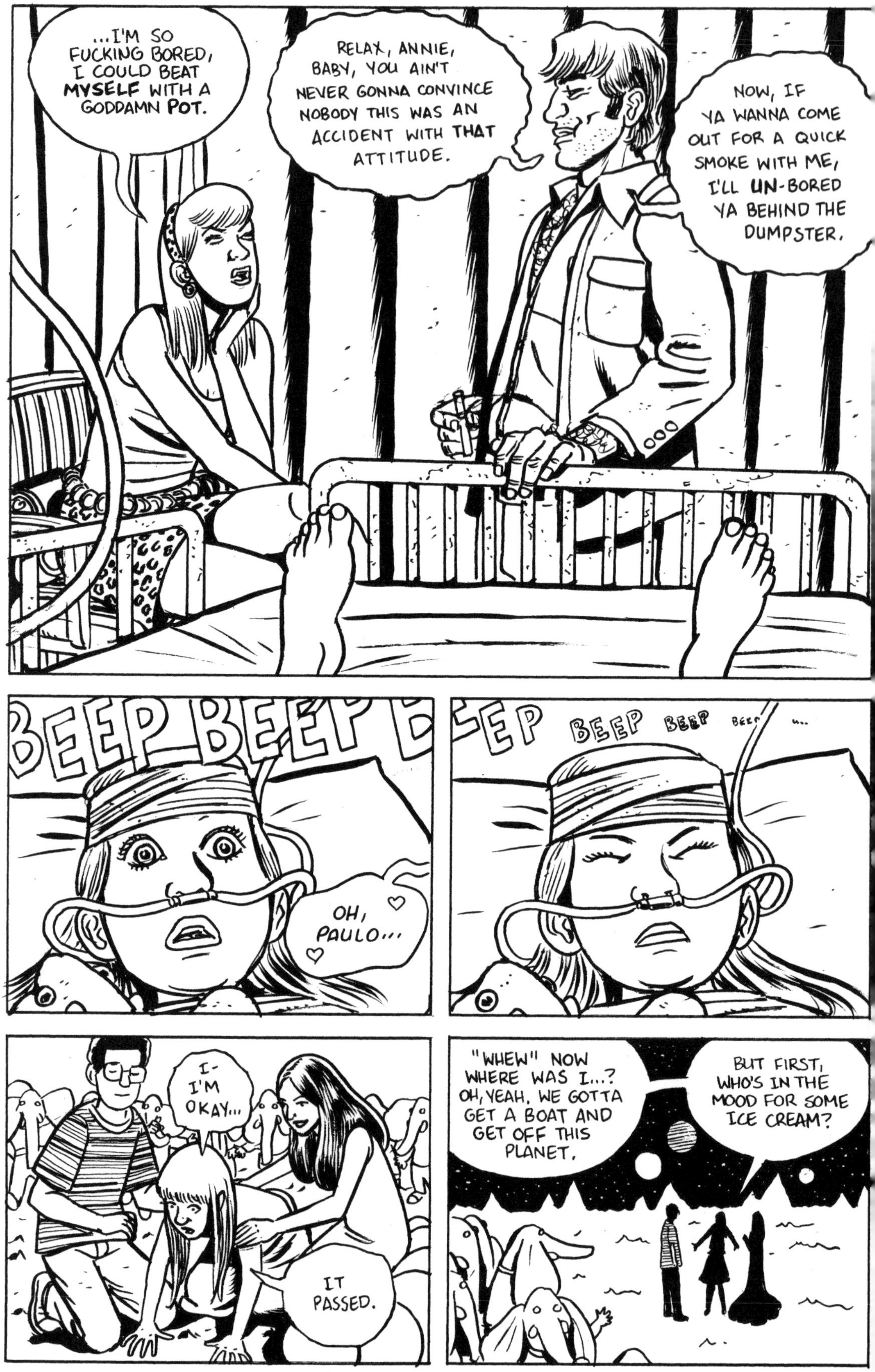
...I'M SO FUCKING BORED, I COULD BEAT **MYSELF** WITH A GODDAMN **POT.**
RELAX, ANNIE, BABY, YOU AIN'T NEVER GONNA CONVINCE NOBODY THIS WAS AN ACCIDENT WITH **THAT** ATTITUDE.
NOW, IF YA WANNA COME OUT FOR A QUICK SMOKE WITH ME, I'LL **UN**-BORED YA BEHIND THE DUMPSTER.
BEEP BEEP BEEP
OH, PAULO...
BEEP BEEP
I- I'M OKAY...
IT PASSED.
"WHEW" NOW WHERE WAS I...? OH, YEAH. WE GOTTA GET A BOAT AND GET OFF THIS PLANET.
BUT FIRST, WHO'S IN THE MOOD FOR SOME ICE CREAM?

THE END...

5
"OTHER PEOPLE"

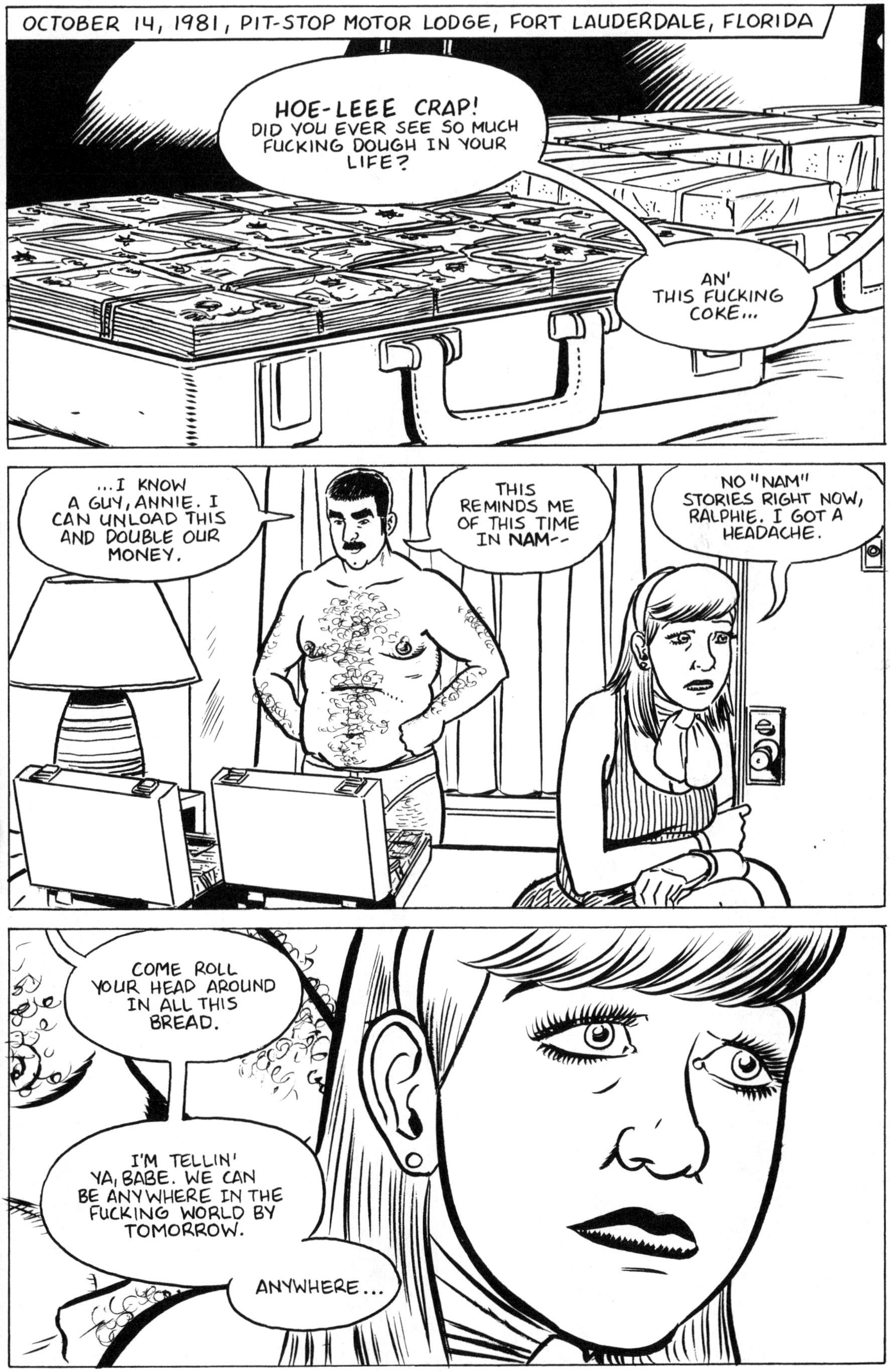
OCTOBER 14, 1981, PIT-STOP MOTOR LODGE, FORT LAUDERDALE, FLORIDA
HOE-LEEE CRAP! DID YOU EVER SEE SO MUCH FUCKING DOUGH IN YOUR LIFE?
AN' THIS FUCKING COKE...
...I KNOW A GUY, ANNIE. I CAN UNLOAD THIS AND DOUBLE OUR MONEY.
THIS REMINDS ME OF THIS TIME IN NAM--
NO "NAM" STORIES RIGHT NOW, RALPHIE. I GOT A HEADACHE.
COME ROLL YOUR HEAD AROUND IN ALL THIS BREAD.
I'M TELLIN' YA, BABE. WE CAN BE ANYWHERE IN THE FUCKING WORLD BY TOMORROW.
ANYWHERE...

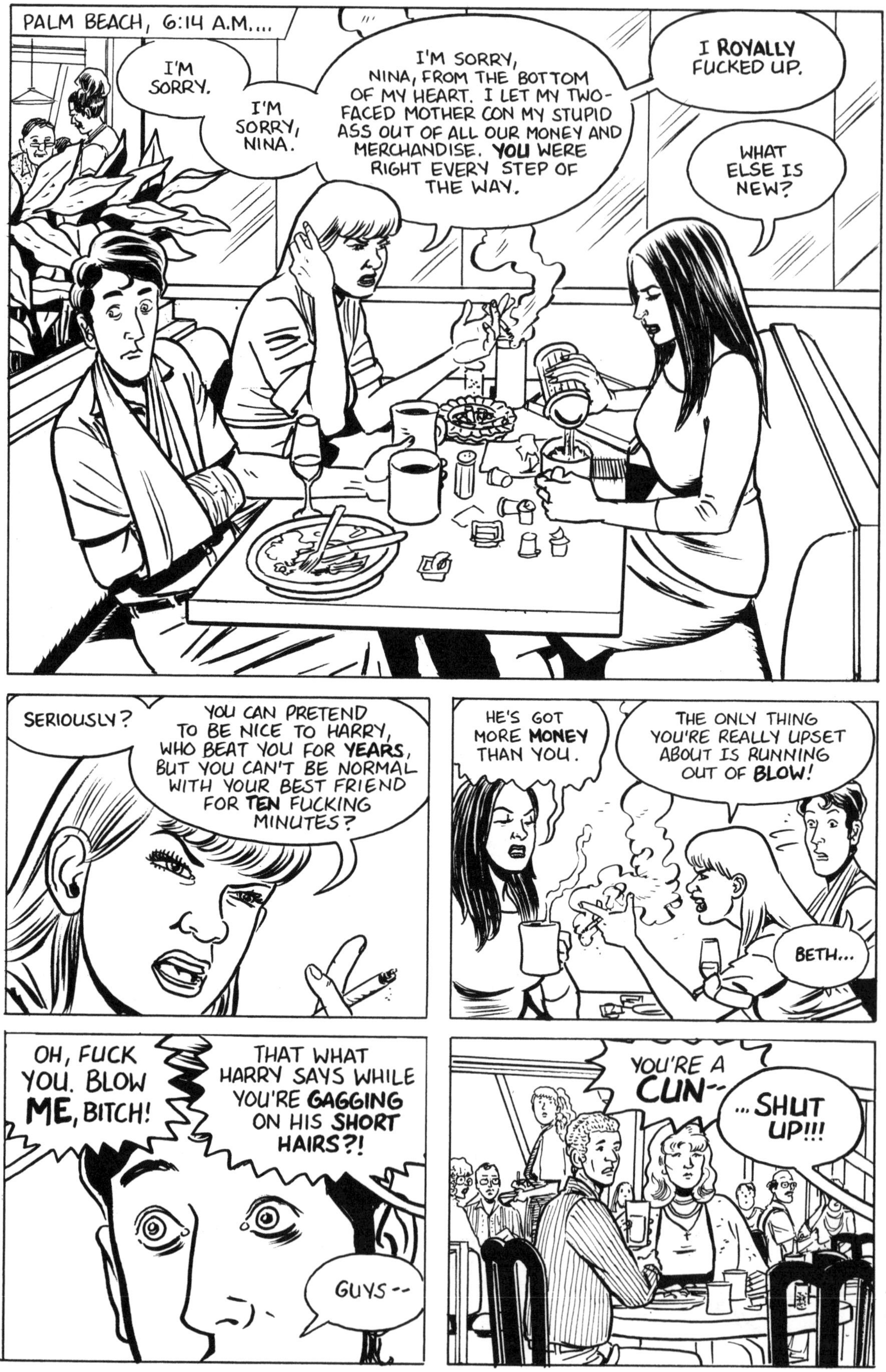
PALM BEACH, 6:14 A.M....
I'M SORRY.
I'M SORRY, NINA.
I'M SORRY, NINA, FROM THE BOTTOM OF MY HEART. I LET MY TWO-FACED MOTHER CON MY STUPID ASS OUT OF ALL OUR MONEY AND MERCHANDISE. YOU WERE RIGHT EVERY STEP OF THE WAY.
I ROYALLY FUCKED UP.
WHAT ELSE IS NEW?
SERIOUSLY?
YOU CAN PRETEND TO BE NICE TO HARRY, WHO BEAT YOU FOR YEARS, BUT YOU CAN'T BE NORMAL WITH YOUR BEST FRIEND FOR TEN FUCKING MINUTES?
HE'S GOT MORE MONEY THAN YOU.
THE ONLY THING YOU'RE REALLY UPSET ABOUT IS RUNNING OUT OF BLOW!
BETH...
OH, FUCK YOU. BLOW ME, BITCH!
THAT WHAT HARRY SAYS WHILE YOU'RE GAGGING ON HIS SHORT HAIRS?!
GUYS--
YOU'RE A CUN--
...SHUT UP!!!

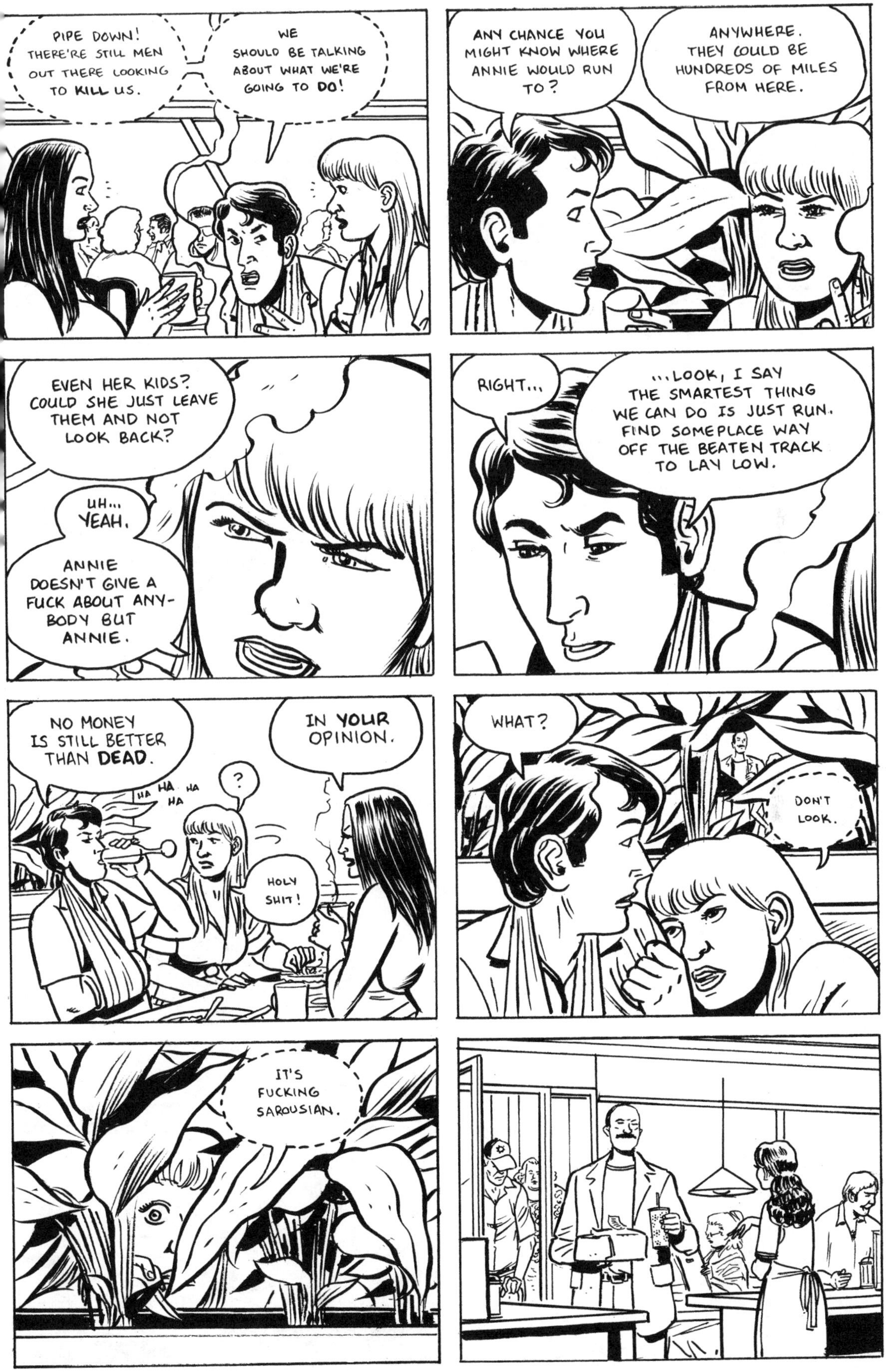
PIPE DOWN! THERE'RE STILL MEN OUT THERE LOOKING TO KILL US.
WE SHOULD BE TALKING ABOUT WHAT WE'RE GOING TO DO!
ANY CHANCE YOU MIGHT KNOW WHERE ANNIE WOULD RUN TO?
ANYWHERE. THEY COULD BE HUNDREDS OF MILES FROM HERE.
EVEN HER KIDS? COULD SHE JUST LEAVE THEM AND NOT LOOK BACK?
UH... YEAH.
ANNIE DOESN'T GIVE A FUCK ABOUT ANY-BODY BUT ANNIE.
RIGHT...
...LOOK, I SAY THE SMARTEST THING WE CAN DO IS JUST RUN. FIND SOMEPLACE WAY OFF THE BEATEN TRACK TO LAY LOW.
NO MONEY IS STILL BETTER THAN DEAD.
HA HA HA HA
?
IN YOUR OPINION.
HOLY SHIT!
WHAT?
DON'T LOOK.
IT'S FUCKING SAROUSIAN.

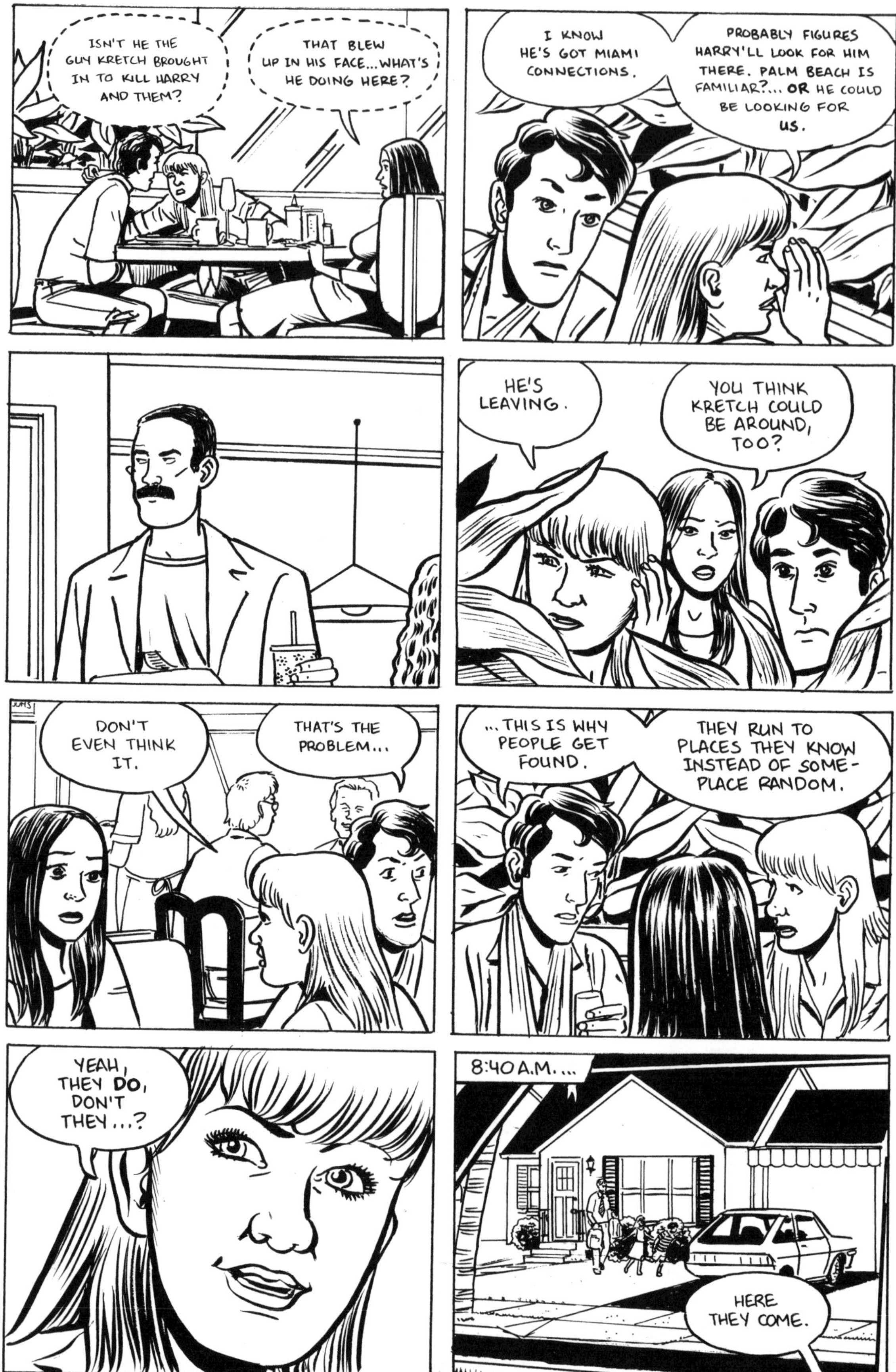
ISN'T HE THE GUY KRETCH BROUGHT IN TO KILL HARRY AND THEM?
THAT BLEW UP IN HIS FACE... WHAT'S HE DOING HERE?
I KNOW HE'S GOT MIAMI CONNECTIONS.
PROBABLY FIGURES HARRY'LL LOOK FOR HIM THERE. PALM BEACH IS FAMILIAR?... OR HE COULD BE LOOKING FOR US.
HE'S LEAVING.
YOU THINK KRETCH COULD BE AROUND, TOO?
DON'T EVEN THINK IT.
THAT'S THE PROBLEM...
...THIS IS WHY PEOPLE GET FOUND.
THEY RUN TO PLACES THEY KNOW INSTEAD OF SOME-PLACE RANDOM.
YEAH, THEY DO, DON'T THEY...?
8:40 A.M....
HERE THEY COME.

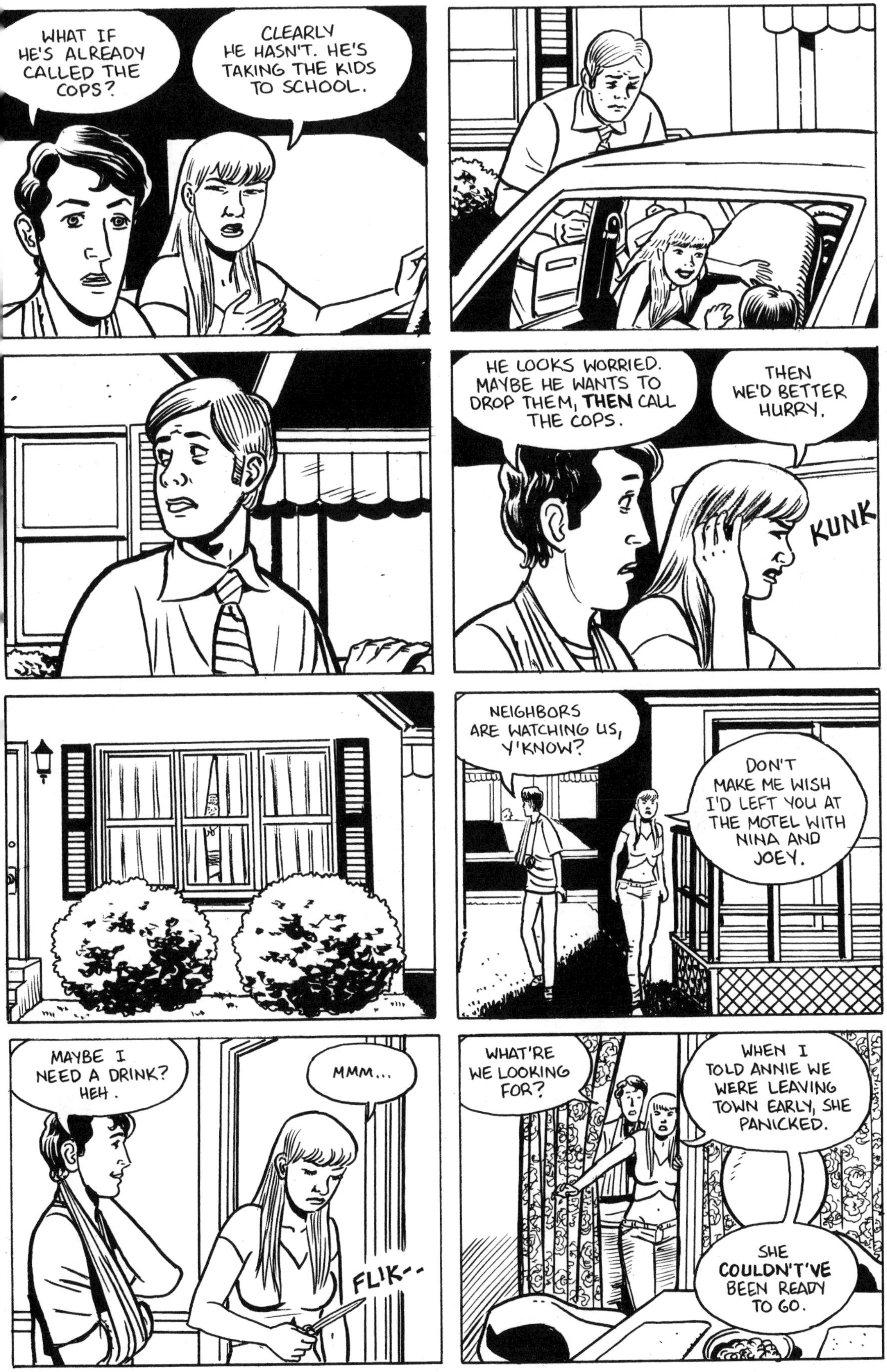
WHAT IF HE'S ALREADY CALLED THE COPS?
CLEARLY HE HASN'T. HE'S TAKING THE KIDS TO SCHOOL.
HE LOOKS WORRIED. MAYBE HE WANTS TO DROP THEM, THEN CALL THE COPS.
THEN WE'D BETTER HURRY.
KUNK
NEIGHBORS ARE WATCHING US, Y'KNOW?
DON'T MAKE ME WISH I'D LEFT YOU AT THE MOTEL WITH NINA AND JOEY.
MAYBE I NEED A DRINK? HEH.
MMM...
FLIK--
WHAT'RE WE LOOKING FOR?
WHEN I TOLD ANNIE WE WERE LEAVING TOWN EARLY, SHE PANICKED.
SHE COULDN'T'VE BEEN READY TO GO.

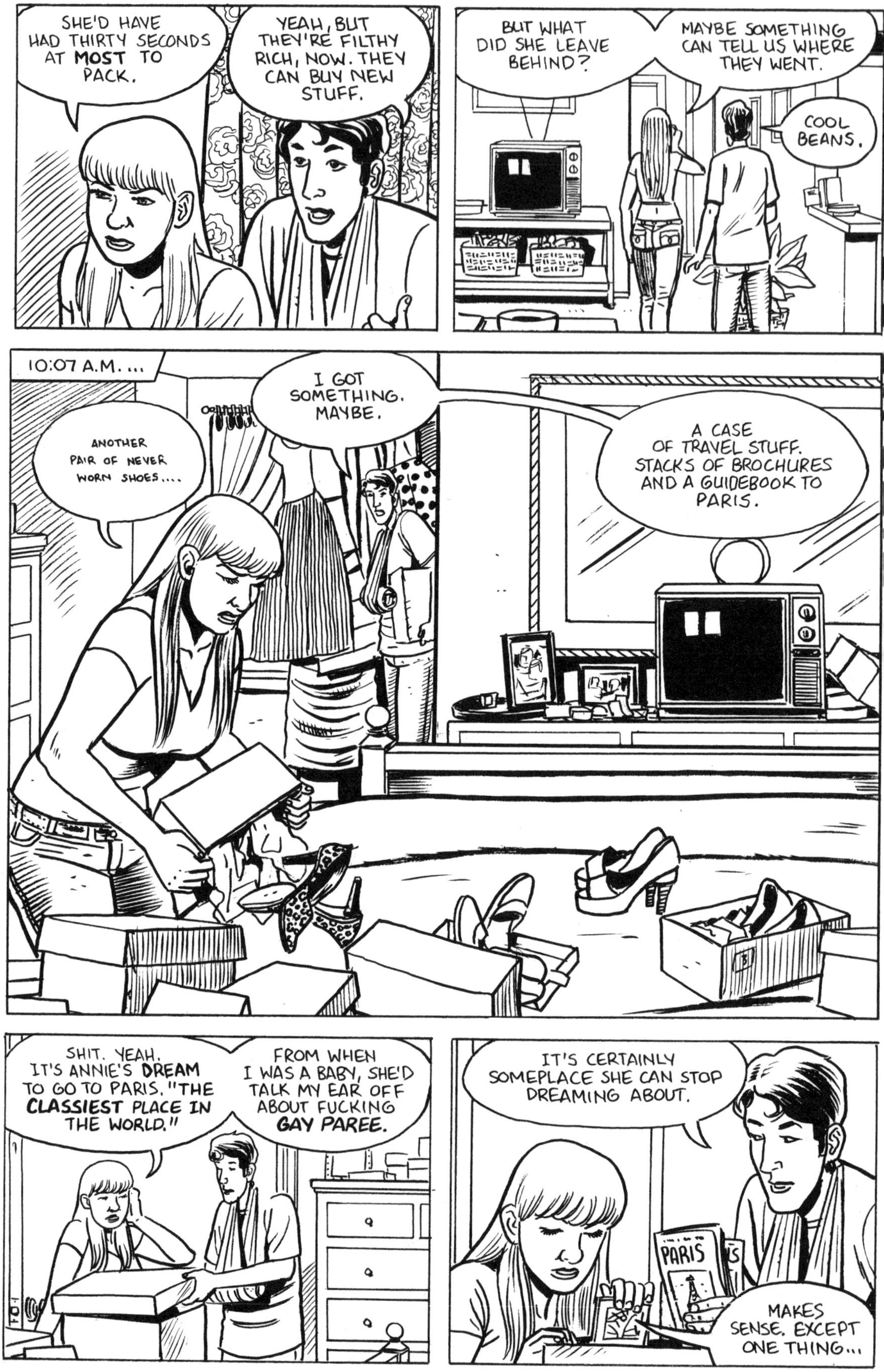
SHE'D HAVE HAD THIRTY SECONDS AT MOST TO PACK.
YEAH, BUT THEY'RE FILTHY RICH, NOW. THEY CAN BUY NEW STUFF.
BUT WHAT DID SHE LEAVE BEHIND?
MAYBE SOMETHING CAN TELL US WHERE THEY WENT.
COOL BEANS.
10:07 A.M. ...
ANOTHER PAIR OF NEVER WORN SHOES....
I GOT SOMETHING. MAYBE.
A CASE OF TRAVEL STUFF. STACKS OF BROCHURES AND A GUIDEBOOK TO PARIS.
SHIT. YEAH. IT'S ANNIE'S DREAM TO GO TO PARIS. "THE CLASSIEST PLACE IN THE WORLD."
FROM WHEN I WAS A BABY, SHE'D TALK MY EAR OFF ABOUT FUCKING GAY PAREE.
IT'S CERTAINLY SOMEPLACE SHE CAN STOP DREAMING ABOUT.
PARIS
MAKES SENSE. EXCEPT ONE THING...

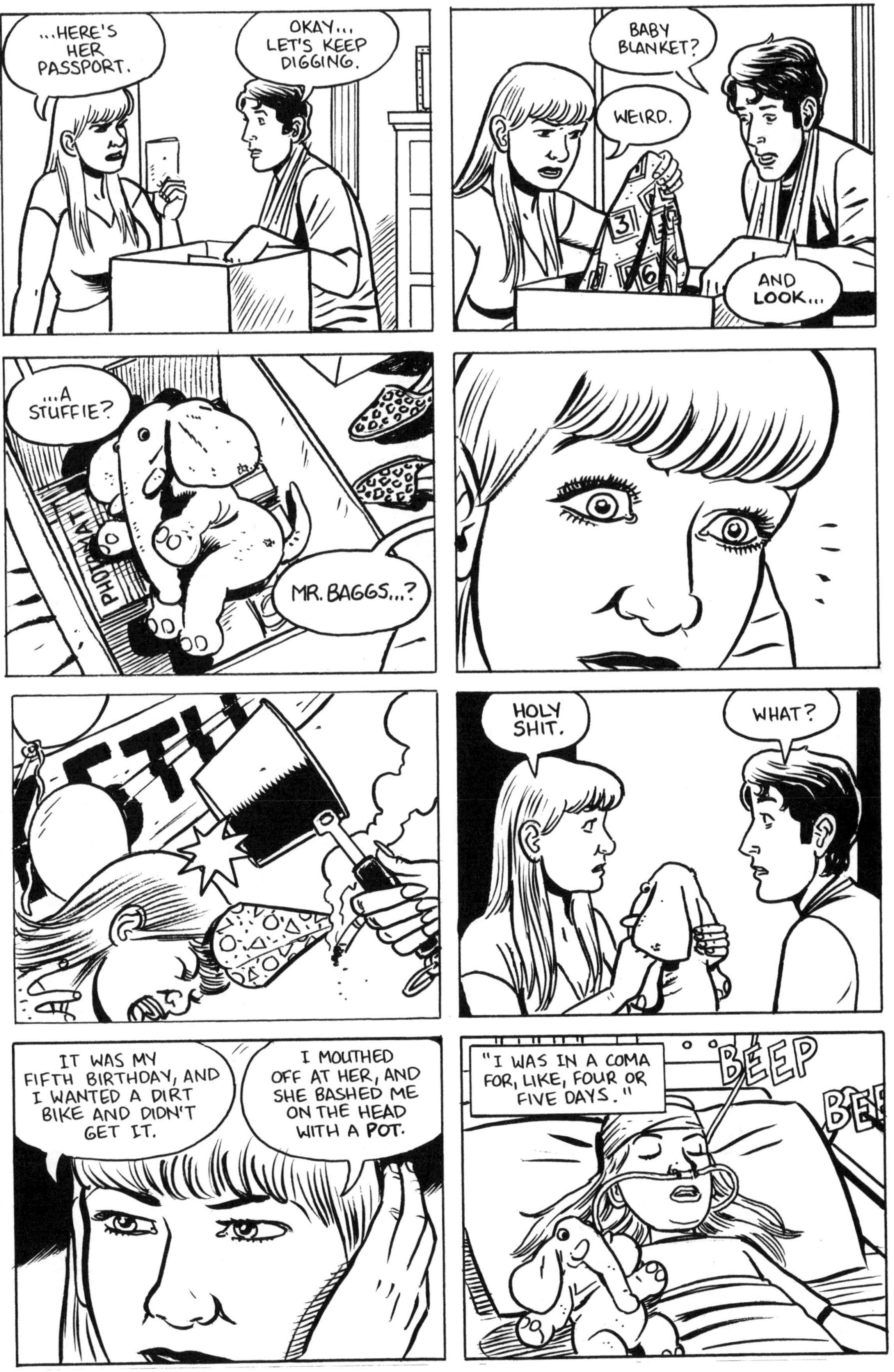
...HERE'S HER PASSPORT.
OKAY... LET'S KEEP DIGGING.
BABY BLANKET?
WEIRD.
AND LOOK...
...A STUFFIE?
PHOTOMAT
MR. BAGGS...?
HOLY SHIT.
WHAT?
IT WAS MY FIFTH BIRTHDAY, AND I WANTED A DIRT BIKE AND DIDN'T GET IT.
I MOUTHED OFF AT HER, AND SHE BASHED ME ON THE HEAD WITH A POT.
"I WAS IN A COMA FOR, LIKE, FOUR OR FIVE DAYS."
BEEP

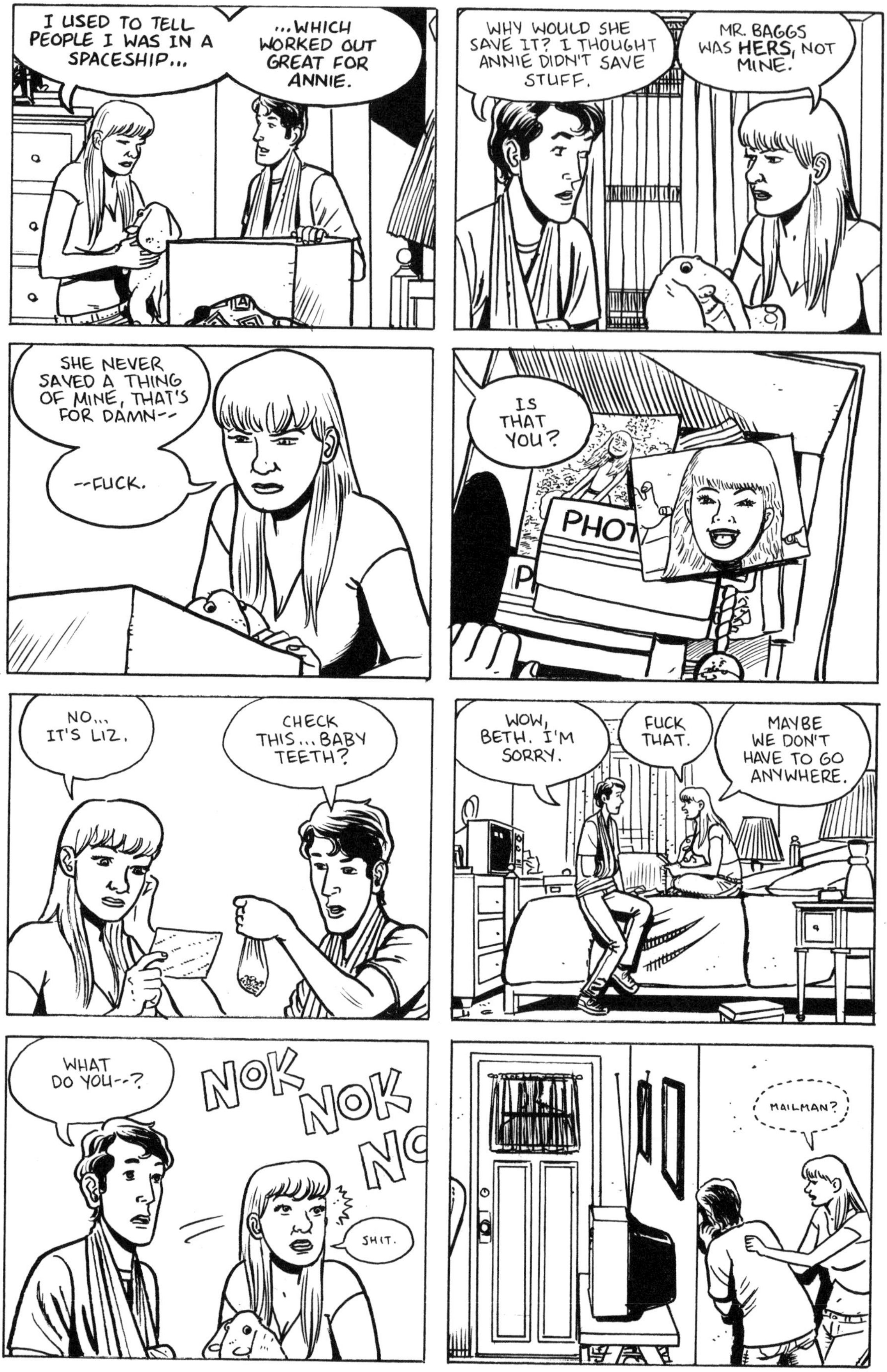
I USED TO TELL PEOPLE I WAS IN A SPACESHIP...
...WHICH WORKED OUT GREAT FOR ANNIE.
WHY WOULD SHE SAVE IT? I THOUGHT ANNIE DIDN'T SAVE STUFF.
MR. BAGGS WAS HERS, NOT MINE.
SHE NEVER SAVED A THING OF MINE, THAT'S FOR DAMN--
--FUCK.
IS THAT YOU?
PHOT
P
NO... IT'S LIZ.
CHECK THIS... BABY TEETH?
WOW, BETH. I'M SORRY.
FUCK THAT.
MAYBE WE DON'T HAVE TO GO ANYWHERE.
WHAT DO YOU--?
NOK NOK NO
SHIT.
MAILMAN?

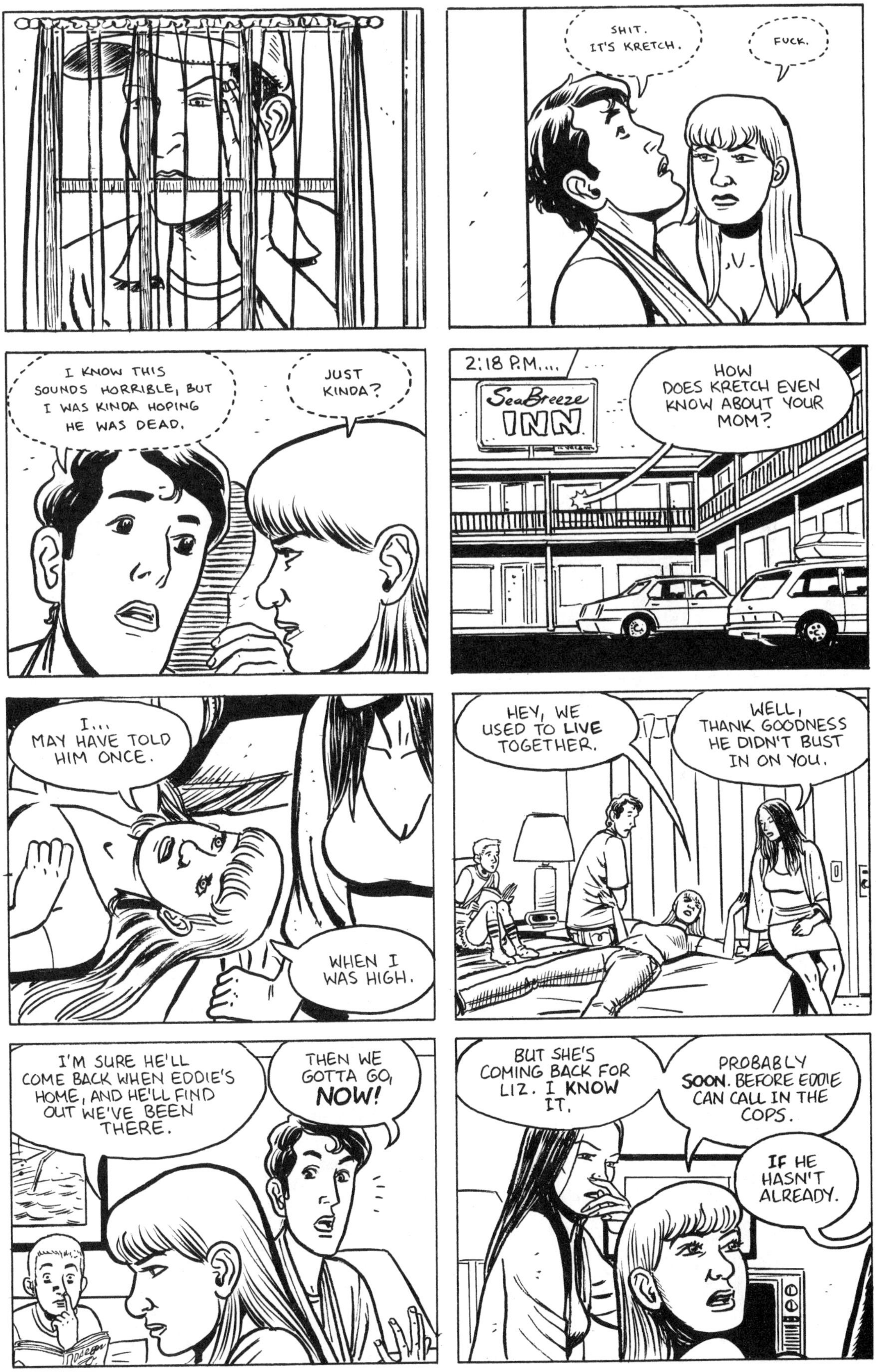
SHIT. IT'S KRETCH.
FUCK.
I KNOW THIS SOUNDS HORRIBLE, BUT I WAS KINDA HOPING HE WAS DEAD.
JUST KINDA?
2:18 P.M....
SeaBreeze INN
HOW DOES KRETCH EVEN KNOW ABOUT YOUR MOM?
I... MAY HAVE TOLD HIM ONCE.
WHEN I WAS HIGH.
HEY, WE USED TO LIVE TOGETHER.
WELL, THANK GOODNESS HE DIDN'T BUST IN ON YOU.
I'M SURE HE'LL COME BACK WHEN EDDIE'S HOME, AND HE'LL FIND OUT WE'VE BEEN THERE.
THEN WE GOTTA GO, NOW!
BUT SHE'S COMING BACK FOR LIZ. I KNOW IT.
PROBABLY SOON. BEFORE EDDIE CAN CALL IN THE COPS.
IF HE HASN'T ALREADY.

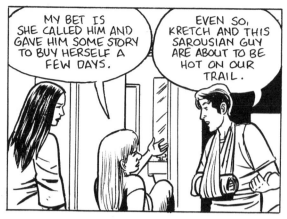

MY BET IS SHE CALLED HIM AND GAVE HIM SOME STORY TO BUY HERSELF A FEW DAYS.

EVEN SO, KRETCH AND THIS SAROUSIAN GUY ARE ABOUT TO BE HOT ON OUR TRAIL.

HOW CAN WE WATCH LIZ WHILE **THEY'RE** WATCHING FOR US?

THAT'S EASY.

WE JUST BECOME **OTHER** PEOPLE...

THREE HOURS LATER...

...SHE EVEN SAVED LIZ'S FUCKIN' BABY TEETH...

JC PENNEY

MAYS

RITE DRUG

...THAT FUCKING BITCH SAVED EVERY-THING.

NOTHING OF **YOURS?**...NOT EVEN THE POT SHE USED TO **BASH** YOUR HEAD IN?

I REALLY THOUGHT I COULD HANDLE HER THIS TIME.

AND FUCK YOU, BY THE WAY.

SERIOUSLY, SHE'S YOUR **MOM.**

PURSE YOUR LIPS.

LIKE ALL MOMS, SHE'S BEEN FUCKING WITH YOUR BRAIN SINCE IT WAS SILLY PUTTY.

AND NOW... YOU **ARE** HER.

HOLY SHIT!

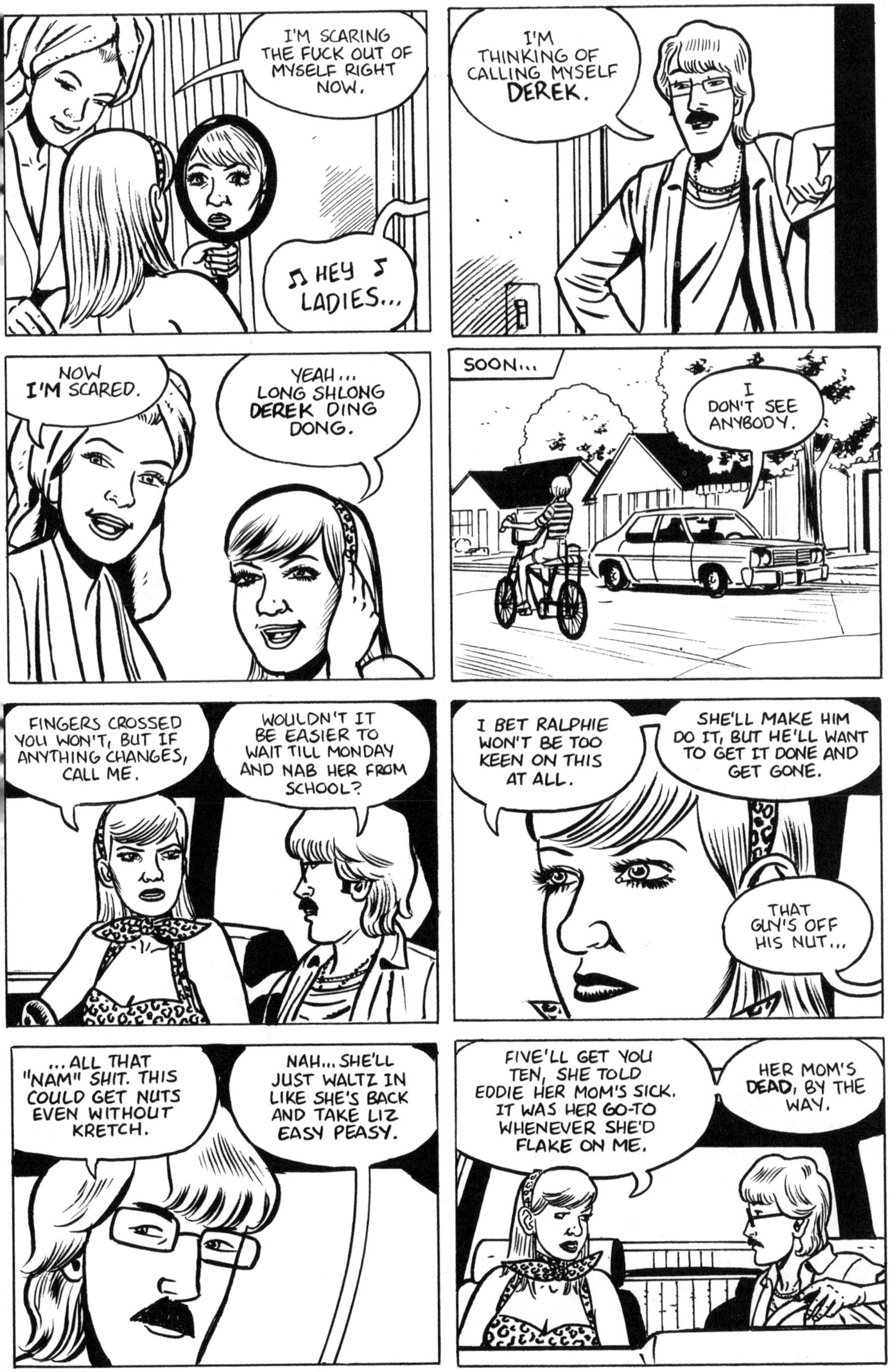
I'M SCARING THE FUCK OUT OF MYSELF RIGHT NOW.
♫ HEY ♫ LADIES...
I'M THINKING OF CALLING MYSELF DEREK.
NOW I'M SCARED.
YEAH... LONG SHLONG DEREK DING DONG.
SOON...
I DON'T SEE ANYBODY.
FINGERS CROSSED YOU WON'T, BUT IF ANYTHING CHANGES, CALL ME.
WOULDN'T IT BE EASIER TO WAIT TILL MONDAY AND NAB HER FROM SCHOOL?
I BET RALPHIE WON'T BE TOO KEEN ON THIS AT ALL.
SHE'LL MAKE HIM DO IT, BUT HE'LL WANT TO GET IT DONE AND GET GONE.
THAT GUY'S OFF HIS NUT...
...ALL THAT "NAM" SHIT. THIS COULD GET NUTS EVEN WITHOUT KRETCH.
NAH... SHE'LL JUST WALTZ IN LIKE SHE'S BACK AND TAKE LIZ EASY PEASY.
FIVE'LL GET YOU TEN, SHE TOLD EDDIE HER MOM'S SICK. IT WAS HER GO-TO WHENEVER SHE'D FLAKE ON ME.
HER MOM'S DEAD, BY THE WAY.

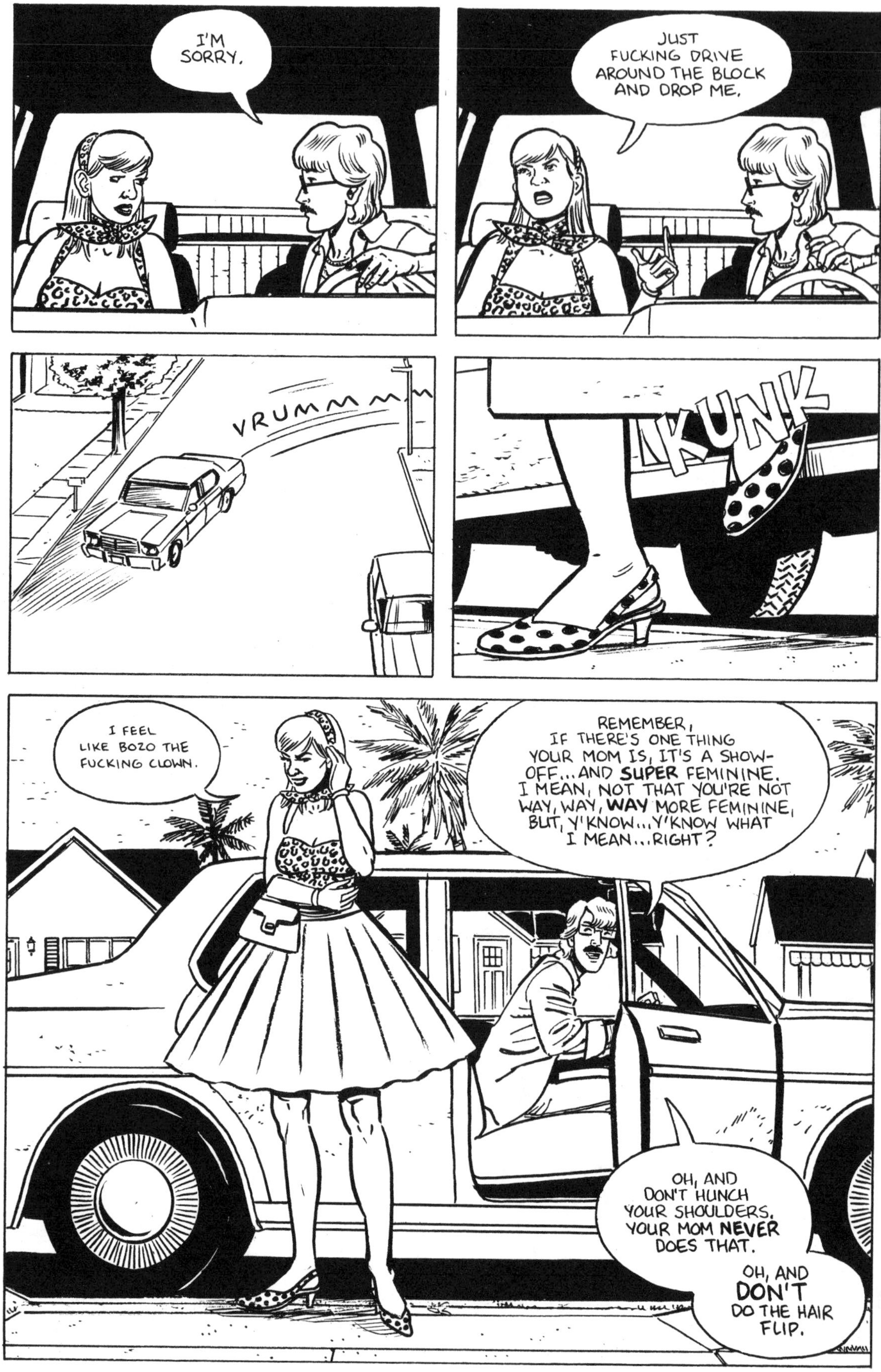

I'M SORRY.
JUST FUCKING DRIVE AROUND THE BLOCK AND DROP ME.
VRUMMMMM
KUNK
I FEEL LIKE BOZO THE FUCKING CLOWN.
REMEMBER, IF THERE'S ONE THING YOUR MOM IS, IT'S A SHOW-OFF... AND **SUPER** FEMININE. I MEAN, NOT THAT YOU'RE NOT WAY, WAY, **WAY** MORE FEMININE, BUT, Y'KNOW... Y'KNOW WHAT I MEAN... RIGHT?
OH, AND DON'T HUNCH YOUR SHOULDERS. YOUR MOM **NEVER** DOES THAT.
OH, AND **DON'T** DO THE HAIR FLIP.

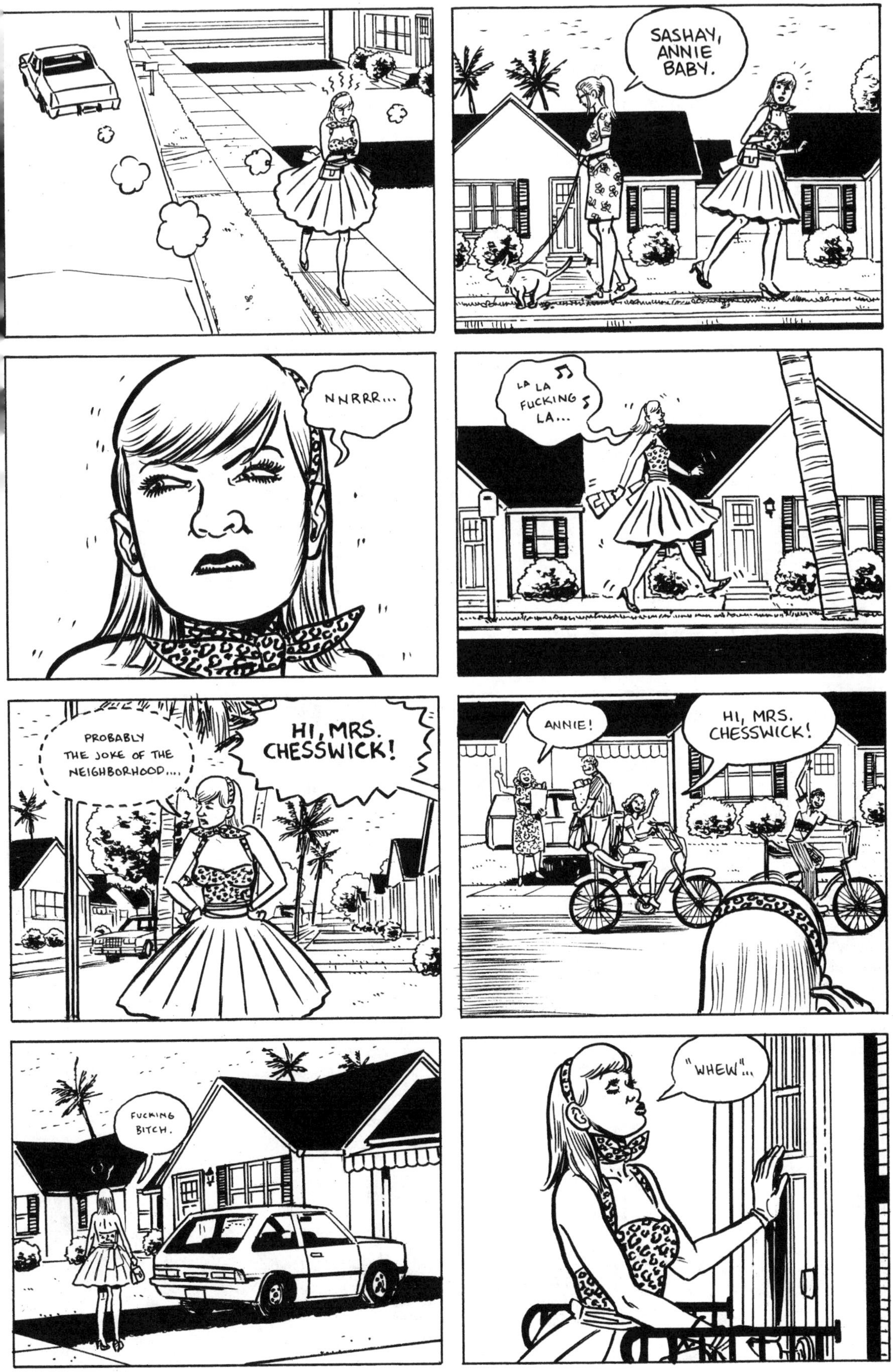
SASHAY, ANNIE BABY.
NNRRR...
LA LA FUCKING LA...
PROBABLY THE JOKE OF THE NEIGHBORHOOD....
HI, MRS. CHESSWICK!
ANNIE!
HI, MRS. CHESSWICK!
FUCKING BITCH.
"WHEW"...

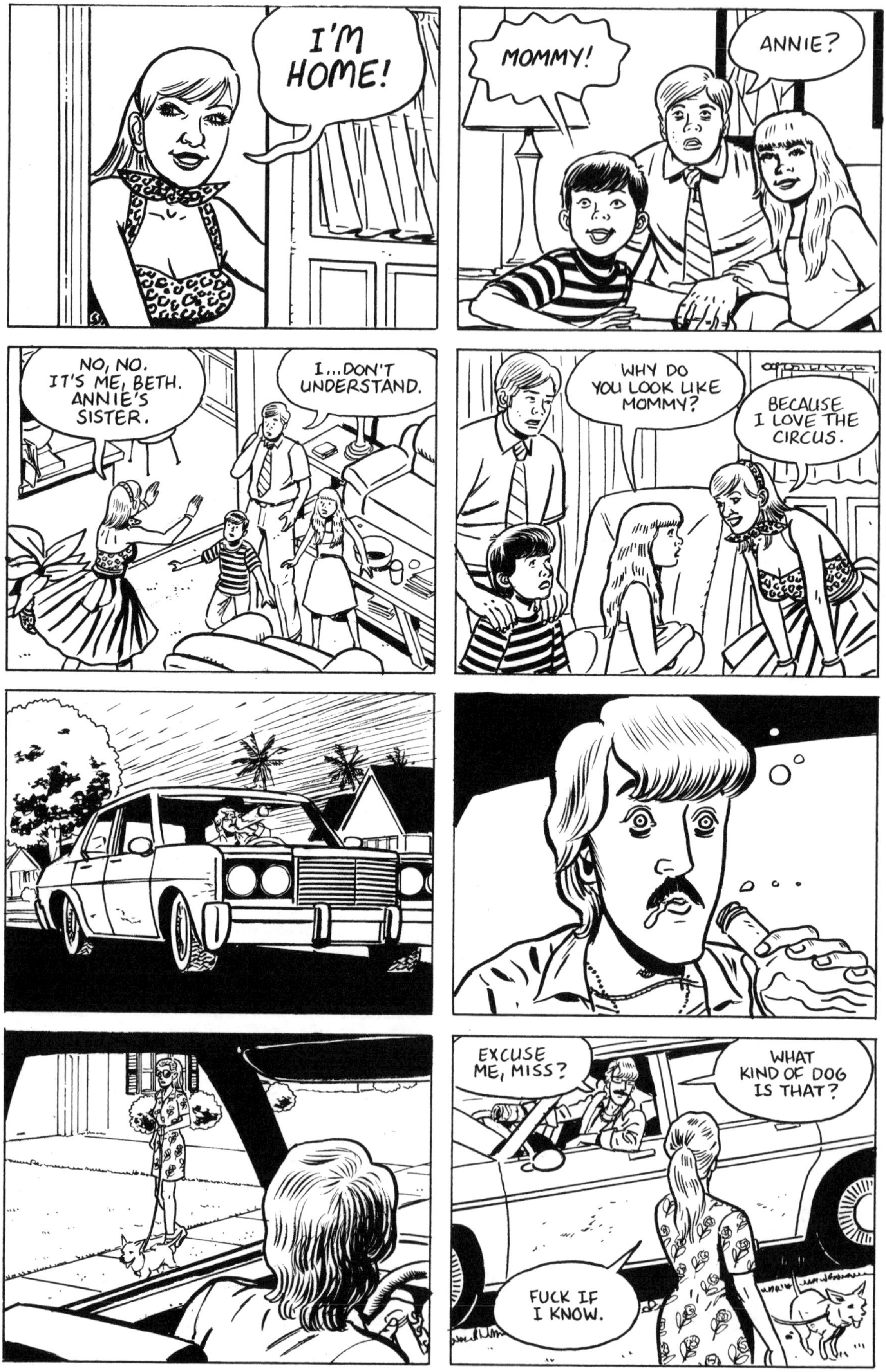
I'M HOME!
MOMMY!
ANNIE?
NO, NO. IT'S ME, BETH. ANNIE'S SISTER.
I...DON'T UNDERSTAND.
WHY DO YOU LOOK LIKE MOMMY?
BECAUSE I LOVE THE CIRCUS.
EXCUSE ME, MISS?
WHAT KIND OF DOG IS THAT?
FUCK IF I KNOW.

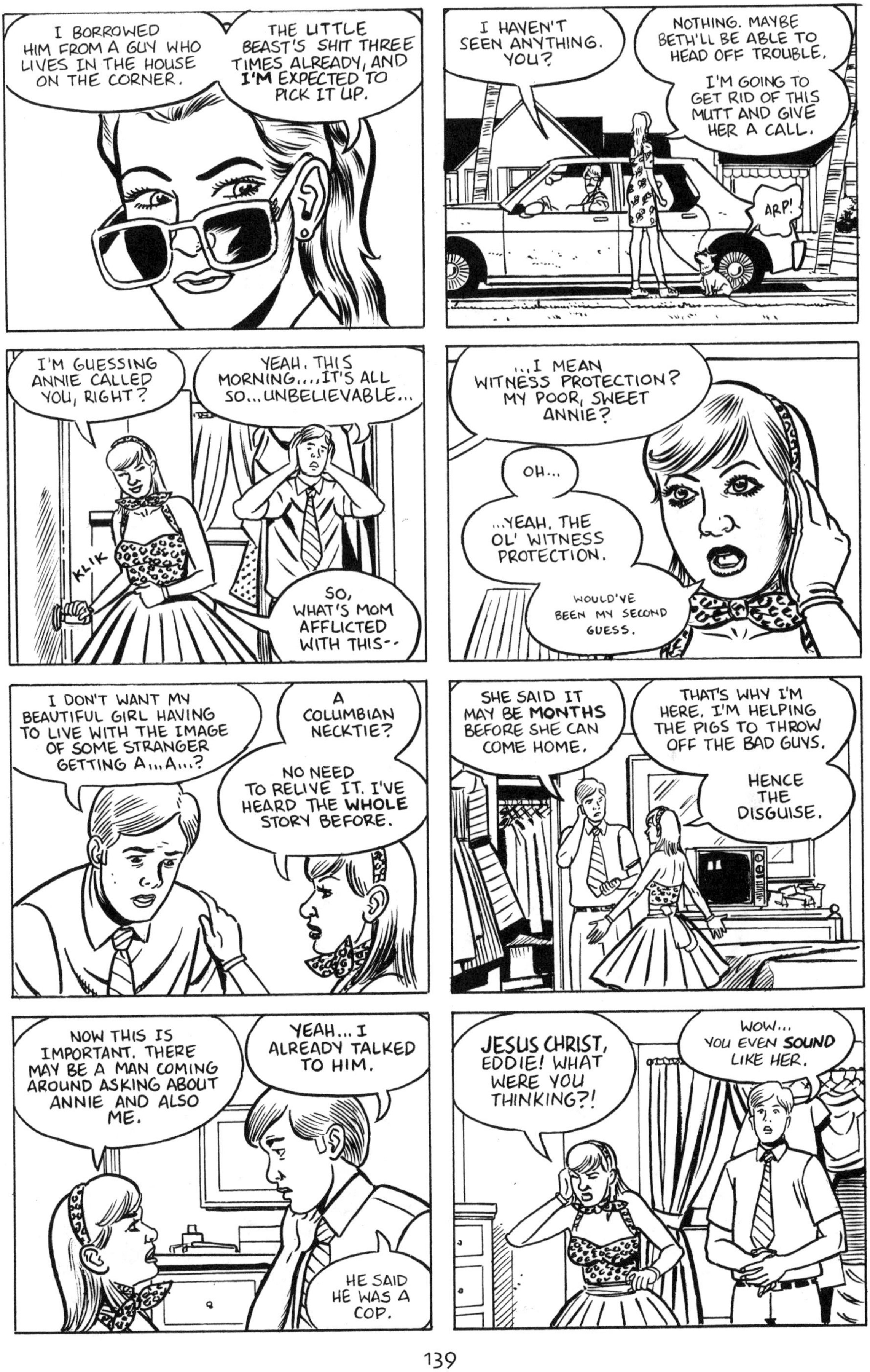
I BORROWED HIM FROM A GUY WHO LIVES IN THE HOUSE ON THE CORNER.
THE LITTLE BEAST'S SHIT THREE TIMES ALREADY, AND **I'M** EXPECTED TO PICK IT UP.
I HAVEN'T SEEN ANYTHING. YOU?
NOTHING. MAYBE BETH'LL BE ABLE TO HEAD OFF TROUBLE.
I'M GOING TO GET RID OF THIS MUTT AND GIVE HER A CALL.
ARP!
I'M GUESSING ANNIE CALLED YOU, RIGHT?
YEAH. THIS MORNING....IT'S ALL SO...UNBELIEVABLE...
KLIK
SO, WHAT'S MOM AFFLICTED WITH THIS-.
...I MEAN WITNESS PROTECTION? MY POOR, SWEET ANNIE?
OH...
...YEAH. THE OL' WITNESS PROTECTION.
WOULD'VE BEEN MY SECOND GUESS.
I DON'T WANT MY BEAUTIFUL GIRL HAVING TO LIVE WITH THE IMAGE OF SOME STRANGER GETTING A...A...?
A COLUMBIAN NECKTIE?
NO NEED TO RELIVE IT. I'VE HEARD THE **WHOLE** STORY BEFORE.
SHE SAID IT MAY BE **MONTHS** BEFORE SHE CAN COME HOME.
THAT'S WHY I'M HERE. I'M HELPING THE PIGS TO THROW OFF THE BAD GUYS.
HENCE THE DISGUISE.
NOW THIS IS IMPORTANT. THERE MAY BE A MAN COMING AROUND ASKING ABOUT ANNIE AND ALSO ME.
YEAH... I ALREADY TALKED TO HIM.
HE SAID HE WAS A COP.
JESUS CHRIST, EDDIE! WHAT WERE YOU THINKING?!
WOW... YOU EVEN **SOUND** LIKE HER.

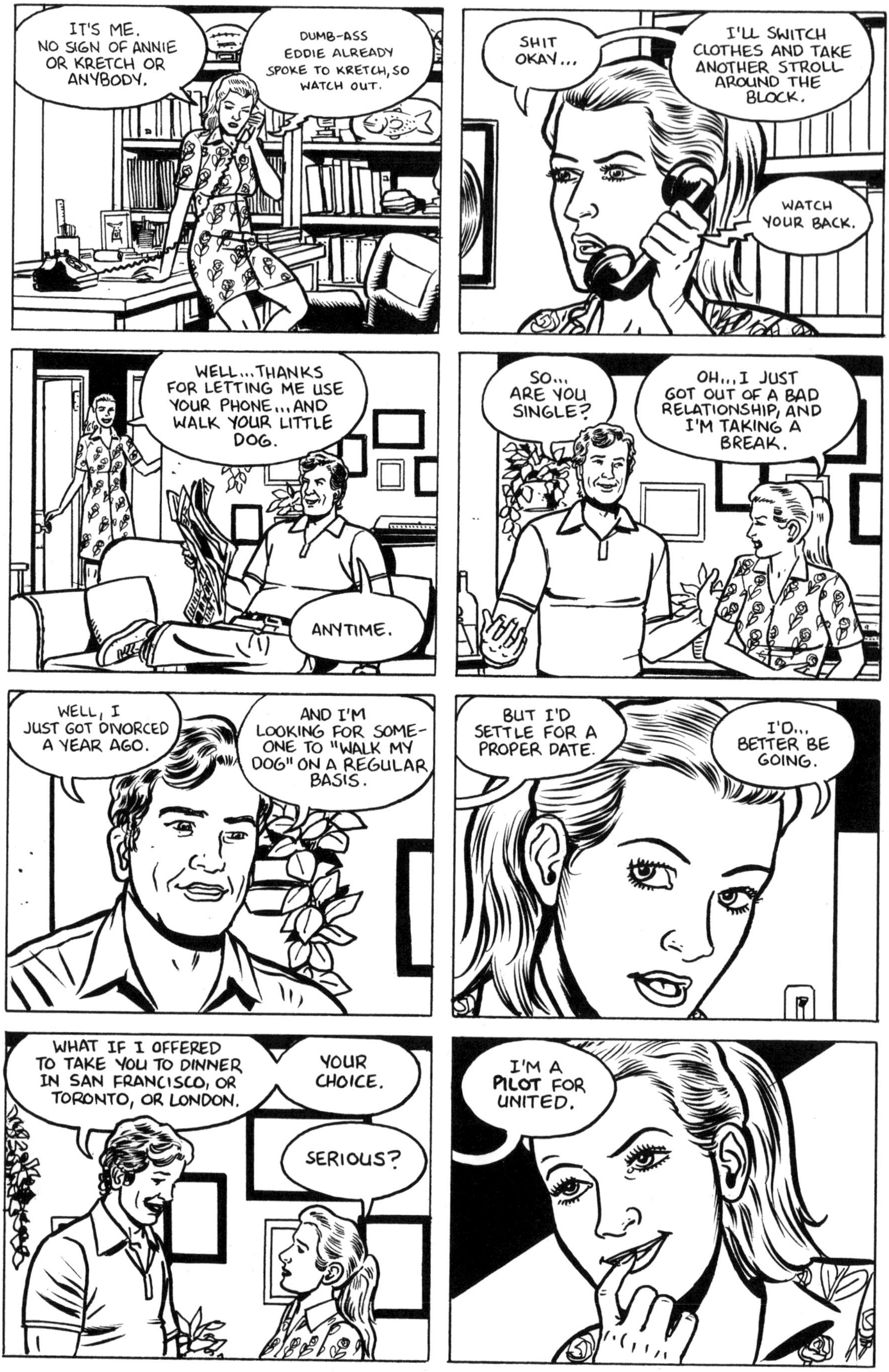
IT'S ME. NO SIGN OF ANNIE OR KRETCH OR ANYBODY.
DUMB-ASS EDDIE ALREADY SPOKE TO KRETCH, SO WATCH OUT.
SHIT OKAY...
I'LL SWITCH CLOTHES AND TAKE ANOTHER STROLL AROUND THE BLOCK.
WATCH YOUR BACK.
WELL...THANKS FOR LETTING ME USE YOUR PHONE...AND WALK YOUR LITTLE DOG.
ANYTIME.
SO... ARE YOU SINGLE?
OH...I JUST GOT OUT OF A BAD RELATIONSHIP, AND I'M TAKING A BREAK.
WELL, I JUST GOT DIVORCED A YEAR AGO.
AND I'M LOOKING FOR SOME-ONE TO "WALK MY DOG" ON A REGULAR BASIS.
BUT I'D SETTLE FOR A PROPER DATE.
I'D... BETTER BE GOING.
WHAT IF I OFFERED TO TAKE YOU TO DINNER IN SAN FRANCISCO, OR TORONTO, OR LONDON.
YOUR CHOICE.
SERIOUS?
I'M A PILOT FOR UNITED.

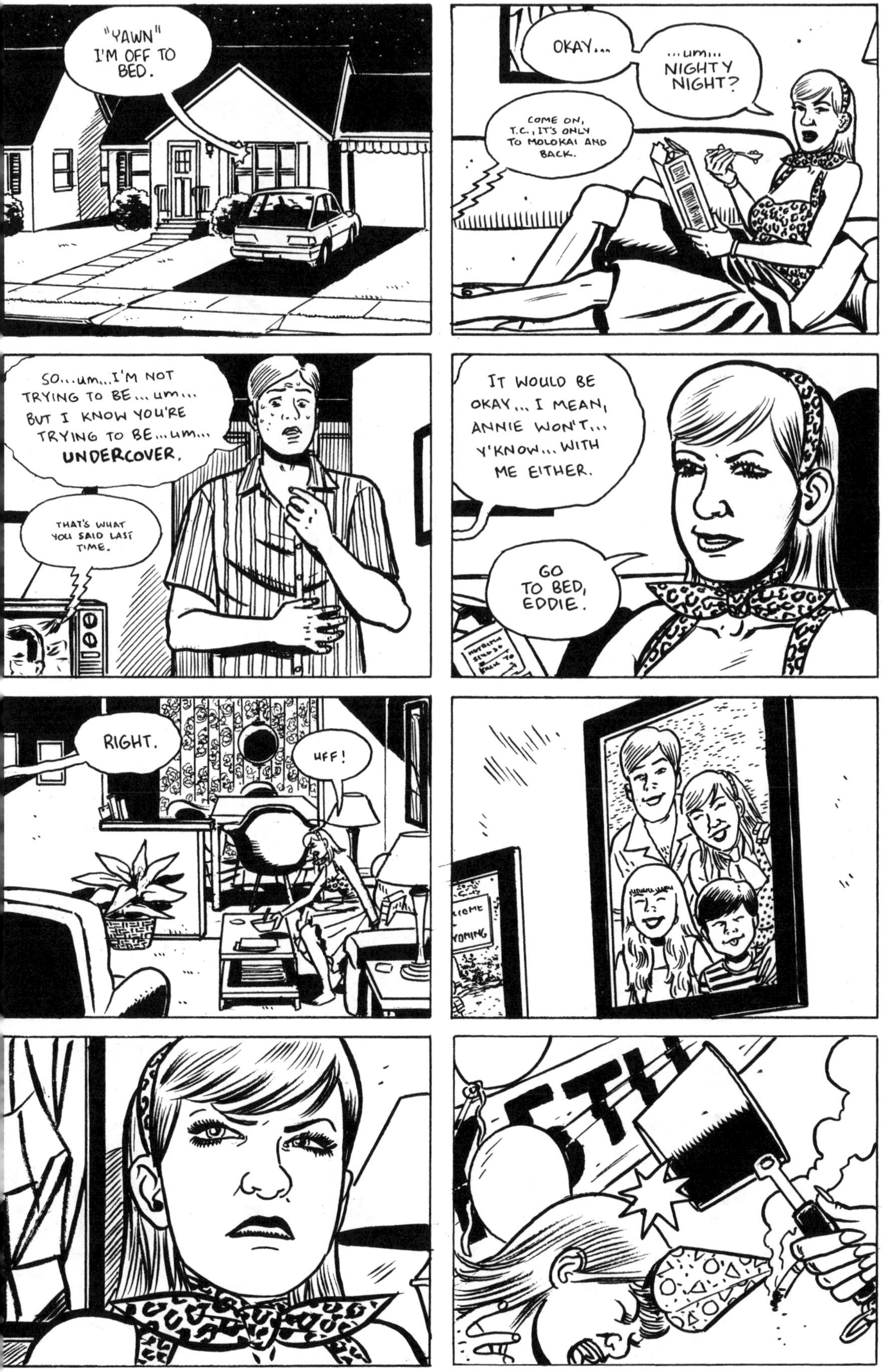
"YAWN" I'M OFF TO BED.
OKAY...
...um... NIGHTY NIGHT?
COME ON, T.C., IT'S ONLY TO MOLOKAI AND BACK.
SO...um...I'M NOT TRYING TO BE...um... BUT I KNOW YOU'RE TRYING TO BE...um... UNDERCOVER.
THAT'S WHAT YOU SAID LAST TIME.
IT WOULD BE OKAY... I MEAN, ANNIE WON'T... Y'KNOW... WITH ME EITHER.
GO TO BED, EDDIE.
RIGHT.
UFF!

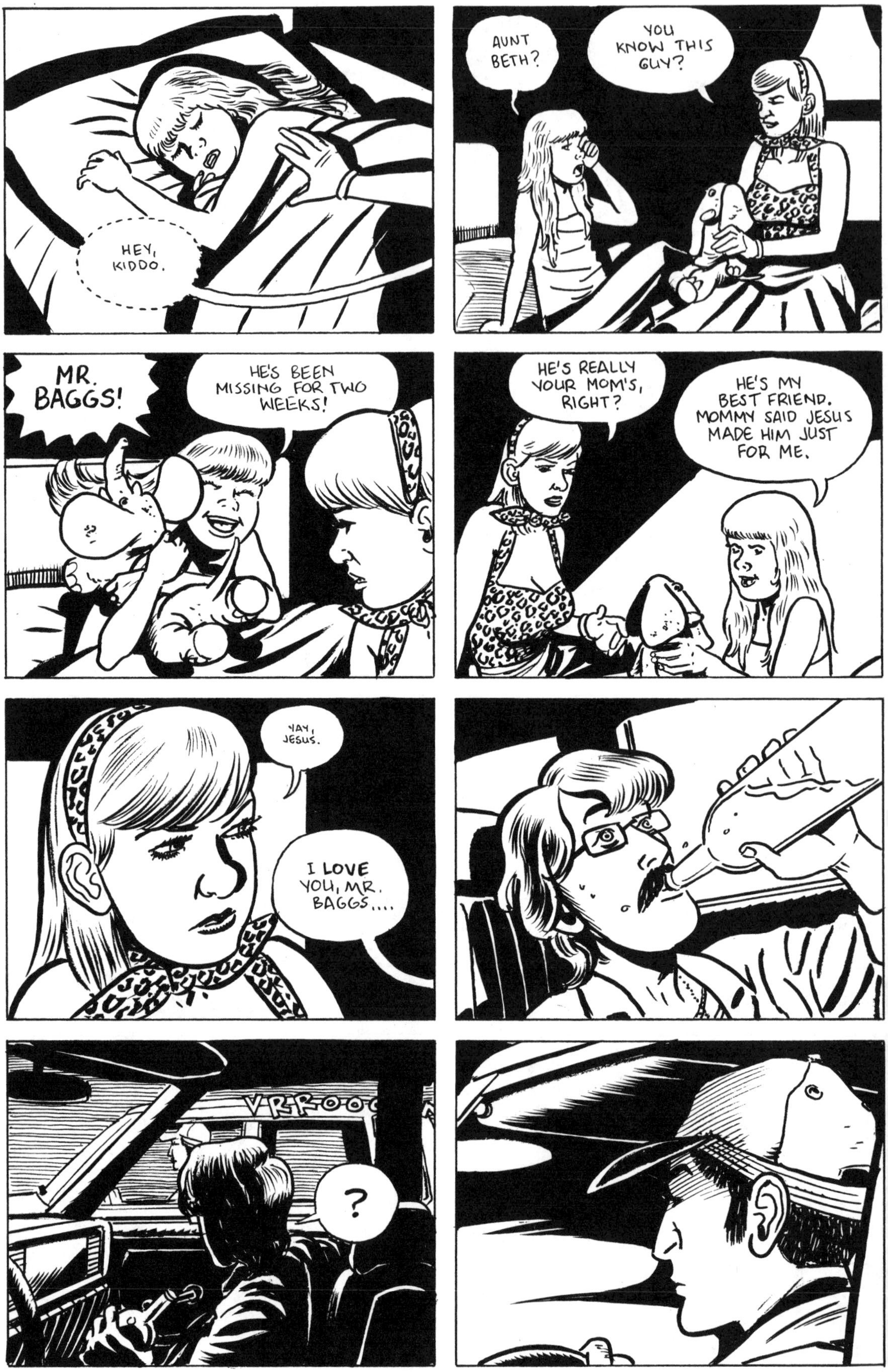
HEY, KIDDO.
AUNT BETH?
YOU KNOW THIS GUY?
MR. BAGGS!
HE'S BEEN MISSING FOR TWO WEEKS!
HE'S REALLY YOUR MOM'S, RIGHT?
HE'S MY BEST FRIEND. MOMMY SAID JESUS MADE HIM JUST FOR ME.
YAY, JESUS.
I LOVE YOU, MR. BAGGS....
VRROOO
?

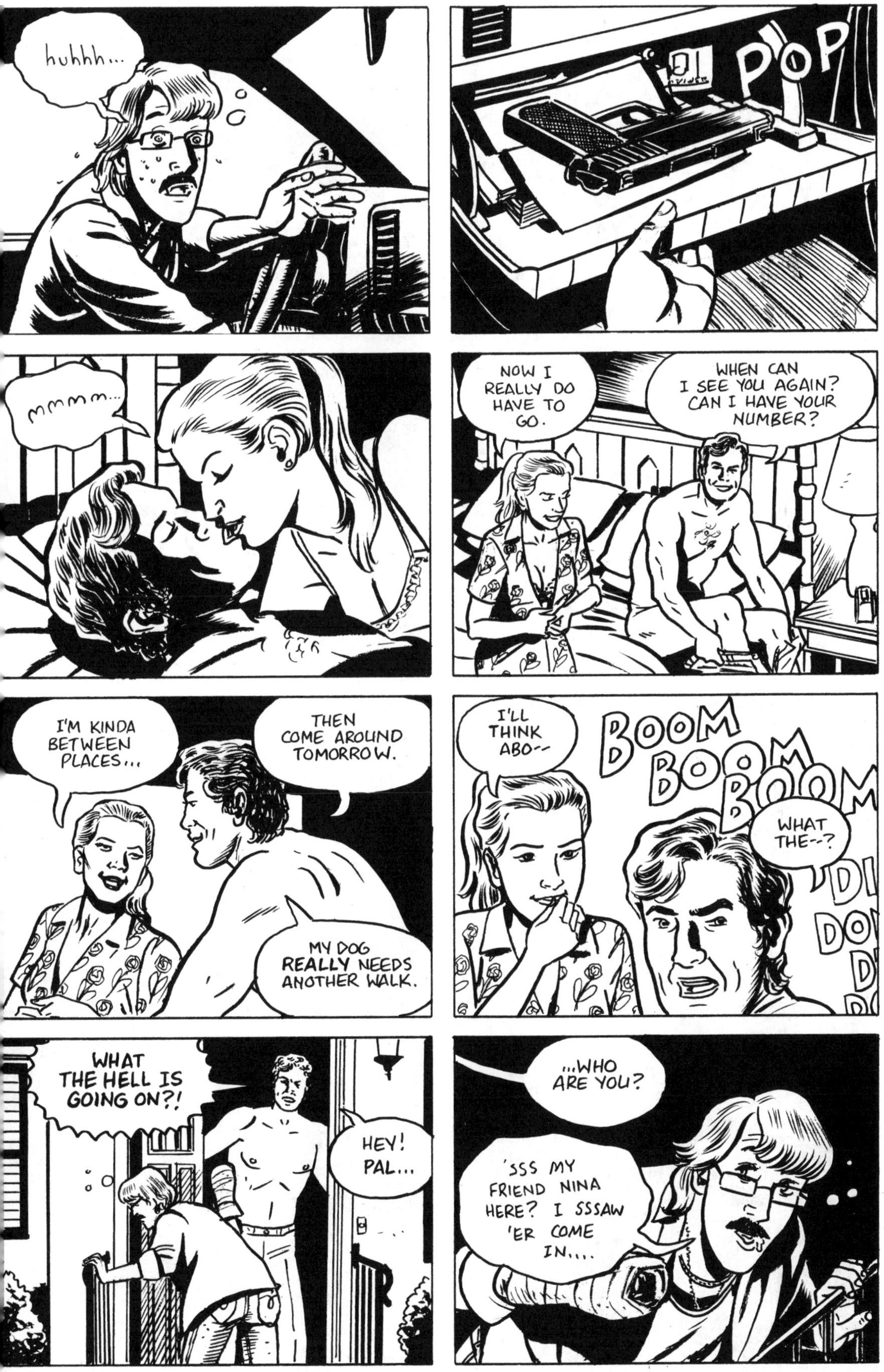
huhhh...
POP
mmmm...
NOW I REALLY DO HAVE TO GO.
WHEN CAN I SEE YOU AGAIN? CAN I HAVE YOUR NUMBER?
I'M KINDA BETWEEN PLACES...
THEN COME AROUND TOMORROW.
MY DOG REALLY NEEDS ANOTHER WALK.
I'LL THINK ABO--
BOOM
BOOM
BOOM
WHAT THE--?
WHAT THE HELL IS GOING ON?!
HEY! PAL...
...WHO ARE YOU?
'SSS MY FRIEND NINA HERE? I SSSAW 'ER COME IN....

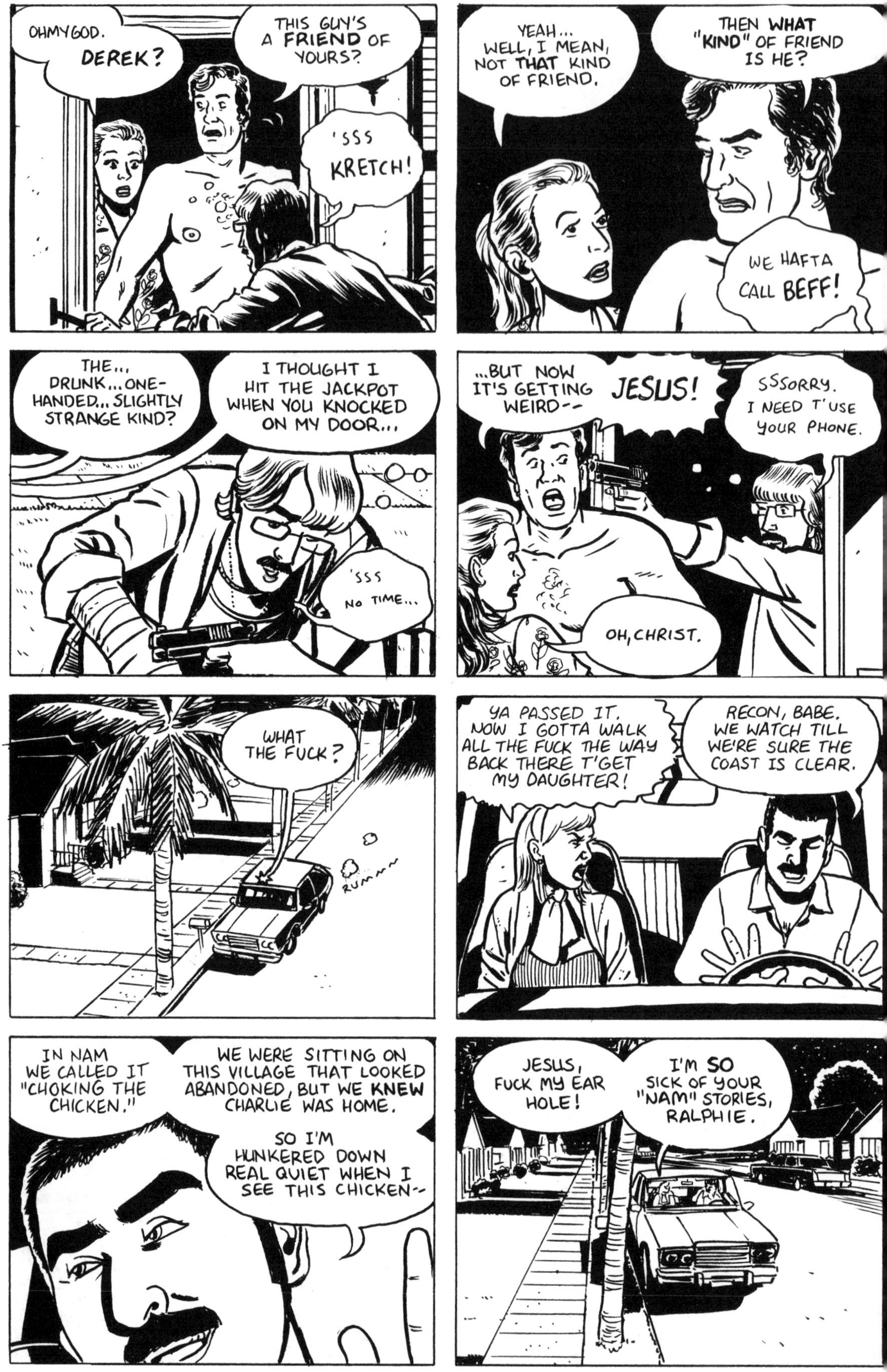
OHMYGOD.
DEREK?
THIS GUY'S A FRIEND OF YOURS?
'SSS KRETCH!
YEAH... WELL, I MEAN, NOT THAT KIND OF FRIEND.
THEN WHAT "KIND" OF FRIEND IS HE?
WE HAFTA CALL BEFF!
THE... DRUNK... ONE-HANDED... SLIGHTLY STRANGE KIND?
I THOUGHT I HIT THE JACKPOT WHEN YOU KNOCKED ON MY DOOR...
'SSS NO TIME...
...BUT NOW IT'S GETTING WEIRD--
JESUS!
SSSORRY. I NEED T'USE YOUR PHONE.
OH, CHRIST.
WHAT THE FUCK?
RUMMM
YA PASSED IT. NOW I GOTTA WALK ALL THE FUCK THE WAY BACK THERE T'GET MY DAUGHTER!
RECON, BABE. WE WATCH TILL WE'RE SURE THE COAST IS CLEAR.
IN NAM WE CALLED IT "CHOKING THE CHICKEN."
WE WERE SITTING ON THIS VILLAGE THAT LOOKED ABANDONED, BUT WE KNEW CHARLIE WAS HOME.
SO I'M HUNKERED DOWN REAL QUIET WHEN I SEE THIS CHICKEN--
JESUS, FUCK MY EAR HOLE!
I'M SO SICK OF YOUR "NAM" STORIES, RALPHIE.

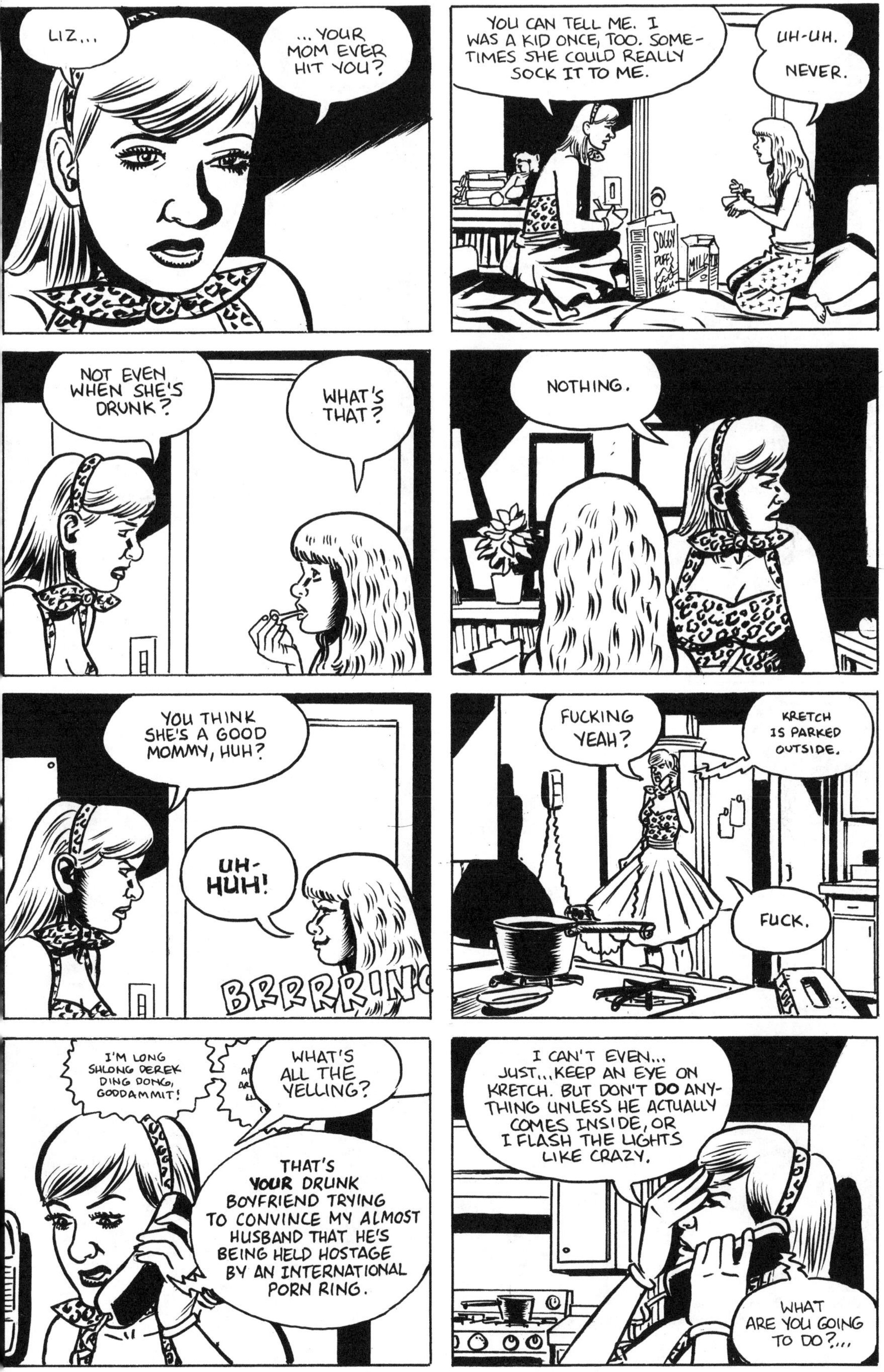
LIZ...
...YOUR MOM EVER HIT YOU?
YOU CAN TELL ME. I WAS A KID ONCE, TOO. SOMETIMES SHE COULD REALLY SOCK IT TO ME.
UH-UH.
NEVER.
SOGGY PUFFS
MILK
NOT EVEN WHEN SHE'S DRUNK?
WHAT'S THAT?
NOTHING.
YOU THINK SHE'S A GOOD MOMMY, HUH?
UH-HUH!
BRRRRING
FUCKING YEAH?
KRETCH IS PARKED OUTSIDE.
FUCK.
I'M LONG SHLONG DEREK DING DONG, GODDAMMIT!
WHAT'S ALL THE YELLING?
THAT'S YOUR DRUNK BOYFRIEND TRYING TO CONVINCE MY ALMOST HUSBAND THAT HE'S BEING HELD HOSTAGE BY AN INTERNATIONAL PORN RING.
I CAN'T EVEN... JUST...KEEP AN EYE ON KRETCH. BUT DON'T DO ANYTHING UNLESS HE ACTUALLY COMES INSIDE, OR I FLASH THE LIGHTS LIKE CRAZY.
WHAT ARE YOU GOING TO DO?...

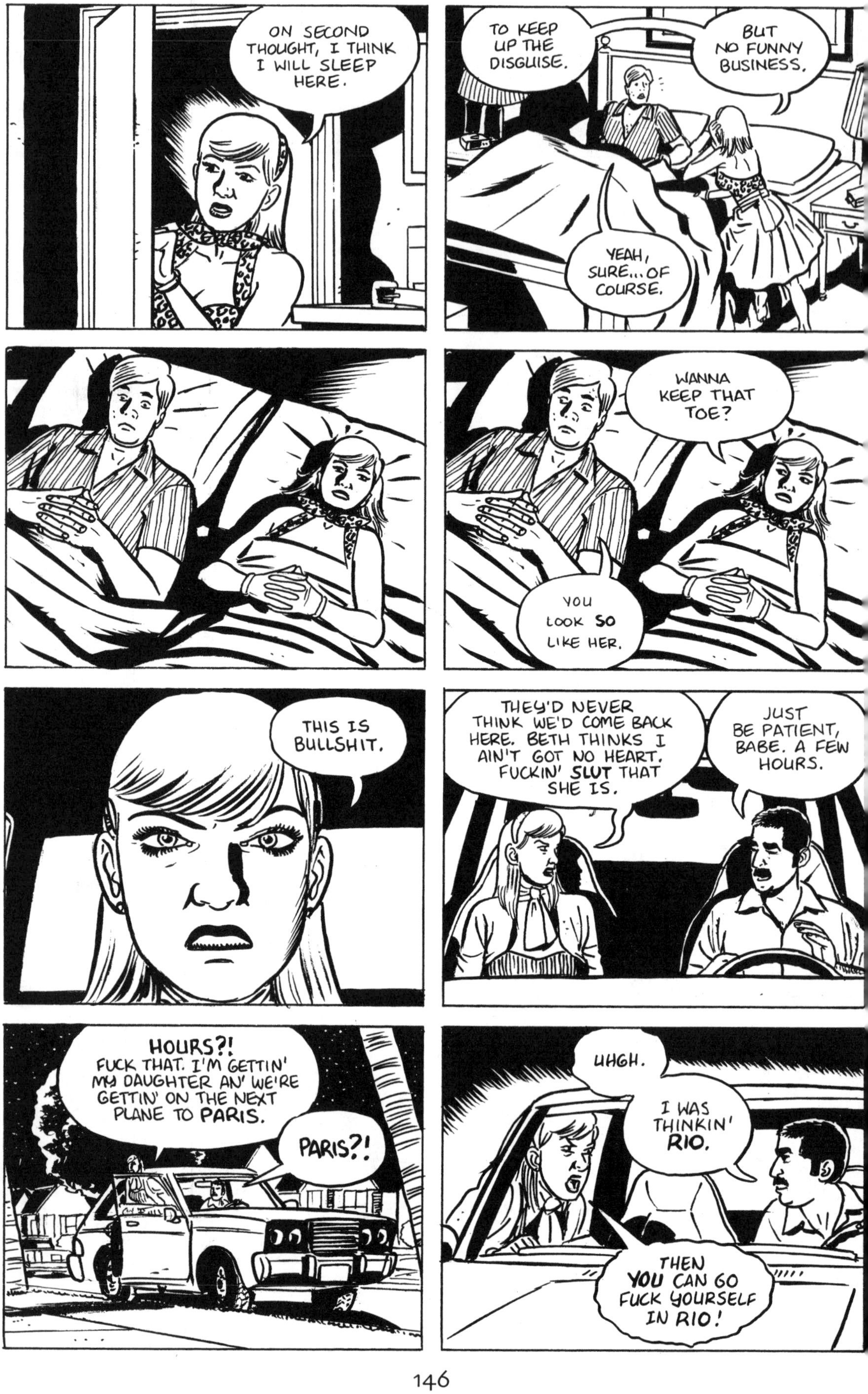

ON SECOND THOUGHT, I THINK I WILL SLEEP HERE.
TO KEEP UP THE DISGUISE.
BUT NO FUNNY BUSINESS.
YEAH, SURE... OF COURSE.
WANNA KEEP THAT TOE?
YOU LOOK **SO** LIKE HER.
THIS IS BULLSHIT.
THEY'D NEVER THINK WE'D COME BACK HERE. BETH THINKS I AIN'T GOT NO HEART. FUCKIN' **SLUT** THAT SHE IS.
JUST BE PATIENT, BABE. A FEW HOURS.
HOURS?! FUCK THAT. I'M GETTIN' MY DAUGHTER AN' WE'RE GETTIN' ON THE NEXT PLANE TO **PARIS**.
PARIS?!
UHGH.
I WAS THINKIN' **RIO**.
THEN **YOU** CAN GO FUCK YOURSELF IN RIO!

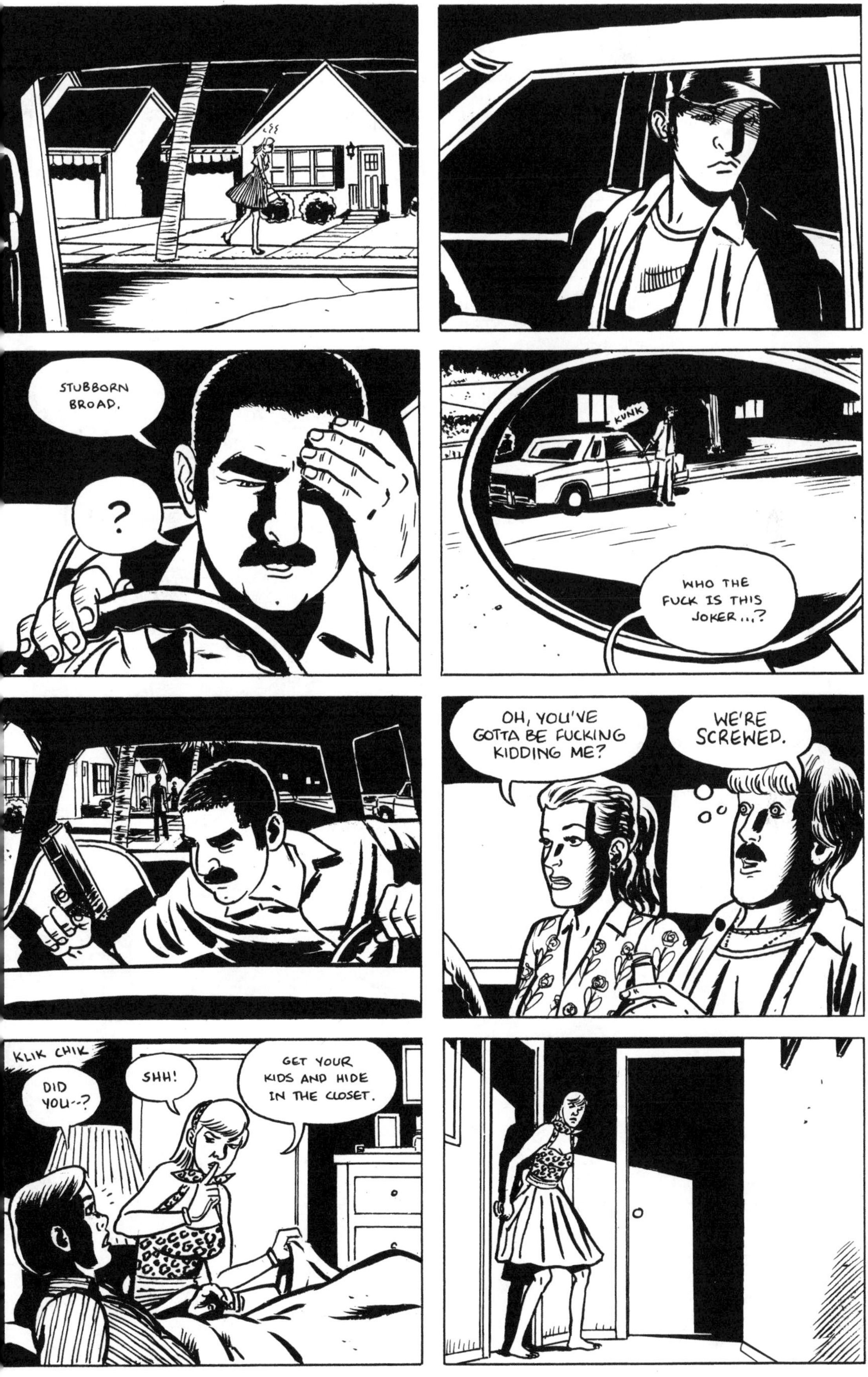
STUBBORN BROAD.
?
KUNK
WHO THE FUCK IS THIS JOKER...?
OH, YOU'VE GOTTA BE FUCKING KIDDING ME?
WE'RE SCREWED.
KLIK CHIK
DID YOU--?
SHH!
GET YOUR KIDS AND HIDE IN THE CLOSET.

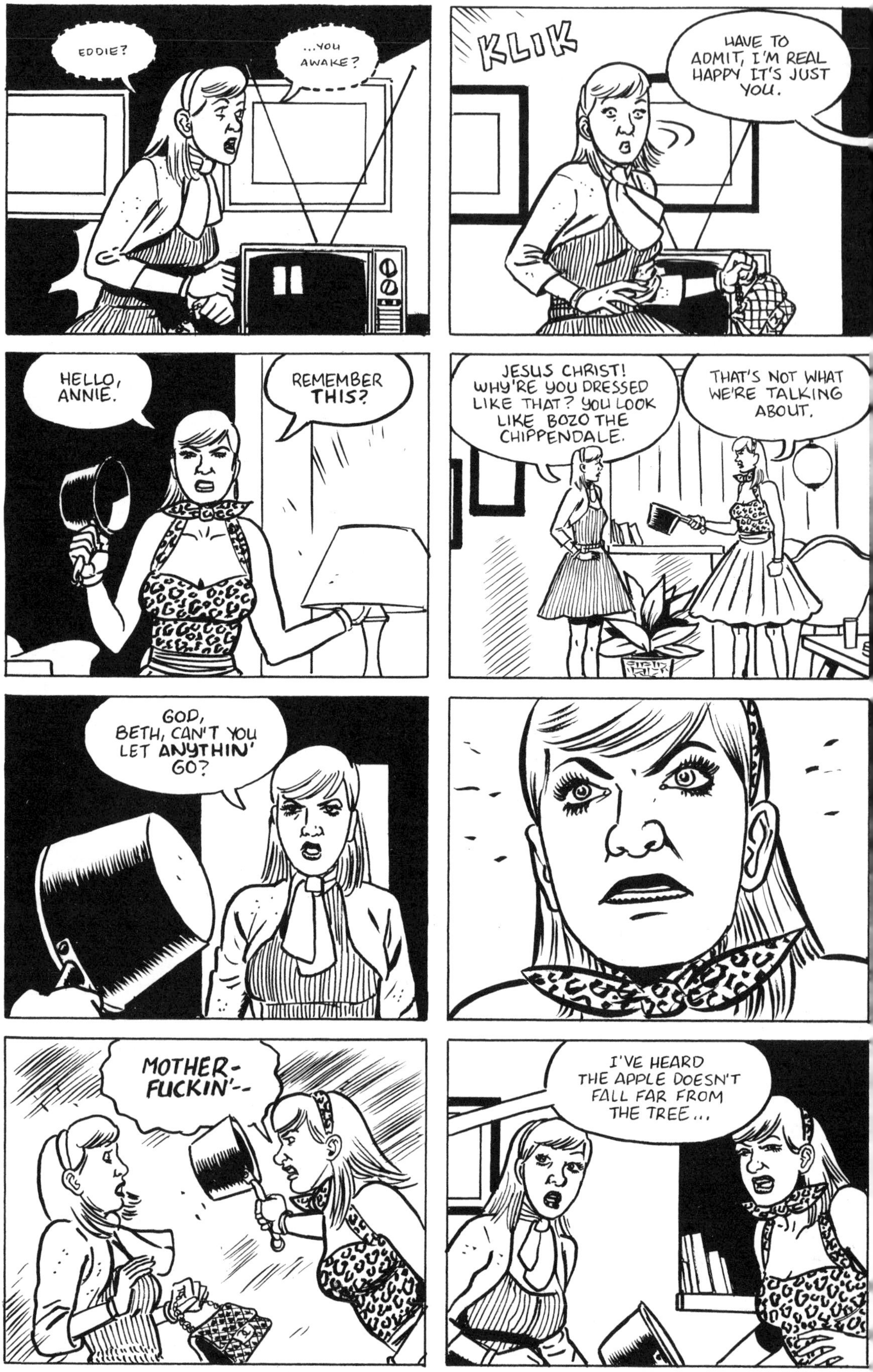
EDDIE?
...YOU AWAKE?
KLIK
HAVE TO ADMIT, I'M REAL HAPPY IT'S JUST YOU.
HELLO, ANNIE.
REMEMBER THIS?
JESUS CHRIST! WHY'RE YOU DRESSED LIKE THAT? YOU LOOK LIKE BOZO THE CHIPPENDALE.
THAT'S NOT WHAT WE'RE TALKING ABOUT.
GOD, BETH, CAN'T YOU LET ANYTHIN' GO?
MOTHER-FUCKIN'--
I'VE HEARD THE APPLE DOESN'T FALL FAR FROM THE TREE...

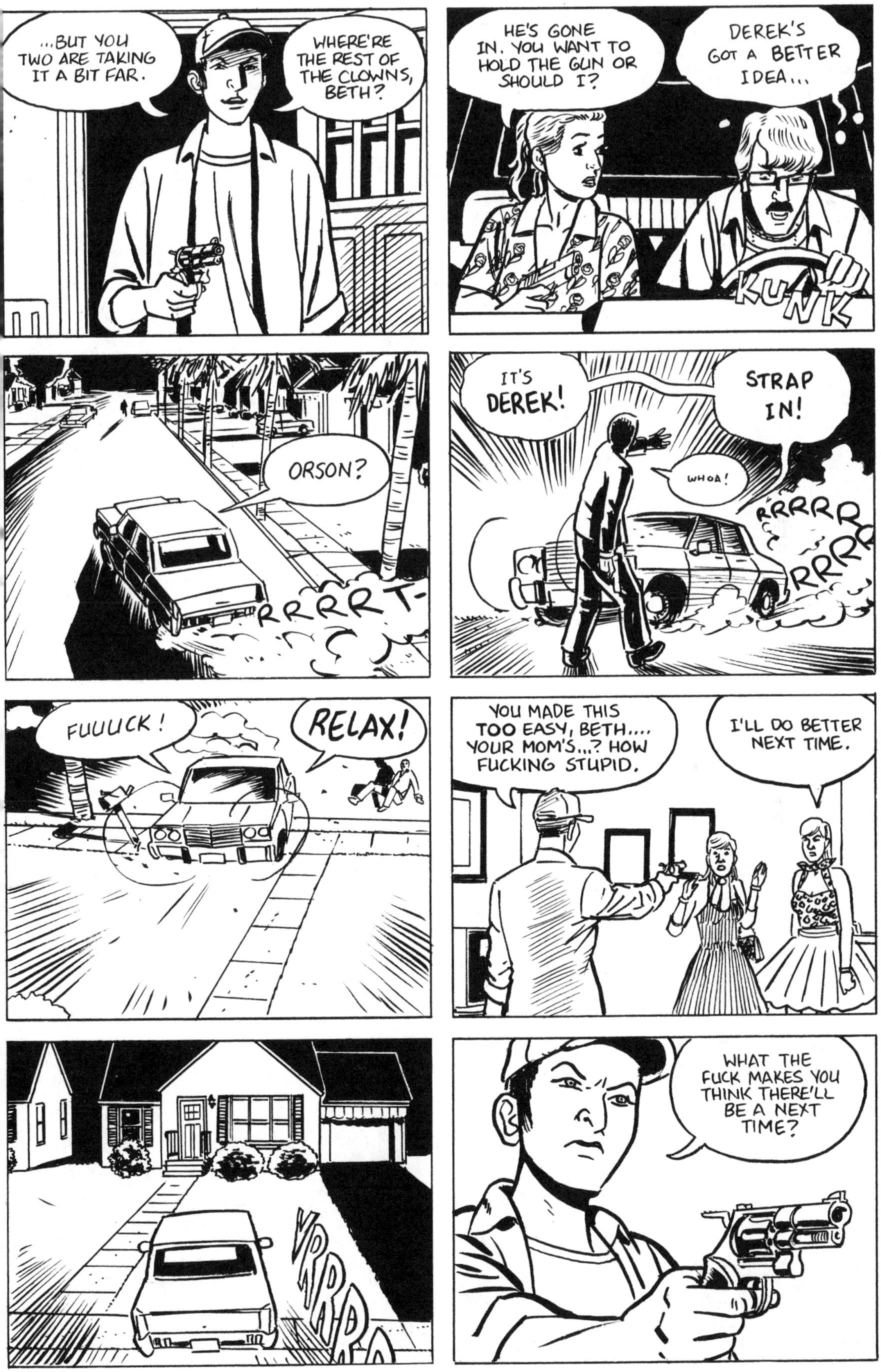

...BUT YOU TWO ARE TAKING IT A BIT FAR.
WHERE'RE THE REST OF THE CLOWNS, BETH?
HE'S GONE IN. YOU WANT TO HOLD THE GUN OR SHOULD I?
DEREK'S GOT A BETTER IDEA...
KUNK
ORSON?
RRRRRT-
IT'S DEREK!
STRAP IN!
WHOA!
RRRRRR
RRRR
FUUUCK!
RELAX!
YOU MADE THIS TOO EASY, BETH.... YOUR MOM'S...? HOW FUCKING STUPID.
I'LL DO BETTER NEXT TIME.
VRRRRO
WHAT THE FUCK MAKES YOU THINK THERE'LL BE A NEXT TIME?

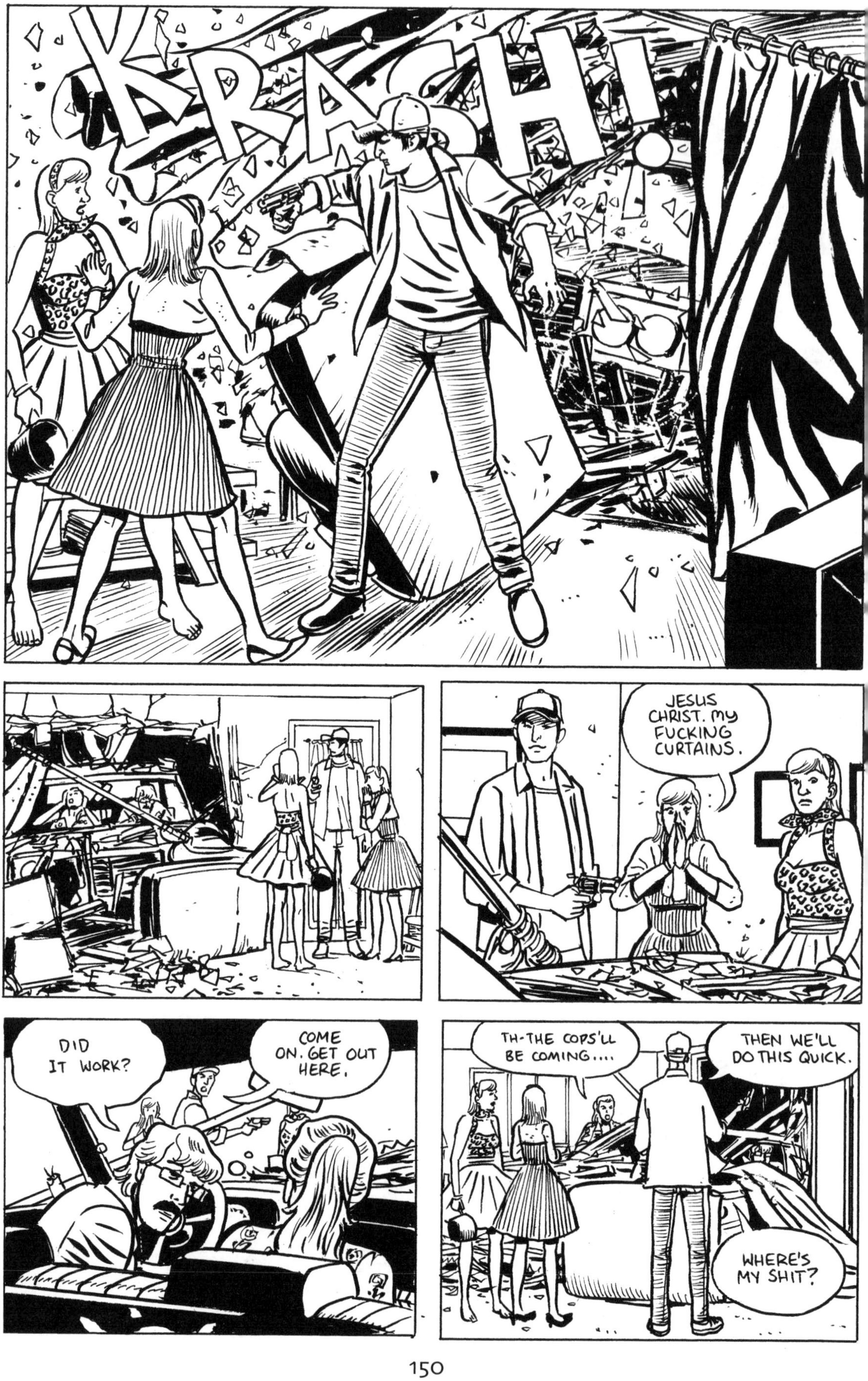
KRASH!
JESUS CHRIST. MY FUCKING CURTAINS.
DID IT WORK?
COME ON. GET OUT HERE.
TH-THE COPS'LL BE COMING....
THEN WE'LL DO THIS QUICK.
WHERE'S MY SHIT?

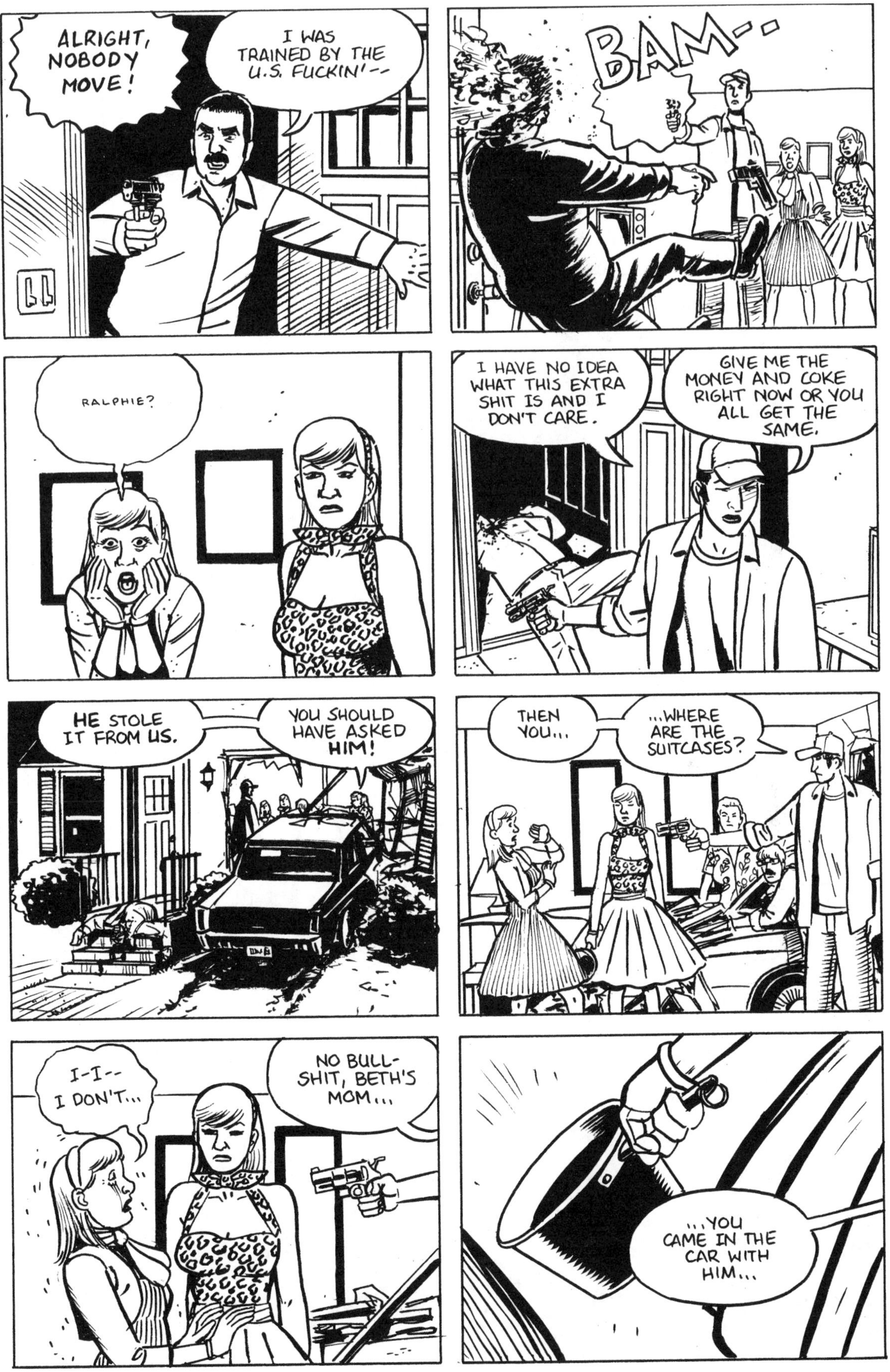
ALRIGHT, NOBODY MOVE!
I WAS TRAINED BY THE U.S. FUCKIN'--
BAM--
RALPHIE?
I HAVE NO IDEA WHAT THIS EXTRA SHIT IS AND I DON'T CARE.
GIVE ME THE MONEY AND COKE RIGHT NOW OR YOU ALL GET THE SAME.
HE STOLE IT FROM US.
YOU SHOULD HAVE ASKED HIM!
THEN YOU...
...WHERE ARE THE SUITCASES?
I-I-- I DON'T...
NO BULL-SHIT, BETH'S MOM...
...YOU CAME IN THE CAR WITH HIM...

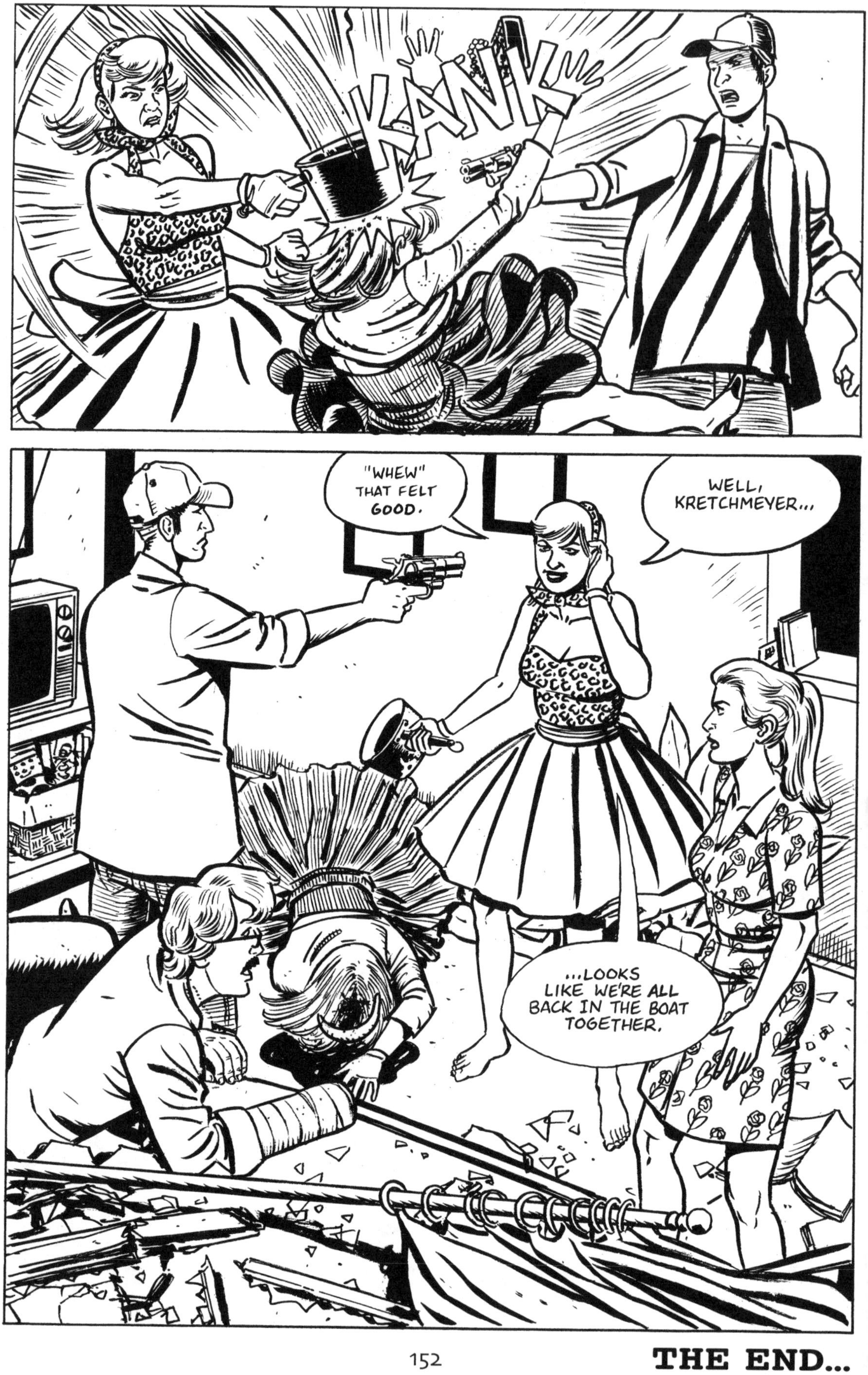
KANK!!
"WHEW" THAT FELT GOOD.
WELL, KRETCHMEYER...
...LOOKS LIKE WE'RE ALL BACK IN THE BOAT TOGETHER.

THE END...

6

"KILLERS, THIEVES, LIARS, AND NUTS"

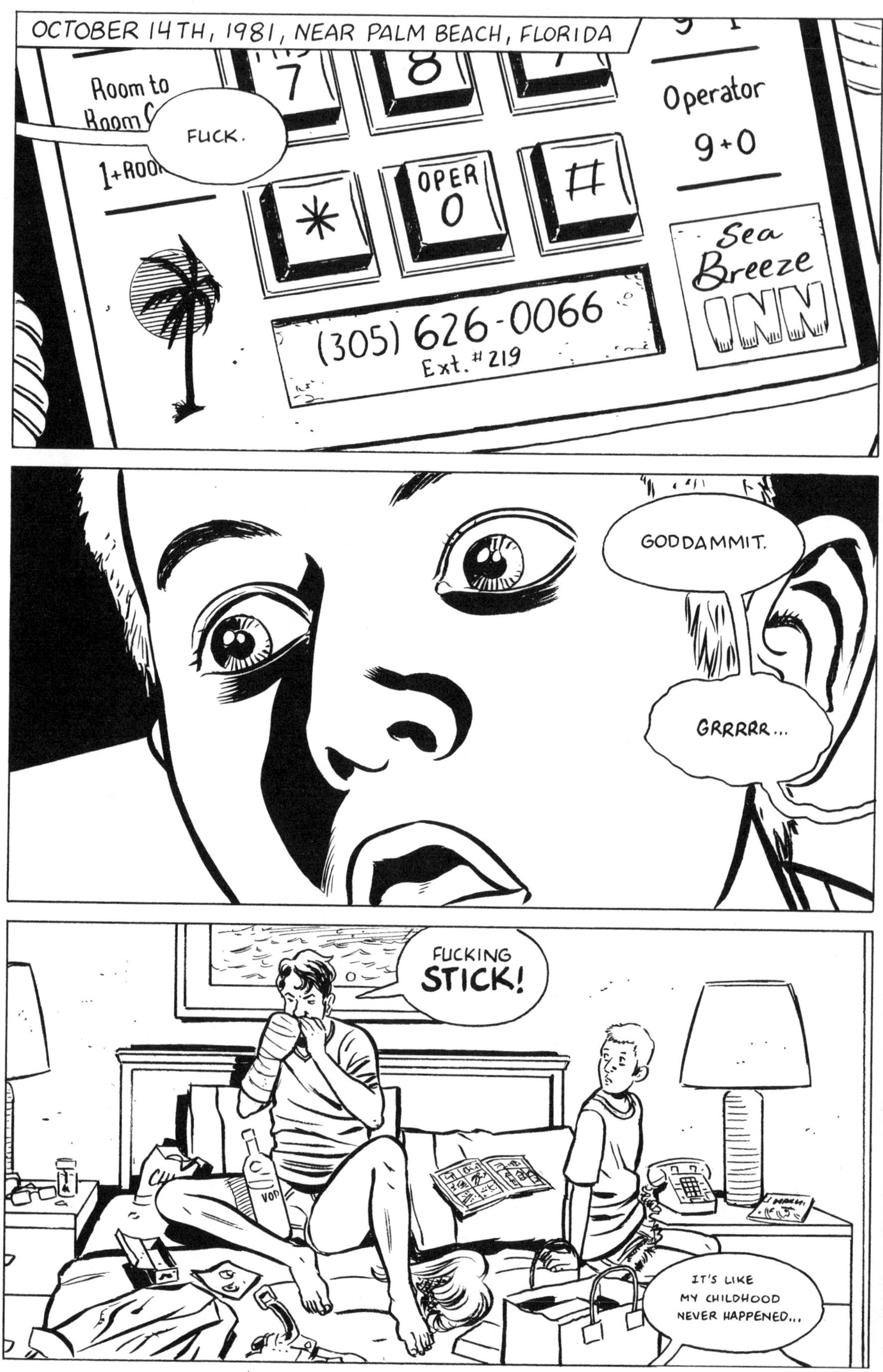
OCTOBER 14TH, 1981, NEAR PALM BEACH, FLORIDA
Room to Room C
FUCK.
1+ROO
OPER 0
Operator 9+0
(305) 626-0066
Ext. #219
Sea Breeze INN
GODDAMMIT.
GRRRRR...
FUCKING STICK!
IT'S LIKE MY CHILDHOOD NEVER HAPPENED...

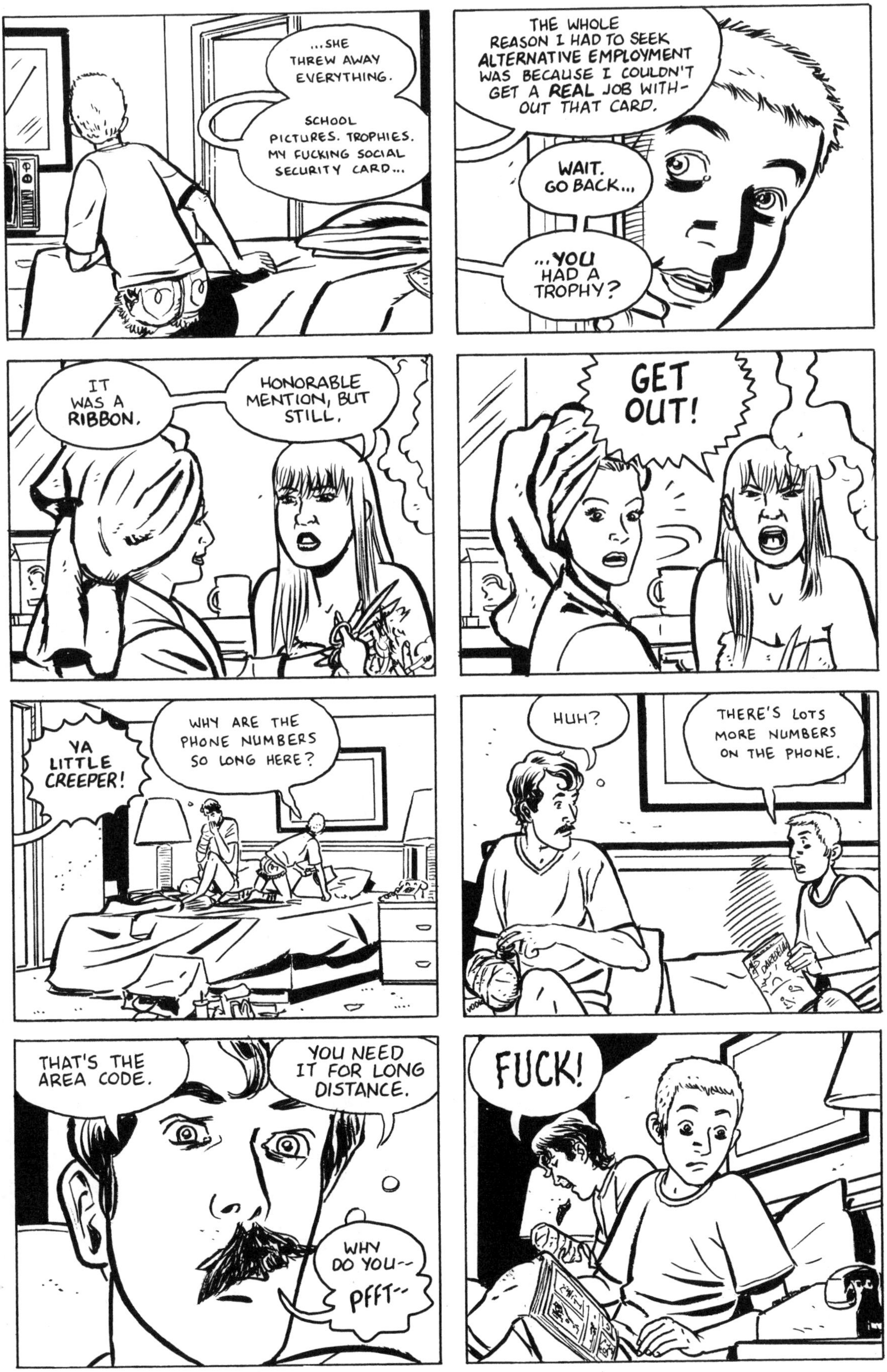
...SHE THREW AWAY EVERYTHING.
SCHOOL PICTURES. TROPHIES. MY FUCKING SOCIAL SECURITY CARD...
THE WHOLE REASON I HAD TO SEEK ALTERNATIVE EMPLOYMENT WAS BECAUSE I COULDN'T GET A REAL JOB WITH-OUT THAT CARD.
WAIT. GO BACK...
...YOU HAD A TROPHY?
IT WAS A RIBBON.
HONORABLE MENTION, BUT STILL.
GET OUT!
YA LITTLE CREEPER!
WHY ARE THE PHONE NUMBERS SO LONG HERE?
HUH?
THERE'S LOTS MORE NUMBERS ON THE PHONE.
THAT'S THE AREA CODE.
YOU NEED IT FOR LONG DISTANCE.
WHY DO YOU--
PFFT--
FUCK!

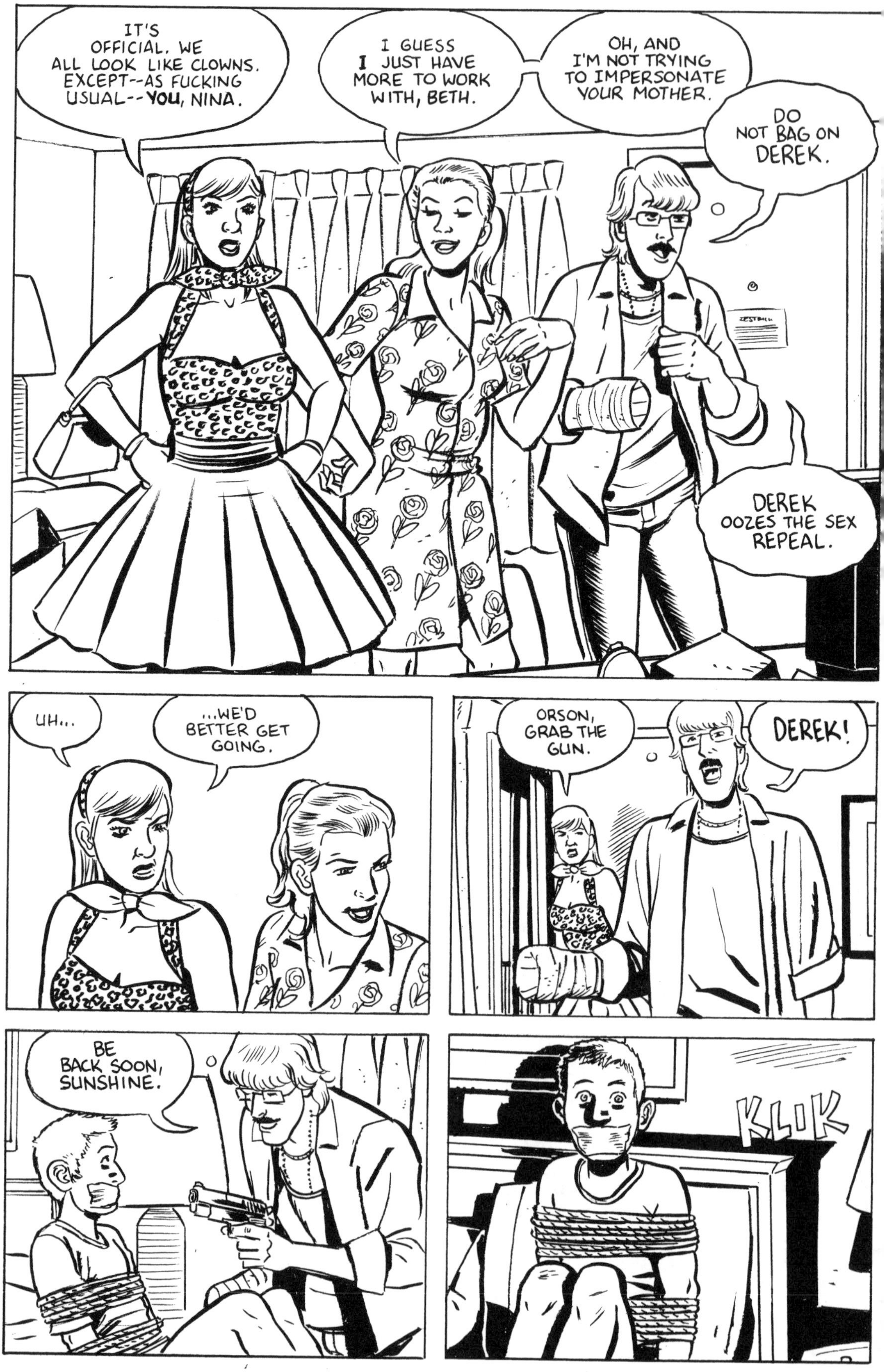
IT'S OFFICIAL. WE ALL LOOK LIKE CLOWNS. EXCEPT--AS FUCKING USUAL--YOU, NINA.
I GUESS I JUST HAVE MORE TO WORK WITH, BETH.
OH, AND I'M NOT TRYING TO IMPERSONATE YOUR MOTHER.
DO NOT BAG ON DEREK.
DEREK OOZES THE SEX REPEAL.
UH...
...WE'D BETTER GET GOING.
ORSON, GRAB THE GUN.
DEREK!
BE BACK SOON, SUNSHINE.
KLIK

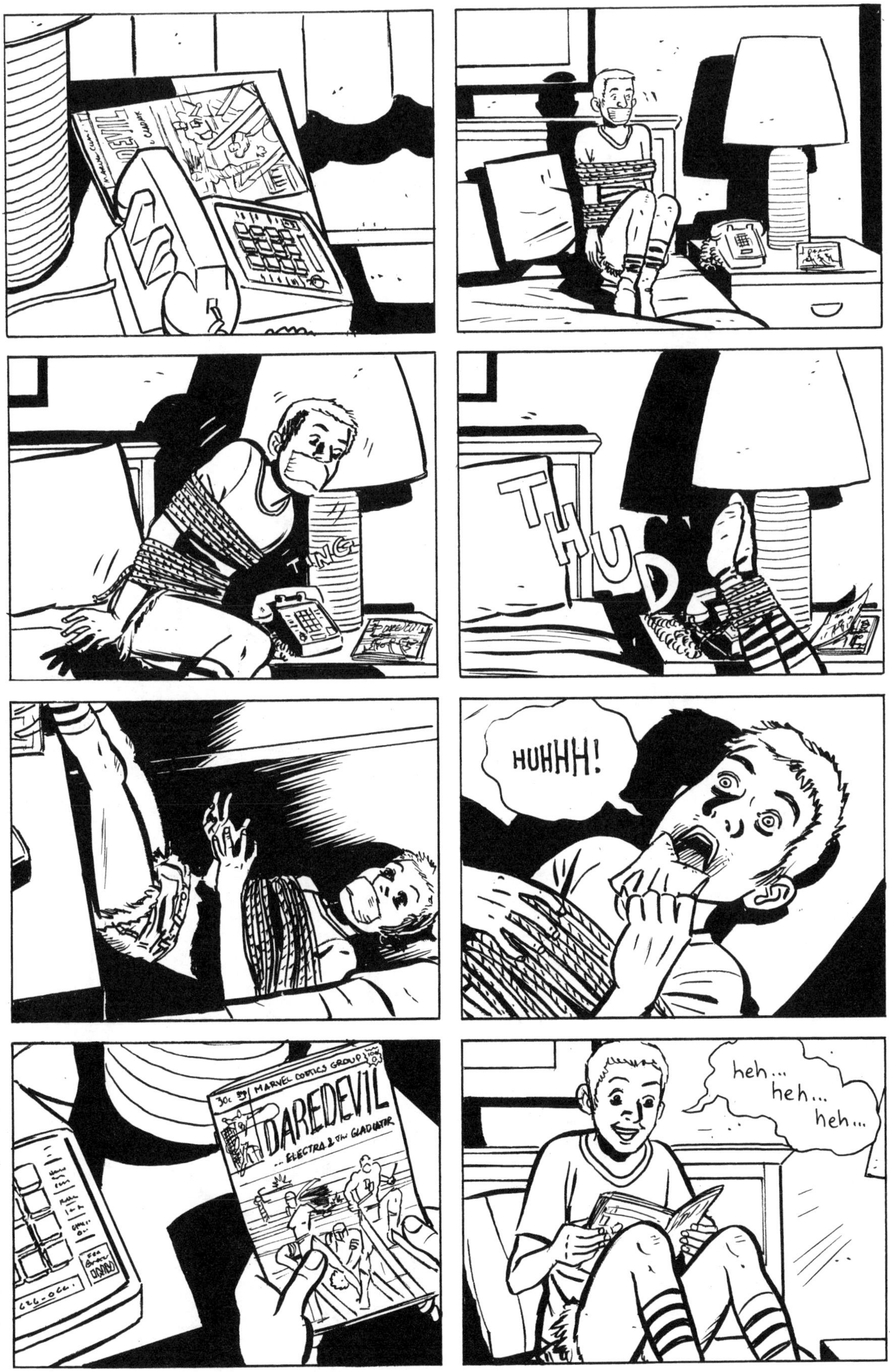

TING
THUD
HUHHH!
DAREDEVIL
heh... heh... heh...

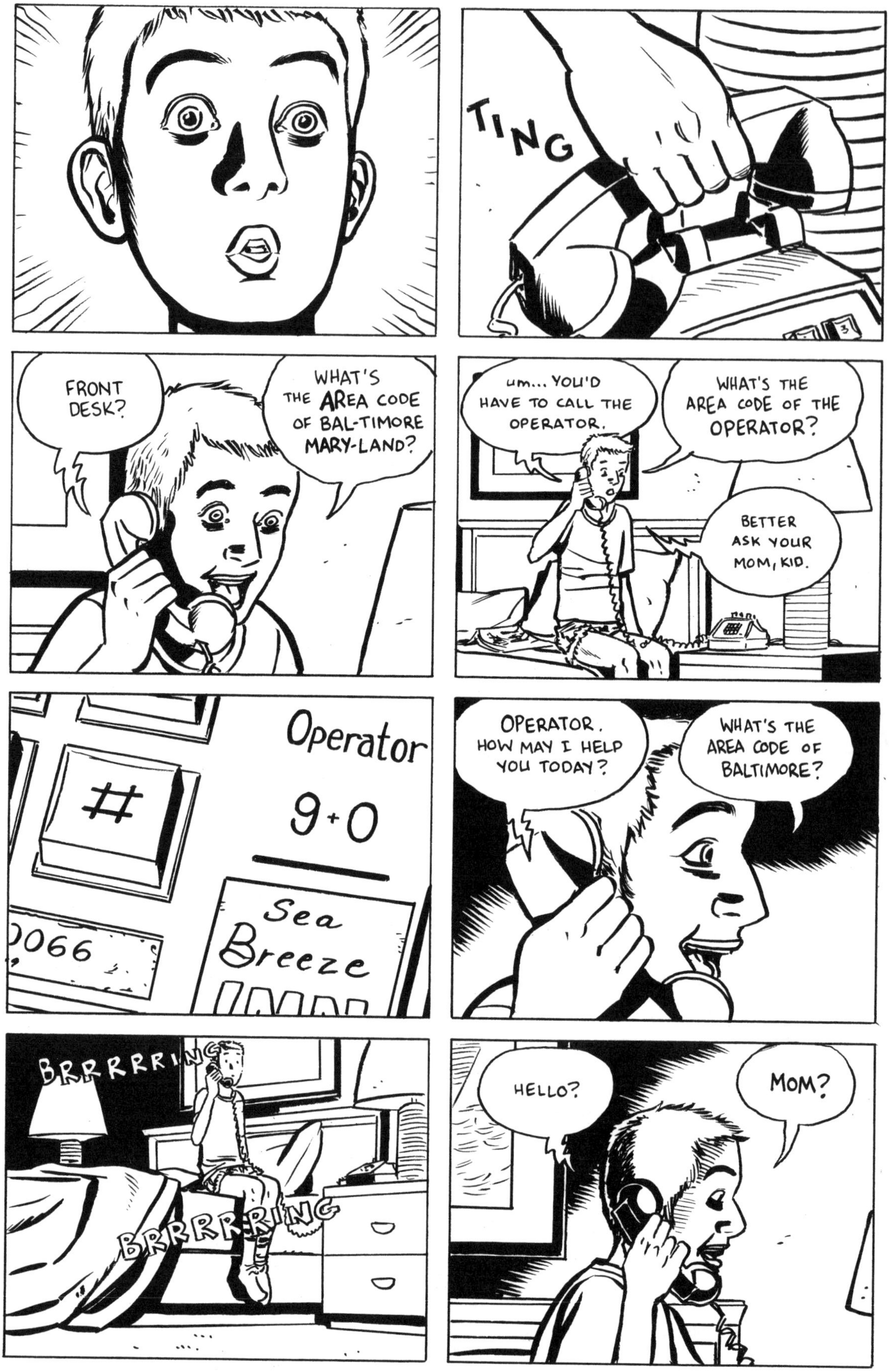
TING
FRONT DESK?
WHAT'S THE AREA CODE OF BAL-TIMORE MARY-LAND?
um... YOU'D HAVE TO CALL THE OPERATOR.
WHAT'S THE AREA CODE OF THE OPERATOR?
BETTER ASK YOUR MOM, KID.
Operator
9+0
Sea Breeze
OPERATOR. HOW MAY I HELP YOU TODAY?
WHAT'S THE AREA CODE OF BALTIMORE?
BRRRRRING
BRRRRRING
HELLO?
MOM?

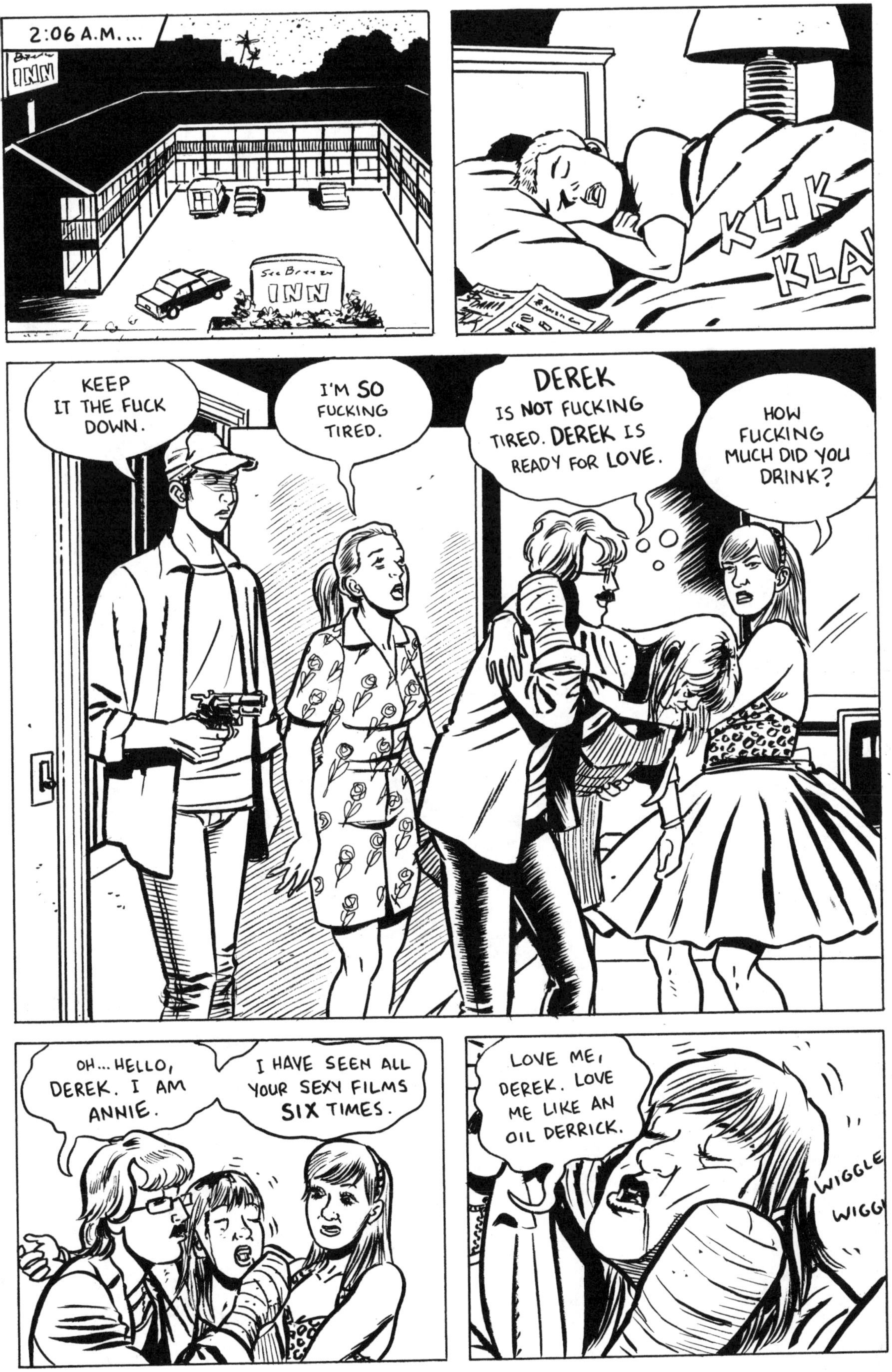
2:06 A.M....
INN
INN
KLIK
KLA
KEEP IT THE FUCK DOWN.
I'M SO FUCKING TIRED.
DEREK IS NOT FUCKING TIRED. DEREK IS READY FOR LOVE.
HOW FUCKING MUCH DID YOU DRINK?
OH... HELLO, DEREK. I AM ANNIE.
I HAVE SEEN ALL YOUR SEXY FILMS SIX TIMES.
LOVE ME, DEREK. LOVE ME LIKE AN OIL DERRICK.
WIGGLE
WIGG

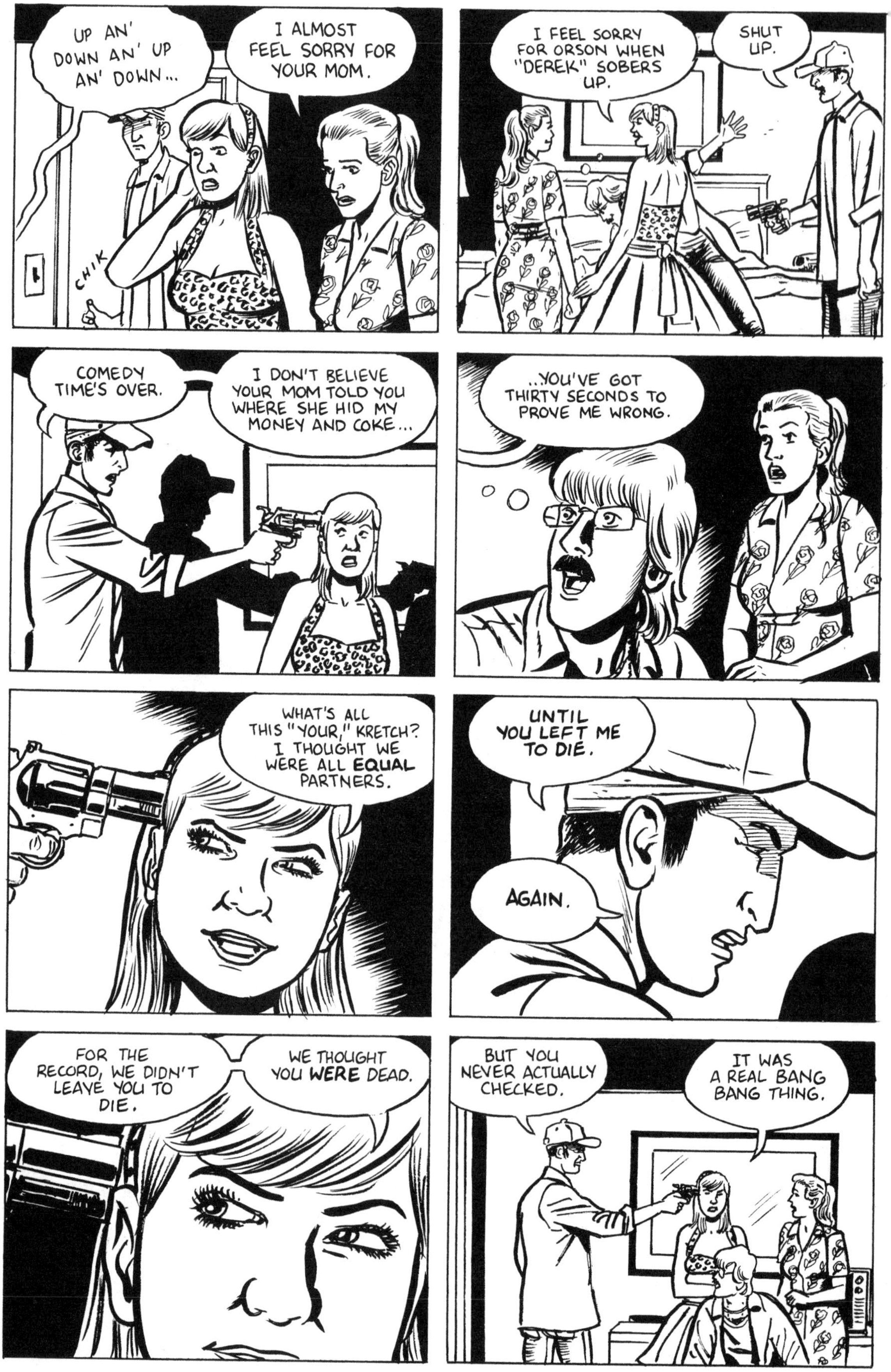
UP AN' DOWN AN' UP AN' DOWN...
CHIK
I ALMOST FEEL SORRY FOR YOUR MOM.
I FEEL SORRY FOR ORSON WHEN "DEREK" SOBERS UP.
SHUT UP.
COMEDY TIME'S OVER.
I DON'T BELIEVE YOUR MOM TOLD YOU WHERE SHE HID MY MONEY AND COKE...
..YOU'VE GOT THIRTY SECONDS TO PROVE ME WRONG.
WHAT'S ALL THIS "YOUR," KRETCH? I THOUGHT WE WERE ALL **EQUAL** PARTNERS.
UNTIL YOU LEFT ME TO DIE.
AGAIN.
FOR THE RECORD, WE DIDN'T LEAVE YOU TO DIE.
WE THOUGHT YOU **WERE** DEAD.
BUT YOU NEVER ACTUALLY CHECKED.
IT WAS A REAL BANG BANG THING.

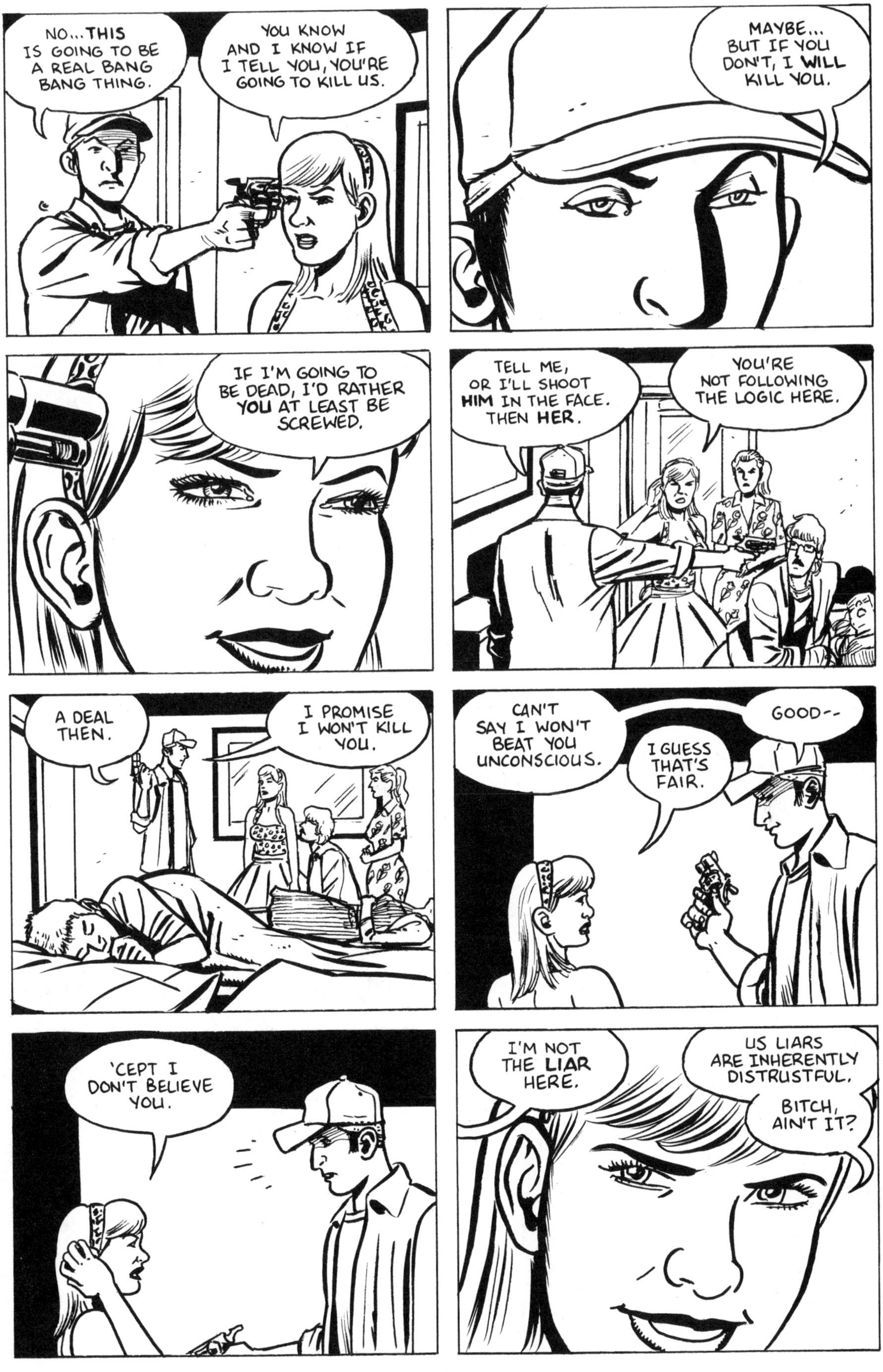
NO...THIS IS GOING TO BE A REAL BANG BANG THING.
YOU KNOW AND I KNOW IF I TELL YOU, YOU'RE GOING TO KILL US.
MAYBE... BUT IF YOU DON'T, I WILL KILL YOU.
IF I'M GOING TO BE DEAD, I'D RATHER YOU AT LEAST BE SCREWED.
TELL ME, OR I'LL SHOOT HIM IN THE FACE. THEN HER.
YOU'RE NOT FOLLOWING THE LOGIC HERE.
A DEAL THEN.
I PROMISE I WON'T KILL YOU.
CAN'T SAY I WON'T BEAT YOU UNCONSCIOUS.
I GUESS THAT'S FAIR.
GOOD--
'CEPT I DON'T BELIEVE YOU.
I'M NOT THE LIAR HERE.
US LIARS ARE INHERENTLY DISTRUSTFUL.
BITCH, AIN'T IT?

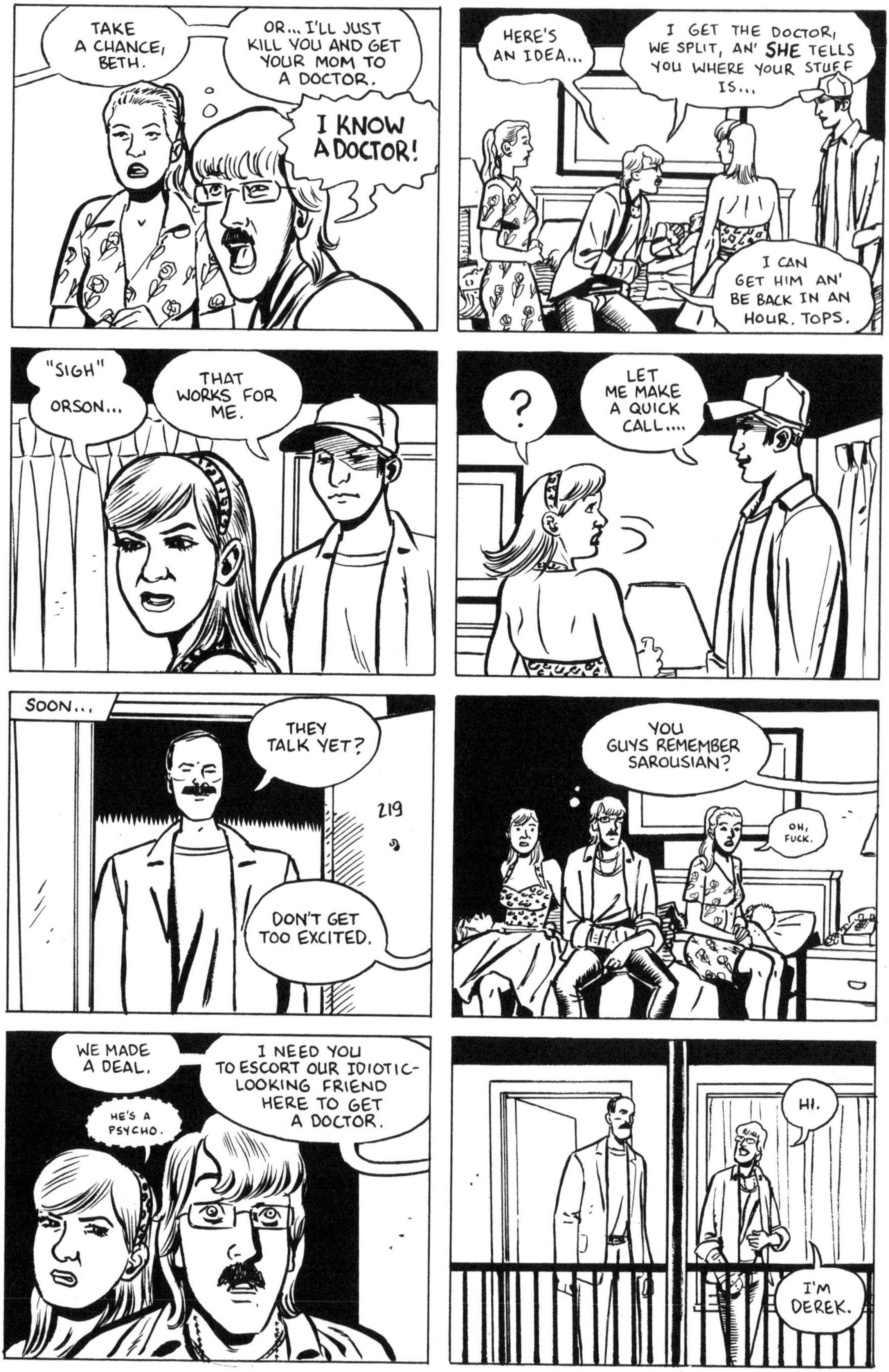
TAKE A CHANCE, BETH.
OR... I'LL JUST KILL YOU AND GET YOUR MOM TO A DOCTOR.
I KNOW A DOCTOR!
HERE'S AN IDEA...
I GET THE DOCTOR, WE SPLIT, AN' SHE TELLS YOU WHERE YOUR STUFF IS...
I CAN GET HIM AN' BE BACK IN AN HOUR. TOPS.
"SIGH" ORSON...
THAT WORKS FOR ME.
?
LET ME MAKE A QUICK CALL....
SOON...
THEY TALK YET?
219
DON'T GET TOO EXCITED.
YOU GUYS REMEMBER SAROUSIAN?
OH, FUCK.
WE MADE A DEAL.
I NEED YOU TO ESCORT OUR IDIOTIC-LOOKING FRIEND HERE TO GET A DOCTOR.
HE'S A PSYCHO.
HI.
I'M DEREK.

ARE WE GOOD? CAN I WATCH TV?
OF COURSE WE'RE NOT GOOD.
I NEEDED "DEREK" TO FEEL GOOD ABOUT GOING TO BRING BACK A DOCTOR.
BUT UNTIL I GET MY SHIT IN HAND, YOU'RE NOT GOING ANYWHERE.
BUT SURE. WATCH TV.
WHILE YOU'RE AT IT, YOU MAY WANT TO THINK ABOUT TELLING ME WHAT YOU KNOW...
...CUZ IF I HAVE TO WAIT FOR HER, I WILL KILL ALL OF YOU.
I'LL TAKE IT UNDER ADVISEMENT.
?
...
...
...
..

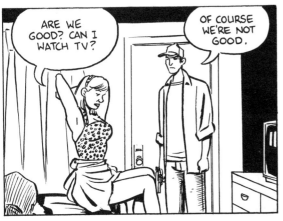

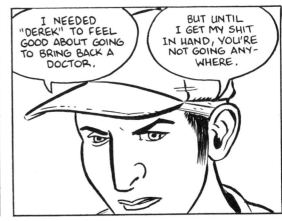

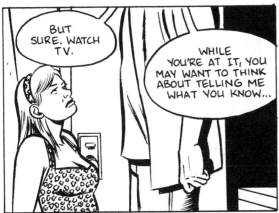

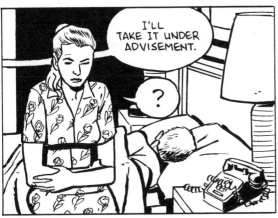

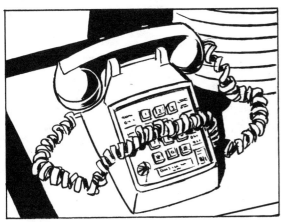

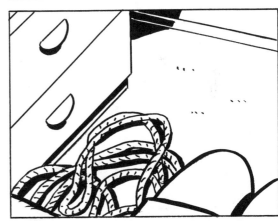

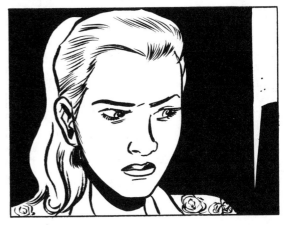

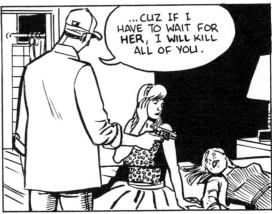

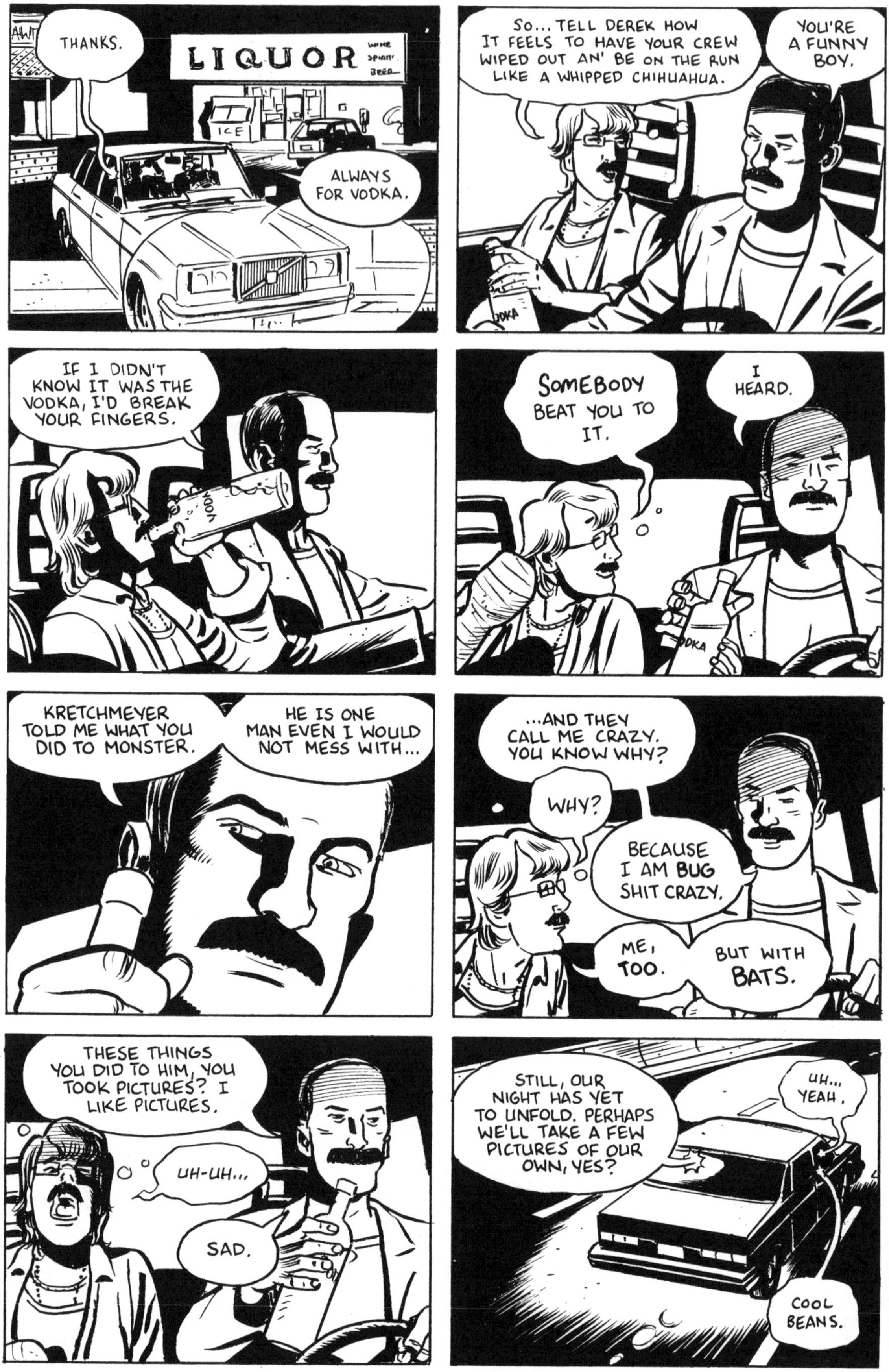
THANKS.
LIQUOR
WINE
SPIRITS
BEER
ICE
ALWAYS FOR VODKA.
SO... TELL DEREK HOW IT FEELS TO HAVE YOUR CREW WIPED OUT AN' BE ON THE RUN LIKE A WHIPPED CHIHUAHUA.
YOU'RE A FUNNY BOY.
IF I DIDN'T KNOW IT WAS THE VODKA, I'D BREAK YOUR FINGERS.
SOMEBODY BEAT YOU TO IT.
I HEARD.
KRETCHMEYER TOLD ME WHAT YOU DID TO MONSTER.
HE IS ONE MAN EVEN I WOULD NOT MESS WITH...
...AND THEY CALL ME CRAZY. YOU KNOW WHY?
WHY?
BECAUSE I AM BUG SHIT CRAZY.
ME, TOO.
BUT WITH BATS.
THESE THINGS YOU DID TO HIM, YOU TOOK PICTURES? I LIKE PICTURES.
UH-UH...
SAD.
STILL, OUR NIGHT HAS YET TO UNFOLD. PERHAPS WE'LL TAKE A FEW PICTURES OF OUR OWN, YES?
UH... YEAH.
COOL BEANS.

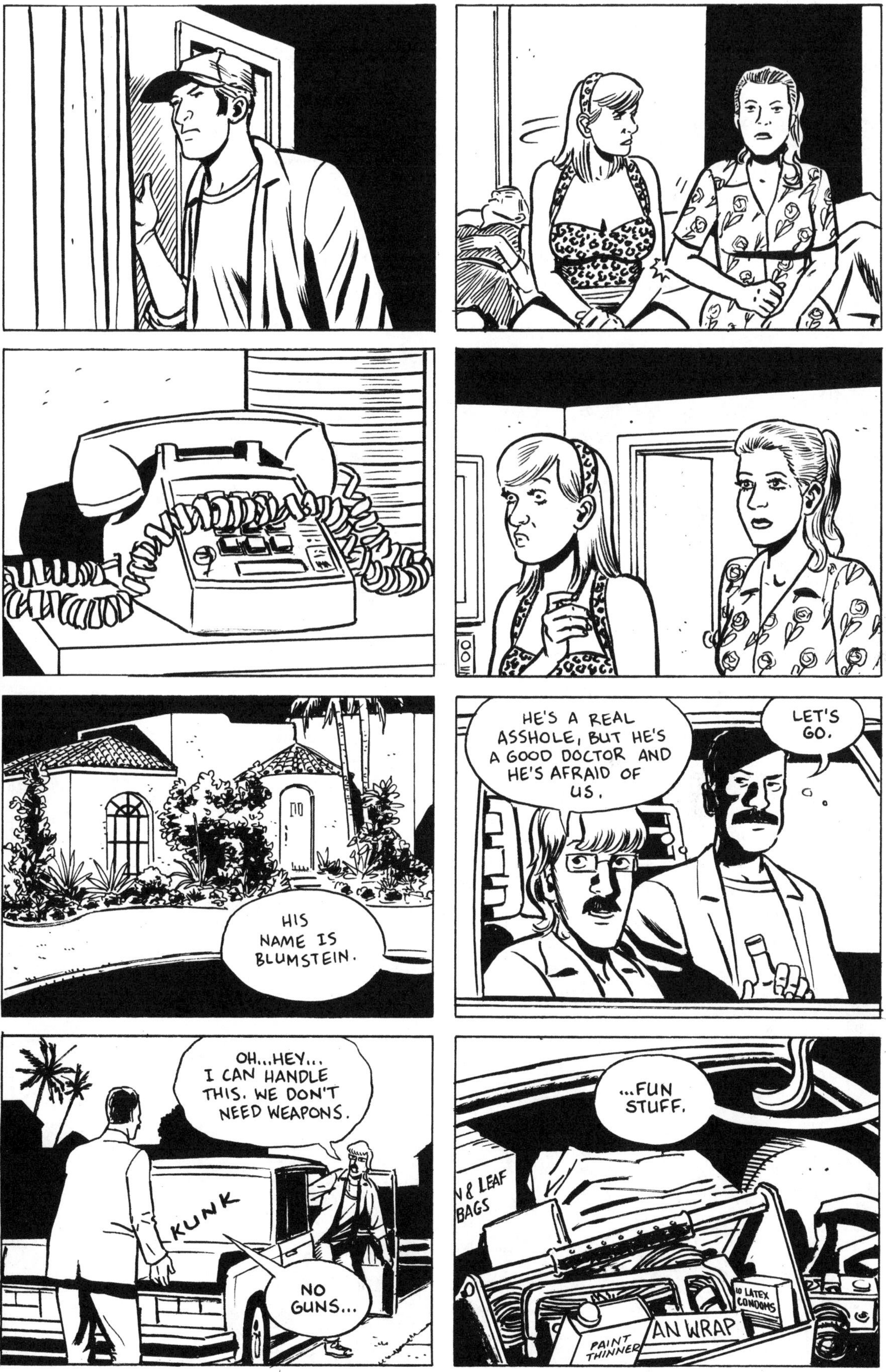
HIS NAME IS BLUMSTEIN.
HE'S A REAL ASSHOLE, BUT HE'S A GOOD DOCTOR AND HE'S AFRAID OF US.
LET'S GO.
OH...HEY... I CAN HANDLE THIS. WE DON'T NEED WEAPONS.
KUNK
NO GUNS...
...FUN STUFF.
N & LEAF BAGS
10 LATEX CONDOMS
AN WRAP
PAINT THINNER

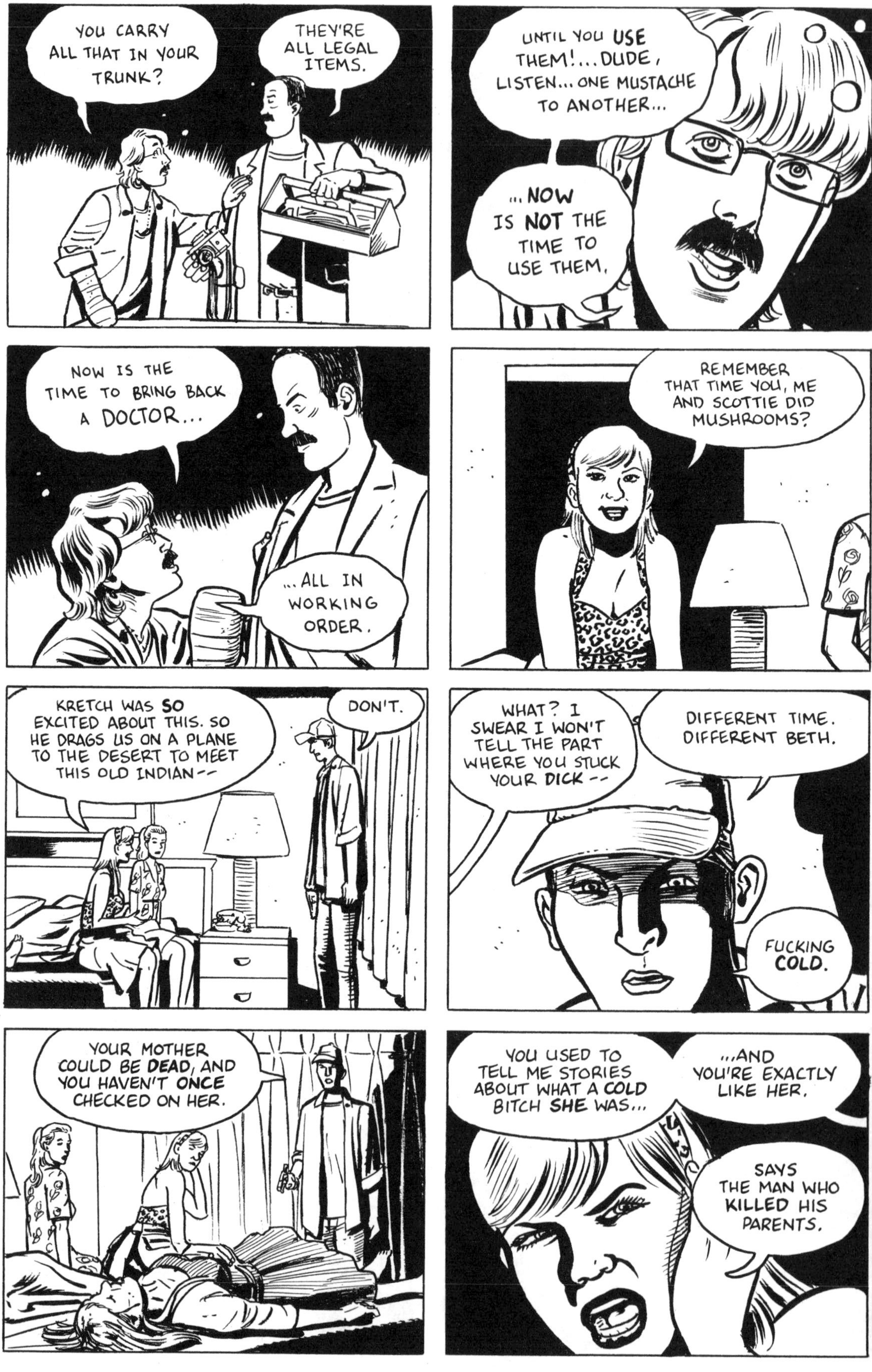
YOU CARRY ALL THAT IN YOUR TRUNK?
THEY'RE ALL LEGAL ITEMS.
UNTIL YOU USE THEM!... DUDE, LISTEN... ONE MUSTACHE TO ANOTHER...
...NOW IS NOT THE TIME TO USE THEM.
NOW IS THE TIME TO BRING BACK A DOCTOR...
...ALL IN WORKING ORDER.
REMEMBER THAT TIME YOU, ME AND SCOTTIE DID MUSHROOMS?
KRETCH WAS SO EXCITED ABOUT THIS. SO HE DRAGS US ON A PLANE TO THE DESERT TO MEET THIS OLD INDIAN--
DON'T.
WHAT? I SWEAR I WON'T TELL THE PART WHERE YOU STUCK YOUR DICK --
DIFFERENT TIME. DIFFERENT BETH.
FUCKING COLD.
YOUR MOTHER COULD BE DEAD, AND YOU HAVEN'T ONCE CHECKED ON HER.
YOU USED TO TELL ME STORIES ABOUT WHAT A COLD BITCH SHE WAS...
...AND YOU'RE EXACTLY LIKE HER.
SAYS THE MAN WHO KILLED HIS PARENTS.

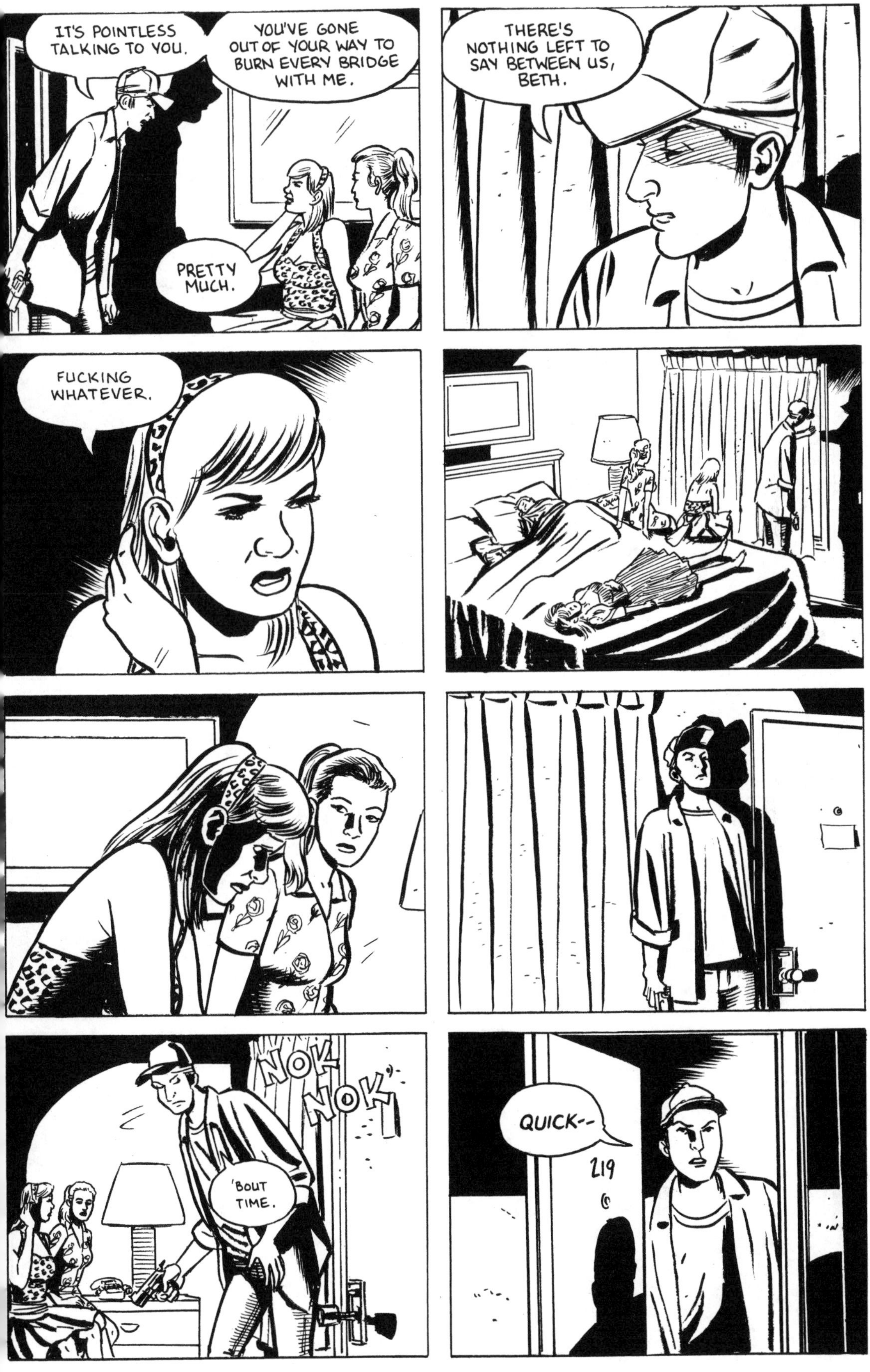
IT'S POINTLESS TALKING TO YOU.
YOU'VE GONE OUT OF YOUR WAY TO BURN EVERY BRIDGE WITH ME.
PRETTY MUCH.
THERE'S NOTHING LEFT TO SAY BETWEEN US, BETH.
FUCKING WHATEVER.
NOK NOK
'BOUT TIME.
QUICK--
219

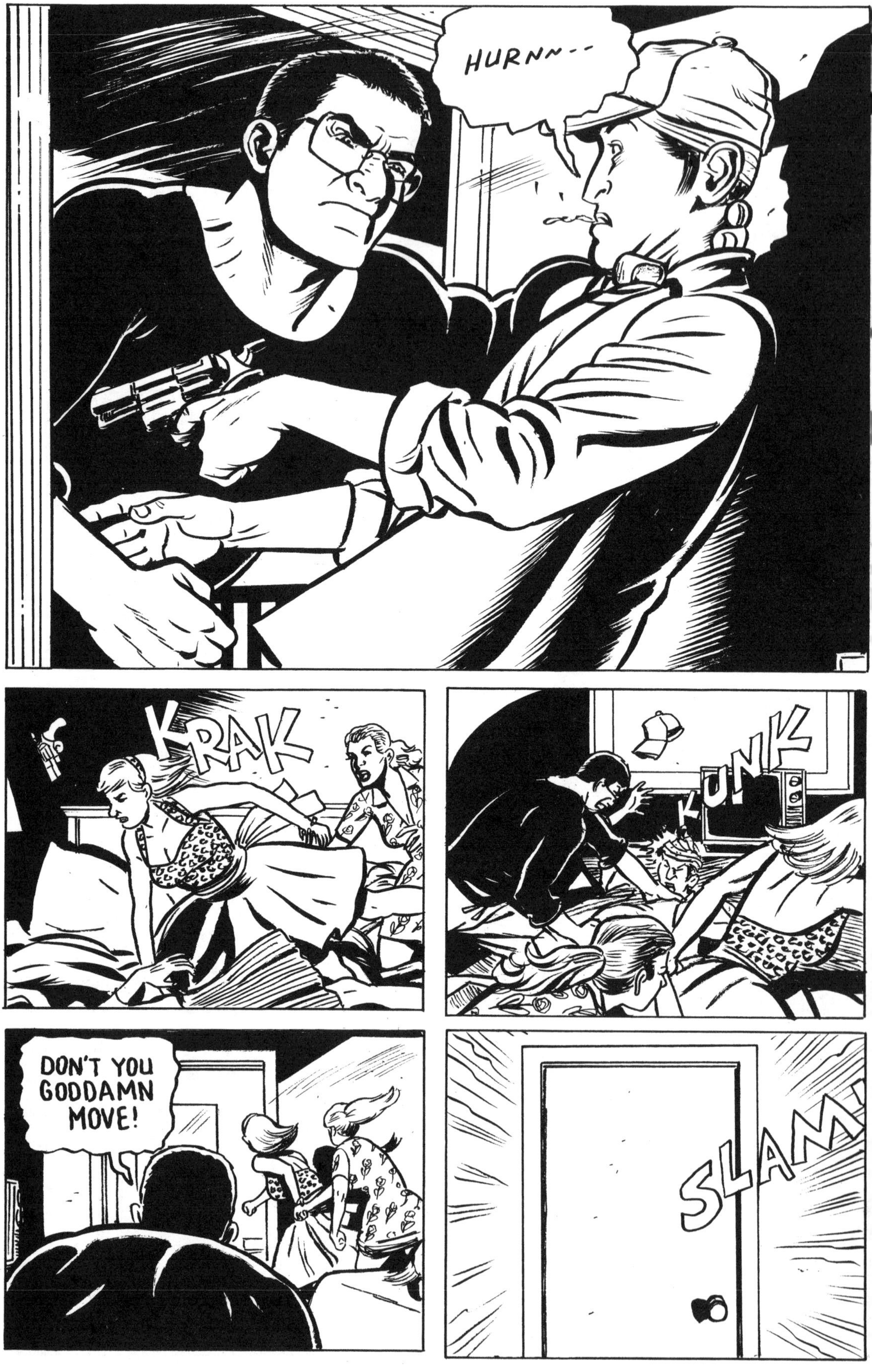
HURNN--
KRAK
KUNK
DON'T YOU GODDAMN MOVE!
SLAM

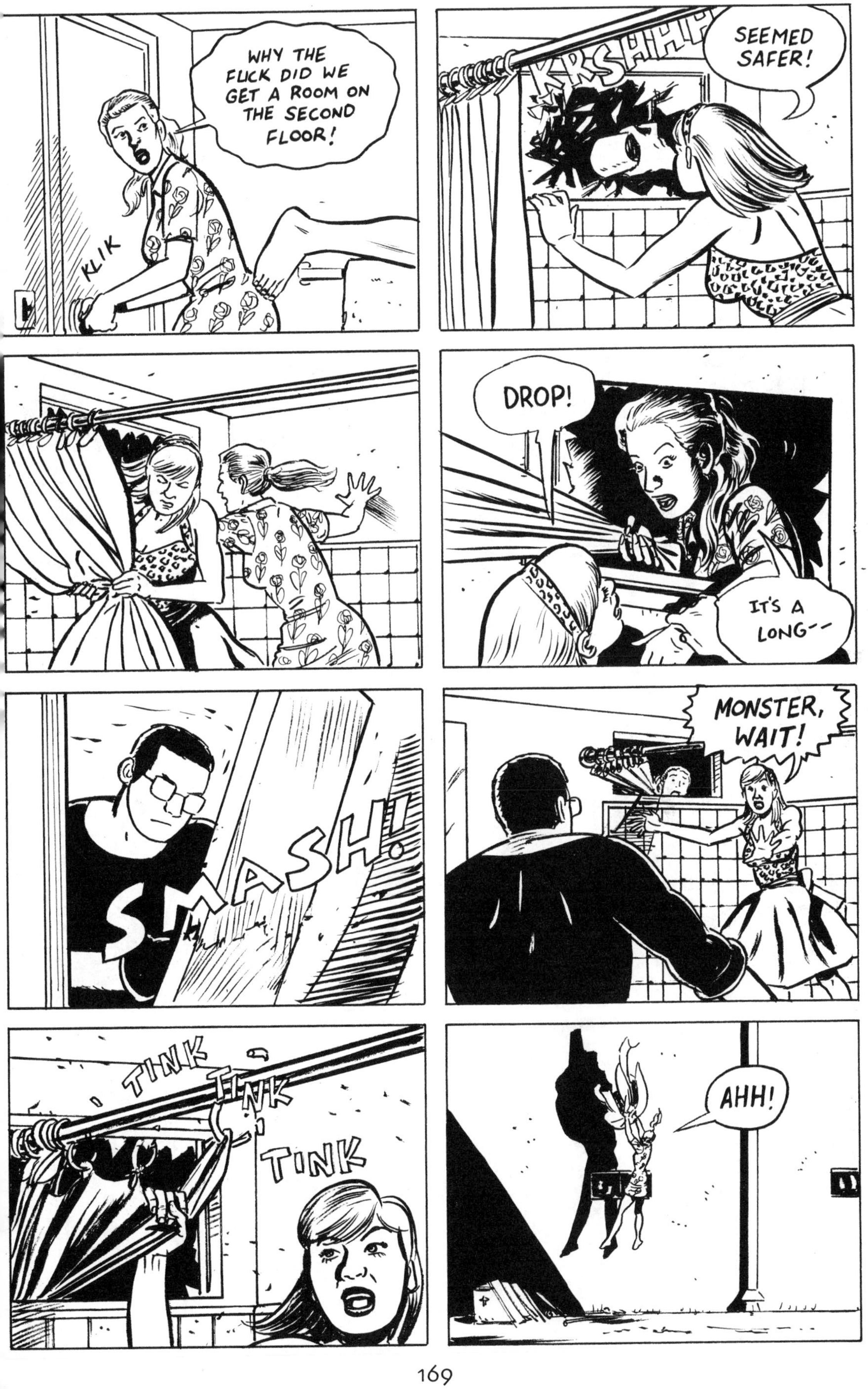
WHY THE FUCK DID WE GET A ROOM ON THE SECOND FLOOR!
KLIK
KRSHHH
SEEMED SAFER!
DROP!
IT'S A LONG--
SMASH!
MONSTER, WAIT!
TINK
TINK
TINK
AHH!

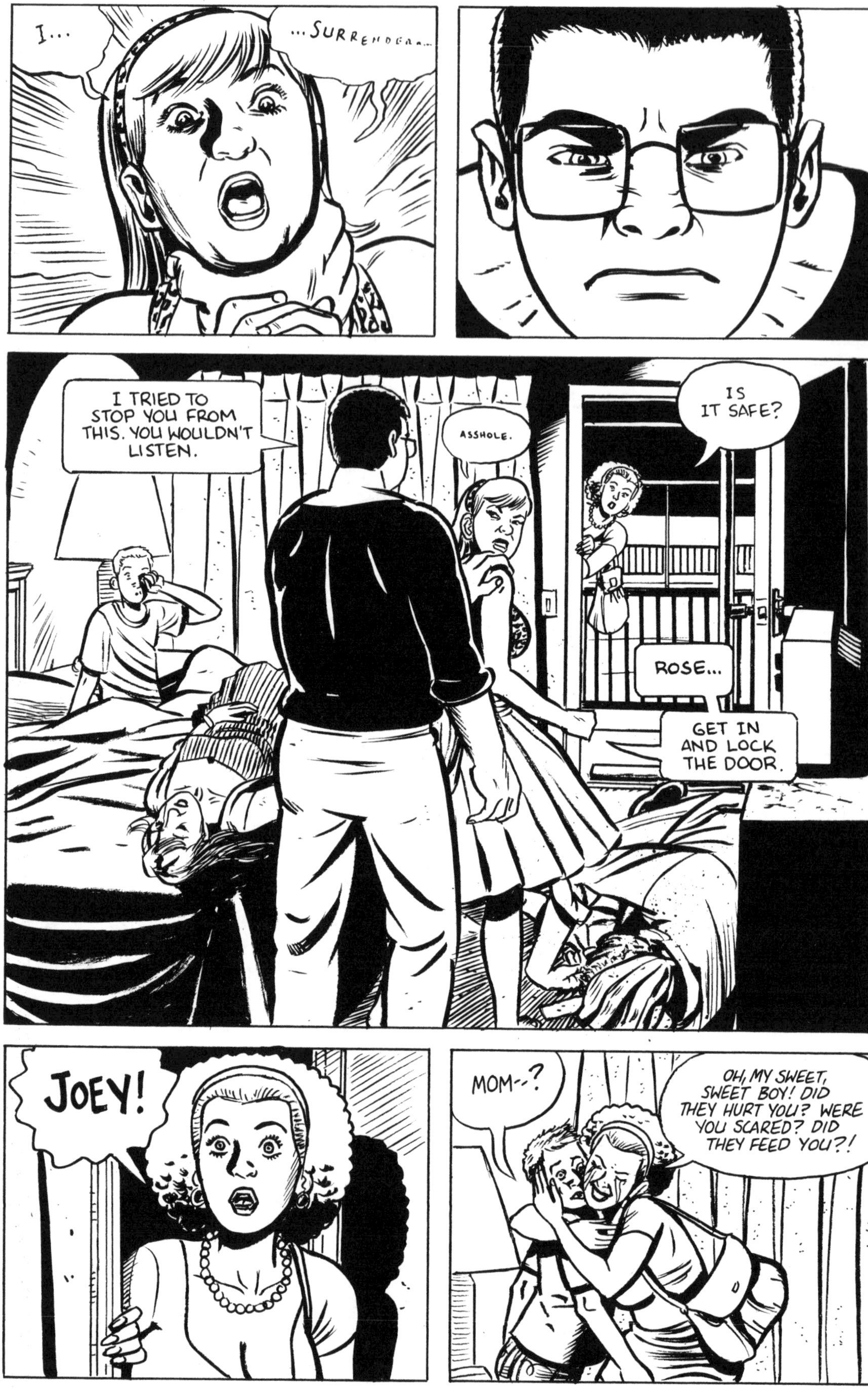
I...
...SURRENDER...
I TRIED TO STOP YOU FROM THIS. YOU WOULDN'T LISTEN.
ASSHOLE.
IS IT SAFE?
ROSE...
GET IN AND LOCK THE DOOR.
JOEY!
MOM--?
OH, MY SWEET, SWEET BOY! DID THEY HURT YOU? WERE YOU SCARED? DID THEY FEED YOU?!

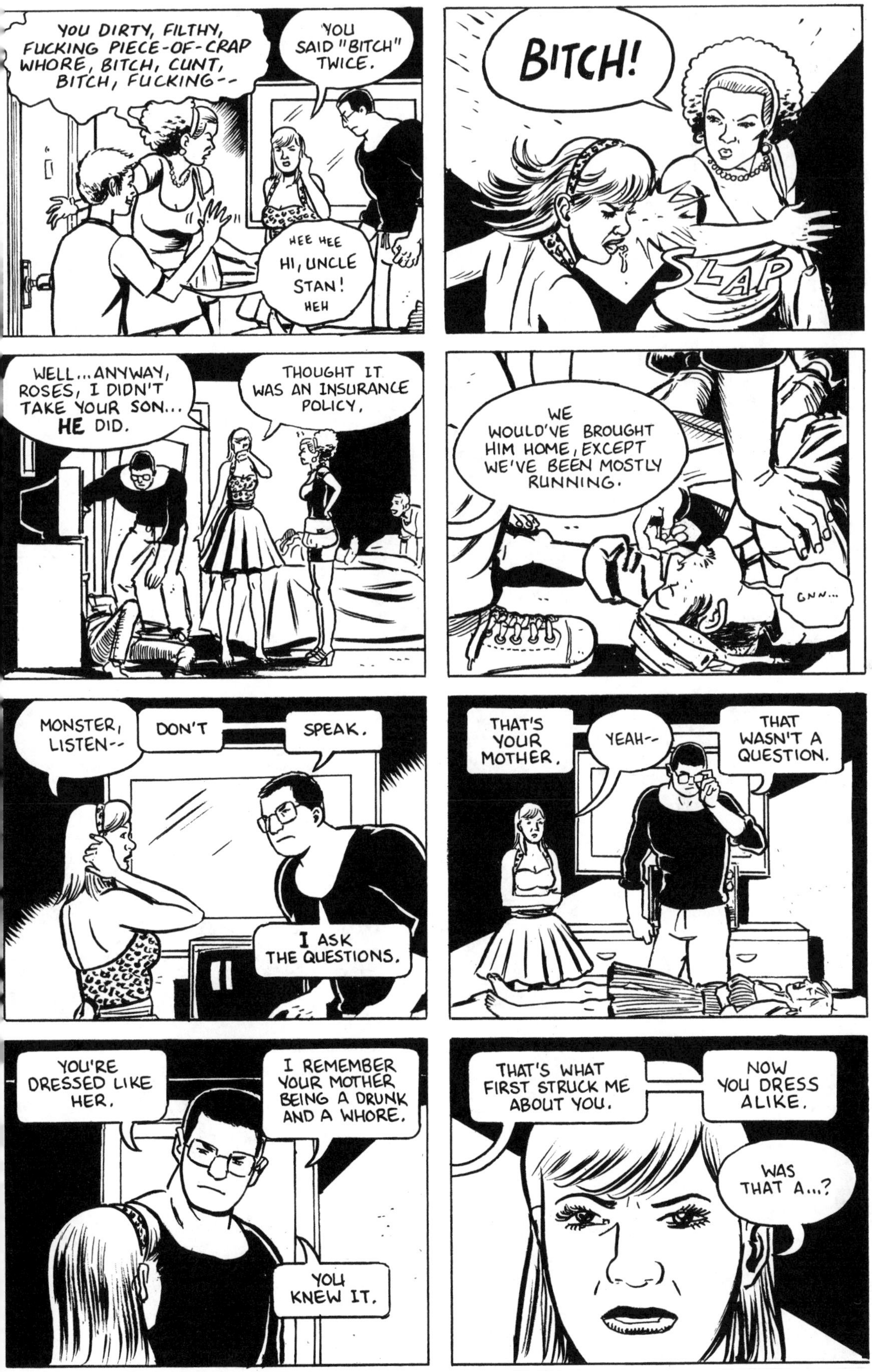

YOU DIRTY, FILTHY, FUCKING PIECE-OF-CRAP WHORE, BITCH, CUNT, BITCH, FUCKING--
YOU SAID "BITCH" TWICE.
HEE HEE HI, UNCLE STAN! HEH
BITCH!
SLAP
WELL...ANYWAY, ROSES, I DIDN'T TAKE YOUR SON... HE DID.
THOUGHT IT WAS AN INSURANCE POLICY.
WE WOULD'VE BROUGHT HIM HOME, EXCEPT WE'VE BEEN MOSTLY RUNNING.
GNN...
MONSTER, LISTEN--
DON'T
SPEAK.
I ASK THE QUESTIONS.
THAT'S YOUR MOTHER.
YEAH--
THAT WASN'T A QUESTION.
YOU'RE DRESSED LIKE HER.
I REMEMBER YOUR MOTHER BEING A DRUNK AND A WHORE.
YOU KNEW IT.
THAT'S WHAT FIRST STRUCK ME ABOUT YOU.
NOW YOU DRESS ALIKE.
WAS THAT A...?

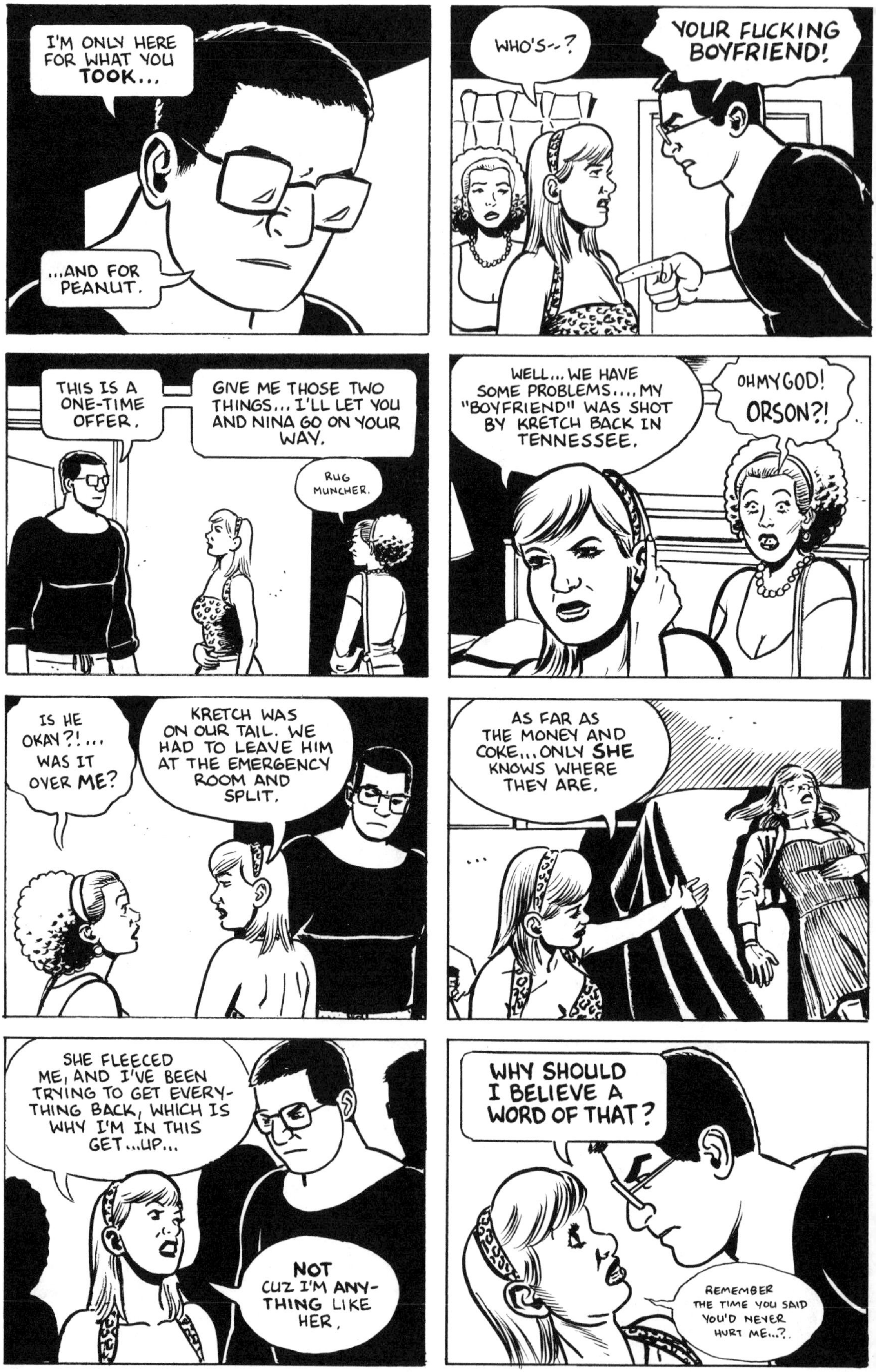
I'M ONLY HERE FOR WHAT YOU TOOK...
...AND FOR PEANUT.
WHO'S--?
YOUR FUCKING BOYFRIEND!
THIS IS A ONE-TIME OFFER.
GIVE ME THOSE TWO THINGS... I'LL LET YOU AND NINA GO ON YOUR WAY.
RUG MUNCHER.
WELL... WE HAVE SOME PROBLEMS...., MY "BOYFRIEND" WAS SHOT BY KRETCH BACK IN TENNESSEE.
OHMYGOD! ORSON?!
IS HE OKAY?!... WAS IT OVER ME?
KRETCH WAS ON OUR TAIL. WE HAD TO LEAVE HIM AT THE EMERGENCY ROOM AND SPLIT.
AS FAR AS THE MONEY AND COKE...ONLY SHE KNOWS WHERE THEY ARE.
...
SHE FLEECED ME, AND I'VE BEEN TRYING TO GET EVERY-THING BACK, WHICH IS WHY I'M IN THIS GET...UP...
NOT CUZ I'M ANY-THING LIKE HER.
WHY SHOULD I BELIEVE A WORD OF THAT?
REMEMBER THE TIME YOU SAID YOU'D NEVER HURT ME...?

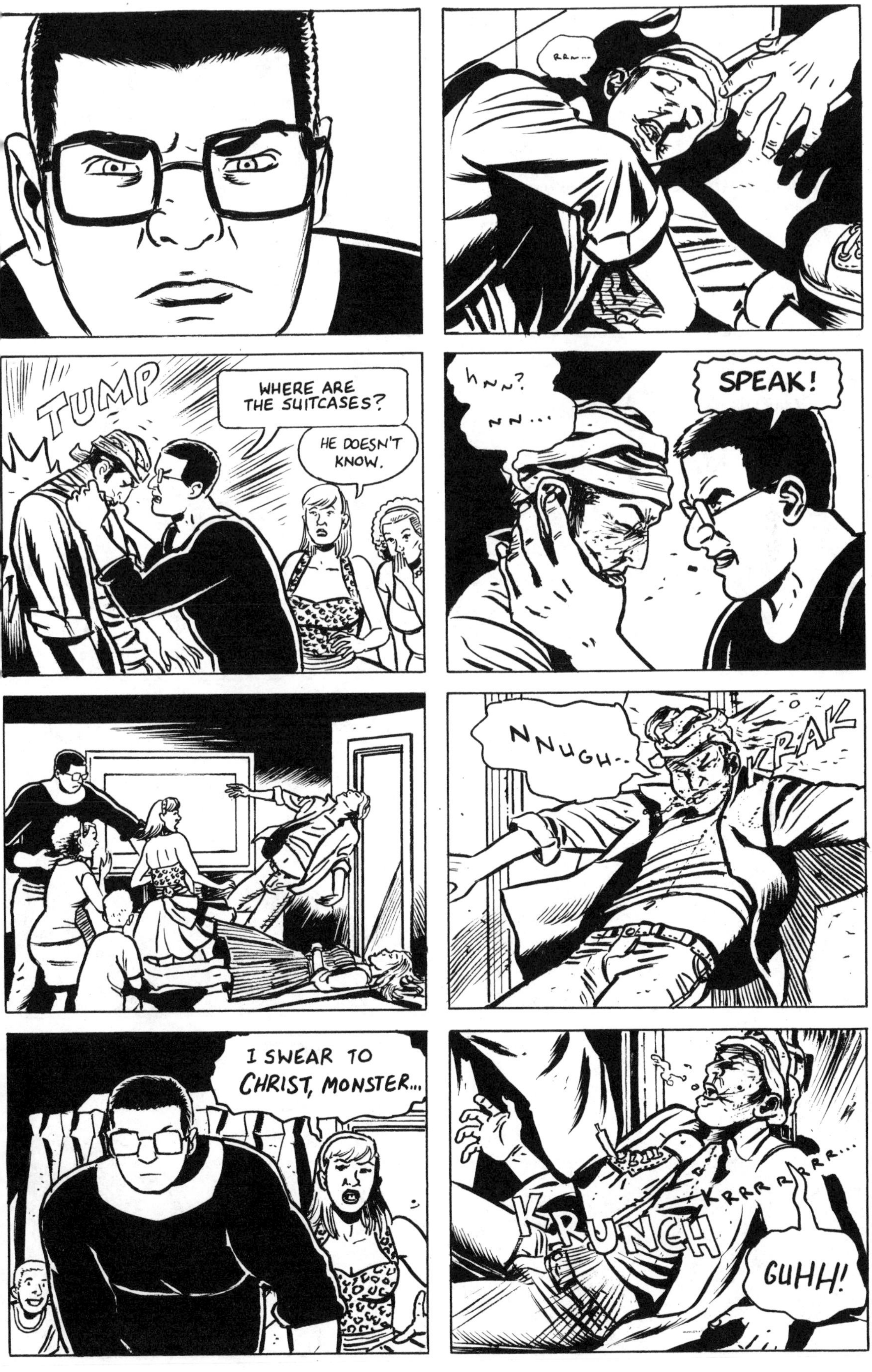
RRN...
TUMP
WHERE ARE THE SUITCASES?
HE DOESN'T KNOW.
hnn?
NN...
SPEAK!
NNUGH..
KRAK
I SWEAR TO CHRIST, MONSTER...
KRUNCH
KRRRRRRR...
GUHH!

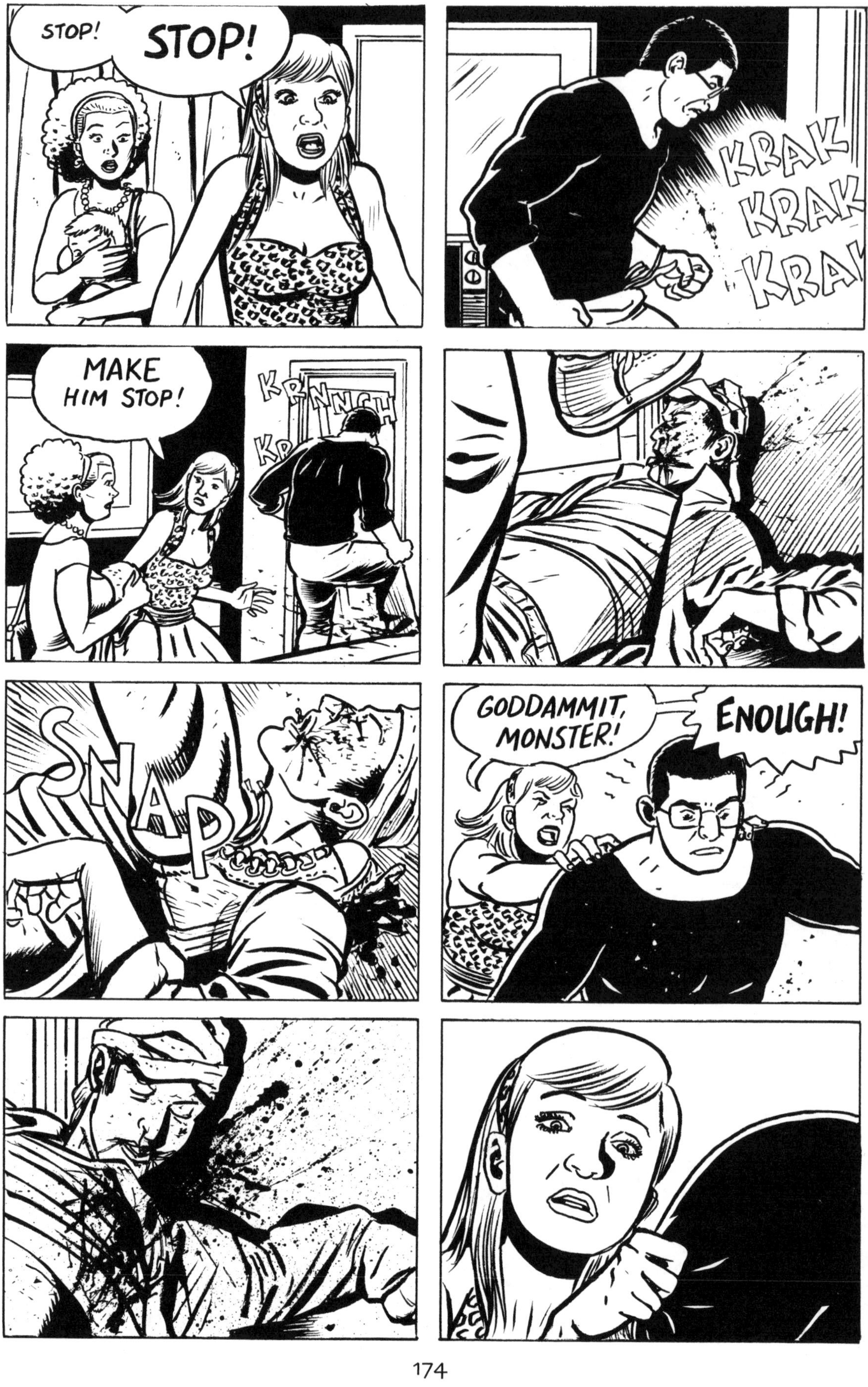
STOP!
STOP!
KRAK
KRAK
KRAK
MAKE HIM STOP!
KRNNCH
KR
SNAP
GODDAMMIT, MONSTER!
ENOUGH!

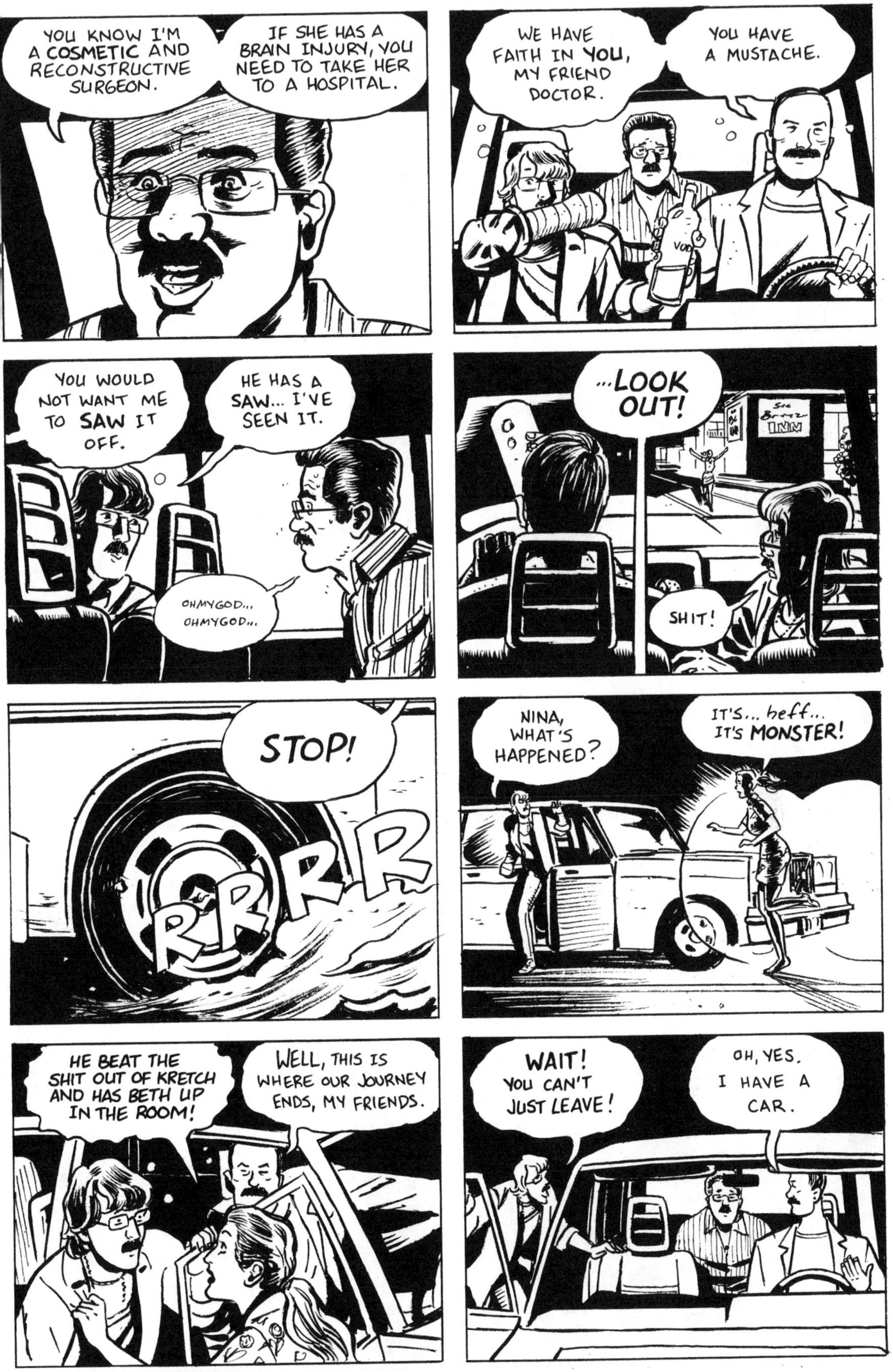
YOU KNOW I'M A COSMETIC AND RECONSTRUCTIVE SURGEON.
IF SHE HAS A BRAIN INJURY, YOU NEED TO TAKE HER TO A HOSPITAL.
WE HAVE FAITH IN YOU, MY FRIEND DOCTOR.
YOU HAVE A MUSTACHE.
YOU WOULD NOT WANT ME TO SAW IT OFF.
HE HAS A SAW... I'VE SEEN IT.
OHMYGOD... OHMYGOD...
...LOOK OUT!
SHIT!
STOP!
RRRR
NINA, WHAT'S HAPPENED?
IT'S... heff... IT'S MONSTER!
HE BEAT THE SHIT OUT OF KRETCH AND HAS BETH UP IN THE ROOM!
WELL, THIS IS WHERE OUR JOURNEY ENDS, MY FRIENDS.
WAIT! YOU CAN'T JUST LEAVE!
OH, YES. I HAVE A CAR.

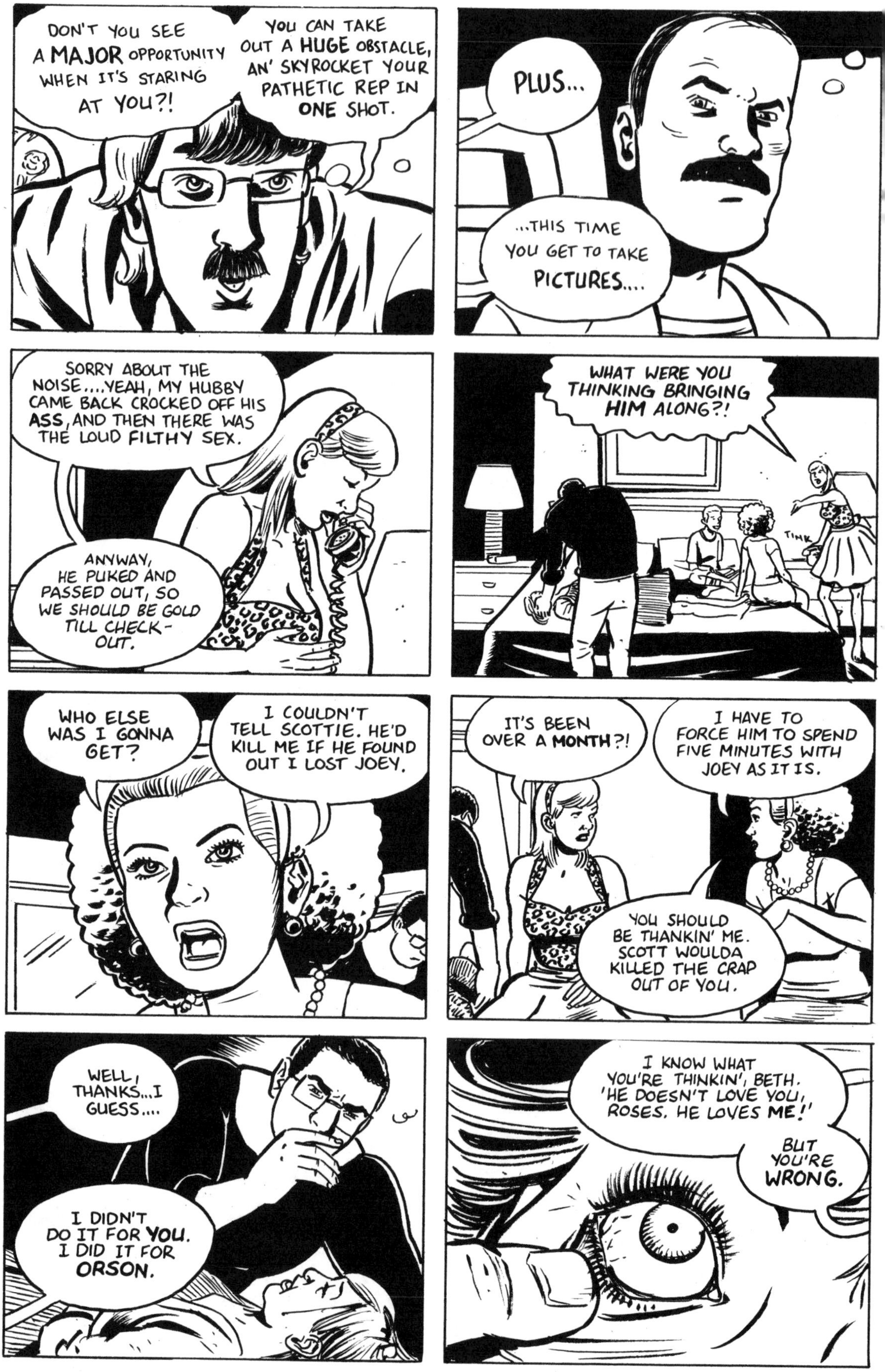
DON'T YOU SEE A MAJOR OPPORTUNITY WHEN IT'S STARING AT YOU?!
YOU CAN TAKE OUT A HUGE OBSTACLE, AN' SKYROCKET YOUR PATHETIC REP IN ONE SHOT.
PLUS...
...THIS TIME YOU GET TO TAKE PICTURES....
SORRY ABOUT THE NOISE....YEAH, MY HUBBY CAME BACK CROCKED OFF HIS ASS, AND THEN THERE WAS THE LOUD FILTHY SEX.
ANYWAY, HE PUKED AND PASSED OUT, SO WE SHOULD BE GOLD TILL CHECK-OUT.
WHAT WERE YOU THINKING BRINGING HIM ALONG?!
TINK
WHO ELSE WAS I GONNA GET?
I COULDN'T TELL SCOTTIE. HE'D KILL ME IF HE FOUND OUT I LOST JOEY.
IT'S BEEN OVER A MONTH?!
I HAVE TO FORCE HIM TO SPEND FIVE MINUTES WITH JOEY AS IT IS.
YOU SHOULD BE THANKIN' ME. SCOTT WOULDA KILLED THE CRAP OUT OF YOU.
WELL, THANKS...I GUESS....
I DIDN'T DO IT FOR YOU. I DID IT FOR ORSON.
I KNOW WHAT YOU'RE THINKIN', BETH. 'HE DOESN'T LOVE YOU, ROSES. HE LOVES ME!'
BUT YOU'RE WRONG.

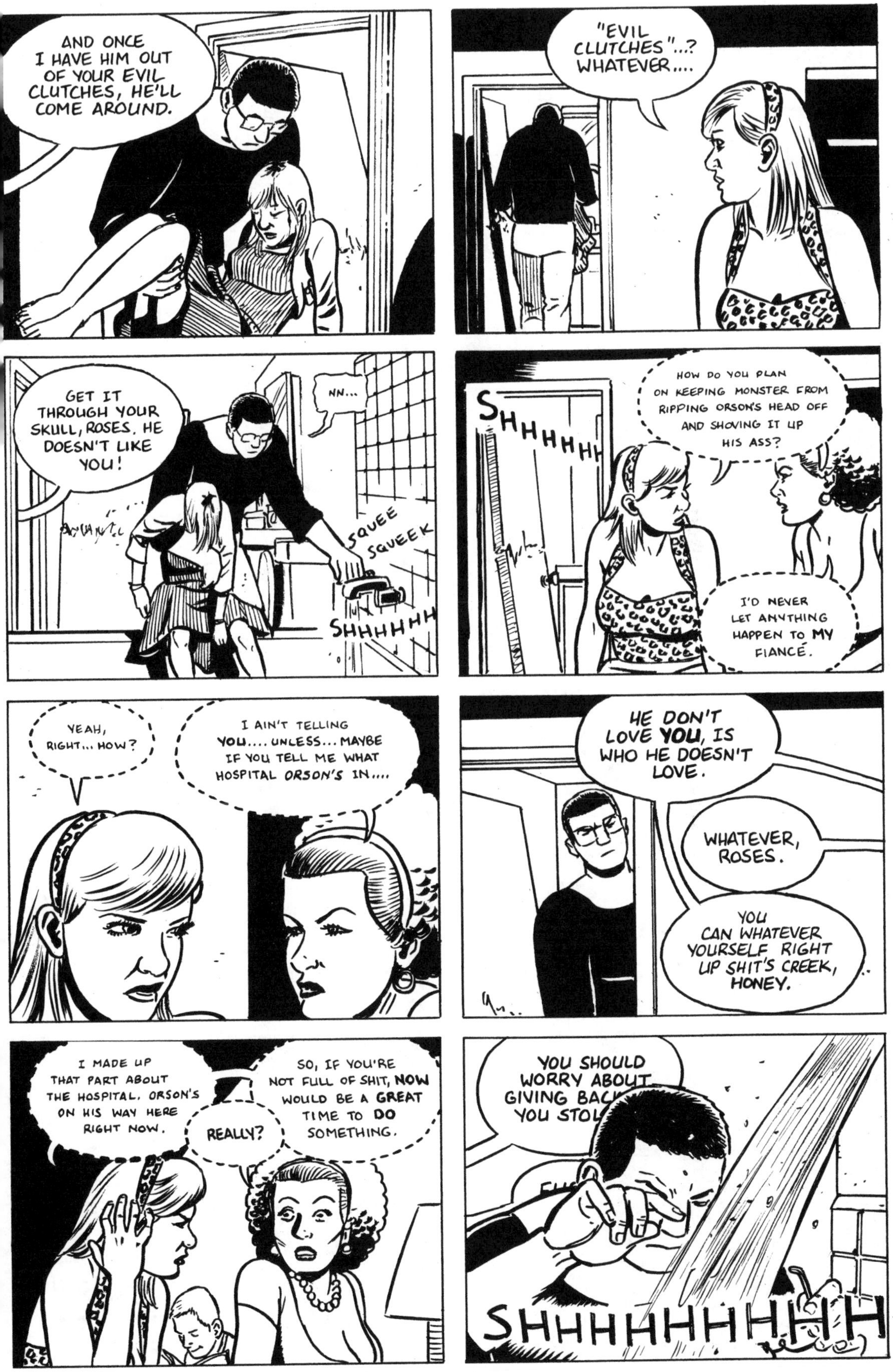
AND ONCE I HAVE HIM OUT OF YOUR EVIL CLUTCHES, HE'LL COME AROUND.
"EVIL CLUTCHES"...? WHATEVER....
GET IT THROUGH YOUR SKULL, ROSES. HE DOESN'T LIKE YOU!
NN...
SQUEE SQUEEK
SHHHHHH
SHHHHHH
HOW DO YOU PLAN ON KEEPING MONSTER FROM RIPPING ORSON'S HEAD OFF AND SHOVING IT UP HIS ASS?
I'D NEVER LET ANYTHING HAPPEN TO MY FIANCÉ.
YEAH, RIGHT... HOW?
I AIN'T TELLING YOU.... UNLESS... MAYBE IF YOU TELL ME WHAT HOSPITAL ORSON'S IN....
HE DON'T LOVE YOU, IS WHO HE DOESN'T LOVE.
WHATEVER, ROSES.
YOU CAN WHATEVER YOURSELF RIGHT UP SHIT'S CREEK, HONEY.
I MADE UP THAT PART ABOUT THE HOSPITAL. ORSON'S ON HIS WAY HERE RIGHT NOW.
REALLY?
SO, IF YOU'RE NOT FULL OF SHIT, NOW WOULD BE A GREAT TIME TO DO SOMETHING.
YOU SHOULD WORRY ABOUT
GIVING BAC
YOU STOL
SHHHHHHHHH

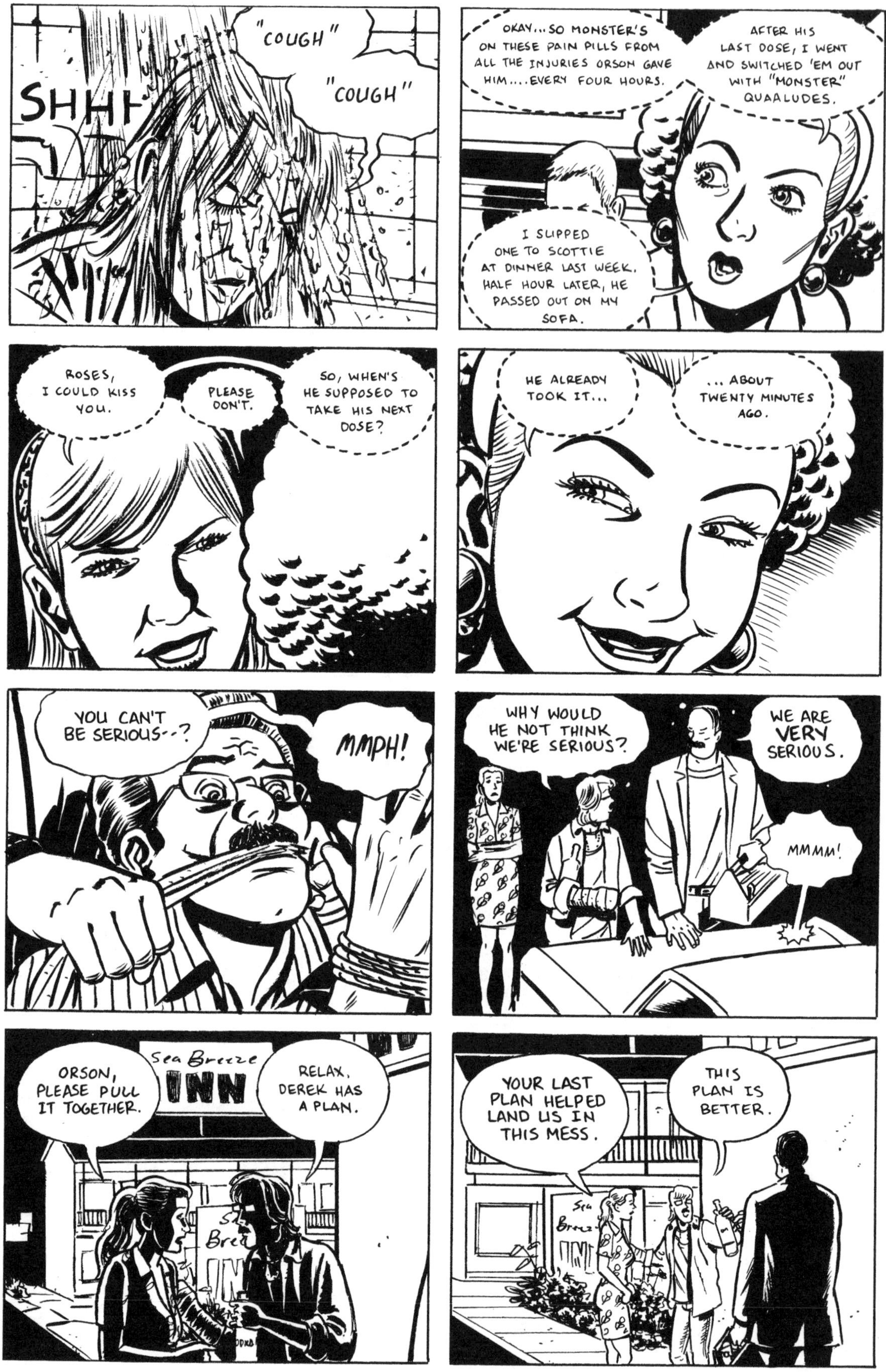
"COUGH"
"COUGH"
SHHH
OKAY... SO MONSTER'S ON THESE PAIN PILLS FROM ALL THE INJURIES ORSON GAVE HIM.... EVERY FOUR HOURS.
AFTER HIS LAST DOSE, I WENT AND SWITCHED 'EM OUT WITH "MONSTER" QUAALUDES.
I SLIPPED ONE TO SCOTTIE AT DINNER LAST WEEK. HALF HOUR LATER, HE PASSED OUT ON MY SOFA.
ROSES, I COULD KISS YOU.
PLEASE DON'T.
SO, WHEN'S HE SUPPOSED TO TAKE HIS NEXT DOSE?
HE ALREADY TOOK IT...
... ABOUT TWENTY MINUTES AGO.
YOU CAN'T BE SERIOUS--?
MMPH!
WHY WOULD HE NOT THINK WE'RE SERIOUS?
WE ARE VERY SERIOUS.
MMMM!
Sea Breeze INN
ORSON, PLEASE PULL IT TOGETHER.
RELAX. DEREK HAS A PLAN.
YOUR LAST PLAN HELPED LAND US IN THIS MESS.
THIS PLAN IS BETTER.

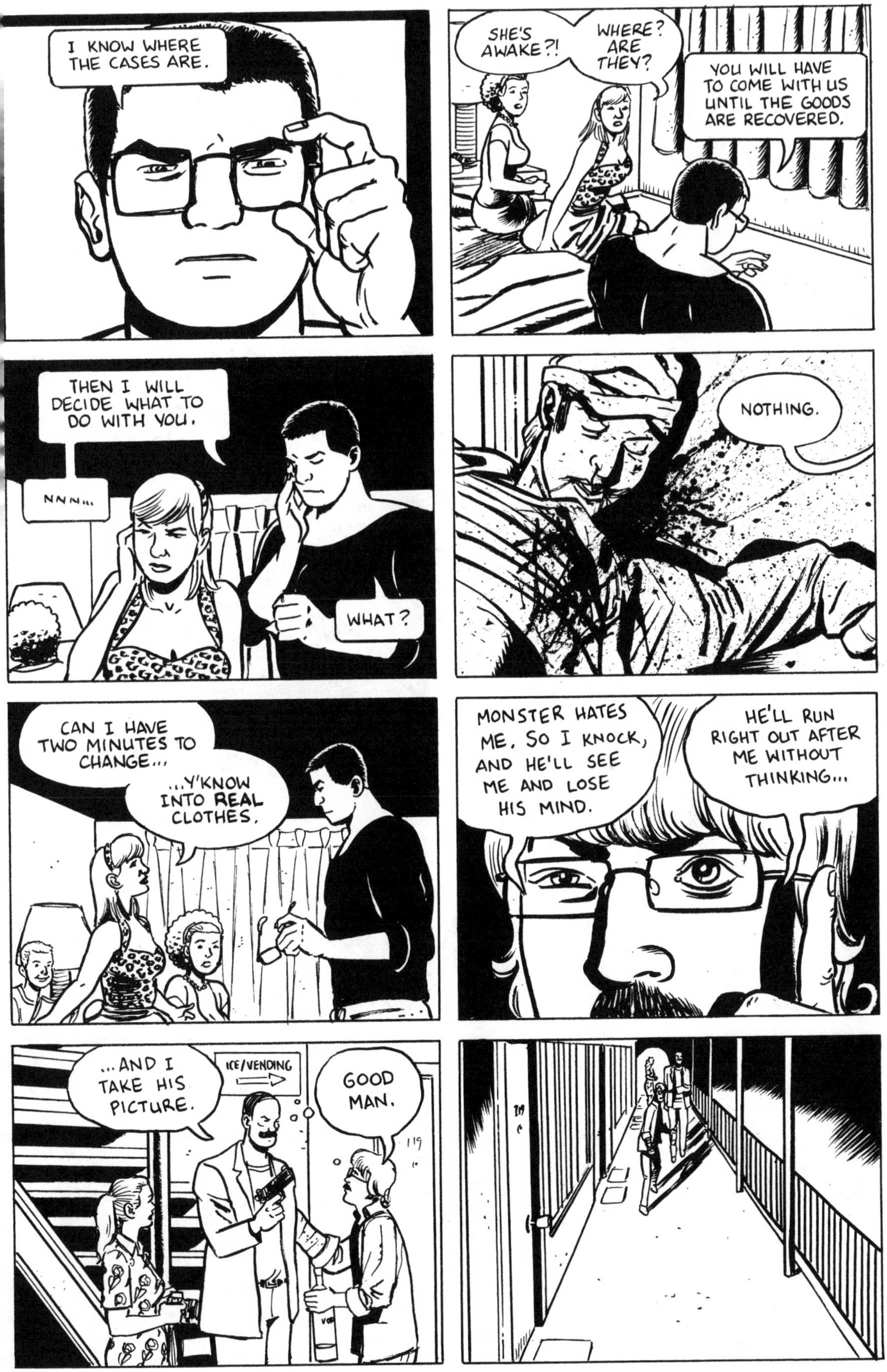
I KNOW WHERE THE CASES ARE.
SHE'S AWAKE?!
WHERE? ARE THEY?
YOU WILL HAVE TO COME WITH US UNTIL THE GOODS ARE RECOVERED.
THEN I WILL DECIDE WHAT TO DO WITH YOU.
NNN...
WHAT?
NOTHING.
CAN I HAVE TWO MINUTES TO CHANGE...
...Y'KNOW INTO **REAL** CLOTHES.
MONSTER HATES ME, SO I KNOCK, AND HE'LL SEE ME AND LOSE HIS MIND.
HE'LL RUN RIGHT OUT AFTER ME WITHOUT THINKING...
...AND I TAKE HIS PICTURE.
ICE/VENDING
GOOD MAN.

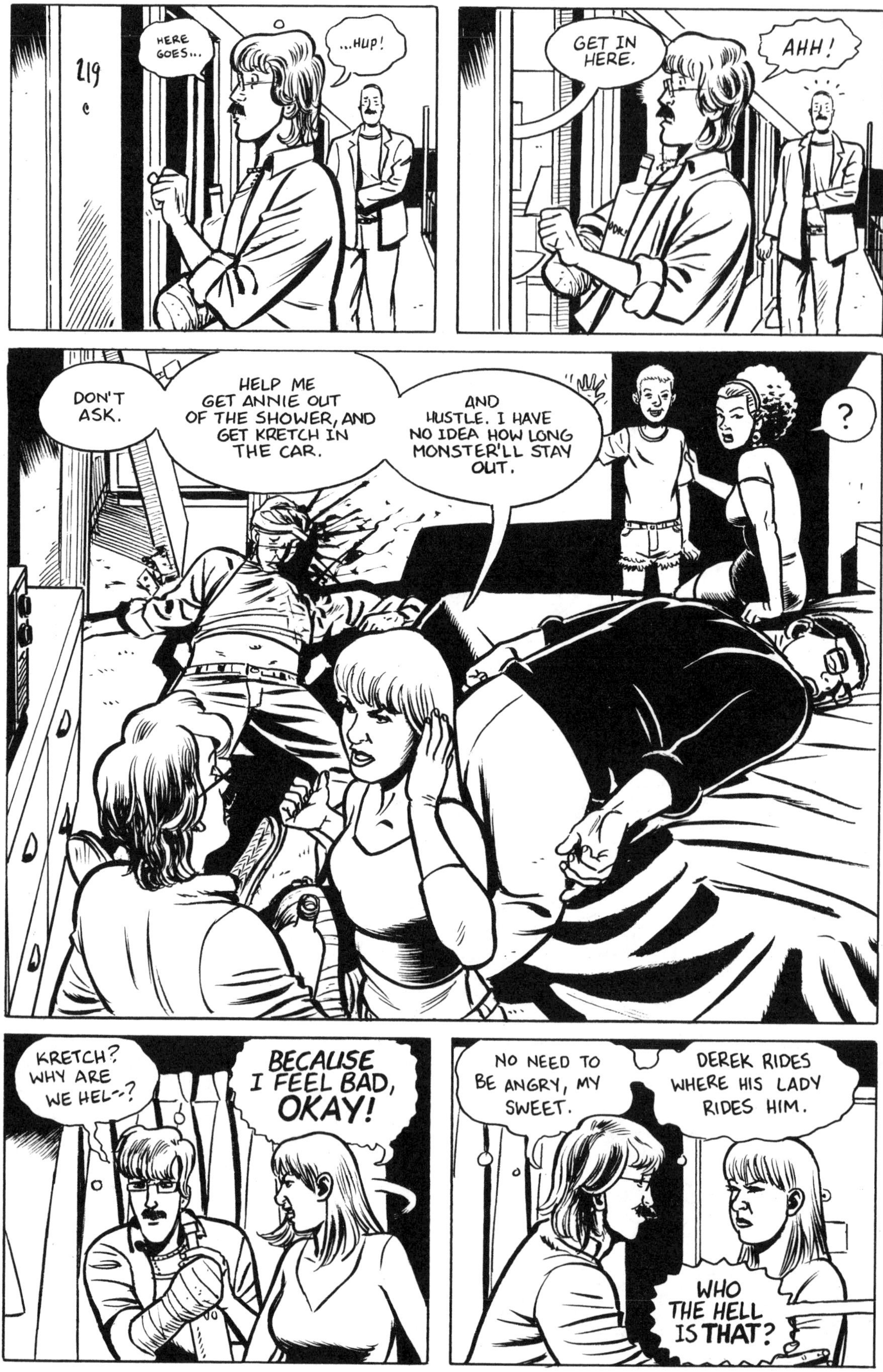
HERE GOES...
...HUP!
219
GET IN HERE.
AHH!
DON'T ASK.
HELP ME GET ANNIE OUT OF THE SHOWER, AND GET KRETCH IN THE CAR.
AND HUSTLE. I HAVE NO IDEA HOW LONG MONSTER'LL STAY OUT.
?
KRETCH? WHY ARE WE HEL--?
BECAUSE I FEEL BAD, OKAY!
NO NEED TO BE ANGRY, MY SWEET.
DEREK RIDES WHERE HIS LADY RIDES HIM.
WHO THE HELL IS THAT?

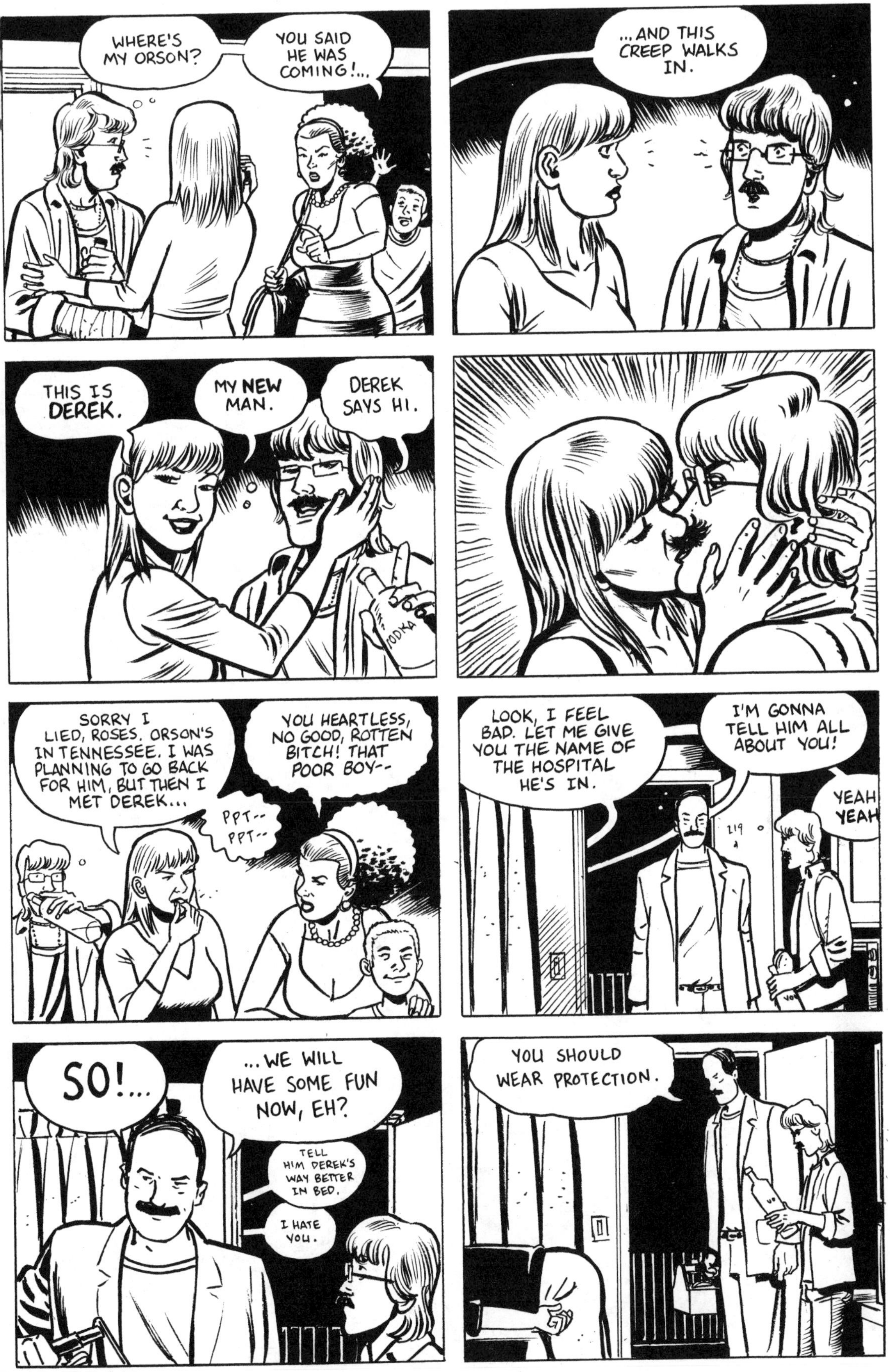
WHERE'S MY ORSON?
YOU SAID HE WAS COMING!...
...AND THIS CREEP WALKS IN.
THIS IS DEREK.
MY NEW MAN.
DEREK SAYS HI.
VODKA
SORRY I LIED, ROSES. ORSON'S IN TENNESSEE. I WAS PLANNING TO GO BACK FOR HIM, BUT THEN I MET DEREK...
PPT-- PPT--
YOU HEARTLESS, NO GOOD, ROTTEN BITCH! THAT POOR BOY--
LOOK, I FEEL BAD. LET ME GIVE YOU THE NAME OF THE HOSPITAL HE'S IN.
I'M GONNA TELL HIM ALL ABOUT YOU!
YEAH YEAH
SO!...
...WE WILL HAVE SOME FUN NOW, EH?
TELL HIM DEREK'S WAY BETTER IN BED.
I HATE YOU.
YOU SHOULD WEAR PROTECTION.

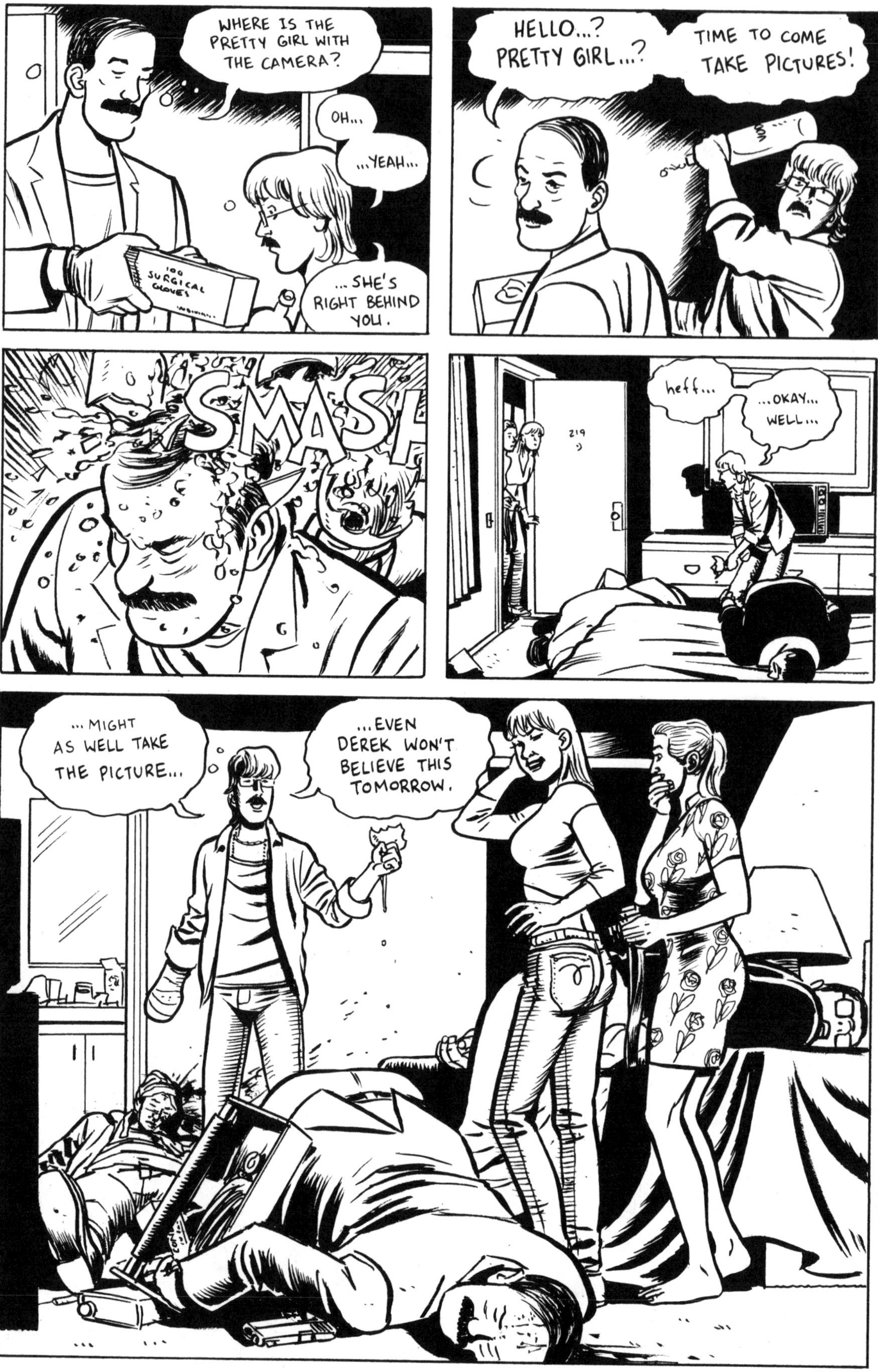
WHERE IS THE PRETTY GIRL WITH THE CAMERA?
100 SURGICAL GLOVES
OH...
...YEAH...
...SHE'S RIGHT BEHIND YOU.
HELLO...? PRETTY GIRL...?
TIME TO COME TAKE PICTURES!
SMASH
heff...
...OKAY... WELL...
...MIGHT AS WELL TAKE THE PICTURE...
...EVEN DEREK WON'T BELIEVE THIS TOMORROW.

THE END...

7

"ME, MYSELF, AND ME"

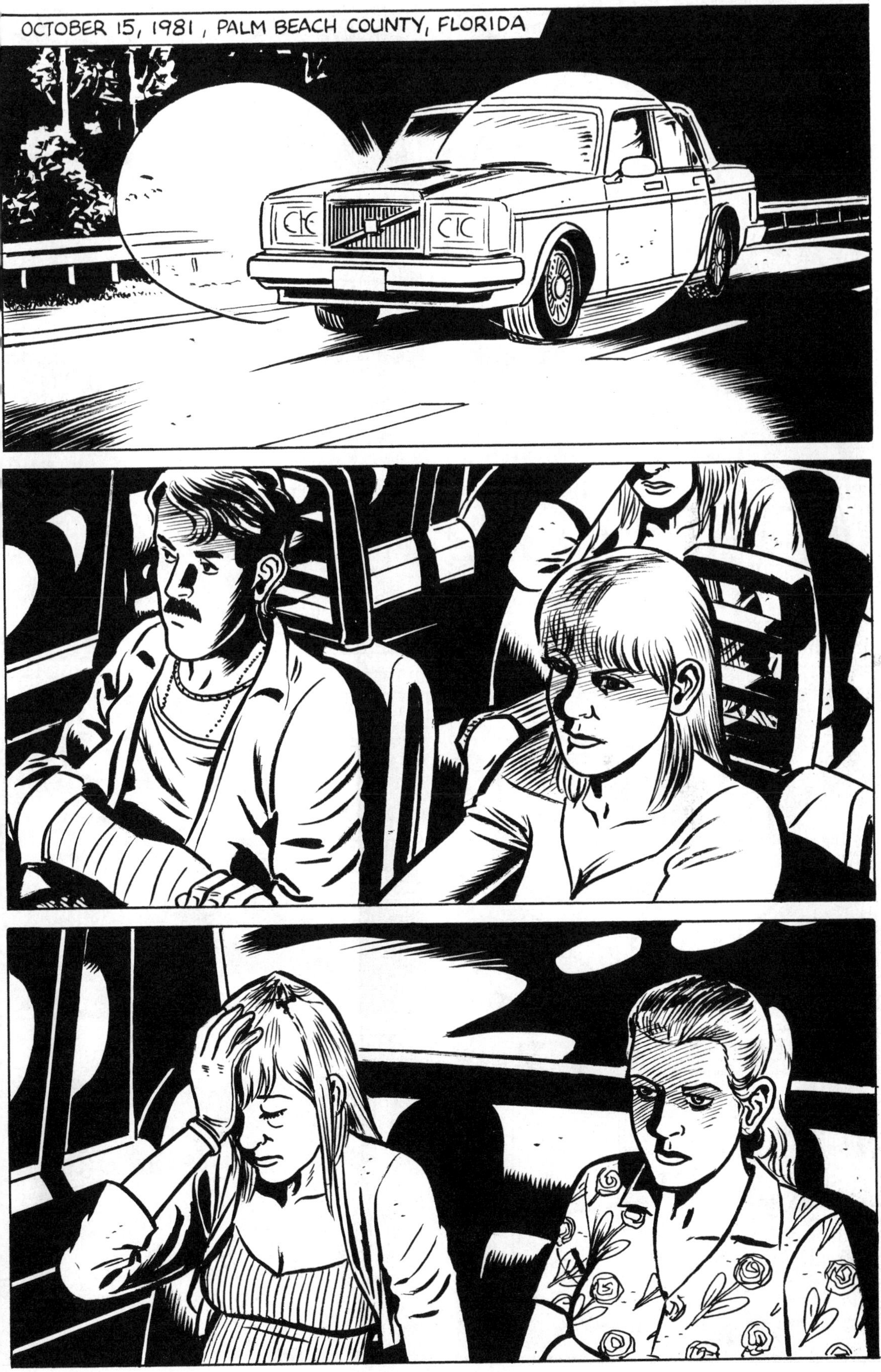
OCTOBER 15, 1981, PALM BEACH COUNTY, FLORIDA

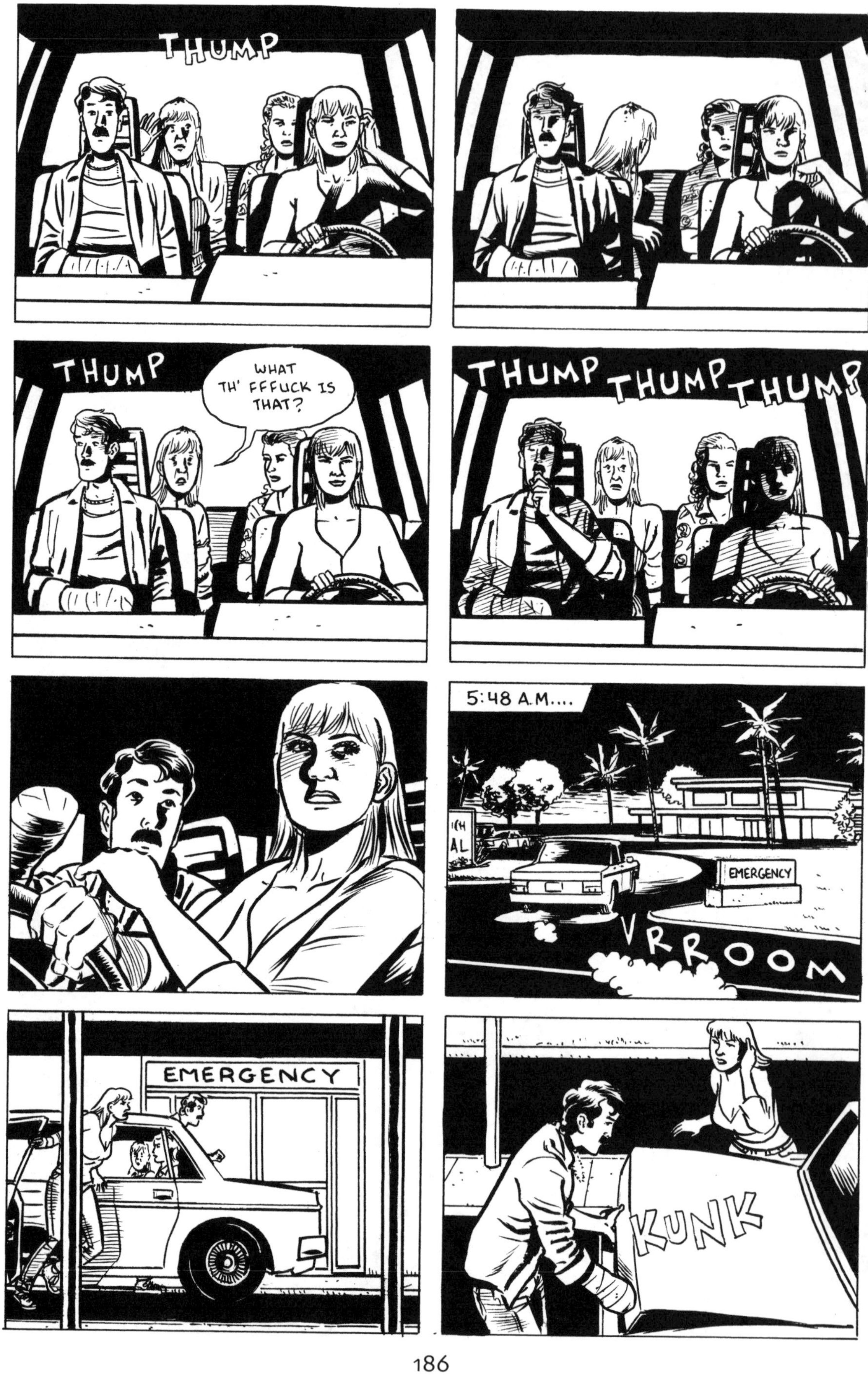
THUMP
THUMP
WHAT TH' FFFUCK IS THAT?
THUMP THUMP THUMP
5:48 A.M....
EMERGENCY
VRROOM
EMERGENCY
KUNK

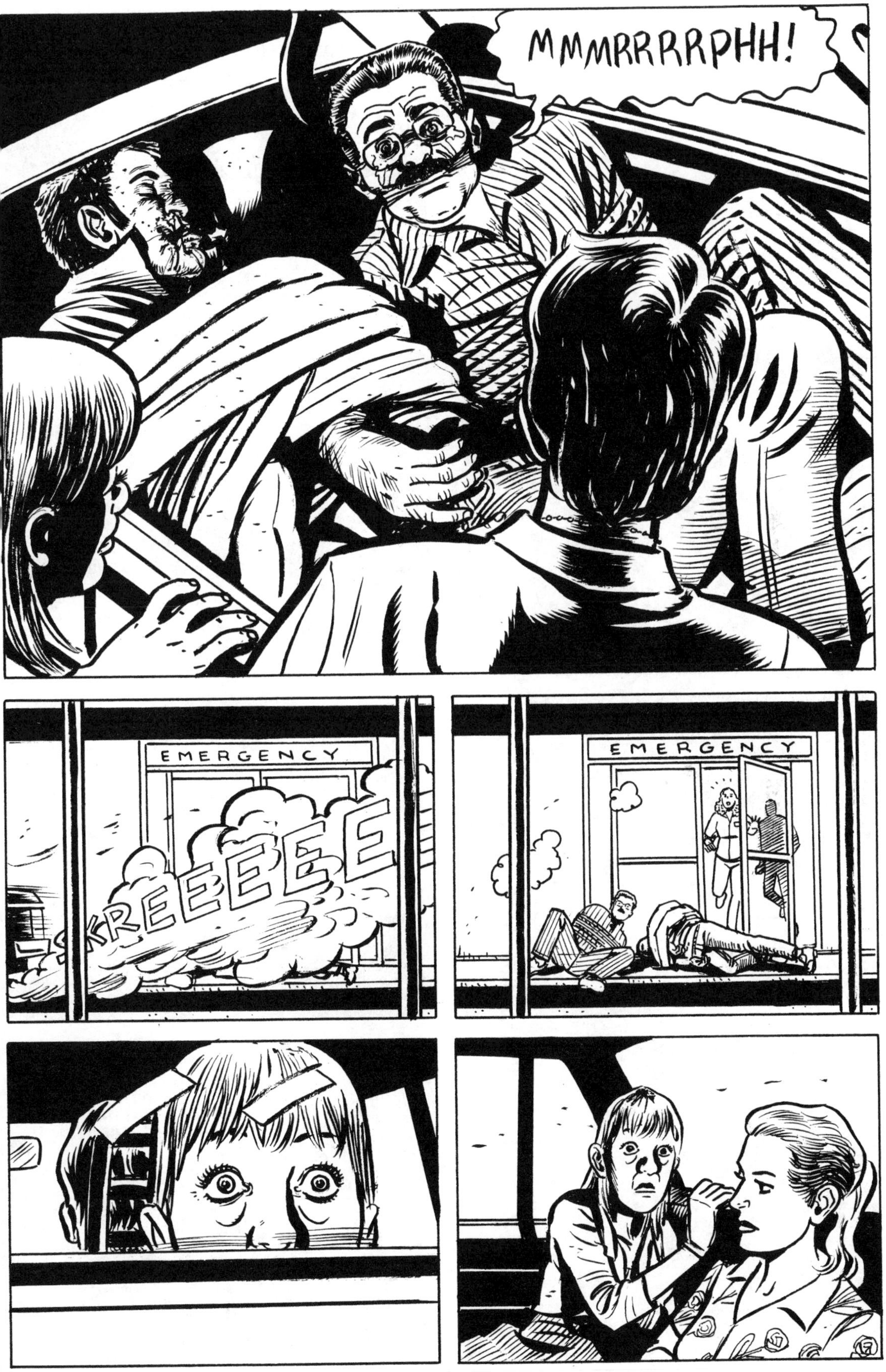
MMMRRRRPHH!
EMERGENCY
SKREEEEEE
EMERGENCY

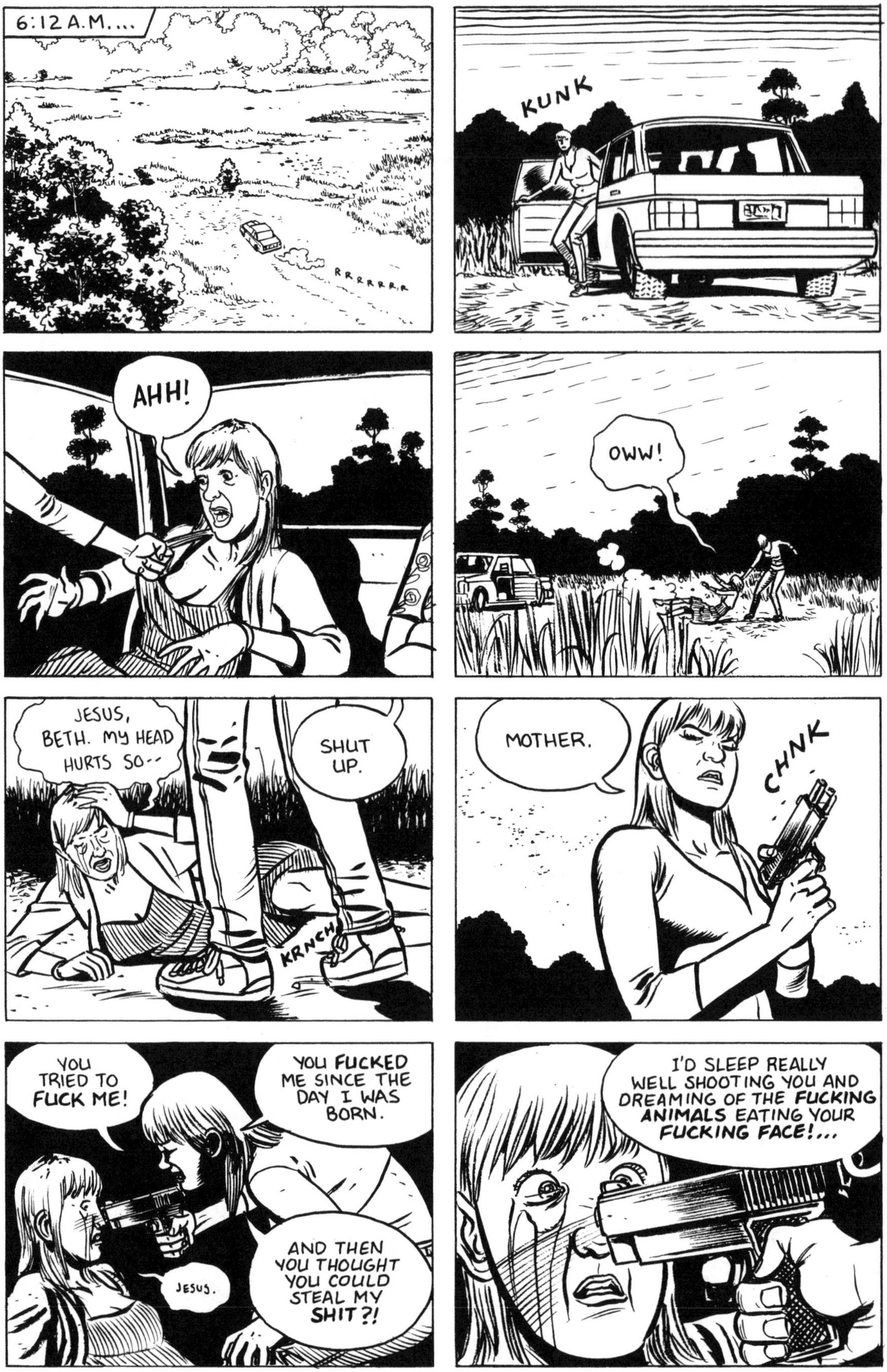
6:12 A.M....
RRRRRRR
KUNK
AHH!
OWW!
JESUS, BETH. MY HEAD HURTS SO--
SHUT UP.
KRNCH
MOTHER.
CHNK
YOU TRIED TO FUCK ME!
YOU FUCKED ME SINCE THE DAY I WAS BORN.
JESUS.
AND THEN YOU THOUGHT YOU COULD STEAL MY SHIT?!
I'D SLEEP REALLY WELL SHOOTING YOU AND DREAMING OF THE FUCKING ANIMALS EATING YOUR FUCKING FACE!...

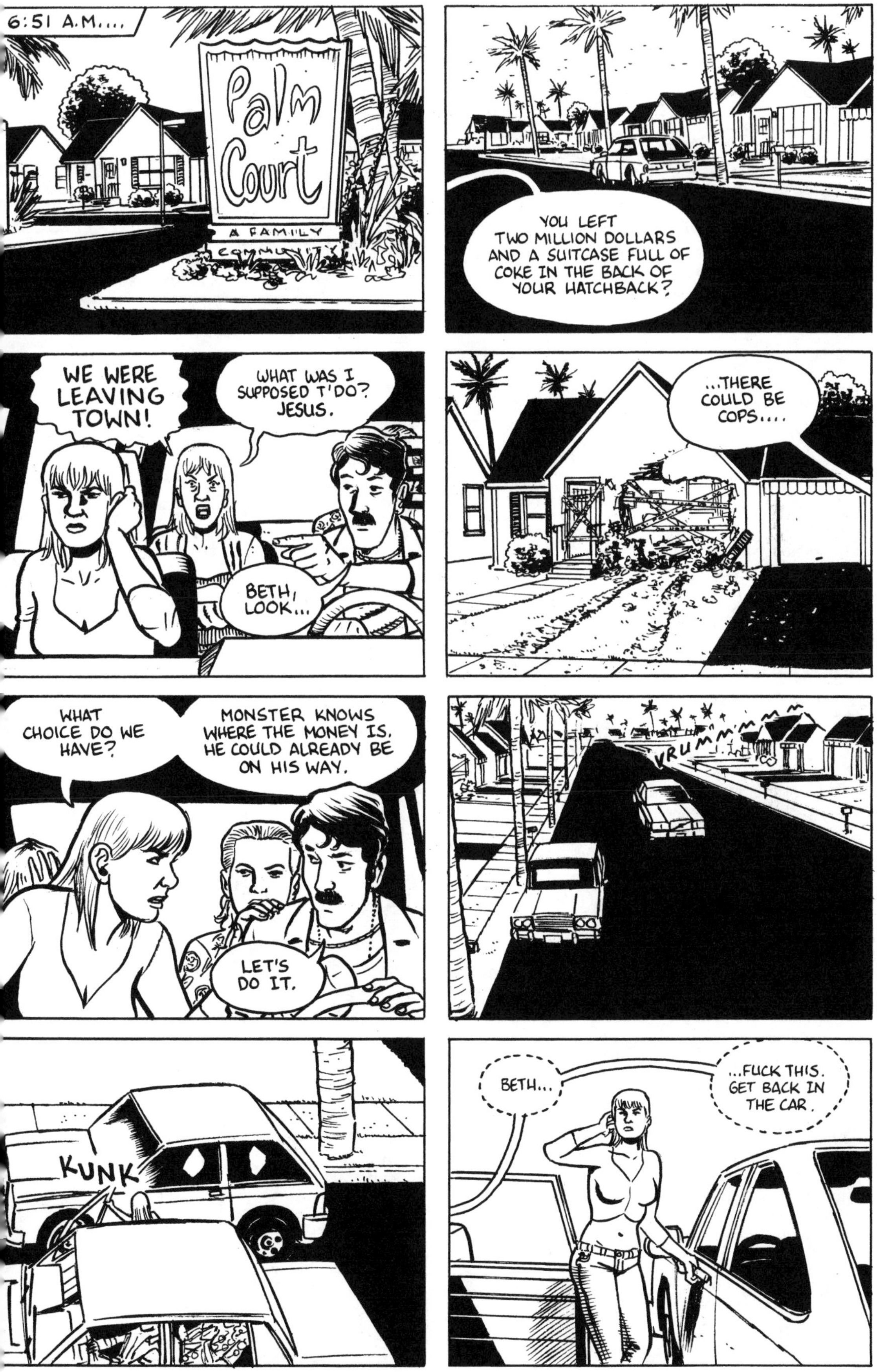
6:51 A.M....
Palm Court
A FAMILY COMMUNITY
YOU LEFT TWO MILLION DOLLARS AND A SUITCASE FULL OF COKE IN THE BACK OF YOUR HATCHBACK?
WE WERE LEAVING TOWN!
WHAT WAS I SUPPOSED T'DO? JESUS.
BETH, LOOK...
...THERE COULD BE COPS....
WHAT CHOICE DO WE HAVE?
MONSTER KNOWS WHERE THE MONEY IS. HE COULD ALREADY BE ON HIS WAY.
LET'S DO IT.
VRUMMMMMM
KUNK
BETH...
...FUCK THIS. GET BACK IN THE CAR.

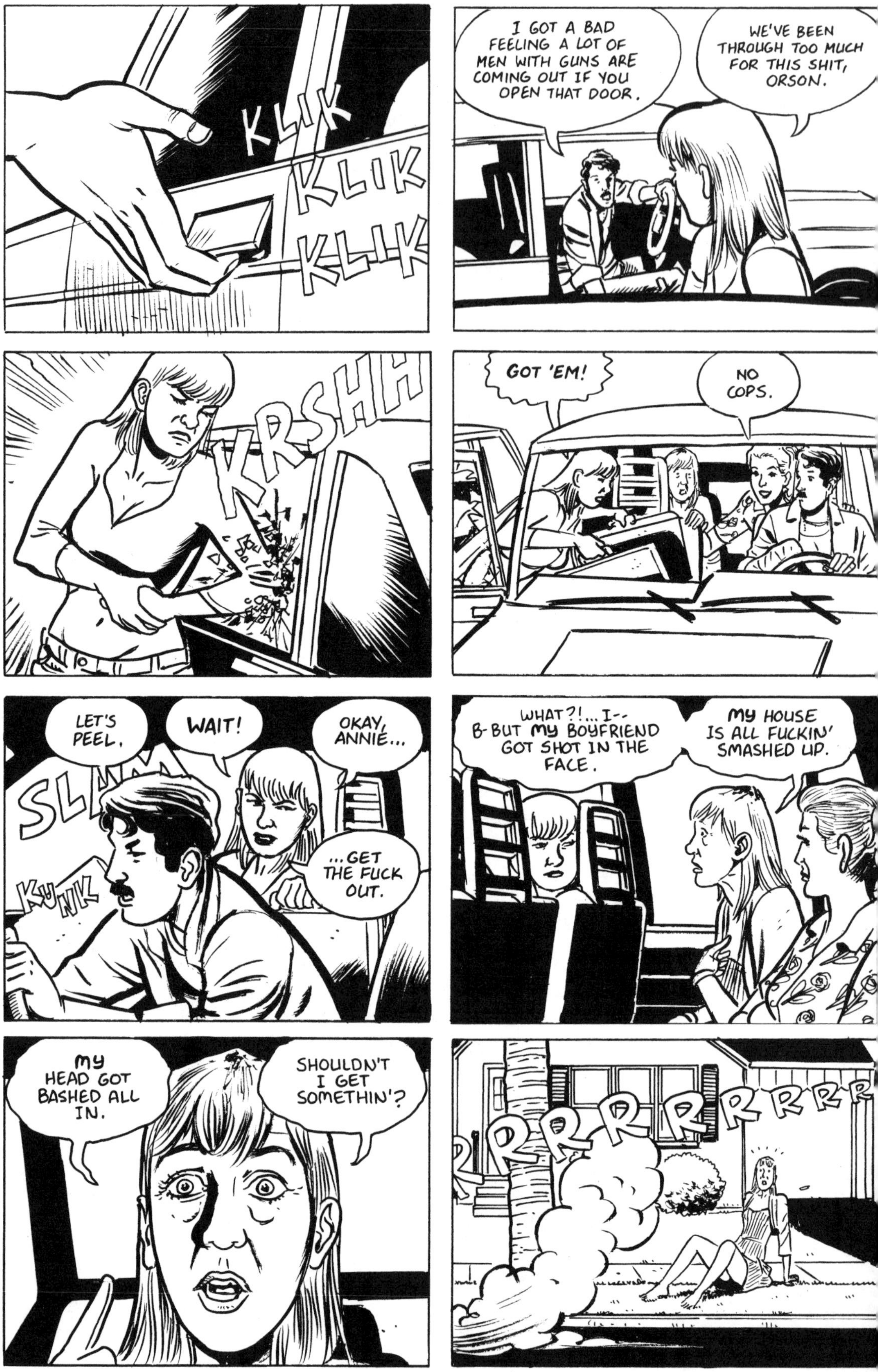
KLIK
KLIK
KLIK
I GOT A BAD FEELING A LOT OF MEN WITH GUNS ARE COMING OUT IF YOU OPEN THAT DOOR.
WE'VE BEEN THROUGH TOO MUCH FOR THIS SHIT, ORSON.
KRSHH
GOT 'EM!
NO COPS.
LET'S PEEL.
WAIT!
OKAY, ANNIE...
SLAM
KUNK
...GET THE FUCK OUT.
WHAT?!... I-- B-BUT MY BOYFRIEND GOT SHOT IN THE FACE.
MY HOUSE IS ALL FUCKIN' SMASHED UP.
MY HEAD GOT BASHED ALL IN.
SHOULDN'T I GET SOMETHIN'?
RRRRRRRRRRR

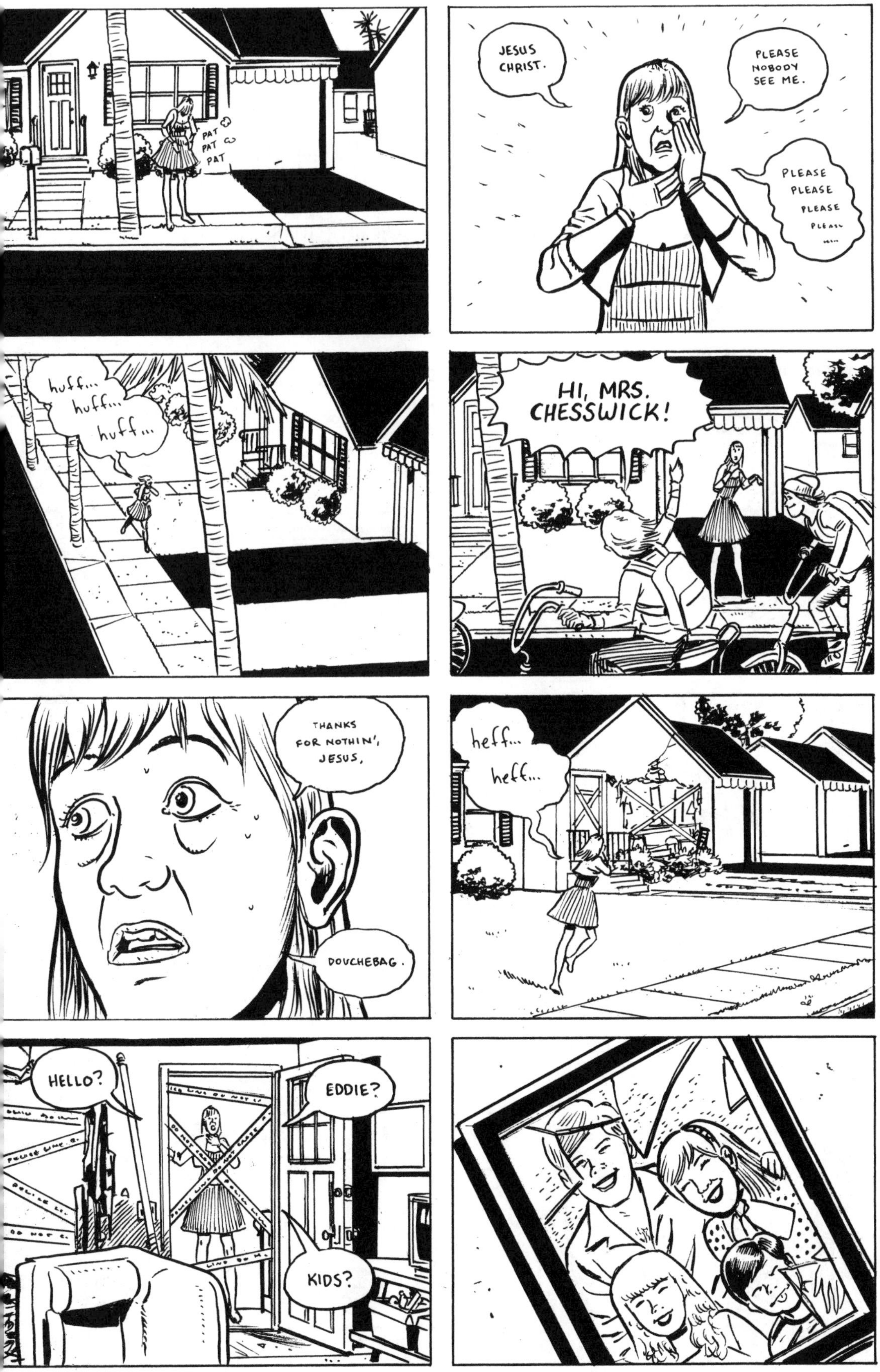
PAT
PAT
PAT
JESUS CHRIST.
PLEASE NOBODY SEE ME.
PLEASE
PLEASE
PLEASE
PLEASE
huff...
huff...
huff...
HI, MRS. CHESSWICK!
THANKS FOR NOTHIN', JESUS,
DOUCHEBAG.
heff...
heff...
HELLO?
EDDIE?
KIDS?

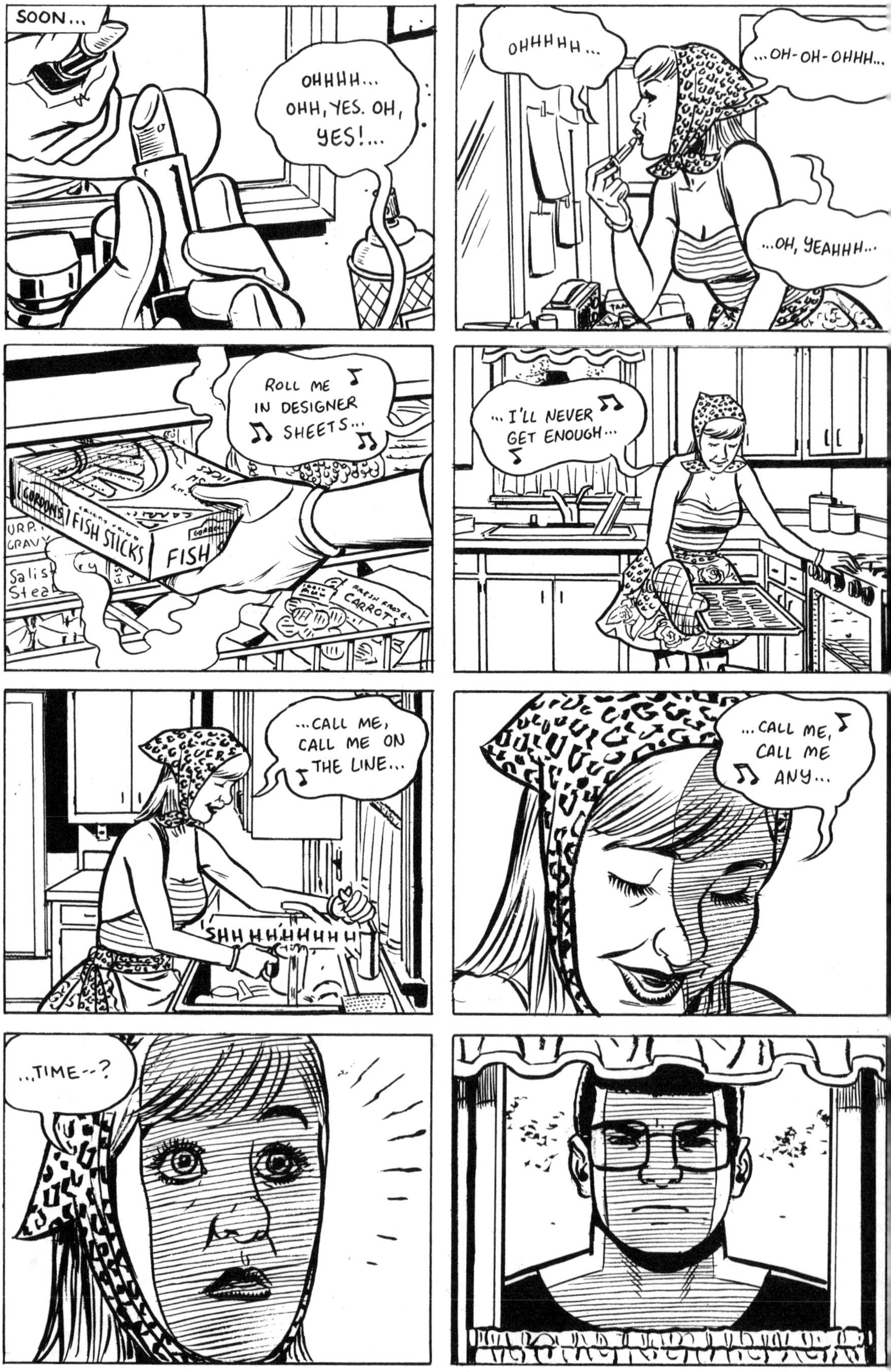
SOON...
OHHHH... OHH, YES. OH, YES!...
OHHHHH...
...OH-OH-OHHH...
...OH, YEAHHH...
ROLL ME IN DESIGNER SHEETS...
GORDON'S FISH STICKS
FISH
CARROTS
...I'LL NEVER GET ENOUGH...
...CALL ME, CALL ME ON THE LINE...
SHHHHHHHHHH
...CALL ME, CALL ME ANY...
...TIME--?

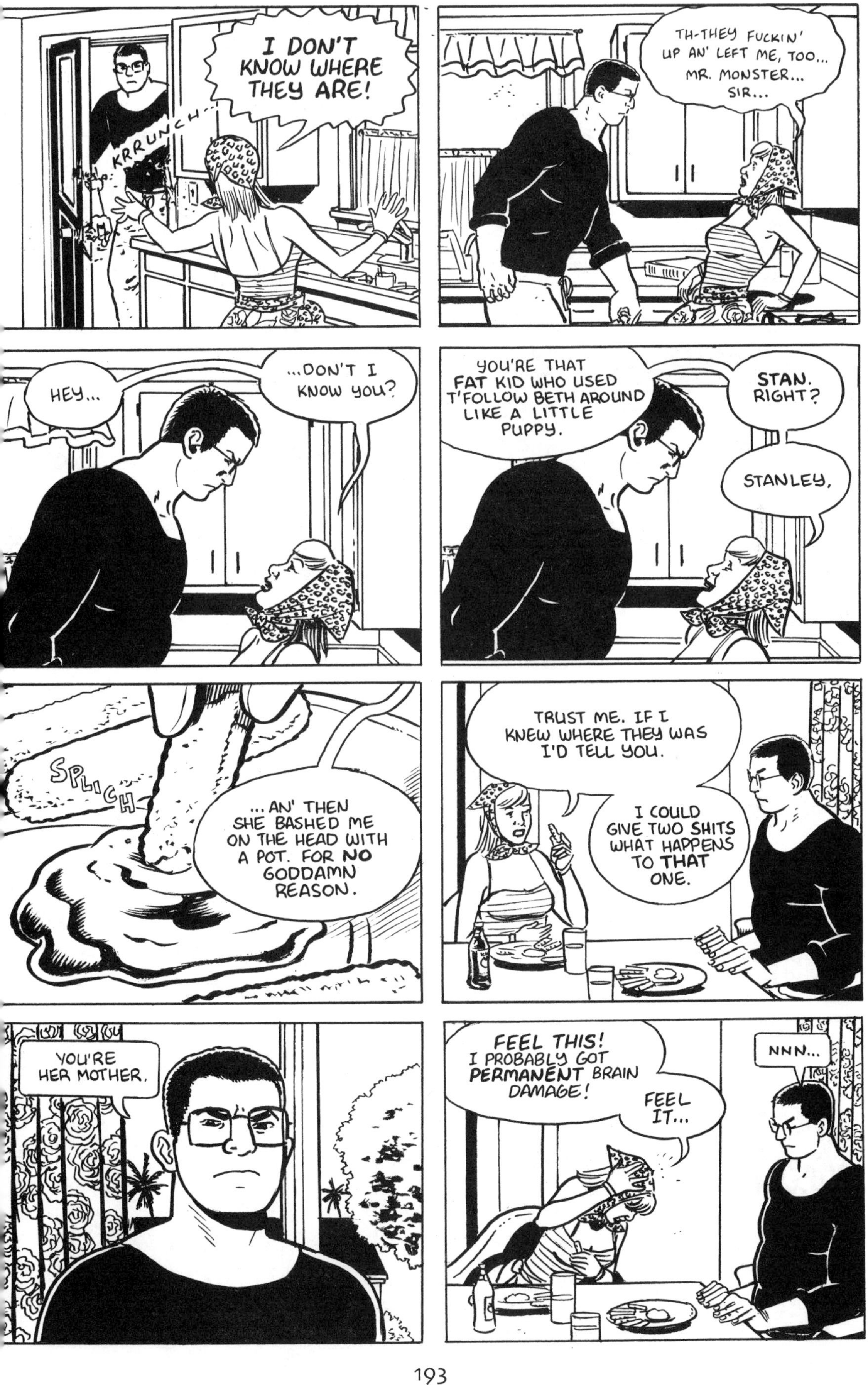
I DON'T KNOW WHERE THEY ARE!
KRRUNCH...
TH-THEY FUCKIN' UP AN' LEFT ME, TOO... MR. MONSTER... SIR...
HEY...
...DON'T I KNOW YOU?
YOU'RE THAT FAT KID WHO USED T'FOLLOW BETH AROUND LIKE A LITTLE PUPPY.
STAN. RIGHT?
STANLEY.
SPLICH
...AN' THEN SHE BASHED ME ON THE HEAD WITH A POT. FOR NO GODDAMN REASON.
TRUST ME. IF I KNEW WHERE THEY WAS I'D TELL YOU.
I COULD GIVE TWO SHITS WHAT HAPPENS TO THAT ONE.
YOU'RE HER MOTHER.
FEEL THIS! I PROBABLY GOT PERMANENT BRAIN DAMAGE!
FEEL IT...
NNN...

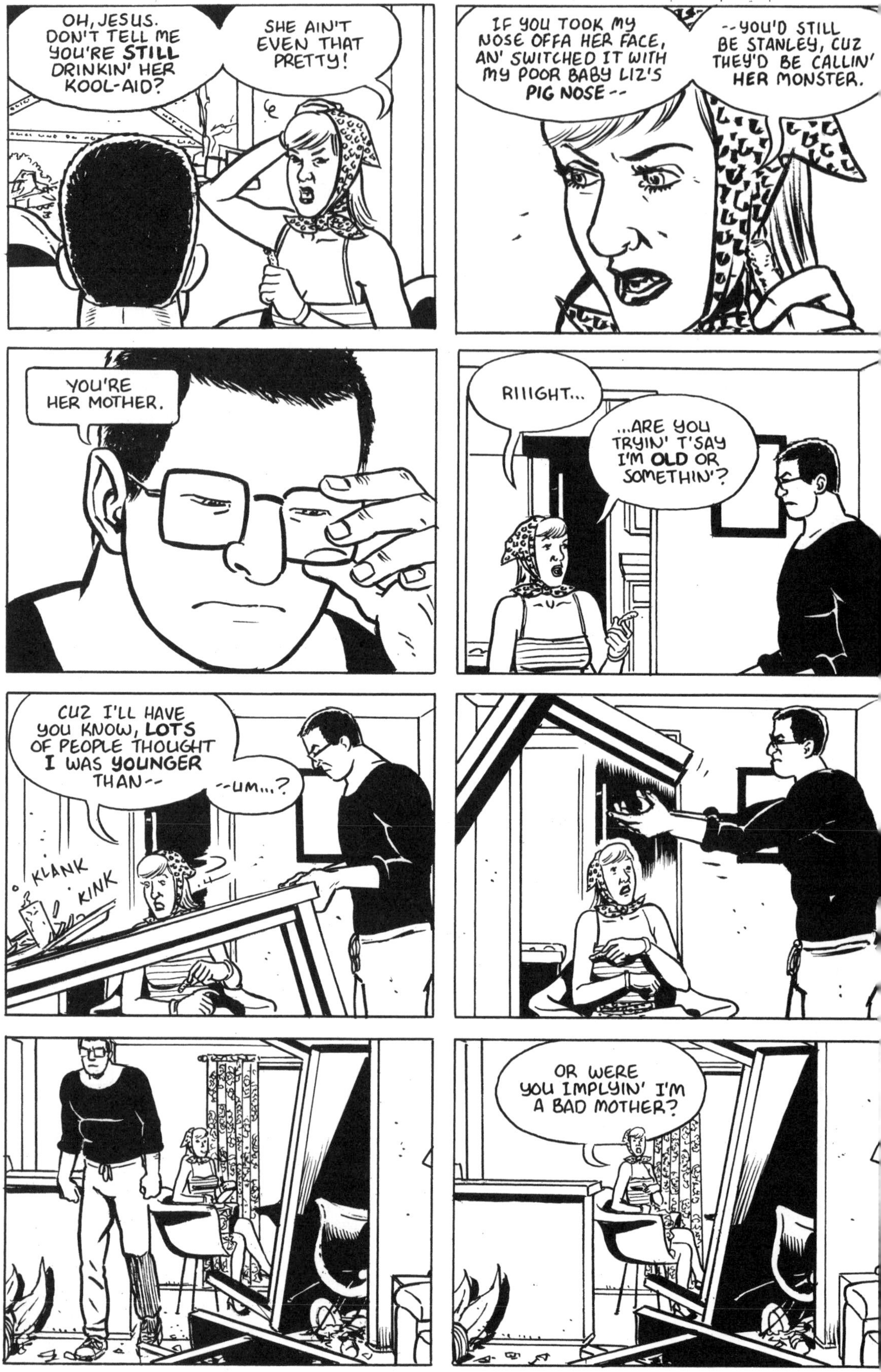
OH, JESUS. DON'T TELL ME YOU'RE STILL DRINKIN' HER KOOL-AID?
SHE AIN'T EVEN THAT PRETTY!
IF YOU TOOK MY NOSE OFFA HER FACE, AN' SWITCHED IT WITH MY POOR BABY LIZ'S PIG NOSE --
--YOU'D STILL BE STANLEY, CUZ THEY'D BE CALLIN' HER MONSTER.
YOU'RE HER MOTHER.
RIIIGHT...
...ARE YOU TRYIN' T'SAY I'M OLD OR SOMETHIN'?
CUZ I'LL HAVE YOU KNOW, LOTS OF PEOPLE THOUGHT I WAS YOUNGER THAN--
--UM...?
KLANK
KINK
OR WERE YOU IMPLYIN' I'M A BAD MOTHER?

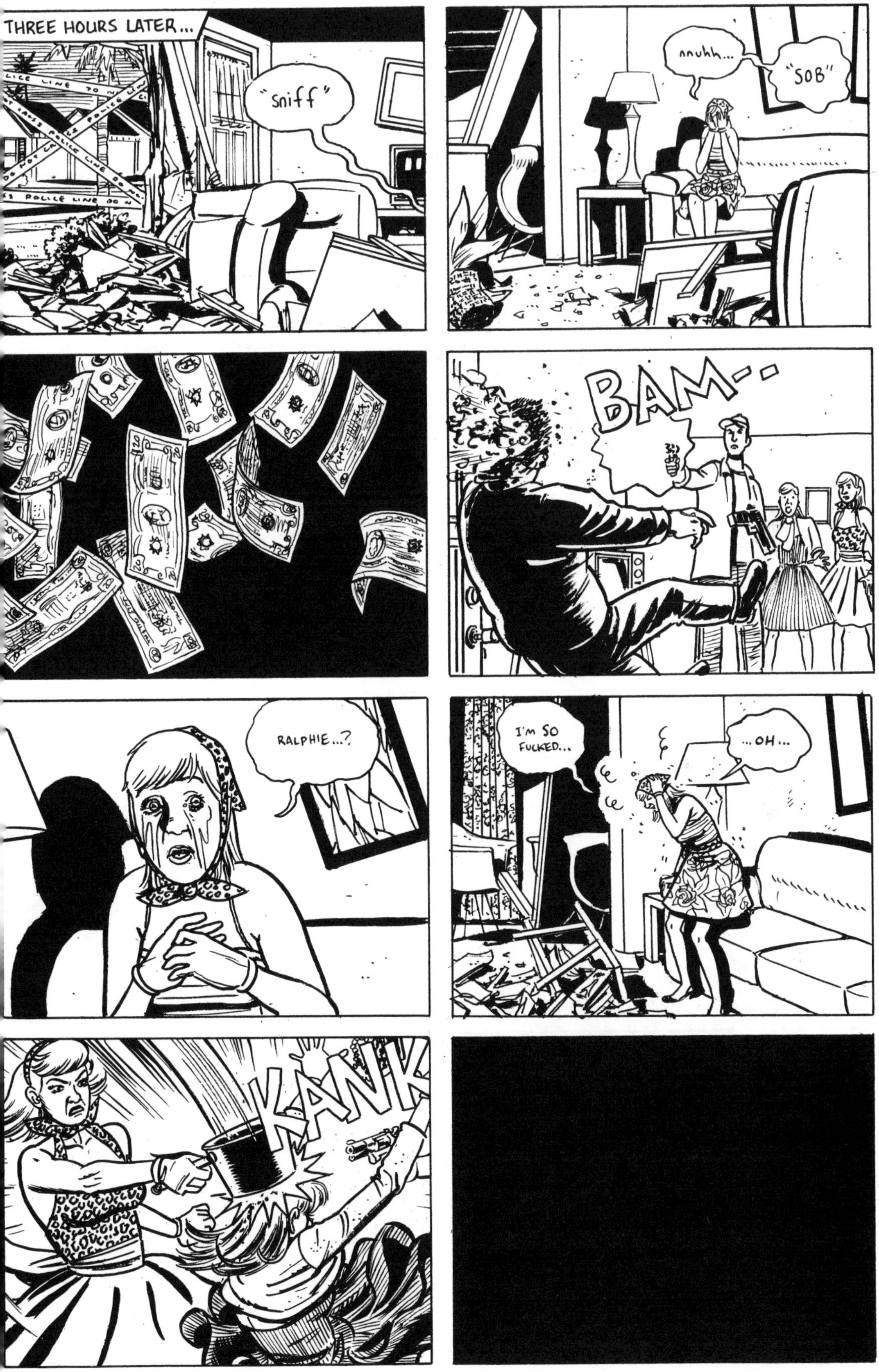
THREE HOURS LATER...
"sniff"
POLICE LINE DO NOT CROSS
nnuhh...
"SOB"
BAM--
RALPHIE...?
I'M SO FUCKED...
...OH...
KANK

CHRIST...

ERMI...

HONE

LTA

AMERICAN AIRLINES

UNITED

TUMP

RESTRICTIONS

TWO TICKETS.

T'PARIS.

ANNIE...

ANNIE!

HUH?!

EDDIE?

CHARLIE UP THE BLOCK CALLED AND SAID HE SAW YOU COME HOME.

HOLY FUCKIN' JESUS, EDDIE! I'M SO GLAD IT'S YOU!

ANNIE! LANGUAGE.

I-I'M GONNA HELP THE KIDS WITH THEIR HOMEWORK, AN' I'LL LET YOU STICK YOUR YOU-KNOW-WHAT THING IN ME...SOMETIMES, AN'...

...AN' I'LL EVEN LEARN HOW T'COOK NON-FROZEN FOOD.

I'M GONNA BE THE BEST WIFE AN' MOTHER IN THE WHOLE WORLD.

I SWEAR!

AWW...YOU ALREADY ARE, SWEETIE.

YOU ALREADY ARE.

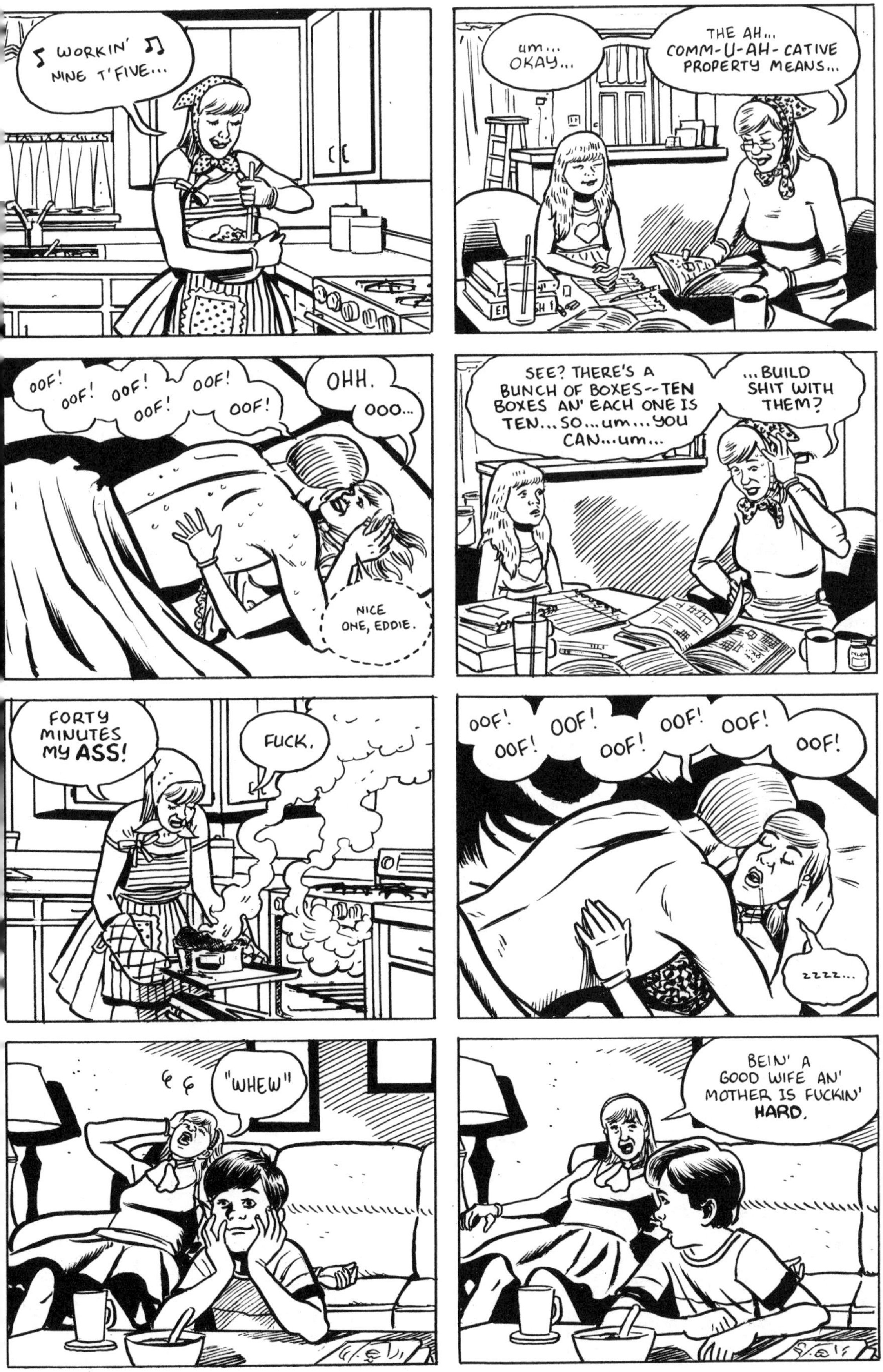

WORKIN' NINE T'FIVE...
um... OKAY...
THE AH... COMM-U-AH-CATIVE PROPERTY MEANS...
OOF! OOF! OOF! OOF! OOF! OOF!
OHH. OOO...
NICE ONE, EDDIE.
SEE? THERE'S A BUNCH OF BOXES--TEN BOXES AN' EACH ONE IS TEN... SO... um... YOU CAN... um...
...BUILD SHIT WITH THEM?
FORTY MINUTES MY ASS!
FUCK.
OOF! OOF! OOF! OOF! OOF! OOF! OOF!
zzzz...
"WHEW"
BEIN' A GOOD WIFE AN' MOTHER IS FUCKIN' HARD.

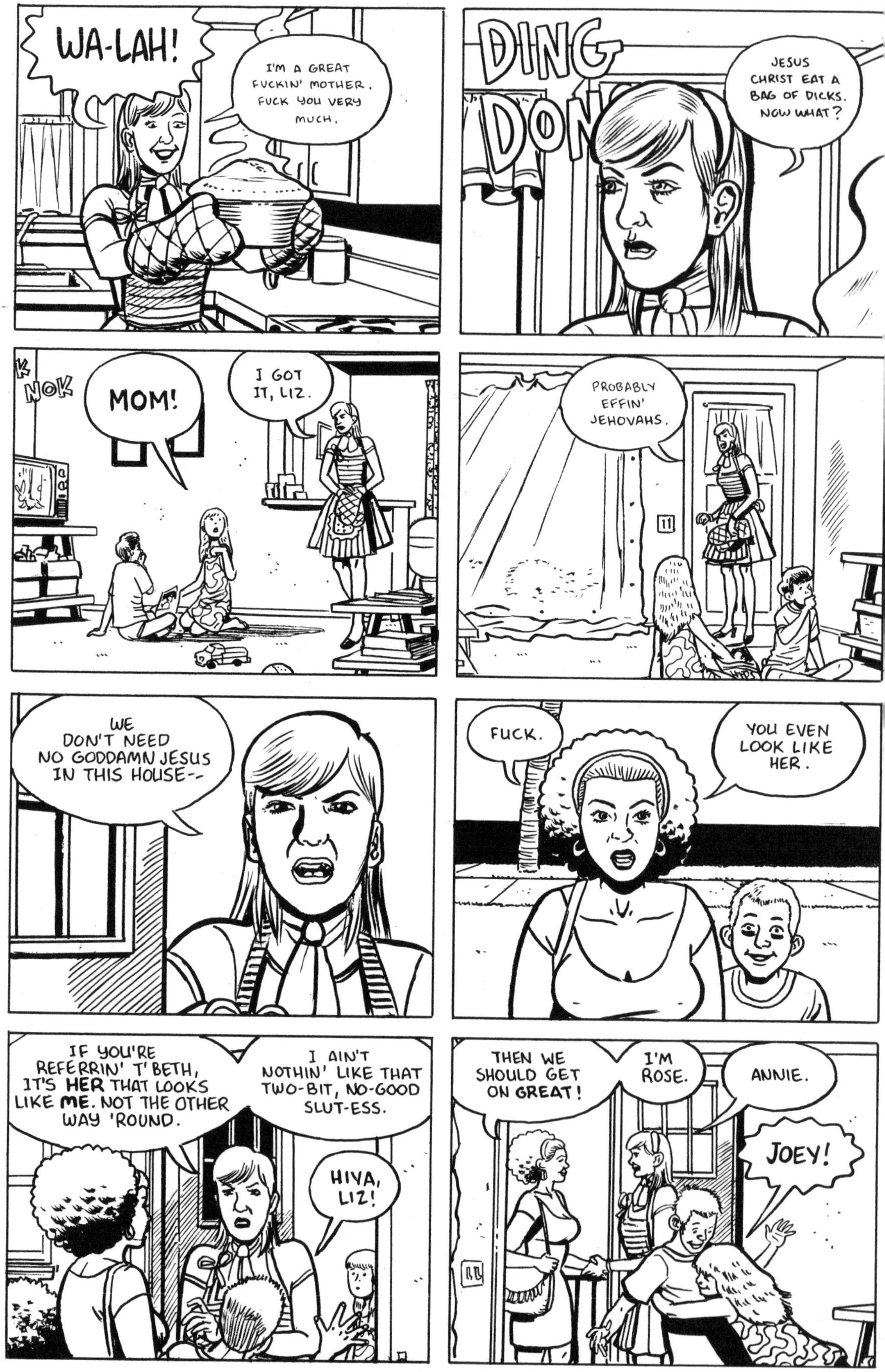
WA-LAH!
I'M A GREAT FUCKIN' MOTHER. FUCK YOU VERY MUCH.
DING DONG
JESUS CHRIST EAT A BAG OF DICKS. NOW WHAT?
K NOK
MOM!
I GOT IT, LIZ.
PROBABLY EFFIN' JEHOVAHS.
WE DON'T NEED NO GODDAMN JESUS IN THIS HOUSE--
FUCK.
YOU EVEN LOOK LIKE HER.
IF YOU'RE REFERRIN' T' BETH, IT'S HER THAT LOOKS LIKE ME. NOT THE OTHER WAY 'ROUND.
I AIN'T NOTHIN' LIKE THAT TWO-BIT, NO-GOOD SLUT-ESS.
HIYA, LIZ!
THEN WE SHOULD GET ON GREAT!
I'M ROSE.
ANNIE.
JOEY!

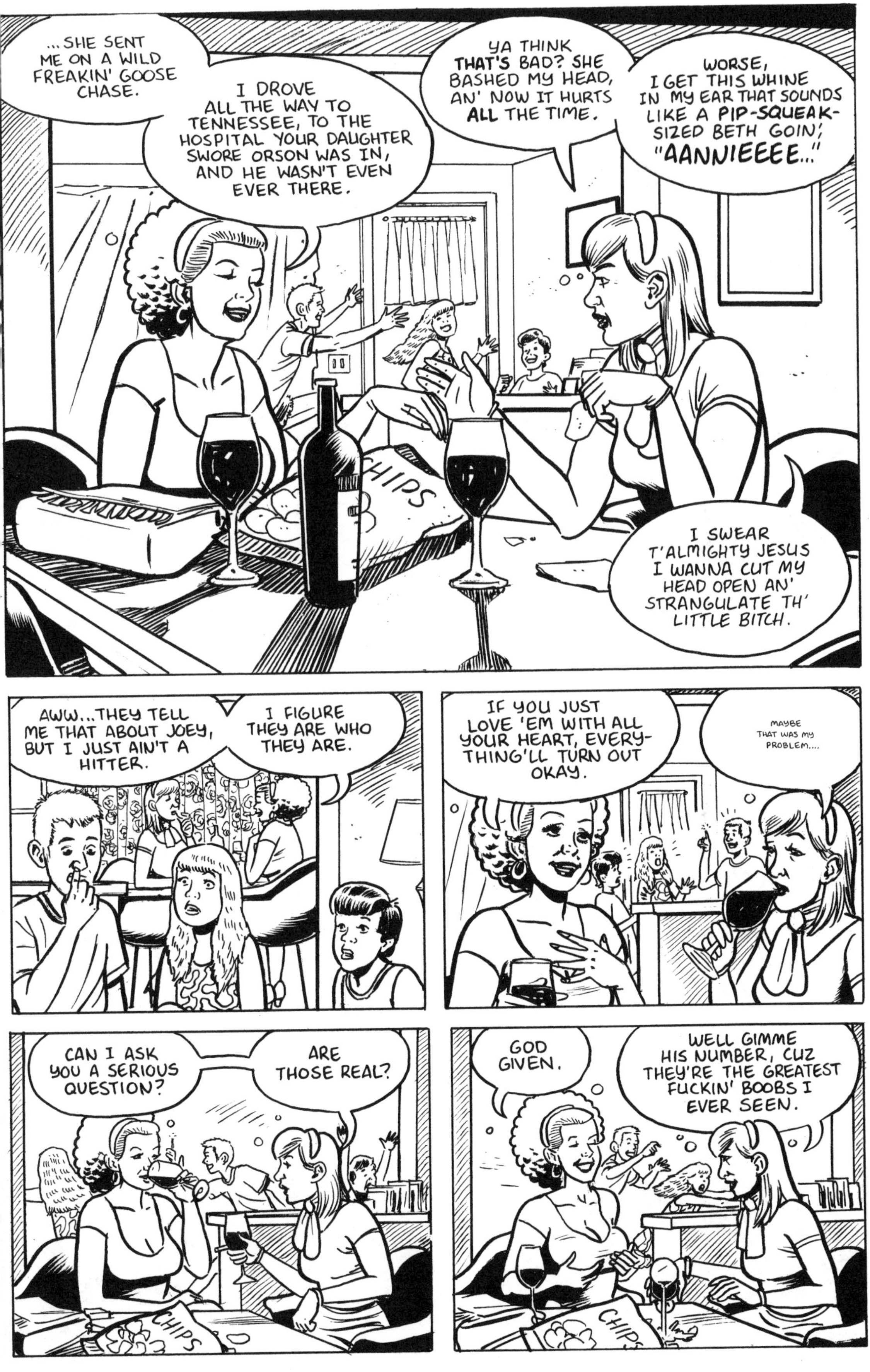

...SHE SENT ME ON A WILD FREAKIN' GOOSE CHASE.
I DROVE ALL THE WAY TO TENNESSEE, TO THE HOSPITAL YOUR DAUGHTER SWORE ORSON WAS IN, AND HE WASN'T EVEN EVER THERE.
YA THINK **THAT'S** BAD? SHE BASHED MY HEAD, AN' NOW IT HURTS **ALL** THE TIME.
WORSE, I GET THIS WHINE IN MY EAR THAT SOUNDS LIKE A **PIP-SQUEAK**-SIZED BETH GOIN', **"AANNIEEEE..."**
I SWEAR T'ALMIGHTY JESUS I WANNA CUT MY HEAD OPEN AN' STRANGULATE TH' LITTLE BITCH.
CHIPS
AWW...THEY TELL ME THAT ABOUT JOEY, BUT I JUST AIN'T A HITTER.
I FIGURE THEY ARE WHO THEY ARE.
IF YOU JUST LOVE 'EM WITH ALL YOUR HEART, EVERYTHING'LL TURN OUT OKAY.
MAYBE THAT WAS MY PROBLEM....
CAN I ASK YOU A SERIOUS QUESTION?
ARE THOSE REAL?
CHIPS
GOD GIVEN.
WELL GIMME HIS NUMBER, CUZ THEY'RE THE GREATEST FUCKIN' BOOBS I EVER SEEN.
CHIPS

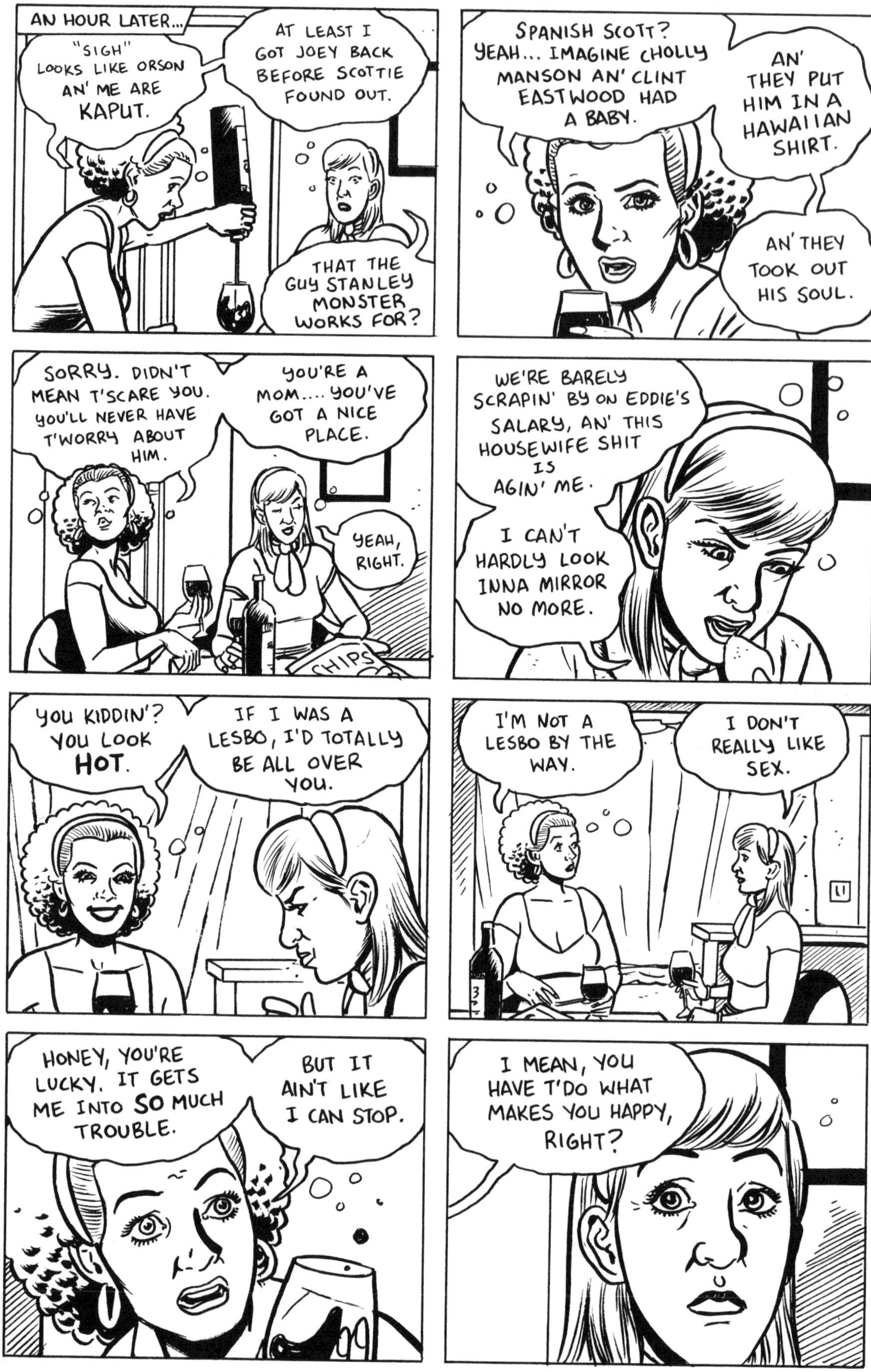

AN HOUR LATER...
"SIGH" LOOKS LIKE ORSON AN' ME ARE KAPUT.
AT LEAST I GOT JOEY BACK BEFORE SCOTTIE FOUND OUT.
THAT THE GUY STANLEY MONSTER WORKS FOR?
SPANISH SCOTT? YEAH... IMAGINE CHOLLY MANSON AN' CLINT EASTWOOD HAD A BABY.
AN' THEY PUT HIM IN A HAWAIIAN SHIRT.
AN' THEY TOOK OUT HIS SOUL.
SORRY. DIDN'T MEAN T'SCARE YOU. YOU'LL NEVER HAVE T'WORRY ABOUT HIM.
YOU'RE A MOM.... YOU'VE GOT A NICE PLACE.
YEAH, RIGHT.
CHIPS
WE'RE BARELY SCRAPIN' BY ON EDDIE'S SALARY, AN' THIS HOUSEWIFE SHIT IS AGIN' ME.
I CAN'T HARDLY LOOK INNA MIRROR NO MORE.
YOU KIDDIN'? YOU LOOK HOT.
IF I WAS A LESBO, I'D TOTALLY BE ALL OVER YOU.
I'M NOT A LESBO BY THE WAY.
I DON'T REALLY LIKE SEX.
HONEY, YOU'RE LUCKY. IT GETS ME INTO SO MUCH TROUBLE.
BUT IT AIN'T LIKE I CAN STOP.
I MEAN, YOU HAVE T'DO WHAT MAKES YOU HAPPY, RIGHT?

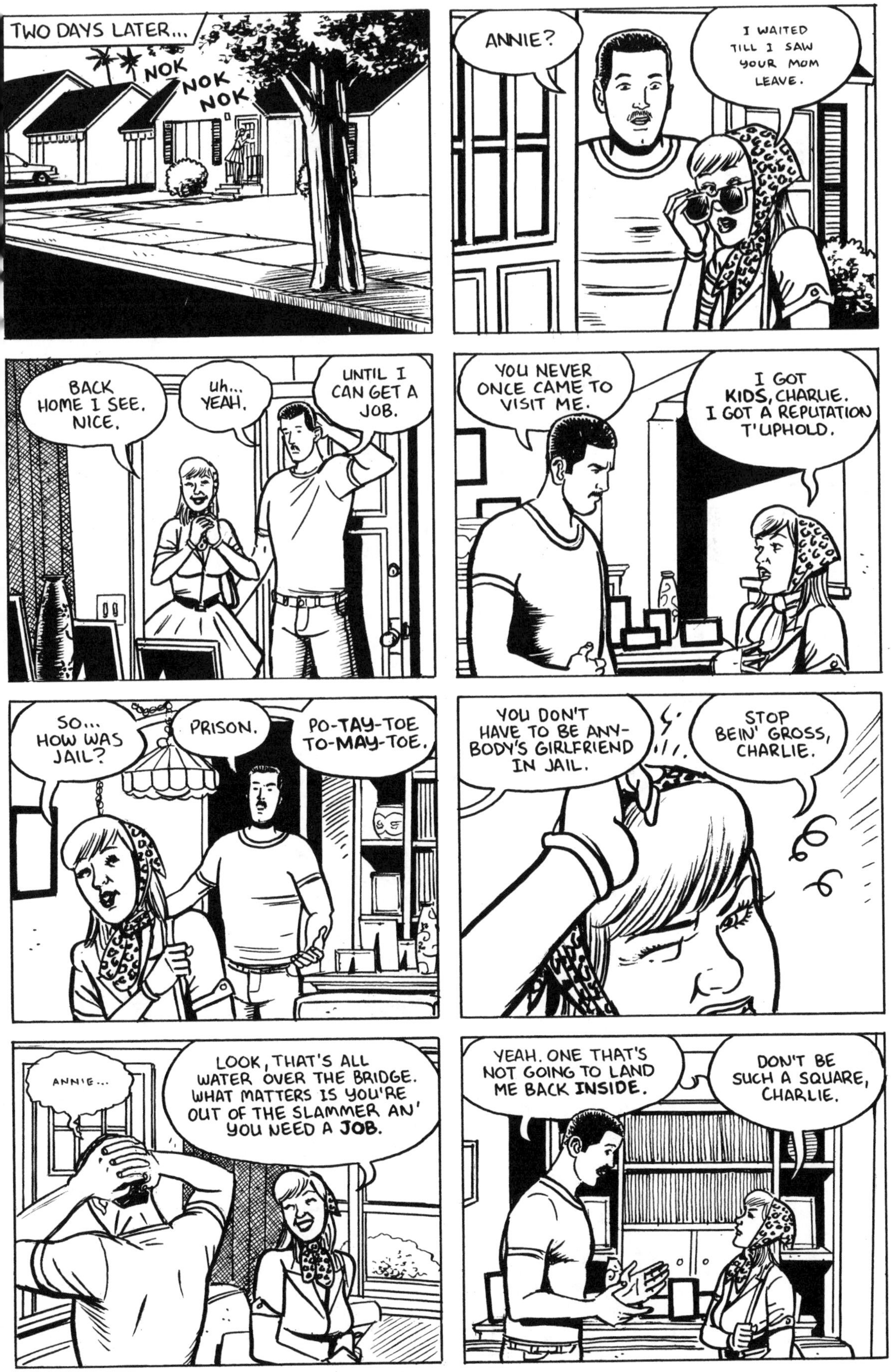
TWO DAYS LATER...
NOK
NOK
NOK
ANNIE?
I WAITED TILL I SAW YOUR MOM LEAVE.
BACK HOME I SEE. NICE.
uh... YEAH.
UNTIL I CAN GET A JOB.
YOU NEVER ONCE CAME TO VISIT ME.
I GOT **KIDS**, CHARLIE. I GOT A REPUTATION T'UPHOLD.
SO... HOW WAS JAIL?
PRISON.
PO-**TAY**-TOE TO-**MAY**-TOE.
YOU DON'T HAVE TO BE ANYBODY'S GIRLFRIEND IN JAIL.
STOP BEIN' GROSS, CHARLIE.
ANNIE...
LOOK, THAT'S ALL WATER OVER THE BRIDGE. WHAT MATTERS IS YOU'RE OUT OF THE SLAMMER AN' YOU NEED A **JOB**.
YEAH. ONE THAT'S NOT GOING TO LAND ME BACK **INSIDE**.
DON'T BE SUCH A SQUARE, CHARLIE.

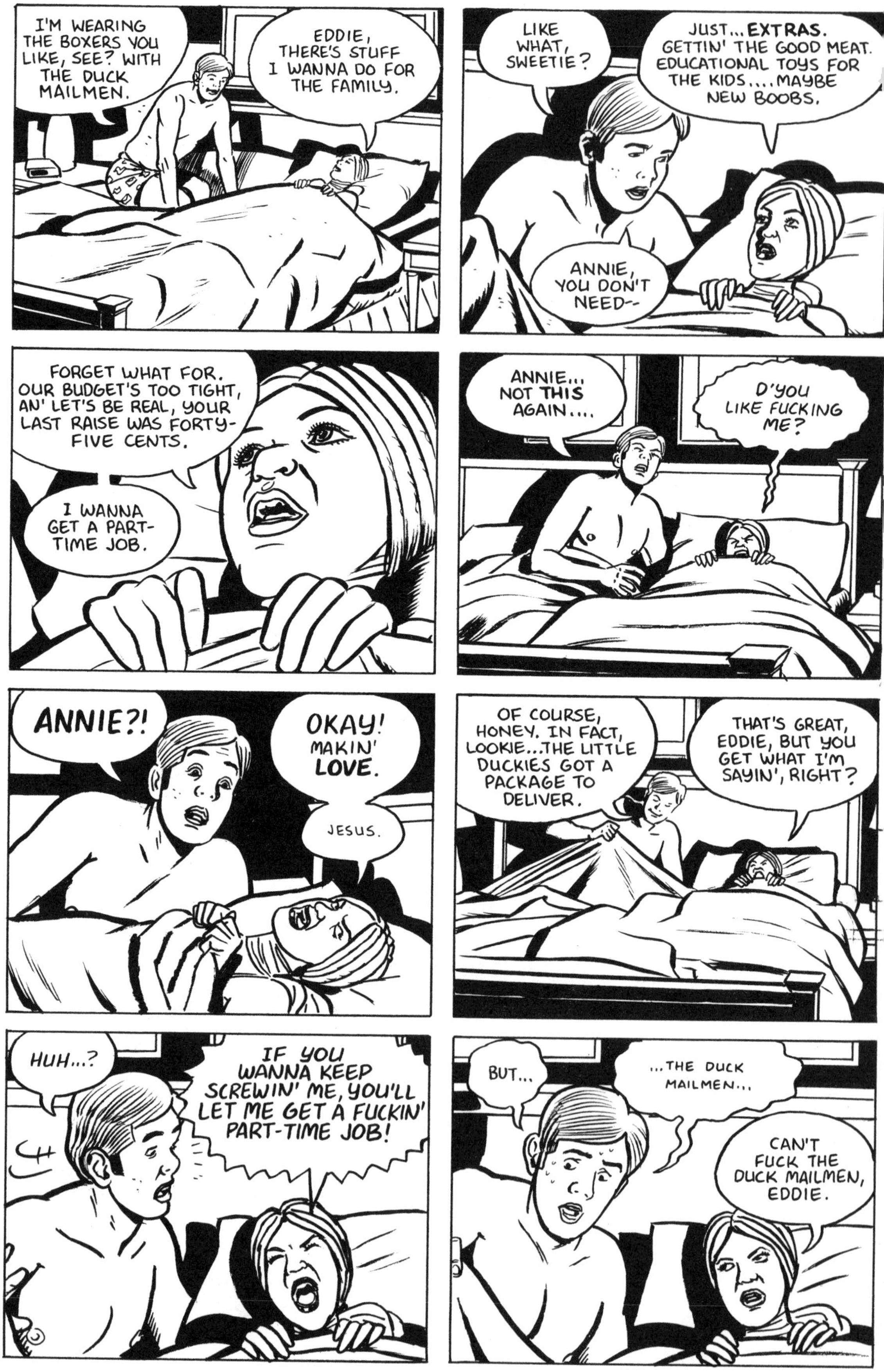
I'M WEARING THE BOXERS YOU LIKE, SEE? WITH THE DUCK MAILMEN.
EDDIE, THERE'S STUFF I WANNA DO FOR THE FAMILY.
LIKE WHAT, SWEETIE?
JUST... EXTRAS. GETTIN' THE GOOD MEAT. EDUCATIONAL TOYS FOR THE KIDS.... MAYBE NEW BOOBS.
ANNIE, YOU DON'T NEED--
FORGET WHAT FOR. OUR BUDGET'S TOO TIGHT, AN' LET'S BE REAL, YOUR LAST RAISE WAS FORTY-FIVE CENTS.
I WANNA GET A PART-TIME JOB.
ANNIE... NOT THIS AGAIN....
D'YOU LIKE FUCKING ME?
ANNIE?!
OKAY! MAKIN' LOVE.
JESUS.
OF COURSE, HONEY. IN FACT, LOOKIE... THE LITTLE DUCKIES GOT A PACKAGE TO DELIVER.
THAT'S GREAT, EDDIE, BUT YOU GET WHAT I'M SAYIN', RIGHT?
HUH...?
IF YOU WANNA KEEP SCREWIN' ME, YOU'LL LET ME GET A FUCKIN' PART-TIME JOB!
BUT...
...THE DUCK MAILMEN...
CAN'T FUCK THE DUCK MAILMEN, EDDIE.

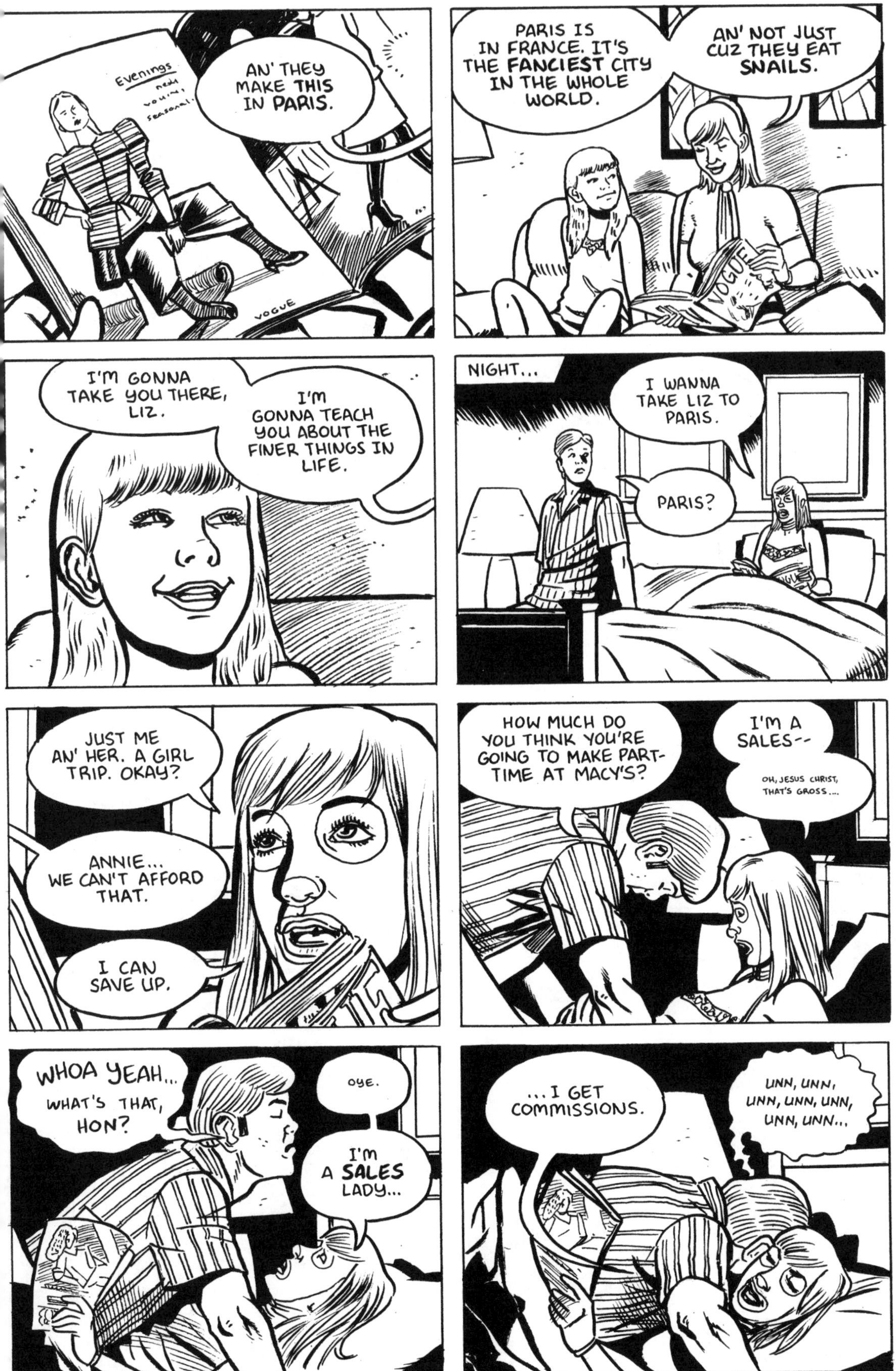
Evenings
VOGUE
AN' THEY MAKE THIS IN PARIS.
PARIS IS IN FRANCE. IT'S THE FANCIEST CITY IN THE WHOLE WORLD.
AN' NOT JUST CUZ THEY EAT SNAILS.
VOGUE
I'M GONNA TAKE YOU THERE, LIZ.
I'M GONNA TEACH YOU ABOUT THE FINER THINGS IN LIFE.
NIGHT...
I WANNA TAKE LIZ TO PARIS.
PARIS?
JUST ME AN' HER. A GIRL TRIP. OKAY?
ANNIE... WE CAN'T AFFORD THAT.
I CAN SAVE UP.
HOW MUCH DO YOU THINK YOU'RE GOING TO MAKE PART-TIME AT MACY'S?
I'M A SALES--
OH, JESUS CHRIST, THAT'S GROSS....
WHOA YEAH... WHAT'S THAT, HON?
OYE.
I'M A SALES LADY...
...I GET COMMISSIONS.
UNN, UNN, UNN, UNN, UNN, UNN, UNN...

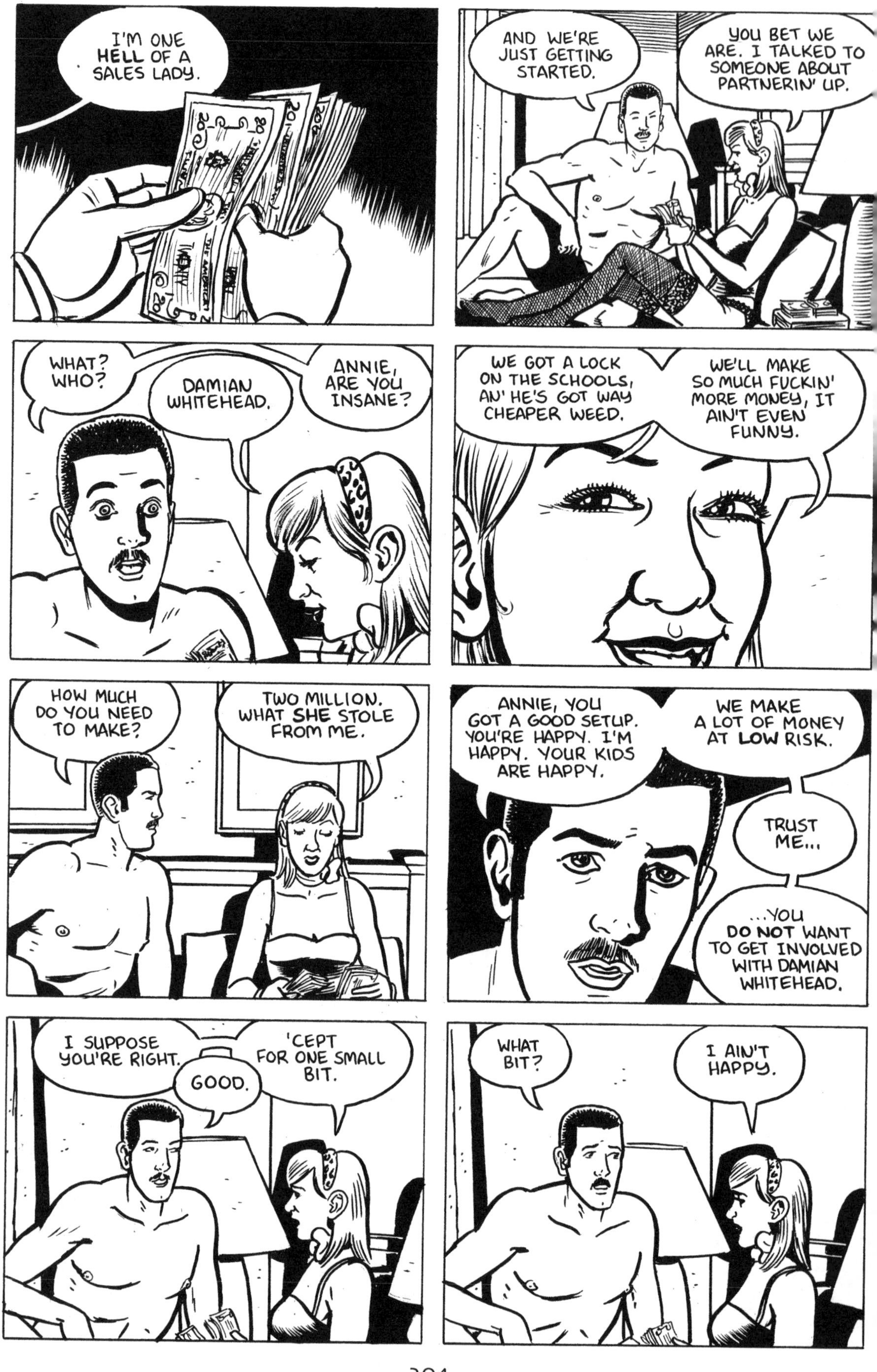
I'M ONE HELL OF A SALES LADY.
AND WE'RE JUST GETTING STARTED.
YOU BET WE ARE. I TALKED TO SOMEONE ABOUT PARTNERIN' UP.
WHAT? WHO?
DAMIAN WHITEHEAD.
ANNIE, ARE YOU INSANE?
WE GOT A LOCK ON THE SCHOOLS, AN' HE'S GOT WAY CHEAPER WEED.
WE'LL MAKE SO MUCH FUCKIN' MORE MONEY, IT AIN'T EVEN FUNNY.
HOW MUCH DO YOU NEED TO MAKE?
TWO MILLION. WHAT SHE STOLE FROM ME.
ANNIE, YOU GOT A GOOD SETUP. YOU'RE HAPPY. I'M HAPPY. YOUR KIDS ARE HAPPY.
WE MAKE A LOT OF MONEY AT LOW RISK.
TRUST ME...
...YOU DO NOT WANT TO GET INVOLVED WITH DAMIAN WHITEHEAD.
I SUPPOSE YOU'RE RIGHT.
GOOD.
'CEPT FOR ONE SMALL BIT.
WHAT BIT?
I AIN'T HAPPY.

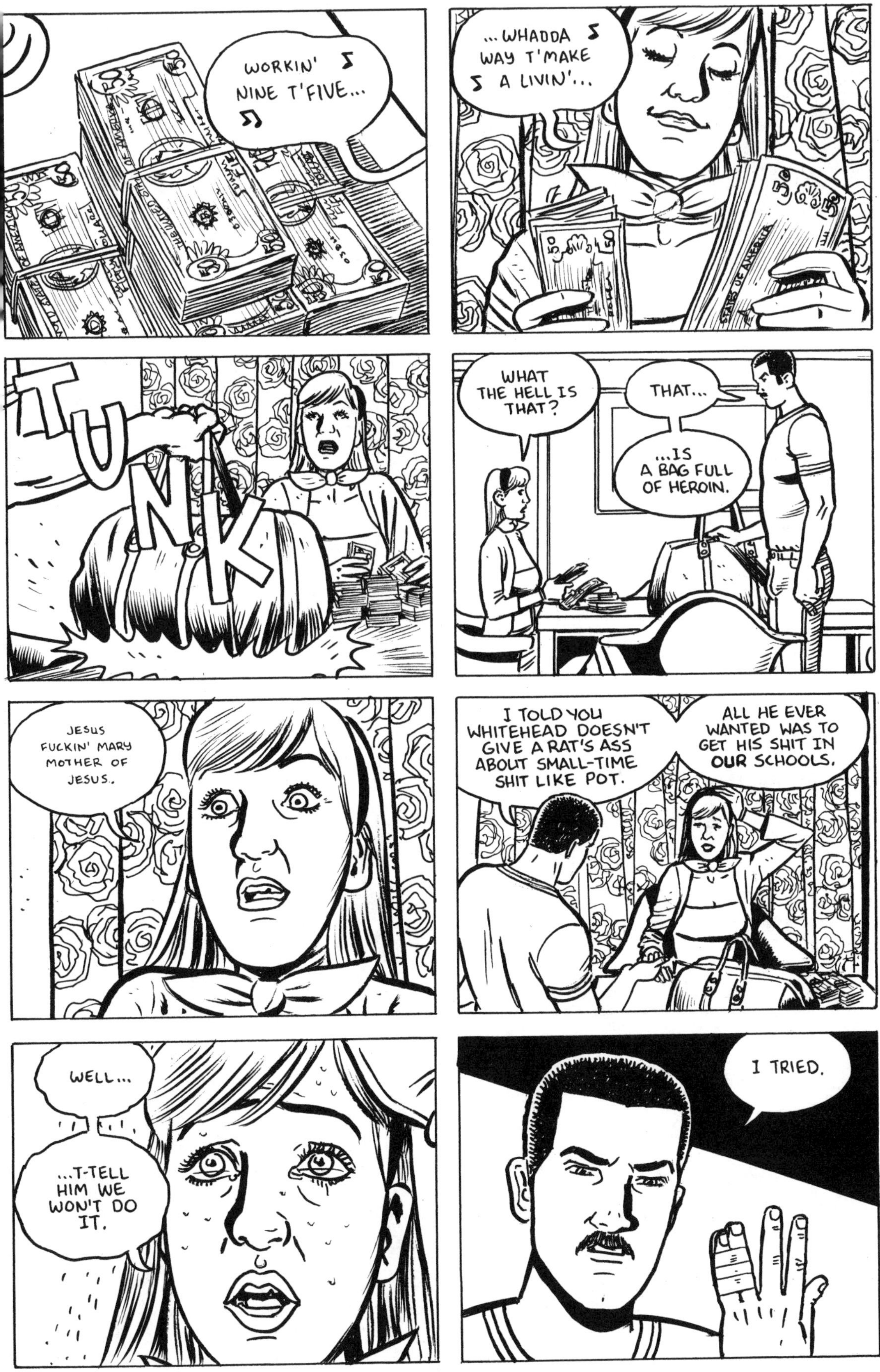
WORKIN' NINE T'FIVE...
...WHADDA WAY T'MAKE A LIVIN'...
TUNK
WHAT THE HELL IS THAT?
THAT...
...IS A BAG FULL OF HEROIN.
JESUS FUCKIN' MARY MOTHER OF JESUS.
I TOLD YOU WHITEHEAD DOESN'T GIVE A RAT'S ASS ABOUT SMALL-TIME SHIT LIKE POT.
ALL HE EVER WANTED WAS TO GET HIS SHIT IN OUR SCHOOLS.
WELL...
...T-TELL HIM WE WON'T DO IT.
I TRIED.

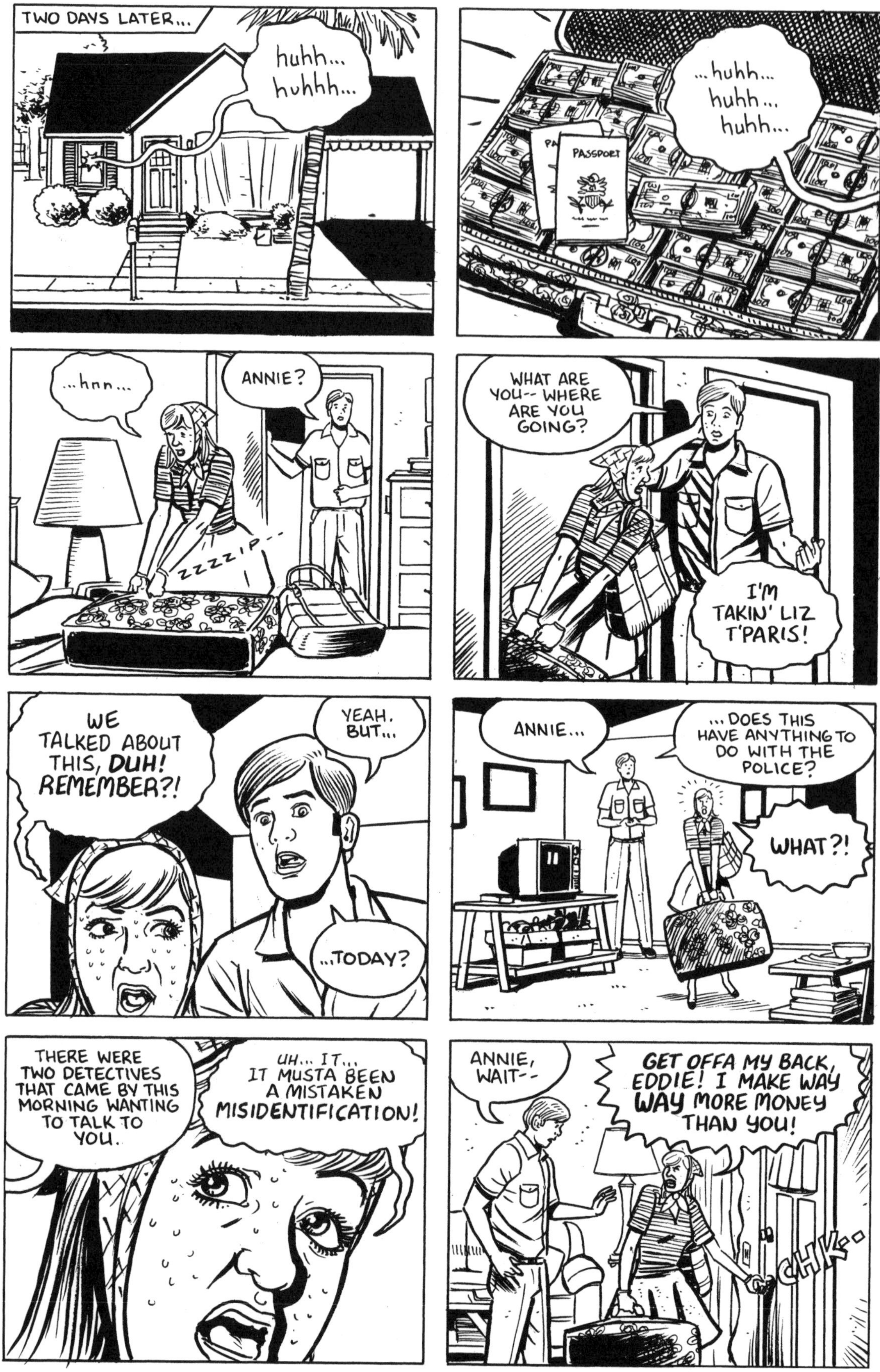
TWO DAYS LATER...
huhh... huhhh...
...huhh... huhh... huhh...
PASSPORT
...hnn...
ANNIE?
ZZZZIP--
WHAT ARE YOU-- WHERE ARE YOU GOING?
I'M TAKIN' LIZ T'PARIS!
WE TALKED ABOUT THIS, DUH! REMEMBER?!
YEAH. BUT...
...TODAY?
ANNIE...
...DOES THIS HAVE ANYTHING TO DO WITH THE POLICE?
WHAT?!
THERE WERE TWO DETECTIVES THAT CAME BY THIS MORNING WANTING TO TALK TO YOU.
UH... IT... IT MUSTA BEEN A MISTAKEN MISIDENTIFICATION!
ANNIE, WAIT--
GET OFFA MY BACK, EDDIE! I MAKE WAY WAY MORE MONEY THAN YOU!
CHK

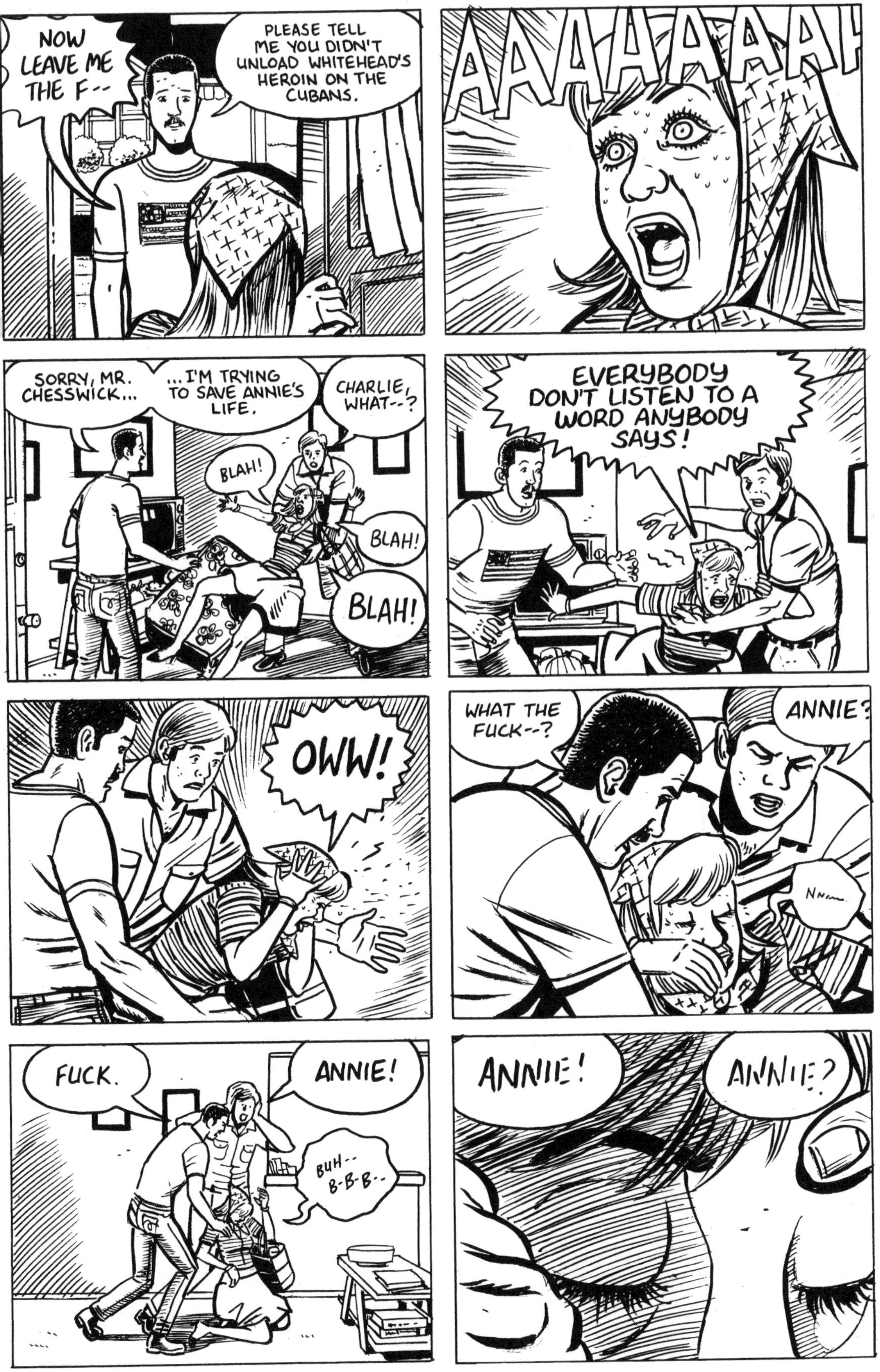
NOW LEAVE ME THE F--
PLEASE TELL ME YOU DIDN'T UNLOAD WHITEHEAD'S HEROIN ON THE CUBANS.
AAAAAAAH
SORRY, MR. CHESSWICK...
...I'M TRYING TO SAVE ANNIE'S LIFE.
CHARLIE, WHAT--?
BLAH!
BLAH!
BLAH!
EVERYBODY DON'T LISTEN TO A WORD ANYBODY SAYS!
OWW!
WHAT THE FUCK--?
ANNIE?
FUCK.
ANNIE!
BUH-- B-B-B--
ANNIE!
ANNIE?

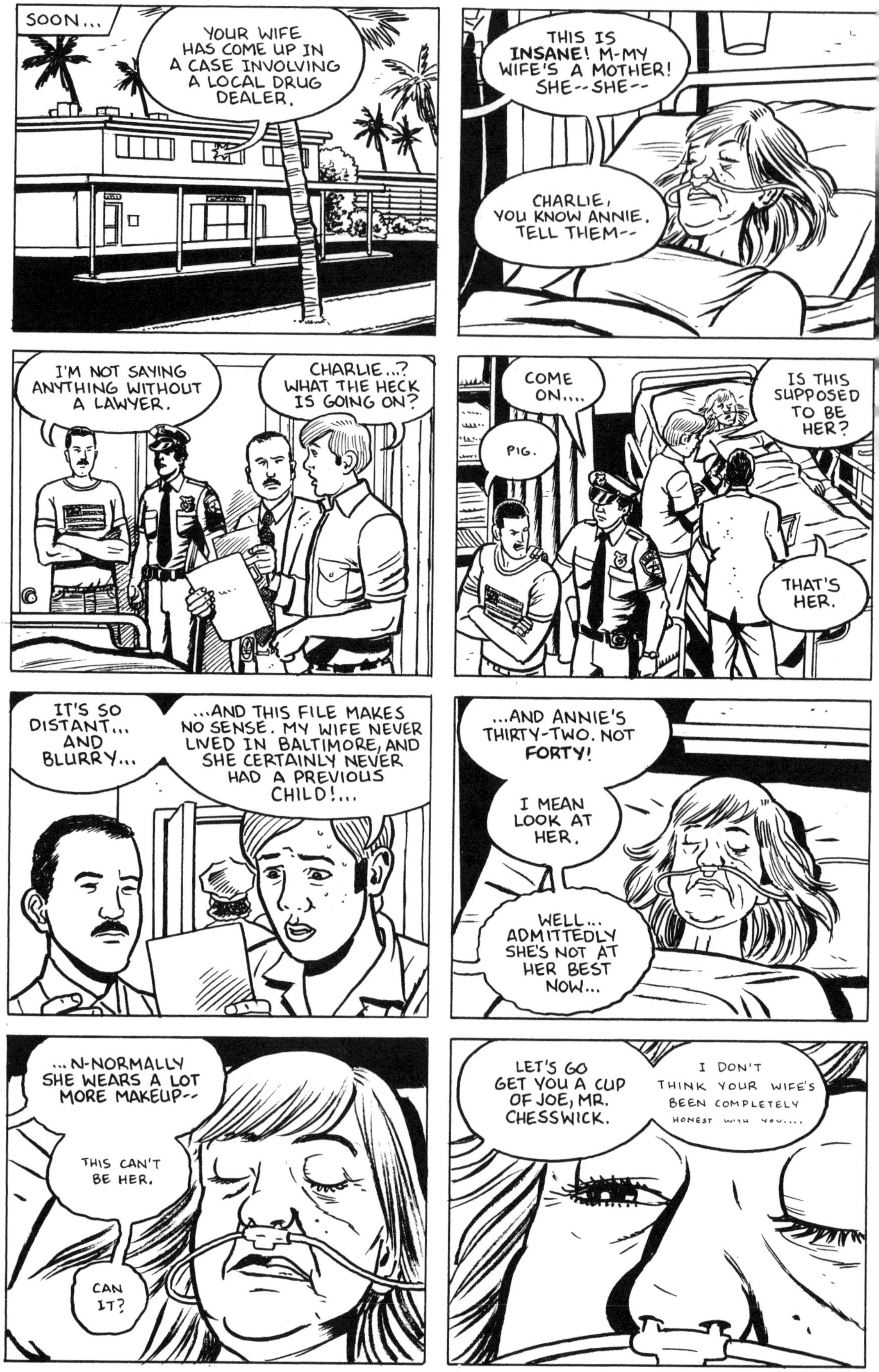
SOON...
YOUR WIFE HAS COME UP IN A CASE INVOLVING A LOCAL DRUG DEALER.
THIS IS INSANE! M-MY WIFE'S A MOTHER! SHE--SHE--
CHARLIE, YOU KNOW ANNIE. TELL THEM--
I'M NOT SAYING ANYTHING WITHOUT A LAWYER.
CHARLIE...? WHAT THE HECK IS GOING ON?
COME ON....
PIG.
IS THIS SUPPOSED TO BE HER?
THAT'S HER.
IT'S SO DISTANT... AND BLURRY...
...AND THIS FILE MAKES NO SENSE. MY WIFE NEVER LIVED IN BALTIMORE, AND SHE CERTAINLY NEVER HAD A PREVIOUS CHILD!...
...AND ANNIE'S THIRTY-TWO. NOT FORTY!
I MEAN LOOK AT HER.
WELL... ADMITTEDLY SHE'S NOT AT HER BEST NOW...
...N-NORMALLY SHE WEARS A LOT MORE MAKEUP--
THIS CAN'T BE HER.
CAN IT?
LET'S GO GET YOU A CUP OF JOE, MR. CHESSWICK.
I DON'T THINK YOUR WIFE'S BEEN COMPLETELY HONEST WITH YOU....

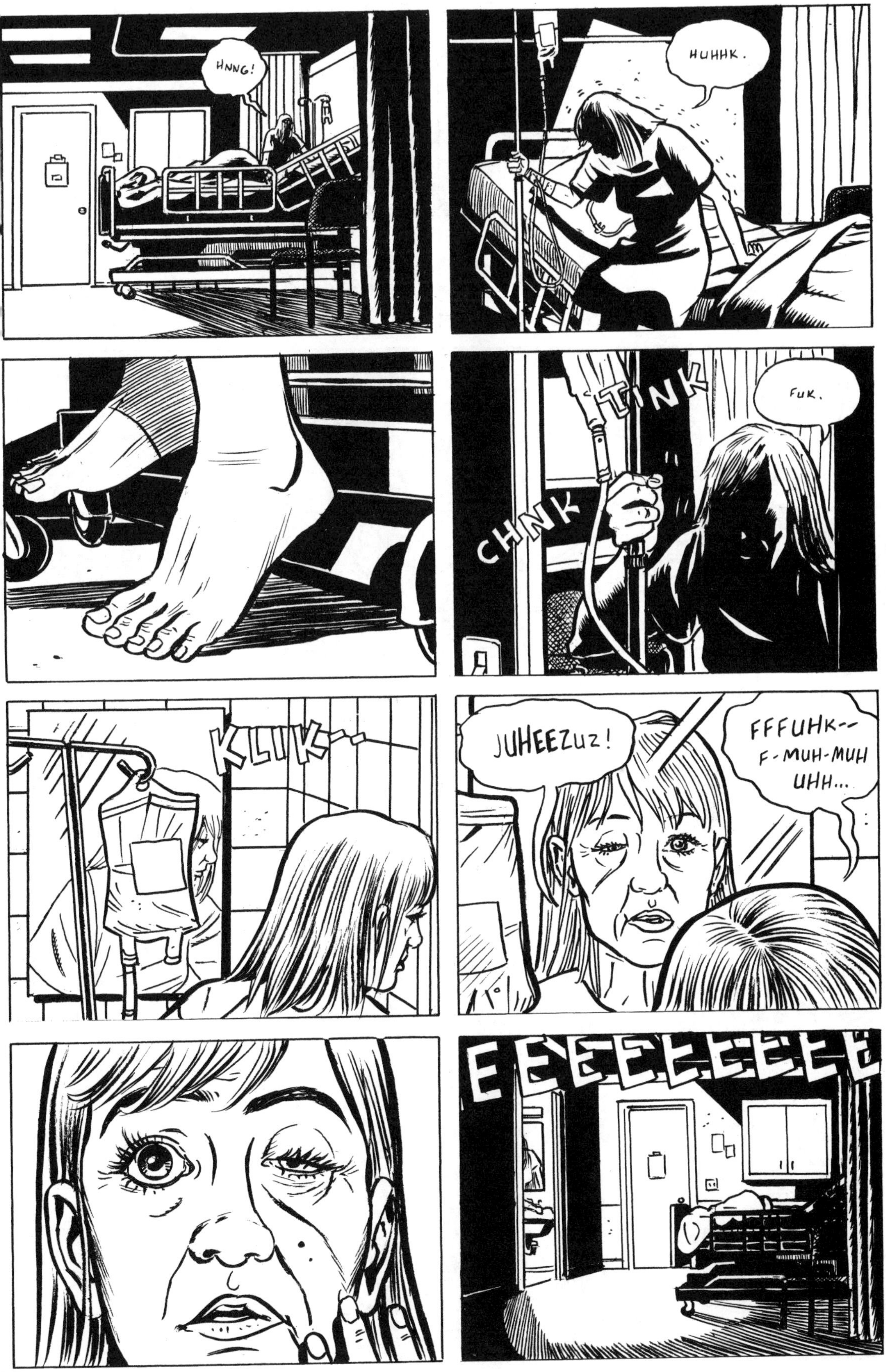
HNNG!
HUHHK.
TINK
CHNK
FUK.
KLIK--
JUHEEZUZ!
FFFUHK--
F-MUH-MUH
UHH...
EEEEEEEEEE

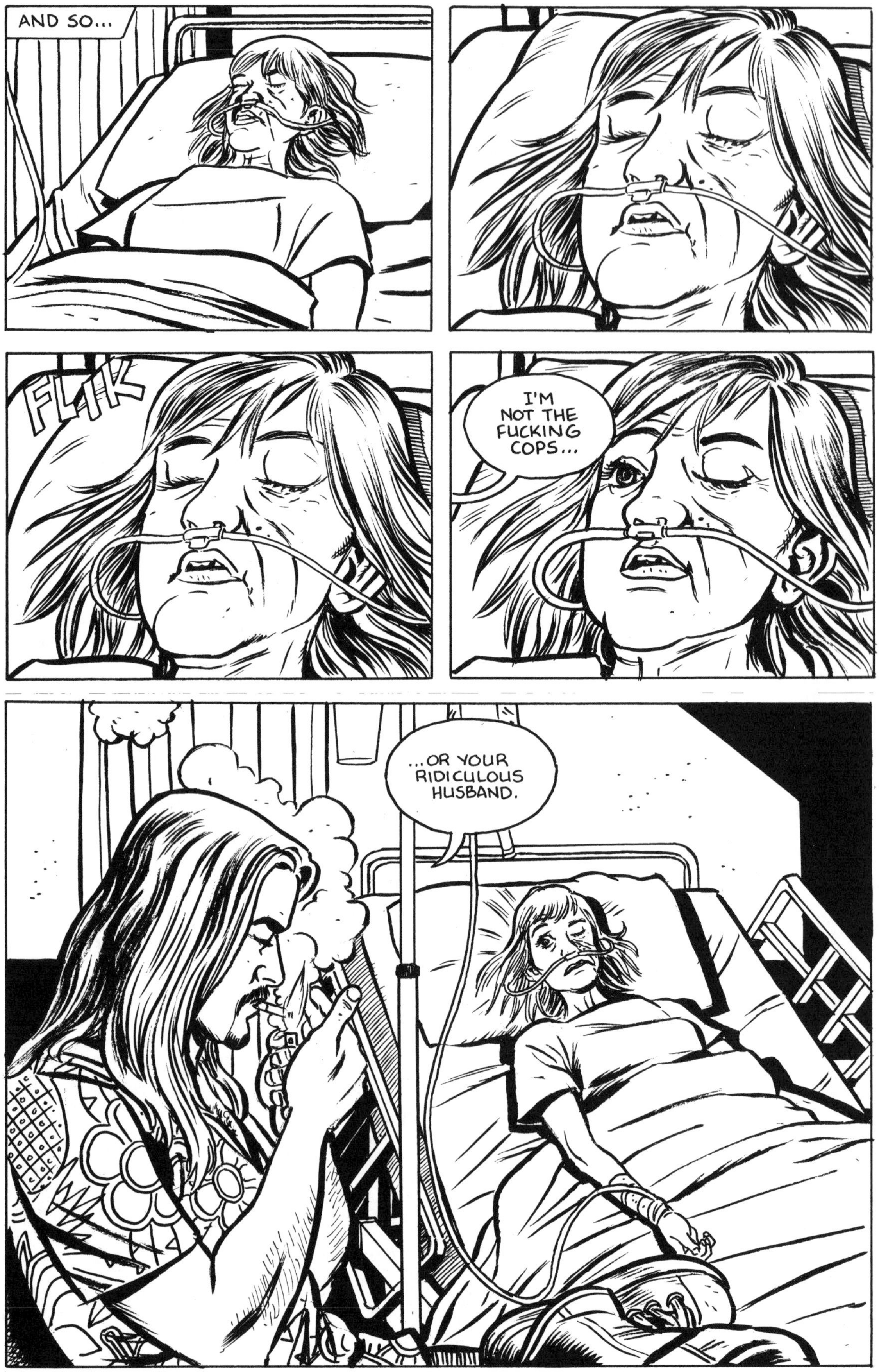
AND SO...
FLIK
I'M NOT THE FUCKING COPS...
...OR YOUR RIDICULOUS HUSBAND.

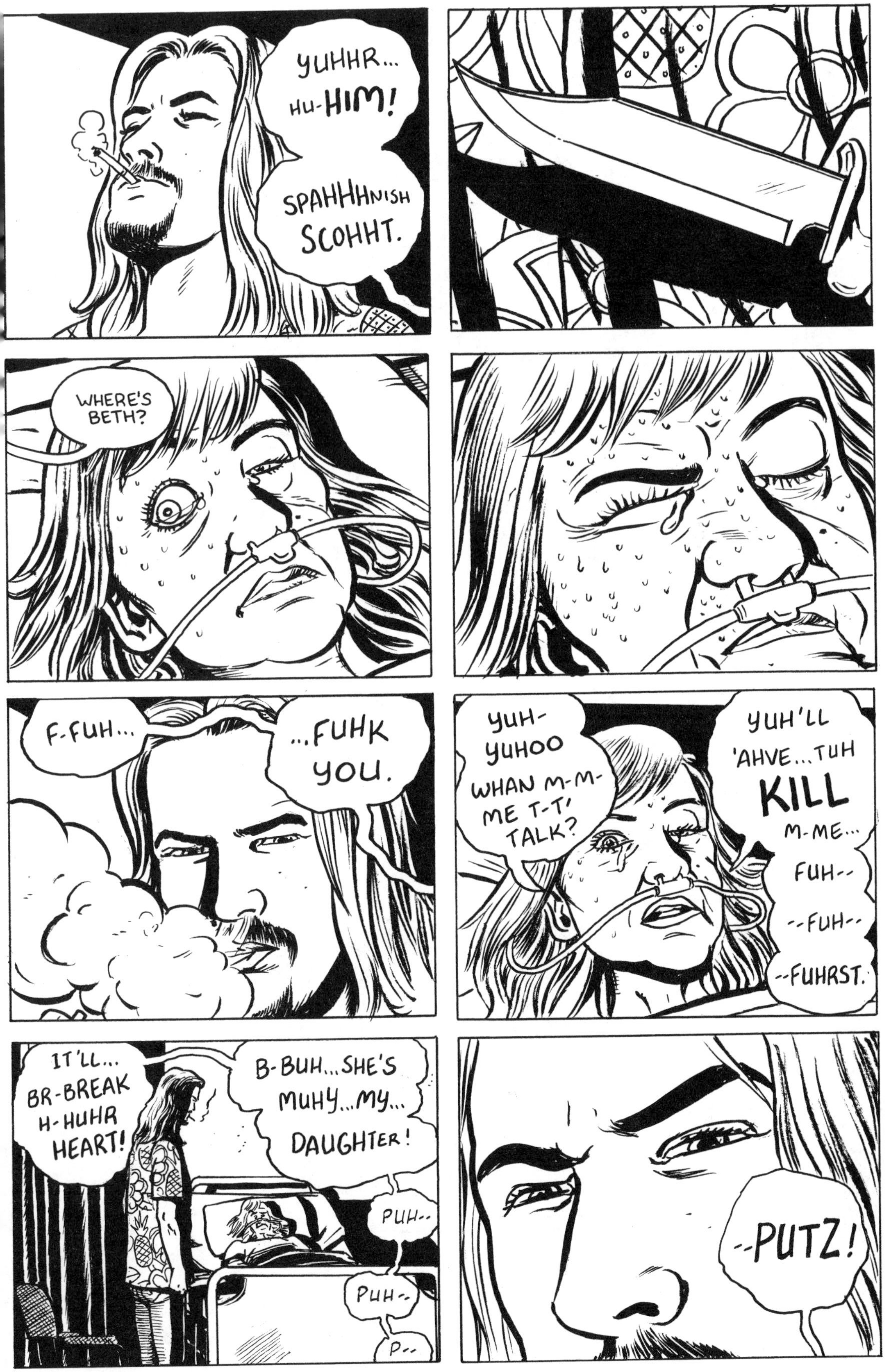
YUHHR... HU-HIM!
SPAHHHNISH SCOHHT.
WHERE'S BETH?
F-FUH...
...FUHK YOU.
YUH-YUHOO WHAN M-M-ME T-T' TALK?
YUH'LL 'AHVE...TUH KILL M-ME...
FUH--
--FUH--
--FUHRST.
IT'LL... BR-BREAK H-HUHR HEART!
B-BUH...SHE'S MUHY...MY... DAUGHTER!
PUH--
PUH--
P--
--PUTZ!

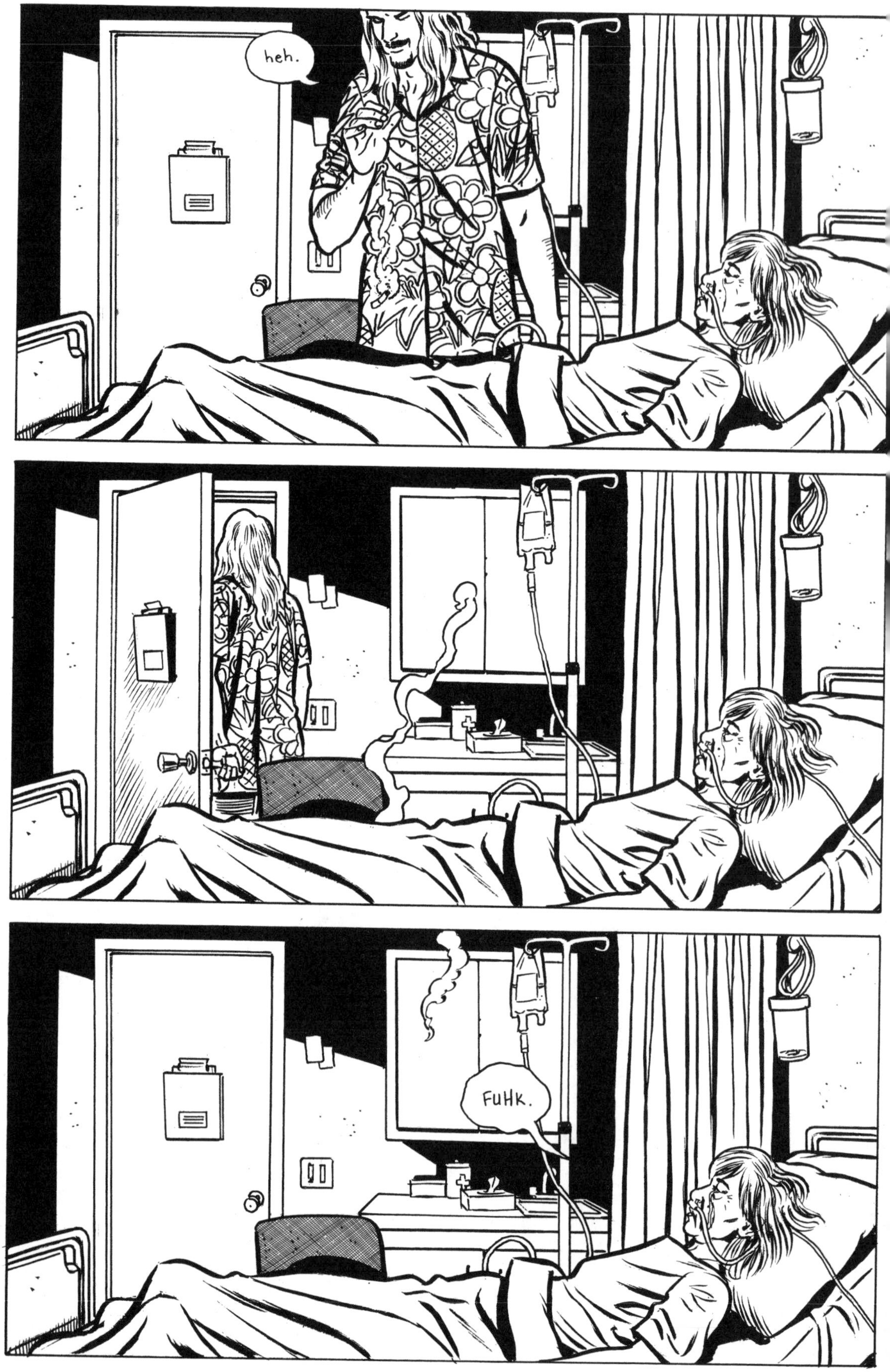
heh.
FUHK.

THE END...

8

"PASS THE MUSTACHE"

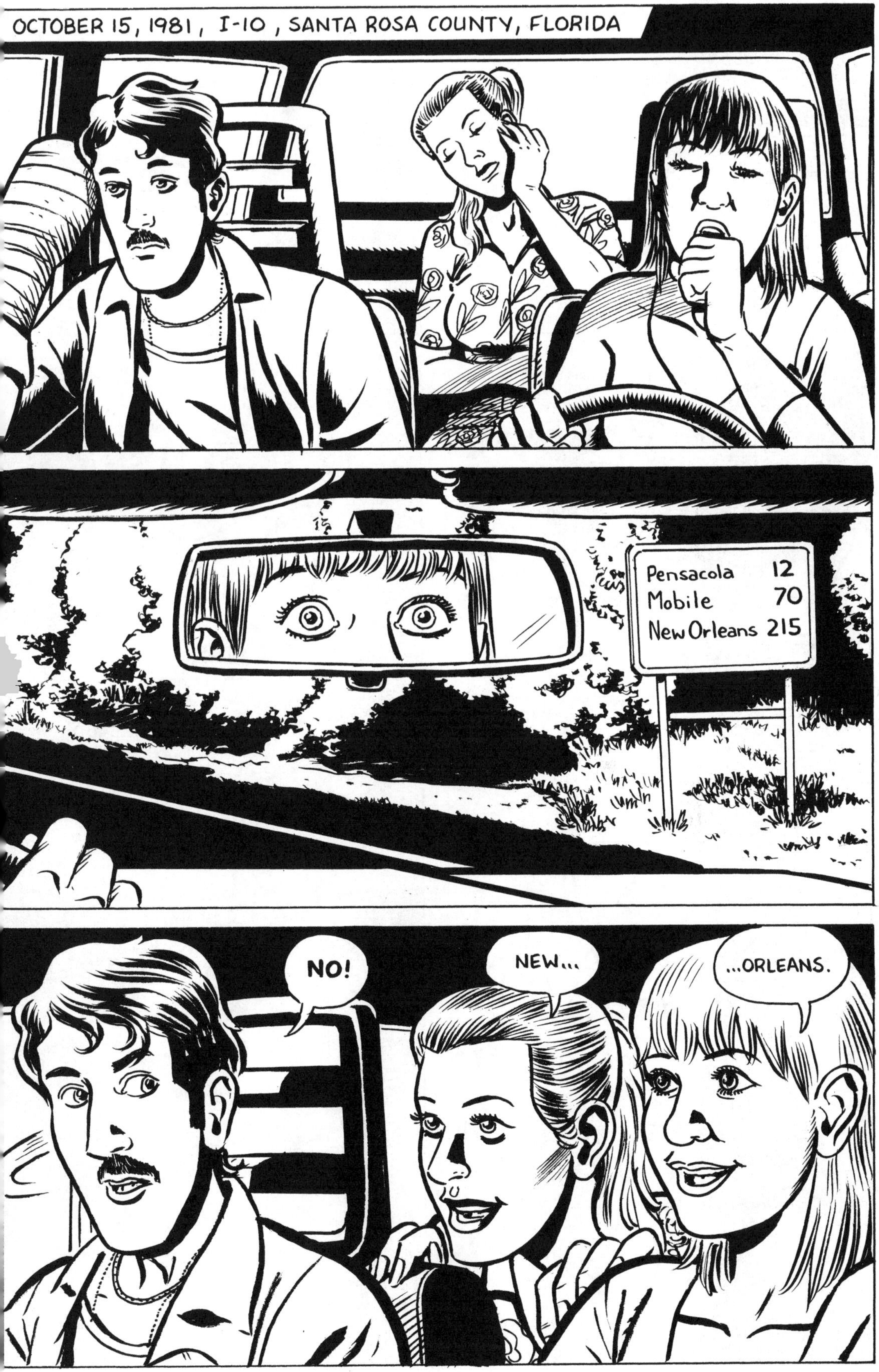
OCTOBER 15, 1981, I-10, SANTA ROSA COUNTY, FLORIDA
Pensacola 12
Mobile 70
New Orleans 215
NO!
NEW...
...ORLEANS.

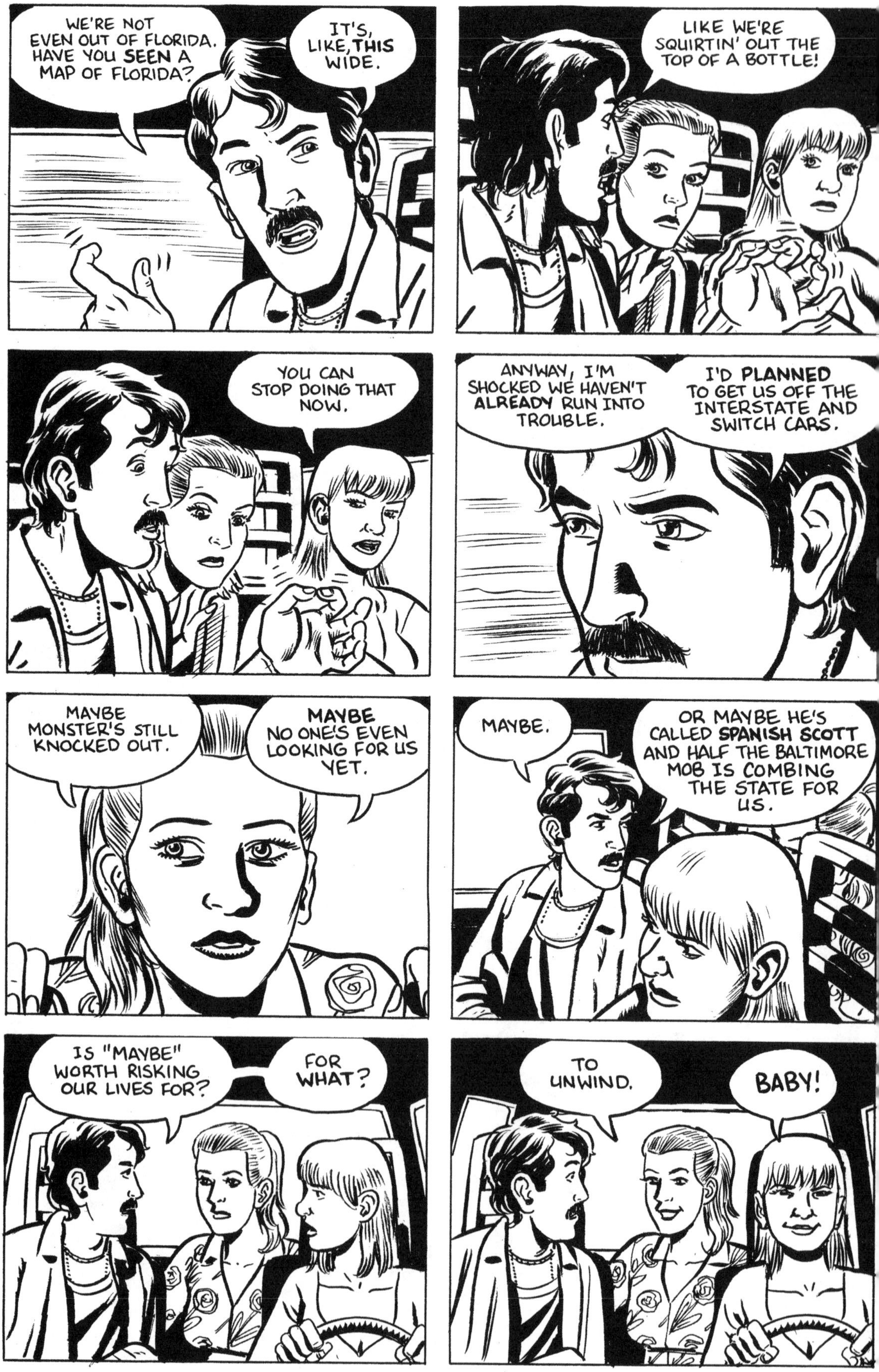
WE'RE NOT EVEN OUT OF FLORIDA. HAVE YOU SEEN A MAP OF FLORIDA?
IT'S, LIKE, THIS WIDE.
LIKE WE'RE SQUIRTIN' OUT THE TOP OF A BOTTLE!
YOU CAN STOP DOING THAT NOW.
ANYWAY, I'M SHOCKED WE HAVEN'T ALREADY RUN INTO TROUBLE.
I'D PLANNED TO GET US OFF THE INTERSTATE AND SWITCH CARS.
MAYBE MONSTER'S STILL KNOCKED OUT.
MAYBE NO ONE'S EVEN LOOKING FOR US YET.
MAYBE.
OR MAYBE HE'S CALLED SPANISH SCOTT AND HALF THE BALTIMORE MOB IS COMBING THE STATE FOR US.
IS "MAYBE" WORTH RISKING OUR LIVES FOR?
FOR WHAT?
TO UNWIND.
BABY!

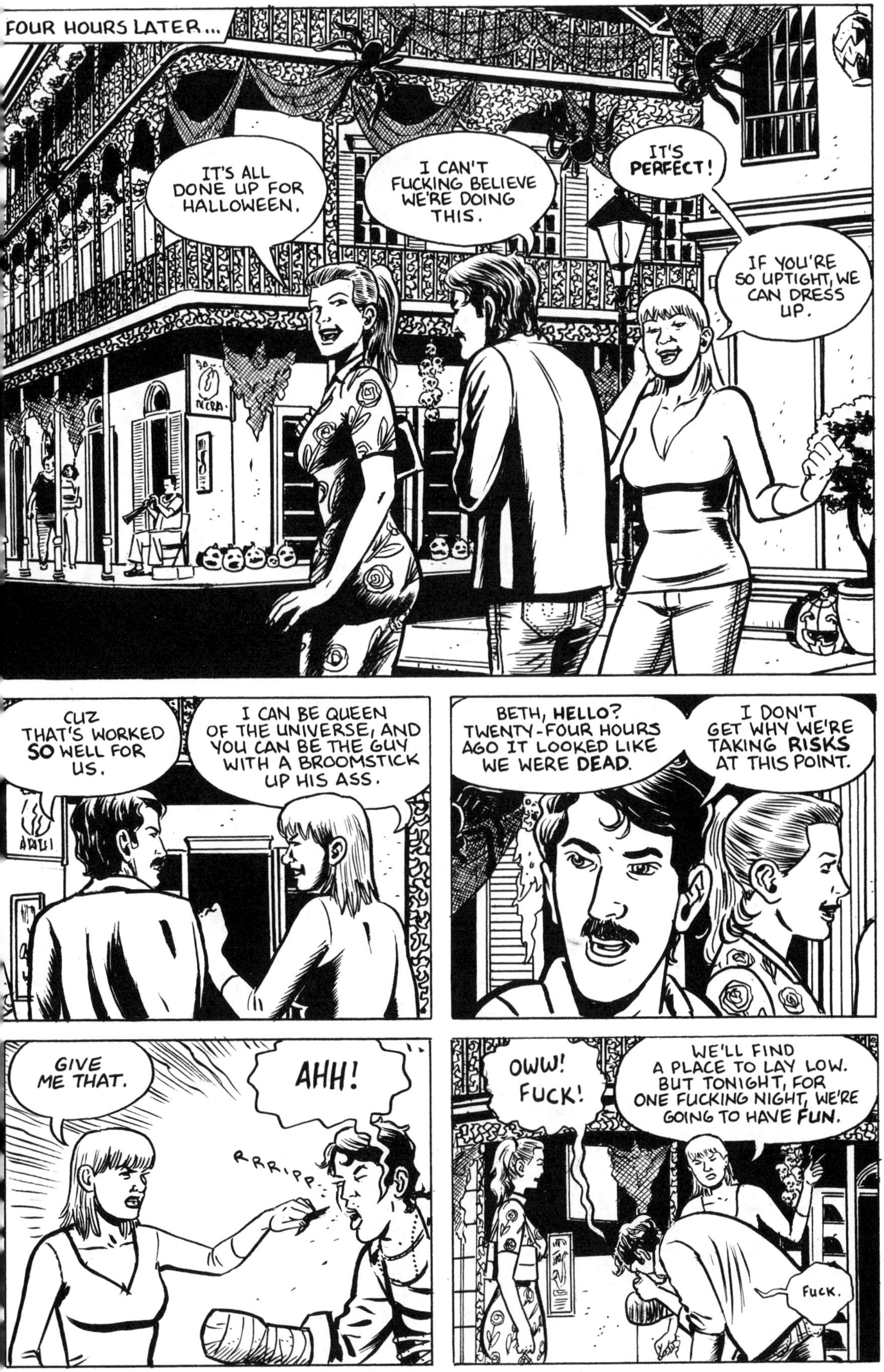
FOUR HOURS LATER...
IT'S ALL DONE UP FOR HALLOWEEN.
I CAN'T FUCKING BELIEVE WE'RE DOING THIS.
IT'S PERFECT!
IF YOU'RE SO UPTIGHT, WE CAN DRESS UP.
CUZ THAT'S WORKED SO WELL FOR US.
I CAN BE QUEEN OF THE UNIVERSE, AND YOU CAN BE THE GUY WITH A BROOMSTICK UP HIS ASS.
BETH, HELLO? TWENTY-FOUR HOURS AGO IT LOOKED LIKE WE WERE DEAD.
I DON'T GET WHY WE'RE TAKING RISKS AT THIS POINT.
GIVE ME THAT.
AHH!
RRRIPP
OWW! FUCK!
WE'LL FIND A PLACE TO LAY LOW. BUT TONIGHT, FOR ONE FUCKING NIGHT, WE'RE GOING TO HAVE FUN.
FUCK.

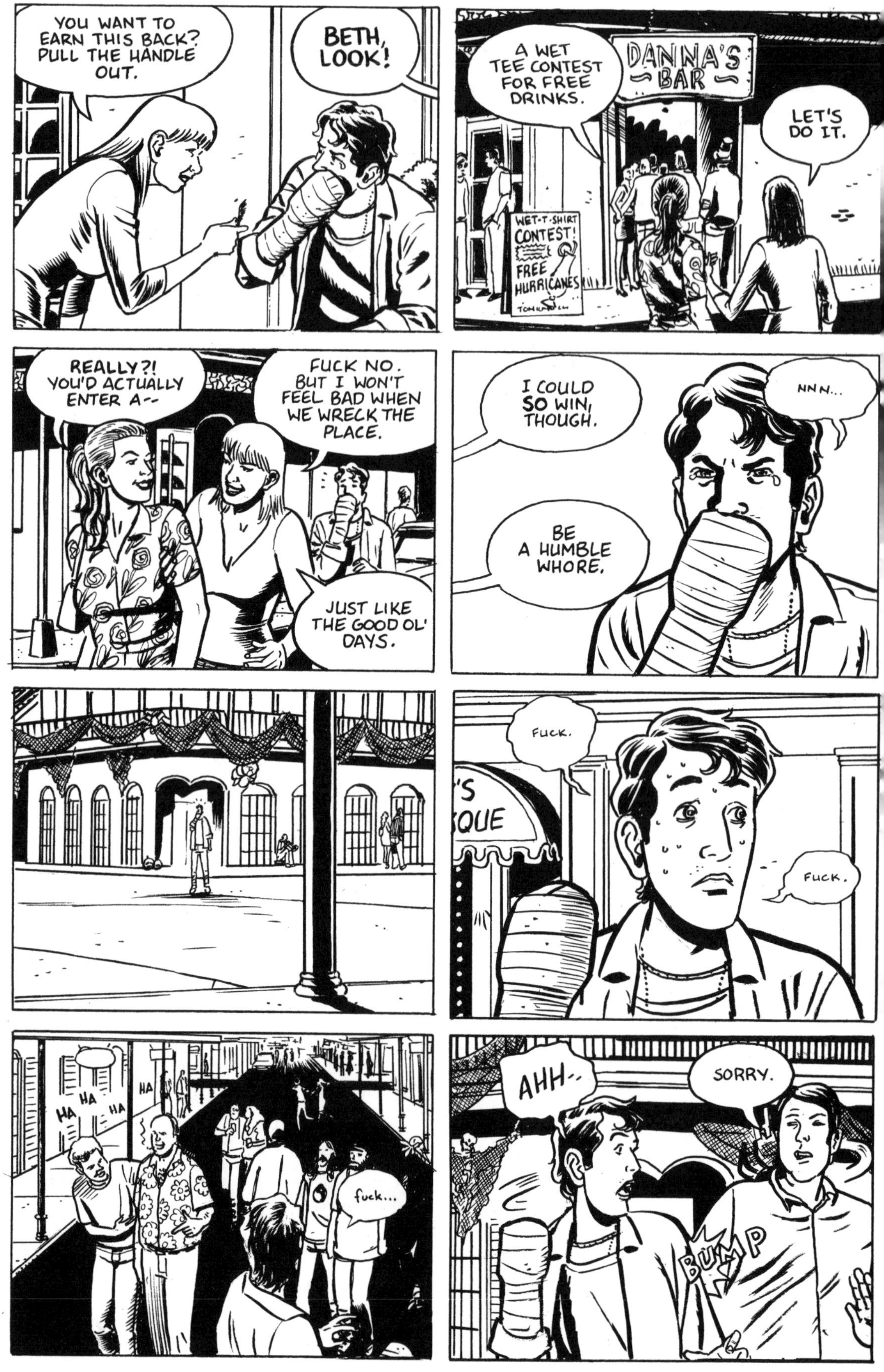
YOU WANT TO EARN THIS BACK? PULL THE HANDLE OUT.
BETH, LOOK!
A WET TEE CONTEST FOR FREE DRINKS.
DANNA'S BAR
WET-T-SHIRT CONTEST! FREE HURRICANES
LET'S DO IT.
REALLY?! YOU'D ACTUALLY ENTER A--
FUCK NO. BUT I WON'T FEEL BAD WHEN WE WRECK THE PLACE.
JUST LIKE THE GOOD OL' DAYS.
I COULD SO WIN, THOUGH.
NNN...
BE A HUMBLE WHORE.
FUCK.
FUCK.
HA
HA
HA
HA
fuck...
AHH--
SORRY.
BUMP

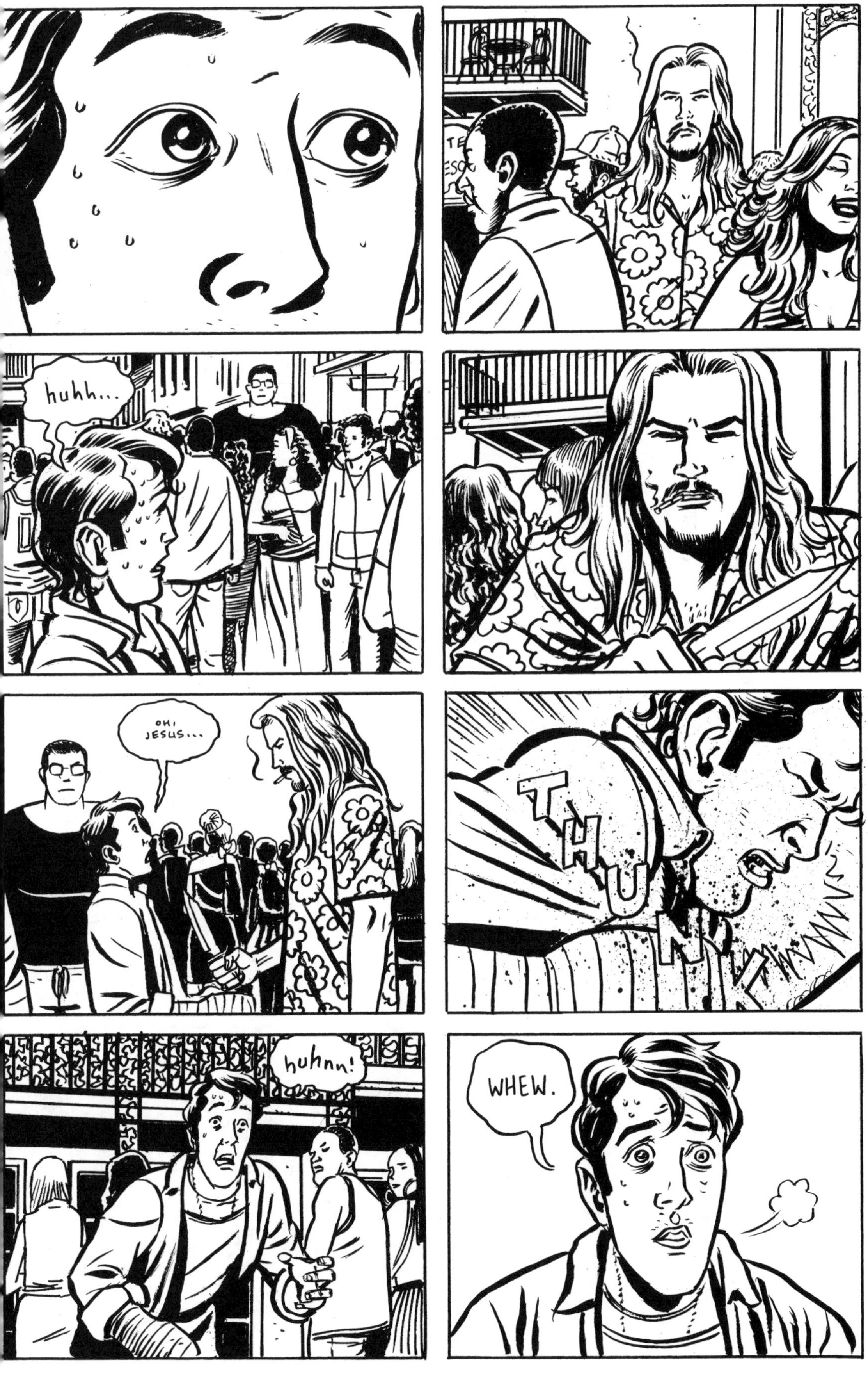
huhh...
OH! JESUS...
THUNK
huhnn!
WHEW.

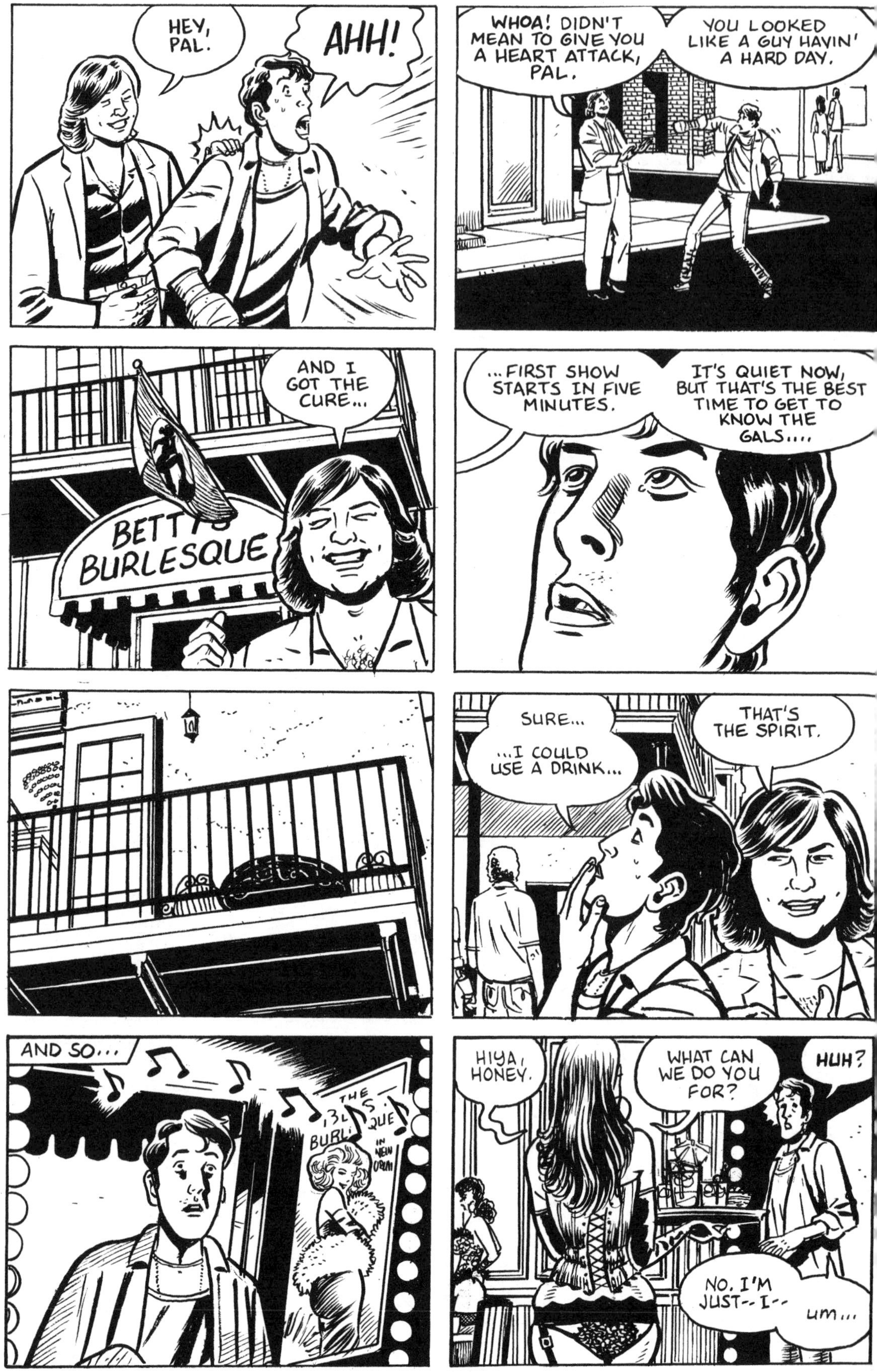
HEY, PAL.
AHH!
WHOA! DIDN'T MEAN TO GIVE YOU A HEART ATTACK, PAL.
YOU LOOKED LIKE A GUY HAVIN' A HARD DAY.
AND I GOT THE CURE...
BURLESQUE
...FIRST SHOW STARTS IN FIVE MINUTES.
IT'S QUIET NOW, BUT THAT'S THE BEST TIME TO GET TO KNOW THE GALS....
SURE...
...I COULD USE A DRINK...
THAT'S THE SPIRIT.
AND SO...
HIYA, HONEY.
WHAT CAN WE DO YOU FOR?
HUH?
NO. I'M JUST-- I--
um...

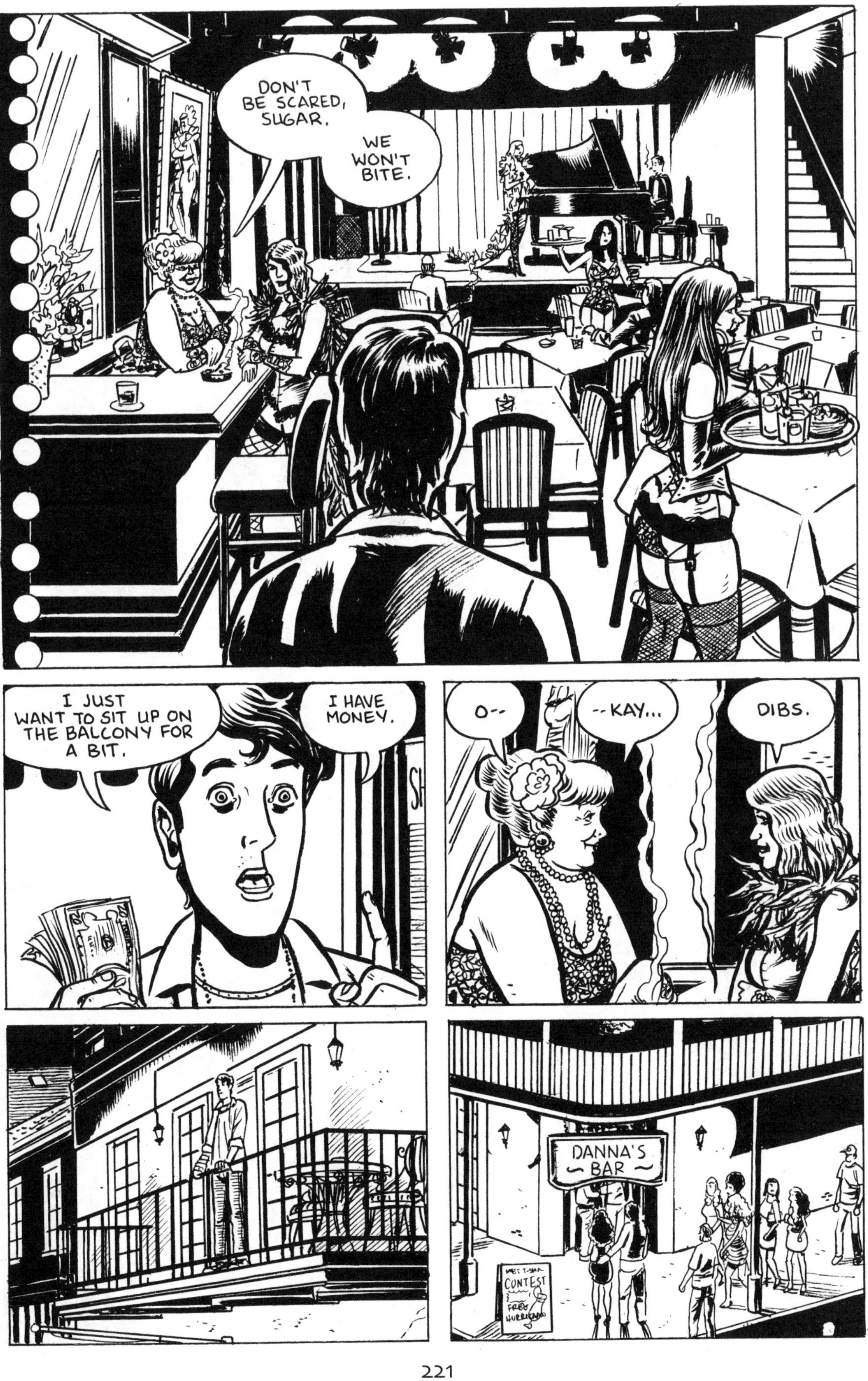
DON'T BE SCARED, SUGAR.
WE WON'T BITE.
I JUST WANT TO SIT UP ON THE BALCONY FOR A BIT.
I HAVE MONEY.
O--
--KAY...
DIBS.
DANNA'S BAR
CONTEST

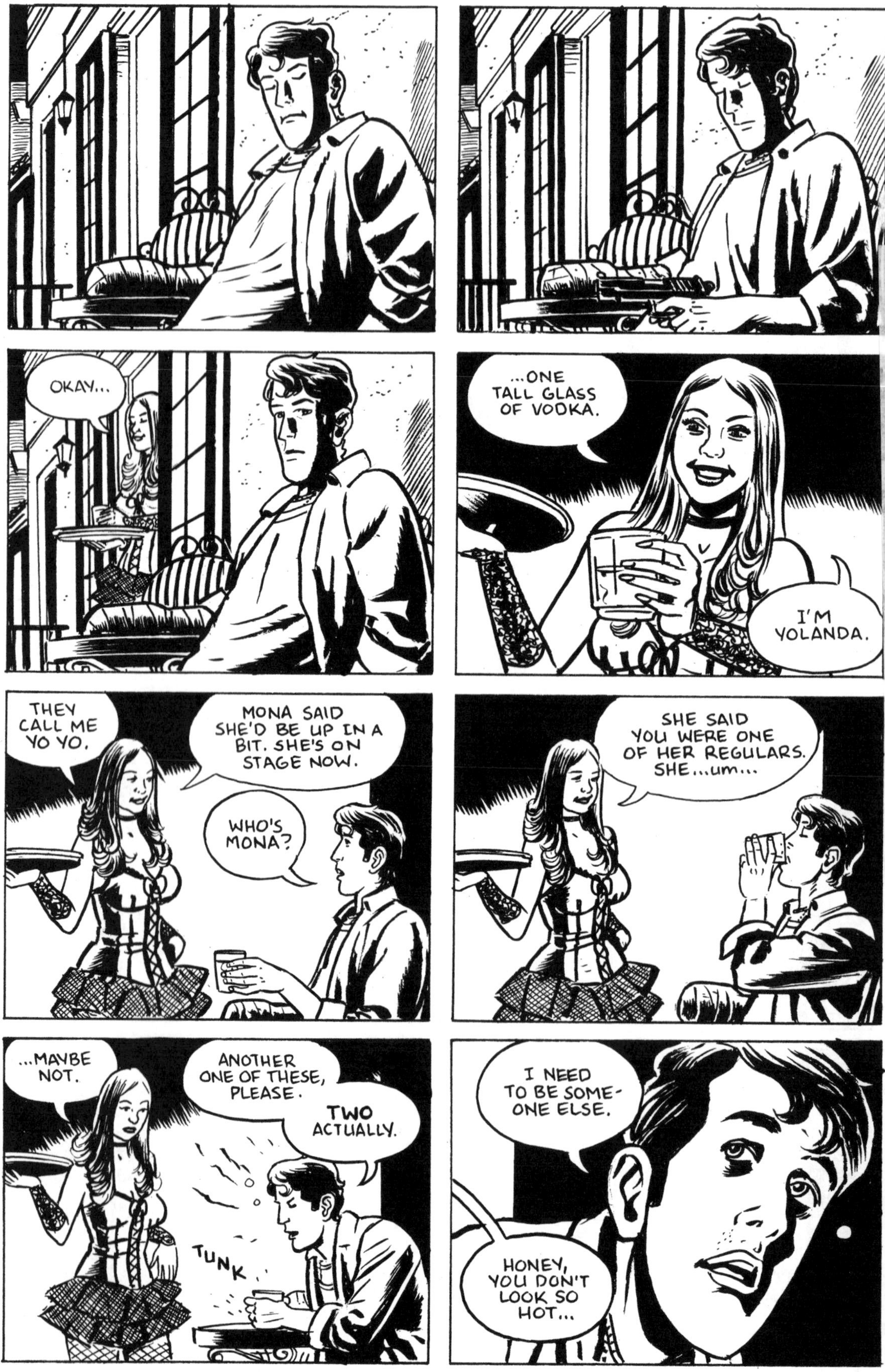
OKAY...
...ONE TALL GLASS OF VODKA.
I'M YOLANDA.
THEY CALL ME YO YO.
MONA SAID SHE'D BE UP IN A BIT. SHE'S ON STAGE NOW.
WHO'S MONA?
SHE SAID YOU WERE ONE OF HER REGULARS. SHE...um...
...MAYBE NOT.
ANOTHER ONE OF THESE, PLEASE.
TWO ACTUALLY.
TUNK
I NEED TO BE SOME-ONE ELSE.
HONEY, YOU DON'T LOOK SO HOT...

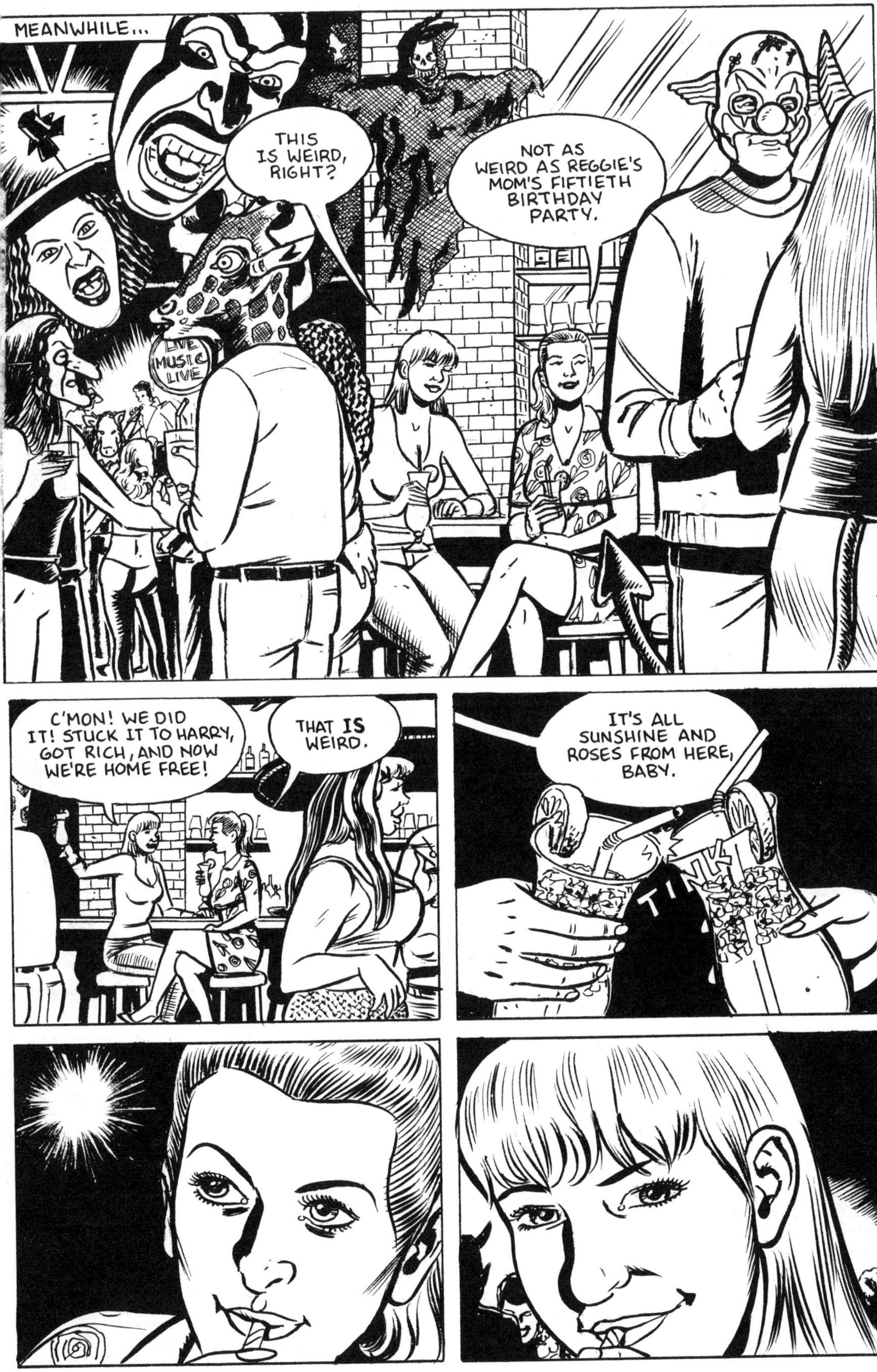
MEANWHILE...
THIS IS WEIRD, RIGHT?
NOT AS WEIRD AS REGGIE'S MOM'S FIFTIETH BIRTHDAY PARTY.
LIVE MUSIC LIVE
C'MON! WE DID IT! STUCK IT TO HARRY, GOT RICH, AND NOW WE'RE HOME FREE!
THAT IS WEIRD.
IT'S ALL SUNSHINE AND ROSES FROM HERE, BABY.
TINK

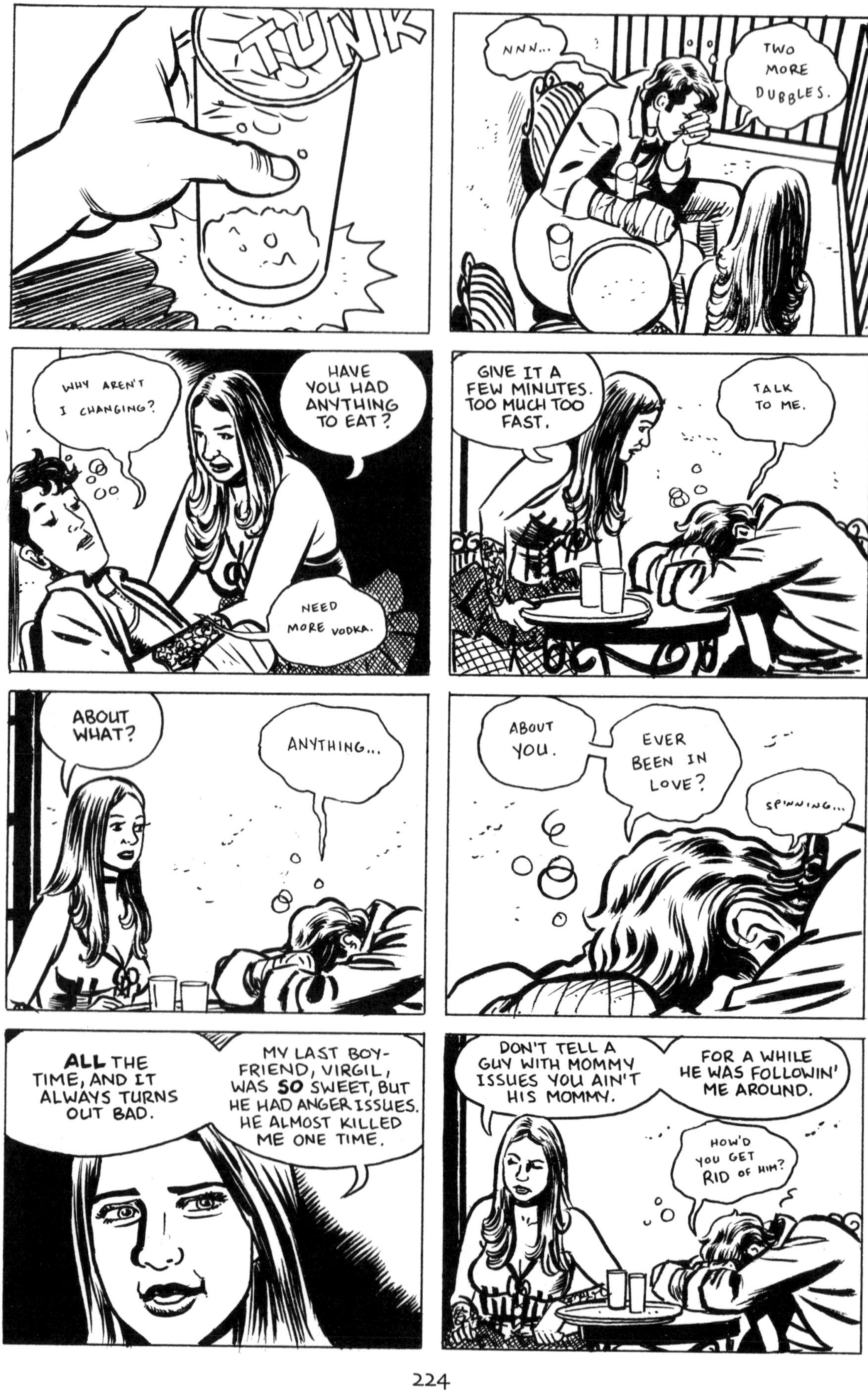
TUNK
NNN...
TWO MORE DUBBLES.
WHY AREN'T I CHANGING?
HAVE YOU HAD ANYTHING TO EAT?
NEED MORE VODKA.
GIVE IT A FEW MINUTES. TOO MUCH TOO FAST.
TALK TO ME.
ABOUT WHAT?
ANYTHING...
ABOUT YOU.
EVER BEEN IN LOVE?
SPINNING...
ALL THE TIME, AND IT ALWAYS TURNS OUT BAD.
MY LAST BOY-FRIEND, VIRGIL, WAS SO SWEET, BUT HE HAD ANGER ISSUES. HE ALMOST KILLED ME ONE TIME.
DON'T TELL A GUY WITH MOMMY ISSUES YOU AIN'T HIS MOMMY.
FOR A WHILE HE WAS FOLLOWIN' ME AROUND.
HOW'D YOU GET RID OF HIM?

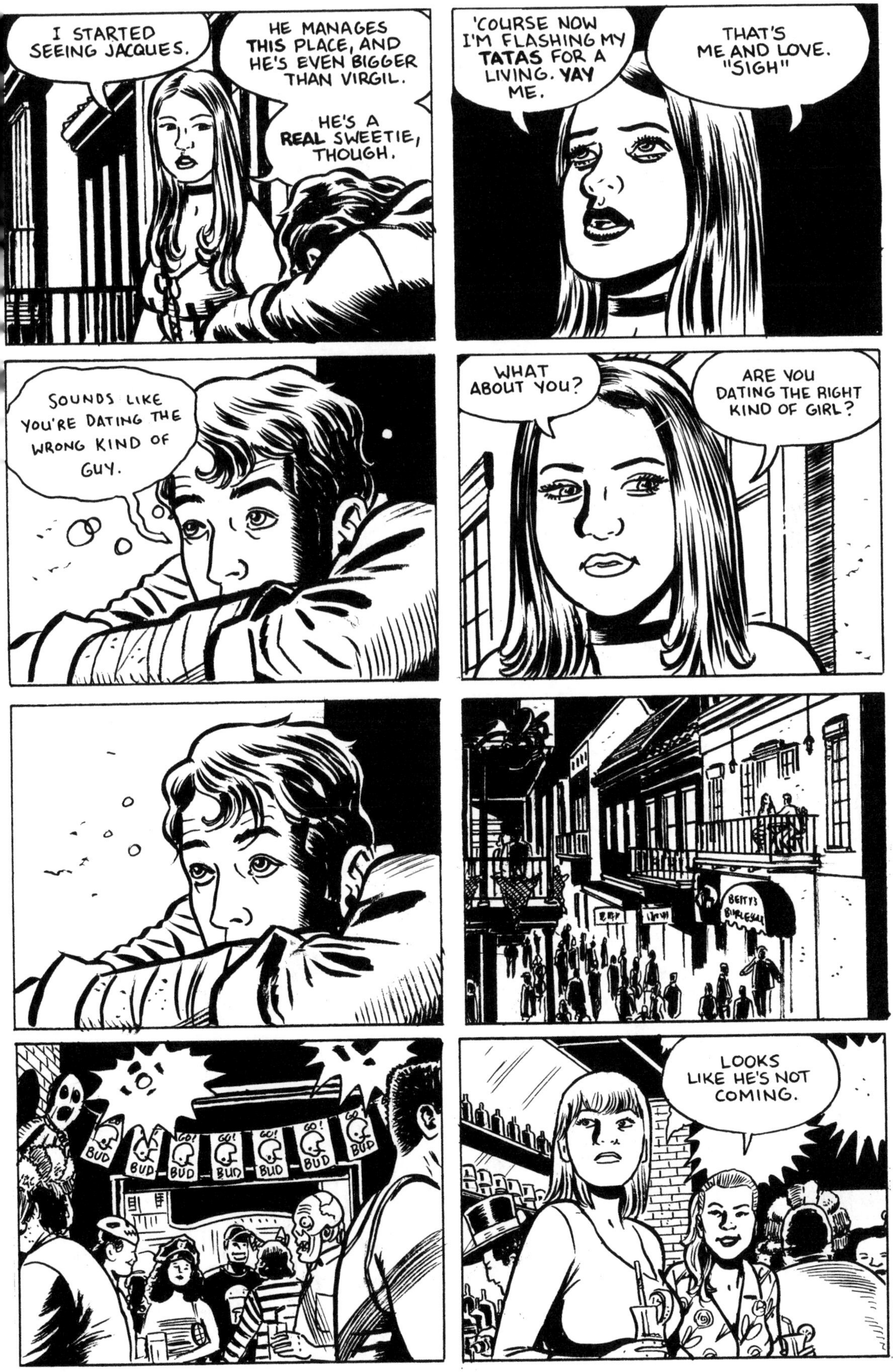
I STARTED SEEING JACQUES.
HE MANAGES THIS PLACE, AND HE'S EVEN BIGGER THAN VIRGIL.
HE'S A REAL SWEETIE, THOUGH.
'COURSE NOW I'M FLASHING MY TATAS FOR A LIVING. YAY ME.
THAT'S ME AND LOVE. "SIGH"
SOUNDS LIKE YOU'RE DATING THE WRONG KIND OF GUY.
WHAT ABOUT YOU?
ARE YOU DATING THE RIGHT KIND OF GIRL?
BETTY'S BURLESQUE
BUD
GO!
LOOKS LIKE HE'S NOT COMING.

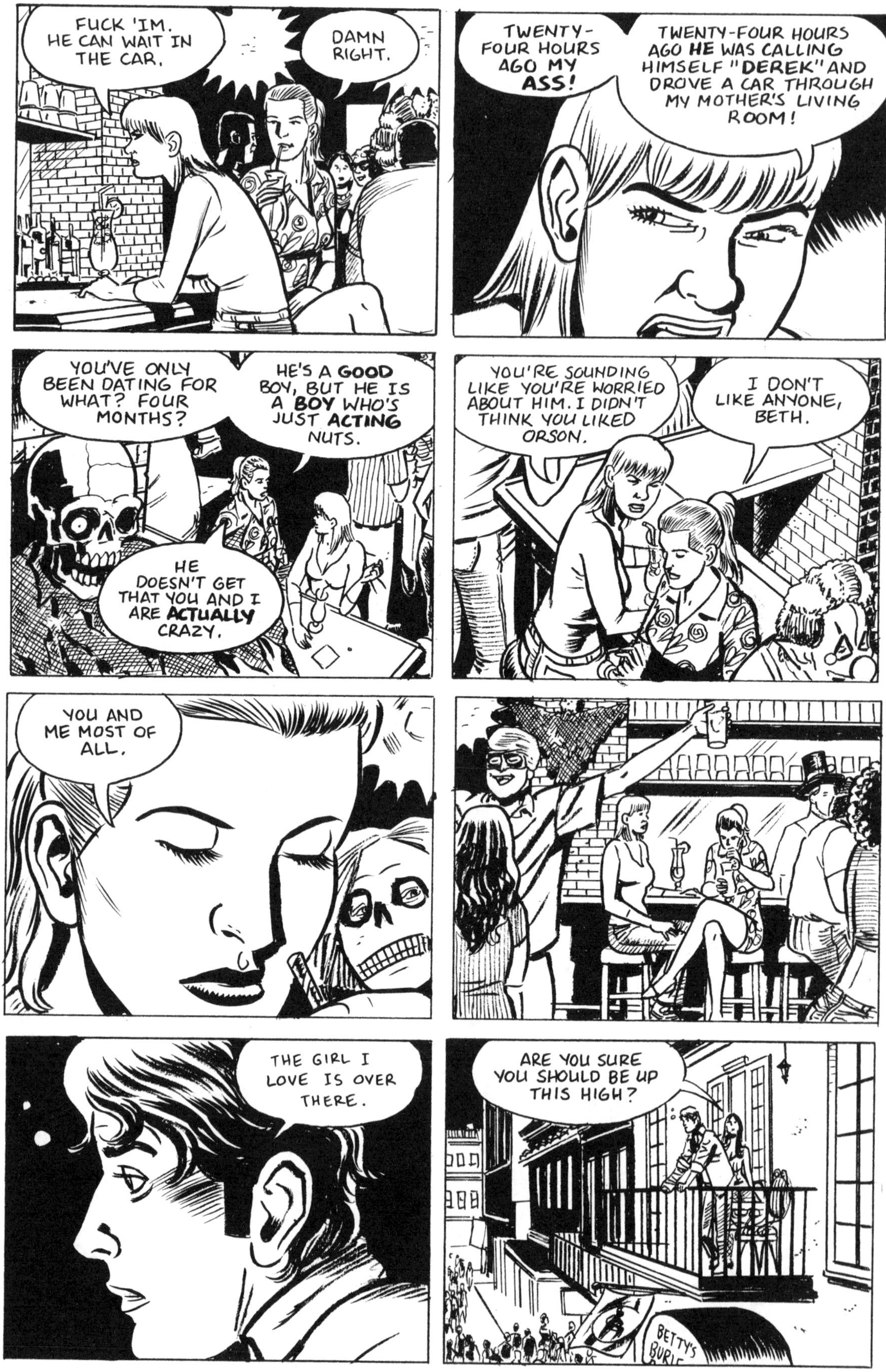
FUCK 'IM. HE CAN WAIT IN THE CAR.
DAMN RIGHT.
TWENTY-FOUR HOURS AGO MY ASS!
TWENTY-FOUR HOURS AGO HE WAS CALLING HIMSELF "DEREK" AND DROVE A CAR THROUGH MY MOTHER'S LIVING ROOM!
YOU'VE ONLY BEEN DATING FOR WHAT? FOUR MONTHS?
HE'S A GOOD BOY, BUT HE IS A BOY WHO'S JUST ACTING NUTS.
HE DOESN'T GET THAT YOU AND I ARE ACTUALLY CRAZY.
YOU'RE SOUNDING LIKE YOU'RE WORRIED ABOUT HIM. I DIDN'T THINK YOU LIKED ORSON.
I DON'T LIKE ANYONE, BETH.
YOU AND ME MOST OF ALL.
THE GIRL I LOVE IS OVER THERE.
ARE YOU SURE YOU SHOULD BE UP THIS HIGH?

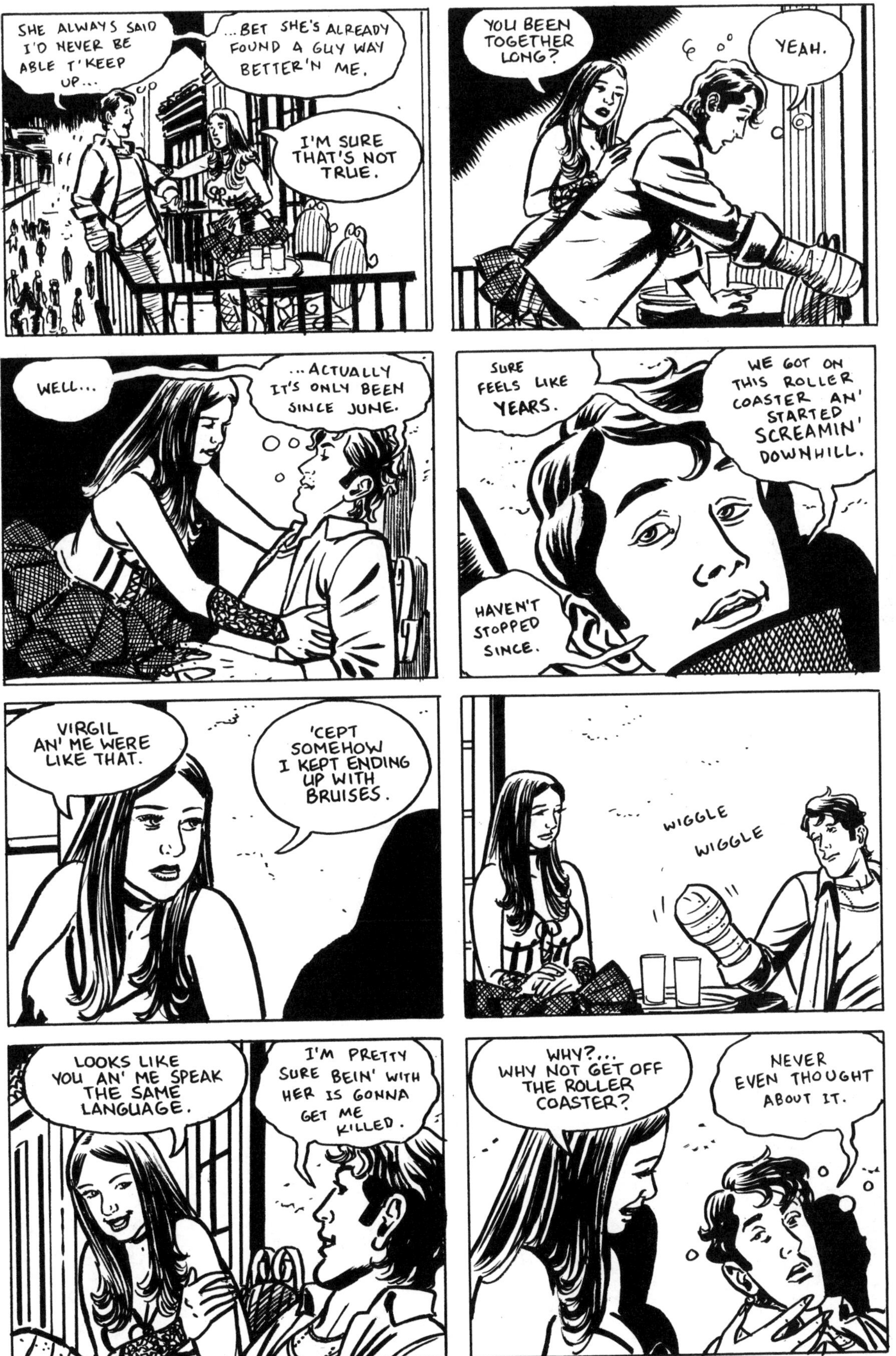
SHE ALWAYS SAID I'D NEVER BE ABLE T'KEEP UP...
...BET SHE'S ALREADY FOUND A GUY WAY BETTER'N ME.
I'M SURE THAT'S NOT TRUE.
YOU BEEN TOGETHER LONG?
YEAH.
WELL...
...ACTUALLY IT'S ONLY BEEN SINCE JUNE.
SURE FEELS LIKE YEARS.
WE GOT ON THIS ROLLER COASTER AN' STARTED SCREAMIN' DOWNHILL.
HAVEN'T STOPPED SINCE.
VIRGIL AN' ME WERE LIKE THAT.
'CEPT SOMEHOW I KEPT ENDING UP WITH BRUISES.
WIGGLE
WIGGLE
LOOKS LIKE YOU AN' ME SPEAK THE SAME LANGUAGE.
I'M PRETTY SURE BEIN' WITH HER IS GONNA GET ME KILLED.
WHY?... WHY NOT GET OFF THE ROLLER COASTER?
NEVER EVEN THOUGHT ABOUT IT.

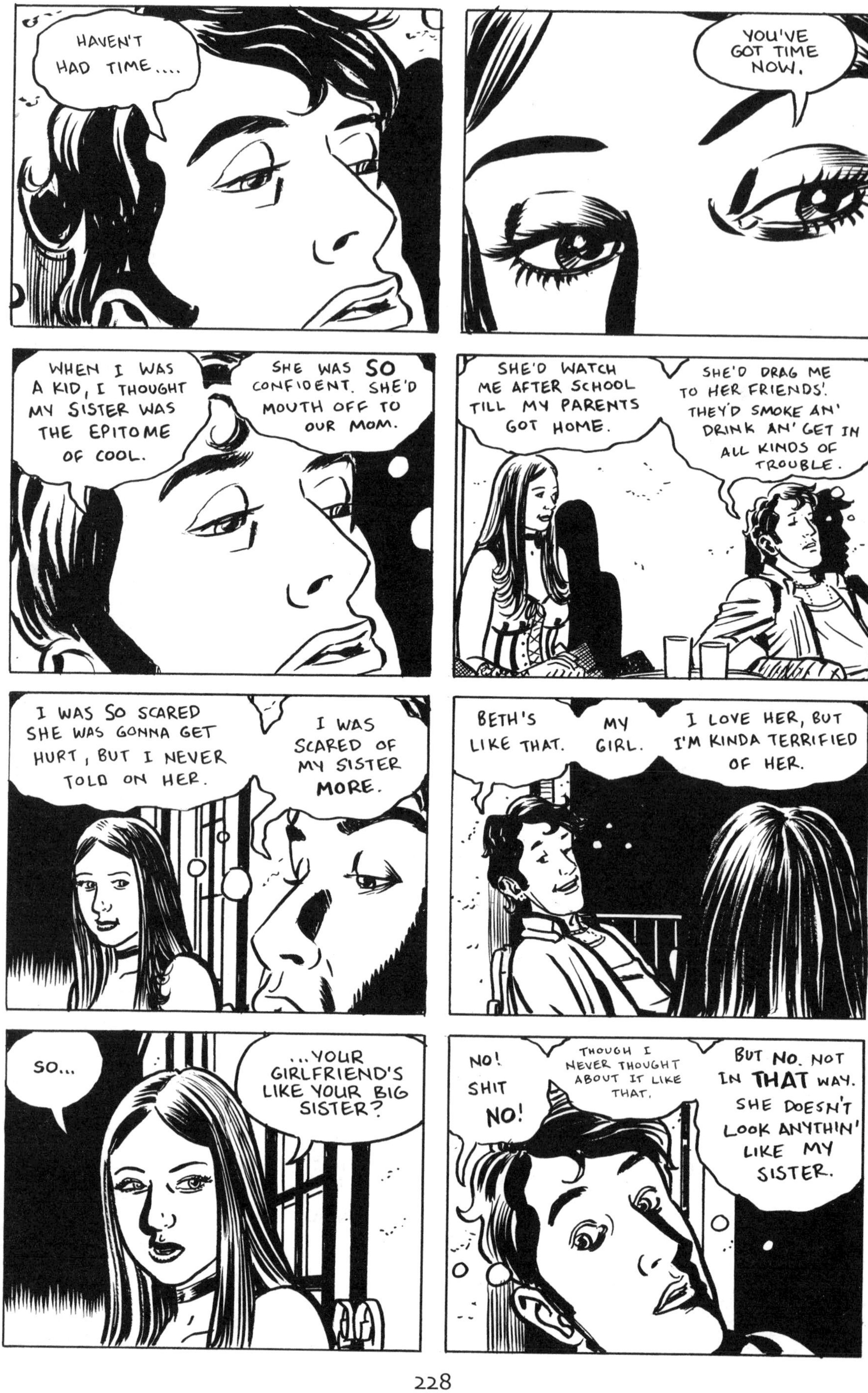

HAVEN'T HAD TIME....
YOU'VE GOT TIME NOW.
WHEN I WAS A KID, I THOUGHT MY SISTER WAS THE EPITOME OF COOL.
SHE WAS SO CONFIDENT. SHE'D MOUTH OFF TO OUR MOM.
SHE'D WATCH ME AFTER SCHOOL TILL MY PARENTS GOT HOME.
SHE'D DRAG ME TO HER FRIENDS'. THEY'D SMOKE AN' DRINK AN' GET IN ALL KINDS OF TROUBLE.
I WAS SO SCARED SHE WAS GONNA GET HURT, BUT I NEVER TOLD ON HER.
I WAS SCARED OF MY SISTER MORE.
BETH'S LIKE THAT.
MY GIRL.
I LOVE HER, BUT I'M KINDA TERRIFIED OF HER.
SO...
...YOUR GIRLFRIEND'S LIKE YOUR BIG SISTER?
NO! SHIT NO!
THOUGH I NEVER THOUGHT ABOUT IT LIKE THAT.
BUT NO. NOT IN THAT WAY.
SHE DOESN'T LOOK ANYTHIN' LIKE MY SISTER.

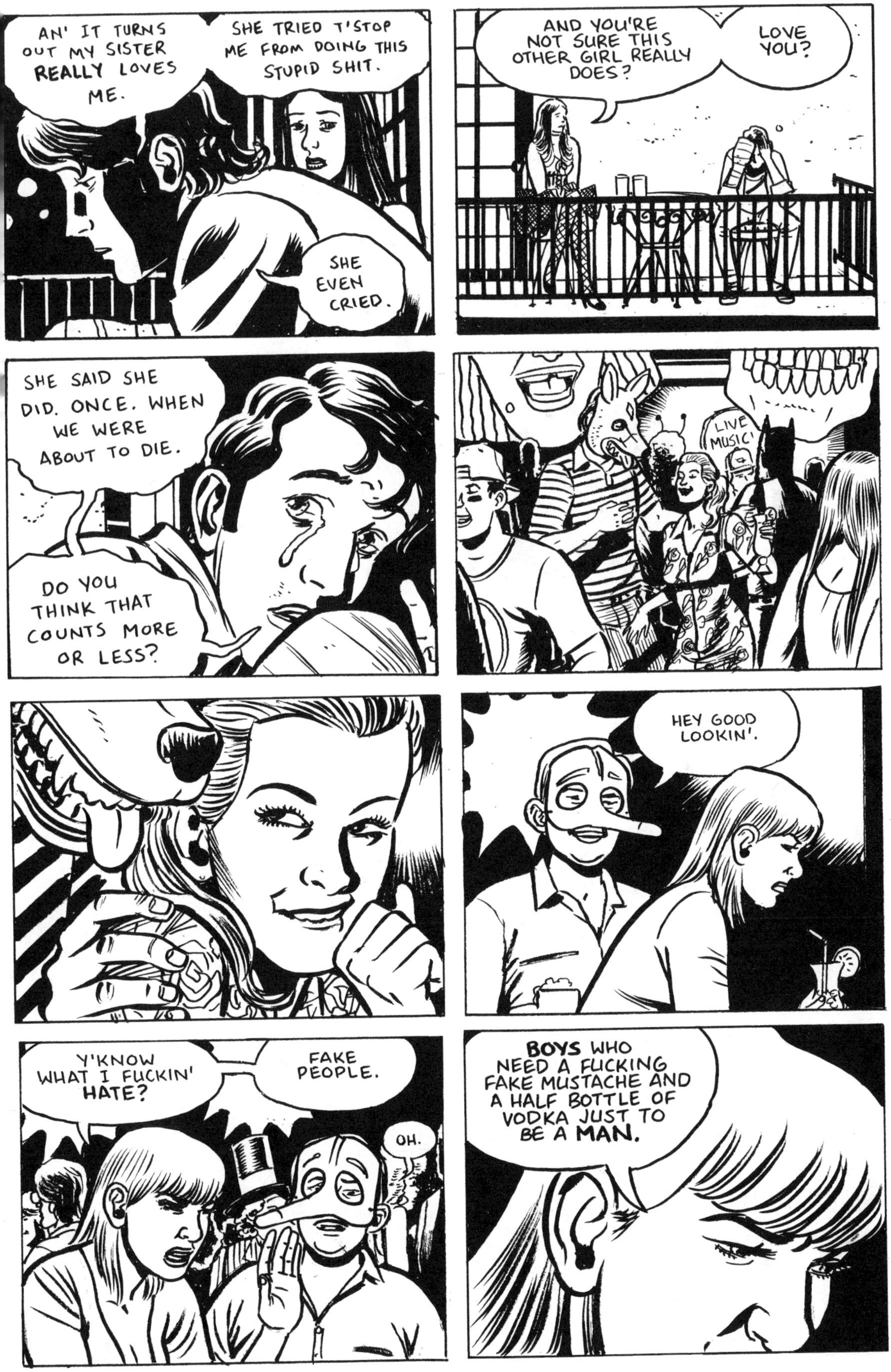
AN' IT TURNS OUT MY SISTER REALLY LOVES ME.
SHE TRIED T'STOP ME FROM DOING THIS STUPID SHIT.
SHE EVEN CRIED.
AND YOU'RE NOT SURE THIS OTHER GIRL REALLY DOES?
LOVE YOU?
SHE SAID SHE DID. ONCE. WHEN WE WERE ABOUT TO DIE.
DO YOU THINK THAT COUNTS MORE OR LESS?
LIVE MUSIC!
HEY GOOD LOOKIN'.
Y'KNOW WHAT I FUCKIN' HATE?
FAKE PEOPLE.
OH.
BOYS WHO NEED A FUCKING FAKE MUSTACHE AND A HALF BOTTLE OF VODKA JUST TO BE A MAN.

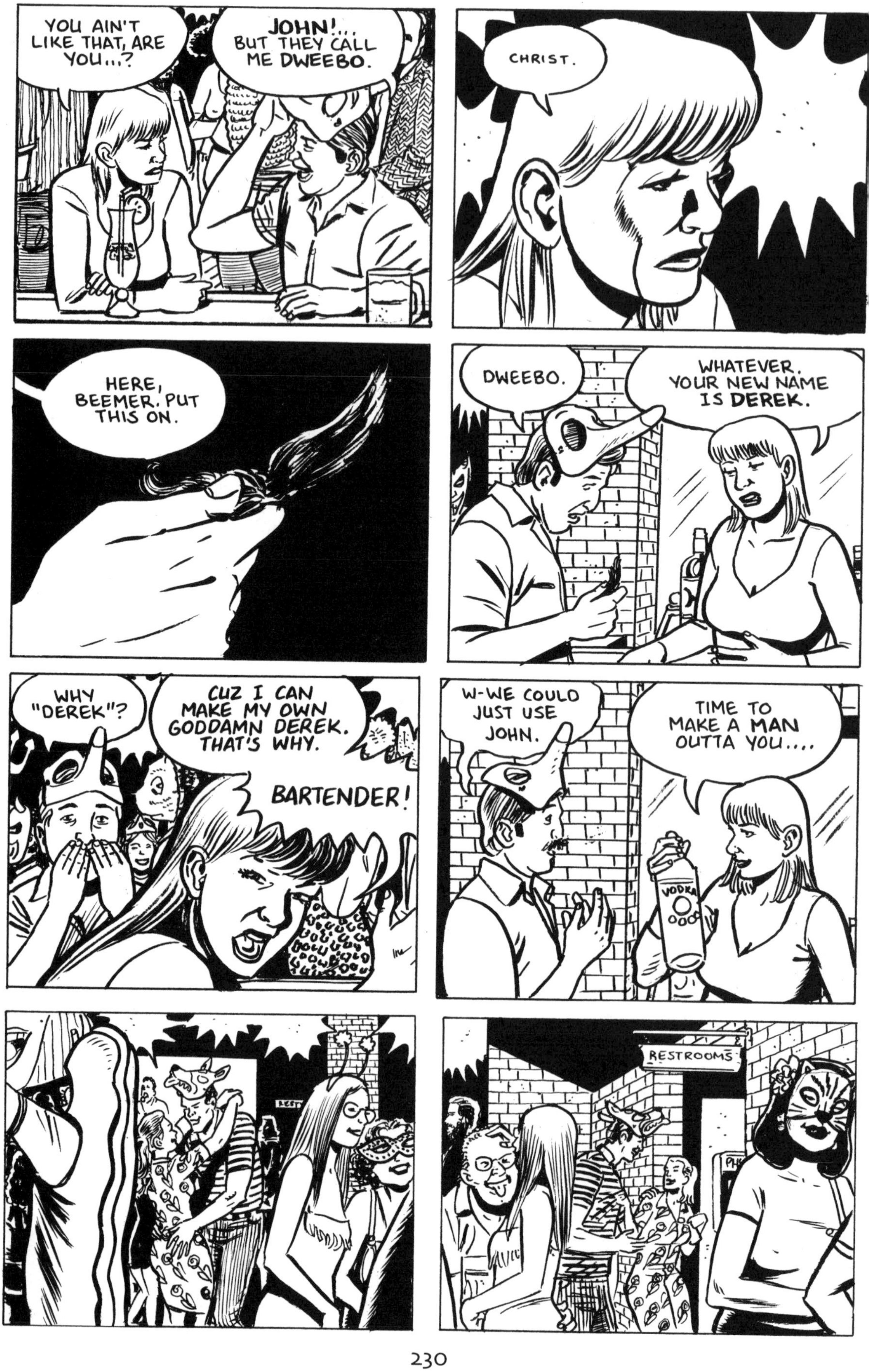
YOU AIN'T LIKE THAT, ARE YOU...?
JOHN!... BUT THEY CALL ME DWEEBO.
CHRIST.
HERE, BEEMER. PUT THIS ON.
DWEEBO.
WHATEVER. YOUR NEW NAME IS DEREK.
WHY "DEREK"?
CUZ I CAN MAKE MY OWN GODDAMN DEREK. THAT'S WHY.
BARTENDER!
W-WE COULD JUST USE JOHN.
TIME TO MAKE A MAN OUTTA YOU....
VODKA
RESTROOMS

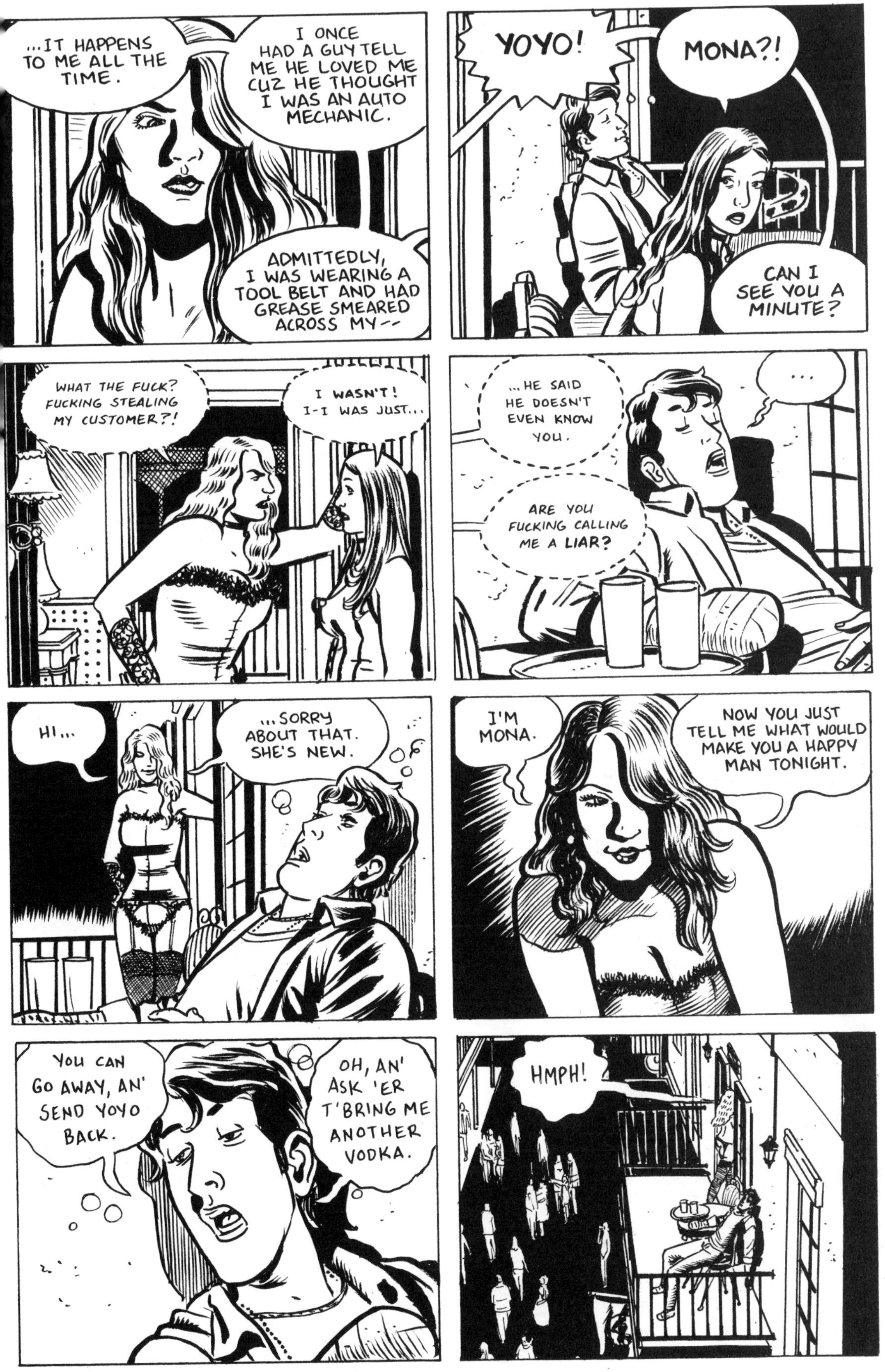
...IT HAPPENS TO ME ALL THE TIME.
I ONCE HAD A GUY TELL ME HE LOVED ME CUZ HE THOUGHT I WAS AN AUTO MECHANIC.
ADMITTEDLY, I WAS WEARING A TOOL BELT AND HAD GREASE SMEARED ACROSS MY--
YOYO!
MONA?!
CAN I SEE YOU A MINUTE?
WHAT THE FUCK? FUCKING STEALING MY CUSTOMER?!
I WASN'T! I-I WAS JUST...
...HE SAID HE DOESN'T EVEN KNOW YOU.
ARE YOU FUCKING CALLING ME A LIAR?
...
HI...
...SORRY ABOUT THAT. SHE'S NEW.
I'M MONA.
NOW YOU JUST TELL ME WHAT WOULD MAKE YOU A HAPPY MAN TONIGHT.
YOU CAN GO AWAY, AN' SEND YOYO BACK.
OH, AN' ASK 'ER T'BRING ME ANOTHER VODKA.
HMPH!

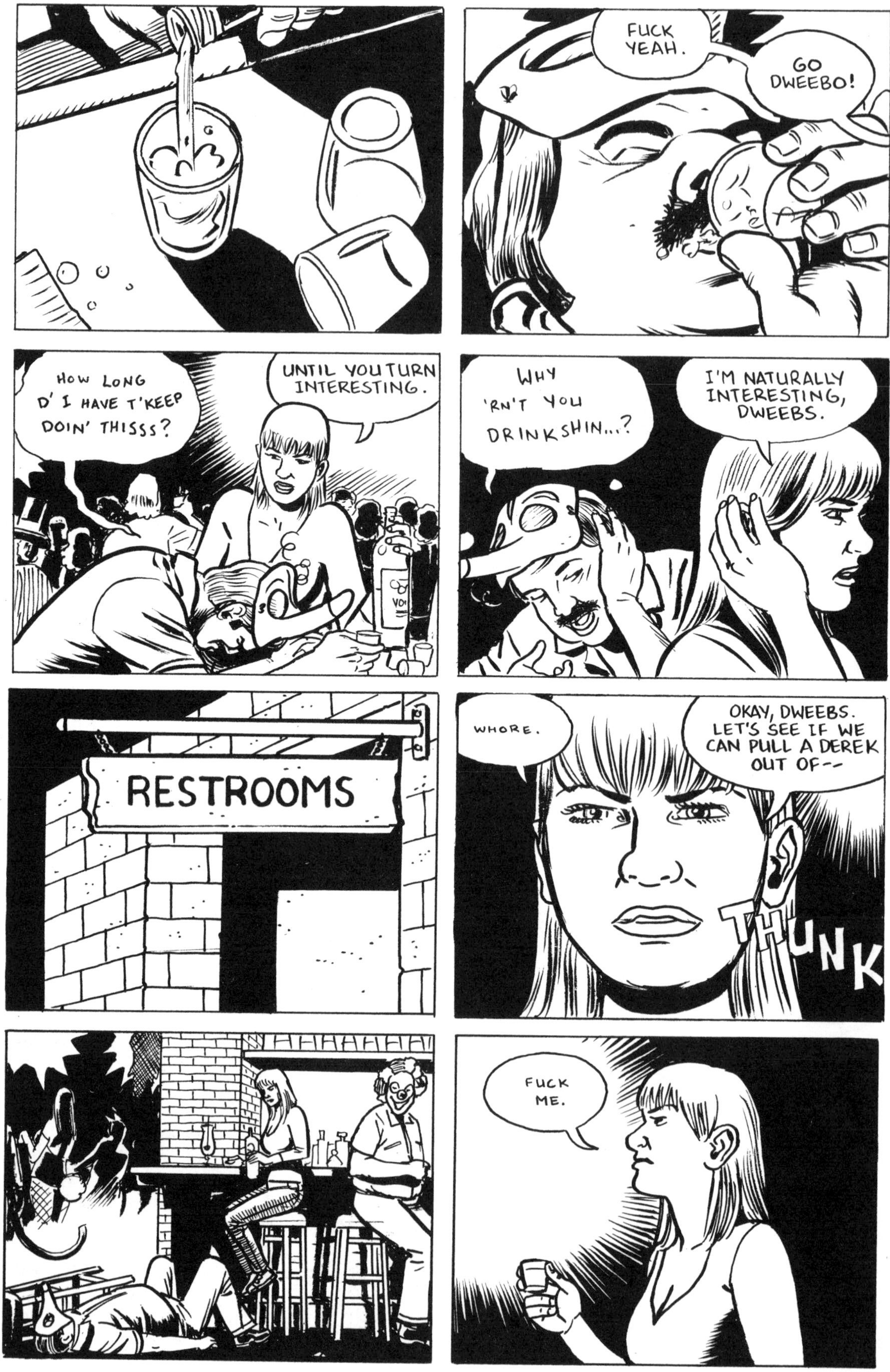
FUCK YEAH.
GO DWEEBO!
HOW LONG D' I HAVE T'KEEP DOIN' THISSS?
UNTIL YOU TURN INTERESTING.
WHY 'RN'T YOU DRINKSHIN...?
I'M NATURALLY INTERESTING, DWEEBS.
RESTROOMS
WHORE.
OKAY, DWEEBS. LET'S SEE IF WE CAN PULL A DEREK OUT OF--
THUNK
FUCK ME.

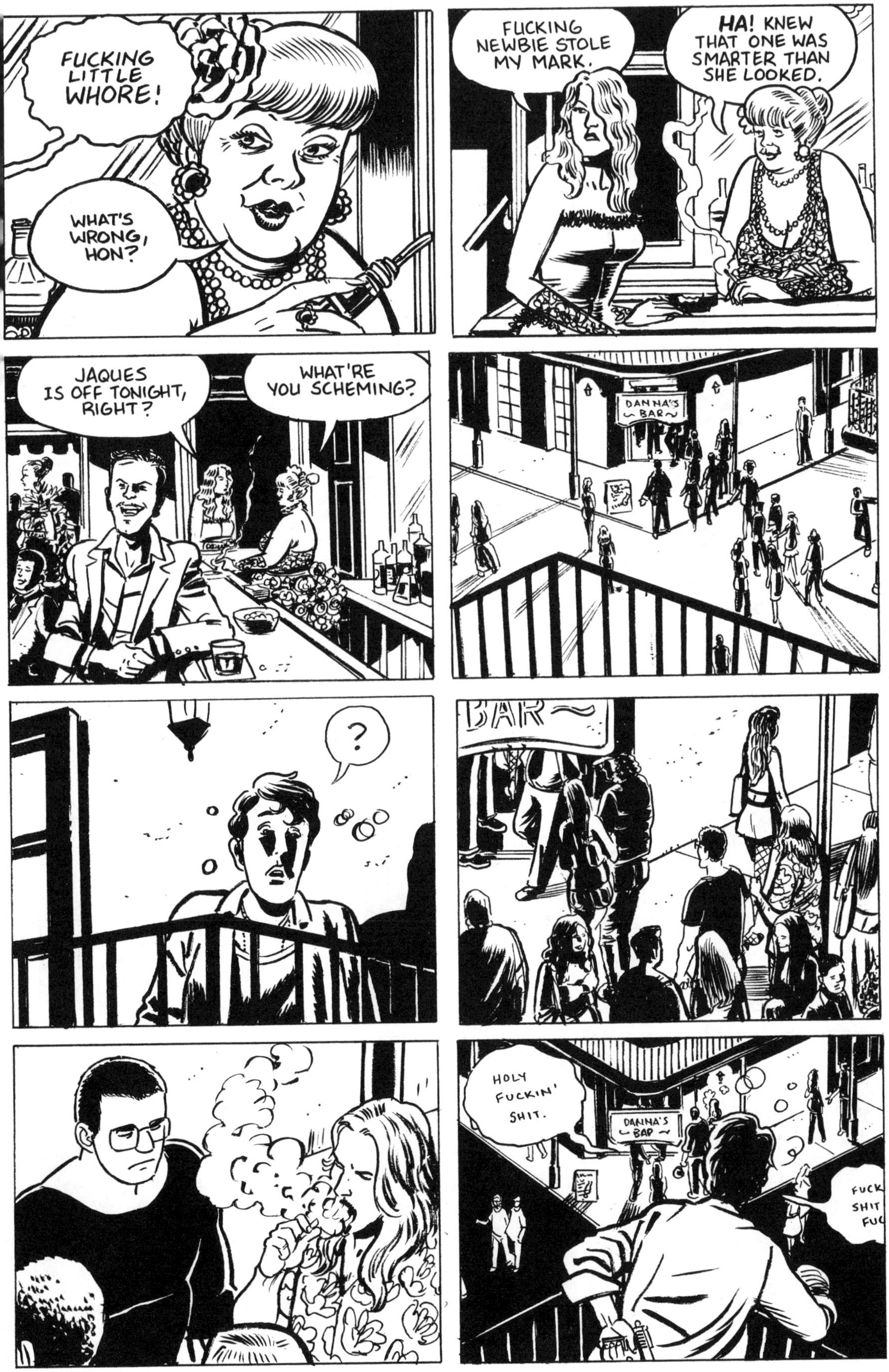
FUCKING LITTLE WHORE!
WHAT'S WRONG, HON?
FUCKING NEWBIE STOLE MY MARK.
HA! KNEW THAT ONE WAS SMARTER THAN SHE LOOKED.
JAQUES IS OFF TONIGHT, RIGHT?
WHAT'RE YOU SCHEMING?
DANNA'S BAR
?
BAR
HOLY FUCKIN' SHIT.
DANNA'S BAR
FUCK
SHIT
FUC

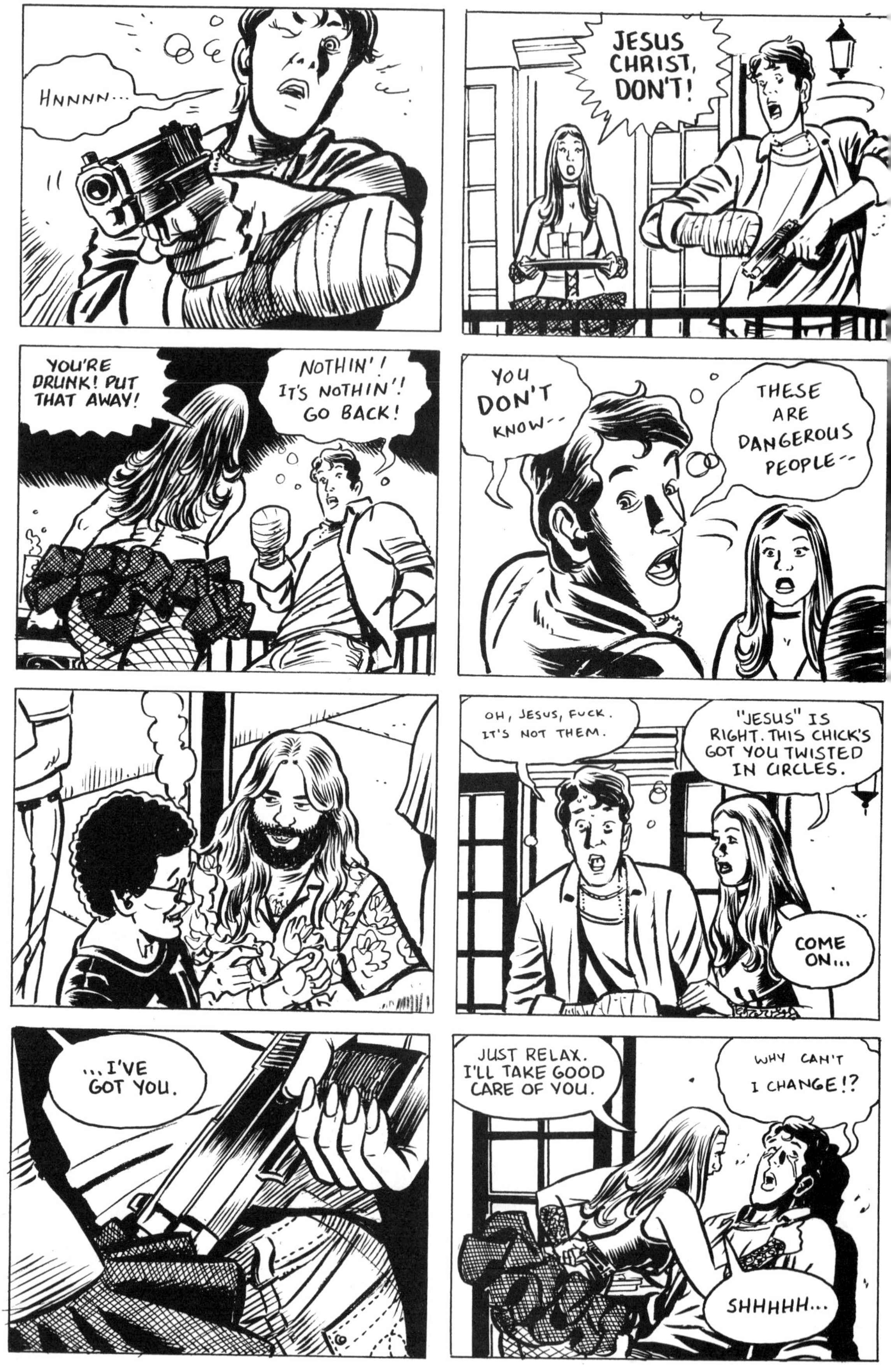
HNNNN...
JESUS CHRIST, DON'T!
YOU'RE DRUNK! PUT THAT AWAY!
NOTHIN'! IT'S NOTHIN'! GO BACK!
YOU DON'T KNOW--
THESE ARE DANGEROUS PEOPLE--
OH, JESUS, FUCK. IT'S NOT THEM.
"JESUS" IS RIGHT. THIS CHICK'S GOT YOU TWISTED IN CIRCLES.
COME ON...
...I'VE GOT YOU.
JUST RELAX. I'LL TAKE GOOD CARE OF YOU.
WHY CAN'T I CHANGE!?
SHHHHH...

I JUST REALIZED... ...I DON'T EVEN KNOW YOUR NAME.

IT'S DEREK.

I'M DEREK.

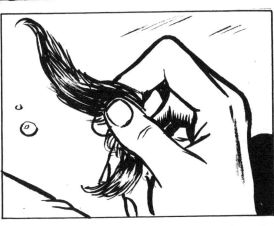

HAVE FUN...?

ASSHOLE'S GOT COKE DICK.

THIS WAS PROBABLY A BAD IDEA.

IT WAS A BORING IDEA.

"sniff"

I DID LEARN ONE THING THOUGH.

WHAT'S THAT?

A MUSTACHE DOESN'T MAKE THE DEREK.

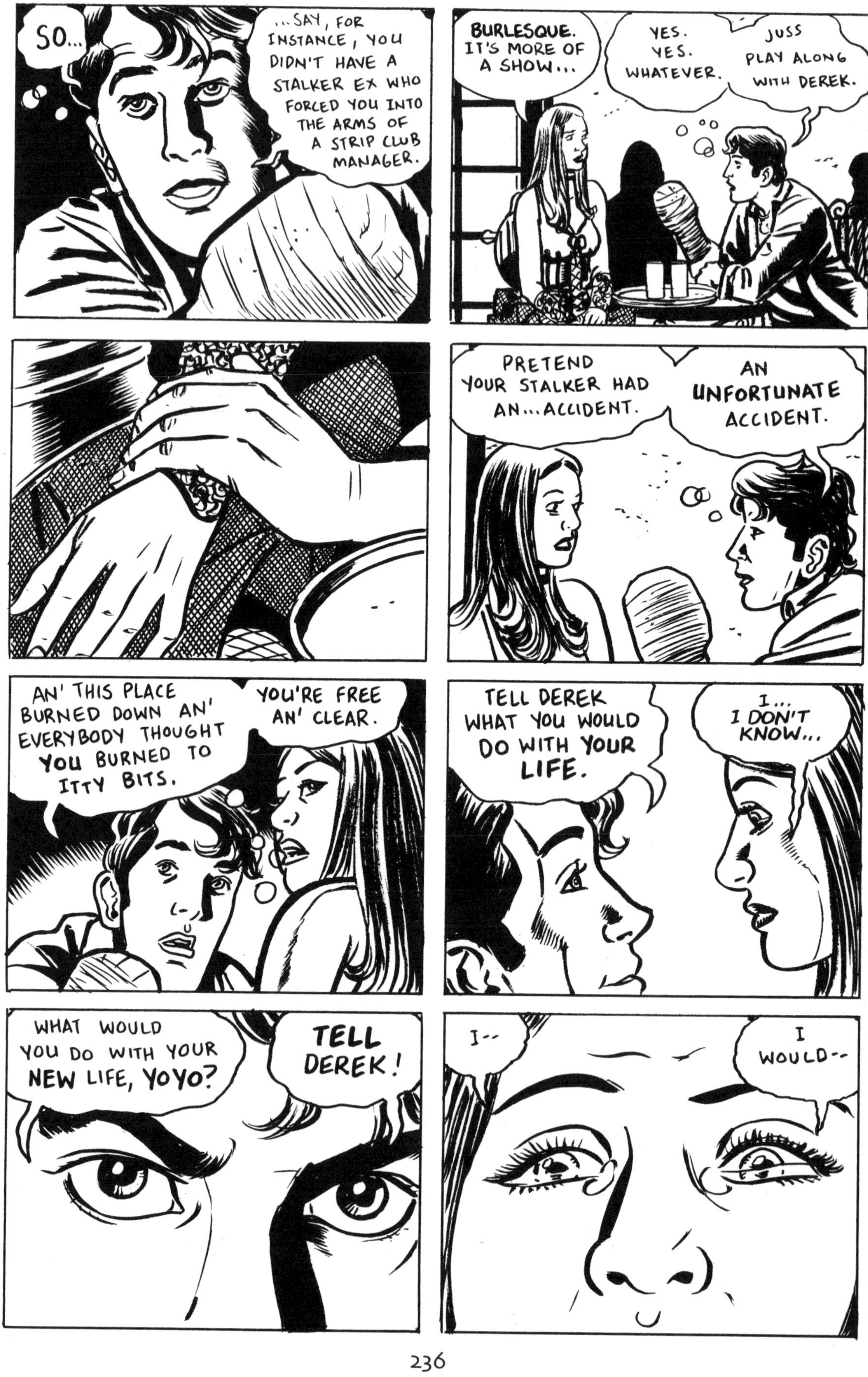
SO...
...SAY, FOR INSTANCE, YOU DIDN'T HAVE A STALKER EX WHO FORCED YOU INTO THE ARMS OF A STRIP CLUB MANAGER.
BURLESQUE. IT'S MORE OF A SHOW...
YES. YES. WHATEVER.
JUSS PLAY ALONG WITH DEREK.
PRETEND YOUR STALKER HAD AN...ACCIDENT.
AN UNFORTUNATE ACCIDENT.
AN' THIS PLACE BURNED DOWN AN' EVERYBODY THOUGHT YOU BURNED TO ITTY BITS.
YOU'RE FREE AN' CLEAR.
TELL DEREK WHAT YOU WOULD DO WITH YOUR LIFE.
I... I DON'T KNOW...
WHAT WOULD YOU DO WITH YOUR NEW LIFE, YOYO?
TELL DEREK!
I--
I WOULD--

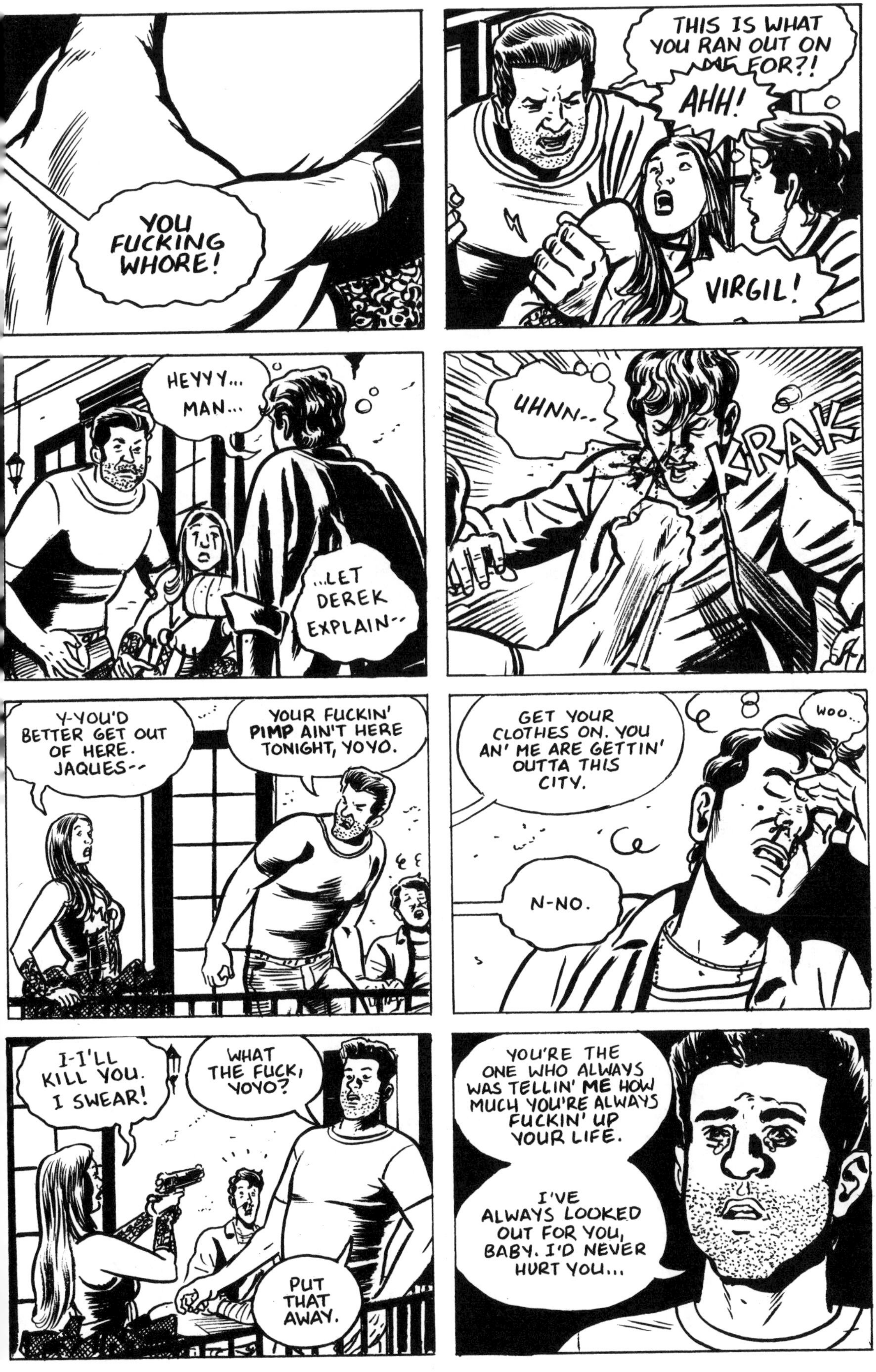
YOU FUCKING WHORE!
THIS IS WHAT YOU RAN OUT ON FOR?!
AHH!
VIRGIL!
HEYYY... MAN...
...LET DEREK EXPLAIN--
UHNN--
KRAK
Y-YOU'D BETTER GET OUT OF HERE. JAQUES--
YOUR FUCKIN' PIMP AIN'T HERE TONIGHT, YOYO.
GET YOUR CLOTHES ON. YOU AN' ME ARE GETTIN' OUTTA THIS CITY.
WOO...
N-NO.
I-I'LL KILL YOU. I SWEAR!
WHAT THE FUCK, YOYO?
PUT THAT AWAY.
YOU'RE THE ONE WHO ALWAYS WAS TELLIN' ME HOW MUCH YOU'RE ALWAYS FUCKIN' UP YOUR LIFE.
I'VE ALWAYS LOOKED OUT FOR YOU, BABY. I'D NEVER HURT YOU...

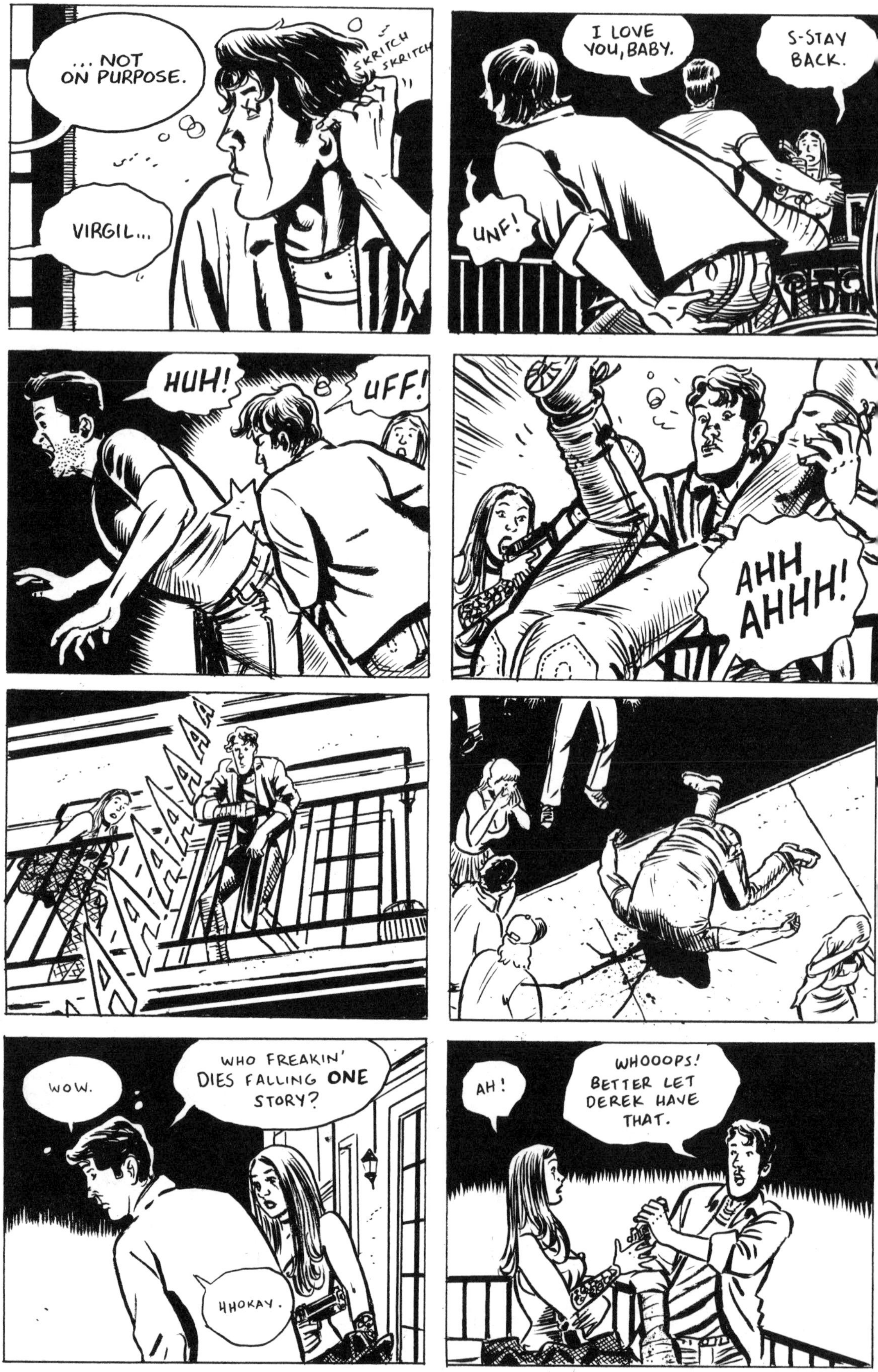
...NOT ON PURPOSE.
SKRITCH SKRITCH
VIRGIL...
I LOVE YOU, BABY.
S-STAY BACK.
UNF!
HUH!
UFF!
AHH AHHH!
WOW.
WHO FREAKIN' DIES FALLING ONE STORY?
WHOKAY.
AH!
WHOOOPS! BETTER LET DEREK HAVE THAT.

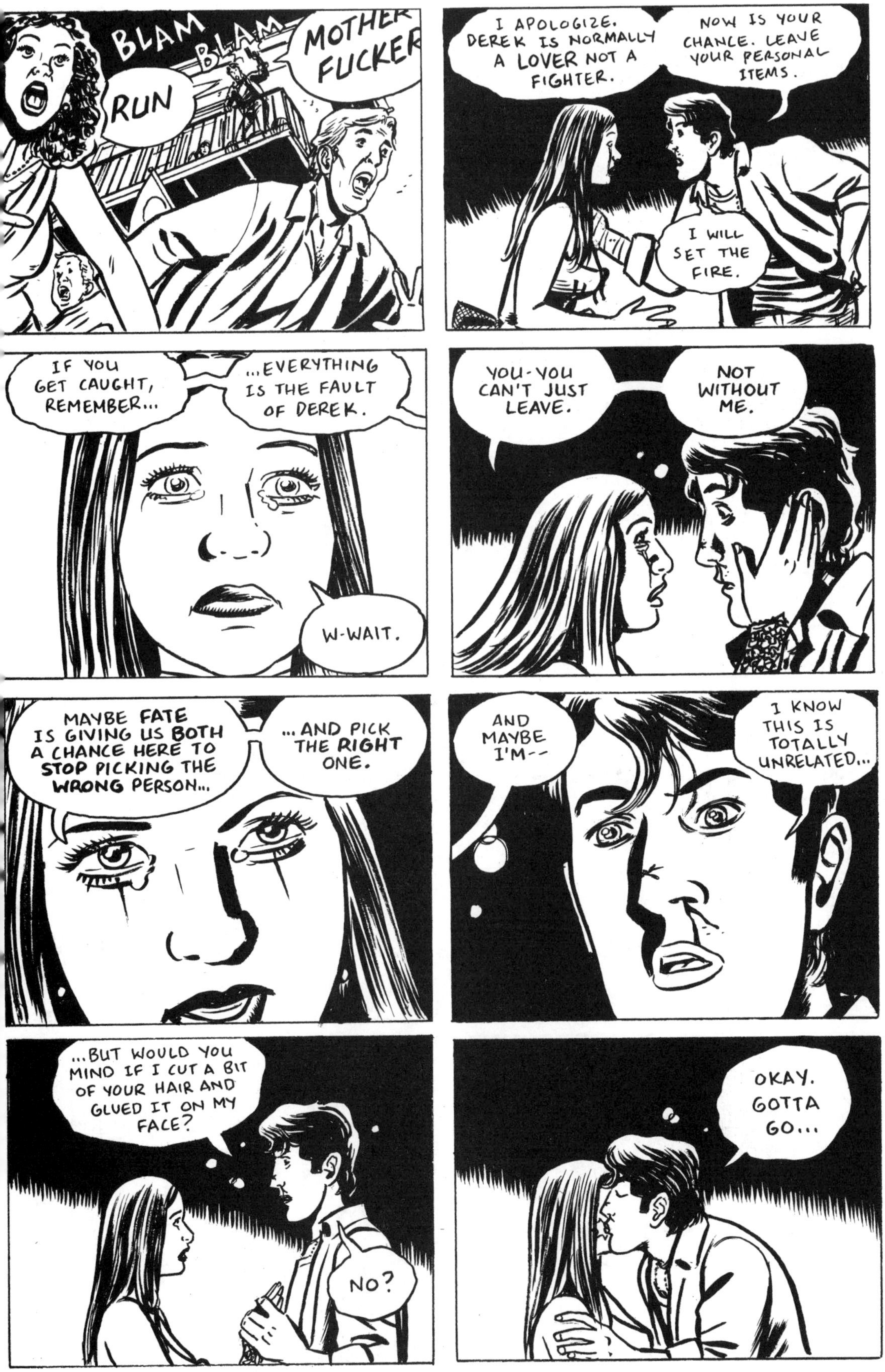
BLAM
BLAM
RUN
MOTHER FUCKER
I APOLOGIZE. DEREK IS NORMALLY A LOVER NOT A FIGHTER.
NOW IS YOUR CHANCE. LEAVE YOUR PERSONAL ITEMS.
I WILL SET THE FIRE.
IF YOU GET CAUGHT, REMEMBER...
...EVERYTHING IS THE FAULT OF DEREK.
W-WAIT.
YOU-YOU CAN'T JUST LEAVE.
NOT WITHOUT ME.
MAYBE FATE IS GIVING US BOTH A CHANCE HERE TO STOP PICKING THE WRONG PERSON...
...AND PICK THE RIGHT ONE.
AND MAYBE I'M--
I KNOW THIS IS TOTALLY UNRELATED...
...BUT WOULD YOU MIND IF I CUT A BIT OF YOUR HAIR AND GLUED IT ON MY FACE?
NO?
OKAY. GOTTA GO...

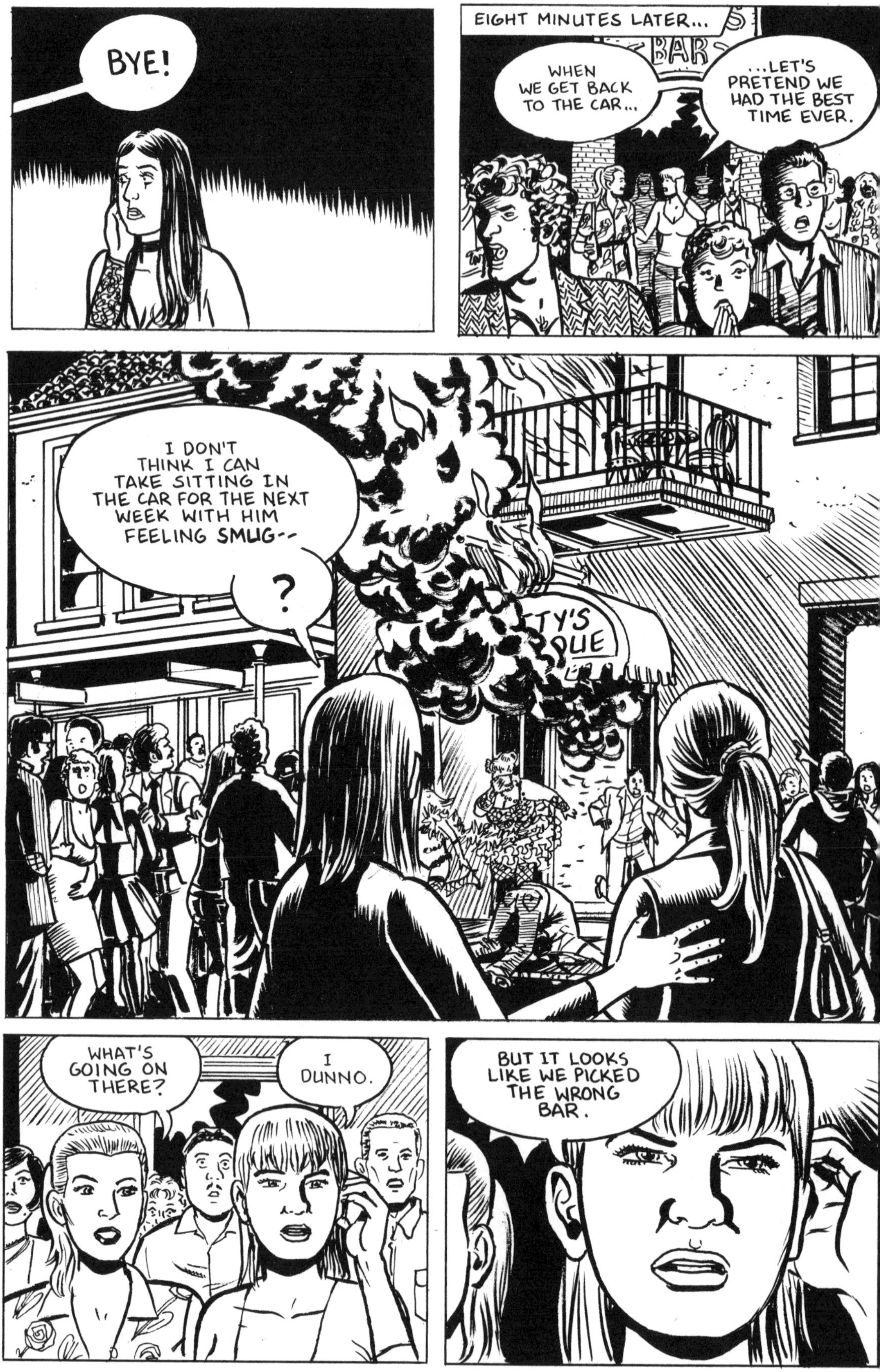
BYE!
EIGHT MINUTES LATER...
WHEN WE GET BACK TO THE CAR...
...LET'S PRETEND WE HAD THE BEST TIME EVER.
I DON'T THINK I CAN TAKE SITTING IN THE CAR FOR THE NEXT WEEK WITH HIM FEELING SMUG--
?
WHAT'S GOING ON THERE?
I DUNNO.
BUT IT LOOKS LIKE WE PICKED THE WRONG BAR.

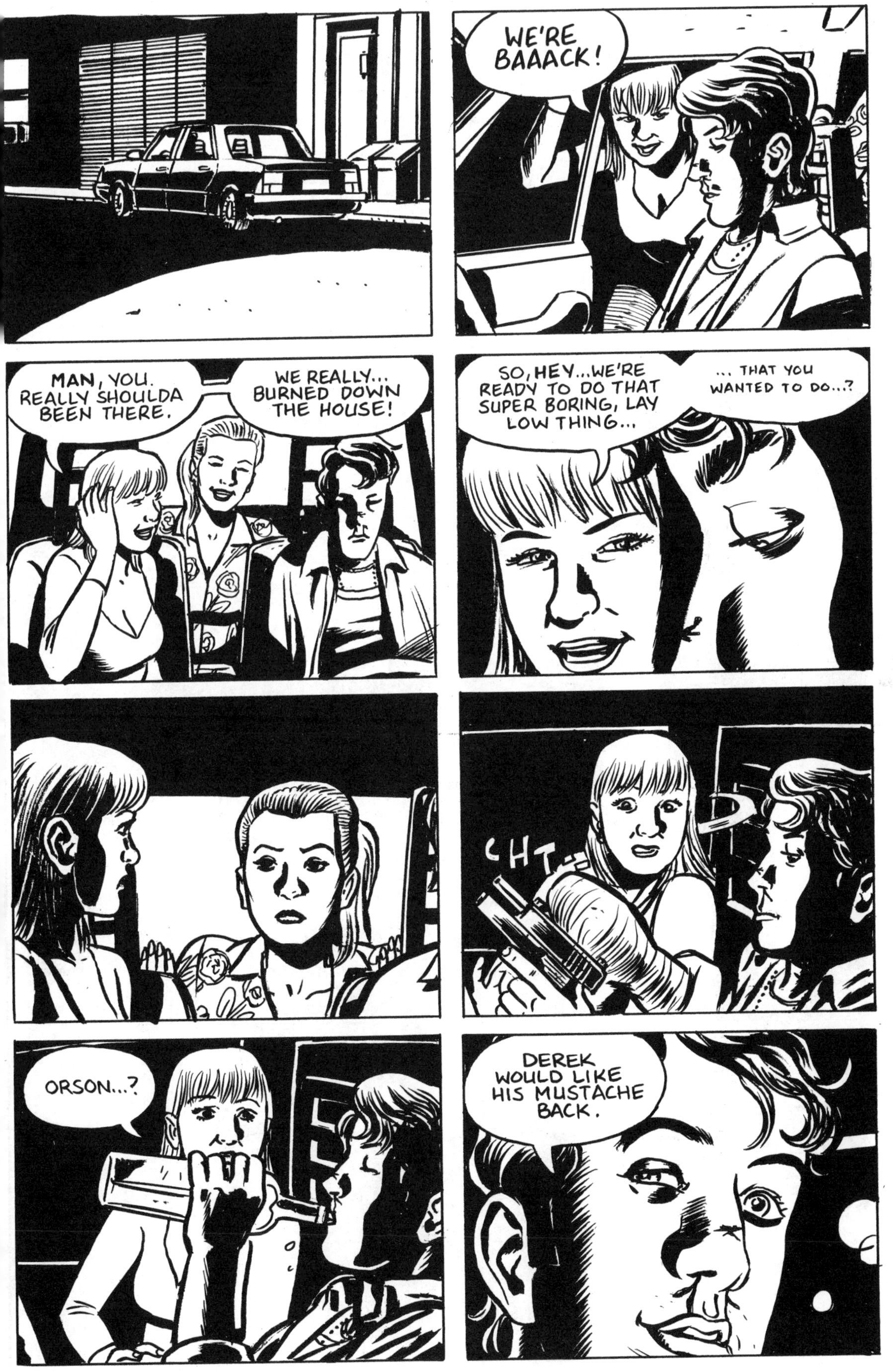
WE'RE BAAACK!
MAN, YOU. REALLY SHOULDA BEEN THERE.
WE REALLY... BURNED DOWN THE HOUSE!
SO, HEY...WE'RE READY TO DO THAT SUPER BORING, LAY LOW THING...
... THAT YOU WANTED TO DO...?
CHT
ORSON...?
DEREK WOULD LIKE HIS MUSTACHE BACK.

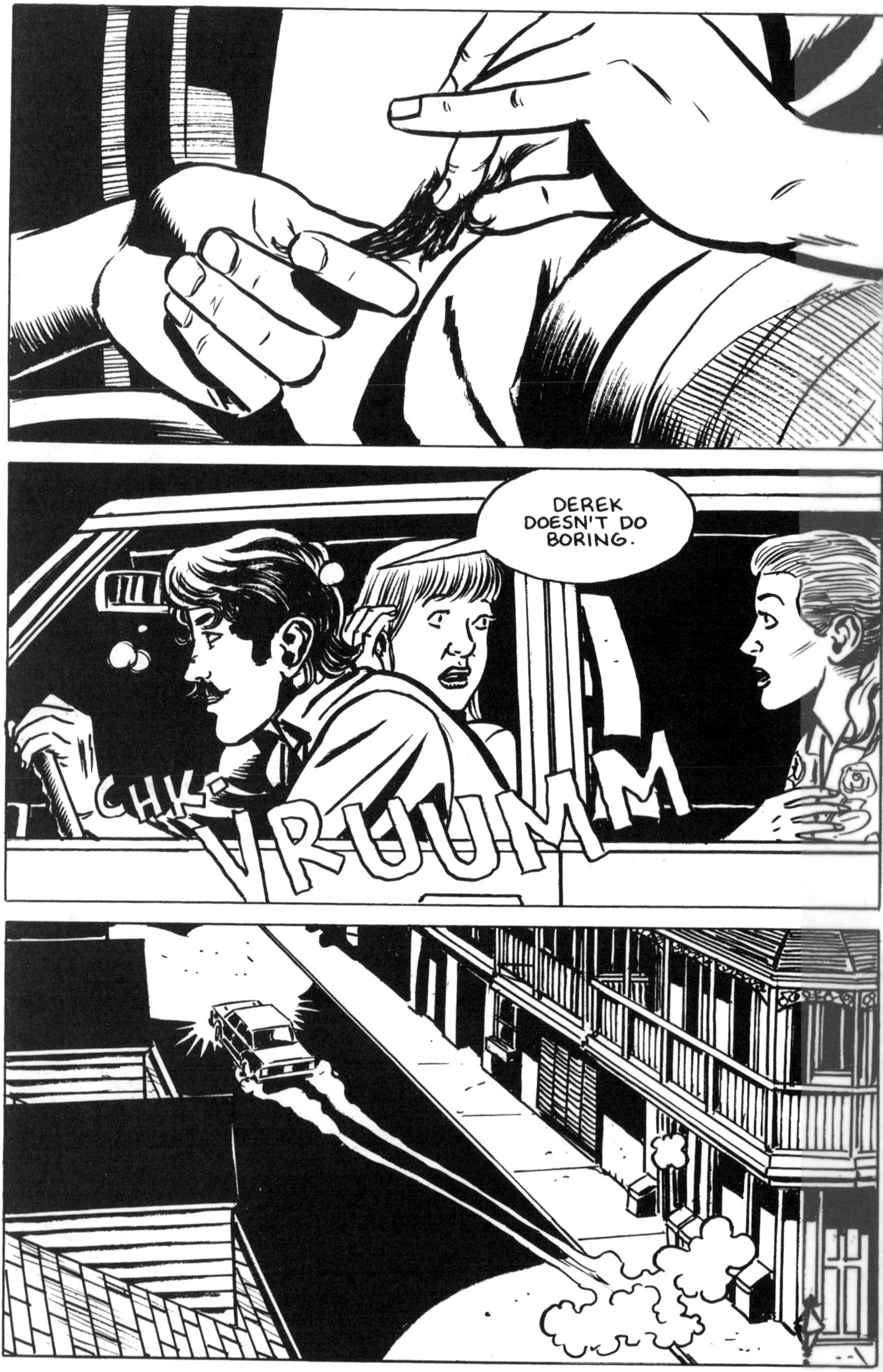
DEREK DOESN'T DO BORING.
CHK-
VRUUMM

THE END...